Praise for Kelly Eileen Hake

Kelly Eileen Hake spins a fast-paced romance set against the backdrop of frontier Americana. Kelly's storytelling skills shine through on *The Bride Bargain*, and I highly recommend you add it to your reading list. I can hardly wait to see what she comes up with next!

—Tracie Peterson, bestselling author
of the Ladies of Liberty series and
the Broadmoor Legacy series with Judith Miller

Should we ever do the wrong thing for the right reason? This is the dilemma Clara faces when she agrees to a scheme that could result in a permanent home for her beloved aunt. Unfortunately, for her to receive the prize, someone will pay a mighty price. . .of matrimony! For a sweet, relaxing read, treat yourself to *The Bride Bargain*.

—Kim Vogel Sawyer, author of
My Heart Remembers

A family feud, love, and history all rolled into a fun and fascinating story that will keep you reading until you've turned the final page.

—Judith Miller, author of the
Postcards from Pullman series

Who would have thought one cantankerous ox and a lonely shopkeeper would conspire to cause double the trouble and double the blessings? In this quirky, romantic tale, Kelly Hake combines unforgettable characters and a plot that tugs at both your funny bone and your heartstrings. *The Bride Bargain* is my favorite Kelly Hake book yet!

—Kathleen Y'Barbo, author of
Beloved Castaway

PRAIRIE PROMISES

Three unlikely romances bring DELIGHT
and HUMOR *to Buttonwood, Nebraska*

KELLY EILEEN HAKE

BARBOUR
PUBLISHING

THE BRIDE
BARGAIN

KELLY EILEEN HAKE

DEDICATION/ACKNOWLEDGMENT

Seven years ago I dedicated my first novella to "the two unstoppable forces in my life: God and my mother!"

Since then, my blessings have grown, and so has the list of incredible people who've supported my writing. I want to personally thank Rebecca Germany and Aaron McCarver, my wonderful editors; and Julia Rich, Kathleen Y'Barbo, and Elsa Carruthers, whose encouragement and prayers meant more than they know.

This wouldn't have been possible without all of you!

CHAPTER 1

Nebraska Territory, Oregon Trail,
two weeks journey past Fort Laramie, 1855

That does it!" Clara Field gritted her teeth and tugged harder on her leather glove, which was currently clamped between the jaws of a cantankerous ox. She didn't know whether to laugh or cry.

"I'll get him in a headlock for you, Miss Field, and cut off his air so he'll open his mouth." Burt Sprouse sauntered over. "That should take care of things quick enough."

"Oh, choking him wouldn't be the right answer." Clara struggled to hide her disgust at the very suggestion. "I have to marvel at how similar animals and humans can be. Neither group likes to be forced into anything, and try as I might, I can't seem to convince him we're trudging toward freedom."

"Well, I reckon I could knee him in the chest to make him let go." Sprouse shuffled closer. "Hickory's got an eye on you."

"Thank you, Mr. Sprouse. I'll handle this." Clara waited until the burly ex-lumberjack wandered away before pleading with the ox. "Your antics are going to get us kicked off the wagon train, Simon!"

At the sound of his name, the ox perked his ears and his mouth

7

went slack, allowing Clara to yank away her glove. How an ox had a taste for leather escaped her, but bovine cannibalism counted as the least of her worries at the moment. She held up the mangled thing and sighed.

Thank You, Lord, that I brought an extra pair just in case I lost one. Her lips quirked at the tooth marks on the leather. *Though I never thought things would come to this.*

Yanking on the length of rope she'd tied around Simon's neck, Clara urged him toward the makeshift corral the trail boss had set up for the night. The obstinate animal refused to budge, his eyes fixed on her glove with a greedy gleam.

"There's lots of good forage and fresh water," she tempted. "And plenty of rest." Oooh, how good that sounded. A verse from Psalms floated into memory: *"He leadeth me beside the still waters. He restoreth my soul."*

For it being a river, the Platte came as close to still water as any running water could ever hope. Wide, shallow, and dark with mud, it was their constant guide and water source. Clara tried not to compare it to babbling brooks, flowing streams, or any other clear, flowing water with a friendly rush of sound.

As for the earlier part of that scripture. . .well, they'd only just stopped for the night. Until she got this last ox to the corral, gathered enough fuel for the campfire, and cooked dinner for herself, Aunt Doreen, and the blessedly helpful Burt, she wouldn't be lying beside anything.

But we're one day closer to Oregon. Eleven miles farther toward a new start. Not even Simon's snacking can take that away.

Tension eased from her shoulders as Simon ambled toward the enclosure. She and Aunt Doreen had already lost two oxen on the trail, and when they settled in Oregon, the remaining stock would be used for food or trade. The sadness creeping over her at the thought explained, at least in part, why Clara wasn't an accomplished driver. Even after weeks on the trail, she couldn't bear to use a whip harshly.

With Simon safely tucked away with the rest of the train's livestock, Clara began hunting for buffalo chips. The tall, dry grass rustled around her skirts as she searched. Typically, the prairie held a large and ready supply of the quick-burning fuel. But the recalcitrant ox had cost her valuable time. The areas closest to the circled wagons were picked over by the other women on the train whose husbands saw to the animals. She needed to go farther, though never too far, to scrape together a fair-sized load.

By the time she got back to camp and started their fire, Aunt Doreen already had vegetables—the same supply of potatoes, carrots, and onions that they'd been using since the stop at Fort Laramie—chopped and in the pot for cooking, and the batter ready for johnnycake. Once the fire burned hot enough to heat the Dutch oven and cook the stew, Clara gratefully sank down beside the makeshift kitchen.

A healthy breeze carried away the smoke from the fire, bringing welcome coolness as the sun faded. The moon came into view, its modest glow bathing the plains in whitish blue light.

"Grub ready yet, Miz Field?" Burt Sprouse's head tilted forward as he sniffed the air like a hopeful bear. In exchange for their cooking, alongside a bit of washing and mending, the ex-lumberjack provided them with fresh meat whenever possible, took on the night watches assigned to their wagon, and lent a hand when he could.

"Not quite, Mr. Sprouse." Apologies wouldn't make the rabbit cook any faster. "I had difficulty finding enough buffalo chips tonight."

"Looked like the oxen gave you some trouble tonight." Burt's voice held no censure as he squatted down. "I'll take on your watch tonight, like we agreed, but Hickory's getting antsy about having you and your aunt in your own wagon. You were last in the row and last to set up camp tonight."

"Sure were." The trail boss, Hickory McGee, stomped over to glower at them. Disgust filled his tone. "Same as every day on this trail. I warned you gals I didn't want to take on two women with no menfolk to shoulder the night watches, wagons, and livestock. You know the law of the trail—pull your weight or be left behind."

"We know." Clara forced the words through gritted teeth. Men who believed women to be inferior in every way put up her back as little else could. *If you spent more time helping and less time harping, things would get done faster. As it is, you accomplish nothing with threats, yet Aunt Doreen and I hold things together in spite of them. A true gentleman—the kind of man a mother would be proud to raise and a woman would be glad to claim as husband—would be respectful and helpful.*

She kept the thoughts to herself. Speaking her mind was a luxury she couldn't afford if it angered the trail boss. A quick prayer for patience, and she swallowed her ire.

"I haven't completely mastered the art of unhitching the oxen," Clara admitted before staring him down. "But Mr. Sprouse makes sure our watches aren't shirked, and you know it." She cast a grateful look at Burt.

"You ain't the ones doin' it," Hickory groused. "No call for a man with his own wagon and responsibilities to shoulder yours."

"I don't mind taking the extra watch in exchange for their cooking," Burt put in.

"Don't recall askin' you, Sprouse." Hickory turned his glare from Clara to the lumberjack. "But anyone causin' problems can be left behind."

"Worse comes to worse"—Mr. Sprouse shrugged—"I can sear some meat. Got an iron stomach, I do."

"Glad to hear it." The guide returned his attention to Clara.

"You're lagging behind as it is. Not being able to control your animals is one more hassle to endanger the train. One rampaging ox can set off a stampede."

"We managed to sort it out." Aunt Doreen tugged a bucket of water toward them. "We always do."

"It didn't put anyone else out." Clara shoved aside her remorse over Mr. Sprouse's late dinner. "We'll be ready to pull out at dawn, same as everyone else."

"Better be." The disagreeable guide punctuated that statement by launching spittle toward their cookfire. It hissed as he stalked away.

When we get to Oregon, it will be worth it, she vowed to herself for the thousandth time since they left Independence and started out on the trail. *The Lord will see us to a new life and a happy home.*

"The johnnycake should be about ready." Clara pushed the ashes off the top of the Dutch oven with her ladle handle, wrapped her hand in a dishcloth, and lifted the lid. The sweet smell of warm cornbread wafted toward them. "Let me slice a piece for you to have now while the stew finishes."

"Mmmph." A moment later, Mr. Sprouse plunked himself down and set to munching the hot bread. His obvious enjoyment didn't soothe Clara as it usually did—not when he'd made it clear that their agreement wasn't as strong as Hickory's warnings.

"Here, Aunt Doreen." Clara made sure her aunt got a large portion. After weeks on the trail, not only did their simple dresses boast enough dust to plant a garden, but the calico also hung from her aunt's thin frame. After a grueling day of travel, any moment they could use for a good night's rest was another small loss her aunt didn't deserve to bear. *Unacceptable.*

Aunt Doreen passed Mr. Sprouse another piece before he asked. Their success on the trail depended on keeping the man well fed. So long as they did that and kept pressing onward, the trail boss couldn't leave them behind.

Clara filled a tin with the steaming stew. Onions came from their supply, greens they'd gathered along the way, and the rabbit came courtesy of Mr. Sprouse's shotgun. If it weren't for their little arrangement with him, she and her aunt would be surviving on jerky.

"Best deal I ever made." His grunt made both of them smile. Burt made no bones about the fact he liked to eat but couldn't cook. Another's misfortune was rarely cause for prayers of gratitude, but. . .

"I was just thinking the same thing." Clara knew Aunt Doreen's reply came from the heart, to say the least.

Until now, Mr. Sprouse was just one more example of how the Lord watched over them and would see them through this arduous journey, which had become more wearing than Clara anticipated. A continuous stream of mishaps drained their supplies and energy. And they'd yet to make it past the prairie to the hardships of the mountains.

"When we reach the mountains, things will go more slowly." She meant the words as a comfort to her own aching bones and her aunt's worries, but Burt Sprouse didn't see it that way.

"Yep. Snow can make us lose days, get off the trail, have so many delays food runs out and animals freeze. Everything's harder once you hit the Rockies."

"Our oxen are too ornery to freeze." Clara couldn't help smiling even as she muttered the words.

"Even so, we'll all probably lighten our loads." Burt shrugged. "I hear the mountains are littered with furniture and heirlooms abandoned by travelers so they can get free of a snow bank or make it up a steep pass."

Her aunt's gasp made Clara wrack her brain for something positive to say.

"After that rough river crossing, we already lost several items."

She quelled the sense of loss that overcame her at the memory of her childhood trunk, filled with her doll and doll's clothes. The last thing her father gave her, lost in the Platte forever. "So we probably won't need to leave anything else behind." She forced a smile.

"For all those reasons, you have to be careful not to get on the trail boss's bad side." Burt waved his spoon in the air. "We won't make it without him, and he's dead serious about leaving behind anyone who causes problems."

He does care. Surely Burt said that nonsense about having an iron stomach just to placate Hickory. She eyed him fondly as he made his way back to his own wagon. Who would have thought a burly ex-lumberjack looking to make his fortune gold mining would be their saving grace?

"You go on ahead and get to bed," Clara encouraged her aunt after they'd eaten their fill. "I'll clean up and join you in a few moments."

Aunt Doreen's lack of protest and grateful nod spoke of her weariness more eloquently than if she'd carped over the long day. Yet the older woman never uttered so much as a word of complaint. Not that she ever had, even throughout the long years of living under Uncle Uriah's thumb.

No matter how many verses her uncle warped out of context, how often he misinterpreted her own words or actions, Clara held firm to the conviction that Uriah's chauvinism was personal prejudice, not truth. Oft-repeated lectures against the frail values and fragile mindsets of the so-called weaker sex only underscored the quiet strength of the woman who'd raised her.

The few months when she'd had Doreen's sole attention soothed her soul, pulling her from the endless cycle of guilt and anger over Ma's and Pa's deaths. Clara owed everything to the self-sacrificing love of Doreen. Then she'd married Uriah Zeph, and their world tilted once more. For the worse.

Hopes ahead; regrets behind. Grandma's saying had become their motto over the years and seemed more appropriate with each passing day. Tonight, as Clara fell into her quilt, she added one more phrase. . . .

And God alongside.

～⚬⚬～

Outskirts of Baltimore

Filth everywhere. Dr. Saul Reed shook his head as he made his way from the room he rented to the area of the Baltimore outskirts that housed businesses. Brackish water and mud splotched the street. The odor of stale urine in the alleyways fought for dominance over the smell of stewed cabbages and onions.

To think, this was the better area of town, where most of the residents had roofs over their heads and cabbage to eat. There were others less fortunate, left to burrow under garbage or be chased away from bridges until pneumonia or fever took them away. The illness he could treat, the neglect of hygiene and sanitation he could fight, but all he could do was pray for the indifference neighbors showed for one another.

That's why he'd chosen this place. A cozy practice in a whitewashed building in the heart of Baltimore would bring affluent clients, respectable standing, and a nice living. Here, though, he could put his knowledge to the best use. These were the areas where people otherwise denied medical attention needed his help.

If only You will open their ears, Lord, he prayed as he entered the post office. His youth became an impediment in the eyes of some, who saw more value in years than in his Edinburgh education. They didn't take into account the school's reputation as he had when making his choice. The university's renown for technological advancement didn't transmit beyond the medical community.

"Letter come for ya, Doc." The post office worker thrust the note at him.

"Any packages?" Saul peered into the cubbyholes behind the desk to no avail. "Those forceps I ordered should be coming in any day now."

"Any day ain't today." The man chewed his tobacco before sending a thick stream of sludge onto the floor beside an obviously oft-missed spittoon. "While yer here an' all, though. . ."

"What's ailing you?" Saul prayed the man wouldn't do as he had the last time he'd asked for help and pull down his britches to display a carbuncle on his hip.

"M' mouth." The tobacco tucked into his cheek, he opened wide.

Holding his breath to avoid the foul blast of air, Saul tilted his head and surveyed browned teeth, yellowed gums, and a sore the size of his thumb on the man's tongue. Saul pulled back to a safe distance and inhaled.

"You've got an open sore on your tongue."

"Heck, Doc, even I knowed that much." The man rolled his eyes. "What can I do about the thing?"

"I'll make you a rinse of witch hazel to clean it out. Be sure to drink a lot of water and use the rinse after you eat anything." Saul set his jaw. "Most of all, you must stop using the tobacco."

"Wha'?" His jaw gaped, treating the doctor to another view of that open sore and losing the tobacco altogether. It landed with a soft thud on the dusty floor.

"Good. The tobacco is what's causing the problem."

"Naw." The man stooped down, scooped up the wad, dusted it off as best he could, and plopped it right back in his mouth.

"Yes." Saul closed his eyes. "Though taking things from the

ground and putting them in your mouth doesn't help, either."

"Dirt don't hurt." Crossing his arms over his chest, he rolled the chaw in his mouth, sending another stream toward the ground. This time it landed perilously close to Saul's boot. "Even a quack'd know that."

"People track in more than dirt." Saul's voice became more stern. "The more you chew, the worse it'll get. Keep on, and you'll see more sores until they spread down your throat and you can't speak."

The man's laughter followed Saul outside—another example of the ignorance that ruled this area. *How can I make a difference if they won't let me? What do I have to do, Lord, to make them see how to take care of themselves? Give me the chance to make a difference.*

As he rounded a corner, a shaky voice sounded. "Young and untouched. I'll give ya a good time, sir."

"No." He made to move on, but her gaunt face stopped him in his tracks. The girl couldn't be more than eleven. Shadows smudged her eyes, and bony wrists protruded from beneath too-short sleeves.

"I swear it's true." She drew closer, obviously misinterpreting his pause for interest. In the brighter light, livid bruises bloomed along her throat. Whether they'd been pressed there by a violent customer or an enraged pimp was impossible to say.

"Stay there." He held out a hand to stay her progress. Between her youth, her assertion of innocence, and those bruises, he couldn't walk away. "What is your name?"

"Whatever ya like." She raised a nervous hand to the marks on her throat. "Whatever ya want."

Enraged pimp then. Saul peered down the alleyway to see if the brute lingered behind. No one there.

"What can you do—no, not that." He stopped her hastily as she prepared to speak. "Can you sew? Cook? Clean?"

"What?" Astonishment replaced the desperation in her gaze.

"I know a lady who runs a boardinghouse and is in need of some help." Saul kept his voice muted. "If you're an honest sort and not afraid of solid work, you might do."

"I sews real fine—it's what he used to have me do." The glow of pride left her abruptly. "He'd find me." The whisper almost floated past him unheard, but when her hand fluttered toward her neck again, Saul understood her fear.

"Where is he now?"

"Pub." She jerked her head toward a side street.

"Come with me now, and he'll never know." Saul shifted his doctor's bag so it came into a more prominent view, hoping the symbol of trusted authority would put her at ease.

"You're one of them what purges babes when one of us gets unlucky?" Suspicion blazed to life in her pinched face. "Like him that came last night? He took the baby, right, but m' sister hasn't stopped bleeding since."

"Absolutely not." Saul closed his eyes at the image she evoked. "Where's your sister?" Obviously the woman needed immediate help—if it wasn't too late.

"Inside." She backed away a step. "Be on yore way, sir. M' sister don't need any more help from no doctors. She didn't want the first one to come, but he didn't give 'er no choice."

"The quack who did that to her was no doctor." Rage boiled in Saul's chest. "If she keeps bleeding, your sister will die."

"And I'll be alone wif"—her gaze darted in the direction of the pub she'd indicated earlier as her voice went hoarse—"*him.*" Though Saul wouldn't have thought it possible, her face became even more pale. "He said he'd take care of us, but he turned Nancy out within a week. After last night he said I'd have to take her place."

"No, you won't. Take me to Nancy."

CHAPTER 2

Panting, she spun and darted back down the alley, shoved open a warped door, and waved him inside. "Nancy's there."

When Saul's eyes adjusted to the dim light, he sank to his knees and examined the poor girl's face. Completely waxen, her skin was cool to his touch. Cold. No breath stirred her chest, no heartbeat pumped life in her veins, and the reason was clear. A dark pool of blood stained the base of the pallet. Saul pulled the worn sheet over the woman's face.

"Nancy!" With a choked scream, the little girl threw herself over her sister. "Wake up, Nancy. Please, Nancy. This gent's going to help us. Just wake up." She dissolved into tears as Saul gently pulled her away, only to spring from his arms, grab her sister's shoulders, and violently shake them.

"Nancy! You come back here," she ordered. "Nancy. . ."

"She can't hear you." Saul pulled her back and kept his grip firm this time. His words carried over the sobs wracking her thin frame. "You need to say good-bye. We have to go now. You aren't safe here."

Eyes widening in fear, her sobs jerked to a stop with the realization. "He'll be back." She tenderly reached out and folded

18

the blanket away from her sister's face. "Good-bye, Nancy."

A few stray tears spilled onto her sister's dress as the little girl unclasped a brass locket from around Nancy's neck and clutched it in her shaking hand. "May the angels welcome you, and may Mama make yore favorite bread pudding when you see her in heaven." Finished, she pressed a kiss to her sister's forehead, raised the blanket once more, and rose to her feet. Shoulders slumped but chin raised, she allowed him to whisk her away.

Hoping to make her feel safe, Saul spoke past the lump in his throat. "I'm Dr. Reed, and we're going to Mrs. Henderson. With a bath and new clothes, no one will recognize you." Seeing the fragile glint of hope in her expression, he added, "She'll keep you indoors for a few weeks to be on the safe side."

"All right then. I'm Midge." She meekly kept pace as he led the way back to Mrs. Henderson's. The farther they walked, the lighter her steps became until she murmured, "I hope she likes me."

"She will." Saul's words must have done the trick, because a small, cold hand slipped into his as they reached the stoop. "And you'll be treated well."

I'll make sure of it.

Clara cupped her hands to her mouth and gave an unladylike bellow. "Si-iimon!" *Where is that stubborn ox?* In a burst of inspiration, she whipped her chewed-up glove from the pocket of her apron. "Here, Simon!"

She moved up a slight rise in the landscape and surveyed the area. Seeing no sign of Simon, she turned back. Perhaps her ox had traveled south? She lifted her skirts as she hurried down the rolling hill and back toward where the wagon train already began to break camp.

A swift journey to the south gave her no more hope than the

north. Clara took several deep breaths before rushing eastward. Without Simon, their wagon was one ox short.

"Lord," she gasped slightly as she spoke, still gripping the ruined glove and searching frantically for the ox, "without Simon, we won't make it in the mountains. Please help me find him before Hickory discovers he's lost!"

Several minutes passed before she had to give up the search and head back toward their wagon. Sure enough, Hickory waited there. A swift glance showed Aunt Doreen was trying not to cry.

"I'm sure we'll find him in a moment." Clara tried not to wheeze and forced a smile. "If you could just ask a few of the men to help, we'd be ready in no time."

"No. We're leaving. Your oxen are your business."

"How did he get out of the enclosure?" It went against the grain to point out someone else's carelessness, but Simon should have been safely corralled with the rest of the team.

"If you were hitched up on time like everybody else, the stupid beast wouldn't have been left back there long enough for it to be a problem. The way things stand right now, you're out."

"You can't do this!" Clara's jaw tightened. "You have no reason!"

"You're slowing down the whole train, and we don't have time to spare." Hickory McGee's glower could singe the fur off a polar bear.

"This is the first time one of our oxen wandered off," she objected then softened her tone in an attempt to placate the man. "Same thing happened to the Jamesons two days past."

"They have a newborn to look after. You don't have any excuse. We're leavin' soon as I git back to the front, whether you and your aunt are ready or not." He jerked a thumb toward the start of the train. "Keep pace or git left behind."

"You know we can't." Though it almost stuck in her throat, she pled with the man. "Without that ox, we can't make it through the mountains."

"Lighten your load." He shrugged. "Others have had to do the same."

"So have we!" Her temper rose as she recalled everything they'd left at home and more lost in a rough river crossing when their spare ox floundered and drowned. "We've the bare minimum as it is, and you know it!"

"I saw you lookin' at a picture album the other day. And from here I can spy a rockin' chair in there." He folded his arms and planted his feet. "You don't need those. . .or that awful flute thing I know you've still got tucked away."

"Yes, we do." Aunt Doreen came alongside Clara. "My grandfather carved that rocking chair for my mother when I was born. My father shipped it to America when they left England, and I won't leave it behind."

"You don't have to leave it." Hot pinpricks of tears stung Clara's eyes. After all Aunt Doreen had done for her, had sacrificed to raise her. . . "The chair stays."

Clara wouldn't defend her decision to bring along the large album full of tintypes. They were the guardians of what few memories she had left of her parents, before the accident. When she shut her eyes, it was the photos she saw now, not the sway of Ma's fancy skirts or the scent of Pa's spicy cologne.

"Necessities. That's all you take. Told you at the start, anything that don't help you holds you back. What you've got is a bunch of sentimental claptrap that won't help you, missy." Hickory's brows knit together. "You can't keep the chair and the pictures and whatever else ain't vital. The sooner you reckon with it, the more chance you have of makin' it. The trail brings enough tears without women fussin' over foolish things."

"Life is more than food and livestock, Mr. Hickory." Clara drew in a deep breath. "We only need a little time."

"What you need is a man to take you in hand and make

decisions. I've said it from the start, and you ain't proved me wrong." The trail boss narrowed his eyes as he looked from them, to their wagon, to the five oxen already yoked to it, to Simon's empty space. "A wagon train can't afford dead weight. You're out. Next town you'll be left behind."

Clara's throat tightened as she struggled not to yell at the man. "You can't kick us out."

"Yes, I can." His assertion came with cold confidence.

"What if I take 'em on?" Burt Sprouse lumbered over from behind their wagon, where he'd been lurking during the argument.

Clara battled between anger over his assumption of responsibility, exasperation that he'd been eavesdropping rather than finding Simon, and hope that this could be a solution. Mr. Sprouse already exchanged duties with them, so a slight modification of the arrangement wouldn't be too onerous.

"You sure you want to?" Hickory glowered at Clara. "Troublesome female you got there. Once you make the decision, you can't take it back, neither."

"I could use a wife." Sprouse shrugged before adding, "And Miss Field is easy on the eyes."

"Wife?" She spluttered at the word.

"See what I mean? Not much in the brainbox." Hickory tapped the side of his skull as he spoke to the other man before turning to Clara. "Sprouse here, against good judgment, is offering to take you two on."

"I heard that. Surely we can work out a partnership between our wagons," she began.

"Already tried that." Sprouse threw a beefy arm around her, tucking her against his sweat-stained underarm. "Only way is for you two to join my wagon."

Clara tried to shift away from the damp fabric and stale odor pressed against her cheek. She couldn't suppress a shudder.

"See? Women are fragile." He clamped her closer. "Even in the heat of the prairie, she's shivering. Go on ahead and get your clothes. Then you and your aunt can settle into my wagon."

"Leave this stuff behind." Hickory thumped the side of their wagon, casually dismissing every last thing they owned.

"I'll get the food," Sprouse finally released her as he turned toward their wagon, eyeing it as though trying to decide which crates held their cooking supplies.

Clara couldn't squeeze any words out until she saw Aunt Doreen's horrified, hopeless expression. "There's no. . .we have no preacher." She straightened her shoulders. "We can't make the change until we find one." *And by then I'll have thought of something.*

"Buttonwood may be tiny, but we'll make it there today. They've got a preacher." Hickory scratched his stomach. "You might be able to sell some of your things in town. Join up with Sprouse before he changes his mind or stay behind. You waste time trying to find that ox and press on, I wash my hands of you."

"She'll marry me." A huge grin split Sprouse's face. "It's the only way."

No. Clara backed away, reaching blindly until she caught Aunt Doreen's hand in her own. She couldn't seem to draw enough air into her lungs. *It hasn't come to this. After seven years, we're not in the same situation where we began. Lord, give me the strength not to fall into the same dreadful trap.*

"Give us a moment, gentlemen." Aunt Doreen drew her away, the rustle of their skirts the only sound until they'd gone far enough to speak in private. "Clara, there will be another way."

"How can you say that?" Tears pricked the back of her eyes. "I failed you, Aunt Doreen. When my parents died, you married Uriah to be able to provide for me so we could stay together."

"Selfish and cruel as Uriah turned out to be"—Aunt Doreen

tightened her clasp—"you know the cost of marriage to the wrong man. I want better for you, Clara."

"How can I do less for you than you've done for me?" Heat pressed against her chest, almost cutting off the words.

"You wouldn't disregard all I've done to give you better opportunities. Together, we'll do what I should have done so many years ago and trust God to provide."

"This is my fault. I brought us here, to the middle of the prairie." Clara bowed her head. "We're supposed to start fresh, not live under the sway of a man because he can make his way in the world and we can't. But it's the same in the middle of the Nebraska Territory as it was back home."

"Not quite. It's not God forcing you to marry Sprouse."

"No." Clara's head came up. "It's Hickory and Sprouse." Her jaw jutted forward. "You're right. They're manipulating the situation to make us do what they want. It's not a sign of my failure or a marker of God's will—it's another example of self-serving stubbornness."

"Are you ready to give up on yourself, stop looking for God's path, and marry Sprouse to stay on the wagon train?" Aunt Doreen drew a deep breath. "Because that's not the niece I raised."

"Marriage isn't an easy answer. We'll press forward on our own terms." Clara lifted her chin. "The only stubborn male we'll be looking to keep today is Simon."

CHAPTER 3

Town of Buttonwood,
between Fort Laramie and Independence Rock

Josiah Reed! What are you doing here?" Kevin Burn plunged a red-hot horseshoe into a water barrel. As it sizzled, he gestured for Josiah to come inside.

"Need a new crowbar, Kevin," Josiah answered, stepping into the heat of the smithy. The forge sat in the middle of the structure, its stone chimney reaching through the ceiling. Orange flames that would be cheery come winter blazed as though to compete with the stifling August weather. "I sold the last one, so just tell me when I can pick it up."

"Take a seat." Kevin's eldest son, Matthew, came from the stables where Josiah assumed he'd been shoeing a horse. He gestured toward the bench in the corner near the door, where visitors could get some fresh air and cool water from the bucket nearby. "A crowbar won't take me long."

"Sounds good." Josiah settled himself close to the Burns so he wouldn't miss anything they said over the clang of iron on iron. "How've things been for you?"

"Good," Kevin grunted as he pounded a piece of metal on his

anvil. "That last wagon train brought lots of business."

"I'd think that will be the last one until spring." Josiah removed his hat in a futile attempt to cool off. "Awful late for a caravan not to have made it to Independence Rock yet."

"Hickory McGee's ornery enough to make sure they get to Oregon before winter hits." Matthew's movements made him shift between the flickering light of the forge and the shadows beyond. "He knows what he's doing."

"That doesn't make it the right choice." Kevin plunged his work into the cooling bath, releasing a hiss of steam.

"Too often we think we know what we're doing when we don't." Josiah used his hat to fan the steam away as best he could, but the Burn men kept working as though the heat didn't register. "And sometimes a man makes a leap of faith and it works out just fine."

"What's on your mind?" Kevin made his way over to the bench. "You're not thinking of leaving Buttonwood?"

"No!" Josiah put his hat down. He'd known Kevin Burn for years even before the blacksmith moved out to the prairie. "You know I'd have come sooner if I could've."

If Gladys wouldn't have thrown a screeching, hollering fit. He squelched the unkind thoughts of his wife. She'd passed on years ago, and he prayed she'd found the peace she denied everyone else during her time on earth.

"All those years of talk, and now we're both settled out West." Kevin grinned. "Glad to hear you're not thinking of turning tail and scampering back East. That'd be a waste, with your store doing so well and that grand house you put up."

Josiah sobered at the mention of his place. Standing at two stories, built of brick and wood, that house took pride of place for hundreds of miles any direction. Oh, he'd started out in a one-room dirt soddy like everyone else, but once he'd set up the store, he'd made a house fit for his family.

Only hitch was, his family didn't come out West to join him.

"Yeah. She's a beaut." Matthew joined the conversation. "Isn't Saul coming out soon, now that he's back from Edinburgh?"

"He's a genuine doctor." Boasting about his son's achievement didn't do much to ease the hollowness of his home. "But he's decided to set up his practice in the outskirts of Baltimore."

"Sorry to hear that, Joe." Kevin clapped a hand on his shoulder.

"Say"—Matthew shifted his weight from one foot to the other as he spoke—"if you ever want to sell, I'd be interested."

"Naw." Even as he said it, Josiah suppressed a sigh. It was a house built for a family—the laughter of loved ones and the thumps of children at play. Unless Saul changed his mind, he'd be rattling around in the place until the Lord called him home. But it wasn't time to give up hope just yet.

"All right. Just keep it in mind." Matthew held out the new crowbar. "Here you go."

"Thanks. You want cash or store credit?"

"Credit."

"I'll be seeing you." Josiah waved good-bye and headed back to his store. In the time it took to put the crowbar behind the counter, he heard someone pull up outside. It sounded like a lot of commotion for a buckboard, so he craned his neck to look through the window.

A lone Conestoga wagon—a prairie schooner—stood outside.

The tinkle of the bell above the door announced customers. Josiah straightened his apron, surprised to see two strange women entering the shop. He didn't see any men with them.

"Afternoon, ladies." He stepped out from behind the counter for a closer look. Beauties, the pair of them, but bearing the telltale signs of the trail. The young gal was enough to turn any buck's head, but Josiah focused on her companion.

Beneath her dusty bonnet peeked swirls of soft mahogany

threaded through with light touches of silver. Eyes that on anyone else would be dismissed as gray echoed the bright glint of her hair. *Now, there's a woman I wouldn't mind seeing every day.*

"Afternoon." The younger gal stepped forward, dark blond hair escaping from beneath her sunbonnet to shine in the daylight. "We were hoping you could tell us whether you've seen Hickory McGee's wagon train?"

"Two days past." Josiah heard a quickly stifled gasp. "You trying to find someone with that group?"

"We *were* 'someones' with that group." The girl muttered the words, but he heard them.

Surely the old coot hadn't kicked a family off the wagon train and left them to face the trail alone? Not even Hickory could sink so low. Josiah glanced out the window to see a lone wagon, oxen still yoked, standing outside. No men in sight.

"Two days." The silver beauty's murmur held none of the bitterness of the other. Instead, it was weighted with despair.

"Did your family start out late, hopin' to catch up?" Josiah craned his neck, looking for a father or brother—anyone—but the street remained empty.

"No." Tears shone in the older woman's eyes. "We got left behind, and if they're two days ahead, I don't see how we'll make it."

"Left behind?" Josiah had to force himself not to bellow. "Where are your men? You'd do better to wait for another train, but I can give 'em some tips on areas to skirt around so you'd have a better chance."

"Would you?" The girl pulled a pencil and a folded-up piece of paper from her worn purse. "We'd be much obliged."

Alarm bells sounded in Josiah's mind at her actions. "It'd be best if I spoke to the driver, ma'am."

She heaved a deep sigh but didn't slouch. "I'm driving."

"The two of you are alone?" He didn't bother to hide his

surprise. "Not even old Hickory would abandon two women."

"Oh yes, he would," the girl muttered again before raising her voice. "We hit a rough patch, but as time is of the essence, we really need to be on our way."

"It's late in the season to still be at this point." Josiah tried to make his words gentle. "Especially with a lone wagon. Truth of the matter, ladies, is that catching up with Hickory is a slim hope. If he left you behind once, he'll do it again." *The rat. Someone needs to teach that low-down snake a lesson or two, and I'd be happy to volunteer.* "Safest bet would be for you to stay here and join another train next summer." He watched as they reached for each other and linked arms as though trying to create a wall.

The younger woman spoke for them both. "We can't."

It didn't take an excess of brains to figure out the problem. Most folks headed West spent their money on the wagon and supplies. Time, then, wasn't the only commodity at stake. Josiah looked at the two, then beyond them through the shop windows at the house beyond.

He glanced at the gal again, affirming his impression that she'd spark an interest in any young man. If his son came to mind the store, the pair could be thrown together if he angled it right. . . . Could this be the answer to his prayers?

Josiah closed his eyes and waited for the Lord to give him that gut-wrenching sensation he always had when he'd made a poor decision.

Didn't come.

Yep. That settled it. For good or ill, he was going to invite these little ladies to stay.

Two days. Those words pounded in Clara's brain with the force of a sledgehammer, striking at her temples and sending a chill down her spine. *Two days. We're two days behind the wagon train after finding Simon and getting stuck in the mud after that rainstorm. Oh, Lord, what are we to do? So far we've clung to the hope that they're just a few miles away. That if we caught up with a full team, Hickory would accept us as part of the train. Now we know the truth.*

"Josiah Reed." The man's voice caught her attention. He gave a small bow. "Owner of Buttonwood General Store."

"Mrs. Doreen Edgerly and my niece, Miss Clara Field." Her aunt introduced them, her voice not betraying any of the worry Clara knew they shared. "Nice to meet you, Mr. Reed."

"My pleasure." The man's gaze lingered on Aunt Doreen appreciatively, making her flush a bit. "It's not often two such lovely ladies come to Buttonwood. And I do hope you'll be staying, though my motives aren't entirely selfless."

"Oh?" Clara's eyes narrowed.

"Yep." His posture slumped as he gestured around the well-kept store. "See, keeping up on everything around here is getting to be a big job. Between this and the house"—he indicated the beautiful two-story brick and wood home she and Aunt Doreen had driven past moments ago—"I could use a hand."

"Where is your family?" Aunt Doreen craned her neck as though certain some grown children and a plump wife would appear momentarily. "Surely they pitch in."

"Gladys passed on years ago, and my children are grown. When I moved here, they opted to stay behind." He brightened with pride. "Hannah's married and in a delicate condition, and Saul's just come back from studying in Edinburgh. He's a doctor." The glow left his features and he slumped once more, heaving what Clara would have called a dramatic sigh. "So I'm alone and would be more than happy to put the two of you up in exchange for some cleaning and good cooking."

"Seems like everything's well in hand." Clara couldn't help but feel Mr. Reed was hamming it up. "And you don't know us."

"Oh, Clara." Aunt Doreen's disapproval came through loud and clear. "If the man says he'd like some help, why"—she faltered for a moment before swiping a gloved hand along a shelf, leaving behind a smudge Clara would have sworn wasn't there a moment ago and triumphantly displaying her dirty palm—"who are we to gainsay him?"

"Exactly so." Mr. Reed beamed at her aunt.

Clara tried to organize the mess of thoughts whirling in her head. If Aunt Doreen was willing to use a soiled glove to convince her to stay, that spoke volumes about her aunt's exhaustion. And desperation.

You failed. Uncle Uriah's voice echoed in her memory. *You couldn't take care of yourself, much less your aunt. Women are weak and need men to look out for them.* She shook away the lump in her throat at the thought he might have been right.

Simple truth of the matter was that they couldn't catch up to the wagon train. Not with the distance so great and their resources so small. *Is this Your answer, Lord? To wait for an early wagon train in spring and start again?*

"You're very generous," she demurred, "but it's a large decision based on such a short acquaintance."

"True." Josiah Reed stroked his salt-and-pepper beard. "I am trusting the two of you with my house, store, and everything I own. But I've learned to be a good judge of character, and there's plenty of crazier things a man will do for some good cooking."

"You don't know for certain that our cooking is any good," Clara pointed out, squelching an impulse to smile at the clever way he turned her doubts back at her. "You might not be able to tell our pot roast from coal. If it comes to that, then where will we all be?"

"Clara!" Her aunt's gasp held recrimination. "I'm an excellent cook, and I taught you everything I know. How could you suggest to this man that I would leave you rudderless in the kitchen?"

"Oh, Aunt Doreen," Clara hastened to mend the breach, "I wasn't saying we can't cook. The point was that Mr. Reed doesn't know one way or another, and he's willing to hire us."

"You wouldn't have made it this far if you couldn't cook." Mr. Reed's pronouncement hit home, making Clara think of Burt Sprouse—the man whose mouth worked only for eating, making unilateral decisions, and denouncing women who didn't go along with them. He didn't bother to speak a word in their defense.

Mr. Sprouse went along with Hickory when it counted, and he'd be sure to do so again. If that happened while they were in the mountains. . .Clara shuddered at the thought.

"What would the arrangements be?" She still didn't know enough to make a decision. Things had to be fair for Mr. Reed, as well.

"I built that house hoping my children would come fill it with grandbabies, so there's plenty of room." He rubbed the back of his neck. "If you take care of the cleaning, laundry, and cooking over there and pitch in over here from time to time, I'd be more than happy to put you up. Might even say you're an answer to prayer. Room and board till the next train comes along, and I'll find a place for your oxen to hole up come winter."

An answer to prayer. The phrase rang in Clara's thoughts long after Mr. Reed stopped speaking. The possibility that this situation was a blessing to everyone involved. . ."Will you excuse us for just a moment?" Clara ushered her aunt out the door for a brief consultation. "We don't know him, and to trust him with everything we own on such short acquaintance seems foolish." *Especially after Uncle Uriah.* The thought hung between them, unspoken.

"I think we should agree." Aunt Doreen looked at her with

wide eyes. "We'll stay together, and he has no legal claim. Besides, Mr. Reed seems a good man. It's a fair deal, he's not handing out charity, and we wouldn't have to use our savings!"

"It seems like a God-given answer to the problem," Clara acknowledged. "Catching up after we found Simon would have been difficult, but there's that creaking from the rear of the wagon. We're going slow and falling farther behind."

"Two days," Aunt Doreen repeated, her expression grim. "And that's *if* the axle holds. Taking the time to repair it means a longer lag, but breaking down in the middle of the plains. . ." Her voice drifted off, but there was no mistaking her meaning.

Clara clasped her aunt's chilled hands in hers. Wisps of hair flew away from her aunt's usually meticulous bun, dark circles beneath her eyes making her older than her thirty-nine years.

They'd given up the house to creditors, almost all their savings to outfit the wagon, and their life in Boston to make a new beginning. But Clara wouldn't allow her aunt's health to pay the price for their passage. Her aunt deserved rest from this grueling pace they'd set trying to catch up, and Mr. Reed's offer would provide that. Better still, they'd have a roof over their heads and access to any foodstuffs they might need.

Haven't I been praying for You to clear the way, to enable me to provide for us on the journey? The answer seems so clear, Lord. As simply as that, Clara made her decision. She gave her aunt a slight nod, gratified to see the smile blooming across the older woman's face as they went back inside.

"Mr. Reed, we'd like to accept your offer."

"Good." Of average height, in nondescript clothing, the shop owner hadn't made too much of an impression at first.

Now that Clara really looked, she could see that Mr. Reed's eyes sparkled and a distinguished smattering of gray adorned his temples and beard. He smiled broadly, a generous stretch with no clamped corners like Uncle Uriah, who constantly pinched away the joy in life. *Maybe this will work.*

"First things first." He pulled a pair of wire-framed spectacles from his pocket and settled them on his nose. "My larder isn't well stocked, so you'll need to have pretty much everything over at the house. Flour, sugar, molasses, beans, and the like are already set aside. You two just add on as needed, and I'll keep a list for my records."

"Truly?" Aunt Doreen's eyes widened at the thought.

"What are your favorite dishes?" Clara realized that Mr. Reed probably wouldn't have a garden or a fully-stocked cellar, so vegetables would be a problem.

"Can't say I'm picky." He grinned. "Though I do have a sweet tooth. What little we do have in the way of canned fruit is over there." He indicated a shelf to their left. "Got powdered milk but not the fresh stuff. Eggs are in the crates in the corner."

He wrote while he spoke, and Clara rushed to pile things on the counter.

Aunt Doreen added potatoes, baking powder, cheese, salt pork, a ham hock, a venison roast, and a side of bacon. She looked around the store twice before declaring she couldn't find vegetables.

"Fresh vegetables come in the spring from farmers hereabouts. Other than that, we make do with whatever gets preserved." Mr. Reed shrugged. "Not a lot we can do about it so far from the railroads. We're lucky if the stage comes through once a month."

"We've plenty in the wagon," Doreen pointed out.

"Anything you use from your own supplies, keep a list," Mr. Reed ordered, "and I'll replace it come spring."

"Thank you." Clara felt some tension in her shoulders relax at his sincerity. She sent up a prayer of thanks.

"If that'll do, leave that stuff behind. I'll haul it over." Mr. Reed headed toward the door. "For now, how 'bout I show you around?"

When he offered his arm to her aunt, Clara's conviction that they'd made the right choice grew. A few steps took them away from the store, leading them to their new home. As they skirted around their wagon, a great crack sounded.

"If you wanted an assurance you made a wise decision," Mr. Reed spoke, staring as the back of their wagon tilted ominously, the oxen pulling frantically against their yokes, "I'd say you just got one."

"Just one more." Saul passed Midge another peppermint. In the week since he'd brought her to Mrs. Henderson's, the little girl had become almost unrecognizable. A good scrubbing revealed Midge's hair to be a deep red rather than the dark brown he'd seen. And she'd already outgrown the hastily hemmed dress Mrs. Henderson unearthed from an old chest and bloomed under the kindness shown her. A few more weeks of good meals and the pale urchin he'd found in an alley would be healthy.

While Midge stood smaller than most girls of her thirteen years and showed the signs of being underfed for a prolonged period, her overall health was good. No signs of illness he would have expected from her poor living conditions—fever, weak pulse, coughing, and the like—seemed to threaten her. People didn't come any more resilient than Midge, who'd born far more suffering than her years should hold and not let it destroy her.

"What color do you want for your new dress?" Saul led her over to the corner where bolts of fabric were stacked to the ceiling. "How about this?" He picked out a bolt of pink cotton. His sisters had always liked pink.

Midge, on the other hand, shrank away from the fabric as though it would bite her, pressing against his side and shaking her head. "The gents like a girl in pink." She was obviously repeating something she'd heard before. "He made Nancy wear it."

Saul stuffed the bolt back in place, jamming it against the wall as his other arm curled protectively around Midge. He stared at the fabric without seeing any of it. *What other simple things have been tainted for her?*

"Maybe the yellow?" She hesitantly pointed toward a yellow and white gingham, tucked high up in the corner.

He swung her onto a sturdy table nearby so she could pull it down. Saul didn't know much about fabric—and far less about little girls—but it seemed soft and cheery. A good choice.

He watched Midge run her hand along it then look down at him. "What do you think?" She chewed on her lower lip as though afraid she'd be denied.

He nodded. "It'll make you look like a ray of sunshine."

"I like it." Midge fingered the gingham as though it were made of golden thread. "This one, please."

"This one it is." Saul handed off the bolt to the store clerk and ordered more than Mrs. Henderson told him she'd need, just in case the hem would need to be let out or some such thing. "Now pick another."

"Really?" Midge's eyes widened until they seemed to take up her whole face. "Two more dresses? I'm to have *three*?"

"That dress was only meant to be temporary." Saul gestured to the old black wool she wore, a leftover from when Mrs. Henderson's first husband had died and her daughter wore the traditional black. "It's too hot for summer."

"I don't mind, Dr. Reed. Honest, I don't." Concern replaced the excitement on her face. "The black is fine and"—she stooped to slide off the table as she lowered her voice—"fitting. Since Nancy passed on and all."

He could hear the tears threatening to overtake her, so he squatted down beside her. "Now, Midge, we talked about this.

36

No one is to know where you came from, so he can't find you. Wouldn't Nancy want you to be safe and happy?"

"Yes, sir." She drew a shaky breath.

"In Nancy's honor, why don't you choose to have a dress in her favorite color?"

"Green." Midge didn't hesitate for a moment. "She loved green."

"Well then, green it is." He straightened as she eyed the fabric once more. "And every time you wear it, you can think of Nancy."

"She'd like that." Midge gave a tiny nod. "I know she would. 'Specially if it was a dark green."

Within moments they'd chosen a length of deep green reminiscent of a lush forest. When Saul paid for the material, he added in a few more peppermints. They were good for the stomach and, besides, Midge liked them.

As they made their way back to the house, they came upon a church. Saul stopped in front of it. "Would you like to say a prayer for your sister before we go back?"

"Naw." She shook her head vehemently. "Don't want to keep Mrs. Henderson waiting." Midge wouldn't even look at the building. Odd for such a curious child.

"Midge, why don't you want to go inside?"

"Prayers aren't worth the time they take." She glowered at the cross on the door. "Nancy prayed every day, didn't she? And see what came of it. She died, and if it weren't for you and Mrs. Henderson, I'd be stuck alone with him, wouldn't I?"

Her ferocity took him aback, but he could see why she had that perspective. It would take time before she'd see otherwise. "But you're not alone with him. That means something, doesn't it?"

"Yes." She stared at him. "And grateful I am, too. But it don't have a thing to do with prayer, Dr. Reed. Rodney was right when he talked about church. I seen it same as him."

"You saw what?"

"Sundays was good days to Rodney." Her brows drew together in a ferocious scowl. "He said customers came fresh from church, all squeaky clean so's they could afford to muck about. There's some as would come straight from church to the alley. Nancy hated Sundays, and all her prayers couldn't change that."

"Listen to me, Midge." He sank down so their eyes were level. "That was the sin of men. The men who came to that alley were wrong, but it wasn't because of church. Nancy knew that, and it's why she kept praying."

"That's what she said." Midge shrugged. "But all I seen is the wrong side, and until I see the good part, praying is a waste of breath." She must have seen the sadness in his face, because she gave him an awkward pat on the shoulder. "Don't be put out by it, Doctor. I know there are good men, too. You're one of them."

"You said Nancy would see your mother in heaven," he pointed out. "If you don't believe in prayer, how can you believe in that?"

"Simple." She raised one brow. "Mama told us, and she were one of the good'uns, too. The way I figure it, if prayers work, it's only after you've gone to meet your Maker. Either way, it don't do much good while we're here."

Her words haunted him throughout the day and into the evening as he paced around his room. With all Midge had seen, her conclusions were logical. Problem was she based her understanding of the spiritual in the physical. How could he make her see how different the two were?

Lord, how do I reach her? If I'd pressed the issue, she would have gone inside and said a prayer. But she would have done it to please me, not because she believed in Your love. She needs to see Your hand in the world, despite the terrible things men do to each other. Here, it seems as though everything, even church, reminds her of the evil she's seen. It's a battle I'm unprepared for.

Between his pacing and the heat of the fire in the grate, he soon grew warm. Saul took off his jacket and laid it over the back of a chair, only to have it slither to the floor in a crumpled heap. He hung it up properly before the envelope caught his eye—the letter he'd gotten the day he found Midge. He picked it up, breaking the seal as he settled in the chair.

My son,

You know your sister is in the family way and I want to be there for the birth of my first grandchild. I'm not getting any younger, and you're not getting married in a hurry, so it may well be my only chance. If it's a boy, they're going to name it Josiah. But if I'm going to be there when my namesake enters the world, someone's got to look after the store.

That's where you come in. I want you to hop on the stage and come to Buttonwood for a few weeks. Take care of things as a favor to your old man now and set up your fancy city practice when you get back.

Who knows? You might find the gal you want right here in town. At the very least, you can breathe some fresh air for a change.

Love,
Your father

Saul smiled. Dad had been trying to get him to settle down for years, never understanding the time it took to train properly. Now that he'd returned to America, his father was more determined than ever to needle him into marriage.

He ran his palm down his face. The building he had his eye on to become his office wouldn't be vacated for another month. And Hannah'd categorically refused to let him deliver his niece or nephew—no matter that he was a trained professional.

A peaceful little town on the Oregon Trail would certainly make for a change of pace. *Midge.* A small town of good people would go a long way toward helping heal her. Propriety dictated he couldn't travel alone with her, but Mrs. Henderson would probably bring her once he'd gotten everything ready.

It'd do Dad good to see Hannah, Saul could certainly watch over the store, and Midge could relax far away from her past. The slow, easy pace of life on the prairie could be just what they both needed. Buttonwood sounded like a godsend.

He rose to his feet, grabbed ink and parchment, and began to draft his reply.

CHAPTER 4

"I never thought to see brick all the way out here." Clara surveyed the large house with curiosity.

"Everyone pretty much starts out in a soddy or a dugout." Mr. Reed led them around the back of the house.

A modest distance away stood an outhouse and one of the earthen homes that dotted the Oregon Trail. Dug straight into the dirt, with a slanted, mud-packed roof over the pit and blocked steps leading down to the entry, it seemed sad and dank.

"I built the big house after the store turned a respectable profit in hopes of talking my son into setting up his practice here." He turned toward a side door to the grander residence. "I special ordered these bricks from an old friend. Shipping 'em all here cost an arm and a leg."

Clara raised her brows and shot Aunt Doreen a glance at his casual mention of such an expenditure. Obviously, Mr. Reed's pockets were deep long before he came to Buttonwood and set up shop. It made a person wonder why he left a comfortable city life to rough it in a dirt hole. Of course, so many people back home wondered why she and Aunt Doreen chose to travel West, she had no room to speculate.

She moved closer as Mr. Reed opened the door to what looked to be a new kitchen, with a open-hearth fireplace in the far corner paired with a generous working table. Across the room, a large hutch guarded a door in the opposite wall. Clara could only assume it led to a pantry.

"Oh," Aunt Doreen breathed as she stepped into the room, trailing her fingers across the sturdy mantel over the hearth. She moved toward the worktable, tilting her head to peruse the shelf above it.

A jumble of items sat together—mixing bowls, sifter, pie tins, roasting pan, measuring cups, and more. If Clara were to guess, she'd say none of it had seen any use. Despite the assortment, the area boasted only one hook with a single skillet adorning the wall. Kettles and pots heaped together beneath the worktable. Slumped against one another in despair, the cookware gave the impression of once waiting in orderly stacks for a purpose that never arrived.

Until now. This muddle of a magnificent kitchen convinced Clara as nothing else could that Josiah Reed genuinely needed their help. She and Aunt Doreen would put his kitchen—and perhaps more—in order before they left.

"Don't say I didn't warn you," Reed reminded as he crossed the room and opened the door to a disgracefully bare pantry. "I would've stocked up before the end of fall, but during the warmer months I don't keep much here when the store's so near."

"May I?" Clara gestured to the closed cabinets of the pine hutch. Up close, she could see the thin veil of dust coating the entire piece.

At his nod, her fingers closed around one smooth knob and she tugged, finding a hodgepodge of dishes littering the shelves. A drawer beneath revealed a clatter of utensils. Forks clashed with knives, spoons bowed timidly away from the fray, and faded paper liner bore the brunt of the battle. Another compartment unearthed the silverware case. The deep depressions in its molded velvet stared up, rich and lonely.

Like Mr. Reed, his untouched kitchen, and his grand, empty house in the middle of the prairie. Clara closed the lid and slid the case away, only to realize the others were leaving. She hastily followed them past the door, to the dining room.

"Your room will be this way, if you like." Mr. Reed didn't linger over the oval table dominating the long, bare room. Instead, he moved into a narrow hallway of sorts. He bypassed the first door with a muttered, "Mud room," and came to a halt beside the other.

"How lovely!" Aunt Doreen exclaimed before Clara got a good look at the space. "Such beautiful windows!" She went over to trace the leaded panes melding waves of glass together.

"Yes." Clara couldn't tear her gaze from the softened view of the prairie. Here there were no parched stretches of land where dirt dried into gray scales and grass grew as brittle as the ends of an old broom. The window blurred the landscape to a mixed mist of browns and green below and blue above—an oasis nursed by the waters of the Platte River.

"There's a door to the outside?" Her aunt pulled it open. "We can get to the kitchen and the washroom from right here!"

"I planned it that way in case of harsh winters." Mr. Reed's voice came from the doorway, where he hovered respectfully. "It's easier to heat just the downstairs and have quick access to the outdoors and such."

"Ingenious." Aunt Doreen looked at Mr. Reed with such admiration he practically beamed.

"There are plenty of empty rooms upstairs but"—he cleared his throat—"I thought you might want to stay close to each other."

"It's also good to be close to the kitchen," Clara agreed. Mr. Reed's decision would maintain propriety. It also dissipated any worries she or Aunt Doreen might harbor were they in separate rooms upstairs.

"After weeks in the wagon, staying in any house seems like a luxury." Her aunt moved toward the dresser on the opposite wall. "Staying here is. . ."

"A great favor to me," Mr. Reed filled in when Doreen couldn't find the words. "Having you two around will make the house less empty, and I won't have to fuss around the place."

"We'll see to everything," Clara promised. Her resolve strengthened as Mr. Reed led them through the rest of the house. An air of abandonment hung over the still parlor. The wood of the stairwell banisters, while smooth, held no cheerful gleam. No flowers, photographs, or art enlivened the walls of the foyer as they climbed to the second floor.

Sheets twisted on the bed, towels slouched over the back of a chair, and thick curtains shut out any glimmer of sunlight in the master bedroom. A guest room bore no signs of occupancy. The worn quilt on the bed sagged toward the floor. One washstand and trunk huddled together on another wall as though joining forces against the sparseness all around.

While Mr. Reed wouldn't open the door to his office, the other two rooms boasted nothing but dust. No furniture claimed space, no hooks or pegs stood out from the walls, and no curtains hung over the windows. The barrenness of it all made Clara itch to weave rugs, stitch samplers, piece together quilts, lug in old bedsteads, sew cushions, and fill the space with signs of love and use.

A swift glance at Aunt Doreen told the same story. Her hands locked together as though clutching an imaginary lifeline. Silently, they made their way back outside.

"First thing we need to do is move your things out here." Mr. Reed's words stabbed at Clara.

"We can't put all that in your house," she declined with more vehemence than she intended. Putting their treasured belongings all over the place would be akin to settling here for good, which wasn't a possibility.

"You wouldn't want to haul everything upstairs." Mr. Reed's thin smile told her he knew there was more to her objection. "I planned to hitch up my buckboard and bring things over to the soddy. That way you can unpack what you'll need, and we'll be able to have Kevin Burn—he's our blacksmith but does a bit of everything—take a look at that axle."

"Perfect!" Aunt Doreen hurried after Mr. Reed, leaving Clara to follow. The two of them stayed at the wagon while he went to get his buckboard and mule from the stables, also managed by the Burns.

"Here we are." Mr. Reed pulled up in his buckboard, but another pulled up alongside it. Three strangers jumped out of the second one to line up alongside Mr. Reed. "This here's Kevin Burn and his sons, Matthew and Brett. Fellows, meet Mrs. Doreen Edgerly and Miss Clara Field."

"Nice to meet you," the father said. His sons quickly followed his lead. "Josiah told us you've hit a spot of trouble and plan to stay for a while, so we thought we'd lend a hand."

"Thank you." Clara couldn't help but compare all four of them to Hickory McGee and Burt Sprouse. Needless to say, the residents of Buttonwood, a town she'd not even known existed a few days ago, made a better impression than the men who'd traveled alongside her for weeks on end. Who, but for God's grace, she'd still be catering to.

The burly blacksmith and his sons unloaded things quickly, until everything she and Aunt Doreen owned stood in the backs of the buckboards.

"I'll drive it over," the youngest of the three Burns volunteered for the job, shooting a smile toward Clara.

She gave him a light nod in return. Encouraging his attention would do no good, since she and Aunt Doreen would be leaving come spring. Instead, she needed to focus on the task at hand. "What can we do about the oxen?"

"I'll take the wagon over to the shop," Mr. Burn explained, "and Matthew will take the oxen over to the Fossets'. Frank's a reasonable man and will probably be glad to take them on for a while. We'll strike some kind of arrangement."

"Perhaps I should speak with Mr. Fosset." Clara spoke softly but tried to remind them just whose oxen they discussed—and who would be obligated by whatever arrangement was made.

"No need for that." Burn shrugged off her concern. "We'll see to it while you and your aunt settle in. Folks look after each other around Buttonwood."

With that, the men were moving again, leaving Clara and Aunt Doreen with little choice but to follow the buckboards back to the dugout. With two of the men looking after the wagon and oxen, it took considerably longer to unload everything.

As the men hefted heavy items into the soddy, she and Aunt Doreen sorted things. The two women set aside any boxes, crates, trunks, and bags they remembered as having things they'd need. Any cookware they hadn't seen counterparts to in the kitchen went in one pile, along with produce and foodstuffs. Their clothing and toiletries sat in trunks, ready to be carried to the house. Almost everything else, from dishes to the rocking chair, went to the soddy.

Another mound of items sat next to her aunt, so Clara went to investigate. Sure enough, she found a stockpile of things obviously squirreled away for the house.

"We don't need this." Clara retrieved a quilt from the pile Aunt Doreen kept adding to. "Or this." She picked up a framed sampler and tucked it under her arm.

"We can put them in our room," Aunt Doreen protested. "It's good to have a touch of home around you."

"That's just it." Clara set down the items and perched on a trunk. She lowered her voice so it wouldn't carry. "This isn't home for us. We have to remember that."

"I know." Aunt Doreen pulled a handkerchief from her sleeve and dabbed her forehead. "But a few things are a good reminder."

"This?" Clara held up the sampler, a verse stitched across the face. " 'As for me and my house, we will serve the Lord,' " she read aloud before looking at her aunt. "This isn't our household, Aunt Doreen. It's Mr. Reed's."

"I don't know what I was thinking." The older woman sighed. "The last thing I'd want is for that kind man to see it on the wall and be offended."

"Yes. I'm more concerned about you growing attached to Buttonwood." Clara stood back up. "It's a nice town, but in spring we'll be heading out to Oregon. If we settle in, well, that'll make things more difficult when it's time to leave."

"Makes sense." Her aunt replaced the lid on a crate. "This winter might be a good time to work on your drawing." The hopeful suggestion made Clara wince. "Mr. Reed says we'll be snowed in a great deal of the time after November, and it'd be nice to leave him something to remember us by."

"We'll see." Clara grudgingly added her own art set to the last mound of things they'd take inside. Why she'd never been able to capture the likeness of things in charcoal was an irksome mystery. She'd learned every other lesson quickly—cooking, sewing, managing a household, dressing appropriately, engaging in light conversation, and playing both the pianoforte and flute—but her list of accomplishments ended there.

"Don't look so glum, Clara." Aunt Doreen smiled. "Try to think of it as another form of expression, like writing in your journal or playing your flute." She cast an anxious glance around. "Have we found it?"

"Right here." At the start of their journey, Clara had taken it out and played a little tune, only to be told by a glowering Hickory McGee that he couldn't abide 'screeching through a metal tube.' He advised her to put it far back in her wagon and leave it there until they'd reached Oregon.

"Oh, good. Mr. Reed seems the type to enjoy fine music." Aunt Doreen braced the small of her back. "Is that everything?"

"I believe so." Clara gathered her flute, sewing kit, and art set before snatching the quilt she'd put aside earlier. If it made her aunt happy, a simple thing like a quilt shouldn't cause any problems. She waited while Aunt Doreen gathered her own art and sewing supplies then walked with her back to the big, empty house.

How awful it would be to have no family nearby. She snuck a glance at her aunt. If Doreen hadn't taken her in after her parents' accident, she'd know that deep loneliness firsthand.

Which is why it's so important to get to Oregon, where the land is fertile for gardening and we can make our own way taking in mending and so forth. Aunt Doreen took care of me; now it's my turn to look after her. She squelched the reminder that she'd already experienced failure. Hickory kicking them off the wagon train made for a harsh blow.

Which was exactly why she had to protect her aunt from further heartache. The more rooms they spread their things about in, the more settled they'd feel. Just like a mother bird tucking bits of fluff into her nest, Aunt Doreen would make herself at home.

Looking around, Clara had to stamp down her own urge to make her mark on the place. It took a stern reminder—the same one she gave her aunt when they packed the wagon. *The more we bring, the more we stand to lose along the way.*

If Clara could prevent it, her aunt wouldn't lose so much as a hairpin during their stay in Buttonwood.

❧ ⌘ ☙

Midge watched as the patch of sunshine grew longer, slanting toward her bed. When it crept up to where her toes made tiny lumps under the blankets, she threw back the covers and leaped onto the bedside rug. Arms over her head, fingers waggling, she gave a mighty stretch on her way to the washbasin. Her new yellow dress hung on a peg by the door, bright and clean.

And just for me.

She pulled it on carefully, tugging it into place instead of yanking it over her head like she had with her old one. That dress didn't exist anymore. Mrs. Henderson said it fell to pieces in the wash, not even fit for the rag bag. Midge didn't miss it.

When she really thought about it, she didn't miss much from her old life. Not the sour-smelling dark room, not the way Rodney slapped her for being in his way, not the way she'd huddled on the cold ground outside while Nancy worked. She only missed her sister.

Her nose tingled like it did when she was about to cry, so she rubbed it. Hard. *Crying never makes no difference.*

Besides, she didn't want to get her pretty new dress all wet. That'd be a fine thank-you when Mrs. Henderson made it special for her—coming downstairs all wrung out and mopey. She gave a great sniff and reached for the apron she'd sewn while Mrs. Henderson worked.

She liked Mrs. Henderson but didn't like the way the woman would look at her sideways, all worried. Mrs. Henderson thought Midge didn't see, but she did.

Those glances started when Midge said she didn't want to go to church. Maybe it would be easier to go. Making Mrs. Henderson and Dr. Reed happy was real important. She nodded. That's what she'd do—tell them over breakfast that she'd changed her mind. If it meant so much to them, it couldn't be that bad. They were some of the good'uns.

Ready for the day, she moved to the small, circular window of her attic room and opened the shutters wide. No matter how bad things got, she could always count on the city to be busy. So full of noise and movement, the streets used to beckon to her to lose herself in them until darkness fell. Today she looked over them as though surveying her kingdom. She still claimed the city but stayed out of its reach.

Soft yellow light flooded her room now, resting on her new dress like she was part of the sunbeam. Midge gave a quick twirl before going to make her bed. She never had a real bed to make before, so she did it extra careful, folding the corners and fluffing her pillow just so before she finished.

Then she made her way down the back stairs to the kitchen, going slow so she wouldn't trip in the dark.

Dr. Reed and Mrs. Henderson were already in the kitchen. She could hear their voices. Midge started to speed up but stopped herself. Adults didn't take kindly to interruptions, so she'd wait a bit.

"You plan to go, then." Mrs. Henderson's words made Midge suck in her breath.

Who? Who was going? Not Dr. Reed!

"If you'll take Midge. . ." Dr. Reed didn't say where, but it didn't matter. Not really.

They're getting rid of me. She plunked down on the stairs, not even caring that her dress might get dusty. What did she do wrong? Was it church? She had to tell them she'd go. Maybe it would change their minds!

Midge bolted to her feet and burst through the door. "Please don't take me away. I'll go to church. I promise!" She grasped Mrs. Henderson's skirts. "Please?"

"What do. . .oh, child." Her hand came to rest on Midge's head, stroking her hair. "You don't understand."

"I came down the stairs and heard you." She hated the quavery sound of her voice, but she'd let them see her cry if she had to. Dr. Reed had already seen her do it once.

"Midge," Dr. Reed knelt beside her as he spoke, "I have to go to the Nebraska Territory for a little while to watch my father's store."

"I don't want you to go." She transferred her hold from Mrs. Henderson's skirts to his jacket sleeve. "Stay here."

"Even if Mrs. Henderson brought you to Nebraska once I had things ready?" His words took a while to sink in.

"You mean. . .we'd still be together?" She darted a glance at Mrs. Henderson. "All of us?"

"I'd bring you to him, dearie, but I wouldn't stay in Nebraska unless absolutely necessary. You'll see me when you both come back."

"We'll come back?" She tugged on the doctor's sleeve.

"Yes. Going to Buttonwood will be like an adventure."

"Buttonwood?" She wrinkled her nose. "That's a funny name for a town.

"It's a very tiny town by a river, with lots of land around it." He straightened up, but she still kept her grip.

"And we'd come back here," she repeated. "Do you promise, Dr. Reed?"

"I promise." He looked like he meant it, so she let go.

"All right then. When do we leave?"

"A couple of days after I go. Because you'll take the stage, it will take weeks for you to catch up, though. Would you want to start out later?"

"The sooner the better." She decided not to tell them what her sister used to say, "The sooner things get started, the quicker they're done."

CHAPTER 5

A motley group of folks pushed toward them after church the next morning. Not that Josiah thought himself one to judge, but even he could tell that the residents of Buttonwood would seem like an odd mishmash to his new guests.

The fact that everyone had gaped at them all through the service hadn't helped any, either. Despite the Burns swiftly settling into the pew behind him, Josiah had to employ his best scowl to keep the worst offenders at bay. Even so, the time of reckoning—one could even say judgment—had come.

Appropriately enough, it began with the parson walking up to them. "Nice to see new faces in the congregation this morning." He waited expectantly for an introduction and, it seemed to Josiah, an explanation.

"Mrs. Edgerly and Miss Field are my new staff," he began. "They'll be taking over my housekeeping, cooking, and lending a hand at the store as needed. They share the downstairs room." Josiah made sure to put a little extra emphasis on the words "share" and "downstairs," just to be clear.

"Pleased to meet you." The parson gave a small bow. "How did you come to Buttonwood?"

"We ran into some trouble on the trail and"—Miss Field paused before finishing—"had to separate from our wagon train."

"Trouble?" Lucinda Grogan shouldered her way into the conversation, eyes agleam with speculation.

"One of our oxen wandered off at an inopportune time, so we fell behind," Mrs. Edgerly elaborated on her niece's statement. "When we arrived in Buttonwood, we met Mr. Reed. He mentioned his need of help, and our axle gave way. It seemed best all around for us to stay. Today's our first full day in town."

"A convenient solution." Lucinda's eyes narrowed as she turned her attention to Josiah. "Though, Mr. Reed, if you needed help, my Willa would have been glad to take on some odd jobs."

Interfering old buzzard. He inhaled sharply before answering. "I figured you needed her at home."

"Mrs. Edgerly? Miss Field?" Kevin brought Frank Fosset to the forefront of their group. "This is Frank Fosset, who's agreed to look after your oxen until spring."

"Thank you, Mr. Fosset." Miss Field looked the man over, and Josiah wondered if she noticed what he always had—with a thick chest, short legs, and a lumbering gait, Fosset resembled nothing so much as the oxen he sold to travelers.

"No trouble," he grunted. "This is my wife, Nora, and my eldest daughter, Sally."

"Welcome to Buttonwood!" Sally reached out to clasp Miss Field's hand. "Opal and Amanda and I are so glad to have another girl here."

"And Willa." Lucinda Grogan all but spat out a tooth with her words. "My Willa will be a good friend to you." Bitter determination edged the statement as she yanked Miss Field's hand away from Sally and pulled her toward Willa.

Josiah stepped back. The women may be new to town, but they'd have to navigate the other hens on their own terms. It'd take a man with less between his ears to step into the path of a warring Grogan. He made a note to tell Mrs. Edgerly and Miss Field about the Grogan-Speck feud that night.

If they hadn't already learned firsthand.

◦◦◦◦

"Those wretched Specks and their friends think they own this town," Mrs. Grogan muttered darkly as she tugged Clara away from her aunt. Obviously, the woman bore ill will toward that sweet Sally Fosset and, Clara decided, some family with the unfortunate surname of Speck.

"Where are you off to in such a hurry, Ma?" One young man broke away from the group they passed and fell into step beside them. He spoke to Mrs. Grogan but kept his eyes on Clara.

"I thought I'd introduce Miss Field here to our Willa." Mrs. Grogan's already firm grip tightened when Clara tried to pull away. "Miss Field, meet my son, Larry."

"We're always glad to see another pretty gal in town." This, paired with something of a smirk, came out loudly enough for the entire town to hear. Larry went a step further by trying to take Clara's arm, but they'd already arrived.

She took the opportunity to pull away from both mother and son to approach the daughter. Miss Willa Grogan wore a patched calico dress and a wary expression. She seemed long used to her family's overbearing ways and tried to fade into the background so she'd be overlooked. Clara's heart immediately went out to this girl who reminded her of a young Aunt Doreen.

"You must be Willa." She gave a heartfelt smile, ignoring the way Larry puffed out his chest when he saw it. "I'm Clara Field. Your mother thought you might be able to help me get settled into things around Buttonwood?"

"Of course." The girl's eyes widened. "Everyone wants to meet you, hear where you're from, and such forth."

"Exactly." Sally Fosset, another young woman in tow, huffed up to them. "It's good for the town to have new blood."

"Maybe put aside old differences," Sally's friend added. Like Willa, she wore a patched, sun-bleached calico dress. There, the resemblance ended. This girl stood straight and tall, a smattering of freckles marched proudly across the bridge of her nose, and she met Lucinda Grogan's hostile gaze without flinching.

Clara liked her immediately, though she sensed this girl's presence was the root of the tension between Sally Fosset and Lucinda Grogan. When they'd walked up, Lucinda had drawn back, her breath sucking in a rapid hiss. Larry alternately leered at Sally and glowered at her friend, while Willa proved Clara right and somehow began to blend into the background.

Clara couldn't resist trying to get to the bottom of the problem. "Old differences?" She echoed the words as though confused, hoping for an elaboration.

"Another Speck trying to stir the pot again." Lucinda all but growled the words, and one of the missing pieces fell into place.

Clara eyed Sally's friend with new understanding. The girl belonged to the Speck family then. *What is the story there?* Wracking her brain for a way to find the answer without deepening the rift, she ran out of time.

"Opal isn't doing anything wrong," Sally defended. "I had to practically drag her over here to meet Clara!"

"Not that I didn't want to welcome you to Buttonwood," Opal Speck hastily added.

"I appreciate it." Clara could barely bite back her smile at the contrast between Sally's indignation, Lucinda's ire, and Opal's exasperation with the entire situation. If the whole mess—whatever it was—weren't tearing people apart, it would be downright funny.

"You should have let her stay with her kin." Larry stopped

leering at Sally to frown at her. He jerked his head toward Opal as though she were a feral animal and spoke slowly. "Specks should stay where they belong." This didn't sound like petty sniping any longer. Larry's tone held a note of warning, perhaps even threat.

Clara's amusement fled as an angry flush colored Opal's cheeks, Lucinda gave a self-righteous nod, and Willa shrank into herself even more.

Clara fought to keep her tone light but didn't bother to hide the conviction behind her words. "I'm pleased to meet Miss Speck and glad to see Miss Fosset again. In fact, it seems to me that all of us young ladies probably share a lot in common and should spend some time together." Who was this man—who didn't even have the pretext of family connection—to order Opal around?

"That sounds like a fine idea." Sally tilted her nose in the air and linked arms with Opal. "Let's go."

"Just a moment." Clara turned back to the Grogans. "Willa, why don't you come with us?"

"Really?" A glint of hope shone in the girl's dark eyes as she looked from Clara to the other girls. "Well, I. . ."

"Have supper to get on the table." Her mama gripped her elbow and began to steer her away. She directed a fulminating glare at Opal. "We won't have slothful ways rubbing off on our Willa."

"Opal ain't lazy." An adolescent boy of about thirteen rushed to her defense, his scowl growing more fierce when his voice cracked and Larry chuckled at him. "She's worth more than a whole passel of Grogans any day."

"Easy, Pete." Opal put an arm around his shoulders, making Clara think he must be her brother. "This is the Lord's day."

"I know it." He squirmed away, his mussed-up hair sticking straight on end. "That's why I said *any* day."

"Watch what you say, boy." An older man pushed his way

through. A sagging hat brim hid his eyes, but Clara could see the set of his jaw beneath a grizzled beard. Mean—just like Uncle Uriah. "There's a price on every word."

Clara shifted, placing herself more fully between the man and the boy. Her head spun with trying to sort out the identity of these people. The only thing that helped was the hair color of everyone involved. From what she could tell, the fiery Speck family boasted varying shades of red locks, while the stormy Grogans sported pitch-black tresses. Something brushed her sleeve, and she was surprised to see Opal moving next to her. The other girl didn't say a word, didn't push her away, just stood beside her.

"Don't threaten my brother." An older version of Pete shoved Lucinda away from the older man, who Clara assumed was Mr. Grogan. "Your wife insulted my sister first."

"I didn't so much as speak her name." Lucinda sniffed before abandoning her show of refinement to reveal the malice beneath. "Why waste my breath on a Speck?"

"Why waste air on breathin'?" A man Clara would have taken as twin to Mr. Grogan, were it not for the fact he stood half a foot taller and a considerable amount of stomach larger, jumped into the fray. A closer look revealed coppery hair that seemed a mark of the Speck family. "Seems like if you kept your trap shut, things would be easier for everyone."

"Don't insult my wife, Speck." Mr. Grogan's hands clenched as he took a step forward. "Even a mongrel like you should know to show respect to a lady."

"I always show respect to a lady." Mr. Speck tipped his hat toward Clara in a show of fine manners before folding his arms over his chest. "Anytime I see one."

By now, folks from town had recognized the disturbance. Clara tried not to be too perturbed that while they gathered round the fighting families everyone else kept a healthy distance. Everyone, that is, save her and Sally. Now that she looked, she realized Sally was stealthily edging away from the fray, and Clara wondered if it would be prudent to do the same. Even Lucinda had wandered toward the fringes with Willa. Only she and Opal stood in the eye of the storm.

"You're gonna eat them words, Speck." Larry began to shrug out of his coat, an ominous sign at best.

"Nope. I'll have a healthy appetite come suppertime." Speck started loosening his collar. "Opal, darlin', why don't you go and check on that while the boys and I take care of this?"

"It's not right, Pa." Opal's voice quavered on the last word, but she stood firm. "This is the Lord's day, and we have new folks in town, and I can't get out of the way so it's easier for you to have a brawl."

"Honor your father, heathen." This from Larry, who looked like he would've said more but stopped when a lone figure rode up on a mammoth horse. The self-satisfied smile on his face didn't make Clara feel any better.

"I knew it would be nothing good when you were late." A tall young man dismounted and stalked into the middle of everything. He gave a swift glance around as though assessing the situation.

Clara didn't have to wonder which family he belonged to. The dismay on Opal's face spoke as eloquently as the smug expression on Larry's. Still, she clung to hope. This man seemed like he might have a smidge of good sense and reason amid tempers.

"Miss Speck," the man took off his hat as he spoke, "I suggest you get out of the way. You, too, miss." His words obliterated Clara's hope. . .and her last shred of patience.

"This is ridiculous." She planted one hand atop her hat and fisted one on her hip, staring at each one of the Specks, the Grogans, and the assorted crowd of do-nothings. "There's no cause for any violence here today."

" 'Blessed are the peacemakers!'" The parson called. . .from afar.

"Ma'am"—the newcomer took a deep breath—"with all due respect, this is about more than you can know. So you and Opal need to get out of the way and let the men settle things."

That did it. Even though Clara had wondered the same thing just moments before, no man would order her around—especially when they hadn't been so much as introduced. And particularly not so he could use fists instead of reason.

No gentleman would engage in fisticuffs with women in the midst of the fray. At least, not with her there. With the animosity between families, she couldn't be so certain about Opal's safety. Fact of the matter was, Clara's presence kept things in check—if only just barely.

"I'm not moving. You're all going to have to be gentlemen enough not to endanger a lady, fight publicly, or break the Lord's day." She lifted her chin. "I'll have to assume that the first one to start the fight represents the family whose reputation has the least to lose."

"And it won't be the Specks," Opal announced loudly. "We're God-fearing folk. Right, Pa?"

After spluttering for a few seconds, he agreed.

Not to be outdone, Lucinda pushed her way forward. "Don't think it will be the Grogans!"

"Excellent." Clara put on a wide smile. "Now, Mr. Speck mentioned supper, and I'd suppose everyone here is more than ready for a good meal at home." She waited a moment, locking gazes with Lucinda and raising her brows meaningfully.

As the crowd broke up, Opal turned toward her. "Thank you."

"It was the least I could do." Clara shrugged. "I gather your families bear tension from a while past but typically avoid each other. Sally wanting to introduce you to me is what caused the entire mess, so I had to try to fix it."

"I've been trying to fix it my whole life." Opal sighed. "I can't seem to get through to my father and brothers though."

"That's the other thing," Clara confided. "When that other fellow told me to move, it set my back up. He doesn't so much as know my name! What makes a man think, no matter what the circumstances, he has the right to tell a woman what to do?"

CHAPTER 6

Fort Laramie, Oregon Trail

Why did women never listen? Saul Reed refused to consider the lack of logic behind his frustration as he tried to reason with the frazzled mother in front of him.

"Now, Mrs. Geer, was it?" He waited for her to nod. Saul only asked to get her to agree with him. If he could begin that pattern, it would bode well for the rest of the visit.

"My name don't matter." She crossed her arms and stood in the small doorway of the narrow room in the far corner of Fort Laramie, where the officers had put her and her children. "You're not going to so much as step inside this door. Last one—army doctor, he was—came in for two minutes, told me I was doing everything possible already, and wanted me to pay him. Threatened to have us kicked from the fort." Her thin frame shook with indignation—or exhaustion—as she spoke. "Go away."

"I don't care about money." He shifted his saddlebag, with its specially designed medical compartments, to his other shoulder and maneuvered closer. "Let me see your son."

"No money?" She blinked. "We got nothing to trade."

"That doesn't matter." Saul heard the sounds of far too many people crammed into a small space. Tiny whispers hurriedly shushed told him that, if what he'd heard was true, more than one child was in danger. "Your children matter."

"Mama!" A sudden jerking of the woman's skirts had her twisting around. "Billy's worse."

"Come on then!" Mrs. Geer threw open the door and hastened to the far end of a miserably hot room, where a small figure lay beside a fire.

"Get the rest of the children out of here immediately." Saul didn't bother softening the order as he knelt at the sick child's side. Billy, a boy of about six, lay on his back, rasping for air. His face flushed with fever; his chest worked desperately for each breath. "Diphtheria. Croup," he clarified, using the more common name for the contagious ailment, which struck without warning, leaving dozens of children dead.

"That's what the other doctor said." Mrs. Geer reached for a small pot of steaming liquid, dipping a quill into it. She tilted her son's head back and prepared to drop the mixture of what Saul already knew would be boiled sulfur or brimstone into his nostrils. It would do no good.

"Stop. That never helps."

"Neither did the earthworm mash." She sat back on her heels, disconsolate, as Saul brushed her aside and inspected the patient's throat.

White membranes blocked the boy's throat almost entirely, the obvious source of his difficulty breathing. This, the most urgent threat, would have to be dealt with immediately. Billy, lost in his fever, hadn't begun to turn blue. The heat in the room suffused his skin with color, but that wouldn't make a difference if it was too late.

"How old is your eldest son?" Saul hadn't made a thorough inspection of the troop rushing out the door, but he thought he'd seen a tall adolescent. The mother, so obviously weakened by exhaustion and worry, wouldn't be strong enough to help.

"Fifteen. Do we need him?" At Saul's nod, she yelled, "Amos!"

He came in so swiftly Saul knew everyone hovered just outside, waiting to see whether or not little Billy would make it. Saul offered a prayer that the child would survive.

"Mrs. Geer, I'll need an empty bucket. Amos, you are to help me hold your brother upside down over the bucket." He picked up the now-abandoned quill. "Amos will hold Billy by the legs while I brace his shoulders and use the feather to tickle his throat. We're trying to make him cough up the blockage. Ready?"

No one asked questions, and in just a moment, Amos held his brother over the bucket Mrs. Geer held below. Saul braced the unconscious youngster's shoulder with one hand and clutched the feather with the other. In this position, the boy's mouth fell open, so it wasn't too hard to hit his gag reflex.

He couldn't do any more to dislodge the membranes than make the boy retch. At first, dry heaves. Then the thin, sour stream of bile. Saul prayed and tried again. If the blockage didn't come out, the boy's chances of survival were slim. This time, a deep, wracking cough produced the desired results.

"That's it!" Together, he and Amos lowered the child back to his pallet on the floor. Saul inspected Billy's throat once more, satisfied to see almost none of the white patch remaining.

Already, the child breathed much more easily.

"You cured him!" Awe filled Amos's voice.

"No, I didn't." Saul shrugged out of his coat, now that Billy wouldn't suffocate before his eyes. "Bank the fire and bring plenty of cool water to help bring his fever down. We need a hearty broth to keep up his strength, too."

"He's still sick?" Mrs. Geer stroked the boy's hair.

"Yes. The blockage in his throat is one symptom, the fever

another. Now that Billy can breathe, we have to bring down the fever." Saul gentled his voice. "Otherwise, his heart will stop."

"No." She turned a stricken face toward him. "Cool cloths, hearty broth. . .what more can I do?"

"Don't keep the room so hot anymore, and give him as much water as he will hold to flush out the sickness."

"Calomel?" She named a well-known diuretic.

"No, nothing harsh. He should wake up as the fever goes down, so no laudanum or opium. Those will keep him asleep so we can't gauge his progress." Saul opened his bag and pulled out a package. He measured some of the leaves into a twist of paper. "This is slippery elm. Boil the leaves into a tea and give it to him to help with the soreness."

"Yes, Doctor." Respect and gratitude warred with worry.

"I'll go check your other children. They need to be kept separated from Billy. If any of them begins to feel ill, starts coughing, or has any symptoms, isolate that one as well. Amos is probably old enough he's not in as much danger, but it's best he stay away, too, unless needed."

"This is our only place." She wrung her hands over her apron. "I have seven children."

"The fort's commanding officer will give you an extra room after I speak with him." Saul could see three other rooms next to the small one occupied by the Geers, none bearing any signs of activity. Fort Laramie's status as a military outpost meant few children—the Geers presence here was temporary. Most importantly, though, it meant Billy's illness wouldn't cause an epidemic.

"Thank you, Doctor."

"We'll see." Saul gathered his things. "I need to look over your other children, and Billy isn't out of the woods yet."

It took the rest of the day to sort out the Geer family, who'd lost their father a while back. None of the other children exhibited symptoms, but Saul knew all too well that by the time diphtheria made its presence known, there was little anyone could do. In truth, there wasn't much to do in any case.

He took care of a bruise from a nasty fall, a cut which should have been stitched but hadn't been, and a rash plaguing a few of the youngsters before he set off to talk with the commanding officer of the fort.

It didn't take long before he was ushered into Major William Hoffman's office. The commanding officer of Fort Laramie sat behind a massive wooden desk, thoughtfully chomping the end of an unlit cigar. No ashtrays or spittoons littered the orderly room, leading Saul to wonder whether Major Hoffman ever actually smoked or if the cigar was for effect.

"Major." Saul waited until the man gestured for him to sit.

"Diphtheria, was it?" He stopped chewing as he waited for the answer. "Hate to think that assistant surgeon is right but hate to think he's treating my men if he doesn't know what he's about."

"Diphtherial croup, yes." Saul considered his words carefully. "The boy almost suffocated today, though he's breathing well now. I managed to expel the membranes blocking his airway, so he has a fighting chance if the toxins don't stop his heart. The main concern, now, is the other children."

"Not a problem, Doctor." The chomping resumed. "We don't have children here now. Some of the officers have wives with them, but this is an operational military facility. Any children belong to the laundresses and stay in the tents outside fort walls. The contagion should not spread."

"Were you not made aware that the Geer boy has six siblings?" He leaned forward to impart the severity of his meaning. "The eldest bears little risk, but the other five could well become afflicted."

"Do you want me to separate the family?"

"I noticed several rooms in the corner. If you could allow the Geers use of another two, the children would be spared further exposure." Saul saw little concern in the mannerisms of the man before him. "Of course, while diphtherial croup most often strikes children, some adults have fallen prey to it. We want to do everything possible to minimize any possibility of outbreak."

"Of course." Blustering, the major got to his feet. "We do all we can to ensure safety at Fort Laramie." He waved his mangled cigar in a dismal arc. "One spark and all the cottonwood would catch aflame, you know. It happened with one of my predecessors, so I only smoke outside. Major William Hoffman, commander of the Sixth Infantry, won't be known as a failure, by heaven!"

"Your men must appreciate that." Saul grinned and made his way toward the door. "I know the Geers will."

◦◦◦

"There you are, Amanda." Clara passed the young woman the flour she'd just bought. "I'll see you soon."

"I've yet to hear you get a name wrong, even though you've only been here for a couple of weeks." Josiah Reed came alongside her. "You and your aunt have a way with folks."

"Buttonwood is a small town, Mr. Reed." Clara bit back a smile. "There aren't too many names to get confused."

"Fair enough, but I still say you notice things other people don't." Mr. Reed walked around the opposite counter. "I could see you were worried that Miss Dunstall ordered so little flour."

"She and her mother depend on that café, and I know business is slow now that wagon trains aren't passing through. Everyone hereabouts seems to do for themselves." Clara couldn't suppress a small frown. "They're good women who work hard."

"Mrs. Dunstall makes sure to put funds aside during the busy time of the year, so they muddle through."

"Amanda mentioned that business this year trickled slowly." Clara polished a scuff on the counter. "I wonder if it isn't that folks feel they have to order a meal anytime they step foot in the place."

"Could be." Mr. Reed raised his brows. "Doesn't mean there's much we can do about it."

"Well"—Clara gave a little cough to clear her throat—"I was wondering if maybe there wasn't a deal to be made." *Please, Lord, let him be receptive to this suggestion. If I approach it right, he won't feel like a woman is telling him what to do.*

"Oh?"

She had his full attention now. "When spring comes around again, you could speak with the Dunstalls about carrying some of their baked goods in the store. People on the trail always come in here, even if they bypass the café." She kept rubbing at the counter, even though she'd removed the scuff long ago. "I'd guess they wouldn't be able to resist some sweets if they're already in the store. Especially something like fruit tarts and the like. After weeks on the trail, travelers are ready for something other than stew and biscuits."

"Miss Field"—Josiah swiped the rag from her so she had to meet his gaze while he spoke—"you come up with wonderful ideas. It'd be another attraction for the store and increase revenue for the café. The only problem I foresee is that I might eat everything myself." He grinned. "Though it's not such a problem so long as you and your aunt keep feeding me like a king."

"Then you might well be adding to the sales." Clara kept her voice gentle as she reminded, "Aunt Doreen and I will be moving on when spring arrives. Oregon awaits."

"We'll see." He all but shrugged off the thought. "There's always hope you two won't want to leave our small town."

"When we came, you kindly offered to put us up until we found another wagon train to join." Clara started sweeping the hardwood floor to keep busy. "We never intended it to be anything but temporary, and we certainly can't stay permanently. At some point in time, we'll need to establish ourselves in our own home."

"Don't see the need." He gave what sounded close to a snort. "I've got all that room just going to waste, and the two of you more than earn your keep. This is one old man who won't be happy to see you leave."

The arrival of the monthly stage saved Clara from answering. Mr. Reed made his way outside to pick up his catalog orders and mail while Clara cleared a space for the goods. Once they inventoried what came, she'd put it away, but her mind was on Mr. Reed's comment.

Reminding Aunt Doreen that they'd be leaving Buttonwood in a few months took a toll, and Mr. Reed's open-ended invitations didn't make things any easier. When she got right down to the heart of things, she and her aunt couldn't rely on a man—however generous—to take care of them. They needed a home and a living of their own.

"Not much this month." Mr. Reed put a few small boxes on the cleared counter before drawing a handful of envelopes from his pockets. "The Burns and Fossets will be in for their special orders, so the packages stay behind the counter."

Clara slid the paper-wrapped parcels into the storage area before he handed her the unclaimed mail. People knew to come to the general store if they missed the stage. Until then, the envelopes would wait in a small basket atop the counter.

"Hmmm." Mr. Reed opened a letter and perused it. "My son wrote back. Says he'll come to Buttonwood for a spell."

"The doctor?" *He should be with his father. Mr. Reed deserves to be surrounded by his family.*

"Yep. Saul's agreed to come watch the store while I go welcome my first grandchild into the world." A smile spread across the old man's face. "I wrote him before you and your aunt came to Buttonwood."

"We'd gladly watch the store for you."

"I know you would, but I couldn't leave the two of you alone and unprotected."

His words made her straighten her shoulders. "We can take care of ourselves. Aunt Doreen and I made it this far." *Though no farther.* Clara swallowed past a lump in her throat as she acknowledged how bad things would be if Mr. Reed hadn't needed their help.

"You're very capable women." His easy agreement let some of the starch from her spine. "All the same, I'm glad Saul's on his way. It'll do him good to get away from city life for a while, and a man can hope his son will decide to settle nearby."

"Buttonwood could use a doctor. It's in the perfect place for him to be able to tend to the sick on wagon trains, too." Clara decided to add Saul Reed to her prayer list. If he came for a while, maybe he'd abandon his stubbornness and stay to give his father some companionship. *That would certainly make it easier for me and Aunt Doreen to leave when the time comes.*

"I'll trust you to bring that up while he's here." Mr. Reed grinned. "Best thing that could happen to Saul, now that he's finished his education, is for him to find a good woman and settle down to raise a family. Of course, I'm selfish enough to want him to do it here."

"It's not selfish to want good things for your family."

"And myself," he acknowledged.

"Yes." Clara smiled. "Joy is always greater when it's shared."

"And burdens lessened." The old man stroked his beard as though thinking. "You know, Miss Field, there's nothing I want more than to have Saul set up practice here. When you get to be my age, you'll know how important family is."

"We all have dreams." Clara resisted the urge to mention Oregon once again. Mr. Reed already looked wistful enough without a reminder that she and Aunt Doreen planned to leave him. "Pray about it."

"I will." He turned a suddenly intense gaze toward her. "Though I wonder if perhaps God hasn't already given me the answer."

"I'm afraid I don't follow."

"Miss Field," a crafty smile spread across his face as he asked, "what do you know about romance?"

"Not much." She could feel her eyes widen. "I'm not in the market for a husband, Mr. Reed." *The last thing I need is another man making decisions for me.*

"The right man will change your mind." He chuckled. "You can stop backing away, Miss Field. Although I'd be proud to have you as my daughter-in-law, I wouldn't try to pressure you into marrying my son."

"Good." The word escaped in a rush of air, and Clara belatedly realized she sounded far too relieved. "Though I'm sure he'd make an excellent husband."

"What I wondered was whether or not you'd make a good matchmaker." Mr. Reed planted his elbows on the counter and leaned toward her. "You know every eligible gal in Buttonwood, and you'll be here while I go to the birth of my grandchild."

"You want me to find your son a bride?" She raised her brows. "I don't even know him."

"He's twenty-five, God-fearing, educated, and he inherited my good looks." Mr. Reed's expression didn't become any less serious. "Any woman could count herself fortunate to snag Saul. Trouble is he's got blinders on when it comes to marriage."

"What do you mean?"

"He's so busy establishing his career, he hasn't taken time to court any girl he comes across. It'll take extra help to nudge him in the right direction. That's where you come in."

"You want me to tell him he should get married." Doubt threaded the words. "Why would he listen to me?"

"You're young, kind, pretty, and hardworking. You can show him what he's missing by not having a wife."

Clara shook her head. "I don't know about that."

"I do." Mr. Reed leaned farther forward. "And you can invite the other girls from town over, dangle them under his nose. Saul just needs to realize he wants a good woman. Once he's gotten that far, it won't take him long to settle down."

"Playing matchmaker isn't one of my skills. I'm going to have to refuse."

"I'd make it worth your while."

"You've done more than enough for me and my aunt." She sighed. "So of course I'll do my best to point the girls out to your son, but I dislike scheming."

"God blessed you with a sharp mind—look at your idea about the café." Mr. Reed straightened up and slapped the countertop. "I have faith you could come up with something to get my son to the altar. All you need is the right motivation."

"Mr. Reed"—she gave an exasperated laugh—"I already said I'd do what I could. Nothing you say will motivate me to push your son into marriage." *No woman should be pushed into a union when the man who holds the power doesn't have a heart softened by love.*

"Listen to my offer before you make that decision." Mr. Reed gestured toward the windows at the front of the store, which looked out onto the house. "If you can get my son married and settled here in Buttonwood, I'll move into the room over my store and give you the deed to my house."

CHAPTER 7

Saul Reed rode faster as he spotted the buildings. *Buttonwood.* It had to be. The trip took less time than he'd anticipated, considering he couldn't wait for the next stage run and had been held up at Fort Laramie. With his saddlebags packed full of medical supplies, food, water, clothing, his Bible, and a bedroll, he traveled as light as possible.

His horse chuffed tiredly. Saul understood. He would be glad to sleep beneath a roof tonight. He wouldn't turn up his nose at a hot bath and a home-cooked meal, either.

The flat planks he led Abe over served as a rough bridge, a convenient way to cross over the sludge of the Platte River. Up ahead stood a small settlement, boasting no more than half a dozen buildings—a church, a smithy, a café, and Reed's General Store among them. The outlying area seemed dotted with fields, so Saul assumed that farmers made up the bulk of the community.

He steered Abe toward his father's business, surprised by its fine construction of wood and brick with storefront windows. Nearby stood a house built with the same materials but created with graceful lines no one would expect to see in the midst of the prairie. *Looks like Dad's done well here.*

Saul smiled as he hitched Abe to the post out front and shouldered his heaviest bags—those containing his medical kit and Bible. Two steps up and he made it through the door, a tinny clang cheerfully announcing his presence. His eyes didn't adjust immediately after the bright day outside, but he could make out the shape of a woman at the counter as he strode forward.

"Good afternoon." He swung his bags onto the counter and rubbed a crick at the back of his neck. When he looked back up, he caught the full view of the young lady before him.

Golden hair caught glints of light, soft tendrils curling about a face too strong for conventional beauty. Her brows arched finely over brilliant green eyes. Her skin bore the tinge of time spent outdoors in the sun. Delicate hands with tapered fingers quickly finished oiling the eggs on the counter.

"What may I help you with this afternoon?" Her gaze lit on him with reserved curiosity, as though she was taking his measure but didn't want him to know it. Her findings remained a mystery to him as she waited for an answer.

"Can you tell me where I can find Josiah Reed?" He watched as her expressive eyes widened, as though she'd fit another piece into the puzzle of his identity.

"Saul." She breathed his name but blushed immediately when she realized he'd heard her.

How does she know my name?

Surprise must have registered in his expression as she quickly corrected herself. "I mean, you must be Dr. Reed." A slight dip of her head, and she clarified, "Your father isn't expecting you for a few days yet. He's over at the café. Says it's his duty to sample everything the Dunstalls bake."

"Sounds onerous." The corner of his mouth kicked up.

"Your father isn't one to shirk his duty." A smile blossomed on her lips, revealing straight teeth. "He's particularly responsible when it involves pie."

"Sounds like I should join him." Saul reached for his bags. "I didn't know Dad hired anyone to help with the store." He waited for her to introduce herself. Such a pretty girl should have a delicate name to match.

"I'm Clara Field. Your father hired my aunt and me to keep house, cook meals, and help out at the store when needed." She made an expansive gesture. "We only. . .arrived. . .recently."

He noticed her slight hesitation and decided to ask his father about it when he got to the café. Obviously there was more to the situation than met the eye. "Nice to meet you, Miss Field." Saul used the title of an unmarried woman though she hadn't used it in her introduction, illogically rejecting the thought she might have a husband somewhere.

"My pleasure." She laid a hand on the strap of his nearest saddlebag. "I'll watch these for you, if you like. The café's right across the street, next to the church. Amanda said today's pie is rhubarb, if that appeals."

"After riding for so long, I'd eat wet leather if someone slapped it on a plate." Saul smiled. "Rhubarb pie sounds far better."

"Amanda's a wonderful cook." She spoke hastily, with an odd intensity. "With a soft spot for your father, since he compliments her baking."

"I'll be sure to thank her for the pie. I'll take my bags with me so I can purchase my slice." He hefted the bags once more. "Thank you."

"You're welcome." Her gaze followed him as he left the building, and Saul got the impression she was waiting for something. He decided Dad must really be looking forward to going to see Hannah and had told Miss Field as much.

He moved across the large stretch of dusty earth marred with the grooves of wagon and stage tracks, coming to a stop before a single-story whitewashed building. The sign proclaimed to the empty street that this was Dunstall's Café.

Saul stepped inside, this time waiting in the doorway for his eyes to adjust. The café's smaller windows didn't let in much light, so it took a moment before he could make out his father. Dad sat with his back to the door, nodding as the young girl beside him offered more milk.

"Afternoon, Dad." Saul clapped a hand on his old man's shoulder when he walked up.

"Saul!" His father shot to his feet and drew him into a big bear hug. "So glad to see you, son. Early, too."

"It doesn't feel early to me." He sank onto one of the wooden chairs and shot a tired smile at the young lady holding the milk. "I'd like some of whatever he polished off."

"Rhubarb pie," the girl answered. Her straight, dark hair fought to slip loose of its pins as she turned and headed for what Saul assumed was the kitchen. She brought out a generous wedge of the pastry and a steaming mug of coffee.

"Thank you. It smells perfect." His words caused her to duck her head in a shy nod. Saul sank his fork into the flaky crust, through the soft filling, and raised the bite to his mouth. "Heavenly." He didn't waste any more time with words but saw a smile spread across the girl's face before she left them. Saul decided to make a note of the fact that good manners went a long way in little Buttonwood.

"That's Amanda." Dad jerked a thumb toward the back room. "She and her ma run this place. Sweet gal with a way around a stove, but times are hard. Her pa passed on a year ago."

"Good to know." Saul frowned at the thought of such hardship then frowned at the thought that followed. "Why are you telling me all that? She can't be more than sixteen."

"Sixteen last month," Dad acknowledged. "If you're going to run the store in my absence, you need to know about the townsfolk.

No sense putting your foot in when I can give you the basics before I head out." He gave a grimace. "I learn from my mistakes."

Saul almost asked what he meant, but Dad kept talking. "Besides, I just made a deal with the Dunstall women, so they're business partners of a sort."

"They're buying part of the store?" Saul took a swig of coffee, finding it strong enough to stand without the mug. "This is the way coffee should be." He drained the cup and went back to his pie, debating whether or not he should ask for another piece.

"No. Come spring, I'll be carrying their baked goods in the store, so even the travelers who don't stop by the café can have a taste of home." Dad nodded toward Saul's now-empty plate. "I like to think it'll be very successful."

"Smart thinking." Saul's stomach gave a growl, half content at the fare, half disgruntled there wasn't more of it. He cast a glance toward the rear of the store. "Did they come to you?"

"Naw. Whole arrangement was Clara's idea." Dad leaned forward. "Did you look for me at the store first?"

"Yes." Saul straightened when the girl came back, a plate of chicken in one hand and the pot of coffee in the other. He snatched his fork from the dirty pie plate as she moved to clear it. "Thank you, Miss Dunstall."

"You seemed like you came a long way and had an appetite to match." Amanda Dunstall watched with obvious approval as he tucked in. "Just give a call if there's anything more you need."

"So you met her." Dad snagged a chicken leg and bit into it.

"You just saw me meet her." Saul shot him a look. "She cooks just fine, but sixteen's too young for me even if I were in the market for a wife."

"She's not sixteen." Dad's glower disappeared as suddenly as it had shown itself. "I meant Clara. If you stopped by the store, she's the one who told you to find me over here."

"The pretty blond," Saul acknowledged. "She knew who I was the moment I asked after you. Clearly, you've told her about me. I can only hope what she heard is good."

"Almost." Dad wore his sly look—the look that meant he was up to some sort of scheme. Like as not, he probably meant to wrangle Saul into the middle of it.

"Almost?" He injected warning into his tone.

"I just told her I wished you lived nearby." Dad widened his eyes. "It's only natural that a father wants to be close to his son. I can't help it that you're so set on Baltimore."

"You're the one who moved from Baltimore." Saul set down his fork. "Hannah and I still live there, and it wouldn't be hard to find a place to rent if you want to be close."

"I've established a store and a place right here in Buttonwood." Dad leaned back in his chair. "Town could use a doctor."

"My office will be cleared out and ready for me to move in soon." Saul downed some more coffee, the heat energizing him. He thought of Midge, bouncing around on the next stage out here. "I have responsibilities in Baltimore."

"Patients?" Dad tented his fingers over his growing stomach. "You can have every patient in town if you stay here."

"Not patients." Saul slapped his hand on the table. "I came here so you could go be with Hannah, not so you could try to talk me into following you to the middle of nowhere."

"The middle's the best part." Dad stood up and plunked his hat on his head. "But I won't push it." He didn't say anything more, but the final, unspoken words of his statement hung in the air between them.

For now.

As soon as Saul Reed disappeared into the café, Clara grabbed a pencil and a sheet of scrap paper. She folded it in half, writing Saul's name at the top of one column and leaving the other side blank for the moment. Now that he'd arrived, she could start watching him, learning about him. Specifically, learning what kind of woman would most appeal to him.

Beneath his name, she wrote the few things she knew about the man—doctor, handsome, polite. The list would grow as she spent more time around him. Frowning, she added, *Baltimore?* It might take some prying to determine just why the young doctor was so set on staying in the city, but Clara would do what she had to.

She looked through the window to the house beyond. All she had to do was marry off this handsome young doctor and she and Aunt Doreen wouldn't have to go to Oregon. No more weeks under a relentlessly hot sun baking the earth, only to have a sudden rain change the land to mud sucking at their wheels and their progress.

Memories of her aunt trudging alongside the wagon day in, day out for weeks on end, only to go collect dried buffalo dung and cook supper before falling onto a meager pallet made Clara's chest ache. Aunt Doreen shouldn't have to face the trail again—not if there were any way possible to avoid it.

If Clara succeeded in this bargain with Mr. Reed, they wouldn't have to face the Rockies. Her aunt could settle in, bring in every item from the old dugout, and never have to say good-bye to Buttonwood. It wouldn't take much to open a few rooms to boarders, and running a sort of seasonal ordinary would bring enough money for them to live on.

No more wagon. No more failure. I can do this. Clara shifted her attention to the empty column and began listing names: Sally Fosset, Willa Grogan, Opal Speck, Amanda Dunstall. She hesitated over that last one. While she could see Amanda being enamored with Saul Reed, at sixteen she seemed a bit young for the twenty-five-year-old.

She added a question mark next to Amanda's name—not counting her out but acknowledging that she was a long shot. By the same token, she wrote Vanessa Dunstall at the bottom of the list. At thirty-one, Amanda's mother might make a better match, and Clara couldn't afford to rule out any prospects just yet. The top three women were eighteen and nineteen, much more appropriate ages and all single. Well, unmarried, at least.

In tiny script, she scribbled *Matthew Burn* beside Sally's name and *Nathan Fosset* beside Willa's. Though neither couple officially courted, that seemed the direction the wind blew. Saul's competition would need to be taken into account.

Opal Speck. She circled the name of the girl whose backbone helped divert the fight on the day they met. Opal's glowing hair and hazel eyes should draw any man out, but there wasn't anyone special at the moment—probably because of the tension between her family and the Grogans. The only woman amid her father and three brothers, Opal should be comfortable around men, too. *Yes, I like that. Opal deserves to have someone appreciate her, and Dr. Reed would be the type to notice all she gives.*

With that settled, she folded the paper into a tiny square and tucked it in her pocket. When news of Saul's arrival hit town, everyone would come to welcome him—same as they had welcomed her and Aunt Doreen. Clara resolved to stand back and watch as the doctor met each of the girls so she could pinpoint who he liked best. From there, it shouldn't be too hard to have the girls over to the house. Visits to the store for little things and weekly church meetings would round out his exposure to them.

Saul Reed's dark, windswept hair and penetrating gaze would make him a sensation in the town. His dark suits and lean frame would stand out against the rougher clothing and more hulking presence of the local men. Clara could scarcely believe her good fortune. Once the girls met him, they'd fall for him and all she'd have to do is let nature take its course. This wasn't going to be nearly as difficult as she'd thought.

As soon as Mr. Reed and his son came back, she all but flew out of the store to go get things ready at the house. "He's here!" Clara rushed through the kitchen door, only to realize her aunt must be upstairs. She found her waxing the banisters of the stairwell.

"Is something wrong?" Doreen clutched her rag close, her brows slanted in worry.

"No. Dr. Reed—Mr. Reed's son—arrived this afternoon." Clara gestured up the stairs. "We'll need to ready the room for him right away."

"That won't be a problem." Aunt Doreen went back to polishing the banisters. "I dusted everything upstairs already, so we'll just need to put fresh linens on the bed then all will be ready."

"I'll do it." Clara made a beeline for the linen cabinet, only to realize her aunt abandoned the banisters to follow her. "Did you want to help?" Clara didn't remember the bed in the room they'd chosen as being particularly high, but perhaps she remembered incorrectly.

"Why are you so anxious?" Her aunt peered at her, suspicion lining her brow.

"I'm not." Clara filled her arms with sheets and pillow slips before shutting the cabinet. "Everything should be ready, that's all."

"Clara, did you meet the doctor already?"

"Of course." She shrugged then compensated as some linen slid toward the floor. "Mr. Reed had gone for some rhubarb pie at the café when his son came to the store. I told him where he could find his father."

"I see." Aunt Doreen's brows nearly reached her hairline now. "Anything I should know?"

"He's here." Clara headed up the stairs. "So we need to make his room as welcoming as possible. You know how important it is to Mr. Reed that his son wants to stay in Buttonwood."

"We owe it to Josiah to make his son comfortable." Aunt Doreen walked into the spare room behind Clara and went to open the window. "You're right."

"Josiah?" Clara deposited the bed linen on a chair and turned to her aunt. Since when did Aunt Doreen call Mr. Reed by his first name?

"Mr. Reed and Dr. Reed sound so similar." Her words belied the blush creeping up her neck as she stripped the mattress. "I, for one, want to know more about the doctor."

"You know as much as I do." Clara moved to the opposite side of the bed and flicked her wrists, sending the sheet billowing across to her aunt. "He's twenty-five, studied in Edinburgh to become a doctor, comes from Baltimore, and Mr. Reed wants him to settle in Buttonwood."

"Facts don't make a man." Aunt Doreen smoothed out a wrinkle in the quilt they laid over the top. "You met him, so tell me your impressions."

"He's tall, dresses like a doctor, seems the serious sort, and apparently works up an appetite when he travels. I ran into Amanda on the way over, and she said Dr. Reed ate pie, chicken, potatoes, and drank a full pot of coffee. I suppose he'll be glad of a good night's sleep, too."

"Clara"—her aunt finished fluffing the pillows before folding her arms over her chest—"that's not what I meant."

"What did you mean?" Clara frowned. "I only spoke with him for a moment."

"Did you like him? Did you find him kind or demanding? Does he set his jaw as though displeased with the world?"

"No, he's nothing like Uncle Uriah," Clara hastened to clarify.

"Dr. Reed asked politely after his father, looked around with curiosity, and spoke pleasantly." This much, she remembered clearly. "He's handsome, with dark hair, brown eyes, and a deep voice. Dr. Reed holds himself still, like he doesn't want to miss anything. You'll like him, Aunt Doreen."

"He's Jo— Mr. Reed's son." Her aunt smiled. "I already knew I'd like him. The question is. . .do you, Clara?"

"Well enough." Clara straightened the curtains before turning around. "He's the type to turn a woman's head."

"Has he turned your head?" Doreen's eyes lit with delight. "A good husband is a blessing."

"But a bad one. . ." Clara's gaze met her aunt's, leaving the thought unspoken. They both knew how miserable a poor husband could make a household.

"Do you think Dr. Reed will be a bad husband?"

"I scarcely know him, but he seems a good man." Unlike Uriah, who'd made Clara's skin prickle the first time she'd met the man. "He gives me no reason not to introduce him to Opal."

"Opal? So you're not interested in him for yourself?" Aunt Doreen's disappointment came through loud and clear.

"We're going to make our own way, Aunt Doreen. Neither of us needs a husband to provide for us out West. We'll establish a home and life without anyone ordering us about." She looked at the woman who'd done her best to raise her. "Just you and me and the land, remember?"

"Yes, Clara." A wobbly smile accompanied the words. "Remember, too, that plans can change. The last thing I want is for you to ignore opportunities because you're so set on one plan. Oregon isn't the only way."

"Believe me, Aunt Doreen"—Clara thought of her bargain with Mr. Reed, and a smile crept across her face—"I'm not ignoring any opportunities."

CHAPTER 8

"What's your arrangement with Miss Field?" Saul waited until he and his father were alone in the store before broaching the subject. As far as he could tell, a pretty young girl like that shouldn't be flitting around his father.

"Arrangement?" Dad cleared his throat and widened his eyes, signaling a secret all too clearly. "With Miss Field?"

"Yep." Saul took a deep breath. If Dad took to echoing him, things were worse than he'd thought. If the girl were planning on gold digging, she'd do better to head for California. Saul decided to probe gently. "When did she and her aunt come to Buttonwood?"

" 'Bout three weeks ago." A gleam of what Saul would have called relief lit his father's gaze.

Obviously, Saul had asked the wrong question. "Did you send for them to be your housekeepers?" Stranger things happened out West, and everyone knew women weren't exactly thick on the ground along the Oregon Trail.

"No. She and her aunt came passin' through on their own. Something needed to be done, so you could say I took them in." He gave a sheepish shrug.

"They're not asking you for money, Dad?" Saul's eyes narrowed. Dad's hand always reached out to give before he groped for help. These women wouldn't be permitted to take advantage of that. "You don't owe them anything."

"I raised you better." His father's thick gray brows met in the middle as a ferocious scowl. "It's every man's responsibility to help a woman fallen on hard times."

"They're in trouble?" His mind whirled with thoughts of sweet-talking swindlers on the lam.

"Ole Hickory McGee kicked those women off his wagon train." The scowl grew more intense.

"Their wagon train booted them out?" Saul slid from horror over this abandonment to suspicion over why anyone would leave two women behind. Sounded like trouble, all right.

"No good reason why he did it, either. He could've spared a few minutes to search for their missing ox." Dad thumped the counter. "Man won't show his face in my store again if he knows what's good for him."

"A missing ox? He abandoned them in the middle of the prairie to get lost or sick, bit by snakes, overrun with bison, or attacked by Indians...over an ox?" Disbelief made the words skeptical.

"Well, Simon's not your average ox."

"Simon...they named their oxen?" Saul's opinion revised once more. It sounded like these women were one ox short of a team, all right.

"I said the same thing." A grin split Dad's face. "They say Simon eats leather and caused more than his share of problems on the trail." The grin faded. "Still no reason to leave the ladies behind. Not with all the dangers of the trail."

"Unthinkable," Saul agreed. "He could have waited until they reached town to cast 'em out. Leaving them on their own, days away from help...it's amazing they found that ox and made it here."

"Miss Field followed the wagon ruts so she didn't get lost. When she and her aunt came in here, I couldn't believe they were alone and asking after Hickory." He shook his head. "The starch left their spines when I told them they were two days behind."

"They knew they wouldn't catch up."

"Yep. When it looked like they were still going to try, I stepped in and asked them to lend a hand around the store and the house until the next wagon train came through."

"Which won't be until late spring." Saul raised a brow. "So they'll be here for the end of summer, all of fall and winter, and part of spring."

"Longer, if I can wrangle it."

"Why?" Doing his duty by a woman in need was one thing; keeping troublesome strangers around was another.

"Mrs. Edgerly—that's Miss Field's aunt—isn't up to taking the trail to Oregon. She's not one to utter a word of complaint, but Doreen's a delicate lady who deserves a stable home."

"Doreen?" These women worked fast if Dad already used their Christian names.

"Mrs. Edgerly." Dad cleared his throat.

"I see." So they weren't on a first name basis. It didn't take much to surmise that Dad wanted to be, though. "In any case, I don't have any room to lecture anyone about taking in strangers."

"Oh? Did you find a nurse?"

"No. I came across a girl in trouble myself," Saul admitted. "There wasn't any way I could leave her there."

"A girl?" Speculation lifted his father's brows. "You're finally settling down?"

"Midge is thirteen." Saul shook his head. "Her sister's pimp was trying to turn her out since Nancy wasn't up to working that day. By the time Midge found me, her sister had died. I couldn't leave that little girl there."

"Absolutely not." Rage mottled Dad's features. "Where's the child now?"

"She's on her way here. Mrs. Henderson—she keeps the boardinghouse where I live—is bringing her. I thought it'd be good for Midge to get away from the city for a while."

"I'm sorry I won't be here when she arrives. We'll have to let the ladies know so they can ready a room." He pointed above his head. "I've got a bed in the storage area upstairs, along with a few other things."

"They won't mind having a little girl around? With Mrs. Edgerly in the house, Mrs. Henderson wouldn't have to stay." Saul thought aloud. "It'd be some extra work for them."

"Those ladies have big hearts and willing hands. They cook, clean, do the laundry, and Clara keeps an eye on the store when I need her to." Dad gave a brief nod. "They won't mind having a little girl around."

"Sounds like a good setup."

"Asking those two to stay just might be the best bargain I ever made."

"Might?" It sounded pretty good to Saul.

"Oh"—Dad rocked back on his heels—"time will tell."

From where Josiah stood, things looked promising. While his son walked the length of the store, getting more familiar with the setup, he thought of all the reasons why the bride bargain he'd struck with Clara Field should go well.

A deal was a deal, and Josiah wouldn't go back on his word if Miss Field managed to match Saul up with Sally Fosset or Opal Speck. But if all went well, it wouldn't come to that. No, he aimed to have it both ways—see Saul settled in Buttonwood and keep the house in the family.

With Miss Field taking note of what a fine catch his son was and trying to match him up, Josiah figured she'd have to get mighty close. The more time she spent with Saul, the more chance nature would take its course. It might not take much, either, since the girl had been so keyed up she flew out of the store the minute he got back.

Josiah hadn't missed how his son identified Clara, either. "The pretty blond." He had to swallow a snort of laughter. No doubt about it—Saul inherited his good taste in women. After the way Saul bolted down Amanda's chicken, Josiah could count on Clara's cooking to catch his attention, too.

Better yet, what woman could resist a man who saved a child from a life of poverty and degradation? Not many he'd met—especially not a woman who'd been orphaned at a young age, herself, like Clara Field. Yes, the little girl his son saved was another sign of Saul settling down.

Only thing left to worry about was whether Clara did her job too well—worked herself so hard Saul didn't have a chance to recognize all her potential. The girl already did more than she should. He'd heard her rustling around the house, organizing things late at night after putting in a full day at the store. She ran on pure determination, but exhaustion tugged at her strength.

Maybe. . . Josiah straightened up as inspiration struck. *The shadows under her eyes, the way she droops when she thinks no one sees her, how grateful she is to sink onto a seat come mealtime. Anyone could see she takes on too much. Surely a doctor would want to keep an eye on her.*

Decision made, he called his son back over to the corner where he kept the books during the day. "Saul? Now that you're here, I'll be leaving so I can spend as much time with Hannah as possible. This will also have to be a buying trip, since I rarely get to the city, and I know I can count on you to look after the store while I'm gone."

His son nodded. "Of course."

"While you're here, folks will ask for your help. There's no doctor around here for days, and even then the soldiers keep the man at Fort Laramie busy enough as is." Josiah took a deep breath and looked away, as though not wanting to add to his son's burden. "I don't want to ask any more. . ."

"Whatever you need, Dad." His son stepped right into the trap as he spoke. "Just tell me."

"Well. . ." This time Josiah's hesitancy wasn't a show. It seemed too easy to maneuver a son who meant well. *But I mean well, too.* "The thing is. . .Hickory pushed Mrs. Edgerly and Miss Field real hard on the trail. You know the journey already takes a lot out of a person, but these women showed up looking done in. Mind you, don't tell them I said so." He fixed Saul with a sharp stare. "They're strong women, but everyone has a limit. Mrs. Edgerly reached hers long before they made it to Buttonwood, and her niece took everything upon herself."

"I see."

"Since they settled in here, Clara Field hasn't stopped for a moment. Every time I turn around, she's dusting or sweeping or polishing something at the house or store, straightening displays, updating inventory, organizing closets, and the like. She pushes too hard."

"Sounds like a hardworking woman." Approval rang in his voice. "I take it her aunt rested up during that time?"

"Yes, she's in fine condition." Josiah didn't even stop to consider just how fine a woman Doreen Edgerly really was as he pressed onward. "Thing is it's taking a toll on Miss Field now. Months of hardship have her running on willpower, but every so often I see her wilt."

"What do you mean? Does she go pale? Any headaches? Dizziness?"

"She's not one to complain, but she'll sink down to sit for a while or leave the room for a moment." Josiah chose his words carefully so as not to lie but to get the point across. "She's not the type to admit anything's wrong. Even if she felt ill, she wouldn't want anyone making a fuss."

"It's good you told me." Saul clapped a hand on his shoulder. "I'll be sure to keep a close eye on her."

Josiah quelled the urge to smile. "That's all I can ask."

"I should have thought to ask what Dr. Reed's favorite foods are." Clara tossed the sliced cubes of meat into the mixture of flour and seasonings, deftly switching pans with Aunt Doreen. While the meat sizzled, she set aside the already-browned onions.

"Have you ever met a man who disliked steak and onion pie?" Aunt Doreen kept an eye on the meat while Clara rolled out the pastry crust. When her aunt judged the time right, she added boiling water and covered the pan.

The next hour flew by as they worked alongside one another in the well-set-up kitchen. While her aunt chopped potatoes and carrots to add to the meat and gravy, Clara tackled dessert. Since both the Reeds ate dinner at the café, she wouldn't attempt a pie. Besides, that would take a little too long.

"Aunt Doreen, do we still have any of that milk left?" The Fossets brought in fresh milk to trade a few days ago, and Mr. Reed gave it to Clara for baking.

"Probably about a cup or so, but it'll have gone sour by now. The bucket's in the well."

"Perfect! I thought I'd whip up some sour milk coffee cake for dessert. The men both had pie at the café earlier." At her aunt's agreement, Clara made a quick trip to the well and brought back the milk. "This will do nicely."

She added the potatoes and carrots to the meat while Aunt Doreen stirred it all in. In fifteen minutes, she'd put the onions on top then pour it all into a casserole dish. For now, her aunt would watch to make sure it cooked evenly.

During that time, Clara worked on the coffee cake. It didn't take long to cream butter and sugar to blend with a beaten egg. Baking soda added to the sour milk dissolved on its own. She sifted together flour, salt, cinnamon, and nutmeg before mixing everything together. She poured the batter into a shallow greased pan, sprinkling brown sugar with cinnamon and melted butter over the top to form a crispy topping.

It went into the Dutch oven just as Aunt Doreen stretched the rolled pastry over the steak and onion pie. She slid it into the heated brick alcove in the left corner of the hearth to bake golden brown. It should finish at the same time as the coffee cake. The next twenty-five minutes was a flurry of cleanup and setting the table.

Clara brushed the ashes from the top of the Dutch oven, using dishrags to remove the hot coffee cake. Then she passed the dishrags to Aunt Doreen, who swept the pie from the oven nook and went to put it on the trivet in the dining room.

After two hours of work, they had everything ready just in time to be eaten in twenty minutes flat. Well, the steak and onion pie, at any rate. The coffee cake still waited in the kitchen, along with a fresh pot of coffee.

"That takes the prize of best steak and onion pie I've ever tasted," Dr. Reed praised. "When my father told me how great a bargain he'd made with you ladies, I still needed convincing. Not anymore."

Clara put down her fork at his casual mention of a bargain. Her gaze flicked to Mr. Reed, whose subtle head shake told her his son didn't refer to the more recent deal they'd made. The fleeting

91

hope that Dr. Reed knew and wanted to find a wife disappeared, leaving behind a nagging guilt. She chose to soothe it with coffee cake.

"Are you ready for dessert?" She rose from the table, gathering dishes to take back to the kitchen.

"I don't see how I can eat another bite."

"You'll manage." Mr. Reed held none of his son's qualms. "What're we having tonight?"

"Coffee cake," Aunt Doreen answered as Clara made her way back to the kitchen with all the plates and utensils. She came through the door behind her niece, arms loaded with the now-empty casserole dish. "I'll get the coffee." She bustled back out to the men, pouring fresh cups while Clara cut the coffee cake and took out four dessert plates.

"Here we are." She brought everything to the dining room, where she served up the treat. Generous wedges filled the small plates, the crispy topping tumbling to the very edges as she passed portions around the table.

"I take it back." Dr. Reed picked up his fork. "Now I see how I can manage." He sliced off a respectable bite and brought it to his lips with an appreciative smile.

"Good." Clara sampled her own piece. "We hope you'll find a lot of things to surprise you in Buttonwood."

"So far, I can't complain." He reached for his coffee. When a lock of his dark hair tumbled over his forehead, Clara almost moved to tuck it back.

Her guilt over planning to find him a wife eased a little more. *If he appreciates one meal so much, he needs a good woman to look after him. Any of the girls in town would be blessed to call him her husband, to run her fingers through his hair and share smiles every night.*

Polite chitchat filled the rest of the time as they lingered over their coffee, and it wasn't until Dr. Reed went to his room to settle in that his father asked Clara for a word.

She wiped her hands on her apron and abandoned the dishes, only to stop Aunt Doreen when she moved to take over. "I'll finish up in a moment." Clara couldn't answer the questions in her aunt's eyes, not when such an important one blotted out everything else in her own mind.

After tantalizing her with the promise of a good home and a way to provide for Aunt Doreen, would Mr. Reed retract his offer?

CHAPTER 9

Y es, Mr. Reed?" She followed him into the parlor but didn't sit down until he gestured for her to do so. Even then, she busied herself smoothing out her apron. Her hands slid over the worn cotton, pressing out folds in the fabric and working through some of her anxiety.

"Since Saul's arrived, I'll be leaving in a couple days. A few things have changed, though, and I wanted to talk with you before I go."

"I understand." Clara took a deep breath to push down the tears. "If you've changed your mind, you've still done far more for my aunt and me than we could have dared hope."

"Changed my mind?" Surprise colored his voice. "Young lady, I'm too old to change my mind. I set it on something and move on, and that's that. The deal stands."

"Oh?" The exclamation held a world of hope. Incredible how attached she'd become to the idea of settling in Buttonwood.

"Yep." He gave her a slanted look. "Unless you're having second thoughts about your ability to see the matter through?"

"No. Any woman in town would be more than proud to call your son her husband." Clara lowered her voice. Just because Dr.

94

Reed happened to be upstairs didn't mean she could afford to be overheard. "He's a fine catch."

"Thought so, but it's good to hear from a young lady." Mr. Reed grinned. "I meant to give you some specifics before he got here, but that's changed. We'll have to strategize now."

So that's what he meant. Relief almost made Clara giddy as she fetched pencil and paper. "I'm ready."

"First thing"—Mr. Reed shifted on the sofa as though uncomfortable, and Clara jotted down a note to fluff the cushions as he kept speaking—"is that a man has to be alone with a woman— or as close to it as possible—to cultivate a romantic interest."

"Absolutely, though the proprieties must be observed." Clara shot him a stern glance. While she wanted the house and everything it promised, she drew the line at compromising anyone's reputation for a forced wedding. Dr. Reed deserved to choose his own bride—from the selection at hand, of course.

"No question. So if it's possible to give the illusion of privacy, that's a good thing. Makes him feel as though he's moving things along instead of the other way around."

"Mmmhmmm." Clara bit her lip to keep from smiling at this obvious advice. "Perhaps you could tell me more about what your son would look for in a woman?"

"He wants a lady, but someone who's healthy. That's important, him being a doctor and all." Mr. Reed shifted on the sofa again. "Maybe there's a way to make the gals in town seem strong by comparison."

"I'm not sure what you mean." She tapped her pencil against the paper. "Most men don't like a woman who's overly active."

"That's to say"—he cleared his throat—"maybe you could mention having had a long day and needing to rest then go sit in the other room. Or that you'd love to work on your sewing or whatnot. Something to underscore how the other gal's full of energy and get them some of that feeling of being alone all at the same time?"

"I understand." She made a note of the plan. "That won't be difficult, to say I'd like to sit down after a long day. You're right. It's a good way to have him spend time with the girls and get to know them, too."

"Excellent. Just excellent." He beamed at her. "Now, for the other thing. If you could let the other gals in town know how much Saul loves apples, that'd be another step in the right direction. So for the church social or corn husking or whatnot, they can bake a pie or cobbler or some such thing that's sure to catch his eye. You and your aunt can make something different to round things out a bit."

"The way to a man's heart is through his stomach," Clara recited the maxim and jotted down the information about apples. "Does he have any other particular likes or dislikes?"

"Eyelashes. He likes to see long eyelashes on a girl. You know how some women can be all fluttery and shylike?"

"Yes." Clara suppressed the urge to roll her eyes and dutifully added the information to her list. While she found it ridiculous when women batted their lashes at a man in an obvious ploy for attention, some men found it appealing. "This information could be very useful, Mr. Reed."

"That's what I thought." A dull flush stained his cheeks, and he wouldn't meet her gaze. "It will all work out for the best."

Saul awoke the next morning with none of the stiff joints he'd found as his constant companion on the journey to Buttonwood. He sat up on the rope-slung mattress, spurred by the strong scent of fresh coffee wafting up the stairs.

Despite his initial doubts, Miss Field and Mrs. Edgerly proved to be welcome surprises. Tired as he'd been, Saul still recalled the taste of supper last night as being more than worth the day's ride. As he moved around the room, washing up and dressing for church, the light of day revealed small touches he also attributed to the women.

Fresh cedar planks tucked in the corner of his wardrobe chased away stale air and moths. Not so much as a speck of dust dared rest on the dresser or washstand, which also boasted a pitcher full of fresh water and clean towels. The windows shone with the morning sun, as though cheery from a good scrubbing, and the sheets he'd slipped under were obviously freshly washed.

He recalled his father's words about how hard Miss Field worked, and a frown crossed his face. The things he appreciated must have taken a lot of time and work then been multiplied to cover the rest of the rooms in the house.

As he deftly swiped his razor blade over his chin to remove the night's stubble, Saul refused to think too much about what state the women had found the house in after Dad had lived here alone for so long. *Worse, I'm asking them to take on more responsibility when Midge arrives.*

The idea of imposing made him uncomfortable, but Midge needed some time away from the grim realities of life in the city. That little girl deserved to enjoy some sunshine and relaxation while they stayed in Buttonwood. Besides, Midge didn't make any demands or cause trouble. He'd broach the subject at breakfast.

A few moments later, they all sat around a table heaped with fried slices of ham, stacks of flapjacks, and crocks of syrup and preserves. After Dad asked the blessing, Saul noticed the women still wore plain calico dresses—another example of how they'd risen early and worked hard to set the table. They wouldn't change for church until after everything was cleared.

As Saul slathered raspberry preserves on a flapjack, he pondered whether there was a way to have Miss Field help Midge but get more rest at the same time. Nothing sprang to mind, but he'd think on it.

"Delicious," Dad commented as he helped himself to another flapjack. "I can't say how much I'll miss waking up to these breakfasts when I'm on my way to Baltimore."

"It won't go to waste," Saul promised. "As a matter of fact, there's something I need to speak about with you ladies."

"Yes?" Miss Field put down her fork and gave him her undivided attention. The intensity in her green eyes sent a jolt through him, and he found himself hoping she'd approve of his decision to bring Midge to Buttonwood.

"When the next stage comes through Buttonwood, in about two weeks. . . ?" He looked to his father for confirmation of the time frame before continuing, "Two friends of mine will be arriving with it, Mrs. Henderson and Midge. I made these plans before knowing you ladies were in residence here."

"I see." Miss Field straightened her shoulders. "With a little time, we'll have cleared out of your way. Since you've already arranged for housekeepers. . ." A slight tinge of doubt crept into her tone.

"No!" Saul realized he'd bellowed the word and lowered his voice. "That is to say, you misunderstand the situation. Midge is a young girl, recently orphaned, who I've taken in. Mrs. Henderson, a respectable old widow, runs the boardinghouse where I live in Baltimore and is bringing Midge out to join me here. She agreed to stay as a favor to me, but with the two of you ladies already here, I hoped you would lend a hand with Midge so I can send Mrs. Henderson home." He took a breath and watched as the two women before him exchanged astonished glances.

"We're to understand you've taken in a young girl? An orphan?" Miss Field, he couldn't help but notice, hadn't blinked in quite a while.

"I arrived too late to tend to her sister, and Midge had nowhere else to go." He purposely glossed over the less savory details. He saw no reason for the little girl to suffer the stigma of a background she couldn't control. "When we return to Baltimore, I'll need to send her to a boarding school," he added. "Midge just turned thirteen, but for now her loss is fresh, and I thought it would do her some good to be away from the city."

"What a wonderful idea!" Mrs. Edgerly exclaimed. "Clara and I will be delighted to look after her during your stay."

"We'll do everything we can." Determination showed in the set of Miss Field's jaw, but her eyes softened. "Thirteen is a tender age to lose one's family."

"I know, dear." Mrs. Edgerly reached over to pat Miss Field's hand, making Saul wonder whether the connection between the two sprang from more than the obvious relationship.

"Thank you both." He leaned forward in his chair. "You should know Midge's upbringing was a bit rough. Her family fell on hard times. She hasn't seen much schooling. In fact"—the idea struck as he spoke, a perfect way for Miss Field to forgo hard work without feeling as though she shirked anything—"I'd consider it a particular boon if you could help with her manners and speech and reading and the like, so she'll have an easier time adjusting to boarding school." Now that he thought on it, Midge would really benefit from the arrangement, too.

"We'll do our best." Miss Field stood up to clear the table. "First, we'll need to set up a room for her."

"I've things in storage above the store," Dad offered. "We'll haul them over tomorrow so it's all in place before I leave." A flash of sadness crossed his features. "After rattling around here alone so long, seems a shame I'm going just when it's full."

No one said anything more, but the genuine longing in his father's voice stayed in Saul's thoughts throughout the morning service.

Unlike the barely avoided brawl caused by Clara and Aunt Doreen's unexpected arrival, Saul's appearance in town seemed easily accepted. This was due, at least in part, to Mr. Reed and Clara spreading word as folks came to the store.

At any rate, families came to worship the next Sunday prepared to welcome the new doctor. Makeshift tables near the church rapidly filled with food pulled from buckboards. Clara added a few dishes—butter-roasted potatoes, scalloped corn and tomatoes, and baked beans flavored with molasses and bacon—to the variety already in place. She and Aunt Doreen knew this impromptu town gathering would most likely occur and had prepared for it after supper last evening.

"So that's Mr. Reed's son?" Sally Fosset appeared at Clara's elbow. "He's better looking than I pictured."

Opal joined them. "Looks aren't everything, Sally."

"Saul Reed bears more than a handsome face." Clara jumped on the opportunity to talk him up. "You both already know he's a doctor. Not one of those self-taught shysters, either. He went to a university in Scotland for a medical degree."

"I heard about that." Opal raised a brow. "Sounds like the type of thing folks get uppity about, though."

"Dr. Reed doesn't care about things like that." Clara hastened to disabuse Opal of that notion. "As a matter of fact, after he arrived too late to help a woman, he took in her orphaned little sister."

"You don't say?" Amanda Dunstall set a berry pie on a nearby table, not even noticing it wobbled precariously close to the edge as she listened to the conversation. "A bachelor like that took in a child?"

"She'll be coming here on the next stage." Clara lowered her voice so they all leaned in. "The little girl just turned thirteen, and he plans to send her off to school when she's ready. I wonder if your sister wouldn't make a good friend to Midge while she's here, Sally."

"Tricia's turning twelve soon." Sally cast a glance at a trio of nearby girls. "I'll be sure to mention it to her, so she'll say something to Alyssa Warren and Lauren Doane. They're all about the same age."

"I'll tell Pete to behave himself." Opal sighed. "It's not much, but it's the best I can do."

Clara couldn't help but laugh at the rueful expression on her friend's face. "A little teasing should make Midge feel at home, I'd think. After the rough time she's had of it in the city, a place like Buttonwood could be precisely what she needs."

"Shame it sounds like the doctor is set on going back to Baltimore," Sally observed. "We could use a doctor around these parts, and I wouldn't turn my nose up at another handsome bachelor to add to the list." She cast a surreptitious glance toward Matthew Burn.

"We have a couple of months to change Dr. Reed's mind," Clara pointed out. "If we put our heads together, we can show him all the wonderful things about this town so he won't want to leave. Sometimes a man just needs the right incentive to settle down."

"Like a good woman?" Amanda's gaze took on a dreamy cast.

"Yes." Clara stifled a pang of guilt over encouraging the girl, who was a bit on the young side for Dr. Reed. "He's already taken in a child and is in the midst of setting up a practice. Now seems to be a good time for the right woman to step in."

"Hmmm." Sally eyed him with new interest.

"I like that he cares about folks beside himself." Opal patted her hair to make sure it was in place. "That's a good quality."

"Dr. Reed carries a man-sized appetite, too." Amanda's voice rang with approval. "He'd appreciate a wife who knows her way around a kitchen."

"Not to mention he has the education and career to provide a fine kitchen for that wife." Sally turned back to face them all. "What do you say, ladies? I think we can convince Dr. Reed to think twice about settling in Buttonwood."

"Why don't you set your cap for him, Clara?" Opal's question cut through the chatter in an instant. "You're educated and don't plan to stay here, too, so why are you so set on having Dr. Reed settle in Buttonwood?"

"Well"—Clara struggled to find an honest answer she could give them without breaking faith with Mr. Reed—"it's because Aunt Doreen and I can't stay here on Mr. Reed's goodwill indefinitely, but he's always talking about how much he wishes he had his family nearby. He says having us around helps the house not feel so empty, and I don't want him to feel abandoned after all he's done for us."

"That's sweet, Clara." Sally gave her a hug. "While we're convincing Dr. Reed, though, we're going to use the opportunity to change your mind about staying, too!"

"Truth be told, I don't want to leave you all behind." Her nose stung as Clara smiled at them. "We'll see what God has in store."

"In the meantime"—Amanda nudged Opal with her elbow—"how about you introduce us to Dr. Reed. Since God already brought him to town, I mean."

"Of course. You know," Clara whispered as they made their way over to where Mr. Reed stood, introducing his son to the other members of the town, "I've been thinking we should have a quilting bee over at the Reed place, since the parlor's so large. It'd be a good reason to have all of you come to visit."

"You're a sharp one, Clara Field." Brushing a speck off her skirt, Sally added a suggestion of her own. "Threshing will start soon, too. Everyone gets together for that."

"Yes." Opal looked back at a point Clara couldn't follow. "You will invite Willa to the quilting circle, won't you, Clara? She always turns down any invitation from Sally or me."

"Shouldn't be so snobby then." Amanda scowled. "I don't understand why she goes out of her way to avoid you when you're always so nice, Opal."

"It's because I'm a Speck. That's all." Opal brushed away Amanda's anger. "I think maybe her mother makes her stay away, too."

"Of course I'll invite her, Opal." Clara didn't mention that she'd already planned to.

"Since Mama passed on so long ago, there's no one for Mrs. Grogan to squabble with." A shadow of grief passed over Opal's face, and Clara reached over to squeeze her arm. The pain of a lost loved one never completely went away.

"I'd say she brings trouble on herself." Amanda's brow furrowed as she nodded toward where Lucinda barged in front of Dr. Reed and waved her arms in the air, pointing toward Willa. "Could she be more obvious in her attempts at matchmaking?"

"Perfect. This gives us the opportunity to rescue him. Smile," Clara directed as they edged within hearing distance.

"You simply must meet my Willa," Lucinda simpered in a high pitch. "I've always said the girl has a healing touch."

"Dr. Reed," Clara raised her voice, not bothering to hide a wide smile. From the look on his face, the doctor knew he'd made a narrow escape. Good. It couldn't hurt to have him owe her a favor. "I'd like you to meet some of my friends. . . ."

CHAPTER 10

Midge kept her hand clamped around the money shoved in the pocket of her skirt, hidden beneath her apron. She darted suspicious looks around every corner, keeping her head high and shoulders back so any thieves lurking around wouldn't think her an easy mark.

With her free hand, she tugged the brim of her straw boater low over her eyes so no one would recognize her. Not that anyone would, what with her being all clean and dressed so nice now, but it was smart to be careful about these things. Fancy clothes, a bath, and a few miles between her and her old life only amounted to so much when a body got right down to it.

She darted across the street after a carriage passed, narrowly avoiding a coal cart. Two more blocks and she reached the open market where a mishmash of sounds, smells, and sights assaulted her. Shrill wives hawked produce, reed-thin voices wavered offers of matchsticks or flowers, and a muddle of accents made it impossible to understand most of them.

Midge wound her way past a shifty-eyed hag rubbing wax into old apples to make them shine, a thickset man who tried to pinch her bottom when she passed his stall of spittoons, and a greasy-haired fisherman who smelled as though he slept near his wares. In times past, she'd dawdle around the market, waiting for an inattentive stall owner to turn away so she could nab a bite to eat.

Wandering around the stalls, looking at everything from pocket watches to manure carts, whiled away many an afternoon when she couldn't wait inside the room with Nancy. The market offered a place to lose herself in a crowd, to become part of the heartbeat of the city until she forgot about how alone she really was. For a while, at least.

Today, though, she'd come to buy salt pork for her trip with Mrs. Henderson to go meet Dr. Reed. Midge ignored the meat stalls closest to the outside, where everything became coated with street dust and soot, and twisted through the rows until she reached old Finnergan. Here, smoked sausages roped along the high beams in merry streams, hanging down just far enough to tease her nose with good smells.

She bought the salt pork and some of the sausages as Mrs. Henderson asked. Many times before, she'd watched him wrap things for other customers but never for her. Sometimes he'd pass her a sausage, not saying a word about it, but never bundling it up like a present. She watched over the counter as, for the first time, he did it for her.

Midge liked the rustle and tear of the thick, brown paper, the way it creased so straight and sturdy until tied off with a bit of string. She slipped the packages into her apron pockets with a muttered, "Thank you," and went back the way she'd come.

Navigating the twisting alleys of the market always seemed to take longer on the way home, and this time was no different. The wind picked up, making Midge wrap her shawl tight around her shoulders so she wouldn't lose it. She ducked her head against the dust as she rounded a corner, clipping a passerby as she moved.

"Sorry," she mumbled, blinking the dust from her vision.

Midge started to move on, but the man reached out and put a heavy hand on her shoulder. She went rigid.

"Can't be runnin' into folks, luv." A familiar voice sent chills down her spine, and she kept her head bowed. He shifted, and Midge could see his big brown boots.

"Sorry." She rasped it this time, staring at the scuff mark on the toe of his left boot. The one Rodney'd gotten when he kicked in the door after Nancy locked it against him and the doctor the night before she died.

"You can apologize better'n that, a pretty little thing like you." He leaned over her, and when his hand moved from clamping her shoulder to reaching for her chin, Midge sprang into action.

"No!" She jammed her elbow into his doughy middle, slapping his hand aside and leaping away. Midge didn't look back to see if he bent over double. The sound of his wheezing breath spurred her to run and keep running.

She dashed around corners, cut through the park, and circled back in a sideways scuttle to make sure he hadn't crept up behind her. Then, only when she was sure he couldn't have followed, did she run home.

Did he recognize me? She didn't think so but had no way to tell for sure.

Midge lifted the latch on the gate and walked around to the back, where she gulped air in quick pants until her breaths came normal again. Then she went inside.

"Glad to see you've returned, Midge." Mrs. Henderson gave her a big smile as she took the packages. "All ready now for our trip out West?"

Midge gave a tight-lipped nod. *If you only knew. . . .*

~⚬⚬~

"How you brought so many things out here, I'll never know." Saul stepped over an upended crate to enter the rooms above the store. "Halfway to nowhere, and you've a storage area full of items!"

"Wait until we find everything we need," Dad huffed. "Then you'll be singing a different tune."

"It looks as if we could spend the day unearthing treasures," Miss Field agreed. "Though I'm glad you asked Aunt Doreen to watch the store. The dust up here would make her sneeze."

"We'll take frequent breaks." It didn't escape Saul's notice that Miss Field already rubbed her nose. He looked around at dressers, washstands, and bedsteads leaning against each other in no sensible order. "What made you decide to order all this furniture, Dad? Shipping it out here must've cost a solid sum."

"No. Most everything up here I took in exchange from pioneers when their wagons came through." Dad shrugged off his own generosity even as he explained, "If they were low on cash or had to lighten the load to make room for supplies and had something too fine to go to waste, I stashed it up here."

Miss Field stared at his father with admiration. "You're a blessing to many, Mr. Reed."

"I just couldn't stand the thought of all those heirlooms dusting the mountains when the going got too rough." Dad rubbed the nape of his neck. "Twice, someone came back through to buy something back. Had a fellow this year who dug through everything to find his great-grandfather's clock in the corner. That probably made both our days, to tell the truth."

"What about the other time?" Miss Field asked the question Saul wondered.

Dad squinted as though it helped him think. "Most of these things aren't necessities around here, so folks don't buy them and I don't bother putting them in the store. I took a fancy spice chest once. Pretty thing. Put it in the store, and the Warrens snapped it up the same day. Well, that lady's son came looking for it. Said his father had made it special."

"Oh!" Miss Field gripped the edge of a nearby server as though anxious for the family to recover its heirloom.

"I sent him to the Warrens'. They sold it off to him for a fair price, and everyone went their way happier for the deal."

"As the town grows, there'll be more need for bigger items." Saul followed his father's lead and shrugged out of his coat, hanging it on a hall tree shoved against a corner. "Keeping these things represents a solid investment as well as a way to help folks right now."

"Well, for now I'm thinking we'll be able to fill one of those rooms in the house with things for Midge." Dad stomped over to a trunk and pushed it aside. "Big things first. She'll need a bed, washstand, and dresser."

"This bedstead looks good to me." Saul shifted a headboard with wooden slats so the others could see. "It has a matching footboard."

"Oh, yes!" Miss Field came over and traced the floral carving on the center slat. "It's perfect for a little girl."

"These iron bars fit into the joists, and here's a bed box that should fit." Saul nudged it with the toe of his boot. "I don't see any mattresses, though."

"Aunt Doreen and I will make one for her." Miss Field stepped out of the way as he and Dad started moving the pieces toward the door. "We don't have feathers, but there are cornhusks aplenty to use for the time being."

"That sounds good." Saul raised the headboard high to avoid hitting a leather trunk. It took them three trips to get all the pieces for the bed down the stairs and to the house. When they came back upstairs, he found Miss Field scooting a chest of drawers toward the door.

"This seems like a good match for the bedstead," she puffed, obviously out of breath.

"I'll get it while you sit down for a moment." He closed the distance in two strides, noting her relieved expression as she moved out of the way and perched on the edge of a crate. *Dad's right. She does take too much on herself.* Saul frowned as he moved the dresser toward the door, realizing it might take more than he expected to get Miss Field to rest.

"If you don't like it, there are others." The nervous lilt in her tone told him she'd seen his frown.

"You picked the right one," he assured her. "I'm just thinking I should remove the drawers so they don't slide out and bounce down the stairs."

Without a word, she waited until he removed them, then she led the way down the stairs with two long drawers while he and Dad took the heavier outer shell. By the time they had it out to the house, she'd brought the two smaller drawers, as well. With the addition of a washstand, they were ready to haul it up to the room they'd earmarked for Midge.

"We'll take it all up." Dad motioned toward the house, where the furniture lay heaped in the parlor. "If you and your aunt want to put up the closed sign and poke around upstairs to see if you can find anything a little girl might like, go on ahead."

"I'd love to!" Mrs. Edgerly's eyes shone with excitement. "It'll be such fun to sit there, going through boxes and seeing what we find. If we run across anything for the store, we'll set it aside, too."

"Or the house," Dad encouraged. "Anything that captures your fancy, ladies. It doesn't do anyone any good gathering dust up there."

Saul didn't say a word, content with the idea of the women settling down to go through boxes. They shouldn't overtax themselves that way, but the two would still feel useful.

Time flew by as he and his father lugged the furniture up the stairs. Sliding the drawers back into the dresser and assembling the bed frame took longer than anticipated, and it was a while before they returned to the store.

"Ladies?" he called, expecting they would be back downstairs by now. A soft thud sounded from the floor above, so he headed for the stairwell. What he found when he made it upstairs made his jaw drop.

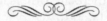

"Oh, Dr. Reed." Clara swiped a lock of hair from her forehead, trying to push it back into her bun. "We didn't hear you come in." She straightened from where she'd just set down a crate of china in the section they'd reserved for kitchenware.

"What have you. . ." He seemed to be experiencing difficulty getting the words out. "What. . .happened?"

"While we went through everything, we decided to organize." Clara beamed. Obviously, the man appreciated their hard work. He was so bowled over by what she and Aunt Doreen had accomplished while they'd been gone, he could scarcely believe it. "Bed frames are in the corner over there, along with the rest of the furniture. We left all that, for the most part." She gestured as she spoke. "You know how heavy it is."

"I've an idea." His voice came out sounding strangled.

His father appeared behind him. "Would you take a look at this place!" Mr. Reed looked around with obvious enjoyment. "You've worked wonders."

"Clara did most of the real work," Aunt Doreen demurred. "I mostly sat here, looking through the contents of trunks and crates and the like. She moved things around."

"Nonsense." Clara waved away her aunt's modesty. "It took both of our efforts." She took a deep breath and tried to ignore the way dust coated her throat. She'd been meaning to go downstairs for a dipperful of water for a while now.

"Furniture in the corner then?" Mr. Reed walked across the room. "What's this lot?"

"Those are things you might want to put out in the store come spring. There's a wagon repair kit, two travel cooking boxes, and the crate has a few lanterns and lengths of rope in it." Clara led him to the next grouping. "These hold finer merchandise—china and silver. People might come back for these or may ask as folks marry or the town grows."

"Excellent." Mr. Reed grinned, while his son still looked stunned.

"These two small crates hold books." Excitement had her lifting off the lid on the top one. "Some have water damage, but altogether they're in wonderful condition. This next to them is a portable writing desk. You lift the top and it has clever compartments for ink, pens, nibs, paper, and wax. It'd be perfect for Midge to work on her penmanship."

"I don't remember trading for that," Mr. Reed admitted.

"Aunt Doreen found it beneath some clothing in one of the trunks. Clothes are over here"—she gestured to one large wooden chest before moving on—"and quilts there. In the portmanteau you have some shoes."

Tears clogged the back of her throat as she finished speaking. The clothes, blankets, and shoes were best clothes. The clothes, families packed away to be worn only when they reached Oregon or California. These items belonged to unfortunate souls who'd been buried in their Sunday best but hadn't survived the trail to wear their finery.

"I never could go through those things." Mr. Reed swept his hat off his head. "It seemed disrespectful."

"Folks can get some use out of them," his son spoke up. "There's no shame in that. By taking them, you helped their families and took away a painful reminder, Dad."

"He's right." Aunt Doreen gave an encouraging nod. "You don't have to sell them unless you want to."

"Did you come across anything more for Midge?" Dr. Reed's attempt to lighten the subject worked.

"Yes!" Clara seized the opportunity. "We found some school supplies to help her get caught up." She opened a box to reveal a slate, chalk, and a primer. "This leather trunk would look good at the foot of her bed to store extra blankets and whatnot, but the best part. . ." She exchanged a glance with Aunt Doreen. "Show them."

"Look!" Aunt Doreen flung open the trunk with a dramatic flourish to unveil a hand-painted tea set too large for a small child but not standard size, either. "Have you ever seen the like?"

"That's something." Mr. Reed hunkered down next to Aunt Doreen. "I recall this, vaguely. The family intended it as a gift for someone in Oregon, but they needed money for a broken axle."

"At thirteen, will Midge feel too old for this?" Clara looked up at Dr. Reed for his opinion.

"She'll love it, I'm sure." His hand dwarfed a tiny cup and saucer. "Midge hasn't had the chance to enjoy the fun little things in life much. I'm glad Buttonwood will help remedy that." His smile when he handed back the cup made Clara's breath catch.

"Buttonwood is like that." She managed to remind herself of her purpose in making Midge and Dr. Reed comfortable here. One glance at Aunt Doreen strengthened her resolve. "We aim to please."

CHAPTER 11

"Please sit down." Saul spoke firmly, reaching to pull his father's saddlebags away from Clara, but the woman batted his hands away and kept on rummaging around.

"I'll break my fast once I'm certain Mr. Reed packed everything he needs. Now where"—her voice grew muffled as she all but stuck her head in the leather—"did he put that. . .ah, here it is." She emerged with a smile and checked something off what seemed to Saul an inordinately long list.

"You've been up since dawn making breakfast and double-checking everything, Miss Field." He gripped her elbow and steered her toward the table. "Those delicious biscuits and gravy are going cold."

"I misspoke when I said I'd break my fast. You see, I nibbled a biscuit earlier and can always eat another later." She turned into the kitchen, out of his grasp, and toward the pantry as she spoke. "Though I do believe your father could use a few more provisions for the journey. . . ."

Saul leaned on the doorjamb to the larder to see her bundling apples, jerked beef, a loaf of fresh baked bread, a crock of preserves, and a chunk of cheese to go with cold chicken and hard tack she'd packed already. Saul barely held back a chuckle, since he'd already seen Mrs. Edgerly flit back and forth, doing much the same thing.

"Between you and your aunt, Dad will be lucky if his horse can walk, much less carry him along with his bags."

"What do you mean?" Miss Field drew up short, arms laden with provisions and green eyes wide. If it weren't for the purple smudges beneath those eyes, she'd be the picture of health. "Is something wrong with the horse? I'm certain Mr. Burn would loan him another—"

"The horse is fine." Saul couldn't stifle his laugh. "Your aunt already added a few bacon sandwiches and extra biscuits to his pack. With all that"—he nodded toward what she carried—"plus what you two packed before, the horse won't be able to budge."

"Oh, that's an exaggeration." She attempted to sidle past him through the doorway but lost the apples in transit. Dismay crossed her features as they tumbled to the floor. "Well, perhaps he won't need those."

"Good thinking." This time, he hid a grin. While she looked at the fallen fruit, he reached out and shifted the load into his own arms. "I'll get this." He carried it out to the entryway, where Dad's saddlebags rested on the big hall table. Before Miss Field could catch up and reevaluate, he stuffed all the food together. "That ought to do it." Saul struggled to fasten each of them shut before shouldering the lot.

"Perhaps I should check one last time." Mrs. Edgerly bustled down the stairs. "Just in case we overlooked something."

"Your niece has it well in hand," Saul assured her, making his way for the door. "Though maybe now you can convince her to take the time to eat a good breakfast!"

"Clara!" The disapproval in Mrs. Edgerly's tone made the

packs seem lighter as Saul walked outside. "You've not eaten?"

"Thanks, son." Dad grabbed a pack, and together they situated everything so the horse was ready to go. "Think you can handle everything?"

"Those two are more than I bargained for," Saul admitted.

"You have no idea." Dad's grin didn't exactly ease his mind. "They're good women though."

"I know. Getting Miss Field to slow down her pace and rest"—Saul whistled—"that's a task more suited to Hercules. The woman seems determined to wear herself out."

"I get the feeling she thinks she has something to prove." Dad's jaw clenched, and his Adam's apple worked hard before he got the next words out. "Mrs. Edgerly raised Clara, but neither of them talks about Clara's uncle much. I get the impression he was a mean sort. Left them both high and dry."

"They do seem extremely close." Saul cast a glance over his shoulder. "Setting out for Oregon after he passed on says a lot about them trying to leave their old life behind."

Miss Field came out on the porch. "Is it time to leave us already?"

"Afraid so, ladies." Dad walked over, and Saul tried to hide his surprise when the women both enveloped his father in a simultaneous embrace. "I'll be back in a couple of months."

"We'll miss you." Mrs. Edgerly's whisper carried to where Saul stood by the horse.

"The time will pass quickly. Remember. . .I'm trusting you to make sure Saul doesn't step between a pair of spitting Specks and Grogans." Dad's smile, when he turned around, bore more than a touch of sadness. He swung into the saddle and took one last look at the three of them. "Knowing you're all here will make coming home a trip worth taking."

With a wave, Dad took off. Saul joined the women on the

porch as they watched him until he faded in the distance; then they went inside.

"Strange how I've only known him a few weeks, but it feels like I'm losing family." Miss Field's whisper floated past Saul, sending a prick of guilt through his chest that he ever thought these women might have set out to take advantage of his father.

"We'll make him proud while he's gone," he promised. "That reminds me...Dad said something about how you'd started taking inventory since he'd fallen behind. You probably know as much about where everything is as he does."

"I wouldn't say that." Rose tinged her cheeks.

"All the same, I'd appreciate it if you'd show me the ropes, so to speak. Muddling around on my own doesn't appeal."

"Certainly. Aunt Doreen? Will you need help making dinner this afternoon?"

"I'll bring it over to the pair of you." Mrs. Edgerly shooed them on. "I made sure she ate well, Doctor. Clara, you go on ahead and show Dr. Reed how things work. If you can have everything in order and inventory done by the time Mr. Reed comes back, so much the better."

Miss Field pulled a shawl off the peg by the door, although the sun had already burned off the morning dew. "Ready?"

"Absolutely." In a moment they'd crossed to the store. It seemed strange to unlock the door without Dad. The counters running the length of the store opposite each other seemed bare without him bustling behind one of them.

"The whole place feels different." Miss Field's comment so closely echoed his thoughts, and Saul glanced at her. A fond smile graced her lips. "Your father has a way of bringing life to a place. I remember my father having the same gift." The smile wavered but held.

"Your aunt raised you?" He made it a question, open enough

for her to tell precisely as much as she wished and nothing more.

"Yes." The glow vanished abruptly. "My parents died after I turned twelve—just about Midge's age."

"If you feel comfortable, you might tell her that. Shared grief makes the burden lighter, and Midge doesn't know anyone who's lost her parents." *And I've never told her about my sister.* He drew a sharp breath at the connection but shoved it away. This wasn't the time to examine it.

"God blessed me with Aunt Doreen, just as He's blessed Midge with you." Her gaze seemed to cut right through him.

They'd moved on, Miss Field showing him the drawers and bins built into the counters which held spices, flour, sugar, coffee, and the like. She seemed eager for the distraction of the store, but he tried to steer the conversation back. He meant to discover more about the shadowy figure of her uncle.

"Your aunt was married when you joined her?" He spoke casually in an attempt to hide the awkward nature of the question. "Mr. Edgerly was already in residence, I mean?"

Miss Field's gaze shot straight to his face, her expression shuttered. "No." The single word fell between them as she turned away.

"The coffee grinder sits here. Just measure in the beans, turn the crank, and the grounds collect here." Clara spoke quickly, retreating into the minutia of running the store. His close proximity made her anxious, the brush of his shirtsleeves against her shoulder seemed to whisper a warning that she couldn't afford to waste any time. "You see?" They'd already looked over the books, writing supplies, and lamps displayed in the left-hand window and moved on to the grocery items.

"Simple." His breath fanned warm against her ear. "Do we use pokes, bags, or gunnysacks for the coffee?"

"That depends on how many pounds the customer orders." She pushed away from the counter—away from him. "It works the same way as the other dry goods, but folks usually order a lot of coffee, so it'll be bags. Gunnysacks are used if they want the beans whole. The only time you'll need pokes is for fine sugar, spices, or candy."

"Good." He pulled away from the large grinder to follow her. "I'm still not convinced I can make a cone out of brown paper and not spill spices everywhere—even if the bins pull out of the counter so handily."

"Don't you put medicinal powders in twists of paper?" She shot him a quizzical glance. "It's the same thing."

"Folding the paper seals it off. Shaping it into a cone leaves a loose end." He looked at the shelves behind one counter, then turned to and surveyed the other length of the store. "That reminds me. . .where are the pharmaceuticals?"

"On the other side, with toiletries and razors and tooth powder." She directed his attention back to the area directly in front of them. "Behind the grinder is the display of dishes and silverware. According to your father, people rarely ask for them, so they're tucked away. She moved farther down the shelves lining the wall to the canning jars, skillets, pots, and other cookware. "Any questions?"

"He displays produce on the countertop, smoked and cured meats sit on the shelves along with eggs, canned goods, and preserves." Dr. Reed leaned back against the counter as he took stock. "Candy's in the glass jars up front to tempt all the customers."

"You don't need me to go over all this." Clara sidled around the counter. "Everything's arranged in sections. Tools and hardware along the back wall." She inclined her head toward the jumble of tubs, buckets, barrels, tools, rope, and lanterns to make her point. "The shelves beneath the other counter hold men's hats, work gloves, and boots leading up to the display of women's bonnets, Sunday gloves, and shoes. The wall behind holds all the yard goods and trimmings for any sewing needs."

"What about this corner?" He moved behind the counter to peer at the shelves in the far corner. "Ah, yes. The toiletries?"

"Yes. Here you'll find soap, combs, and brushes next to the irons and washboards. Your father was clever to put those next to the fabric, I think."

"Hmmm?" He'd plucked a small bottle from the shelf and squinted at it. The morning light didn't reach through the windows to the far wall yet. "I suppose so. When I asked, I meant these liniments and things. Is this all the town has for a pharmacy, Miss Field?"

"It must be."

"We'll start that inventory list right here then." He crossed the store to take the biggest lamp from the window display and bring it back to the dim corner, dropping that bottle in the trash along the way. "Please fetch pen and paper, Miss Field. We'll need to place an order at once so the town doesn't continue to lack essential medical supplies."

"All right." Surprised by his switch from easygoing shopkeeper to intense physician, she hastened to get the logbook. When she had what she needed, she skirted around him, laying the ink and records on the counter. "First, shall we record what we do have?"

"It won't do much good." He pulled away from the shelf and raked a hand through his dark hair. "Most of these aren't worth the bottles they're in. We'll have to dispose of them."

"Why?" Clara caught herself nibbling on her lower lip and immediately stopped. Dr. Reed knew medicine better than she.

"Some are out and out quackery. Look at this." He passed her a small box.

" 'Colden's Liquid Beef Tonic,' " she read aloud, " 'for treatment of alcoholic condition.' Well, I'd think that could be useful to some people, Dr. Reed."

"Look here." He moved to stand beside her, his hand closing over hers. "Read this small print at the bottom of the box."

"Twenty-six percent alcoholic content." She gasped. "Surely that's a mistake! You don't drink spirits to overcome a dependence upon them!"

"Precisely." He swept the box from her hand and plunked it on the counter. "This goes, as does anything proclaiming miracle cures or bearing a high alcohol content. They temporarily mask symptoms and prevent the patient from seeking treatment until it may be too late."

"Look at all of them!" Dozens upon dozens of small boxes and bottles marched in neat rows upon the shelves. "Will any remain?"

"Some." Dr. Reed rolled up his sleeves, exposing strong forearms lightly dusted with dark hair. "We'll make three piles. One for things I'm certain are genuine, one for hoaxes, and the last for tonics to evaluate later."

"Oh." Clara tore her gaze from his arms and snatched the first box she saw. " 'Hostetter's Celebrated Stomach Bitters.' " She turned it over, scanning over promises until she came to a shocking number. "Forty-four percent alcohol by volume!" It started the garbage pile.

They worked in silence, dust motes dancing in the glow of the lantern and the increasing light stretching from the window as time passed. Occasionally they'd stop to read a particularly overblown or ridiculous claim.

" 'Dr. C.V. Girard's Ginger Brandy, a Certain Cure for Cholera, Colic, Cramps, Dysentery, Chills, and Fever,' " Clara mused. "With a wonder like this, it's incredible we even need doctors nowadays."

"That, Miss Field"—an amused sparkle in his eyes belied the gravity of his tone—"is because we of the medical profession wage a war on poor health. And no one understands this better than the estimable Mr. Scott." He whipped a box off the shelf, holding it up as though it were a pistol yet carefully leaving the side free so she could read the print on the side. Dr. Reed announced, " 'Scott's Emulsion: A cough or cold is a spy which has stealthily come in the lines of health: SHOOT THE SPY.'"

Clara clamped one hand over her mouth to muffle her laughter. Between his antics and the dramatic script, the Scott's Emulsion box proved the best entertainment she'd seen in months. "Oh, can we keep that one? Even if we don't sell it?"

"As a matter of fact"—Dr. Reed tapped the box—"it's made with lime and powder, which can temporarily help clear the airways in case of a cough or cold. It's not a cure but could provide some relief." He placed it in the disgracefully small pile of boxes they'd be keeping.

"At a guess, I'd say Pink Pills for Pale People probably don't work so well." Clara held up the light pink box and gave it a shake, the tablets inside crashing against each other.

"Do you know anyone particularly pale?"

"My uncle Uriah used to be so pale it seemed as though the colors ran away from him." She gave a strangled gasp when she realized she'd said it aloud.

"It's all right, Miss Field. You're a truthful sort."

"Yes, but it's never proper to speak ill of the dead, Dr. Reed." She pushed the pills onto the counter and clasped her hands together. "He passed on a little over a year ago."

"Is that what made you decide to go to Oregon?" He leaned close. "To leave behind the memories?"

"How did you—" Her head snapped up and she stared at him for a moment, wondering how he knew she and Aunt Doreen sought to leave the dreadful memories of Uncle Uriah behind forever. Then she realized the innocent nature of the question.

Many people felt haunted by good memories when someone died, that a house carried too many remembrances of happy times long passed. She chose her words carefully. "It's always difficult when a family member dies."

"Should you ever need to discuss it, Miss Field—"

"No, thank you." She softened her words. "It's still too fresh."

He looked as though he wanted to press further, but the tinny brass bell over the door jangled.

The tinkle of that bell sounded the death knell to Saul's fledgling interrogation. Just when he'd gotten her talking about her uncle, a customer had to come striding into the store. That rankled. Particularly since Dad's suspicions seemed correct.

The way Miss Field paled at the thought of her uncle—something was wrong there. Saul didn't know what, but when the sparkle in a woman's eyes died like a doused fire, something caused it. He hadn't missed what she meant by leaving behind the memories, either. Despite her cautious words about fresh pain and difficulty losing a family member, she'd not said a thing about a loved one.

The man striding up to the counter didn't know what he'd walked into. Trouble was, Saul couldn't be exactly sure himself. Only Clara knew, and guarded as she'd been, it might be a long time before he'd be able to get her talking again.

"What can I get you today?" Saul recalled meeting the tall man at church the Sunday before. "Mr. Grogan, isn't it?"

"Call me Adam. I need some baking powder."

"Sure." Saul moved across the store, tore off a strip of thick, brown paper, and rolled it into a cone. Then he shoved in the tip for good measure before opening the baking powder bin. "Say when." White powder poured from the scoop for a good while before Adam Grogan was satisfied.

"Do you need anything else?" Miss Field had risen from the low stool where she'd been sitting, digging through bottles of tinctures and cure-alls.

"No, ma'am." Adam hastily removed his hat. "Except to apologize for that hullabaloo when you first arrived. If I'd been around when the whole thing started, maybe I could have put a stop to it. As it was..." A shrug finished the statement.

"Yes." Miss Field held herself ramrod straight, and Saul wondered at the "hullabaloo" Adam referred to. "I did wish you would've made more of an effort, but I also understand you have family loyalties and the situation goes deeper than I know. All that matters is we averted the crisis."

"For the moment."

"What crisis?" Saul decided not to wait until dinnertime to ask the ladies. The longer trouble brewed, the stronger it became and the more people got hurt.

"There's bad blood between us Grogans and the Specks, you might say." Adam shifted his weight. "Sometimes it boils to the top and spills over on unsuspecting folk like Miss Field."

"Opal Speck and I averted a minor scuffle on my first Sunday in town," Miss Field clarified. "Mr. Grogan here came into the picture too late to avoid trouble altogether."

"I'd stayed home from church that morning when Sadie first showed signs of being ill." Adam reached for the poke of baking powder. "I hope this'll settle her stomach."

"She's been sick for weeks?" Saul snapped to attention. "What are her symptoms?"

"Sadie's always been energetic, but she got real tired, eyes went dull. She stopped eating and didn't want to drink much." Adam sighed. "It seemed after a while she was on the mend, but it started all over again, and now she's starting to bloat."

"Why didn't you come for me sooner?" Saul headed for the door. "I'll grab my kit. We'll go right away."

"You don't mind, Doc?" There was no mistaking the hope in Adam Grogan's tone. "I thought it'd be beneath a college-educated fellow like you.

"Dr. Reed," Miss Field interjected, "you might want to stop a mo—"

"No time to stop now." Saul could scarce credit her interruption. "Not if the girl's been without treatment for so long. Of course I'll help Sadie, Adam."

"I'm sorry I doubted you, Dr. Reed." He followed him toward the door. "I sure appreciate you taking a look at Sadie."

"Every life is sacred." Saul grabbed his jacket from the peg beside the door.

"Sadie's special, too. She's our best milking cow."

CHAPTER 12

Fort Laramie, Oregon Trail

After days on end of being cramped in the bumpy stage and endless stretches of grassy plains taunting her from the small cutout windows, Midge needed to stretch her legs.

She itched to tear off her bonnet and go racing across the earth, leaving her boots and all their buttons behind her so the long grass tickled her toes and cushioned her feet. Midge wanted to run until she gasped for breath, taking great gulps of wind and sky until she forgot the feeling of being trapped in a tiny coach, bouncing over every rock hidden on the prairie.

"We'll stop by Sutton's General Store for a few supplies while the stage trades horses." Mrs. Henderson swept toward the wooden structure, obviously intending for Midge to trail along behind.

Instead, Midge edged along the uneven, gapped cottonwood walls and buildings of Fort Laramie until she reached the far corner. Here, no soldiers marched or drilled or yelled. Mrs. Henderson, bless her for the caring soul she was, kept a gimlet eye fastened on every move Midge made unless Midge took the opportunity to break away from the scrutiny. No, this area away from the bustle of the store suited her better. It seemed quieter, as though not as

125

much in use. Farther off, behind another structure, she heard the giggles of children.

Children? I thought only soldiers lived at forts. Her immediate reaction was to pick up her pace and head toward them, hopefully have some fun before the stage changed out horses and she had to leave again. Something caught her eye—most doors were thrown open in the heat as though trying to tempt a breeze.

Only one stood shut, as though guarding a secret. A furtive glance showed nobody about, so Midge headed to explore the mystery. Her hand closed over the knob, the door gave beneath her slight pressure, and she moved to step into the darkness within.

Just then, a strong arm roped about her middle from behind, pulling her against a wiry body while the man slammed the door shut and dragged her away, toward another. Toward danger.

Midge did as Nancy taught her long ago and went limp, letting the full weight of her body sag against her attacker's arm. Sure enough, the unexpected tactic caused him to falter for a moment—long enough for her to grind her heel into the fleshy part of his foot, dig her elbow under his ribs, and jerk away in a swift movement.

She lunged for the door, shoving it open with all the force of her escape, determined to slam it against her assailant and wait him out. No such luck. He caught her before she could get behind the wood, this time wrapping his arm around both of hers and heaving her away.

To her surprise, he didn't hold her but let go, leaving her to spin like a top with the strength of his movement while he yanked the door shut once more. Midge caught her breath and backed away, taking his measure before she budged.

Tall, the boy had more years than she'd seen and verged on manhood. The anger in his hot gaze didn't translate to his stance. He'd already proved his strength, his speed, but nothing about him suggested he'd pounce on her if she ran. Which meant he wasn't interested in hurting her so much as defending whatever hid behind the door.

Now that she had her breath back, and Midge could be fairly certain her heart wouldn't burst from her chest in panic, she could recognize the heat enveloping her as anger. "Do you normally go around grabbing girls like that?"

"Do you normally go off on your own to snoop?" His voice came out deeper than she expected.

"The other doors are open." She shrugged. "Gentlemen don't manhandle ladies."

"That wasn't manhandling." He gave a snort but eyed her like he might know what she meant.

"You came up behind me, grabbed me, and dragged me backward." She huffed. "What's a girl supposed to think?"

"She should be more careful where she pokes her pretty little nose." He crossed his arms over his chest and leaned on a wooden post. "And I didn't hurt you any. You can't say the same."

"You're lucky." His lack of apology rankled, in spite of that offhanded 'pretty' remark. "I could've given you a bloody nose."

"You could've come out much worse." His frown made a wrinkle between his eyebrows. "And I would've just told you not to go there, but when I came around the corner you'd already opened the door. It was too late."

"Oh." The small concession took her aback. "What's in there?"

"Nothing at the moment." He shrugged. "But my brother Billy got sick, then Dr. Reed came and saved him, and—"

"Dr. Reed?" Midge moved closer. "You saw Dr. Reed? When?"

"Couple of weeks ago." The boy smiled for the first time, showing a slight gap between his front teeth. "He saved Billy's life."

"Then why can't I go into the room?" Midge planned to ask how Dr. Reed saved Billy's life, but first things first.

"Billy's sickness was catching, and the fort doctor hasn't cleaned out the room yet."

"Oh." She moved a little closer. "Thanks, then, and I'm sorry I stomped on your foot."

"And elbowed me in the ribs?"

"That one you deserved." She gave a little smile. "I'm Midge. I'm going to Buttonwood to meet up with Dr. Reed."

"I'm Amos Geer, and I'm sorry I grabbed you without warning. Your Dr. Reed saved my brother's life, and probably my sister's, too."

"Seems like there's no one he won't save. . . ."

"*Cow?*" Saul stopped, still gripping the door handle. "Did you say this Sadie is a cow?"

"Yes, sir." Adam plunked his hat back on his head.

"Their best milking cow." Laughter underscored Miss Field's helpful reminder from behind the counter. "Remember. . .you don't have the time to stop since she needs treatment right away." She bustled down the length of the store as though to shoo him along. When she came close, a mischievous glint shone in her green eyes.

"You meant to tell me—"

"That's right." She gave a sage nod, letting him know that if he'd just listened he could have avoided this whole mess.

"Now, Mr. Grogan"—Saul tried to maintain his dignity—"you do realize I'm not trained in bovine medicine or veterinary arts?"

"I appreciate it." Adam Grogan couldn't look more serious if he tried. "A fancy doctor like you coming to look after a milk cow is a favor I wouldn't have thought to ask."

"We're blessed to have a man like Dr. Reed who honors his word." Miss Field brushed past to open the door. "I hope everything turns out all right."

With that, Saul couldn't back out. Not with Miss Field talking about his honor, Adam Grogan full of hope and respect, and a sick creature suffering out there.

In under ten minutes, he stood in a small, musty barn, looking at a decidedly unhealthy cow. The manger stood full of hay. Green slime spreading up the sides of a full trough told of water standing for too long. In the dim light, Saul could see the cow's dangerously distended abdomen. "Let's get her outside so I can take a better look."

It took both of them to coax the listless animal outside. Eyes dull, coat lackluster, stance placid, Sadie didn't so much as bow her head to inspect the grass at her feet. Flies settled on her face, but she couldn't seem to muster the energy to flick her ears and chase them away. Her pink nose, cracked and dry, told of dehydration.

"It's gotten worse since I left," Adam remarked after surveying the cow's bloated stomach. *Stomachs,* Saul reminded himself. Cows have four.

"Last time she seemed sick, did she look the same?" If so, Saul decided they'd start from what worked before.

"She was tired and dull like this, but no bloat." Adam thought a moment. "And she had the slobbers all over the place."

"How did you treat it before?"

"Shut her up in the barn so she could rest, brought her hay and silage so she'd bulk up. In a couple of weeks she seemed better, so we let her out again." Adam patted her side. "Now she's worse."

"If she continues to bloat, her heart will stop." Saul shook his head. "I've heard of baking powder for humans and horses, but not for cows. At this point it's worth a try."

"We've tried it, but it hasn't helped yet. Do you have any other ideas?"

"Since we don't know what caused it, it's harder to treat."

"Since she got better while in the barn and worsened when she went in the open, Pa's taken to the notion that the Specks are poisoning her." Adam's eyes narrowed. "It hasn't happened before, so there has to be a solid reason."

"I doubt they're poisoning your milk cow." Saul tried not to sound like he discounted the idea out of hand but stayed firm that it wasn't likely. "She's probably eaten something that disagreed with her. Right now she needs to release some of the gas."

"If she dies, Pa will take it out of a Speck's hide." Adam's warning came low and grim, a revelation that Saul might save more than a cow.

"Best thing I can suggest at the moment is elevating her front end." Saul looked around for a good spot. "Put her on a hill so her front legs are higher and hope the gas rises out. Unless you know another way to make a cow burp, that's about the only advice I can give you."

"There's an old wives' tale that if you scare a cow, chase it around, it can help release bloat." Adam hooked his thumbs in his suspenders. "I never thought it held much truth."

"Wait." Saul considered it for a minute. "Walking Sadie might not be enough to get things moving, but running might jostle her into it. The idea makes sense, if you think about it."

"Would chasing her uphill help any?"

"I don't see how it could hurt." Saul grinned then looked at Sadie, who stared at him with big, dull brown eyes. "She doesn't look like she's going to move for anything less than a butcher knife."

"Here." Adam disappeared behind the barn and came back with a spade and a hoe. "Bang these together and on the ground to direct her toward that western rise. I'll come at her from this end."

"All right." Saul ignored the thought that his fellow doctors would howl with laughter if they could see him now. "Go!"

In a burst of movement, they rushed the cow. A tangle of waving arms, banging implements, flying dust, and hoarse shouts, the pair of them would have terrified a pack of wolves into running over that western rise.

But all their efforts didn't budge one exhausted cow. The entire Grogan family, armed with skillets and spoons, pots and lids, earned no more than a quizzical glance. Mr. Grogan's whip, a last resort, got her to shuffle to the side a few paces before heaving a beleaguered sigh.

"I know!" One of the children, a young boy with more gums than teeth, raced out of sight. A flurry of indignant cackles told Saul the youngster went to the chicken coop, and sure enough, the boy returned with a rooster tucked beneath each arm.

"Here!" The child thrust one of the birds at Adam then gifted Saul with the other squawking mass of feathers and spurs.

"Sadie's scared of 'em since that one flogger got loose and tore up her flank."

Sure enough, once Saul had his bird under control, he noticed Sadie stealthily putting distance between herself and the roosters. He exchanged a single nod with Adam before they moved in tandem.

A glorious cacophony of shouts, shrieks, squawks, and frantic lowing sounded as men, roosters, and one long-suffering cow made a mad charge up the western hill.

"It worked!" Clara announced as she came through the door. "Lucinda Grogan didn't want Willa to come over while Opal was here, but when I told her we were all pitching in to make things ready for Midge, she yielded."

"Wonderful!" Aunt Doreen clasped her hands together. "With all the help, we'll have everything ready within the day."

"Midge will be tickled when she hears her arrival has folks laying aside grievances to work together." Dr. Reed grinned, and

Clara shoved aside a stab of remorse for the real reason she'd invited all the young women over to the house.

"Lucinda's reasoning had more to do with you than Midge," Clara admitted. "Even Willa said after the sight of you and Adam brandishing roosters and chasing that cow over the hill, her mama wouldn't be able to deny you anything."

"I hold out hope Sadie will prove one of my most difficult patients." The doctor reached for his hat, clearly on his way to the store. "Though I can't claim much of the credit for her recovery, a doctor won't argue with success."

"You're overmodest, Dr. Reed," Aunt Doreen chided. "Be prepared to tell the tale over dinner, too. The ladies will ask."

"I wouldn't want to get in your way. Should I eat dinner at the café?"

"No!" Clara blurted then softened her voice. "Sally, Opal, Willa, and Amanda agreed to spend the day working on Midge's room, and it'd be a poor return to deny them your company."

He frowned. "I'd only thought to spare you the task of making a large meal, but you're right. It could be perceived as ungracious."

"We'll send someone over this afternoon, when it's time to eat."

A breath of relief escaped her when Dr. Reed left. For a moment, her plan had teetered on the brink of ruin. How would she ever convince Dr. Reed to marry one of the local girls unless he got to know them? She'd schemed to invite all the prospects over so he could spend some time with each one, and the man almost evaded them!

Clara rubbed her temples, reminding herself of the brilliance of this day's work. Not only would Dr. Reed see Opal, Sally, Willa, and even Amanda, he'd see the best of what they had to offer a husband. The comfort a wife would bring to a home and her willingness to love his children should prove appealing lures to someone like the good doctor.

A knock sounded on the front door, announcing Sally and Amanda's arrival. Clara ushered both inside, gesturing for them to set their sewing kits in the parlor. No sooner had they removed their bonnets than Opal and Willa appeared.

"Morning, Willa." Opal made the first attempt at conversation. "I like your shawl."

"Thanks." The other girl gave a tentative smile. "I've always admired your pin."

"Oh?" Opal's fingers fluttered to touch the carved jet bar on her collar. "It belonged to Mama."

Sensing that faint note of grief, Clara stepped in. "Every girl should have something pretty. That's why I'm glad you're all here to help make Midge's room welcoming."

"Oh yes." Aunt Doreen rested a hand on the first banister. "Would you like to see it before we get to work?"

"Please!" Sally moved forward. "We've never really seen the inside of this house, you know."

"It's beautiful," Amanda breathed. "Even if I lived in a regular house instead of a soddy, I'd still think this one was special."

"Yes." Clara followed everyone up the stairs, her gaze lingering on the small details carved in the banister. *Special because it represents a home we can be proud of, a way to support ourselves, an end to the searching and struggling. All it takes is one of these girls marrying Dr. Reed. . . .*

She pushed back the thought that her new friends weren't surveying the house out of polite interest or idle curiosity—it was only reasonable to assume that Dr. Reed's wife would become mistress of the home. Though Clara disliked the idea, she misled them by not directly admitting her bargain. The deal was to be held in strict confidence between herself and Mr. Reed.

Besides, any girl who married Dr. Reed might well expect to go back to Baltimore or to help him build a home and a practice here in

Buttonwood. There's no use making assumptions.

While the girls admired the spacious room and carefully selected furniture, listening as Aunt Doreen explained the projects planned for the day, Clara reminded herself that Dr. Reed would build a fine house for his bride. She needn't worry about him providing for his family.

An odd clenching sensation in her stomach sent her back to the kitchen for a drink of water. The rumbling of footsteps coming downstairs gave her enough time to smile before everyone appeared.

"Look at all this space!" Opal hung back at the door, taking it in.

"Perfect for baking." Amanda ran her hand lovingly across the worktable. "Though I'd keep the pie tins below with the pots...."

"It was arranged differently before we arrived." Clara rested her hand protectively atop the shelf, where she'd placed the pie tins beside the measuring cups.

"Arranged might be a kinder word than strictly truthful," Aunt Doreen admitted with a smile. "But I've never seen a finer kitchen."

Clara noted the speculative glance on Amanda's face as she eyed the worktable anew, as well as the curiosity behind Sally's fascination with the expensively carved hutch. One of these girls could be the way she'd succeed.

Her gaze returned to Aunt Doreen. *Then you'll never have to leave this kitchen.*

CHAPTER 13

"G ood morning," Saul greeted the older Speck brother as he wandered into the store just before noon. "What can I get you?"

Elroy meandered about for a while before selecting a spade and some lard. By the time Saul finished the transaction, Matthew Burn strode into the store. While they pored over a catalog, choosing a new leather apron for the young blacksmith, the Speck boy lingered. Not one to make assumptions, Saul decided Elroy must be waiting to meet someone. But who?

"Yep, Doc." Matthew thumped the ad with a work-roughened hand as he chose the largest apron available. "That one."

"A fine choice." Saul wrote up the order for Burn. "The leather should offer excellent protection."

When Larry Grogan sauntered in, the store went from busy to crowded. Too crowded. Instead of backing out to let Speck pass or moving out to return later, Larry blustered inside as far as he could. Eyes slid to slits as Elroy sized up the invading Grogan.

Granted, Saul couldn't claim an overabundance of experience in feuds or fights of any kind, but common sense revealed Larry's mistakes. What man, unprovoked, strutted up to a long-standing adversary, ignored his only exit, turned to cut himself off from it, and trapped himself between the two counters of a general store filled with an abundance of sharp and breakable items?

Saul already moved from behind the counter, ready to minimize the damage as best he could, when the bell over the door clanged again.

Nathan Fosset assessed the situation at a glance. "If you're about to get into it, go outside."

"He's not." Adam Grogan bypassed Fosset, fisted his hand around his brother's collar, and jerked him backward. "Larry's got things to tend to at home."

"I'm just going to check on Willa," the whelp whined, pulling away from his older brother. "And maybe stay for lunch, if the ladies ask me to."

Ah, that's his plan. Saul swallowed a grin when Elroy became very interested in his boots. It looked like Larry wasn't the only one angling for an invitation to lunch with the town's marriageable ladies. Of the men in town, they'd all know since their sisters made up part of the group. Which meant Fosset probably didn't have an urgent need for that coffee he stared at so blankly.

"What ladies?" Suspicion colored the blacksmith's tone. "What lunch?"

Adam looked around the store at the assorted bachelors, giving Saul the missing piece. "He's the only one who doesn't have a sister."

"Some of the ladies in town, including all of the sisters of these good fellows"—Saul made a wide gesture—"generously agreed to spend the day helping Miss Field and Mrs. Edgerly prepare a room for Midge, who will be arriving on the next stage."

"The orphan," Larry muttered.

"The young girl I've taken as my ward," Saul corrected. There was to be no mistake—everyone would treat Midge with respect, not pity. "The women are sewing and such forth at my father's house today."

"All of them?" Burn's eyes were wide as he processed this. "Miss Fosset, Miss Speck, Miss Grogan, and Miss Dunstall, all over with Miss Field?"

Elroy gave a brief nod. "Yep."

"With Mrs. Edgerly," Saul added to be fair.

"So you all showed up around noon." Burn's eyes narrowed as he looked at the men around him. "You didn't even tell me?" This last he gave in a loud whisper to Nathan Fosset, who Saul assumed to be a close friend.

Nathan managed an unrepentant shrug before pinning his gaze on Saul. "Guess we've been caught hoping for an invite, Dr. Reed."

Embarrassment gave way to purpose as heads came up, shoulders went back, and jaws squared. Every bachelor in Buttonwood eyed Saul as Larry gave voice to the challenge in the air. "So what do you say?"

"The more, the merrier." Clara could hardly believe her good fortune.

"Are you sure?" Mrs. Dunstall set down the pan nervously. "I only meant to bring by the raisin bread, not stay for lunch."

"You've said yourself the diner's not seen a customer since Dr. Reed arrived," Clara reminded her. A striking young widow of only thirty-one years, Mrs. Dunstall had married and borne Amanda very young, which left her in the ranks of eligible women for Dr. Reed. This golden opportunity wouldn't slide out of Clara's hands. The more women, the better. "We'd be more than happy to have you at the table! Please join us."

"I suppose it wouldn't hurt." A smile spread across Vanessa

Dunstall's face. "Let me run back to the café and bank the fire."

"Absolutely." Clara returned to the parlor, where the newly repatched quilt lay folded on a table and the women worked on a matching sham. "How goes the project?"

Aunt Doreen sifted through the remaining squares. "We'll need more yellow and green fabric. Would it be any trouble to pick out a little when you fetch Saul for dinner?"

"I'll come with you!" Sally stuck her needle in her corner of the quilting and rose to her feet. "It'll be a good chance for me to look over the fabric in stock anyway."

"The same thought crossed my mind," Amanda admitted.

"That tea set cries out for a tablecloth," Opal added. "If we can add that to the list. . ."

"And napkins to match!" Willa's shy smile blossomed. "I could help pick out the material, if you want."

Every one of them wants to fetch Dr. Reed and catch his eye. It's working!

"All of you go." Aunt Doreen made shooing motions. "Dinner's all ready and I can put it on the table. Bring back what we need and we'll enjoy a nice meal."

"Vanessa Dunstall will be by in a moment to join us," Clara announced. "She brought raisin bread."

"Ma's raisin bread could make a stubborn mule behave," Amanda promised. "You'll love it."

"Would it work on a stubborn ox?" Thoughts of glove-eating Simon danced in Clara's mind as she led the troop of girls to the store.

Her small flock of women patted their hair, angled their bonnets, dusted tiny specks of lint from their bodices, and studiously avoided any damp spots in the street as they made their way to the shop. Their obvious preening told Clara more clearly than any words could that any one of her friends would be happy to marry Dr. Reed. Each woman would make a good wife.

Distracted by the thought, Clara opened the door to the shop before realizing she'd never seen it so full. . .

Of men. Tension crackled in the place.

"Elroy?" Opal moved past her to stare at her brother. "What are you doing here?"

"Larry?" Willa slid over to implore her brother. "You're not causing trouble?"

Clara shot Dr. Reed a pleading glance. Hostilities between the Specks and Grogans couldn't erupt now—not when Willa and Opal were getting along, and especially not when she was so close to pulling off this crucial luncheon!

"We were having such a nice day," Sally fretted, drawing close to Matthew Burn and looking up at him through her lashes.

"They won't ruin it, miss." Mr. Burn puffed out his barrel chest and lowered his voice. "I won't let them."

"Neither will I." Nathan Forrect moved to stand in Willa's line of vision. "Don't you worry, Miss Grogan."

"Larry's on his way back to the farm." Adam Grogan's gaze found Opal's and held fast, a silent promise not to double-team her brother even Clara could read.

"We have things well in hand," Elroy Speck directed his assurances to Amanda.

Just like that, Clara watched every young woman she'd rounded up for Saul's selection be claimed by a Buttonwood bachelor. Admiring glances flew in coy exchanges across the store. Men cleared their throats and straightened their posture while the girls patted their hair and smoothed their skirts. They paired up as though facing the gangplank to Noah's ark.

No. No, I can salvage this. Clara's thoughts raced past the avoided fight, the almost catastrophic interlude unraveling before her very eyes, and straight to the one stronghold in her plan. *Dinner.* Just

Saul and the ladies and *no other men.*

"Your assistance was greatly appreciated, gentleman." She spoke loudly enough to garner everyone's attention. "I'm afraid the store must close for a brief while. We came to tell Dr. Reed it's time for dinner."

"Dinner does sound good." One of the men put a hand over his abdomen, and several swiftly followed suit.

"Had they known there'd be such an"—Dr. Reed glanced around, obviously taking note of the same things she had—"influx of business, the women would have been glad to make extra food and invite everyone. As it stands, there surely won't be enough for so many strapping men."

"No." Clara fought to look regretful of the fact. "I'm afraid not, gentlemen."

"I reckon I'll go to the café." Elroy Speck's tone matched his hangdog look, which should have made Amanda bristle at the implied insult.

"Oh, you can't!" A wide smile spread across her face. "Ma's joining us for dinner. Isn't that right, Miss Field?" She didn't wait for Clara to answer before adding excitedly, "We keep extra food on hand and can rustle things up really fast when needed. With Ma's help, we'll be able to have everyone over."

A chorus of eager agreement sounded from the men—sung in round by the women, who seconded the "fine idea."

Clara searched desperately for a way to veto the suggestion. "Such a generous suggestion, Amanda, and I know you don't mind the trouble"—she paused while every one of her potential matches promised to help in the kitchen—"but we can't take the business away from your mother's café like that if these men planned to be paying customers."

She relaxed at the remorse on the faces surrounding her as they took that into account. By hook or by crook, she'd get things done, and business was the one thing she could fall back on as an excuse.

"Oh, I'll gladly pony up for a fine meal and better company." Matthew Burn stepped forward. "There's no reason for Mrs. Dunstall to miss dinner with her friends or the business to her café if we can bring them together."

"Couldn't have said it better m'self." Nathan Fosset nodded.

"My brother and I will pass, if it's all the same. We've got a lot of work on the farm." Adam Grogan, the one who'd rode up late that first Sunday and told her and Opal to move, caught his troublemaking brother by the arm.

"Surely you can stomach a meal with a Speck, Adam Grogan?" Opal's voice held quiet determination. "Your sister's strong enough to be civil."

Adam froze, his grip tightening on his brother's sleeve as Larry tried to whirl around. "Go." He shoved Larry out the door. "Tell Ma I'm staying to have dinner with Willa while you see to things at home." Only after Larry stomped off did he turn around and give Opal a quirked smile. "We'll see what I can stomach."

"Two Specks, two Grogans, one big meal." Opal seemed to belatedly realize she'd taken the arrangements for granted. "If it's all right by you, Dr. Reed?"

"So long as Mrs. Dunstall doesn't mind." Dr. Reed's approval brought smiles all around. . . .

Except for Clara. No sense trying to deny it—she'd be eating her plans for lunch.

"That worked out well," Saul commented to Miss Field as everyone headed toward his father's house, arms laden with dishes from the diner.

A strangled sound came from her throat, causing him to look

at her in concern. Dad's talk about how the woman wouldn't be one to admit to feeling poorly flashed through his mind. "What's wrong?"

"Oh, nothing." She stayed back while everyone tromped through the mud room and into the house. "My throat went dry for a moment. I'll be sure to drink some water."

"With Mrs. Dunstall adding to the meal, and the other women helping, you should take a moment to rest." He held the door for her. "Since you've done so much to arrange everything."

"How could I let my invited guests work in the kitchen while I laze about?" She shot him an incredulous look.

"Mrs. Dunstall will be reimbursed for her efforts," Saul pointed out. "Besides, only so many women can cook in a single kitchen."

"I'll be one of them. In addition to which"—she lowered her voice and leaned toward him, green eyes snapping—"I invited Mrs. Dunstall. Her willingness to work on what was meant to be a respite is a favor. I'll come alongside her."

An unsettling suspicion wormed its way into his thoughts. "Miss Field," he, too, spoke quietly, as if the loud group spread out in the parlor and kitchen would overhear them, "would you have preferred I sent the men home?"

"I'd rather have kept the day simple." The admission cost her a bit of resolve. "But there weren't many options."

"They were rather determined." Saul chuckled. "I couldn't see any other way to earn Mrs. Dunstall some much-needed business and keep myself and my father's store in good standing with all those gentlemen. Dinner seemed the easy way to avoid ugliness between the feuding families and also set up a happy arrival for Midge this next week."

"You're right." She moved past him to the doorway. "If you could make a special effort to let the women know you appreciate all they've done, it would be wise."

"Of course." Saul went to join the men as she disappeared around the corner.

"Nice place your father built here, Saul." Matthew Burn, the one man Saul knew from childhood, steered the conversation to deeper waters. "He built it hoping you'd come set up your practice in Buttonwood and fill the place with grandbabies to dandle on his knee."

"Dad knew what he gave up when he left Baltimore." Regret tugged at his heart, and resentment boiled from his stomach as Saul made his decision clear. "I've a practice to finish setting up and plans for back home."

"I'm not sure he's convinced." Burn shrugged. "I offered to buy the place if he was interested in selling, but he turned me down flat."

Nathan Fosset goaded his friend. "Looking to settle down, eh, Burn?"

"Don't spit in the wind, Fosset," Adam Grogan spoke up from where he leaned on the mantel. "You pushed for an invite to lunch with the ladies, too." Ignoring the dirty looks cast his way by a few other bachelors, he directed his next statement to Saul. "Doc, you could do plenty of good here. You traveled the trail and saw the graves. Wagon trains come all through late spring and summer with everything from ailments to epidemics. We've been all right so far, God be praised, but the day can't be far off when Buttonwood's gonna need a doctor."

"My decision stands, gentlemen." Saul wouldn't discuss the matter any further. The poor of Baltimore lacked medical care just as much as the pioneers traveling West, who'd chosen the treacherous trail. Hannah and his niece or nephew-to-be lived in the city.

Then, too, he'd promised Midge they'd return, and he wouldn't rob her of the scant comfort of familiarity. She'd go to school close enough so he could visit her regularly. No, his resolve couldn't be frittered away like dust on a breeze. They'd return to Baltimore, as he planned.

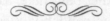

My jaw hurts. Clara raised a hand to rub the soreness before she resumed brushing her hair. Gnashing may be too strong a term, but she'd ground her teeth all through dinner yesterday and beyond. Otherwise, the smile dropped from her lips, and she couldn't explain her frustration over what seemed such a *successful* gathering.

Successful. Clara didn't consider herself the sort to dwell on unpleasant matters, but there came a time when every woman needed to reevaluate. She thrust her hairbrush back on the bureau hard enough to make a dull thud. The loose bun she'd worn at breakfast proved too loose, so she settled on a strict style. Clara divided her unruly golden waves into sections, twisting them with short, hard jerks into a tidy French braid. If only she could direct Dr. Reed as easily as she ordered her hair. After tying off the end with a jaunty blue ribbon which would peek from beneath her bonnet, she set about buttoning her shoes.

A perfect plan. Dr. Reed enjoying a fine meal with four—five, with Mrs. Dunstall joining them—prospective brides the day before the whole town would go to the Fossets' for threshing. He'd get to know the ladies one day, have the opportunity to see them among the community next, and with each visit he'd grow more involved until he settled on one. Having five unmarried women at the table with one bachelor was the marital equivalent of trying to hit the broadside of a barn.

What Clara presumed impossible turned out to be merely improbable. Not only could the plan miss, so to speak, it backfired spectacularly. How else could she explain hosting the most successful matchmaking meal ever seen in the Nebraska Territory?

Not one of her friends, sweet young maidens all, caught Dr. Reed's eye, while focusing instead on the town bachelors.

Dr. Reed, unlike the other men, seemed no closer to courting any of the women. The thought of her failure made her swipe at her nails until the buffer squeaked and her fingertips glowed.

With a deep breath and a prayer for patience, she left the room to join Aunt Doreen, who'd been wrapping a loaf of bread, a plate of biscuits, and a bowl of sweet potato pudding to take to the threshing today. The Fossets would provide the heartier fare, and the women in the town would help cook it once they arrived, but baking took more time and finesse than the occasion allowed.

"If you're both ready, the wagon's waiting outside." Dr. Reed ducked inside, the open door revealing early morning's shy glow.

With her cloak snug around her shoulders and the pudding bowl in her arms, Clara followed Dr. Reed to the wagon. She settled in the back with her aunt, cushioned by old blankets and surrounded by dishes.

A cleverly designed saddlebag, unhooked from its accompanying harness, rested beside them. Clara knew from Dr. Reed's descriptions that it held his medical instruments and powders in small compartments which would fold out when needed. Sturdy brown leather and the ability to convert from portable bag to weatherproof saddlebag made its versatility unmatchable.

He'd paid the princely sum of twelve dollars for the convenience of his unconventional "little black bag"—a detail Clara needed to work into the conversation among the women of the town to underscore how well Dr. Reed would provide for his family. Discussing financial details bordered on vulgarity, but Clara was in no position to overlook any marital incentive when it came to finding Dr. Reed a wife.

They pulled to a stop near the Fosset house, where other wagons dotted the area. Women in full skirts flocked to the house with hurried steps, eager greetings, and home-baked goods. Small children raced around a hastily fenced-in yard. Others played jacks and took turns with hoops. The men gathered in clumps around the farm—some loading a deep wagon with loose sheaves of cut grain, most working to connect heavy iron tumbling rods or set up wooden sweeps to harness the horses who'd power the thresher all day. Frost softened to dew sparkling in the sun, leaving the farmers and helpful tradesmen to do the day's work without interference.

As Clara reached back into the wagon for one of the dishes, she noticed Sally and Opal heading toward the wagon. Toward Dr. Reed. Her first real smile of the day teased the corners of her mouth.

Another day, another chance to repay Mr. Reed's kindness and secure Aunt Doreen's future.

CHAPTER 14

"Glad to see you, Dr. Reed." Nathan Fosset clapped him on the shoulder. "Today we'll return a little of your hospitality."

"I don't recall making you work for your dinner." Saul grinned to take the bite from his words.

"Depends on what you call work." Adam Grogan strode up to join them. "They danced around the issue long enough to work up a sweat."

"You shouldn't be so keen to talk about dancing." Fosset's gaze held a glint of anger. "The way you and the Specks've been circling each other, I expect to see buzzards on the horizon."

"Mind you don't stir things up," Saul broke in.

"We all enjoyed dinner yesterday." Elroy Speck gave a nonchalant shrug. "I see no reason to forget that."

A short nod was all the approval he needed from Adam. Anything the Specks and Grogans agreed on put the other party squarely in the wrong.

"Right," Fosset muttered.

"We've got the power set up," Matthew Burn announced, gesturing toward where his father hitched the horses to the cylinder. "Band-cutting tables are hooked to the separator, and the straw carrier's ready. As soon as the horses set up a rhythm and everyone's in position, we'll be in business."

As one, they headed for their stations. Frank Fosset hopped atop the power, giving the cry of "Teams on!" The horses began to move, sending the rods tumbling with dull clangs like blunt wind chimes. Individual teeth in the thresher awoke and stretched, hastening until they became a steel blur keeping time to the cylinder's constant hum.

Saul, who'd never before seen the process, waited to relieve one of the men who sacked the threshed grain. Free to observe, he drank in the scene, reveling in its unexpected complexity. So many men performing various steps, all working in harmony to complete one job. He'd never seen anything close to it in the city.

Workers stood atop wagons filled with hay, forking bundles onto the band-cutting tables, where the burly Burn scooped the sheaves. One swift, graceful motion sliced the band and unrolled the wheat into an even belt entering the maw of the machine. This kept on in a constant course of cooperation, underscored by the whir of the power and the smothered snarl of the separator itself.

Saul heard both from where he stood. The strong yellow stalks entered the machine, where metal teeth ripped and slashed, spewing straw and chaff into the air for two younger boys to rake into some semblance of order. The pieces drifted everywhere, tickling noses and scratching beneath collars. Saul couldn't imagine trying to stack the itchy stuff.

All of this work, in addition to the plowing, sowing, and harvesting that came before the threshing, for something he'd taken for granted all his life. Saul watched as the threshed grain came pouring out of the machine, filling sack after sack, which were put to the side to be sewn shut. This would later be ground into flour to make bread. *So much work, and I never appreciated any of it.*

The time for mulling it over soon passed, and his arms and back soon appreciated just how much work threshing took. He hefted bag after bag of grain under the hot sun, breathing in the smell of his own sweat, the prairie dust, and the heady quality of the fresh grain. There weren't words to describe the grain, exactly, though it had an earthy feel much like some nuts and a hint of tang that made for good biscuits, but Saul would recognize it the rest of his life. The steady rhythm, sound, smell, and movement meshed into a smear of exertion until the gears ground to a halt.

Dinnertime. After the parson said grace, Saul headed for one of the metal tubs set out as washbasins for the men, choosing a far one that stood in the shade of the barn. He reached it first. The cool water closed over his arms, so refreshing that Saul followed the lead of other workers and dipped his head beneath the surface. Sliding down his face, dripping down the back of his neck, the water provided instant relief from the heat.

Saul mopped it up with his bandanna, finger combing his hair before putting his hat back on. He surrendered the basin to the next man, moving to take a drink from the smaller bucket and lingering in the shade a moment more. The moisture trickled past his parched lips, a measure of coolness he felt clear down to his stomach, which gave a loud roar.

By the time he reached the tables of food, he brought up the rear. A second growl chided him for waiting in the shade, but Saul ignored it. He turned to move to the back of the line and just about ran into Miss Field. How a man could do that when she looked so fresh and pretty in her soft blue dress, Saul didn't know, but he caught himself by placing his hands on her shoulders.

She stared at him, silent, with wide eyes.

"Miss Field?" When she still didn't speak, worry jolted through him. "Is something wrong?"

⟨≈⟩ ∞ ⟨≈⟩

Clara almost walked right past Dr. Reed. The man barely resembled the man she sought, and then only in his face.

No, Dr. Reed wore dark slacks, a matching vest with pocket watch fob, a well-cut jacket, and collared shirt. On Sundays he added a silk tie. He stood a bit taller than other men without making one feel awkward, his dark eyes kind beneath severely parted hair that rarely strayed out of place.

This man, on the other hand, wore no jacket. No somber vest constrained his strength. A cotton shirt, sleeves rolled up and collar slightly unbuttoned, stretched across shoulders far broader than Clara recalled. His time in Buttonwood lent golden color to his skin, and for the first time, his hair kissed his brow in a bid for freedom.

When her hand moved to brush it beneath the brim of his hat, Clara fisted her fingers and moved her gaze away from his face, staring fixedly at her own eye level to regain composure. Unfortunately, her eye level reached the base of his throat, exposed by the two undone buttons of his shirt. The sun lavished radiance on a lone drop of water clinging to his collarbone.

The words caught in her throat as that droplet winked at her, the heat of his hands on her shoulders spreading down her spine. She watched in fascination as his Adam's apple moved, and the rumble of his voice washed over her.

"Is something wrong?"

You look different. She kept the thought to herself, not through any prudent decision but because her mouth wouldn't form words. A dry swallow didn't loosen her tongue, but the weight of his gaze made her flush with embarrassment.

"Is the heat bothering you?" He ran the backs of his fingers over her forehead and down her cheek, the light pressure making her tingle with intensity.

"Yes," she managed to croak over her own mortification. "It is overly warm."

"Let's sit you down." He tucked her arm into the crook of his and steered her toward the leafy cover of the cottonwood tree.

Since that's where Aunt Doreen and all the girls waited for her to bring Dr. Reed so he could sample their cooking, Clara didn't protest. The area beneath the tree cooled her hot cheeks, and she hoped her blush faded as she sank to the grass near her friends. She kept her head bowed, waiting for everyone to distract him while she regained her composure.

"The heat's gotten to her."

"Clara, are you all right?" Aunt Doreen's concern prompted her to give a nod, but it seemed she wouldn't escape further scrutiny.

Dr. Reed hunkered down beside her, one large hand reaching beneath her chin to tug the ties of her sunbonnet. He ignored her muffled squeak of objection but used her surprised movement to glide the bonnet off completely. Its ribbons danced in a breeze she barely felt as Aunt Doreen put it to the side.

"Is that water?" He spoke as he reached for a mug, the cotton of his shirt brushing her hair and sending shivers dancing across the back of her neck. "Drink this." His grasp folded over hers.

She swallowed every drop before registering he'd given her a command, not a kind offer of refreshment. Dr. Reed didn't look after her as a gentleman concerning himself with a lady's comfort but with the determination of a physician caring for a patient. Curiosity surged to replace awkwardness as Clara considered the difference.

He let go of the cup and continued to study her.

"Thank you." She turned the empty cup in her hands. "I feel much better."

"Any dizziness?" The intensity of his gaze made her breath hitch for a moment. "Shortness of breath?"

A wry smile tilted her lips as she shook her head. "I'm quite recovered. There's no need for agitation any longer."

"Let me be the judge of that." Words that might have made her bristle came with no browbeating, only determined humor. "You'll eat something before I'm persuaded."

"I'll get something light to start, along with more water." Amanda took the cup and left.

"You took on too much." Opal rested beside her. "There wasn't any need to take Mrs. Warren's turn at the cookfire just after your own."

"Her babe needed attention," Clara pointed out. "I'm fine now, thanks to Dr. Reed's swift treatment." She made sure to fix in everyone's minds how thoughtful he'd been. It didn't take much to see what a considerate husband he'd make.

"Honestly, I don't know how you men work the thresher for hours on end with the sun beating down on you." Clara noticed Sally eyeing Dr. Reed's shoulders and knew her comment had succeeded not only in drawing attention away from her little difficulty but toward Dr. Reed's manly contribution to the day's work.

"We don't battle the constrictions of women's fashions." His response alluded to the corsets they all wore, tightening their lungs and shortening their breaths. Thankfully, he'd too many manners to humiliate them by mentioning them directly. "Heatstroke is a threat to be taken seriously by all."

"After so much hard work, you deserve a hearty meal." Willa passed him a plate heaped with food.

"Thank you." Dr. Reed accepted it and looked around. "Where are your plates?"

"The men eat first. We go after, since we've had the opportunity to taste all morning." Sally handed him a fork. "We knew the others would storm the tables, and since this is your first threshing, we wanted to be sure you got some of everything. You're the only one who doesn't have anything to gain by being here today."

"I wouldn't say that." He started to eat. "The Burns don't have a farm for folks to return the help, nor do the Dunstalls."

"No, but the Burns repair the thresher and shoe the horses and take part in the community same as everyone else," Opal reminded.

"And everyone pitched in to build our café." Amanda said as she returned with the water and gave it to Clara. "Were they telling you why we saved you a plate?"

"Yes." Dr. Reed smiled at everyone. "I'm so glad you did. Ladies, I've never enjoyed a meal more."

"Good." Clara handed him the water. "Let there be many more."

Chapter 15

Y ou gotta stop hoggin' the ladies, Doc." Larry Grogan's nasal tones invaded their haven scant moments before he plunked down beside Miss Field with an overblown grin.

"He does no such thing." Her indignation made her fine brows beetle slightly. With her chin raised, clear green eyes flashing, Miss Field made up for Larry's irritation. "Dr. Reed merely sought to help when I didn't feel well." A faint hint of rose swept her cheeks at the admission of her own weakness.

Dad's assessment of Miss Field's reluctance to let anyone trouble himself over her couldn't prove more accurate. Here she sat, moments after suffering from the heat, rising to his defense like a mythical Valkyrie. Dappled sunlight flirted through the leaves to gleam in the gold of her hair.

"Grogan's words may be blunt as a mallet," Matthew Burn settled next to Miss Fosset, carefully balancing two plates as he spoke, "but you can't fault him for wanting to join you." What Saul assumed to be fodder for the blacksmith's huge frame turned out to be pure cunning. His old acquaintance silently held out one of the plates, along with a fork, to Miss Fosset.

"Thank you, Mr. Burn." She accepted the offering with a

delighted smile. "How thoughtful!"

Saul smothered his amusement as he watched the fallout of Matthew's courting. Miss Dunstall and Miss Grogan both gave small sighs at the gesture, which didn't go unnoticed by the two other bachelors approaching their group. Nathan Fosset and Elroy Speck, each holding only one plate, headed back to the tables to rectify their mistake.

Most interesting, though, was the reaction of his fellow observer, Miss Field. She watched the entire proceedings first with an obvious air of approval at Matthew's gesture then apparent disgust at Larry's gaping mouth. These swiftly faded to a soft look of seeming wistful disbelief warring with frustration.

Two facets captured his curiosity. Could the wistful shine be a longing for a sweetheart of her own? He'd not seen her encourage any man's interest. And that hint of frustration he glimpsed, so uncharacteristic from what he'd seen, could only be ascribed to Larry's intrusion. Even as he deciphered the expression, her eyes changed again, slanting a concerned glance toward Miss Speck.

The only one of Miss Field's friends not to have a steady admirer present, Miss Speck would be left to fetch her own plate. With the problem pinpointed, Saul immediately stood up.

"Miss Speck, I plan to claim another biscuit and some of that honey if there's any left. Is it true your family cultivates it?"

"Yes." A smile flitted across her face, transforming her for a brief moment. "I keep the bees."

"Fascinating. Would you accompany me to the tables and tell me about it?" Saul didn't miss the pleased look on Miss Field's face as he extended the invitation to her friend.

"Certainly."

From there, the respite of lunch passed quickly. Saul stood at the thresher once more, now in the heat of the afternoon with the weight of a full belly. His muscles groaned until he found the rhythm again. Fill, close, haul, repeat, all to the steady drone of the machine. Everyone moved to the same pulse, shifting and pulling in a seamless pattern as hours melded to bushels filled.

When the golden brown tones of grain turned darker, the metal chutes glowing orange then blue, everything scraped to a halt. The final bag held more air than grain, and Saul asked if he should put it aside for tomorrow.

"That's it." Nathan Fosset slumped on a stack of sacks sewn shut. "We didn't just quit for sundown. We're finished. Since we raise oxen, we grow more in the way of corn for fodder and silage than we do grain."

Saul trudged to the washbasin before supper, cleaned up, thanked God for the meal and the parson for a short blessing, and sank onto the nearest bench with a plate full of whatever had been within reach. No one spared the energy to talk, focusing solely on the food.

After the first plate, Saul's aching muscles had gone blissfully numb. He helped himself to a mug of coffee strong enough to fell an ox, downed it in two swallows, and filled it again before going back to refill his plate. Only now could he appreciate what the women worked on all day.

Every man in town had already gobbled several heaping plates worth of food today, and these tables still swelled with bounty. Fried chicken, roast duck, ham hocks, beef stew, thick gravy, and platters of chops filled one makeshift table. Another bore biscuits, rolls, sliced sourdough, cornbread, and more salads than he could describe, from potato to coleslaw. The final stand held pies, cookies, puddings, and cakes to tempt any appetite.

Saul drained the coffee again, revitalized and ready to enjoy this fine cooking instead of bolting it down. He helped himself to another plateful and refilled his mug before swiping an empty seat next to Adam Grogan.

"You put in a hard day's work," the farmer commented between bites of his own feast.

"Everyone did."

"This is different work than you're used to." Adam's gaze held respect. "And nothing you profit by."

"I'm glad to help."

"Are you handy with a needle?"

"Are you injured?"

"No. Old Mr. Doane's slower than he was last year, and we've got a lot of sacks to sew shut before we leave." A grin stretched across Adam's face. "Think you can ply a needle through burlap?"

"Figures you'd be trying to arrange a sewing contest, Adam." Scorn dripped from Larry's tone as he addressed his older brother.

Saul itched to teach him some respect. He left Adam to handle his own business, as he'd more than proved himself capable of reigning in his scoundrel of a sibling.

"Sewing takes a great deal of skill." Miss Field shot Larry a look of reproof. "After a long day of threshing, your brother and Dr. Reed are to be admired for volunteering to work into the night."

Several girls sent both of them appreciative glances to punctuate that statement then turned expectantly toward the men with whom they'd shared lunch.

Saul shifted uncomfortably.

"I don't know what Larry's thinking, making knuckleheaded comments like that." Matthew Burn held up his ham-sized hands. "Needles seem to stick in all the wrong places, if you ask me, but I'm game to try."

"He probably doesn't want to compete." The jeer came from Elroy Speck, who hastened to add, "I won't back away from the challenge."

"The more of you who sign on, the fewer bags left for me to

stitch shut." Fosset grinned at his lessening workload but spared a grimace for Larry.

"I never said I wouldn't do it," Larry muttered the words but maintained a mutinous scowl. "Contest usually means there's a prize for the winner."

"Shut your mouth and listen to my father's announcement," Nathan Fosset warned, "before you say something even more foolish."

Frank Fosset stood before the wall of the barn, a large fire casting his shadow into prominence over the sacks of grain, the two looped off corners of each bag sticking out like a set of cow's ears. "You all know we got to such a pace today we fell behind sewing the bags shut. For those interested, we're fixing to have a contest to see what man can sew 'em off the fastest."

"What's the winner get, Pa?" Nathan hollered the question, shooting a smug glance at Larry. Silence fell as the entire town awaited the answer.

"The team, and yes, I said team—one man to stitch the bags, one man to haul 'em to the barn—that does the most earns a summertime treat from my daughter, Sally. The very last of our stockpiled ice from last winter will make ice cream for those hardworking men, to be enjoyed fresh at the next threshing."

His stomach might not be able to hold another bite right now, but Saul knew without a doubt that come noon the next time he worked a threshing, he'd want that prize. He wouldn't have thought anyone had an icehouse. And even if someone did, every last shard usually vanished by August.

Just imagining the sweet coldness sliding down his throat, a welcome relief after inhaling scratchy bits of hay and grain dust all day, practically made his mouth water. He looked around for a partner and found Matthew's eyebrows raised.

Saul gave a nod. His stitches would save Burn his clumsy jabs with the needle, while Matt's strength would spare Saul from hauling the sacks to the barn. A slow smile spread across his face as he gauged the other teams. There was nothing like a little rivalry to bring out the best in a man.

So many men couldn't compete without things getting ugly. Clara suppressed a groan as squabbles over partners broke out, followed hard with bickering over who would sew and who would carry.

"You take the haulin'," Larry directed his brother. His obvious attempt to squirm out of the heavy lifting, particularly after his derision of sewing, made Clara turn away.

"I'm rooting for Matthew," Sally confided. Color bloomed high on her cheeks as she looked at the young blacksmith, who spoke with Dr. Reed. "Even when he's not threshing, he spends the day beside a blasting furnace. If anyone deserves some ice cream, it's one of the Burns."

"I see." Clara didn't need to mention that Matthew's father and brother made up a separate team. After witnessing the fledgling couple over lunch for two days in a row, she saw how the wind blew.

Though she hated to lower her own odds of success, Clara no longer listed Sally among Dr. Reed's prospective brides. A wedding loomed large in her friend's future, but it would be a matter strictly between bride and groom in that case. No house would make Clara stand in the way of Sally's happiness.

Which made it a blessing the two men formed a team. "I'll be cheering them on, as well." She'd encourage Matthew and Sally's budding romance but expected the focus of this contest to fall on Dr. Reed. Outdoing every other man in town would go a long way toward recapturing the attention of the remaining ladies.

After his kindness to her this afternoon, Clara would have

cheered him on even if there were no bargain. He'd put in a hot morning's work then focused on taking care of her. Sally was wrong. If any man in town deserved a treat, it was Dr. Reed. Clara craned her neck as the teams took their places.

The "haulers" stood next to the stash of bags, each one loosely wound shut with twine. Any dropped sack resulted in a penalty. Any lost grain cost the team two sacks from their final count. The "threaders" sat on benches arranged horseshoelike around a jumping fire so they could see what they worked on.

At the call of "Ready. . ." the whole town caught its breath, causing a stillness broken only by the pop of the fire, until "Go!" made the men spring into action. The haulers grabbed sacks, moving them to the threaders as fast as they could.

The weakest lifted their bags like large children, clasping them to their chests and waddling forward to deposit them before their teammates. Others scooped the sacks up, using their arms like shovels to get the job done. Some swung a sack under each of their arms and hustled toward the fire as though ready to knock down anyone in their paths. These men moved the fastest and grabbed the most sacks, but they dropped the most, too.

Clara processed all this scrambling, cheering along with everyone else, but swiftly turned her attention to Dr. Reed. Sitting on the end of one of the benches, boots planted firmly against the ground and a sack of grain braced between them, he looked to have a good start.

The firelight flickered reddish orange over his shirt, lending his skin a golden cast as he deftly threaded the large needle, knotted the end, and pinched the edges of the sack. Concentration furrowed his brow, bringing his hat down to block his eyes from her view as he pushed the needle through the burlap. He moved with grace, skill, and careful expertise.

Slowly.

Shaking her head, Clara looked again to be sure. Dr. Reed eased the blunt needle through the rough weave of the burlap as though expecting more resistance from the fabric. As though time didn't concern him and this wasn't a competition. As though precision mattered more than finishing and a neat row of stitches held importance.

Understanding flooded her. He stitched like a doctor suturing a wound. Others moved on to bags four or five, and her chosen contestant finally looked up after accomplishing his first. Shock flitted across his features as he witnessed the burlap butchery practiced by the other contestants, who jabbed their needles in and out without bothering to pull the thread taut or attempt any semblance of straight stitches.

Only intense pressure from her teeth sinking into her lip kept Clara's giggles from spilling out as she took in the scene. Matthew, the only man to master the fine art of carrying three bags at once— one over each shoulder but both held at the base of his neck with one hand, and a third sack slumped in his free arm, had all but built a fort around Dr. Reed. Only the area before him, needed for the firelight, remained open.

Beyond the makeshift structure, the elbows jabbed the air and needles punched through bags as though chasing personal vendettas. Haulers shifted from claiming more sacks for their teams to piling sewn bags in the barn, smirking at Matthew as he cradled the sole mark on his tally sheet and made his way to the barn.

Her smile faded at those smirks. Matthew toted more bags than any one of those men, and while Dr. Reed lacked speed, he did a fine job. Were she to purchase a bag of grain, she'd choose his over any other, certain no bugs would have wormed their ways inside between slapdash stitches.

Clara noticed she wasn't the only one to resent those smug glances. Dr. Reed took the next sack, readied his needle, and tipped off his hat. He pointedly set it atop the vast mound of bags Matthew earmarked for him and fell to stitching with renewed vigor.

His moves became sharper, less fluid. The stitches lengthened but remained strong and rigid as he thrust the needle in and out in a more steady rhythm. Gaze unwavering in the dancing light, he tied off the sack and reached for the next. He still made more stitches per bag than any other man, and kept them firmer and more even, yet Dr. Reed exhibited great determination.

"You can do it, Matthew!" Sally cheered loudly as Mr. Burn hefted another bag.

He gave her a saucy wink as he toted it toward the barn, a hint of a strut in his step as Saul's sewing steadily caught them up. His economy of movement, deftness, and skill more than made up for his scruples over quality. The indiscriminate techniques so arrogantly displayed by the others became more haphazard as the contest wore on and they sought to save time.

"Hurry up!" A red-faced Larry shoved a bag of grain at his brother, who'd been waiting for him to finish. The slipshod stitching ripped apart from the strain, spewing the contents of the bag all over his feet. The acrid smell of burned wheat tainted the air as some hit the flames licking farthest from the center of the fire.

Saul didn't so much as look up from his work while the other teams halted to jeer at the Grogans' misfortune. Tempers raised as paces slowed, eyelids drooped, and shoulders slumped. When the fire burned low and the men finished, consulting the numbers seemed more a formality than anything else.

Clara made a beeline to congratulate Dr. Reed, only to find that Amanda Dunstall and Willa Grogan, who'd shot Larry a haughty glance at that final embarrassment, had beat her to it.

She pulled up short. *It worked!* She watched as several other townspeople blocked him from her vision. *He's recaptured the attention of the girls!* Success couldn't be far behind.

CHAPTER 16

"Mornin', Dr. Reed." Adam Grogan greeted him as they set up to thresh the Grogan grain. "I'm glad to see you're on hand to help out."

"After working the Fossct place, you should've dropped like a fly," Larry grunted as he toted two water pails past them. "If you don't have to work, why keep showing off?"

"Showing up ain't the same as showing off." The rebuke came in a tone low enough to rival a growl. Elroy Speck jerked a nod toward Adam. "Your brother knows it. After the way you flapped your gums last night then couldn't stitch two sides of a sack together, you should have learned the difference."

"Sewin' ain't the test of a real man, Speck." The jeer slid from Larry's face as his brother rounded on him.

"No, but his behavior sure is." Adam loomed over his brother. "Stuff your pride or I'll tan your hide to remind you."

The threat stole some of the swagger from Larry's step as he walked away—the first sensible thing Saul had seen from the young man. At his defection, everyone else breathed easy until the real work of the day began.

The thresher whirred to life, a heady tempo that pulsed in

the veins of every man on the job. Sheaves rained down, bands burst apart, straw belched through the air to mingle with dust and sweat. One task flowed to the next, an unbroken cadence sending grain surging down the chutes to the bags below.

A mighty screech pierced the rhythm, wrenching them from their tasks as everything scraped to a stop.

Saul stepped back, tilting his hat brim to better gauge the problem. Mr. Speck, Opal's and Elroy's father, crouched on the platform and peered in the opening. He shifted to the right then the left before straightening again.

"Feeder's blocked." He yanked on thick work gloves before hunkering down again. Nothing happened while men got the horses under control, ensuring no power fed into the machine whose powerful jaws could snap off a limb or mangle a man so badly he bled to death.

Saul edged closer as Mr. Speck assessed the workings before him and reached in, drawing out a hunk of chewed straw wound into a lump dense enough to clog the machine. A few more cautious swipes assured Saul that the man bore enough respect for the power of the contraption to exercise great caution, and some of the tension left his neck.

"Try 'er now." Upon Speck's order, the horses were let go, the great rods starting their slow dance of climb-and-plunge until the gears of the thresher kicked into action. For a moment, it seemed to function properly. Then a second screech, louder than the first, ruptured their hopes.

Desperate to escape the sound, horses tried to buck free of their traces. Men who'd been leading the horses now dodged sharp-edged, flailing hooves. In a show of bravery and strength, these men kept hold and fought for control of animal and machine. Dust whirled around them, a brown mist shadowing every movement, hiding any injury.

Saul whipped off his gloves, edging around the chutes for a closer vantage point. He scanned for anyone on the ground, any men holding an arm, a shoulder, or limping away from the area. The dust cleared to reveal none of his fears.

Mr. Speck stooped on the platform once more, tilting his chin as though to explore every angle. "Looks like one of the wheels got tilted by the blockage," he announced. "I'll have to pull it back and realign it." He shifted his weight from the balls of his feet to his knees to gain more stability, taking another look before he did anything.

"Get on with it." Larry Grogan stalked up next to the platform. "Time's wasting and we have more acres than most."

"Do a job right and you don't have to do it twice." Speck's wisdom came with the vigor of fighting words.

"Stop slowing us down." Larry jumped atop the platform and crowded the older man. "You're stalling so we Grogans don't get all our grain threshed, Speck."

"Careful." Speck held his ground as Larry tried to edge him out. "The belt attached to the wheel's stretched tight, and you have to know your way around what you're doing."

"Move out of my boy's way." Larry's father shoved his way forward, pitchfork jabbing the air as he spoke.

"I'll have her going in a minute." Speck rose to his feet, bristling at the order. "Tell your fool of a son not to mess with things he can't manage."

"Don't call me a fool." Larry shouldered Speck hard enough to make the man stumble.

"Stop right there." Saul gripped the center tine of the pitchfork and pushed it away from the platform. "Mr. Speck might have fallen onto this if he didn't have such a good sense of balance. This has gone far enough."

"I won't risk my neck for an ungrateful Grogan." Mr. Speck left the platform to Larry.

"And I'll show you that we could've been working this whole time." Larry squatted down, reached inside, and pulled back the wheel with a fierce yank. A victorious grin hadn't even stretched across his face when a loud *snap* sent something smacking into his chest with enough force to knock him clear off the platform. Larry flew over his father's head, landing facedown yards away. He didn't move.

Saul did. He made it to the boy's still form before most others processed what had happened. Blood seeped around a rock embedded in Larry's right cheek, high enough it might have struck his temple. Saul pressed his fingers against the carotid artery, finding the pulse strong and urgent even as he noted Larry didn't struggle to breathe. Cupping his hands, Saul checked to see if light pressure made the skull compress then quickly ran his hands along the arms and legs. So far no fractures, but ribs. . .that would be a different story.

Adam fell to his knees beside his brother. "What can I do?"

"Keep his head and neck steady while I turn him over." Saul waited until Adam was in position. Then dozens of calloused hands helped him get Larry on his back. Seeing no change in the boy's breathing, Saul murmured, "Good."

"Good?" Mr. Grogan croaked hoarsely as he surveyed the blood streaming from his unconscious boy.

"The stone wasn't high enough to crush his temple." Saul leaned forward, thumbing the patient's eyelids open. Larry's pupils constricted sluggishly beneath the onslaught of the sunlight, but they didn't remain dilated. "Pupils are responsive, another good sign. I'll need my medical bag."

"Here." Clara hefted his altered saddlebag to his side. "What else can I do?"

He flashed her a look of gratitude. "I'll need some cool water and a compress. . .as cold as you can possibly make it." Saul eyed

166

Mr. Grogan. "You'll need a well-sprung wagon lined with any blankets you can spare to get Larry to my father's house, where there's enough light for me to see to his wounds."

Several townspeople rushed to help carry out his orders, most remaining a respectful distance away as they watched him draw a thick band of cotton from his bag and fold it into a pad. "Adam, I need you to place this here," Saul laid it over the deepest part of the cut on Larry's cheek to demonstrate as he spoke, "and apply firm, even pressure against it."

With that in Adam's hands, Saul quickly checked Larry's chest. When he cautiously felt around the left side of Larry's rib cage, he could easily detect two fractures. Miraculously, they hadn't punctured his lungs because he wasn't gasping, turning blue, or foaming at the mouth.

"Larry!" Lucinda collapsed in the middle of the scene, throwing herself over her son's legs. "My boy!"

"Get her off of him." Saul still didn't know whether Larry'd done any major damage to his spine.

Mr. Grogan pried his wife from his son, but Lucinda continued to wail, making a mighty racket. It seemed as though nothing would get her to stop caterwauling, until Saul gave Adam fresh cotton and changed out the blood-soaked compress. At the sight of the gash across her son's cheek, Lucinda sagged against her husband.

"Take her out of here and keep her away."

Lord, I can stitch the slash on his face, give him ointment for his bruises, rest for his body, and binding for his ribs, but the rest lies in Your hands.

Clara ran to the well. She leaned over the edge, lowering the bucket to reach the coolest depths before bringing it to the surface.

Willa rushed into the soddy and brought out freshly washed rags and a pail for the water when Opal sprinted forward to join them. Sally followed hard on her heels, apron folded up as though holding something.

"The ice," she panted. "Opal reminded me." She barely got the words out before all of the women hurried back to where Saul tended Larry.

Clara saw Aunt Doreen working alongside Lucinda to pad Mr. Burns's best wagon with hay and blankets so Larry wouldn't be jostled during transport. They passed several women clustered around the parson, heads bowed in fervent prayer.

Men busied themselves clearing the area so the wagon could pull up. Others unhitched the horses from the thresher, determined to avoid any more accidents. Older children marshaled their younger counterparts away from the scene both to spare them worry and keep them from getting underfoot.

When they reached the doctor, Clara took the largest rag, dipped it deep in the water pail, and folded it around one section of the ice. Sally had already broken it into two chunks. Opal quickly mimicked her, layering cloths soaked in the cool water about the ice to prevent melting.

Saul took the first from her, the warmth of his fingertips a fiery jolt as he brushed her hand. His gaze shot to hers at the cold of the compress.

"The last of Sally's ice," she explained, placing the second compress in the chilly pail for safekeeping. "As cold as we can make it."

"Excellent." He removed the blood-soaked cotton from Larry's face, laying the compress over the wound as he directed Adam, "Keep applying pressure to slow the bleeding."

"So much blood." Willa's face was pale as though she'd lost an equal amount of her own.

"Head wounds bleed more than others," Saul stated. "It looks alarming but isn't as bad as it seems. Adam's managed to slow it down enough that I'll be able to stitch the wound when we've carried him back to my place."

Clara stood back with the other women as the wagon pulled forward. She watched Saul lead Matthew and Adam, carefully lifting Larry into the bed and cushioning him around the sides to prevent movement. The compress blazed an angry red before they'd gotten him situated, so Clara brought forward the replacement.

"Matthew, drive the buckboard. Adam, keep the compress on his cheek and hold him down if he tries to stir. I'll ride here, too." Saul's commands came out crisp and clear. "Clara, who remembered the ice?"

"Opal."

"Mr. Grogan," Saul ordered, "take Clara and Miss Speck to my house. You'll make it before we do since we'll go slow. We can't jostle Larry around. Ladies, I'm counting on your help. Clear off the kitchen table. Make sure there is as much light and as many clean cloths as you can find ready for use." Only after he'd finished his instructions did Saul realize Mr. Grogan hadn't moved. "Go!"

"She's a Speck." Grogan whispered the words almost apologetically, as though sorry to have to point out the doctor's mistake.

"I'm aware of that." Saul turned his back on the man, giving his attention to Larry once more. "Get going."

The wagon rolled away, slowly covering ground so as not to jolt Larry and worsen his injuries, leaving them no choice but to follow Saul's orders. Grogan stomped off, muttering to himself.

"Opal?" Clara didn't use more than her friend's name, but the question came out clear for all that.

"I'll come." A stubborn spark lit Opal's gaze. "Larry's as ornery a fellow as I've ever seen, but if I can help, I will. Mr. Grogan won't scare me off."

"Thank you." Willa put a hand on Opal's arm, unshed tears thickening her words. "For thinking of the ice. For ignoring Pa."

Then it was time to go. Mr. Grogan drove like a madman, which, Clara reflected, was as apt a description as any. The sole bit of consideration he showed was to veer wide around his son's wagon so as not to kick up dust. Otherwise, he showed no regard for rock, ditch, bump, or rut as he raced to the house.

She and Opal hunched low in the back of the wagon, clinging to the sides and riding it out until he jerked to a stop. Neither of them waited for any help out of the wagon, scooting to the end and making inelegant leaps for solid ground. They hit the earth running, burst through the doors, and set to work.

"We'll need hot water to clean up the mess and wash the bandages afterward. I'll draw and boil water and scrub the worktable while you get the rags and lamps"—Opal pulled two large pots from their storage places and hooked them over the hearth as she spoke—"since you know where things are and I don't."

By the time the men arrived, the women had done just as Saul asked. Clara opened the curtains wide to let in sunlight and lit lamps in any dark corner where no one would knock them over. Stacks of clean linen stood beside fresh-drawn water while the pots heated. For a brief moment, the kitchen shone.

Then everything became a blur of motion. Matthew and Adam carried Larry in and stretched him on the table. Matthew left the room to wait outside with Mr. Grogan—on Saul's orders, Grogan was to stay outside. Adam moved toward Larry's middle. He'd be ready to hold his brother down if he woke up or tried to move while Saul treated him. Clara and Opal retreated toward the hutch, prepared to bring cloths and water as needed.

"Ladies, I'll have to ask you to step outside for a moment."

Saul began opening Larry's shirt. "I need to check for bruises from internal bleeding."

The next minutes were tense as they waited for Saul to call them back, but he finally did. It seemed Larry had no hard spots on his stomach indicating blood rushing to the surface, and Dr. Reed could treat the cut on his face.

From where she stood, Clara could see everything. The gash in Larry's cheek still oozed blood, but nothing like before. Saul flushed it with cool water several times until the wound ran clear, mopping up the area with towels she passed him.

"He's got at least two broken ribs," Saul spoke as he took out needle, thread, and a bottle of Gilbert and Parson's Hygienic Whiskey for Medical Use. "Best thing is for him to stay out. If he wakes up or tries to move, grab him by the shoulders to keep him down. Stay away from his left side, but be ready." He uncapped the whiskey and held the bottle over the cut, which still sent a thin ribbon of blood down Larry's neck. "This will burn and he might jerk."

"Wouldn't the liquor do more good inside him?" Opal's whisper to Clara carried farther than she intended.

"If he could swallow it under his own steam, I'd give him a belt for the pain." Saul peered at them. "There's some proof alcohol helps prevent infection." With that, he tilted the bottle.

Immediately, Larry hissed, throwing his head back and twisting to avoid what had to be a painful sensation. Adam placed his forearm across Larry's sternum—his elbow applying pressure against his brother's right shoulder—using his hand to immobilize his head. After a few moments, Larry stopped moving. Adam maintained his position as Saul readied his needle and bent close, blocking most of Clara's view.

She considered it a blessing, as the first stitch tore a ragged moan from Larry. His head and upper body held in place, Larry began to kick, the movement radiating upward and making Saul stop his work.

"He's still unconscious; he won't keep calm by willpower." Saul didn't need to say another word.

Clara and Opal darted to the table, each grasping a worn leather boot and leaning their weight to still his thrashing limbs. Their efforts, combined with Adam's, held long enough for Saul's exacting stitchwork.

"I'll say this much," Saul mused as he washed his hands, "it seems he sustained no neck or spinal damage. No paralysis."

"He'll be all right then?" Adam's tone lay in odds to the question.

"There's no paralysis," Saul repeated. "His cheek should heal well, too. Beyond that, I can't say until he wakes up."

"What else could be wrong?" Opal moved forward, between Clara and Adam, to get a better look. "Beside his ribs, I mean?"

"That's the biggest problem. He doesn't have any big lumps or fractures to his skull, so I'd think he would wake up. The other big danger is if one of those broken ribs pierced any organs." The planes of Saul's jaw seemed severe in the bright light of sun and lamp. "If he's bleeding internally, I didn't sense it. There's nothing more I can do."

"Where's my boy?" An earsplitting shriek sounded outside the door as Lucinda caught up with them. "Let me in!"

Larry instinctively reacted to the soothing tones of his mother. His eyes fluttered open as he gave a piteous bleat. "Ma?"

"My angel!" Lucinda Grogan burst through the door and across the room to her son's side.

Angel? Saul didn't give voice to his doubts, instead standing his ground beside his patient as Larry's mother clucked over him.

He shot a glance toward Mr. Grogan, who ducked his head and wouldn't meet his gaze. At least the man had enough shame to know he should've kept his wife out of the house. . .and sense enough to see he couldn't do it.

"What happened?" Larry struggled to sit up and immediately abandoned the effort. He winced and used one arm to brace his bandaged left side. His other hand crept up to gingerly trace the tenderness around his stitches. "I remember I fixed the thresher."

"That's right." His mother stroked his hair as though Larry were a drowsy cat. "You fixed the thresher when that useless Speck couldn't, but a strap snapped and knocked you off the platform."

Her conveniently abridged version of events didn't sit well with anyone. Adam snorted at his mama's doting, Miss Speck's hands—just moments ago wrapped around Larry's right boot to help hold him down—curled into fists at the affront to her father, and Clara's eyes shot green fire.

"No." Saul pulled Lucinda's hands away, stepping between her and his patient. He looked Larry in the eye. "Mr. Speck worked to clear the machine, but you grew impatient and all but pushed him off the platform. After you disregarded his warning about how tight the belt was stretched, you yanked the wheel loose. The belt snapped free, struck you in the chest, and sent you flying."

"No need to be quarrelsome." Lucinda weaseled her way forward. "He was just trying to help the farm and got hurt."

"Yeah." Larry's gaze clouded when he tried to shift his weight. The pain from his broken ribs and other injuries had to be getting to him. "What's wrong with me?"

"You've broken two ribs and taken a gash to the face from a rock you landed on." Saul measured drops of laudanum into a glass of water and held it out. "This will dull the pain."

Matthew and Mr. Grogan held Larry up. He downed it without asking another question, giving a faint gasp as he lay back down. His eyes drifted shut as he waited for the medicine to take effect.

"It will make him drowsy, Mrs. Grogan, but he'll sleep comfortably." Saul moved to his bag and poured some of the liquid into a smaller vial. "Mix a couple of drops of this in a cup of water and give it to him when he hurts. Try not to give it to him unless he truly needs it." He handed the medicine to Mrs. Grogan, whose eyes narrowed while she accepted the instructions.

"What's she doing here?" Her beady gaze stayed fixed on Miss Speck.

"I told your husband to bring Clara and Miss Speck ahead to ready things." Saul kept his tone light. "Miss Speck remembered that Miss Fosset brought ice to make ice cream. It was her quick thinking to grab it to help relieve inflammation and slow Larry's bleeding. She has a good head in a crisis, so I asked her to come assist me and help Clara."

"He's my son." The disagreeable woman rounded on him. "I should have helped."

"Your emotions would have clouded your judgment, Mrs. Grogan. I needed someone to help hold Larry down so I could stitch his wound. You wouldn't be able to do that for your son."

"I'd be able to do anything he needed." Lucinda raised her chin. "And better than that Speck gal. If her father fixed the block right the first time, Larry wouldn't have had to step in."

"Larry didn't need to step in at all, Ma." Adam shifted to stand alongside Miss Speck. "He shoved his way in and paid the price. After the way he treated Mr. Speck, we owe this woman special thanks for all she did."

"I ain't thanking no Speck." Lucinda all but spat out the words.

"You're welcome." Miss Speck looked only at Adam, head held high as she said the words. "I'll be going now."

"And I'll accompany you." Clara linked arms with her friend

as they swept toward the door. She stopped to address Mr. Grogan as they left. "I suggest you take your son while he won't feel the ill effects of the ride home, Mr. Grogan."

Saul bit back a grin at the flummoxed expression on Lucinda's face. "I'll second that prescription. It's time you take Larry home and keep him there until he's fully recovered."

"Yes." Matthew Burn looked solemn as he chimed in. "Even if it takes a long time. Peace and quiet are important."

"For any recovery." This time, Saul had to turn away. The grin just wouldn't stay hidden.

Chapter 17

I remembered what you said about how Dr. Reed likes apple desserts." Willa Grogan sidled up to the counter where Clara was looking over the condition of the bolts of fabric and slid a pan toward her. "This cobbler's to thank him for helping Larry."

Cinnamon teased Clara's nose as she nudged the dish back toward Willa. "How thoughtful of you!" She kept her voice low and encouraging. "Go on ahead and take it to him. Your appreciation will mean a lot."

"Couldn't you just mention I brought it by?" Willa darted a shy glance toward where Saul pored over catalogs, filling out orders for the medical supplies he deemed necessary for the town. "The last thing I'd want to do is disturb him."

"Nonsense!" Clara stifled a sigh, hovering halfway between amusement and exasperation. She settled for raising her voice to capture Saul's attention. "He'll want to hear all about how Larry's recuperating."

"Hmmm?" Saul looked up from the catalog, gaze focusing on Willa. "Miss Grogan!" A welcoming smile crossed his features before a businesslike frown slid into place. "How is your brother?"

"Same as ever." A dry note entered Willa's voice, signaling

to Clara that Larry as a semi-invalid hadn't become any more gracious than his usual cantankerous self. "He says his stitches scratch, and he's got a powerful thirst."

"If he picks at those stitches, his scar will be worse. The wound might even become infected." Saul pulled his medical bag from behind the counter and began rummaging around. He scooped some salve into a small vial. "Use this gently, sparingly if it troubles him anymore. As for the thirst, it's a good thing. He should drink lots of water, and the more he's able to get up without overtaxing himself, the better."

"Thank you, doctor." Willa tucked the vial into a pocket and hesitated a moment. "Though. . .Larry ain't thirsting for water."

"Oh?" Saul's gaze snapped back to meet Willa's, and Clara wondered whether her friend could feel the heat of his intensity all the way to her toes. "I take it he doesn't want milk or coffee, either?"

"Whiskey. Ma gives it to him for the pain."

"I sent home doses of laudanum, which acts as a pain control and sedative." Saul braced both hands on the counter. "Larry doesn't need alcohol when he's dosed with a narcotic."

"Thank you. I'll tell Ma you said so." Gratitude shone in Willa's face as she turned to grab the cobbler then delivered it to Saul. "I baked this apple cobbler for you, as a thank-you for all you done for my brother."

"Thank you, Miss Grogan." Surprised pleasure painted his features as he watched Willa leave the shop, but he didn't so much as take a deep whiff of his treat. He went right back to his catalogs.

Clara didn't give it much more thought, since they'd had breakfast not long ago. She merely went about inspecting the bolts for water damage, brittle spots, pulled threads, faded areas, uneven weaves, and anything that might need to be sold as sale goods or quilting scraps. Yard after yard of fabric unrolled across the counter. Soft cottons, thick merino wool, bright ginghams, cheery flower prints, and bold solids all graced the area before her as she went through.

The bell on the door chimed to announce Sally Fosset, carrying what looked to be a pie in each hand. A smile played about the corners of Clara's mouth as her friend marched right up to Saul. Sally didn't claim a shy bone in her body, particularly now that she'd fixed her attentions on Matthew. All the same, the hints Clara dropped to the girls about rewarding Dr. Reed for his hard work with one of his favorite treats had obviously borne fruit.

"Apple," Sally boasted. "We can't replace the ice until winter, and by then you'll be plenty cold enough and wanting hot cider, instead of the ice cream you were due. So I made an apple pie for you and a peach pie for Matthew. I'll be dropping his off next."

"Thank you very much." Saul accepted the pie, sliding it on a back shelf along with Willa's cobbler. "I know Matthew will appreciate it just as much as I do—if not more."

"I hope so." With another smile, Sally sailed out the door and off to see the young blacksmith.

Clara hummed under her breath as she jotted down the lengths of cloths she cut away. If the way to a man's heart was through his stomach—though an educated doctor might disagree with the anatomical basis of the adage—then the ladies of Buttonwood were well on their way.

When Opal bustled through the door, Clara gave a final snip to the last bolt in the top row and set down her scissors with a merry little click. Sally might be earmarked for Matthew, but both of the other girls burst with potential. Willa's admiration for Saul's kindness and skill, and the way Opal had been spending time with him these past few days showed promise.

"Good morning, Clara." Opal spared her a smile as she passed the counter with a cloth-wrapped plate. "Dr. Reed, I brought you something this morning."

"Oh?" Saul raised his head slowly, as though unable to believe so many women would be so thoughtful.

Well, Clara thought smugly, *that's because you haven't been in a place with people as wonderful as this. By the time we're though, you'll never want to leave Buttonwood.*

"Apple fritters." Opal set the plate in front of him.

"I see." Saul looked from the plate, to Opal, to Clara, and back to the plate. "That sounds wonderful, Miss Speck. I wonder if you would humor my curiosity?"

"What?" Opal spoke aloud the question knocking about Clara's mind.

"After I asked you to help me tend a man who'd shown your father disrespect, why would you bring me apple fritters?"

"Because you asked me to help." Opal's answer clearly didn't satisfy Saul any more than it did Clara, and she must have realized it because she went on. "I liked what you said about me having a good head in a crisis. You didn't see me as a Speck or a Grogan—just saw that I was willing and able to lend a hand."

"Then I'm honored to take your apple fritters." Saul gave her a wide grin. "It's not every woman who appreciates getting roped into holding a man's dirty boot while he tries to kick her."

"It's not every man who appreciates a capable woman," Clara called out. *Saul and Opal really are well suited.* She smiled about it long after her friend left.

"You're looking pleased with yourself." Saul's observation gave her a guilty start.

"I'm glad to be getting things done." Clara swiftly turned the conversation back on him. "That's quite a stockpile of sweets you have there."

"Yes." He gave the assortment an assessing look. "Though I'm beginning to become suspicious."

Oh no! They shouldn't have all come this morning. Clara could have kicked herself. *Three unmarried women bearing desserts to the new bachelor in town? Of course he's becoming suspicious!*

"Of what?" She pasted a smile on her face.

"Miss Field, I'm going to ask you a question." His tone became somber. "And I need you to answer it honestly."

"Of course," Clara squeaked past the lump in her throat. *Saul is a smart man. Has he figured out that I'm trying to marry him off?* "Ask away."

~~~~~

"This many baked goods makes a man wonder." Saul leaned forward, fighting to maintain his serious expression as Clara's eyes went wide and round. "Does Buttonwood harbor a secret?"

"A secret?" she repeated the word innocently.

Too innocently. *What if I asked what secrets you hold, Clara? Would you tell me?* He pushed the thoughts away when the silence stretched too long, like brittle taffy. "A hidden orchard perhaps?" He straightened up, creating more distance between them. "Some undisclosed location where the women of this town grow apples to satisfy their demand?"

"What do you—" Confusion gave way to merriment as she caught on to his joke. Laughter spilled from her lips, lighter and sweeter than any of the confections gracing his shelf.

He wanted a second serving. "Is there a reason no dish seems complete without this particular fruit?" Saul gestured to the row of offerings on the shelf. "Apple cobbler, apple pie, apple fritters—that's more than a coincidence."

"You've eaten many meals here with no apples," she protested. But no giggles peppered her words. Clara, for all her denials, hid something. Even more intriguing, she wasn't good at it.

Saul decided to dig a little deeper. "Then is it some sort of holiday I'm unaware of? A day wherein we celebrate apples?"

"That's ridiculous." The words came out in a small huff, causing a saucy tendril to dance at her forehead for a moment.

"Is it?" *More ridiculous than wanting to wind that springy curl around my finger and give it a tug?*

The bell over the shop door shattered the silence, not the first time a customer provided an unwelcome interruption. Saul's humor came flooding back when he saw who'd arrived.

Amanda Dunstall minced up the center of the store, carefully balancing a large, covered plate as she made her way toward them. "Good morning!"

"Lovely to see you, Amanda!" Clara's obvious relief over the change in conversation made him all the more determined to get back to it.

"What do you have there, Miss Dunstall?" He made a great show of peering at the dish then sending a quizzical look toward Clara.

"Crumb cake." Her cheery answer almost disappointed him.

"If I didn't love crumb cake so much," he admitted, "I'd be saddened to hear it wasn't apple."

"Everything in town can't be made with apples." Clara's triumphant tone matched her grin. "It isn't as though we have a secret orchard."

"Of course not." Miss Dunstall sent Clara a concerned look. "The only trees around here are cottonwood and black walnut."

"We know," he broke in. "It was just a joke about the apples. We were having a conversation about them when you came in."

"Oh yes!" She brightened. "Well, no worries, Dr. Reed. It's apple crumb cake."

"You don't say?" His smile proved a direct counterpoint to the defeat written in Clara's expression, but he held his peace until

Miss Dunstall left. Then he let loose. "'*Apple* crumb cake,' she said. I wonder what the odds are of four women each baking a dish and all of them having to do with apples?"

"I'd be more likely to wonder how often a man finds himself in a town where the people are so thoughtful." She served him a pointed glare. "Why don't you enjoy your food, thank the ladies for their kindness, and finish filling out your orders?"

"That would be a fine idea," he agreed, "if I liked apples."

"Of course you like apples!" She tapped her foot in impatience.

"What makes you think so?" Saul sensed they were getting to the meat of the matter.

"Everyone likes apples!"

"I don't." He plunked the crumb cake on the shelf beside the other dishes. "Which seems an awful waste."

"There's no reason to joke about something like that." Clara's glower wouldn't scare a chipmunk from an acorn. She looked too cute, but Saul could see she meant business. "Those women worked hard to make those for you, and you'll need to tell them how much you enjoyed their efforts."

"No one's disputing that. I'll enjoy watching you and your aunt eat them."

"Oh, I admit it!" She held up both hands, palms outward. "I told the girls it was a shame you'd missed out on your ice cream and that you liked apples."

"Did you?" Chuckles broke free at her earnest expression. "Well, even if you made a wrong assumption, it's good to know your friends trust your judgment."

"I didn't assume anything." Her brow furrowed in puzzlement. "Your father told me when I asked him what you liked to eat."

"Dad told you I like apples?" Saul stopped laughing. Either Clara misheard, wasn't telling the truth, or Dad had forgotten.

"Yes, I'm sure of it." She squinted at him. "You're certain you don't?"

"Absolutely." A muscle in Saul's jaw jumped. "I haven't eaten an apple I didn't have to since I was seven."

"What changed?" Clara knew she had no right to ask, no reason to expect an answer. But the question tugged at her heart so insistently, she had to try.

"What makes you think something changed?" Saul's voice went low and gruff, a warning she delved too deep.

"You said you haven't eaten an apple you didn't have to since you were seven," Clara spoke softly. "That means you ate apples before because you wanted to. Something changed."

"My sister." He thrust his hands in his pockets, eyes staring past Clara.

She got the sense he stared past the shelves, past time itself, as the memory unwound around him.

CHAPTER 18

My sister. Nellie loved apples." Saul's eyes grew bright then dimmed. "She started to feel sick, but no one listened. I didn't listen." His jaw clenched for a long moment. "Until she wouldn't eat the apple bread at dinner. Then I knew Nellie was sick."

"It wasn't your fault," Clara whispered. The reminder of her presence seemed to jerk him back to reality. "I'm sorry."

He pulled his hands from his pockets, blinking hard. "There's nothing you can do about it. Nothing I could do." Saul drew a ragged breath. "I can't believe Dad forgot. Apples."

"Is Nellie the reason you became a doctor?" It fit so perfectly and made Clara wonder, too, about Saul's need to help an orphan like Midge.

"I'm finished talking about it." The words came out clipped as he turned away, moving from behind the counter and toward the door.

"Wait." She reeled from the abruptness of how he'd pulled away. "I didn't—"

"Clara." The sound of her name on his lips halted her apology. "The stage is here."

"The stage?" She struggled to make the transition, not wanting the connection to be broken.

"Midge." His stride grew longer. "Come meet Midge!"

~~~~~~~

"Dr. Reed!" Midge couldn't break free of the stagecoach fast enough. She ran, flinging her arms around his middle in a great hug. "I'm so glad to see you!"

"I'm glad to see you, too." He wrapped his arms around her, tight and safe, before straightening up. Dr. Reed smiled, just like she remembered, and Midge knew she'd be all right in this dusty little town.

She hung back while he talked with Mrs. Henderson, drinking in the space. Her gaze flicked from where the stage master unloaded her luggage to a small wooden building that looked like a restaurant. Midge's grumbling stomach made her hurry her observation of the stables, the smithy, and a fine house that looked as though a giant plucked it from a grand city and plopped it on the prairie.

Just in front of her was the general store, its windows bright in the midday sun, dust already invading the clean-swept boards of the porch. But what really caught her eye was the lady who stood out front, watching. Midge cocked her head to the side and looked straight back.

The woman looked older and taller than she was—about the same age as Nancy. Midge felt a horrible pang at the thought then tried to ignore it by concentrating instead on the other girl's steady scrutiny. With her golden hair all up in a bun and a light blue dress and soft apron over it, she looked normal enough. But it was her smile—nice but not trying too hard, like some folk when they heard Midge was an orphan—that made her stick out in a good way.

Well, that and the way she'd snuck happy glances at Dr. Reed before she saw Midge keeping track. Yeah, the lady seemed the sort she'd like. The town—though "town" seemed almost too long a word for a place so small—was short on buildings but big on room to run. Midge could slip away and stretch her legs and thoughts when she needed to in a place like Buttonwood. She liked that, too.

"Midge"—Dr. Reed gestured for her to come over—"Mrs. Henderson will go back to Fort Laramie with the stage, if that's all right with you. My father hired two ladies to help with the house and the store, so Mrs. Henderson can get back to Baltimore unless you want her to stay."

"That's all right," she assured her traveling companion. After spending every waking moment with Mrs. Henderson for days on end, hardly ever escaping her watchful eye and critical comments, Midge was ready to part ways. "I'm here safe and sound. Thank you, Mrs. Henderson."

"I do miss the city," the older woman confessed. "And it seems God's provision that the stage master found a letter slipped down between the cracks like that and needs to go back to Laramie right away. Bless you, Dr. Reed. Mind you behave, Midge."

"Yes, ma'am." With that settled, Midge turned her attention back to the woman with the yellow hair, who'd drawn closer.

"I'm Miss Field, one of the women Dr. Reed mentioned who helps with the store and the house." She stooped a little so she stood eye to eye with Midge. "You can call me Clara."

"You probably already know I'm Midge." She'd see how Clara responded before making any decisions. Midge might not have any family left, but she wouldn't play the poor little orphan girl for anybody. Not even Dr. Reed.

"Yes"—Clara's smile widened—"Dr. Reed told us how smart you are. We've readied a room if you'd like to see it."

Midge shot a glance at Dr. Reed, making sure he nodded

before she agreed. "All right."

"My aunt is at the house." Clara walked toward the fancy building Midge noticed earlier. "Her name is Mrs. Edgerly, but she'll want you to call her Doreen."

"You must be Midge!" An older lady with dark brown hair shot through with silver met them at the door. "Come in!"

"They'll take you upstairs," Dr. Reed told her. "I'll see to your luggage while you look around." With that, he was gone.

Midge tried not to gawk too much as she went up the stairs and passed several rooms before everyone came to a stop. Clara and Mrs. Edgerly didn't go inside, but she figured this must be hers, so she edged around the doorframe.

"Oooh, it's beautiful." She just stood against the wall, taking the room in little sips to make it last longer. Wispy buttercup curtains danced in a breeze from the open window, beckoning her close to a small table complete with two chairs, a fine linen tablecloth, and a tea set.

"For me?"

"All yours," the older lady promised.

Midge extended a hand toward the teapot, waiting for their agreement before she picked it up. The porcelain felt cool and smooth beneath her fingertips as she traced strands of buttercups and greenery. She set it down gently, careful not to let it clink against the teacups or saucers as she moved toward the bed.

"It's so tall." The top of the mattress reached as high as her hip, the dark wood of the headboard stretching higher. Someone had carved flowers on the center post, and she traced the grooves before brushing against the softness of the quilt. "Green and yellow are two of my favorite colors."

"Dr. Reed told us so," Clara said from the doorway.

"I—I'd better go see if he needs help with my things." Midge pushed past them. She hurried down the stairwell, rushed through the door, and didn't pause for breath until she stood in front of the general store.

It was a good thing nobody caught her, or even tried, because Midge didn't have any good reason for running off like that. How could she explain that when she looked at that room, decorated so perfect just for her, a corner of her mind had started whispering thoughts she'd considered long dead. Thoughts about growing up in a normal house, with a family who knew her favorite colors and cared enough to choose them. Thoughts about what it'd be like to have a real home.

And Midge had seen enough to know where hopes like that led.

Disappointment. Clara watched the hated emotion unfold on Aunt Doreen's face, sweeping away the startled expression of a moment before when Midge raced past. *Not again. Aunt Doreen's had too much disappointment recently.*

"Midge didn't like it."

"She's overwhelmed." Laying a hand on her aunt's arm, Clara tilted her head. "Let me bring her back." She waited for the older woman's nod then hastened down the steps. Following Midge didn't take much, as the girl stood on the porch in front of the general store.

Clara made sure the sound of her voice reached the girl before she did. "Dr. Reed probably carried your things in through the kitchen entrance."

"Why?" Midge's shoulders hunched up, crowding the brim of her bonnet into a calico barrier.

"It's closer."

"No." The girl spun around, eyes wary. "Why are you being so nice?

"Why wouldn't I be?" Clara didn't come closer. Midge's posture and question were walls to protect the girl. But from what?

"That's not the way the world works." She pressed her fingers to the locket at her throat. "Folks are only nice when they have a reason. What's yours?"

"What do you think it is?" Clara read pride in Midge's gaze and thought she knew the answer, but she wanted to hear it.

"I don't need anyone to look down on me." Her hand dropped to her side.

"Good." Clara moved past Midge to sit on a bench outside the store. She waited for the girl to turn and join her. "I don't."

"You and your aunt didn't make those curtains and set up my room so nice out of pity for the orphan?"

"Why waste time on something as useless as pity?" She adjusted her skirts to leave more room on the bench for Midge and patted the area beside her. "I feel compassion for you, not pity. Never mistake the two."

"What's the difference?" She edged closer but didn't sit.

"Pity almost implies a person is looking down on another, which doesn't help either one of them. In fact, it's a bit insulting for the person being pitied, don't you think?" Clara fixed her gaze on Midge as she explained. "Compassion, on the other hand, means that maybe we aren't the same—no two people are—but I can try to understand how you feel and respect how difficult things are."

"That is a big difference." Perching on the far edge of the bench, Midge mulled it over. "All right then. What did you decide?"

"About what?"

"When you were trying to understand how I feel," she clarified. "I'm wondering whether you came close or not, if your way will work any better than Mrs. Henderson feeling sorry for me."

"I thought that after everything you've lost, it'd be important for you to feel like we wanted you here. That knowing we were excited to meet you and tried to make you comfortable would go a long way toward easing any feelings that you didn't belong." Clara shrugged, using the movement to make sure Midge's gaze followed her. "I know it was important to me when I lost my family and came to live with Aunt Doreen."

"You're an orphan, too?" She scooted closer. "Your aunt took you in and fixed up a room for you like you did for me?"

"Yes." Shutting her eyes for a moment helped push back the pain from remembering the day she'd left home. "My mother and father left me behind to go on a business trip." Clara left out how she'd begged to go, too. How Daddy had laughed and said his little girl would be in the way and he'd see her later. "They both died in a carriage accident."

"I'm sorry." Midge slid her hand in Clara's and squeezed.

"Ah, but you're not sorry for me?" She squeezed back. "You wish it hadn't happened, understand that it hurt, but don't pity me or think you're better than me because I had a hard time?"

"No." A shy smile tugged at the corners of Midge's mouth.

"Then I appreciate your compassion, just as I appreciated the time Aunt Doreen spent to make me feel welcome in her home." Clara looked Midge up and down. "I was only a little younger than you at the time." No matter that she'd looked older than Midge did now. The girl before her was a late bloomer, but when she blossomed, she'd be a sight to see. Clara stifled a pang at the thought she wouldn't be around to see it.

"So that's why you're nice—not because of pity but because you *do* understand." The girl sucked in a breath. "I love my room, and I'm sorry I was rude."

"Thank you for the apology, but it was Aunt Doreen whose feelings were hurt." Clara stood up. "It'd make her feel better if you told her how much you like everything."

"I will."

"Dr. Reed mentioned you lived with your sister." Clara delicately felt around the topic, only now realizing how little she knew about this young woman. "I don't know much else, but he's asked us to help with your schooling and such while you're here."

"Anything he wants, I'll do my best." She sounded so serious that Clara was torn between smiling and crying. Midge obviously wanted to please the man who'd saved her.

"Then here's your first lesson. The next time you're upset, don't scamper off." Clara opened the door and followed her charge inside. "You never know what you're missing when you run away from a conversation."

CHAPTER 19

Saul rounded the corner as the girl bounded up the stairs. "Your aunt said you'd gone to talk with Midge."

"Yes." Clara seemed a little lost in her own thoughts, making him wonder where they led her.

"I could use some insight, if you wouldn't mind sharing." He grasped her elbow through the soft cotton of her dress and steered her toward the parlor. "What I know about girls wouldn't pack a tooth."

"You were close with your sister." Her murmur wasn't a question, precisely, but it hung in the air like a challenge.

"Midge, I'm sure you'll agree, can't be compared to anyone else." He sidestepped the trap, adamantly refusing to be drawn into the conversation he'd so narrowly avoided earlier. *I won't talk about Nellie.*

Clara's voice rescued him from the memories. "I received the impression she's lived a hard life."

"What did she say?" Saul paced behind the settee to mask his expression. He'd been careful not to give any details of Midge's background but hadn't cautioned the girl to do the same. Mrs. Henderson should have warned Midge not to tell others about

Nancy's circumstances, lest she be judged for a situation beyond her control.

"Nothing specific. Nor did I ask." She paused as though hoping he'd volunteer information. When he didn't speak, Clara twisted in her seat to peer up at him. "I trust you would fill in any missing information we'd need to be able to help her."

He wouldn't have Midge tarred with the same brush as her sister, and that meant keeping her past firmly in Baltimore. "If she said nothing, how did you gather she's had a difficult time?"

"Her general wariness and mistrust say enough, though her comment that people are never nice unless they have good reason made me ache for the life she must have led." Clara's gaze held censure for his secrecy and sorrow for Midge's suspicions. "For one so young to believe people only do things to benefit themselves. . ."

"I know." Saul moved to take the seat opposite her. "Most don't learn that lesson until much later in life."

"It's not a valid view, no matter one's age," she corrected. "In Midge, it's merely more jarring to see such a jaded perspective since she's so young."

"Clara"—Saul passed his hand over his face—"I'll grant the idea is disheartening, but that doesn't make it invalid. It's true— the majority of people won't lift a finger unless they reap a reward for their efforts."

"We'll have to disagree on that." She sat so still and straight a casual observer could be forgiven for thinking her spine had frozen stiff. "Not all people in the world think solely of themselves."

"Of course not—often they act on behalf of the people they love." His initial agreement made her relax before his final words hit her with the force of a physical blow.

"And caring for those one loves is selfish?" Clara's voice came out taut and brittle, like a piece of leather stretched too thin and baked in the sun.

"You mistake my words. Caring for others is the antithesis of selfishness, but when you look at the decisions people make every day, my point stands. What they do is chosen, almost without exception, to benefit themselves or those close to them."

"Then you see even an act of love as a sad truth of humanity." She refused to see herself that way. "I suppose, then, it's not the actions themselves but the lens through which one views them. Perhaps yours need changing."

"Perhaps yours need cleaning. A rosy tinge can only last so long, Clara." He clasped his hands together as though preparing to deliver a lecture. "Midge knows reality, and you won't reach her with platitudes."

"Since you've come to Buttonwood, have you not seen people look beyond themselves to help others?" Her voice gathered strength as she proved him wrong. "To welcome you and Midge, for instance, or thank you for something you've done on behalf of a neighbor? These are hardly platitudes, Dr. Reed. These are people living good lives and spreading kindness as best they can."

"The people here have big hearts, but I'm in no rush to place them on a pedestal." His words came out as unyielding as his argument. "The Specks and Grogans mill around each other waiting for an opening, tempers grow short when the days stretch long, and no one cultivates patience along with that grain. They help each other, knowing when the time comes their neighbors will return the favor. It's a system just like any other."

"I disagree. They work together to accomplish what they can't achieve alone. Admitting they need help and appreciating the skills others have to offer are virtues to be applauded." Clara stood up, measuring the length of the room with her strides. "Why do you have to narrow it down to materialistic loss and gain statements without taking into account the gracious spirit of the town?"

"Why does it disconcert you that people ultimately do what's best for themselves, and that Midge and I acknowledge it?"

"Because no one deserves to be seen as grasping or opportunistic for taking care of themselves or the ones they love." Clara came to a halt, fingers digging into the brocaded back of the settee. "Not when it takes everything they have just to try."

"I didn't mean you." His voice moved closer, though Clara kept her gaze fixed to the velvet beneath her fingertips. "It takes courage and conviction to come out here and try to provide for your aunt. Selfishness doesn't come into the equation."

Even if I'm trying to marry you off to one of the local girls so I can earn this house? Guilt clumped in the back of her throat, behind her eyes, gathering in tears as she realized what she'd done. *To take care of Aunt Doreen, I'm nudging you into one of the most important decisions you'll ever make—and you don't even know it.*

"Clara," his warm breath fanned against the nape of her neck as he spoke, "I'm wrong."

"No." She raised her head and pulled away, putting as much distance between them as she dared. "You're right, Dr. Reed. If you look closely enough, every decision has its roots in what a person wants. Scratch the surface, and you'll find a reason behind any action."

"Reason is one of the gifts God gave mankind," Saul agreed. "There's no shame behind using logic so long as it's combined with conscience."

"And compassion." Clara forced herself to meet his gaze. "That's what I spoke with Midge about—the difference between pity and compassion. We discussed the mistake of looking down on people less fortunate and the value of trying to understand their feelings."

"She doesn't want to be pitied." His jaw clenched, a protective gesture that shot straight to Clara's heart.

"No one does. Just as no one wants to think that behind every action lies self-centered thought." She took a deep breath. "But both are realities to be faced. Dr. Reed, Midge will face pity so long as she is an orphan under the care of a bachelor. Your motives for taking her in will be questioned by those whose own intentions are less than altruistic."

"A moment ago you protested this idea and said that people deserved better." He moved to stand at the mantel. "Why the change?"

"Because you don't plan to stay in Buttonwood, Dr. Reed." Clara paused to let that sink in. "Because these are the suspicions you will face in a big city. But most of all"—she closed her eyes before admitting the last—"because perhaps I have a few motives of my own."

"Such as?" His palm pressed flat on the mantel, Saul waited for Clara to open her eyes.

When she did, he saw the tumult of her thoughts. Vulnerability yielded before resolve, conviction warred with regret, and the velvety softness of hope held firm against the harsh edges of doubt. "I want you to stay."

His breath left him in a great *whoosh* at the determination in her words. *She wants me to stay. Here. With her?* An unexpected elation washed over him at the thought. Waiting for her to continue, the silence grew until he could no longer stand the delay. "Why?"

"For what your father has done in helping Aunt Doreen and me, I owe him whatever I can do to bring him joy." She took a step forward, her expression as she spoke of his father wanting him to stay—not her own wishes—painfully earnest. "He wants you near him, longs to share the rest of his life with family, needs to see you happy. You can make that happen."

"My work lies in Baltimore." He took his arm off the mantel and straightened up. "There are many in need clustered around the city, overlooked by the medical community."

"Has the medical community made provision for Buttonwood?" She glanced around as though searching for spare doctors. "For any of the outposts on the Oregon Trail or frontier towns in the wilderness? The town's residents need care, and in spring many others will pass through. You'll find need wherever you look for it, Dr. Reed."

"It came to me in Baltimore." He struggled to keep his tone even. "Midge's sister is just one example of thousands of poor living piled atop one another, unable to afford help and told they're not important enough to warrant assistance. The people coming west make the choice to try for a new life. They had the ability to pick up and move on. Others don't possess the means for such a change."

"With all the tales of epidemics plaguing travelers, many are dissuaded from trying. Help along the way means more successes, more hope, less crowding in cities." Clara didn't so much as blink at his protests, instead countering with points so clear, he found himself considering the possibilities.

"I have a responsibility to Midge," he stated. "She's lost everything she knows, and I'll not break my promise to return to the city where she's spent the whole of her life until now."

"Have you asked Midge what's most important to her—staying in Baltimore or staying close to you?" She tilted her head. "I should be surprised if her answer would be Baltimore."

"Midge needn't choose. She's had too much wrenched from her. I won't take anything else. I'll establish my practice in Baltimore as planned." He moved past the settee, heading toward the door in an obvious signal the conversation had ended.

"If that is your choice, you will lose Midge to the city." The quiet certainty in her voice stopped him when desperation or histrionics wouldn't have. She sat down again while she waited for his answer.

"Improbable." Saul turned, lifting a single brow to show his dismissal of the idea. "She'll be well cared for."

"But not by you." Each word hammered into him. "When you return to Baltimore, keeping her in your home would lead to unsavory rumors and reflect poorly on her moral character and your professional ethics."

"We've already established she'll go to school." Saul rested on the arm of an overstuffed chair. "It's been seen to."

"Precisely." Clara laid one hand atop the other in her lap, all angles and finality as she continued. "Midge's lack of family and education will cast her to the fringes there, and while you may live mere blocks away, you'll not be part of her daily life. The isolation inflicted by her status as an orphaned young woman of a family with no status at an elite institution will stifle her spirit and strength."

"I will find a way." The words fell flat even to his own ears. Clara would know far better than he the expectations and petty distinctions drawn among schoolgirls.

"Staying in Buttonwood *is* a way." Her gaze implored him to see things as she did. "The only way to keep Midge close without the unforgiving speculation of high society and to maintain a connection with your father."

"How can that be?" *How dare you tell me to stay when you aren't going to.* "When you and your aunt join another wagon train come spring, Midge's presence with two unmarried men would still be cause for conjecture."

"Not to the same extent as it would be in the city," she conceded, "but that is true. That brings me to the solution I hope you'll consider despite it going against your plans."

"What?" Saul knew he invited disaster, but his curiosity wouldn't let him walk away.

"I'm asking you to look beyond your own reasons—beyond personal gain—to see how what I'm about to propose would be the best course of action for everyone involved."

"Stop hedging." He shifted closer, noting that she fidgeted but didn't pull away. "What solution?"

"Dr. Reed." She drew a deep breath and met his gaze squarely. "Consider how a wife would solve several of your problems."

"A wife!" He sprang from the chair. "Every sane man knows that the more women added to an equation, the more complex it becomes." Saul shot her a pointed glance. "You prove it."

"For now I'll ignore how that statement rankles." Clara remained seated, every inch rigid with icy disdain. "Should you remain in Buttonwood as a married man, Midge's presence wouldn't raise so much as an eyebrow. She'll stay secure and accepted, and you'll fulfill your father's dearest wish. You'll have patients aplenty to tend and epidemics to halt in their tracks. Far from complicating matters, marriage offers an expedient resolution."

"Marriage is more than a contract of convenience. I needn't look beyond that of my own parents for a perfect example of why such arrangements fail." Saul shook his head. "Hasty weddings create problems only funerals can resolve."

"I know." Sorrow crept into her voice, pulling him from the memories of his tension-filled childhood home.

"Do you refer to your uncle?" Saul moved to stand beside her.

"Aunt Doreen married him to be able to support me, and not a day went by I didn't wish she'd found another way." When Clara looked at him, sadness leached away the color in her cheeks. "But that needn't be the case here. Several girls in Buttonwood would make fine wives for you and kind mothers to Midge, if you opened yourself to the possibility."

"Girls in Buttonwood?" The enormity of what she'd said crashed over him all at once, making it impossible to speak aloud all the realizations clashing in his head.

She'd brought her friends over to ready Midge's room, insisted he come to lunch to show his appreciation, and seemed upset by the addition of the other men. Her approval when he asked Miss Speck to join him at the table wasn't due to relief over her friend's avoidance of embarrassment. The apple desserts trickling in all morning after she'd told them it was his favorite treat. . .

"You've been trying to match me with your friends." In his exertion not to shout, the words came out in a deceptively soft tone.

"I've made efforts to give you the opportunity to know them." Her admission only fanned the flames of his anger. "By now I'd hoped you'd have narrowed your interest to one or two."

"You're to be congratulated, Miss Field." He clasped his hands behind his back and turned to face her. "The effectiveness of your plot will astonish you, I'm sure."

"Oh?" Her entire visage lit up with such hope and joy that Saul almost regretted his next words.

"Yes. I've come to know the young ladies in a variety of situations—aside from church and the threshings—thanks to you. I have seen enough of the women to determine how I feel and have narrowed down my interest"—he paused and waited until she leaned closer—"to none of them. You will cease your matchmaking efforts immediately."

CHAPTER 20

She's trying to marry off my Dr. Reed! Midge could scarcely believe what she was hearing through the cast-iron grate in the floor of her room. She'd come upstairs to apologize to Mrs. Edgerly, but the older woman had gone off to clean something, she supposed.

That left Midge alone in the cheery yellow and green room, where she'd edged up to the bed and fluffed herself down upon it to see if it felt as soft as it looked. It did. But more importantly, from where she lay she could hear Clara and Dr. Reed talking in the parlor.

She's trying to marry him off, all right. Incredible as the thought seemed, more unbelievable still came the following realization. *And she's botching it. How can anyone* not *find a wife for a man as kind and smart and handsome as Dr. Reed?* That boggled her brain, but she decided to be thankful. *If Dr. Reed married, where would that leave me?*

A few moments later, Midge sucked in a sharp breath as Clara explained exactly where that would leave her. Or, rather, where she'd wind up if Dr. Reed didn't marry. A boarding school? Dr. Reed hadn't mentioned sending her away to a fancy all girls' school, but there was his voice, agreeing with the plan.

Even after Clara's warnings about those places. There the other girls would pity her, or laugh at her, or look down on her, or be cruel because she wasn't born into a rich family that was still alive. She'd have to trade Dr. Reed for all those snooty little princesses? *Nuh-uh, I'm not getting stuck at a boarding school.*

The other choice sounded much better. Since Baltimore didn't seem safe anymore, especially if she'd be trapped at some fancy school, she wasn't so keen on going back. If getting Dr. Reed hitched meant she could stay with him and not pretend to become a prissy nose-tilter, that's the choice she'd make.

Not that she'd let Dr. Reed marry just anybody. When Midge met everyone in town, she'd be keeping both eyes open for the right woman. Then, with a few nudges and some sneaky scheming, it shouldn't be too hard to make things go the way they ought.

Dr. Reed's voice interrupted her schemes when he forbade Clara to keep trying to marry him off. *Well, he doesn't have to be so stubborn about it.* Disgruntled, Midge swung her feet over the side of the bed and sat up. *What would it hurt him to think it over?* If Dr. Reed wanted to be difficult, she'd have to be especially clever about finding him a bride.

She didn't have time to dawdle, either. Midge waited until she heard the front door close. She scurried down the stairs to find Clara still in the parlor, sitting on a plush sofa, looking sad. Sad wouldn't get them very far, but something else flashed across her new friend's face when she glimpsed Midge—determination. Ah, now that was an emotion Midge could understand. . .and, better yet, use.

"I couldn't find your aunt."

"Dr. Reed said she went to the Dunstalls' café for a moment." Clara gave a tight smile, the kind held in place by tense edges and an unwillingness to reveal one's upset. "Did you see that he'd brought your things up?"

"Yes." Midge waited a moment before settling on the sofa beside Clara. "Clara? Sometimes it's not so bad to have reasons to do things. So long as they're good ones." She snuck a quick glance and saw some of the tightness leave her friend's smile.

"I'm glad you see the difference."

"Yeah, so I was thinking I could help you marry off Dr. Reed, because I listened and you have good reasons." Midge sat real straight on the sofa, finding it harder than it looked. "Your voices came up through the grate in my room."

"I see." Clara looked shocked and horrified. "You heard everything?"

"About Baltimore and boarding schools and people Dr. Reed can help here in Buttonwood and making his pa happy?" Midge nodded. "I heard all of that. I don't want to go to one of those schools, and I think Dr. Reed takes care of enough people. He needs a good wife to take care of him."

"You're right, Midge." Clara sighed. "He didn't take my advice very well."

"And now his guard's up." Midge scooted a little closer. "That's why we'll have to work together and catch him by surprise...."

⟨～⟩

Time slipped by in drips and drabs, days Clara whiled away teaching Midge to read and write or finishing the inventory for the store. With no moment left unfilled, more than a week passed before Clara refocused on ending Dr. Reed's bachelorhood.

"Summer's almost gone." Midge turned mournful eyes from the window, where she'd been staring outside. "And Dr. Reed's father will come back in a couple of weeks."

"Yes." Clara checked the spelling words scrawled across the slate before passing it back to her pupil. "You've been in Buttonwood for a couple of weeks now. Are you certain staying is what you want?"

She didn't want to press, but Clara had to know. If Midge's deepest desire was to return to Baltimore, Clara couldn't go through with the scheme to marry Dr. Reed off. Too many lives would be changed, and Mr. Reed would understand her decision. Neither of them had known about Midge when they struck the bargain. Worse, he'd left too soon after they found out for them to discuss the ramifications of it.

"It depends on Dr. Reed." The younger girl set the slate down on the tabletop with a sharp click. "I want to stay with him, but I want him to be happy, too. It's hard."

"Yes." Clara put an arm around Midge's shoulders for a moment. "My hope is you could both be happy here, and that would please Dr. Reed's father, as well."

Midge took a deep breath, almost as though swallowing her doubts. "The way I figure it, the man has to propose, so we can't rope Dr. Reed into anything he doesn't choose, anyway. All we can do is guide him in the right direction."

"True. Enough time has passed since our first. . .erm. . . conversation," Clara glossed over the disagreement and pressed on, "that I doubt he'll suspect we still harbor any hopes."

"Take him by surprise, like I said. So I'll ask him to come gather walnuts with us this afternoon." Midge tapped the edge of her slate with anxious fingers. "You've already asked the others?"

"Yes. Opal, Willa, Sally, and Amanda will all be there, along with us and Aunt Doreen." Clara smiled. "It will be the perfect opportunity, if we can leave him with the right women."

"Amanda's nice but too young." Midge's fingers stopped tapping. "And Matthew Burn has already spoken for Sally. That leaves Willa and Opal."

"It shouldn't be hard to split into groups. If you go with Amanda, I'll maneuver to be with Aunt Doreen and Sally." Clara kept her voice to a whisper so her aunt wouldn't overhear their scheme. "So Dr. Reed will be with Opal and Willa, which is fine since he's trying to get the Specks and Grogans to stop fighting."

"He can't resist trying to fix things." A somber nod accompanied this wisdom. "It could work."

"As long as we're subtle." Caution wasn't exactly Midge's watchword, but Clara needed to give one last reminder. "If he suspects a plot, that's the end of it."

"Right. I'll go get him for lunch then." Pushing away from the table, Midge pursed her lips. "We're all ready?"

"As ready as we can be." Thin assurance, Clara knew, but the best she could honestly offer. Since her ill-fated conversation with Dr. Reed about the possibility of marriage to a Buttonwood bride, he'd walked a fine line between pointedly avoiding the ladies and remaining sociable.

Please, Lord, Clara prayed as Midge left, *let this work. I followed You to Buttonwood. I followed Your guidance to stay here. Josiah's offer can't be anything but the next step on the path You laid before me. Help Saul see that this is right. His marriage will make Josiah happy, give Midge the family she deserves, enable me to support Aunt Doreen, and allow us all to stay close together. Jesus, I don't want to leave my friends.*

She raised her head when she heard the door open, signaling Midge's return. In a few moments, they all sat around the lunch table. Clara looked at the faces surrounding her, from Aunt Doreen's gentle smile to Midge's puckish charm and Saul's chiseled features. *It feels right to have friends so close, a home to call our own.*

"Did you have a busy morning at the shop?" She knew full well only a trickle of customers wandered in—most of the townsfolk were too busy with harvesting to spare any time.

"Not a soul in the place but me." Saul cut into a thick slice of ham. "If it weren't for taking inventory, I'd have nothing to do."

"Good." Midge seized the opportunity without a second thought. "Then you can come with us this afternoon. It'll be fun! Clara's going to take us to collect walnuts."

"That's a wonderful idea!" Aunt Doreen unwittingly played her part to perfection. "You're tall enough to shake higher branches that we could only hope to reach."

"I'd be glad to help." He swiped another biscuit from the basket set before him. "Why the sudden interest in walnuts?"

"The time is right." Clara passed him some of Opal's honey. "Besides, walnuts make delicious additions to coffee cake and breads."

"What better reason could there be?" His grin showed enthusiasm at the prospect of Clara's promised baking, but the question stung.

Midge slid a swift glance her way before giving a careless shrug. "You never know what you'll find when you're out and about."

<hr />

Never know what I'll find. The words thrummed in Saul's mind as he surveyed the bevy of females lurking among the trees. He spotted no other men in the vicinity, a surefire sign he'd been duped. The corners of his mouth tightened, and he slowed his pace, letting Midge and Miss Edgerly pass him.

"Where's the parson?" he gritted out when Clara drew abreast of him. The guilt stamped across her features did nothing to restore his good humor.

"Perhaps he doesn't have a taste for walnuts." Her blithe reply was at odds with her stiff posture.

"Clara," he growled her name as his hand curled over her elbow. Ignoring the heat searing his fingertips, he pulled them both to a stop. "Give me one good reason why I shouldn't turn around and go back to the store."

"Is it so awful?" Her wide eyes pled with him to deny it. When he held his silence, a wistful sigh escaped her lips. "You'll stay because you won't disappoint Midge."

"Dr. Reed!" Almost as if on cue, Midge's voice came piping back to them. "These branches are so full all you'll have to do is tap them!"

"If I weren't so angry at that underhanded tactic"—he started moving toward Midge as he spoke, never relaxing his grip on Clara's arm—"I'd almost admire your aptitude for diabolical scheming."

"There's nothing diabolical about gathering walnuts," she hissed. Clara tried to disengage her arm, but Saul wouldn't allow it.

"Allow me to make one thing clear—under no circumstances will you or Midge leave my sight this afternoon. I'll not be maneuvered into a sham courtship."

"Then don't let it be a sham." Despite her fixed smile, the words uttered from the side of her mouth were underscored in steel as she pulled her arm free. "Oh, Sally! Midge and I have been wanting to ask about the pattern of your green dress. Why don't we gather the fallen walnuts over there while Dr. Reed shakes these branches?"

"Then these will need to be collected." Saul wasn't about to let her disregard his orders.

"Oh, that's not a problem. We'll remain in your sight while the others stay here." Her smile could have sweetened lemons. "Opal? Willa? Amanda? You won't mind helping Dr. Reed over here, will you?"

"Of course not!" The other women drew close, boxing him near the wrinkled bark of a nearby trunk.

With a triumphant glance over her shoulder, Clara took Midge, Doreen, and Sally far away, leaving him behind. With the three eligible women of Buttonwood.

Saul climbed the tree at record speed, wrapping his fingers around the thinnest parts of the branches and shaking with all his might. Walnuts rained down upon the earth, striking grass and dirt with thuds not nearly loud enough to appease his frustration. A few of the green pods knocked the girls about their heads and shoulders, giving a brief flash of satisfaction before remorse had him calling out apologies.

"That's to be expected!" came the cheerful replies as all three women stooped to gather the harvest.

"It's the reason Ma lets me come do the collecting, instead of asking too many questions." Willa Grogan stiffened as soon as she said the words, avoiding the gazes of the other girls as she stooped. She didn't say much else as everyone worked.

When he moved on to the next tree, Saul bellowed for Midge to come join them. From his vantage point, shadowed in the yellow-green of the autumn walnut leaves still clinging to the branches, he could see her laughing with Clara.

Why isn't she here with the other unmarried women? The realization that Clara didn't see herself as one of his prospects rankled. *Out of all the women in town, she's the only one I'd want to spend time with alone. And just look how well she gets on with Midge....*

Since he'd last seen them, they'd flung decorum to the winds and abandoned their bonnets—obviously certain they'd ventured far enough to be shielded from any disapproval. Both of them hunched in the cool shade, squirreling out the soft green husks of ripe walnuts and adding them to bulging sacks. The trees veiled Clara's smooth white skin from the sun's rays, and Midge's freckles soaked up every drop whether she wore a hat or not. The two wore matching smiles as they worked together.

And pretended not to hear his calls.

Understanding rushed him with enough force to knock the breath from his lungs. This afternoon's interlude with the ladies wasn't just another stage of Clara's matchmaking attempts. No, this latest machination, executed with the precision of practiced surgery, had blinded him to a crucial truth.

Midge is in on it.

CHAPTER 21

"He's yelling pretty loud now." Midge tilted her head toward the direction of Saul's shouts. "I think he wants us to know that he knows we can hear him."

"Nobody likes to be ignored." Clara deposited a handful of husks into her sack. "After the way he disregarded my advice, he needs a good reminder."

"Since he's with Opal and Willa now, we've done what we can." Midge shuffled toward another heap. "At least for today."

"We'll see how things unfold, but we fulfilled the basic goal." Clara picked up their bonnets and followed. A cool breeze lifted the ribbons, sending them dancing in the air. It felt good to stand in the quiet shade for a moment. "You said just the right things at the perfect times."

"Good." A smile flashed across Midge's sun-kissed face before worry lit her gaze. "He'll know I helped."

"Hopefully that will help make him see how important it is and get him to change his mind."

"Him marrying is important to me." Midge set down her sack. "But I haven't figured out why it's so important to you. Why are you trying to marry off Dr. Reed, anyway?"

Clara thought for a moment and chose her words carefully. "Do you remember how I told you that Aunt Doreen and I got kicked off our wagon train just a little ways from Buttonwood?"

"By that no-good Hickory McGee." The fierceness of the girl's glower warmed Clara's heart. "You could've been hurt or gotten lost or something terrible, and he didn't care."

"Well, he made a decision. . .that much is certain. My point is Dr. Reed's father took Aunt Doreen and me in. Oh, he said he wanted some help, and he was glad to have us making his meals, but he didn't have to ask us to stay. We owe it to him to do anything we can to make him happy."

"And Dr. Reed marrying someone here and staying nearby would make his father happy?"

"Yes." Clara leaned against the rough, wrinkly bark of a nearby trunk. "So that's one reason."

"I remember the part about the boarding school." Midge kicked a small stone, sending it tumbling across the grass. "Clara? Do you think having a wife and staying in Buttonwood will make Dr. Reed happy?" Eyes made big with worry stared up at her.

"If she's the right wife, yes. Dr. Reed wants to help people, and he could do a lot of good right here. He wants to make sure you're happy, and staying here would keep you close, too. So there's all of that and getting to see his father every day." Clara nodded. "I'd say a good home in a nice town with plenty of friends and family should make anyone happy."

"You're right." Midge eyed her speculatively. "So you do want Dr. Reed to be happy."

"Of course." Clara frowned at the idea she'd want anything else. "He's a good man."

"So you like him, even if he doesn't listen to you and he's probably very mad at us both right now?" The sidelong glances Midge kept sending her while she tossed more walnuts into her bag began to make Clara uncomfortable.

"Yeeeees."

"That's interesting." Her friend didn't say anything more.

"Why is it interesting?" Clara knew she'd regret asking but couldn't stand the way curiosity niggled at the back of her mind while Midge calmly continued with the chore at hand.

"Well, did you ever stop to think that maybe you could fix all of your problems if you just went ahead and married Dr. Reed?" Midge abandoned all pretense now, clutching her bag of nuts and staring intently at Clara to gauge her reaction.

"No! I mean, no." Heat swept up Clara's neck and to her cheeks. "The thought never crossed my mind."

"Huh." With no more than that grunt, Midge dismissed the topic.

Clara stayed rooted to the spot. *Me? Marry Saul?* The idea made no sense, not when she worked to get the house for Aunt Doreen. *But Midge doesn't know about the house.* Shame streaked through her at the reminder of her mercenary motive. True, making Josiah—and now Midge—happy was part of it, but caring for Aunt Doreen and gaining her independence were primary.

Marry Saul—the thought had no business buzzing around her head.

"Why not?" Midge's voice drew her back.

"Why not, what?" Clara shook her head as though to reorganize the muddle of her thinking.

"Why didn't you ever think about being Dr. Reed's wife?"

"Because marriage isn't the solution to a woman's problems." Uriah's grim features as he cut a switch from the tree in the yard flitted across her memory. "Never forget that, Midge. Don't marry because you think it will make life easier."

"But that's why you want Dr. Reed to marry." Midge gaped at her. "Why is it different for you?"

212

"When a man marries, he gains a wife at his side, a helper in his home, and a mother for his children." Clara struggled to explain. "He keeps his profession, his property, his name, everything but his bachelorhood. Can you understand that?" She waited for Midge's nod. "A man still makes his own way in the world, his own decisions, and his wife is expected to follow him. She leaves her home to join his. That's the difference."

"Then they make a life together," Midge pointed out.

"In a sense. Think about it this way—a woman gives up her name and leaves her family and home. Everything she owns and who she is now belongs to her husband. Her clothes and jewelry aren't hers anymore, but his. Her husband makes the decisions for the rest of their lives, and for the most part she has to live with that."

"And if she marries the right man, they'll agree most of the time." Midge's face took on an obstinate look. "Or she makes him listen."

"But if she marries the wrong man because she needs money, or her family needs the connection with the other family, that woman is bound to her husband for the rest of her life. And in the eyes of the law and society, he rules her."

"I don't like that." Midge's face scrunched into a frown. "There's a big difference for men and women in marriage."

"You have to be sure you marry for love and respect when the time comes, Midge, so you can avoid all those other problems." Clara forced a smile. "And remember that Dr. Reed will make a wonderful husband, so Opal or Willa will be lucky to have him."

"Dr. Reed is a good'un." A wide smile broke across Midge's face. "And since you've gotten to know him better, now maybe you can think about him being a wonderful husband for you."

Time to bring in reinforcements. Saul made a quick getaway, using

Clara's disappearing act to his advantage for the first time all afternoon. While the women laid their harvest on flat areas in the stone outcropping beside the meadow, Saul went to fetch a few extra hammers. Husking the walnuts would take a lot of work. Enough work that he might be able to persuade a few other men to lend a hand.

Mouth curled in a smile, Saul headed straight for the blacksmith's shop, where Matthew and his brother seemed eager to help. It didn't take long before Nathan Fosset and Elroy Speck swelled the ranks, and the whole group of them trooped off to meet the girls at the meadow.

Clara's eyes widened when she caught sight of him, and even at a distance Saul knew they'd darkened with simmering anger. When he drew close enough, the stormy jade of her gaze proved him right. Her lips thinned in a grimace of a smile which raised his spirits more than the merry greetings of the women surrounding her.

"Things seemed uneven this afternoon," he drew out the words, "so while I picked up the hammers, I rounded up a few more men to level things out."

"Shared burdens make the load lighter." Amanda Dunstall's singsong comment couldn't have been better timed.

"Exactly." Saul watched Clara's hands clench into fists. "Here you go." He passed her a hammer, relishing the way her fingers curled around it as though longing to throttle something—or someone.

She turned away, straightened her leather work gloves, and began pounding away at the hapless walnuts before her in what should have been an obvious attempt to vent her ire.

At least her motive shone through to Saul as she hefted the mallet and struck the hulls again and again. It didn't take too much guesswork to imagine she likened his head to those obdurate casings.

214

Well, it'd take more wiles than she and Midge can summon and combine to weaken my resolve. Jaw set, Saul went to work. Dull thuds of hammers against nuts—punctuated by the sharper clang of metal against rock after an occasional miss—filled the afternoon. Inky brown stained the rocks, everyone's gloves, the hammers' heads, and the sacks filled with walnuts still encased in thick shells, and everyone continued to work.

Even Midge's glee at the demolition eventually wore off, but others in the group still found reason to smile. Saul made a point of staying between his ward and Mrs. Edgerly, keeping far away from any of Clara's friends. The other men practiced no such restraint.

According to established pattern, Matthew Burn sought out Sally Fosset's company. Elroy Speck maneuvered to work alongside Amanda Dunstall while Nathan Fosset paired up with Willa Grogan. That left Matthew's younger brother, Brett, to cozy up to Opal Speck.

Instead, Brett edged his way in next to Clara, who initially brushed off his occasional comments. The youngest Burn blacksmith didn't seem deterred but kept on cracking casings with deft blows of his hammer and sliding smiles her way whenever he could.

Saul made a point of moving to the side. "Come over here, Midge, and give Brett some more room."

Clara's disgruntled glance earned her a smug grin. *You have no room to complain,* his expression told her. Though she gave an exasperated huff, he knew she acknowledged the truth in it when she looked away.

As the day wore on, young Brett's attentions toward Clara became less amusing. His arm would brush hers, his gloved hand rasped across her wrist when reaching for another walnut. The boy's bulk crowded Clara, letting him get too close. The longer Saul watched this progression, the more it chafed.

Still, Clara did nothing. No frowns chased away the insolent suitor. No widening of her stance forced him to retreat. Clara didn't encourage him, but she didn't discourage him, either. In short, she carried on as though she didn't notice Brett's advances.

Everyone else ostensibly detected his interest. When the young blacksmith wrapped his fingers around Clara's under the pretext of showing her how to better grip the hammer, Saul shouldered his way between them. "That's it. We're done." He cast a pointed look at their bags. "Everyone else goes home to full families and should get a larger share."

"No one will argue with you about that, Doc." Elroy hefted a sack as though judging its weight. "Amanda here gets the same as everyone else since she and her ma will use them in the diner."

"We certainly will." Amanda flushed with pleasure.

"I'm building some shelves for the medical supplies I ordered for the store." Saul handed half-filled bags to Mrs. Edgerly and Midge, lifting a large one to carry.

"It seems a shame to leave now." Clara made one last effort to salvage the afternoon, and Midge opened her mouth as though to support her.

"We came early," Saul reminded her. "And Midge needs to keep up on her lessons."

"All this has left me a bit tired," Mrs. Edgerly admitted. That did the trick like nothing else would have.

"Are you all right?" Clara moved with lightning speed, slipping her arm beneath her aunt's elbow to offer support.

"Let me take that, Mrs. Edgerly." Saul took the bag back.

"I'll be fine so long as you start to call me Doreen." She gave a tight smile. "With Midge and Clara calling me by my Christian name, you're the lone hold out. I never cared much for Edgerly, anyway."

"Doreen, it is." Saul let that last enigmatic comment slide, not pressing her as to whether she meant the sound of the name or the husband who'd given it to her.

Clara said a flurry of good-byes and sidestepped a crestfallen Brett Burn, and they all headed home. Midge and Doreen kept up a constant stream of chatter, but it couldn't mask the tension underlying the walk.

When Clara made as though to go to the kitchen, Saul snagged the door to keep her outside with him. "We need to have a conversation, you and I."

"After today, we've both made our aims quite clear, Dr. Reed." She lifted her chin. "There's nothing more to say."

"I disagree." He crossed his arms and leaned against the doorjamb, blocking her entry. "You specifically disregarded my instructions today."

"Midge and I stayed in sight," she countered. "With you up in the trees, you could see for miles on end."

"Those aren't the instructions I meant, though you didn't keep to the spirit of those orders, either."

"Dr. Reed, you may not have noticed, but I'm not one who does well with orders." She folded her hands together primly. "Not without good reason, and not without proper authority."

"I forbade you to meddle in my affairs and told you to stop matchmaking." A muscle worked in his jaw. "As this pertains to my future directly, my reasons are none of your concern and my authority is absolute."

"Had I shown up with a parson in tow and a loaded shotgun in hand, I might concede your point." Her nostrils flared slightly. "As it is, arranging situations where you spend time in the company of others can't be deemed a hardship."

"In the company of women." Saul uncrossed his arms. "Unmarried women." He leaned forward. "With no other men around."

"The arrangement presented itself as ideal for you to further your acquaintance with the ladies," Clara acknowledged.

"I tire of this game." Saul stepped away from the door, leaving her avenue of escape clear. "So I'll get to the point. What if I told you this afternoon gave me second thoughts?"

CHAPTER 22

An icy shiver tingled down Clara's spine, flooding her senses and making her mouth go dry. Where was the warm rush of elation, the heady flush of success she expected to feel?

Missing. Clara's brows lowered as she realized the reason for her odd reaction. "Dr. Reed, I'm in no mood for jokes. I prefer your irritation, which at least is in keeping with the serious nature of what is at stake."

"What makes you think I'm not serious?" The surprise in his voice left no doubt as to his sincerity, but the mysterious tilt to his grin left her unsettled.

She'd tread softly to start. "Who caught your interest?"

"Due to your *foresight*," he lingered over the word, obviously refraining from using a less flattering description, "I've spent considerable time getting to know the women of Buttonwood. While I'm not about to propose, I've decided to consider the option."

Relief surged through her nerves. *Thank You, Lord!* "You don't know how happy I am to hear you say so." She inched closer and looked up at him. "Which girl?"

"That's what I wanted to discuss. Your knowledge of the women in town ranges farther than my own, and I'd like your input. Will you walk with me?" He offered her his arm.

"Certainly." She laid her fingers on his strong forearm without hesitation, the bolt of heat an indication that her victory was sinking in. "I'll help in any way I can."

"Nothing could please me more than to hear you say that." His sidelong glance sent her stomach aflutter.

"Oh?" Reborn suspicion put a damper on her enthusiasm.

"When choosing a wife, a man needs to have all the information possible at hand. It makes sense to start at the basics. Miss Reed, what qualities did you look for in the prospective brides?"

"Wouldn't it make more sense to discuss the aspects of the women you're currently considering?" Clara itched to know who stood the best chance. *Opal, most likely.*

"No. *You* may have started the process weeks ago, but *I'll* begin anew." He leveled a look of admonition. "Preferably with your cooperation to ensure nothing is overlooked."

"Very well." Clara quelled her resentment over the implication she might have overlooked something. Obviously, Saul needed to feel he'd taken control, so she'd do her best to be gracious. After all, he'd come around to her way of thinking. "After discerning essential eligibility—"

"Ah, ah, Miss Reed. We'll apply scientific principle from the offset. How did you determine eligibility?"

"You know the fundamental criteria as well as anyone." She didn't bother to hide her annoyance but decided to humor him regardless of it. "The women cannot bear direct relation to you or already be married, but must be of suitable age for matrimony without having an understanding or engagement with another man. Additionally, her reputation must be in good standing to reflect well on her husband-to-be."

"Very thorough," he praised. "I agree with every requirement listed and am now prepared to move on to personal qualities and wifely attributes."

"How gratifying to hear I didn't overlook anything thus far." Clara straightened her shoulders. "Any wife of yours must be a godly woman with integrity and intelligence. Caring for her family and loved ones is of utmost importance, and she'd not be one to shirk her responsibilities. Essentially, the woman you marry will be a good mother to your children, a helpmeet in your home, and assist with your patients."

"Excellent." Saul gave a firm nod. "I assume that includes all the skills to run a household. Your advice holds merit."

"Any of the women would make a good wife to you and a loving guide for Midge," Clara urged. "Your father would be so pleased to hear you're considering staying in Buttonwood!" *And so will Aunt Doreen, if all goes as planned!*

"Wait." He jerked them both to a stop. "I said I'm considering a wife. Did you hear me say anything about staying in town? This is precisely the type of assumption that can derail the best-laid arrangements."

"But. . .why wouldn't you stay?" Clara dug in her heels as he started to walk again, making him remain at her side. "If you marry one of the women here and can have Midge stay with you while you keep close to your father, why would you leave?"

"Marriage will allow me to have Midge stay in my household regardless of its location." His calm observation cut through her hopes like a dagger. "Remain focused on the issue at hand."

"You'd ask your wife to leave behind her home and family— everything—to follow you to Baltimore?" Her heart sank at the thought. Not only would she not earn the house and Josiah not know the happiness of keeping his son close, but one of her friend's joy would be mingled with wrenching sorrow.

"I will not discuss that now." Saul strode ahead, and Clara

moved with him, too lost in thought to protest. "Let's review the women who met the criteria we've both agreed upon."

"The initial candidates included Sally Fosset, Amanda Dunstall, Vanessa Dunstall, Opal Speck, and Willa Grogan." Clara ticked off the names, concentrating on the current issue. Once Saul chose a wife, she'd work with the woman to get him to stay in Buttonwood. For now, she'd take his interest as a step in the right direction. A sizeable step."

"The Dunstalls?" His brow furrowed. "How do they fulfill your standards?"

"To be truthful, I always felt Amanda seemed a bit young for you." The admission didn't cost her much, as the tone of his voice made it clear he held a similar view. "Yet I couldn't exclude her from the gatherings. Elroy Speck will be a much better match for her, should things progress in that direction."

"Agreed. And her mother, the Widow Dunstall?"

"While Amanda's mother, Vanessa, is still young enough to make a good wife since she married early, the obstacle there has more to do with her continued mourning of her husband." Clara's voice softened. "He was her true love, and even after fourteen months, she's not ready to move on."

"I wouldn't want to compete with a previous relationship or show disrespect to the memory of her first husband." Saul patted Clara's hand as though to assure her he agreed with that assessment. "So that leaves Misses Fosset, Speck, and Grogan on your list."

"Yes. Sally met all the requirements, but in the past weeks it's become clear to me that Matthew Burn cares deeply for her." She slanted a glance at Saul to make sure he wasn't disturbed by the comment. If Sally were the woman he'd settled on, there'd be trouble ahead. "What do you think?"

"I expect their wedding to come before my father returns from Baltimore." Saul's easy acceptance of the fact belied her qualms.

"They'll make a good couple."

"Indeed." Her stomach flopped a little as Clara realized they'd finally come down to it—the two women Saul was seriously considering as his wife. "That leaves Opal and Willa."

His nod, unaccompanied by any statement, was frustratingly noncommittal.

"Both women are God-fearing, strong, loving, and kind. Either would make a fine wife and mother," she pressed. When he still didn't respond, she pushed harder. "So what do you have to say about Buttonwood's prospects?"

"I'd have to say, based on our specifications"—Saul's gaze bored into hers as he finally answered—"you overlooked someone."

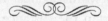

Saul watched as Clara's brow furrowed at his comment. To her credit, she didn't immediately dismiss his statement. Instead, she caught her lower lip between her teeth in dismay at the very thought she'd failed him in such a manner.

He hid his amusement as she tilted her head to the side as if running through the names of every woman in town, considering and discarding potential applicants for the position until her shoulders slumped in defeat.

"I can't think of anyone else. If Amanda's too young, everyone else already married or spoken for. . ." She looked up, so adorably disgruntled he couldn't hide his smile for another minute. "Oh, you're pulling my leg!" Outrage darkened her features. "After all your talk of scientific process, you make a jest just when we get down to the nitty-gritty of things."

"This is no joke." Saul reached down, clasping both her hands in his as his chuckles faded. "Can't you think of at least one other single woman in Buttonwood, Clara?" He drew out her name, relishing the sound of its soft syllables.

"Me?" The word came out in a squeak, her brows raised so high they disappeared beneath the brim of her bonnet.

"You're single, not related to me, and of the proper age." He stroked his thumb across the back of her hand with each point he made. "We get along well when you're not trying to foist me on any other woman in town."

Her eyes had softened to the color of spring moss as he spoke, but at that last comment Clara yanked her hands away. "How dare you," she hissed.

"How dare I what?" He reached for her, only to have her back away, eyes snapping. "Clara, you have to admit you belong on my list of possibilities." Saul attempted an engaging smile.

"No. Don't turn my words against me." She backed farther away as he tried to shorten the distance. "Be as annoyed as you like at my interference, but don't pull me into it to toy with my thoughts. To pretend you would be interested in me—to want to marry me—mocks a lifetime commitment. This is beneath you."

"Is that what you think?" Saul came to a halt, lowering his hands to his sides. Anger flared to life, lending heat to his words. "That I'd toy with you? When have I ever been less than honest?"

"Never." Fury formed tears of frustration in her eyes as she glowered at him. "You've been clear about your intention to leave from the start. I should have known something was afoot the moment you told me you'd had second thoughts."

"Because you're so unyielding, you assume the same of others." He stood his ground. "You take my words and twist them."

"No, you led me into this conversation, step by step, guiding me to form a list of qualities you could turn on me." Her words came out thick, heavy. "It's despicable you'd resort to such a tactic. You tried to humiliate me by drawing me into this ruse, but you've only shamed yourself."

"You honestly believe that." The realization struck a nerve

deep inside. "I meant what I said, Clara. If you stop and think about it, we're well matched to each other. Any man would be proud to take you as his wife"

"It's a ploy to make me stop trying to meddle." Her breath rasped out in bursts. "Well, I'll tell you this much, Saul Reed. . . it won't work. You need a wife, and I intend to see that you get one—if not for your own good, then for everyone else's." With that, she whirled away and hurried back in the direction they'd come.

"Good!" He called after her. "Just remember the list is longer, now, Clara Field! And if I marry one of those women, it may very well be you!"

"No, it won't!" Clara didn't even stop to yell the words back, but from where Midge stood behind a cottonwood tree, she saw Dr. Reed's face when he heard them.

He wore the look of a man issued a challenge.

Midge didn't need any more prompting to go fan the flames. As soon as Clara vanished behind the door to the house, Midge sprang into action. She reached Dr. Reed's side fast enough to see his eyes still shooting sparks. Good. If he was going to convince Clara to be part of their new family, he'd have a fight ahead of him.

"I'm real sorry that didn't work out, Dr. Reed." She put on a mournful face and peeked up at him.

"Humph." The grunt was his only response.

Not good. He'd need more fire than that if he was going to win—and Midge had already decided Dr. Reed needed to win. She thought for a minute and tried again. "That's all right. I'm sure you can get Opal or Willa." She waited a beat. "Probably."

"What?" He looked at her like she'd insulted him, which, come to think of it, had sort of been the point.

"Well, sometimes folks have to settle."

"I choose Clara," he told her, "but I wouldn't say having either Miss Speck or Miss Grogan for a wife would be settling."

"Oh, I didn't mean *you'd* be settling." Midge flashed him a bright smile as he went reddish purple. "Just that since Clara turned you down, you're already passed-over goods."

"She did not turn me down." The words came out all stiff. "I haven't asked her to marry me."

"But she said she won't marry you," Midge pointed out. She shrugged to grind the rejection in a little deeper. "That's the same thing."

"No, it is not the same thing." He peered down at her, eyebrows scrunched together in one long line. "It's not the same unless I ask her."

"But she'd say no."

"She says she'd say no. That's a different matter entirely," Dr. Reed corrected. "If I asked her, she'd say yes."

Midge fought to keep from smiling. Now she had him right where she wanted. She gave a teensy snort to make sure he knew she didn't believe it. "But you're not ever going to ask."

"Scamp!" He burst out laughing so loud, she jumped.

"What?" She stared up at him, wondering if she'd overdone that last bit.

"You pushed too far, Midge." Dr. Reed smiled at her, all that determination she'd worked to provoke gone in a second. "You're trying to goad me into proposing to Clara."

"It almost worked," she grumped. "Tell me the truth—it was the snort that did me in, wasn't it?"

"That. . .and you were starting to look smug." He tapped his index finger on her nose. "So you like the idea of my marrying Clara, eh?"

"Yep."

"Clara in particular, or anyone? I know you helped with her matchmaking this afternoon."

"You're not mad?" She held her breath while she waited for his answer.

"I was," he finally said. "But I could use a little turncoat to help convince Clara to marry me. What do you say?"

CHAPTER 23

Saul Reed doesn't know what he unleashed. Clara's desire to thwart the doctor grew with each passing hour. Today the whole town would turn out for a picnic and taffy-pulling to mark the end of ensiling. She still wasn't clear on what all the process of ensiling entailed. It involved cutting down stalks of corn before they dried and fermenting them into silage for cattle, but the precise method didn't interest her.

The celebration, on the other hand, presented a day full of sweet opportunities to pair Saul with Opal or Willa. Taffy-pulling, conveniently enough, required two sets of hands, and Clara couldn't think of a better way to stick Saul far away from her. The mere memory of how he'd played on her sincere attempts to find him a good match made her blood boil.

If he thinks his ploy yesterday will distract me from marrying him off to one of the other girls, he'll soon regret his gambit. Her eyes narrowed as she recalled how he'd held her hands when he declared his intent to court her. *My opponent may be devious, but my cause is righteous.*

With that last reassurance, she set out to find Midge. Right or not, Clara would take all the help she could dredge up to win the war. She found her young ally still in her room, tugging the green

228

and yellow honeycomb quilt up and smoothing it over her bed.

"Good morning, Midge." She waited outside the doorway until Midge gestured for her to come inside. "Are you looking forward to the taffy-pull?"

"Who doesn't like taffy?"

"My Uncle Uriah didn't like taffy." Clara fingered one of the small teacups sitting on Midge's tabletop. "I always thought perhaps if he ate more sugar it would improve his sour disposition."

"Maybe." Midge giggled. "Everyone in town will be there, won't they? Especially the girls?"

"Exactly. Can I count on you to help me make sure Dr. Reed is paired with one of the girls to pull taffy?"

"Absolutely." Midge's eyes sparkled. "I'll ask him to be my partner then I'll call you over for some reason and say I can't do it."

"Then we'll arrange a last-second switch so he can't finagle his way out of it." Clara hugged Midge. "Brilliant!"

"Clara, did you fix up this quilt?" She walked back to the bed and traced one of the hexagonal pieces of fabric. "It's been repaired real nice, and I wondered who took the time."

"I found it in a trunk above the store, but all of us girls worked together to make it ready for you. Opal, Willa, Amanda, and Sally all came over, and we spent a morning stitching it back together." As she drew closer, Clara saw Midge rub at her nose.

"Thanks. I like it. All of you are so nice to me, I know Dr. Reed won't regret his wedding." Her friend's voice came out hesitant and concerned. "You don't feel guilty sneaking around though? Like you're fooling someone you care about and it's wrong?"

"Not over something so simple as a partner for pulling taffy," Clara reassured her. "Especially when it's for his own good. Sometimes, when people won't listen, you have to nudge them in the right directions."

"All right then." Her smile back and brighter than ever, Midge headed for the door. "I'm willing to nudge. And if that means eating lots of taffy, so be it!"

"I'm not sure I see the connection." As they made their way down the stairs, Clara gave up trying to link eating taffy with getting Saul safely married and settled in Buttonwood.

"A girl can only hope." Midge skipped over the last step. "Maybe if I give up my partner, I'll somehow end up tasting everybody else's batches?"

"If there's a way to wrangle it, I'm sure you'll manage." With that, Clara went to join Aunt Doreen in the kitchen. She gathered the dishes they'd contribute to the picnic and passed a few for Midge to carry before they left.

As they neared the church, she saw Saul with the other men. He'd come early to help set up the makeshift tables and scattered cookfires, which suited Clara straight down to her bones. The less she had to speak with him directly, the better. As it was, getting through the day without the whole town suspecting she wanted to tar and feather the man would be a difficult feat.

"Good morning, Clara!" Opal bustled up to join them. "I hear the men will be patching the roof on the church while we start the taffy boiling."

"An excellent use of time." *And another reason to stay far away from Saul. I never imagined tar would be so readily available....*

Clara made a note to ask Opal to take Saul some water later on. Any pretext to throw the two of them together was an opportunity not to be overlooked.

The morning whirled by as they boiled huge pots full of sugar, vinegar, water, and butter until spoonfuls of the mixture formed hard lumps when tossed into cold water. To these batches, they'd add vanilla or honey flavoring as they poured them into cooling pans. For the molasses taffy made with sorghum, the flavor was already set.

While the pans cooled, everyone flocked together for an

informal lunch. The men came over after finishing repairs to the church, jockeying for position as they heaped their plates full of everything within reach.

"Midge, why don't you show Dr. Reed that seat over there." Clara indicated the bench where Opal sat.

"Will you be there to help?" Midge cast a quick glance around. "In case he tries to leave?"

"Yes." She suppressed a surge of irritation that she had to watch over every move Saul made. It wasn't Midge's fault the man's behavior was erratic. "I'll join you in a minute."

"All right then." Midge headed off to fetch Saul, leaving Clara alone for a moment to ready herself for the trial to come.

"Miss Field?" Brett Burn appeared at her elbow, holding out a mug. "Would you like some cool cider? It looked awful hot over those taffy fires."

"Oh. . ." Clara was about to refuse when the fine hairs on the back of her neck prickled. A swift turn, and she saw Saul staring at her, brows beetling as he took in the blacksmith's presence. "Thank you." She accepted swiftly. "My friends and I will be eating over there, if you'd like to join us."

"I'd like that." His eager smile sent a pang of guilt through her. Obviously, young Mr. Burn read more into the invitation than she meant.

"Excuse me." Clara drifted toward Opal, resolving to be more careful in how she handled her suitor. She welcomed him as a barrier between her and Saul, but as nothing more.

"Seems as though you've picked up a stray friend." Saul's comment sounded innocent enough, but his gaze spoke volumes as she walked up to join him, Opal, and Midge.

"Mr. Burn's offered me no insult." If she stressed his name slightly for Saul's benefit, no one would blame her. "Here he comes now."

"Miss Speck, Dr. Reed." The young blacksmith sank down on the grass beside the bench, balancing a full plate on his knees. "Miss. . ."

"Midge. Everyone calls me Midge."

Clara shot her friend a censorious glance. Obviously she'd need to have a chat with Midge about certain proprieties. At thirteen, the girl wore her hair up, her skirts long, and needed to be addressed by her surname as any other respectable lady.

"Miss Northand," Saul corrected. "This is Mr. Burn."

By all rights, Clara should have applauded Saul's swift handling of the situation. Instead, she noticed the sharpness of his tone, as though he deliberately sought to make the other man feel distanced from the rest of the group.

"Brett," she added, "runs the blacksmith shop along with his father and older brother." A zing of satisfaction at the peeved expression on Saul's face faded when she saw the delight written across Brett's features.

Oh no. What have I gotten myself into now?

❧

A mess. No matter how he tried, Saul couldn't see the goopy pan of sticky candy smeared with butter as anything but one huge mess.

"I don't see the appeal," he told Midge.

"You're a doctor." She rolled her eyes at him. "Of all people, you know that to get the job done sometimes you have to get your hands dirty."

"Not that—I meant I don't see how this is considered romantic." Saul frowned at the glop before him. "Spending the afternoon yanking on tacky candy won't win Clara's heart."

"It's not about the candy. . .though eating it at the end doesn't hurt," Midge whispered. "Think of it this way—if you don't ask her, she'll spend the whole time with that blacksmith she brought over at lunch."

That galvanized him. "She won't say yes. We'll have to think up another way."

"Just leave it to me." Midge waited for a few moments, until the taffy-pulling contest was about to begin. "Clara!" she shouted loud enough that everyone heard her. "Clara!"

"Yes?" Sure enough, Clara came running—with Brett hard on her heels. "Are you all right, Midge?"

"I think I ate too much at lunch." Saul watched in fascination as Midge's eyes drooped and she laid a hand over her stomach. "I'll be fine, but I don't want to leave Dr. Reed without a partner. Will you take care of it?"

"Of course." Her quick capitulation made sense—Clara had always been one to think of others before herself. "I'll make sure Dr. Reed has a partner."

"Thank you." Midge put on a brave smile. "I think I'll go sit in the shade for a little while and watch."

"Would you get her some water?" Clara asked her oversize suitor, nipping about her heels like a big puppy. Of course it worked, and Brett went loping off toward the water bucket.

"I would have seen to it," Saul told her now that he didn't have to leave her alone with the blacksmith.

"Yes." She gave him the first genuine smile he'd seen from her since yesterday morning. "You're good to Midge—to all your patients. I haven't forgotten that."

"Especially the ones I like." He raised a brow.

She immediately retreated to polite conversation. "But how often does a big-city doctor get to have all the fun of a taffy-pull?"

"Rarely," he acknowledged. Saul shot Midge a big smile to let her know everything was working perfectly. "So what now?"

"First. . ." Clara craned her neck as though searching for

someone. "Opal!" She gestured for her friend to come over.

Saul listened in stony silence as Clara explained the situation, relaxing only when Opal gave an apologetic shrug. "I already have a partner." With that, she left them alone again.

"Working with you would be an honor." Saul stepped closer.

"Hmmm." Clara's lips tightened to a thin line. "Willa!" She waved her arms wildly until she caught Miss Grogan's attention.

"Yes?" Willa waited during Clara's quick clarification of the problem then ventured a quick glance at Saul. Apparently, that one glance told her everything she needed to know, because she beat a hasty retreat.

"Now will you be my partner?" His patience wore thin, but since Clara had no more maidens to call over, he could keep things pleasant.

Brett returned, complete with menacing frown. "She's already agreed to be my partner."

"That's true." Clara looked from him to Brett and back again.

"Take your places. The contest is about to begin!" the parson called out to everyone. "Remember that the pair with the best consistency and most pleasing design will win, so be as thorough as possible!"

"We belong over there." Brett's hand curled around Clara's elbow, making Saul step forward.

"But she promised Midge she'd see to it I had a partner," Saul pulled out his trump card.

"What's wrong?" As if on cue, Midge appeared at his side. She kept one hand pressed to her stomach.

"I couldn't find a partner for Dr. Reed, and I already told Mr. Burn I'd work with him this afternoon." Distress raised Clara's voice. "Someone will have to do without."

"Oh, but Dr. Reed was so looking forward to his first taffy-pull!"

At Midge's statement, Saul put on his best hangdog expression. But it was too late.

Clara's eyes narrowed as she looked at the pair of them. Without her eyes drooping, her shoulders hunching, or her hand over her stomach, Midge looked the picture of health. Saul knew it, and Clara wouldn't miss the truth.

"Oh, how silly of me!" When Clara spoke again, the words came out loudly. She reached for Midge's hand and drew the girl close. "The answer is obvious. I'll look after you this afternoon, since Mr. Burn and Dr. Reed are both so anxious to pull taffy." She seared Saul with a malevolent glare as she tugged Midge away. "They can partner up with each other!"

CHAPTER 24

Clara sat pressed up against the end of the pew the next morning, Aunt Doreen a comforting presence on her other side. She'd not said more than a handful of words to Saul or Midge since the taffy-pull and wasn't about to relent now.

The unmitigated gall of the man! She twisted her gloves in her lap as she thought of how he'd not only continued this ludicrous pretense of courting her but had hoodwinked Midge into helping him. *It's bad enough to make sport of my emotions, but to cavalierly raise the hopes of a young orphan longing for a family?* One of the buttons popped off her gloves and pinged to the floor below.

When Saul bent to retrieve it, she eyed him wrathfully and refused to accept the fastener. *I won't take anything you offer, Dr. Reed. Not when I know your manners for the facade they truly are.*

It wasn't until the congregation began to sing that Clara shook free from her ruminations. Bowing her head, she listened for a moment to identify the hymn so she could join in. Within the first line, she recognized it and raised her voice.

"Safely through another week
God has brought us on our way;

Let us now a blessing seek,
On th' approaching Sabbath day;"

The verse rang true. How else could she have struggled through such a trying time, if not for God's grace? More importantly, she would need His blessing if she were to continue to press on in the face of such opposition. At the reminder she didn't face the challenge alone, Clara's voice grew stronger.

"While we pray for pardoning grace,
Through the dear Redeemer's Name,
Show Thy reconciled face,
Shine away our sin and shame;"

She silently asked forgiveness for her frustration and impatience as well as how she'd tried to creep around to accomplish her goals. Clara snuck a glance at Saul's profile as he sang in a husky baritone, suddenly regretting her short temper. Trying to manipulate him was wrong, no matter how much it rankled to admit it, and she owed him an apology for the way she'd handled things.

The parson launched into the next hymn, the familiar melody washing over Clara in a mingle of regret and hope.

"Guide me, O Thou gracious Savior,
Pilgrim through this barren land.
I am weak, but Thou art mighty;
Hold me with Thy powerful hand."

The song continued, and she sang along by rote, but the words of that last stanza occupied her thoughts. *Lord, I am a pilgrim in this land—a traveler. You brought me to Buttonwood, too weak to provide for Aunt Doreen despite my determination. That we made it*

*even this far is a mark of Your might and power, not my own. Why,
then, have I tried to strong-arm Saul into bending to my will?*

Saul turned his face toward hers. Their gazes caught and held.
The intensity of his scrutiny made her chest go tight with shame.
By all rights, Saul should be furious with her plot to marry him
off. That maneuver yesterday, leaving him with Brett Burn as his
taffy-pulling partner after she failed to match him with Opal or
Willa, should have him smoldering.

Instead of censure or anger, his brown eyes held apology. Clara
tilted her head in a small show of acceptance. Her own actions
had forced him to resort to using Midge as a buffer between him
and the other women of the town.

Clara sank back onto the pew as the sermon began, grateful
for the support. Drained of her fiery resolve, she realized for the
first time in a long while just how tired she felt.

"Now we reap the harvest of all the work we've done and lay
in stores for the hard winter to come." The parson straightened
his spectacles while he spoke. "As summer draws to a close and
autumn changes the land around us, it is tempting to mourn the
bright days passing away. In the third chapter of Philippians, we're
reminded that we're to keep our focus on Christ."

Tears pricked the back of her eyes as Clara listened and realized
the awful truth. *I've focused on getting the house, not following Your
way.* Regret clawed at her. *How can I make it right, Lord?*

"Just a moment. . ." The parson ran his finger down the thin
parchment of the pages in his Bible until he came to the proper
place. "'But this one thing I do, forgetting those things which are
behind, and reaching forth unto those things which are before, I
press toward the mark for the prize of the high calling of God. . . .'"

*This is the end of my machinations to make Saul wed a Buttonwood
girl,* she decided. *When Josiah returns, I can tell him in all honesty
that I gave it a valiant effort but failed.* Peace settled over her at the

thought. *I'll follow His word and forget what's behind, reaching for what God has in store. The future has never been in my hands.*

～～◦○◦～～

Saul's grip tightened around the small button he'd retrieved from the floor. It never failed to amaze him that words written dozens of centuries ago spoke so clearly to his heart.

" 'I press toward the mark. . . .'" The parson's reading resonated with such depth, Saul wondered whether he intended today's message to affect his parishioners so personally.

The significance of the passage wasn't lost on Clara, either. Her earlier nod after the uplifting hymns had given him hope that she softened toward him, and the contentment on her face now bolstered his anticipation. Together, they'd put the mistakes of the past weeks behind them.

And Saul would see to it that everything went smoothly from there on out. New tactics were called for. No more antagonistic plotting or chesslike opposition would be employed. Instead, he'd make her understand he hadn't spoken lightly about courting her.

He squared his jaw. Today marked a new beginning. Oh, Clara would need a lot of convincing, but by the time he finished, he'd have her eating out of his hand. As the parson moved on, Saul refocused his attention to make sure he didn't miss anything.

"Today we'll close with one last hymn." With that, the preacher led them in a rousing chorus of one of Saul's favorite praise songs.

He rose to his feet and lifted his voice along with the others, relishing the purpose behind the words.

> "Forward! be our watchword,
> Steps and voices joined;
> Seek the things before us,
> Not a look behind. . ."

When they left the church to walk home, Saul kept his gaze fixed firmly ahead, to where Clara spoke with Midge.

"You're not angry with me anymore?" Hope shone through Midge's guarded tone.

"No." Clara reached out and grasped the girl's hand. "And we're not going to try to make Dr. Reed marry anyone. We're finished pushing him when it's his choice to make." She peeked over his shoulder as though to be sure he was listening.

"Good." He flashed her a wide grin as she and Midge hurried out of earshot and began whispering.

"Is that what's been afoot?" Doreen's murmur took him by surprise. "I wondered why everyone's been so quiet lately."

"Your niece is of the opinion I should marry a Buttonwood girl and settle down near my father." Saul looked down at the older woman whose hand rested on his arm. "Despite my explanations that I had different plans, she's insisted on throwing me in the company of her friends."

"I suspected as much," she admitted. "I'd held out some hope it might work. Your father longs to have you stay."

"My practice is based in Baltimore." He didn't offer further explanation, instead choosing to change the subject. "Though Clara's efforts have piqued my interest in marriage."

"Oh?" Doreen's bonnet brim nearly caught him in the eye as she turned. "Is that why she won't be matchmaking any longer? I find that easy to believe—it's unlike Clara to abandon any undertaking unless she's already succeeded."

"Determined women such as your niece are rare."

"Yet you find yourself in a house with two of them." Doreen raised a single eyebrow. "It's uncanny how alike Clara and Midge are when it comes to pure strength of will."

"Perhaps that's why they get on so well." Saul thought about that for a moment. "For all that, the two of them are very different. Perhaps if Midge hadn't grown up in such difficult circumstances..."

"I won't pry," the older woman assured him. "You mean their perspectives differ even if their personalities run parallel."

"Exactly." He searched for words to describe it. "Midge is all sharp angles hewn by hardship. Clara's strength seems. . .softer somehow. But that's not the right word."

"The edges of her past are worn smooth from weathering," Doreen supplied. "In time, love will level out Midge's rough spots, too. But the sheer force or character it took to withstand their losses will always be the foundation of their worlds. Everything becomes shaped by how they perceive it."

"All this time, you've kept such wisdom to yourself." Saul stared at the woman whose quiet presence he'd taken for granted. "I should have asked sooner."

"You wouldn't have heard it." She sat down on the bench before the general store and gestured for him to join her. "It took you this long to realize you should be wooing my niece."

"How do I go about it?" Saul rubbed at the tension in the back of his neck. "When I tried to tell her, she decided my declaration was a ploy to stop her from matchmaking anymore."

"She's never seen her own value." Grief and remorse flashed across Doreen's usually calm face. "My husband saw to that."

"Why?" Saul's jaw clenched. "What did your husband do?"

"Uriah made it clear from the start that he saw women as inferior to men in every way and expected both of us to cater to his every whim." Doreen's eyes lit with fury, her words coming out faster. "Clara, in particular, he deemed useless. 'A penniless orphan brat,' he called her."

"If it weren't for the Lord's mercy softening my heart, I'd consider the man fortunate to have died." The words came out low and harsh, from his very gut. "Had I ever met this Uriah, he would have rued the day."

"The worst of it is I married him so I could take care of her. My inheritance wouldn't support both of us, so I needed a husband." Doreen drew a shaky breath. "If you want Clara, you'll have an uphill battle convincing her. She'll never marry for less than genuine love and respect."

CHAPTER 25

"How's that?" Midge peered over Clara's shoulder and waited for the verdict on her penmanship.

"Beautiful." Clara set down the slate. "We'll move on to pen and ink soon. In fact, I'll bring some back from the store this afternoon."

"Thank you." She scooped up the slate and took it from the table. "I'm glad you and Dr. Reed are getting along so well."

"Now that I'm not pestering him about getting married, things go much more smoothly." Clara stood up. "Today I'll be emptying and rinsing all those bottles of useless tonics. That way we'll have vials for powdered medicines when the new supplies arrive."

"Dr. Reed says you're real smart to have thought of that." Midge slid out of Clara's way and followed close. "He likes having you around to come up with ideas and help organize things."

"He's kind to say so." Red color climbed up Clara's neck and spread across her cheeks in a telltale sign of pleasure.

"One of the things I like about Dr. Reed is that he doesn't say anything he doesn't mean." Midge clasped the slate to her chest. "Like he told me back in Baltimore he wouldn't make me go to church if I didn't want to, and he meant it. I go while we're

243

here because it would make him sad if I didn't, and I don't want to disappoint him, but he would keep his word if I tried to stay home."

"Yes, he would." Clara paused, one hand on the doorknob. "Why wouldn't you want to go to church, Midge?"

"Sometimes I forget that you've only known me for a little while." She rubbed her finger over the rough splinter on the right side of her slate. "You know, you and Dr. Reed and Aunt Doreen are all so wrapped up in church and prayer and everything, sometimes you forget other people don't think the same way."

"Midge, does it bother you when we pray?"

"No. I like the way we all hold hands around the table." She released the slate when Clara tugged it from her hands. "And the songs in church are real nice, too. They remind me of ones my sister used to sing to me."

"Nancy." Reaching for her hand, Clara led Midge to the parlor and sat down on the settee. "I remember you said she prayed a lot."

"Yeah, but she still lost her baby and died." Midge kicked the settee's leg with the heel of her boot since she couldn't say what she wanted to—that Rodney beat down the door and choked her when she tried to get in his way. That the man in the dirty suit shoved Nancy on the ground and took away the child growing inside her, making her bleed until she died. That Midge hadn't been able to stop it, and all her sister's cries didn't help, either. "Like I told Dr. Reed, it may sound good, but praying doesn't work."

"I've never heard anybody talk about it like that before." Clara's voice jerked Midge back. "Is that what you think? That prayer has a job to do, and if nothing happens, it's useless?"

"Well. . ." *Yes.* But the wonder in her friend's expression stopped Midge from saying so too fast. "It makes sense."

"I can see why you'd think so. Let me try to explain it another way, and you tell me if you understand what I mean. Okay?" Clara waited for her to nod then went ahead. "Do you remember when you wanted more taffy on Saturday evening and you asked for another piece?"

"You said no because it would spoil my supper," Midge recalled. A thought struck her. "Do we have any taffy left?"

"I'll look in a minute." Clara didn't seem very excited by the idea. "When you think about that conversation, do you look back and say that talking to me is a waste of time?"

"No, talking to you isn't a waste of time." Midge could hardly get the words out fast enough. "Even if you never give me another piece of taffy again, I'd still talk to you."

"I'm glad to hear it." A smile stretched across Clara's face. "You know, a lot of times I'll ask God for things and I don't get the answer I want."

"Oh." Midge looked down at the toes of her boots. "You mean you prayed."

"I prayed for God to see Aunt Doreen and me safe to Oregon before winter," she pointed out. "But if that happened, I wouldn't have stayed in Buttonwood and met you."

"What you're saying is that even if you pray and you don't get what you ask for, it's not a waste of time." Midge heaved a sigh. "But it's not the same as talking to a person, Clara."

"No, because you're talking to God. Time spent praying is never wasted, Midge, even if you don't like the answer."

"Then I still don't see what good it does."

"Will you try something for me?"

"Depends on what it is." Midge snuck a glance at Clara out of the corner of her eye.

"You know how when you talk with people you say 'please' *and* 'thank you?'"

"Yes. That's just being polite."

"Have you ever been polite to God?" Clara raised both eyebrows when she asked. "Or have all your prayers been 'please' without any 'thank you?'"

"When I could talk to Him, I concentrated on the important stuff." Midge's nose tingled, so she kicked the sofa leg again. "If God has the whole world, why waste time on a 'thank you' from me when He could've saved my sister?"

"I don't have all the answers." Clara reached over to fold her in a hug, but Midge hopped up off the sofa.

"Well, neither do I." She headed for the door but stopped long enough to say one last thing. "And neither does prayer."

"Where's Midge going in such a hurry?" Saul kept one hand behind his back as he walked into the house.

"She needs time to think a few things over." Clara absently ran a fingertip over the thick velvet of the settee. "My talk about prayer upset her."

"And you, from the looks of it." He strode into the parlor and pulled the gift from behind his back with a flourish. "Perhaps these will cheer you up?"

"Oh, Dr. Reed, how lovely!" Clara took the bouquet of purple flowers he'd gathered and raised them to her nose. "Aunt Doreen will be so pleased to see them on the table."

"I picked them for you, Clara." Saul settled next to her. "To show how much I appreciate the time you've spent making our stay in Buttonwood a time to cherish."

"You'll have me thinking I should apologize more often"—she fingered a petal of one of the delicate blossoms—"if this is how you make amends after our battle over trying to get you married off."

"These humble flowers are meant as more than amends." He

246

reached to take one of her hands in his. "I hope you're ready to hear me when I tell you there's only one woman in Buttonwood I'd consider courting."

Her lips parted in a small O of surprise, the flowers tumbling to her lap. "You. . .I. . ." She took a breath and started again. "The evening after the walnut gathering, when you said you'd put me on the list. . .?" her voice trailed off in a question.

"As true then as it is now." His pulse kicked up a notch at the shy hope flitting across her face.

"Midge was right. Just this morning she told me you don't say anything unless you mean it." She gave his hand a tentative squeeze. "I'm ashamed I even suspected otherwise."

"We'll put it behind us and move forward." Her mention of Midge made him remember his charge's hasty departure a moment before. "What else did your conversation include this morning?"

"She mentioned your promise not to force her to go to church, and she revealed her disbelief in prayer." Clara's gaze sought his. "Saul, curiosity ranks among my vices, but I've refrained from asking about Midge's past. I hoped you or she would come to tell me in your own time, but it seems she connects her sister's death with God not answering prayer."

"That's true." He tightened his grip yet didn't reveal more. "What else did she tell you?"

"Nothing particular." Tears shimmered in her eyes. "That girl's heart is still raw with grief for her sister, and the thought she has neither faith nor family to sustain her makes me ache."

"We stand as her family, and our faith will bolster hers." Saul prayed it would be so. "The loss of life is never easy to understand or accept."

"She mentioned a baby." Clara sat bolt upright, her hand sliding from his grasp. "Did she watch her sister die in childbirth, along with the infant? Such a tragedy would test anyone's character, and she's so young."

"Clara, I intend to ask you to become my wife." He held a finger to her lips when she would speak. "Don't answer now. I tell you this so you know what I say is in hopes you'll join me and Midge to make our little family complete. To do that, there are things you need to know."

"I'm listening." Her expression gave no hint to her thoughts, forcing Saul to continue.

"When I told you I took Midge in after I arrived too late to save her sister, I spoke the truth. This is all most people need to know, all they can know if Midge is to have the kind of life she deserves." He rose to his feet, measuring his words with steps. "What you've earned the right to hear is the part of the tale I omitted to protect her reputation."

"Whatever her past, she needs us now." Clara's selfless response proved, as nothing else could, that he'd made the right decision in telling her. In choosing her.

"Midge found me after her sister's bully sent her out on the street for the first time." He chose his words carefully, pausing to make sure Clara understood his meaning. "To sell herself." Saul hated having to say the words, but she had to understand the full horror of it.

"No." She went white. "Midge didn't—"

"She found me." He cut off the words, wishing he could cut away the ugliness. "Filthy, skin and bones, dress too small, Midge looked to be no more than ten. I stopped and offered to find her respectable work. That's when I saw the bruises around her neck. From what I gather, Midge's older sister took up with a bruiser named Rodney, who forced Nancy into prostitution. When Nancy found herself in a delicate condition, Rodney hauled in a quack to terminate the. . .problem."

"The baby?" Clara's whisper scarcely floated to his ears.

"Yes. Nancy resisted but couldn't stop them." Saul began pacing again, the words coming low and furious. "When Midge tried to intervene, Rodney all but choked the life out of her before sending her out to take her sister's place. By the time I got there, Nancy had passed away."

"Oh, Saul."

The strangled sob drew him right back to Clara. Tears streamed down her face as he lowered himself onto the settee and wrapped his arms around her. He held her for long moments, until her cries softened and her breaths returned to normal once again.

"I'm sorry I had to tell you." He kept one arm around her waist while he handed her his handkerchief.

"I needed to know." She dabbed the linen beneath her eyes. "Thank you for telling me. Thank you for saving Midge and bringing her here."

"Thank you for understanding." He reached out to cup her cheek in his hand. "I'm blessed to have found you. Once we return to Baltimore, the three of us will be able to move forward."

Clara slowly lowered his handkerchief, her hand covering his and bringing it away from her face as her brows knit together. "Baltimore?"

"Hello?" A feminine voice preceded a knock at the door. "Dr. Reed? Do you have anything for a toothache?"

CHAPTER 26

"**B**altimore!" Opal's gasp of indignation went a long way toward soothing Clara's exasperation.

"Yes! After all this time, how can he not understand that I won't drag Aunt Doreen back East? That we traveled all this way to prove we can make something of ourselves, start fresh, and he wants us to forget all about that?" The words came out in a huff. "He didn't even consider it. . .just informed me we'd be going."

"He did bring flowers." Opal's eyelids, made heavy from the laudanum she'd taken to dull her toothache, drifted shut. She snuggled deeper into Midge's quilt, making herself comfortable on the settee as she spoke with Clara. "How romantic. It must be nice to have a man be romantic like that."

"That part was nice," Clara admitted. *And Opal doesn't have an inkling how wonderful Saul truly is because I can't tell her about Midge. Not many men in this world would disrupt their own lives to care for an orphan.* "It makes no sense how he can seem so thoughtful and kind one moment, and be a tyrant the next."

"Mmmmhmmm." The drowsy agreement signaled Opal's descent into sleep. Hopefully, the ache would be gone by the time she awoke again. If not, Saul would have to pull the bothersome tooth.

Clara tucked Midge's quilt tighter around Opal, remembering how proud and pleased the girl had been to share it. Belying everyone's expectations, Midge's favorite item in her yellow and green sanctuary wasn't the dainty porcelain tea set, but the quilt she so carefully tugged into place each morning and curled under each night.

A swift glance out the window didn't show any sign of the girl, who must still be on the far side of the meadow, cracking walnuts on the flat rocks. Aunt Doreen had just left to tell Saul it was time for the noon meal, so Midge should turn up at any minute.

An acrid tinge of smoke tickled Clara's nose. The Dunstalls' trash burning had lasted longer than usual this week, leaving a sulfuric trace still strong in the air. As Clara made her way to the kitchen to check on lunch, the odor of burned food grew stronger until she opened the kitchen door.

She stood rooted to the spot in horror at what she saw. Greedy flames engulfed the worktable. When the shelf above it collapsed in a shower of sparks and cinders, Clara slammed the door shut and raced to the parlor, where Opal slept on.

"Wake up!" Grasping her friend's shoulder, Clara gave a violent shake. She pulled Opal to a sitting position, only to have her friend sag back onto the settee. "Opal, the house is on fire!" It was no use. The laudanum kept her friend locked in sleep.

There wasn't time to get help. Tendrils of smoke curled around the doorway. With so much wood in the house, the flames would reach the parlor before Clara returned with anyone strong enough to carry Opal out.

"Lord, help me!" Desperate, she jammed her shoulder into Opal's stomach, trying to lift her friend. Her knees buckled before she got Opal off the settee, sending them both crashing to the floor.

Gasping for breath, Clara wriggled out from beneath Opal's

weight, kicking off the quilt which had tangled about her legs. At the flash of an idea, she seized the blanket, tugging, shoving, pushing, and pulling to get it beneath Opal as a makeshift travois.

By now, everything had turned a murky, grayish haze. Clara grasped the edges of the blanket, sliding it—and Opal—across the floor in a frantic bid for safety. Coughs wracked her as she fought for every inch. Flames danced around the edges of her vision, crowding out the darkness as she stumbled.

"Clara!" Strong arms wrapped around her waist and hauled her toward air so clear it hurt her chest. "Clara, honey, breathe." Saul carried her far from the house, bracing her shoulders.

"Opal," she managed to croak before the coughs overtook her again. "Still. . .inside." Clara struggled to see beyond Saul's face. Fire engulfed both stories of the house now.

"I have her." A familiar voice came from beside her, but Clara couldn't place it.

"Opal," she murmured, trying to turn her head to see that her friend had made it out. She couldn't twist far enough, so she reached out, grasping hold of some fabric nearby. Clara yanked it as close as she could, throat dry and aching so she couldn't speak.

Beneath the soot and smoke, her fingers rubbed enough grime away for Clara to see the green and yellow of Midge's quilt. It was enough to let her know they'd saved Opal. What could be more important?

◦⟨∞⟩◦

"Clara, look at me," Saul ordered as he set her down a goodly distance from the house, propping her back against a large stone. "Breathe deep for me."

She looked up at him through eyes made bleary with tears, obediently drawing a deep breath of untainted air as Adam laid Opal beside her. Coughs wracked Clara's frame as she did as he urged, expelling some of the smoke from her lungs. Her shoulders drooped, head lolling to the side in exhaustion.

"Water." He spared only the one word for Adam as he crooked a finger beneath Clara's chin and tilted her face upward once more. "Look up, sweetheart." Saul ran his hands over her sleeves and skirts, checking for telltale scorch marks or any tenderness to indicate injury. He found nothing.

Thank You, Lord.

"Opal," she rasped after the spasms subsided once more.

"I'll check on her." Saul shifted, looking for the first time at the other woman pulled from the fire.

Still under the effects of the laudanum, Opal Speck lay curled on one side, partly bolstered by the quilt twined around her. Though her breath came in slight wheezes, no coughing or gasping plagued her. Obviously, she hadn't breathed in as much smoke.

"Here, Doc." Adam set down a bucket of cool water and crouched beside him. He slid an uncertain glance toward Clara, who still coughed. "She all right?"

"I pray so. She seems to have taken in more smoke and ash than Miss Speck." Saul dipped his handkerchief in the water, wrung it out, and moved toward Clara. "Don't move."

He used the cloth to wipe soot away from her eyes, already cleansed by the tears, to lessen the stinging. Only after she'd sipped from the tin cup he'd given her did he turn back to Opal and repeat the process.

"How come she's out like that?" Adam stayed close to Opal but didn't touch her. "Did she hit her head? She was on the floor when we got there."

"She came to me for help with a toothache." Saul closed his eyes at the memory of his frustration over her interruption. "I gave her some laudanum to dull the pain, so she'll sleep for a while yet. You say you found her on the floor?"

"Yep, all twisted in that quilt." Understanding flashed across his friend's features. "Miss Field was trying to drag Opal out of there."

"Couldn't." The word came out in a husky scratch as Clara's eyes filled with tears again. She reached out to put a hand on Adam's sleeve. "Thank you."

"Don't talk anymore, Clara." Saul refilled the cup and passed it to her. "Just deep breaths, then small sips of water. That's better. Easy does it."

"Why isn't Opal coughing?" Adam looked from Clara to her friend and back, his brow furrowed.

"She was on the floor, below the smoke. Clara was standing, trying to pull them to safety, so she breathed it all in." Saul swallowed at the thought of it.

Behind them, everyone in town or near enough to see trouble formed a bucket brigade. Midge stood in line with the others, her return with the shelled walnuts at the moment he and Doreen discovered the fire a blessing in and of itself.

Otherwise, he'd be tearing the place apart searching for her, just in case the collapsing second story had trapped Midge. Bucket after bucket of water hissed as they clashed with the flames, slowly vanquishing the destructive force.

Saul knew Dad's house was ruined, but it didn't matter. As long as Clara's lungs weren't scorched and she suffered no permanent damage, he'd praise the Lord for this day's work. They'd lost no lives, and the fire hadn't spread to the dry prairie grasses to devastate the town and surrounding farms. Overall, a crisis had been averted.

Why, then, Saul wondered as he braced Clara through another paroxysm of coughing, *does it feel as though everything has changed?*

Ruined. Even if her throat weren't raw and aching, Clara wouldn't have been able to speak as she surveyed the smoldering remains of

Josiah's once-fine home. *Everything is ruined.*

Jagged talons of guilt slashed at her, cutting off the air Saul kept insisting she breathe. She gasped at the sharp pain in her chest, tears stinging her eyes though she'd thought them all spent. Thick coughs bent her double, blotting out the thoughts of her failure for a blessed moment.

Saul shifted beside her, warm and solid, one arm bracing her back so she could inhale more easily. How was he to know regret tainted every breath, scraping her throat and bruising her heart?

She closed her eyes against the sight of charred bricks heaped in smoking ashes. *Why, Lord?* Against thoughts of what Midge had suffered before Saul found her. *Why?*

Memories long held at bay rushed forward, sliding like storm clouds one atop the other until their rumbling deafened her to everything else.

"Not now, Clara. Mommy and I will be home in a few weeks. You'd be in the way on this trip. . ." The last words her father spoke to her before he and her mother died in the carriage accident.

"Useless," Uriah's voice hissed. *"Penniless orphan brat. There's no place in my house for a willful woman."*

The verses he'd made her memorize, write over and over, recite nightly as a reminder she'd be nothing but a burden her entire life.

"'It is better to dwell in the wilderness, than with a contentious and an angry woman.' 'A foolish woman is clamorous: she is simple, and knoweth nothing.'"

His favorite proverbs from the Word resounded in the passageways of her mind, striking at her every decision. Anger over his unfair judgments filled her with a desire to prove herself. Settling in Oregon seemed the perfect opportunity to stand on her own, provide for Doreen, and be a burden to no man.

Or was it pure foolishness that drove her to bring them to

the middle of the wilderness? After a lifetime of rejecting Uriah's prejudice, her own actions had come to epitomize the worst of it.

Clara slumped into the crook of Saul's arm, sobs merging with coughs she couldn't control until black spots danced in her vision. And still the tears came.

I failed us all.

CHAPTER 27

Midge stared at what was left of the house. Only the brick husk of the first floor remained in place, the wooden second story having collapsed in the blaze. Smoke still hung heavy in the air, steaming bits of broken house still sending tendrils upward.

Tears streamed down her face from the stinging smoke and the new layer of loss. Her fingers closed around the locket she'd not taken from her neck since the day Nancy died, squeezing tight as though to hold on to the only thing she had left.

Things. Midge straightened. *Memories count, too.* Blinking, she turned away and looked toward where Dr. Reed tended Clara. She stumbled a little as she headed toward them, until a soft hand smudged with soot reached out to clasp hers.

Aunt Doreen didn't say anything, didn't try to smile or pretend everything was all right. She just held Midge's hand in a firm grip as they made their way over to Clara and Dr. Reed. That made her feel better than any slick smiles or shiny promises could have.

Midge dropped to her knees beside Clara, still keeping hold of Doreen's hand. She released her clutch on the locket to reach out and comb her fingers through her friend's hair. There wasn't much to say, nothing good to tell, so she settled for the obvious. "We're here now."

"Good." Clara's voice sounded far away and gravelly from all the smoke and coughing. Her eyelids sank low, but she still moved to draw Midge close to her side.

All of her worries merged with the smoke she'd breathed to clog Midge's throat as she snuggled close. Aunt Doreen settled on her other side, between her and Opal, who hadn't woken up yet from the laudanum. At least, that's what Dr. Reed was saying.

"She'll be fine." He had his arm around Clara's waist and looked down at her while he spoke. "Clara will need to take it easy since she breathed in so much smoke. It doesn't seem as though she scorched her lungs, but we can't be too careful."

They all sat for a moment, huddled together. Them, against this terrible thing that had almost taken Clara away. The thought brought fresh tears to sting Midge's eyes, and she swiped at them with the back of her hand.

Not Clara. She scowled and looked overhead. *Or Dr. Reed or Aunt Doreen, either.* No matter how hard she rubbed her eyes, the tears kept coming, so she just let them. *You've already got Mama and Nancy and Nancy's baby up there in heaven.*

No answer came. No voice sounded from the heavens or whispered in the wind as the rest of the town doused the rubble of the house one last time. The silence rushed in her ears until it became an unbearable taunt.

Midge held on tighter to Clara and Doreen and finally asked the question that had plagued her since Nancy died. *How am I supposed to believe in You, and all Your love and goodness, if You keep trying to steal everything I love?*

"Saul?!" Josiah bellowed as he burst into the shop, the acrid stench of smoke and ashes spurring him forward in the darkness. "Doreen?" Receiving no immediate answer, he pounded up the stairs.

The icy hand of fear clamped around his heart, making it hard to breath, hard to move. He moved anyway, not stopping until he ran into his son at the top of the steps. Josiah wrapped Saul in his arms and held tight for a moment to assure himself his son was safe and sound before he let go. "Where are Doreen and Clara?"

"In the dugout with Midge." Saul led him into the crowded room. Everything had been shoved against one wall, making room for a mattress and washstand near the stairwell. "I insisted the girls sleep here, but. . ." A gesture at the cramped space finished the statement for him.

"No one was hurt? They're all fine?" Josiah's pulse kicked up a notch when Saul hesitated.

"Clara inhaled a lot of smoke, and I can't get her to rest as she should." A frown furrowed his brow. "Her coughing has lessened in the two days since it happened, though I'd be more satisfied if she'd stop sifting through the remains of the house, trying to salvage things. She needs to recover fully."

"And Doreen?"

"She was with me in the store when the fire started." Saul's assurance drained some of the tension from Josiah's shoulders. "Midge came back from the field to find the house aflame, so neither one suffered any injury."

"What trapped Clara inside?" *I thought the place safe, but if something collapsed and endangered her, I'll never forgive myself.*

"Opal Speck." Saul's expression softened. "I'd given her laudanum for a toothache, and she'd dozed off in the parlor. Clara wouldn't leave her behind."

"She's a good woman."

"A stubborn woman." He turned away so Josiah couldn't see his eyes. "She tried to drag Opal out on a quilt. When Adam and

259

I burst in, she'd all but collapsed mere feet from the door. Praise God we were able to save them."

Rage and gratitude warred in his son's voice, and Josiah knew the emotions centered around a woman. *But which one?*

"You carried Opal out of the house?" He kept his tone casual to hide the importance of the question.

"I reached Clara first. Adam managed Opal."

"She seems to have made quite an impression since I left." Josiah kept the observation neutral.

"You could say that." A wry smile tilted the corners of Saul's mouth. "Clara understands I intend to marry her."

For the first time since he'd seen the skeletal brick outline of his house, smelled the ashes of charred wood and tang of over-heated metal, Josiah grinned. *Clara. My boy inherited my good sense after all.*

"Fine." He dragged off his hat and leaned against the wall. "Fire doesn't matter then. No harm done."

"No harm?" Saul gave a short bark of laughter. "The house burned down. The women lost their clothes and belongings."

"We'll rebuild from the bricks and replace everything lost." Josiah squinted at the glower on his son's face. "That's one of the advantages of owning a general store."

"It's more than that." Saul paced three steps, executed a tight turn in the narrow space, and kept going. "Since the fire, Clara's changed. It's not just that her throat hurts so she doesn't talk a lot." He gave a helpless shrug. "I don't know how to fix what's wrong."

"Well, it makes sense she takes the loss of the house personally." Josiah moved over and sank onto the mattress on the floor, stretching out his feet. "The only thing she wanted was a way to provide for Doreen and give her a good life. It was underhanded of me to use that against her, but how else could I have gotten her to agree to our little bargain?"

"What bargain?" Steel edged Saul's words.

Now I've gone and stepped in it. Josiah didn't move a muscle, too busy trying to figure out how to squirm out of the mess he'd made without twisting any more of the truth.

"What bargain," he parroted his son. "Good question."

"Dad, what did you do?" Saul loomed closer.

"Sit down, son." Josiah waited as Saul silently debated whether or not to give ground, finally settling next to him. "The easy answer here would be to remind you of the deal I made with Doreen and Clara when they first showed up in Buttonwood. In exchange for room and board, they'd cook the meals and keep house."

"Keep house," Saul muttered. "I know she feels responsible because you left them to take care of the house while you were gone, but it goes deeper. Tell me the rest."

"It's going to stick in your craw, but every man learns that when it comes to women, he has to swallow his pride."

"Go on." Saul stared straight ahead like a man bracing for a firing squad.

"In the letter I wrote asking you to come, do you remember me mentioning that you might find a wife while you were here?" Josiah knew that wasn't enough warning for what he'd done, but he'd bring up whatever points he had in his favor.

"You hadn't even met Clara when you wrote that." Saul pinned him with an impatient glower.

"You might not have been set on finding a wife, and Clara skittered away like a gun-shy mare at the very idea, but I'm not fool enough to miss an opportunity like that when it walks right into my store."

"Skittered away at the idea? She could have at least met me before ruling out the possibility."

"You're a fine one to speak." Josiah bit back a grin at the disgruntled note in his son's tone. *Maybe this talk won't go too badly.*

"Did you come willing to consider the girls you met during your stay?" The silence between them was answer enough to suit him. "So I decided you needed some guidance, a nudge in the right direction."

Saul snorted. "You expect me to think that's all of it?"

"Yep." Josiah stretched, trying to end the conversation right there. "That's all." He threw in a yawn for good measure. "What say we turn in?"

"Not so fast, Dad." Saul didn't budge. "You put Clara up to all that matchmaking, didn't you? I have my own father to thank for her incessant attempts to throw me together with every unmarried woman in Buttonwood the entire time you were gone?"

"If you knew what she was up to, why pry it out of me?" Josiah yanked off a boot. "The whole thing worked in the end. I counted on you to pick Clara, you know."

"That I believe." Saul shook his head. "You're crafty, Dad, setting it all up that way. And since it's Clara you chose, I'll forgive you." He got up, walking to the kerosene lamp as though about to put it out.

"Good. Now maybe we can get some shut-eye and put this whole thing about the house behind us. With you marrying, Clara, she doesn't need it anymore."

Saul froze, hand still reaching for the lamp. "The house?"

"It was the only way to get her to play matchmaker, son. As much as I hate to admit it, I was devious enough to offer her the house if she could get you married off and settled down."

"Why?" His arm fell to his side.

"All that girl wants is to be able to provide for Doreen. After Hickory kicked them off the wagon train, it looked like they couldn't ever make it." Josiah stood up. "I offered her a home if she could give me my family."

"And if she doesn't marry me?" Saul swung around to face him.

THE BRIDE BARGAIN

"What then? You knew I wouldn't wed any of the other women here. Now she and Doreen can't even stay to keep house for you. Clara isn't marrying me because she wants to, Dad." His voice went hoarse. "She has no other choice."

CHAPTER 28

"Good morning." Clara's subdued greeting the next day tightened the vise around Saul's chest.

Sleep evaded him the night before, and now words played the same trick. He rubbed some of the grit from his eyes. "Why are you doing laundry? You should be resting."

"I feel much better today." She kept at it. "After all, there isn't much laundry left since everything burned."

"Take it easy," he ordered. "My father came home last night."

"Home?" Her lips trembled, and she stopped stirring the laundry she heated in a large pot. "I'll go explain."

"You have nothing to explain." His hand shot out and caught her by the wrist, drawing her away from the laundry. Saul's jaw set. "At least, not to my father."

"He trusted me to look after his house." The green of her gaze darkened. "I failed."

"In more ways than one." The harsh statement came out before he could stop it. "What about marrying me off to a Buttonwood girl? Dad's more disappointed about that than the house."

Clara tried to tug her hand away. "I promised him I'd try, and I did. But after the walnut gathering, and the message that Sunday,

264

I couldn't keep forcing you into those situations. Your father will understand that it didn't work. As for the house. . ." She lifted her chin. "I'll pay him back in time. Somehow. Turn loose of me, Saul. I need to go to him. He deserves an explanation."

"*I* deserve the explanation, Clara." Saul stepped closer, refusing to let the feel of her soft wrist beneath his fingers or the rosy blush of the morning sun on her hair sway him. "Why didn't you tell me about the bargain?"

She paled. "That was private. It wasn't my place to break a confidence, although you knew I was angling to see you wed. What more did you need to evade my efforts?"

"The truth," he all but growled it. "I needed to know that the time you spent with me meant nothing more than gathering information. That the way you made me and Midge feel welcome all had to do with your ambition to get this house. I needed to know your *real* motive behind it all."

"Why?" This time she snatched her hand from his grasp. "Why did you need to know that if I saw you happily married, your father delighted to have family nearby, I could make a home for Aunt Doreen and myself?" Her eyes shone bright and fierce. "Would you have married one of the other girls out of charity for us? What would it have changed?"

"I would have known that you were using me from the moment I came to town." He spoke low, shadowing her steps as she backed up. "I would have known better than to start looking for you in a crowd, to wait for your hair to escape your bonnet and gleam in the sun. I would have known it was a waste of time to watch how your eyes change color according to how you feel, and that for all your big heart and kindness, you calculated every step of the way."

"No, Saul," she whispered the plea.

"Most of all, I would have known why you never put yourself

on that list of brides-to-be. You never wanted to marry me. You still don't." He reached toward her face but curled his fingers back before he touched her. If he touched her, he'd be lost. "Isn't it ironic how you wanted to marry me off and I swore to avoid it, but now I'm going to be the one taking you to the altar?"

"How could you still want to marry me?" Wonder filled her face. "In spite of the bargain I made with your father?"

"Because you didn't trick me into choosing you, Clara." He took a deep breath. "I did that on my own."

"It's not too late to fix that mistake." Anger flared to life in her gaze as she crossed her arms over her chest. "Neither of us is bound by any promise."

"But you will marry me."

"No." She uttered the syllable as though it were an immovable mountain.

"Don't be foolish, Clara."

"I won't be." Her lips pressed in a thin line. "Only a foolish woman would marry a man who didn't want her. Who said he'd been tricked into it."

"It's my decision." He closed the distance between them so his boots brushed against her skirts.

"Marriage vows take two people, Saul Reed." She unfolded her arms to plant her hands on her hips. "So it's my decision. And I say no." Her voice caught. "I won't marry a man who'll resent me for it."

She thinks I don't really want her anymore, that I'm just going through the motions out of a misplaced sense of obligation.

"The only thing I'd resent"—he wound one arm around her waist as he spoke—"is your refusing to be my wife. We'll have a good life, Clara."

"Then why all of this?" She pressed against his chest in a bid for freedom.

"We're not leaving anything out this time." Saul kept one arm at her waist and reached up to trap her palm against the beat of his heart. "No more secrets."

She stared at their joined hands, "Are you sure?"

The heat of their contact seared him. "Never doubt it." He leaned to press a kiss on her brow before freeing her hand so he could tilt her chin up. Their gazes held. "And I'll spend the rest of our lives convincing you that you made the right choice."

He lowered his head to hers, his mouth pressing against the softness of her lips for a long, heady moment. *Marrying me may not be her first choice, but I'll make sure she never regrets it.*

"I never suspected you could be so persuasive." She touched the tips of her fingers to her lips and gave him a shy smile.

"From now on, Clara, there will only be one bargain. You'll become my bride, and together we'll give Midge the family she deserves. It'll be a new start for us when we return to Baltimore."

"Baltimore?" Her echo made the memory of their conversation the day of the fire resurface. Just before Opal came, hadn't she said the exact same thing—with that same look of mulish stubbornness?

"Where I'm establishing my practice," he reminded. "The city that's the only home Midge has every really known."

"Oh, Saul." She pulled away from him, tears sparkling in her eyes. "After everything we've been through, how could you think I would go to Baltimore? I can't go back East."

"It's the only way." He caught one of her hands in his. "Be sensible, Clara. In Baltimore, I can provide for you and Doreen. The loss of the house here doesn't matter—Dad can live above the store. You won't have to wait for a new wagon train or endure the hardships of the trail ever again, and Midge will finally have the family she deserves. It's the perfect solution to every problem."

"You're wrong." She pulled away for what seemed like the last time. "Marriage is never the solution for a woman."

With her head bowed, Clara almost ran straight into Josiah.

"Chin up," he warned. "Or I might think you're unhappy to see me."

"Never," she promised. The now-familiar guilt speared her. "I'm so sorry about the house, Mr. Reed." Her throat ached with memories of helplessness. "By the time I found the kitchen aflame, I couldn't stop it."

"It's not your fault." Saul came behind her and tried to put his hands on her shoulders, but she stepped aside.

"All that matters is all of you came out fine." Josiah craned his neck. "Where's that aunt of yours?"

"Inside, cleaning up after breakfast." Clara saw his hesitation. "Go on ahead. She'll be happy to see you."

"Will she?" His murmur almost slid past her, but Clara heard it as Josiah Reed went down the steps of the dugout.

Saul blocked her when she would have followed. "Our conversation isn't over."

"I will not marry you for convenience. I will not go back East." She looked up at him, searching for an answer—any answer—for the question she had to ask. "What more is there to say?"

"Morning, Dr. Reed!" Midge came bouncing out of the dugout. "Your pa brought me a peppermint from the store."

"He's looked forward to meeting you." Saul's smile strained around the edges. "Is he talking with Doreen now?"

"Mmmmhmmm." Midge answered around the minty candy. "Aunt Doreen said I should see if I could help you with anything."

Clara cast a last look at Saul. His stony expression smashed her last fragments of hope. *He doesn't have any other reason. Saul doesn't want to marry me because he loves me—it's just the easiest way to make things work out for him and Midge.* Hot tears pricked behind her eyelids, but she blinked them back, forcing a smile for her young friend.

"I have a surprise over here." Clara reached out and grasped Midge's hand, tugging her toward the pot where she'd been laundering the quilt. "Opal stopped by this morning with something for you."

"What is it?" Midge's jaw dropped as she peered into the steaming pot. Her voice came out in a whisper. "My quilt?"

"That's right." Clara used the wooden paddle to pull the bed covering out of the hot water and deposit it in a cooling rinse. "She'd already washed it once, but I could still smell the smoke. I thought I'd give it another wash before you used it tonight."

They swirled it in the rinse water, watching as yellow and green melded in a whirl of color. It took both their efforts to pull the heavy quilt from the pot and try to coax the excess water out.

A shadow fell over the fabric, lending a bluish hue to the greens as large hands reached to help them. Saul didn't say a word as he wrung the fabric in the middle so she and Midge needn't do a delicate balancing act to keep it from dragging in the dirt. He didn't look at Clara even as he spoke.

"I can see why this is special to you, Midge, since it's the only thing that made it out of the fire."

"No, it's not." The young girl's hand crept up to the locket she always wore about her neck, only to hastily catch up her corner of the quilt when it sagged toward the earth. "I mean, that's not what makes it special."

"She loved this quilt before the fire," Clara agreed. "As an act of kindness, she fetched it for Opal that day. One good deed deserves another, and that's why she still has it today."

"Well, fair's fair." Midge carefully tugged her end over the rigged clothesline and pinned it in place. "Opal helped fix it for me, so she deserved to use it."

"Is it the color?" Saul's voice came out low and serious. "The green reminds you of Nancy?"

"Partly. Nancy's favorite was green and mine's yellow, so it's like both of us together." Midge pursed her lips as she looked up at him. "Do you want to know what's really so special about this quilt, Dr. Reed?"

For the first time that day, Saul said the right thing. "Of course I do. If it's important to you, it's important to me."

"All right." Midge traced her fingertips along the wet fabric, outlining the honeycomb pattern as she spoke. "It's more than the colors and more than it coming out of the fire. When I came here and saw it waiting for me, I thought it was real pretty and nice, but it didn't matter all that much."

"What changed?" Clara had to know. She'd been wondering about the significance for a long while.

"That first night, I laid down and thought about what you said. You remember coming after me that day?" At Clara's nod, Midge kept on. "No one had ever been excited to meet me or done anything nice like fixing up a room for me. I liked that. And when I woke up, I looked at the pattern because I hadn't seen the same one before. That's when I saw that it'd been repaired. Someone put a lot of time into making it beautiful again."

"I can see why you'd appreciate that." Saul clapped a hand on her shoulders. "That'd make it special to anyone."

"No." A frown creased Midge's features as she stared up at her hero. "A lot of people would have thought it was junk and thrown it away or wanted something new. They'd say it was a waste of effort for something old and worn."

"Such a shame," Clara sighed, "when people can't recognize the value of what lies right in front of them." She stared at Saul as she spoke, willing him to hear the meaning beneath the words. *Look at me, Saul. Ask me to marry you because you love me. Ask me to make a home with you here, in Buttonwood, where we've already shared so much. See what's right in front of you.*

"Exactly." Midge walked around Saul to loop an arm around Clara's waist. "You saw that quilt and knew it had been through a lot. Maybe somebody loved it to pieces, and somebody else gave it a good thrashing, and it wasn't much to look at when you found it. But you saw that it could be made whole and beautiful again, and it was worth saving." She reached out and curled her other hand around Saul's forearm. "Just like I was when Dr. Reed found me."

Oh, Lord. . . Clara gave up trying to stop the tears. There were only so many times per morning a woman could be expected to hold them back under such circumstances. *Is this the same girl who came to Buttonwood defiantly asking whether I pitied her? She's not accepted Your love yet, but I see Your hand at work. Thank You, Jesus.*

CHAPTER 29

*N*either of us is bound by any promise. . ." What he'd give to have extracted Clara's pledge of her hand in marriage before everything had gone wrong.

Fragments of his conversations with Clara and Midge rang through Saul's mind the rest of the day, giving him no peace.

"That's not what makes it special." Midge's frown chastened him as she revealed the depth of her loving heart.

"Such a shame when people can't recognize the value of what lies right in front of them." Clara's gaze was full of meaning, but the words did not follow due course. It made no sense.

He was good at recognizing what stood in front of him. He'd found Midge. He'd asked Clara to marry him. Fisting his hands at his temples, Saul leaned on the counter for a moment while Dad went up to the room overhead. *What more can Clara want?*

"Whiskey." Larry Grogan's voice broke through the muddle of his thoughts. "Where's your whiskey, Doc?" The man's blood-shot eyes scanned the shelves. His wrinkled clothes and the stubble on his cheeks, bisected by the still-angry pink of his scar, spoke of days of neglect.

"We only sell medicinal whiskey here, for cleaning wounds

and such." Saul straightened. He purposefully omitted mentioning whiskey's other use for muting pain. Larry was long past suffering from his injuries. "You know that, Larry."

"I know." He slapped some crumpled money on the counter. "Two bottles, and make it snappy."

"Who's hurt?" Saul reached for his medical bag even as he asked the question. If Larry looked this bad, even after his ribs and face had healed, the sick family member must be far worse off.

I've been too preoccupied with Clara and the fire to have paid attention. He tamped down the surge of remorse. A doctor didn't have time for such things in a crisis.

"What?" Larry's astonishment would have been more at home on a cartoon caricature. "Nobody I know of. Why?"

"I see." Saul put back his bag and placed both palms flat on the counter. He took in his customer's disheveled state with new eyes. "Then it's best you leave, Larry."

"Soon as I get m' whiskey." The fool gave the counter an imperious thump. "Better make it three bottles."

"We only sell whiskey for medical use," Saul rephrased his earlier statement, speaking slowly to clarify his meaning.

"Yeah, that Gilbert and Parsons stuff." Larry grimaced. "Don't matter much though. After a few belts you can't taste the difference anymore. Bring it out, Doc."

"No." It would have been amusing to watch Larry try to figure out what he meant, but today Saul was in no mood for it.

"No?" The man sounded incredulous.

"No."

"You can't do that!" Outrage beetled Larry's brows. "You can't turn down a paying customer!"

"What are we turning down?" Dad came down the steps just in time to spare Larry from being escorted to the door by Saul's hand on the scruff of his collar.

"Josiah! Come tell your boy how men handle things in Button-wood." Larry puffed up like one of the roosters his family used to terrorize Sadie the cow.

Saul, for one, would rather deal with the animals.

"Keep your hat on, Larry." Dad approached slowly. "My son's got five years and a medical degree on you. Buttonwood's the same as anyplace else in that you show respect."

Trust Dad to put that little weasel in his place with a few words when I was ready to toss him on his ear.

"He won't sell me any whiskey." The petulance in their customer's voice grated on Saul's nerves. Sober, Larry acted like a spoiled brat. Drunk, he could be dangerous. Saul shouldered his way between his father and Larry.

"We only sell the hygienic stuff." Dad's repetition of Saul's warning didn't sit too well with Larry.

"I know, and I want to buy three bottles." He jabbed his money with a grubby finger. "So what's the holdup?"

"There's no reason under the sun why you'd need three bottles. . .unless you Grogans have finally had it out with the Specks?" The look Dad shot him meant that was a question.

"No." Saul crossed his arms over his chest. "It seems Larry's developed a taste for the stuff."

"This isn't a saloon, Grogan." Dad's growl made Larry back up against the counter. "We've worked hard to keep that sort of thing out of Buttonwood, and you won't get it from my store. Saul's right—you can take your money and leave."

"One day, you Reeds'll be sorry you crossed me." Larry scooped the money into his pocket. "Same as those Specks." He kept muttering as he stalked out the door.

"What a piece of work." Dad shook his head. "The Grogans and the Specks are fairly good bunches as long as you don't mix them, but that Larry seems to have gotten all the rotten in his batch.

What happened to his face?"

"I stitched him up after a threshing accident where he just about got himself killed. As for the others, Adam and his sister are fine folk," Saul agreed. "And I'd say the same for Elroy and Opal Speck. Larry, on the other hand, attracts trouble like a trash heap attracts maggots."

"Let's not think about that." A grin spread across Dad's face. "I've got some good news to tell you."

At least one of us is having a nice day. Saul lounged against the counter. "What's your news?"

"You're getting married?" Clara repeated dumbly, staring at her aunt as though she'd gone mad. Which, come to think of it, was as good an explanation as any.

"Josiah asked me this morning." Aunt Doreen's eyes shone with suspicious moisture in the dim light of the small dugout. "I said yes."

"How could you?" Clara sank onto the bed, her knees unable to keep her upright. Sitting didn't ease the cramped feeling of walls and the earth itself crowding down around her.

"How could I not?" The woman who'd raised her looked astonished by the question. "After all that's happened. . ."

"After all that's happened," somehow she managed to choke the words past the lump in her throat, "you're giving up?"

"What am I giving up by choosing to marry Josiah?" Doreen's weight made the mattress dip slightly. "Think of all that I'm gaining."

"Just as you thought of what you'd gain when you married Uriah?" The words shot out of Clara's mouth before she could bite them back. Before she could decide if she wanted to.

"The two have nothing in common."

The vehemence in Aunt Doreen's tone spurred the roiling frenzy in Clara's heart. "Even their names are similar," she snapped. "Both men seek your hand only after you've withstood devastating change, preying upon you in a difficult time."

"How dare you say such things about Josiah!" Aunt Doreen rose from the bed, gray eyes darkening to the color of thunderclouds. "He's offered nothing but kindness, and you equate him with your *uncle*?" A long pause filled the room before sorrow softened her gaze. "Can you honestly not see the difference?"

"I see a difference," Clara admitted. "Else I would have pressed onward until we caught up to Hickory or found Oregon on our own rather than accept his help."

"Josiah knew it, too. Without even knowing us, he went out of his way to make us feel needed, although the trade was never a fair one."

Her point didn't ease Clara's mind at all. "Why is that? Why take in two women he just met, know them for only a few weeks, and suddenly return with a proposal?" She set her jaw. "It doesn't sit well, Aunt Doreen. You don't have to accept his offer."

"It's my choice, Clara."

"I don't accept it." Clara reached out, holding her aunt's shoulders. "You needn't marry Josiah to see us through. You'll never need to make such a sacrifice again." Tears couldn't seep through her determination this time. Nothing would.

"Oh, Clara." Her aunt reached out to stroke her face. "Is that what you think? That I'm marrying Josiah because we didn't make it to Oregon?"

"And I didn't stop the fire." Shame made her voice as hollow and dark as the depressing place where they now lived. She hung her head. "I failed us both."

"No, Clara." Doreen pulled her close and wrapped her in a tight embrace. "I told Josiah I'd marry him because I want to."

276

"Don't pretend for me. We'll find another way." She babbled now, trying to withdraw but unable to because she'd backed against the bed. "Marriage isn't the solution. That's what I told Saul when he asked me to marry him and said it would fix everything. We'd go to Baltimore because that's where Midge wants to live, and the house burning down wouldn't matter."

"I'm not marrying him to solve anything. We could stay in this dugout through spring and go on to Oregon, Clara." Doreen finally eased back to look her in the eye. "I'm engaged because I want to be. The way Josiah looks at me makes me feel beautiful and cherished."

"Hurrying into anything would be a mistake. Can you have a long engagement, get to know each other better?" *Give me more time to grow accustomed to the idea?*

Silence spooled between them as Doreen eased down beside her once more. When she spoke again, it was almost a whisper. "He says he loves me."

Clara saw her aunt touch the third finger of her left hand briefly and belatedly noticed the sparkle upon it. "You deserve to be loved. Did he give you that as an engagement ring?"

"Yes." Doreen's face flushed with pleasure as she splayed her fingers to better display the finery. "Isn't it lovely?"

Clara looked at the rose gold ring set with small diamonds and seed pearls. It looked like something she would have chosen for her aunt, had anyone sought her opinion. "There's no question Josiah has good taste. He chose you."

"Won't you be happy for me?" The vulnerability in her aunt's gaze proved Clara's undoing.

This is about her, not me. Aunt Doreen's given up so much for me through the years, so long as she's not tying herself to another man for the wrong reason it's time for me to let go of my own plans. She took a deep breath and found a small smile. "I'll try."

Midge backed away from the dugout slowly so she wouldn't make any noise. The roof raised in a hill-like mound, with the stovepipe poking through it. The last thing she needed was for Clara to know she'd heard everything.

Aunt Doreen is marrying Dr. Reed's father, which means she'll stay in Buttonwood. Midge walked briskly, stomping out her thoughts and her energy as she went along. *That'd be fine if Clara married Dr. Reed and we stayed, too.*

She paused to aim a savage kick at an unsuspecting rock. *But Clara won't marry Dr. Reed because marriage isn't for fixing problems and she doesn't want to go to Baltimore. Well, neither do I. Why can't we stay with Aunt Doreen and Opal and everybody here? And why can't Dr. Reed just come out and say he wants to marry Clara for Clara?*

An exasperated huff sent some wisps of hair around her face dancing. She shoved them behind her ears and kept walking. *And what was that about me wanting to live in Baltimore? Nobody asked me. I'd have told them even if we have to stay in the dugout where dirt sprinkles into our food in the morning and on our noses at night I'd stay. It's worth it for the open space and the big sky and not running into Rodney on the street.*

When she reached the river, she made an about-face and marched back the way she'd come. *Clara wants to marry Dr. Reed, but only if he wants to marry her. Dr. Reed wants to marry Clara, but somehow bungled it up so she thinks he proposed to fix everything and she said no. And now that Dr. Reed's father is back, we'll go back to Baltimore on the next stage.*

Midge flopped to the ground, plucked a blade of dry grass from the stalks surrounding her, and placed it between her lips. A puff of air made it hum. A good blow and it whistled. She pulled it to her lap and stared at it for a second.

Maybe. . .just maybe Clara and Dr. Reed were like this blade of grass. When they met, things started humming, but it wasn't enough to get things off the ground. They needed something to knock them into shape and make it work.

The longer Midge sat, the more the prairie grasses poked through her skirts and jabbed her legs, prickling until she had to get up. It was like the land itself was shoving her away, ordering her to get going. *But where?*

Suddenly, she knew what she had to do. It shouldn't take much, but if she handled things right. . . .

Midge whistled as she headed for the general store.

CHAPTER 30

"Why aren't you marrying my son?" Josiah's abrupt version of "good morning" took Clara aback the next day when she went to get a few eggs from the general store.

"Excuse me?" She could hear herself spluttering but couldn't manage to exert more dignity than that.

"You heard me." He rapped his knuckles on the counter. "The first night I came back, scared half to eternity that everyone had died in a fire, Saul told me you two were getting married. Then, yesterday, the bottom fell out. So while he's out taking a look at the Specks' sick cow, I'm asking for an explanation."

Clara raised an eyebrow at his high-handed speech. "That's between your son and me."

"The way I look at it, since I'm marrying Doreen, that makes you family." The smile spreading across Josiah's face at the thought of marrying her aunt went a long way toward softening Clara's reaction. "So I'm asking, as family, what went wrong?"

Clara took a moment to study this man who'd swooped into their lives, given them a home, and recognized her aunt for the treasure she was. Josiah didn't so much as bat an eye when his grand house burned to cinders, but as a concerned family member, he'd brook no obstacle. *He's a good man, Lord. Thank You for that.*

"Saul only wants to marry me because he thinks I'm in a bad situation, out here alone with just my aunt." Pain streaked through her chest as she spoke the painful words. "Your son just can't resist trying to fix things, but I won't marry a man who doesn't love me."

"Who'd have thought my son would've inherited all my good taste without a lick of sense to go with it?" Josiah's snort shook Clara from her melancholy. "He hasn't told you he loves you then?"

"No." She sniffed back the surge of emotion his thoughtless words caused. "He told me the truth—marriage is the perfect solution."

"That's Saul's way of saying he loves you." Josiah shook his head. "Though he's foolish not to realize you wouldn't see it that way."

"I'm afraid you're mistaken." Clara abandoned the eggs and began inching back toward the door, hoping to leave before the tears caught up with her.

"Don't run off now." He tugged a handkerchief from the display and waggled it at her. "Listen to me for a minute so we can clear this up."

Clara kept moving. "I need to go." A few more steps. . .

"What do you know about Saul's sister?" The words stopped her cold.

The image of Saul's expression on the one day he'd mentioned Nellie flashed through her mind. The raw grief, the sorrow mixed with helpless rage she recognized all too well, had struck a chord she still couldn't deny.

Clara walked back to Josiah and took the hankie. "That she loved apples, and he only realized she was really sick when she wouldn't eat apple bread." Her tone softened. "You told me he liked apples, but that was wrong. You got him mixed up with his sister."

"No, I told a falsehood." Creases around Josiah's eyes grew more pronounced as he winced at the memory. "I knew if you had the other gals bake apple desserts but made something different, yourself, he'd notice yours."

"A side scheme all along?" Funny how she couldn't even work up much indignation over it. Not when she was so close to finding out the reason behind Saul's drive to be a doctor. "What happened to Nellie, and why does Saul blame himself?"

"She was his twin, you know." Josiah's eyes clouded over as he looked past her to years long gone by. "Saul wanted to go to the park. Nellie said she felt sick, but he told her not to be a baby. So she went. The next day she was worse and wouldn't eat anything. By the time the doctor came, it was too late. She died that night."

"No," Clara breathed. "It's not Saul's fault."

"He's always believed he should have listened to her and asked for a doctor earlier, that she would still be alive if he'd cared enough to fix the problem." Josiah mopped his face with a bandanna before turning a gimlet eye on Clara. "When anyone he cares about—anyone he *loves*—has a problem, there is nothing Saul won't do to fix it."

Understanding dawned. "You mean—"

The jangle of the bell above the door interrupted her as Doreen rushed into the shop, waving a piece of paper. "Josiah! Clara!" She ran up against the counter, breathing hard. "Midge has run away!"

Saul returned from the Doane farm after setting their youngest boy's broken arm. When he entered the store, he found Clara, Doreen, and his father gathered around one of the counters.

Obviously agitated, everyone spoke at once.

"What's the problem?" Saul strode up to see a slightly blotchy letter lying there, so he plucked it up and began to read.

Dear Everyone,

I'm sorry for all my bad habits. Eavesdropping is hard to stop. I heard Clara and Aunt Doreen talking through the stovepipe in the dugout. I know that Aunt Doreen is going to marry Dr. Reed's father and stay here. Dr. Reed thinks I want to go back to Baltimore. Clara won't marry him just to fix problems.

I'm going to go away awhile. Dr. Reed, you can marry Clara and she won't think it's for me. You both stay in Buttonwood with Aunt Doreen and your father.

Love,
Midge

"Where would she go?" Saul stared at the loopy writing scrawled across the note, heart clenching. "Why would she leave?"

"We'll find her." Clara put her hand on his forearm, her warmth seeping though his sleeve and easing some of the tightness in his chest. "As for why she left, she says it right here. She didn't want us to get married just because of her."

"But we weren't!" Saul's grip tightened, crushing the paper.

"We weren't?" Hope and wariness flickered in her gaze. "Was it so Aunt Doreen and I would have a home?"

"No." He shook his head as though to clear it. *Had everyone gone mad?* "I chose you because you're the only woman I'd want for my wife, Clara Field." Saul returned her gaze, willing her to accept his meaning. Accept him.

"You're the only man I'd want for my husband." A shy smile blossomed across her lips before horror flashed across her face.

"Midge wouldn't try to go to Baltimore?"

"Surely not," Doreen protested. "It's too far. She has no money and no direction. Midge has more sense."

"But isn't that what her letter says?" Clara tugged it from his fist, scanning it with anxious eyes. "Yes, she's going away so we can stay in Buttonwood, because she wants to go back to Baltimore."

"She can't have gone far. We'll find her and bring her home," Saul promised. He reached out to tuck a tendril of Clara's soft blonde hair behind her ear. "She'll learn to love it here."

"You mean. . . ?" The woman he'd make his bride didn't finish the question, but the sparkle in her eyes said it all.

"I know you won't leave your aunt, and I've done a lot of thinking. Adam Grogan is right about Buttonwood needing a doctor. I can do just as much good right here as I could in Baltimore." Saul reached out to draw her close. "Midge will just have to learn to live with that."

"Good!" His precocious ward's voice rang down the steps moments before she appeared, a triumphant smile across her face. "I like it here, too!"

"Then why the letter?" Clara brandished the missive. "You frightened us all!"

"I'm sorry about that." Midge bit her lip. "I really do want to stay in Buttonwood with Aunt Doreen and Opal and everyone, but that wasn't the big reason. It seemed like the two of you might get married just for me, and I wanted to be sure that you were in love."

"Clara knows I love her." Saul slid an arm around her waist. "Don't you, sweetheart?"

"You never said so." Her blush tattled of doubts, but the way her hand rested on his forearm told him he had the power to dispel them.

"Forgive me, Clara." He put his other arm around her to draw her close, relishing her warmth. "Let me tell you now that I love you and intend to marry you as soon as you'll say the word."

"I'm sorry it took me so long to trust you and trust that God had brought someone so wonderful to me." Her smile shone bright and tender, promising years of joy. Her light touch as she reached up to tuck an errant lock of hair behind his ear sent shivers through him. "I love you, too, Saul."

"It's about time!" Midge's exclamation made everyone laugh.

"Yes, it is." Doreen slid a glance at his father. "We could have a double wedding, if you like."

"Yes." Saul couldn't stop grinning at the feel of Clara in his arms at last. "I don't want to wait any longer than necessary to make good on this bride bargain."

Discussion Questions

1. Clara and Doreen arrive in Buttonwood facing the loss of a dream. Have you ever had to face a bitter failure? How did you overcome it?

2. Saul comes to Buttonwood with his mind made up that he's not going to stay, but in the end he realizes what he'd be missing by not following the path the Lord laid before him. Have you ever closed yourself off to an opportunity God might be presenting you? How do you make sure that choices you make aren't a result of your own stubbornness?

3. Why does Clara so desperately want to have a home, and how does that shape her decisions? How is it tied up in her spiritual struggle?

4. Several characters in the novel make choices they aren't comfortable with in order to get what they need; Doreen married Uriah, Josiah pushed Clara and Saul together, Clara took on the Bride Bargain, and even Midge pretended to have run away—just to name a few. Do you think the ends justified the means for any of these decisions? Why or why not?

5. Have you ever wanted something badly enough that you made the wrong decision? Why do you think we, as humans, do this time and time again? How is it linked to our relationship with God?

6. Who are your favorite and least favorite characters in the book and why? Is there something about either one that reminds you of yourself?

7. Buttonwood is a small community where everyone knows each other and each other's business. They come together to offer support, but when there's a problem (like the feud between the Specks and Grogans), it affects everyone. Would you want to live in such a close-knit town? Why or why not?

8. Think for a moment about the members of the families involved in the feud—Adam, Lucinda, Larry, and Willa from the Grogan family and Opal and Elroy from the Speck clan. What do you think about each of these people individually? As families? As neighbors? Does your perception of some of these people change when you take their relationships into consideration? Why or why not?

9. One of the key issues in this novel is respect. How does this come into play with Clara and the trail boss? With Clara and Saul? With Saul and his father? With Midge and Clara when they first meet? With the Specks and Grogans? Why do you think respect is so fundamentally important to all of us?

10. Midge narrowly escaped being forced into prostitution but has seen and lived through things no little girl should. As a result, her ability to believe in the unconditional love of God was severely shaken. By the end of book one in the Prairie Promises series, how has Midge's outlook begun to change from her first conversation with Saul in front of the church? Why do you think that is?

THE BRIDE
BACKFIRE

CHAPTER 1

Nebraska Territory, March 1857

N ot again!" Opal Speck breathed the words on a groan so low her brothers couldn't hear her—a wasted effort since the entire problem lay in having no one around but Larry Grogan.

Even Larry, despite having the temperament of a riled skunk and a smell to rival one, kept the oily gleam from his eyes when the men of her family were in sight. No, the appraising leers and occasional advances were Opal's private shame. Hers to handle whenever he tried something, and hers to hide from everyone lest the old feud between their families spring to life once more.

"Figured you'd come by here sooner or later, since Ma and Willa are making dandelion jelly." Larry levered himself on one elbow, pushing away from the broad rock he'd lounged against. He gestured toward the abundance of newly blooming dandelions bordering Speck and Grogan lands, but his gaze fixed on her as he spoke. "Let's enjoy the sweetness of spring."

"No." Opal kept her voice level though her fingers clamped around the handle of her basket so tightly she could feel the wood bite into her flesh. Letting Larry know he upset her would only give him more power, and false bravery to match. *Lord, give me strength and protection.* "Not today."

"Look ripe for the plucking to me." Larry sauntered closer, but Opal wouldn't give an inch. Everyone knew that when animals sensed fear, they pressed their advantage.

"Dandelion jelly may be sweet, but it takes a lot of work to make it that way. Do it wrong, it'll be bitter."

"I like a little tang." He reached out and tweaked a stray strand of her red hair as he leaned closer. "Keeps things interesting."

Opal fought not to wrinkle her nose as his breath washed over her. Instead, she tipped her head back and laughed, the note high and shrill to her ears as she stepped away. "Then I'll leave them to you, Mr. Grogan."

"Wait." His hand snaked out and closed around her wrist, but it was the unexpected note of pleading in his voice that brought her up short. "Won't you call me Larry?"

"I—" Opal couldn't have found any words had they been sitting in the clearing. She and Larry both stared at where his hand enfolded her wrist. "I don't think that's wise."

"We can't always be wise." With a wince, he used his other hand to trace the long, thin scar bisecting his cheek. His hand dropped back to his side when he noticed her watching the motion, but something softened in his face. "You must like me a little, Opal. Otherwise you would've left me to die like everyone would expect a Speck to do."

Not really, no. She didn't speak the words, her silence stretching thin and strained between them. Larry's sly innuendos were a threat Opal expected, but Larry Grogan looking as though he cared what she thought of him. . . How could she be prepared for that? *Why didn't I notice his advances only began after his accident— that Larry must have interpreted me helping Dr. Reed patch him up as something more than kindness?*

Surprise softened her words when she finally spoke. "I would

292

have helped anyone thrown from the thresher." Opal's reference to the incident didn't need to be more detailed. The man before her would never forget the cause of his scar, just as she'd never forget it was his animosity toward her father that caused him to mess with that machine in the first place.

"Even a Grogan?" He shook his head. "I don't believe you."

She would've backed away at the desperation written on his face if she could. "Believe it, Larry."

"What if I don't want to?" His grip turned painful, bruising her arm. "I know you'd do anything to protect your family. Even deny your own feelings." Larry moved closer. "And I can prove it with one kiss."

"My family would kill you." She tried to tug her wrist free, only to have him jerk her closer.

"We both know you wouldn't tell them." Darkness danced in his eyes. "This is between you and me."

Panic shivered down Opal's spine at the truth of his words. The one thing she could never do was put her family in danger, and if she told Pa or her brothers, blood would flow until there wasn't a Speck—or a Grogan—left standing. She stayed still as he leaned in, his grip loosening slightly as his other hand grabbed her chin.

"No!" Exploding into action the second she sensed her opportunity, Opal sent a vicious kick to his shins with one work boot. A swift twist freed her wrist from his grasp, letting her shove her basket into his stomach with all her might.

She barely registered the crack of wood splintering as she sprang away, running for home before Larry caught his breath enough to catch her.

"Pa ain't gonna like this." Nine-year-old Dave poked his head around the stall partition like a nosy weasel sniffing out trouble.

"That's why you're not mentioning it to him." Adam didn't normally hold with keeping things from one's father, but telling Diggory Grogan that another one of their milk cows had fallen prey to the strange, listless bloat that had plagued their cattle for the past few years without explanation would be akin to leaving a lit lantern in a hayloft. The resulting blaze would burn more than the contents of the barn.

"But didn't he say that the next time one of those Specks poisoned one of our cows he was goin' to march over there an—"

"We don't know that anyone's been poisoning our cows, Dave." Adam pinned his much younger brother with a fierce glower. "But we do know the Specks have had sick cattle, same as us. The last thing either of us needs is to start fighting again."

Confusion twisted Dave's features. "When did we ever stop fighting?"

"There's different kinds of fighting, squirt."

"I know!" Dave scrambled after him as Adam left the barn to go find the meanest rooster he could catch. "There's name-calling and bare-knuckles and knock-down drag-outs and slaps—"

His list came to an abrupt end when Adam rounded on him. "That's not what I meant." He squatted down so he could look his little brother in the eye. "There's fighting for what you believe in, fighting to protect what's yours, and there's fighting just because you like fighting. That's never a good enough reason, understand?"

"Kind of." Dave squinted up at him when Adam straightened once more. "How come we fight the Specks, then?"

"A mix of all three." Willa's voice provided a welcome interruption. "Our granddaddies both thought the east pasture belonged to them. Then each of our families believed the other was wrong, and now we're so used to fighting that we blame each other when anything goes wrong."

"Like the cows?" Dave processed their sister's explanation so fast it made Adam proud.

"Yep." He didn't say more as the three of them each chased down a chicken, ignoring the angry squawks and vicious pecks as best they could. When everyone's arms were loaded down with feathers and flailing spurs, they headed back to the barn.

"Then I guess it's a good thing Pa and Larry are out hunting today." Dave spat out a stray feather. "So we can scare some of the bloat out of Clem before he finds out and blames the Specks?"

"That's right." Willa set her jaw. "Because no matter what Larry says or how Pa listens, the Specks aren't poisoning our cows. And the last thing we need is for him to stir things up over nothing!"

That was the last any of them said for a while, as everyone knew it was useless to try to talk over the sounds of a cow belching. Since Dr. Saul Reed had first tried the treatment two years ago on Sadie—when the bloats began—the Grogans had perfected the process to a fine art.

If a cow grew listless, went off her feed, stopped drinking water, and generally gave signs of illness, they watched for signs of bloat. When baking soda didn't help, the last hope for expelling the buildup of gas before it stopped the animal's heart was to get it moving at a rapid pace. On the Grogan farm, that meant terrorizing the cattle with riled roosters.

Dave darted toward the stall and thrust his bird toward the back, spurring Clem to her feet for the first time that whole morning. She rushed out of the partition, heading toward a corner plush with hay, only to be headed off by Willa, whose alarmed chicken made an impressive display of thrashing wings to drive the cow out the barn door.

From there it was a matter of chasing her around the barn-yard and up the western hill—the theory being that elevating her front end made it easier for the gas to rise out—until the endeavor succeeded or the entire group dropped from exhaustion. Thankfully, they'd yet to fail.

To an outsider, Adam Grogan would be hard-pressed to explain why leading a slobbering, stumbling, belching cow back to the barn would put a smile on his face, but Willa and Dave shared his feeling of triumph. Sure, Clem might not look like much of a prize at the moment, but she'd been hard-won. Better yet, they'd averted having Pa and Larry ride over to the Speck place with fired tempers and loaded shotguns.

Much the way Murphy and Elroy Speck were riding toward them right now. Adam tensed, taking stock of the situation. With Pa and Larry out for the day, it was up to him to take care of things.

"Stay here." He snatched the shotgun from the wall of the barn and rolled the door closed, pushing Dave back inside when he tried to squirm out. "I said stay. And don't go up in the hayloft either, or I'll tan your hide later." With the door shut, Adam slid the deadbolt in place, effectively locking his sister and younger brother in the barn. . .and hopefully out of trouble.

He strode to meet the Specks, intent on putting as much distance from their stopping place and his family as humanly possible. While Adam didn't hold with the idea of a feud and did everything in his power to maintain peace, he wouldn't stake the safety of a single Grogan on any Speck's intention to do the same.

"Ho." Murphy Speck easily brought his horse to a halt, followed closely by his second-eldest son. The two of them sat there, shotguns laid across their saddles, silent as they looked down on Adam.

Adam, for his part, rested his firearm over his shoulder, vigilant without being hostile, refusing to offer false welcome. Specks had ventured onto Grogan land; it was for them to state their business. Adam wouldn't put himself in the weaker position by asking, and only a fool would provoke them by demanding answers.

Good thing Larry's not here. The stray thought would have earned a smile under any other circumstance.

"Where's your brother?" Murphy's gaze slid toward the corners of his eyes, as though expecting someone to sneak up on him.

Not a good beginning. He sure as shooting wasn't about to tell two armed Specks he was the only grown Grogan around the place. Adam just raised a brow in wordless recrimination at the older man's rudeness.

"What Pa means to say," Elroy's tone held a tinge of apology, though his stance in the saddle lost none of its steel, "is that Pete's seen your brother on our land a few times this past week."

"Oh?" *I knew he'd been up to no good when he hadn't been helping fertilize the fields. Something else stank.* Adam's jaw clenched.

"Some of our cattle have the bloat." Murphy's statement held accusation, though his words didn't. The man walked a fine line.

"Ours, too." Adam lifted his chin. "Must be a common cause."

"Common cause or no, seemed maybe a reminder was in order." Elroy's level gaze held a deeper meaning.

His father wasn't half so diplomatic. "The next time a Grogan steps foot on Speck land without express invitation, he won't be walking away from it."

Adam ignored the sharp drop in his stomach at the irrefutable proof tensions were wound tight enough to snap. "Good fences make good neighbors." He gave Speck a curt nod.

"Fences and family, Grogan." Murphy's parting words came through loud and clear. "Watch yours a bit closer."

CHAPTER 2

"What did you see, Pete?" Opal fought to keep her voice steady when she tracked down her younger brother.

"When?" At fifteen, Pete had shot up to top her by a solid two inches, his limbs long and coltish as he turned to face her.

"Whenever it was you saw Grogan on our land." Opal chose her words carefully. As of now, all she knew was Pete had seen Larry skulking around this week and diligently reported it to Pa, who'd gone over to Grogan land this afternoon to address the issue. Her heart skittered at the thought of Pa and Elroy riding onto Grogan lands for any kind of confrontation, but since she'd only found out after they returned home safe and sound, there were more urgent things to focus on.

Like whether Pete had seen Larry following her or had heard their exchange by the clearing that morning. If so, why he hadn't told Pa about it? *And how can I keep it that way?*

But these were questions Opal couldn't fire at her brother outright—not if all Pete had seen were glimpses of Larry hanging around. As long as none of the Speck men knew the real reason for Larry Grogan's visits, she could keep their blood safely in their bodies. So she didn't say another word, just waited for Pete to spill what he'd seen and what he'd said about it.

"Two days past I saw someone in the brush bordering the southeast field but couldn't make him out. He beat it too fast for me to get a good look, but this morning I saw him again." Pete's young face hardened, making him look older. "Caught a glimpse of his face, and it was Larry Grogan. Like I told Pa, I could tell he was spoiling for a fight and he'd made it past the meadow."

He followed me. Opal sucked in a sharp breath, drawing an approving nod from her younger brother.

"He turned back when he saw my gun, but that's too close to the house." Pete jerked his chin toward their soddy. "We don't want the likes of Larry Grogan getting anywhere near you, Opal."

A humorless rasp of laughter scraped her throat. *He doesn't know. They can stay safe as long as I don't tell them.* She closed her eyes for a precious second as the knowledge flowed over her. *Thank You, Father, for protecting them. Thank You, too, for having Pete see just enough of Larry to make Pa warn him away. . . .*

"You did well to put a stop to it." She stretched out to net Pete in a swift hug before he squirmed free. "I'm so relieved Diggory and Larry didn't try to start something when Pa and Elroy went over to discuss it." Another not-so-minor miracle to add to her praise list that night.

"You and me, both." The martial light in her brother's eyes took her aback for a moment. "I didn't like it when Pa told me to stay home in case things went sour. If it wasn't for him saying he needed to know one of us was here to protect you, I would've followed 'em."

I can take care of myself! The fierce need to make the men in her life understand she didn't need their protection—particularly not when it endangered them—welled up with such force she choked on the resentment before she could say so. Another blessing.

"Thank you." Opal said the words so Pete could hear, but in her heart they went to God. The important thing was Pete stayed home when he could have been in danger. She'd swallow every ounce of pride she possessed in exchange for his safety. *But what a pass we've come to, when we're all so busy protecting each other we don't talk about it first.*

The familiar wash of regret pulled at her, almost making her miss Pete saying the Grogan men hadn't been on the farm.

"What do you mean Diggory and Larry weren't there?"

"We figure they must've been out hunting or something." Pete shrugged. "Course, now the problem is once they hear that Pa and Elroy went over and gave that warning, they might get furious enough to make everything worse."

Cold swept from Opal's ears to her fingertips, making even her lips numb as she registered the danger. "Tell me they didn't speak to Lucinda!" Surely Pa knew better than to deliver bad news to Mrs. Grogan in the absence of her husband—any harsh words had to be spoken among men. "You know the Grogan men would take that as a threat to their women!"

"I dunno. She's Larry's ma and should keep him in line." Pete's sudden, mischievous grin dissolved when he saw the look on her face. "Naw, don't fret, Opal. Everyone knows this is a matter among men. They talked with Adam."

"Adam," she whispered his name. Her blood started moving again, warming her cheeks, making her lips tingle. It was a mark of how distressed she'd been that she could ever have forgotten about Adam Grogan.

Memories of murky darkness, crackling heat muffled by thick smoke, the acrid tinge of burnt wood creeping into her nose rose before her as if it were yesterday. Half-asleep from the morphine Dr. Reed had given her for her toothache, limbs heavy and eyes refusing to open, she'd never even registered Clara's attempts to pull her from the burning house two years ago. Even now, the recollections of smothering soot were hazy at best.

Until Adam. Even drugged by the doctor and half-choked by the thick blanket of smoke, Opal's awareness of Adam Grogan's deep voice calling her name had been clear as spring water on a sunny day. Not even the wearing of time had dimmed her memory of his cradling her against a solid chest as he swept her into strong arms she knew would carry her to safety.

"They talked with Adam," she repeated, relief leaving her knees weakened. "He'll talk with Larry, then. Adam will make it right."

"Yeah, Adam's always been the one with a level head." Pete rubbed the back of his neck. "If he weren't a Grogan, I'd even say I liked him."

"Me, too."

Pete raised a brow at her quick agreement.

"I mean, if he weren't a Grogan."

~~~ ⌘ ~~~

"Grogans don't stand for this kind of disrespect!" Larry's roar the next morning could've deafened an elephant. In Africa.

"We sure don't." Anger lined Pa's jaw, making Adam's gut churn.

But now wasn't the time to protest. Not until he heard Pa's line of thinking so he could reason him right back out of it.

"Specks coming onto our land. . ." Larry's words came fast and furious as he paced the small room he shared with Adam. "They got no right. If they think they can just push their way over where they don't belong and ain't wanted, they need to be taught a lesson."

"Agreed." Pa's outstretched arm brought Larry to a halt. "Any man who trespasses is asking for trouble."

"So what are we waitin' for?" Shifting his weight from one foot to the other, Larry glanced at Adam from the corner of his eye. "They've brought this on themselves. Let's take care of those Specks once and for all!"

"Thing of it is," Adam spoke slowly, careful to keep his voice thoughtful and free of force so as not to encroach on his father's position, "that the Specks have never come here before. Even today, they never raised their guns—just made it clear that it's best all around that we respect the boundaries."

"And that's what's troubling me." Pa swiped his hat across his brow. "I've known Murphy Speck my whole life. I don't like him, don't agree with the man, and wouldn't trust him as far as I could toss our heaviest draft horse. But he's never crossed our lines without cause. No matter how I try to avoid it, him bothering to come today means something stuck in his craw."

"And that something is me?" Disbelief, heavy and false, rang in his younger brother's voice, confirming Adam's suspicion that Larry had, indeed, breached boundaries on Speck land and brought this upon them.

"That's what they say." Adam struggled to keep his voice non-accusatory. Setting up Larry's back any more than it already was would only worsen things. And it looked like his younger brother was bent on doing his crooked best to stir up more trouble than any of them could handle.

"Were you over there, son?" Pa's eyes narrowed. "Much as I can't abide the thought of Specks on Grogan land, they're more than within their rights if they caught you."

If they caught him, not just if he was over there. Adam shut his eyes at his father's logic. To Pa, the problem didn't lie in breaking trust; it lay squarely in being found out. With that kind of creaking foundation, it wouldn't be long before the tenuous peace they'd built with the Specks came crumbling around their ears.

"Has anyone thought about what those no-good Specks are trying to do here?" Larry's demand conveniently neglected to provide an answer to the question at hand. "We all know Murphy's eldest is coming back here—failed at the mines, didn't he? So now he'll be wanting some good farmland close to home, and what's better than ours? They're laying the groundwork to get rid of us, and we shouldn't let them get one step closer!"

"Ben's coming back?" A flash of fear struck against the flint of his father's eyes. "With Ben home, they outnumber us."

"Hardly." Shaking his head, Adam tried to calm the storm. "Pete doesn't make much of a man yet. If anything, Ben just evens things up again."

"The odds are still better for us now." Larry kept on pressing. "And even a stupid Speck can count high enough to see it. That's why they didn't man up and do anything today."

"Makes sense."

"No, it doesn't." His disagreement came out too blunt, so Adam took another track. "It would make sense if you, Larry, and I had all been here. Instead, with just one, they would have been fools not to pick me off while they had no other opposition. If Diggory Speck wanted to end this feud once and for all, that would have been the strategy to use."

"No one ever said the Specks were smart." Larry's sneer didn't have Adam doubting anyone's intelligence but that of his brother.

"They're smart enough for that, or Pa wouldn't waste the effort worrying over what they might plan." When Pa's eyebrows went up, Adam knew he'd scored a point. "Grogans don't concern themselves with unworthy adversaries—especially not for generations."

"Adam's right." Pa plunked his hat back on his head. "You should know that, Larry. The Specks are just canny enough to be a threat."

"If you say so, Pa."

"I say so, all right. And, son?"

"Yeah?"

"*I'm* canny enough to know that you not answering about being on Speck lands means they were right." Pa's observation had Adam biting back a grin. "Which makes you the stupidest in the whole lot of us. Stay away from the Specks, son, or Murphy will have every right to make good on his threat. Trespassin's a shooting offense."

Adam started to breathe a prayer of gratitude that Pa wouldn't be deciding to saddle up with guns blazing anytime soon when Larry's mutter floated past him.

"Next time, I'll make sure they don't see me."

CHAPTER 3

"I see you!" Opal swooped to the floor, nudging her face close to the baby's. "You're such a pretty girl, Matilda." She crooned to keep the ten-month-old from crawling away with the surprisingly quick speed she'd developed.

"Got her, did you?" Clara laughed when Opal, Matilda snug in her arms, settled onto the parlor sofa.

"For now." Opal ducked her head, pressing her cheek against the downy softness of the baby's hair. The gesture hid a sudden tug of sadness at the thought she wasn't anywhere close to having a child of her own. She breathed deep of Matilda's sweet, powdery scent. "You'll make me give her back, won't you?"

"Eventually, though I find most folks more than willing to return the loan without any urging when she needs changing." Leaning closer, Clara lowered her voice. "What I long for is conversation."

"You can converse with just about anyone." Snuggling the baby a bit tighter, Opal kept the accompanying thought to herself. *Someone to cuddle, now that's a different matter!*

"I know, but Saul is kept busy with his doctoring calls, and

Josiah doesn't need me at the store these days. In any case, it seems all my time gets taken up keeping things in order around here." Clara cast a satisfied look around her newly rebuilt house. After the fire two years ago, the Reeds had recreated it as both a home and doctor's office for her husband. "That's part of why I'm always so glad to see you visit! I know Midge will be disappointed she missed it."

The mention of Midge, an irrepressible fifteen-year-old Saul had adopted just before coming to Buttonwood a few years ago, where he met his match in Clara, doused Opal's gloom. She'd held a particular fondness for Midge ever since the younger girl brought down her most prized possession—the old honeycomb-patterned quilt the women of the town had worked to restore in preparation for Midge's arrival—to comfort Opal during the treatment for her toothache.

When Clara realized the house had caught fire and that Opal, largely unconscious, couldn't leave under her own steam, she laid out Midge's quilt as a makeshift travois and dragged Opal toward the door. She owed her life to Midge's generosity and Clara's determination every bit as much as Adam Grogan's remarkable bravery.

"Where is Midge today?"

"At the Warren place, making candles." As she spoke, Clara wrinkled her nose and waggled her brows, eliciting a giggle from her little daughter. So the sudden seriousness of her next expression warned Opal the next thing her friend said would be important. "She and Alyssa are turning into quite the young women, and the boys in town are starting to notice."

"Pete stands straighter when they walk by." Opal didn't bother to repress a little snort. "And he's not yet sixteen!"

"But Midge is—and looks every bit as old as Alyssa, who boasts sixteen. It's something for us to keep an eye on." A burp cloth appeared as if out of thin air to be dabbed against Maddie's chin. "Thought I'd mention it while you were here, but what I really want to talk about. . ."

Opal tensed as her friend leaned back in a pose of relaxation, her pale eyes snapping with mischief. Clara looked far too pleased with herself for anyone else in the vicinity to be comfortable.

"Who's been chasing after you, Opal Speck? Shame on you for not telling me what was going on!"

"How did you know?" Somehow, she worked the words around the lump in her throat. Pete hadn't known Larry was chasing after her that day, and she wouldn't breathe a word to any soul, so there could only be one explanation. *How can I control the damage if Larry's spreading rumors?*

"Buttonwood doesn't rank as anything but a small town, Opal. Folks watch carefully and talk about what they see. You didn't expect to keep his interest a secret?"

"I hoped to." A snuffly wail penetrated her preoccupation, alerting Opal that she'd clutched baby Maddie too tightly.

"Nap time." Clara swept her daughter into her arms and bustled up the stairs, dispelling Opal's hopes that time would stop long enough for her to figure out a solution to the problem before her.

She returned to the parlor as swiftly as she'd left. "Opal?" Clara's brow furrowed as she sat down. "You don't look at all well. Saul should be back any time now. We'll have him take a look at you."

"No, thank you." *The doctor can't fix what's wrong. No one can.* Tears burned behind Opal's eyes, the first of many she'd feel before this all ended. She had no way out. Unless Larry was saying his intentions were honorable—then she'd have a choice: Refuse, and spark the feud to slaughter her family, or marry Larry Grogan, tying herself to him for life.

It wasn't much of a choice, but she'd marry the lout before she let him destroy her family. If that was Larry's plan, she needed to find out. *Now.* "Why did he tell you, Clara?"

"He didn't say anything!" Her friend seemed taken aback, though whether it was the question or the desperation with which she asked it, Opal couldn't tell. "Like I said, there's plenty to see if you watch."

"So he hasn't said anything? It's just what you think you've seen?" Hope, tantalizing and intoxicating, made her head light. "Do you think anyone else noticed anything?"

"Observant as I am, it's possible I'm the only one to have marked his attention." Clara's brow furrowed. "I take it you don't want to encourage him, then?"

"Of course not! I want nothing to do with the man!" Opal twisted her hands in her lap. "And so long as you're the only one who suspects, we can stop it before it becomes a real problem."

"I never thought you'd feel this way." Her friend shook her head as though puzzling over something she'd never understand. "What did Brett Burn ever do to make you dislike him so?"

"Brett Burn!" Now Opal stared in confusion. "Who's talking about the blacksmith?"

"Me." Straightening her skirts, Clara leaned closer. "At least, I thought I was. Opal Speck, are you trying to tell me there are two men looking your way and you never breathed a word of it? Who's the objectionable one, then, if you're not talking about Brett?"

"Erm. . ." The way her head spun, Opal was starting to wonder whether maybe she shouldn't have Dr. Reed take a look at her after all. "That's not important, since the entire point is to ignore him." Outrage and obstinacy melded in her friend's face, calling for immediate diversion. "Now, what is it you were saying about Brett?" She injected a measure of wistfulness into her tone. "I hadn't noticed any partiality."

"Don't think I'm finished asking about the mystery man, but

you know I've always preferred to deal with possibilities instead of closed doors." Clara tucked her feet up under her and proceeded to recall all the times she'd—supposedly—seen the youngest of the Burn blacksmiths mooning over Opal.

"I don't have eyes in the back of my skull, so I'll have to take your word for it if he's sneaking glances during church." In spite of herself, Opal began to entertain the notion. "He never talks to me or walks me home or brings me tokens or anything to indicate he'd be interested in courting me, though."

"He asks about your beekeeping, Opal! And you ask about his work, too." Clara's list grew. "Maybe he's just waiting for a sign you'd be happy to accept his attentions."

"I ask about his work because he mends our tools and knows the latest advancements to help on the farm," Opal defended. "That's not talking; that's business."

"When your father and brothers talk with him, it's business." The correction came soft but firm. "And when he talks with you about your hives, that's not even a valid excuse. Those bee boxes of yours are made of wood!"

"There's such a thing as just being friendly."

"Even to a good-looking, hardworking bachelor the same age as you?" With romance on the brain, Clara drove her point home. "Don't you think you might make a good couple?"

"Never thought about it." Opal chewed on the inside of her lip and looked at her now-empty arms. *But I'm going to.*

~~❧~~

"I can't think what happened to all my baking soda." Ma's fretting made Adam bolt his dinner.

"Done." He pushed back his plate. "I'll drop by the general store and pick some up for you, Ma."

"Thank you, son." Lucinda Grogan sent her eldest a fond smile.

"But I can walk over there as well as anyone, and I know you've plenty to do in the fields."

But I used your baking soda on a sick cow and forgot to replace it. "I need to head into town anyway. Dusty's picked up a rock and bent one of his shoes something awful. One of the Burns will need to have a look at it."

"We'll go together." Ma beamed. "Willa can pick out whichever flour bags she likes best for her next dress."

Adam smothered a groan as his sister perked up. Who knew how long it would take the women if the trip involved more than staples? He'd planned on keeping a sharp eye on Larry for a good while yet, but that wouldn't be happening this afternoon.

It was worse than he thought. By the time Adam dropped the women off at Josiah Reed's General Store and headed toward Burn's Blacksmithing, he could've finished the entire trip alone twice over. With time to spare.

"Afternoon, Adam." Matthew Burn came up to greet him, his father and younger brother working at the forge.

"Good to see you, Matthew." Adam tilted his head back toward the massive draft horse he was leading. "Dusty here ran into a rock this morning and bent his shoe. I was hoping one of you Burn men could take a look."

"Sure thing." Taking the lead from Adam's hand, Matthew led Dusty into the stable enclosure attached to the smithy. He patted the horse's shoulders, murmuring softly to soothe him. Even the most placid horse disliked the noise, heat, and smell of a smithy, so putting the large creatures at ease came as part and parcel of the job before a smart smith would go anywhere near a set of massive hooves.

Some folks held the opinion that three blacksmiths in one small—though growing—town ranked as excess if not downright foolishness. At least, that was the argument every Burn—and whatever townsman happened to be within hearing range—had ignored from almost every wagon train to pass through Buttonwood. No one blamed the pioneers for trying to secure a skilled blacksmith for their new homes, but Adam often had reason to be glad the Burns stayed in Buttonwood. There probably wasn't another town within a thousand miles where he could've gone to get Dusty taken care of that same afternoon—even if he lived there.

With Matthew fully engrossed inspecting Dusty's hooves—which he and Adam both agreed were due for a fresh shoeing anyway—not much chitchat went back and forth. That they held no penchant for gossip or babbling ranked as another reason Adam liked the Burn men. In a town as small as Buttonwood, most people made it their business to know everyone else's.

Ma sure does. Adam stifled the thought but didn't dispute the truth of it. If he walked over to the general store this minute, he'd find Ma talking up a storm at anyone who walked inside. Between Ma's surplus of talk over at the Reed store and Matthew's lack of it at the Burn smithy, Adam had plenty of time on his hands.

Too much time, for a man accustomed to seeing daylight hours as a commodity every bit as valuable as a good horse or plow. Spring days, when the earth smelled rich with sprouting green shoots and the sun shone brightly without the punishing heat of summer, called to the farmer in him. Back home, fields waited to be cleared, ploughed, harrowed, and sown.

Unable to stay still, Adam wandered closer to the smithy to exchange greetings with Kevin, Matthew's father. The older blacksmith didn't hear him as he continued shaping red-hot iron. Metal on metal produced a rhythmic *clang*, the craftsman carefully bending what should have been impossible to his will.

If only forging a lasting peace with the Specks were so easy. The thought of Larry's escapade sparked a heat that had nothing to do with the smithy and everything to do with anger. *Pity you can't actually pound good sense into someone.* But Larry was too blind to see the danger he should keep away from.

A prickling at the back of his neck made Adam turn toward the entrance, where a woman stood backlit by the sun, her face hidden in shadow. It didn't matter. Wisps of soft hair teased away from her bonnet to catch the sun behind her and glints from the forge before her, giving her a burnished crown. Opal's fiery locks proclaimed her identity as surely as though she wore a sign saying "Speck."

Adam's mouth went dry as she stepped into the shop, lissome and lively. With her pale yellow dress and red hair, she could have been a sunbeam sprung to life. As it had for years now, reminding himself of the danger she presented took more of an effort than Adam would like to admit.

Fire proved a worthy association for Opal, and not just because of her hair. How many times had Adam witnessed her fiercely protecting her family by trying to avoid violence? The warmth of her spirit reflected in the smile she gave readily to everyone else. Still he'd kept a distance, knowing he shouldn't notice her.

Until the day a real fire threatened to extinguish her life.

When Saul Reed raced for his house, yelling that Clara and Opal were inside the burning building, Adam didn't think twice. He didn't regret saving the girl he'd never managed to think of as his enemy, but the action still carried a heavy toll.

The feel of cradling her close as he swept Opal away from the house was seared into his memory like a brand. It served to reaffirm what he'd always suspected—Specks were trouble, but Opal was downright dangerous.

CHAPTER 4

Midge Collins drew in a deep breath for a friendly holler when she saw Opal walking down the street, only to swallow it when her friend ducked into the smithy, of all places.

Ah well. Polite young ladies don't raise their voices anyway. A rueful grin crossed her lips at the idea that Aunt Doreen's and Clara's tutelage might be rubbing off on her. Midge bore no intention of acting a stick-in-the-mud at the age of fifteen, no matter how she wanted to please the makeshift family she'd come to love.

Polite young ladies don't snoop, either, she reminded herself as she slowed her pace, sidling up on the smithy. But in Midge's experience, informed women kept their eyes and ears open. She wasted no breath on gossiping, but *knowing. . .*now that was a different story.

Saul said knowledge made the difference between helping and hindering, and Midge didn't respect anyone's opinion more than that of the doctor who'd saved her life just over two years before. As a matter of fact, she reckoned that God, if He existed like everyone in Buttonwood insisted He did, would understand

Midge's constant status as lookout. After all, God could see and hear *everything*.

Not being so fortunate as that, Midge resorted to lingering in doorways when the need presented itself. Like when a friend who never stepped foot in the smithy marched in, wearing her favorite dress, the day after she met with Clara. Oh, it didn't take much to weasel things out of Clara, who'd confessed to watching Brett Burn's growing interest in Opal.

As though Midge hadn't noticed that *ages* ago. The one who bore watching, to her way of thinking, was that shifty Larry Grogan.

Casually peering around the doorframe into the smithy, Midge spotted her friend's yellow dress, brightened by the forge's firelight, and squinted to get a better look. Sure as a sharpshooter never missed and told, Opal stood in deep conversation with Brett Burn.

Oh, she brandished a battered metal something-or-other, but if Clara's chat with Opal yesterday hadn't prompted this visit, Lucinda Grogan took tea with the Queen of England every Thursday. This trip to the smithy didn't fall under the category of business, no matter if it involved some careful calculation.

Midge eased back, unwilling to be caught spying when there would be at least two other Burns around the place. Yet she lingered when she should've left—a sense she'd missed something making her glance back into the smithy.

This time, she ran her gaze over every nook and cranny until it caught on a subtle movement in the stable annex. *There. That's what I missed before.* Her smile came back full force as she took in the entire scene a second time, with the missing piece in place. Midge recognized the figure as Adam Grogan, and she followed his sightline to find out what he was gaping at.

Her eyes widened. *Oh, now* that's *interesting!*

"Ben!" Opal rushed down the church steps that Sunday, Pete and Elroy hard on her heels to greet their eldest brother. She pulled to a halt with the help of a big hug. "You're early!"

"Good to see you, sis." He tucked her to his side and pulled their brothers close. "You, too, Elroy." Ben made a show of tilting his head, over-long carroty curls spilling from under his hat as he peered at the youngest Speck. "This can't be little Pete?"

"Not so little anymore." Pete puffed up in protest, gaze sliding toward where Midge stood several yards away.

"I can see that."

"Four years makes a difference, son." Pa came up to them all with a smile broader than the sky above. "Glad to have you back home."

"Especially now." The lowered tone didn't stop Pete's whisper from carrying as more than one Speck cast a quick glance toward the Grogans.

Or rather, where Larry and Willa stood. Opal didn't spot Lucinda or Adam nearby. Still, their fleeting looks constituted enough of a cue for Ben to follow suit.

He peered over, a frown darkening his face for the first time since Opal spied him. "That Larry Grogan stirring the pot again? We'll sort him out as needed, though I thought after his threshing accident he'd learned to settle down."

"So you *did* get my letters." Opal couldn't hold back the grumble. After all, it wouldn't have done him any serious harm to write back more often.

"Sporadically." Ben's apologetic smile turned appreciative as he continued to look toward Larry. "Who's the girl? Don't tell me old Larry's nabbed himself a pretty little wife while I was gone!"

Opal just about swallowed her tongue at the realization Ben's appreciation focused on none other than Willa Grogan. Willa had, now that she thought about it, blossomed during his absence. But in the after-church swell of greetings, folks had moved around just enough to confuse the rest of her family.

"Who? The blond?" Elroy shook his head. "Nah, that's Clara Reed—Dr. Reed's wife."

"Never bore any partiality toward blonds," Ben denied. "The brunette—looks sort of quiet but with a spark waiting to come out."

"That's Midge." Pete thrust his jaw forward. "Now, you may be my elder, but I've got an eye on that one. You can't just come waltzing in here and decide you're interested in her spark when I've been fired up about her for—"

"That's enough, Pete!" Opal stepped in before her brother worked himself into a lather over nothing. "Since when would you describe Midge as quiet anyway?"

"Well. . ." Loyalty warred with truth and Pete settled for a shrug. "He don't know her."

"Yet." Ben dropped the word like a gauntlet, biting back an obvious grin as Pete tensed up again. "So why's she standing next to Larry?"

"Because you're not looking at Midge." Opal shot a pointed glance at Pete before laying a warning hand on Ben's arm. "The pretty brunette with the quiet air and the attachment to Larry? That's Willa Grogan."

"Willa!" Astonishment rang in four male Speck voices, setting off a chain reaction.

"She grew up nice," Ben mused amid Pa's spluttered warnings.

Elroy and Pete craned their necks and gaped as though seeing Willa for the first time in, well, about four years.

The whole tableau would have earned a roll of the eyes and a sigh from Opal at any other time, but as things stood, she swiftly separated herself from the Speck men. After the thunder of her family's joint exclamation, how could the Grogans not stir up a storm?

Sure enough, Larry's and Diggory's darkening expressions signaled trouble.

Lucinda, never one to smooth ruffled feathers, bustled over to throw protective arms around her only daughter and glower at Ben.

Opal fixed her gaze on Adam—whose face mirrored the resignation in her own heart. "Sorry," she addressed her apology to him. "Ben didn't recognize your sister is all."

Diggory shouldered forward. "He shouldn't have been looking."

"Hold on." Ben held up his hands, palms out in the universal signal of avoiding trouble. "I meant no disrespect. It's been years and my family needed to bring me up to speed on the new faces."

"I'm not new." Puzzled curiosity arched Willa's brows, making her eyes seem brighter than usual.

"No, Miss Grogan"—Ben swept off his hat and gave a little bow—"though I didn't recognize you alongside Mrs. Reed and some others. The years bring changes."

"So I see." Surely that wasn't *interest* tingeing Willa's agreement? A faint pink flushed her cheeks as she glanced at Ben in a way Opal would've pegged as admiration.

An admiration sure to invite adversity.

Opal bit her lip. Why, oh why couldn't Ben have noticed Amanda Dunstall? Or even Midge. As much as it would mean chaos with Pete, she'd rather deal with that than goading the Grogans!

Larry stepped in front of his sister. "Not enough changes for you to forget your place, Speck."

"My place is in Buttonwood, same as yours." Level and logical, Ben's words did nothing to soothe the situation.

"Maybe you should pick another place. I liked it better when you jaunted off for years."

"You would!" Pete's jaw pushed forward as he addressed Larry. "Ben's the better man, and you wouldn't want any comparisons."

"Don't insult Willa's brother." A swift dip of his hat accompanied Ben's words. "No need for insults. Every man stands on his own merit."

"True." His sister's agreement with his enemy pushed Larry's patience over the edge.

"You don't get to stand anywhere near her, Speck!"

"Strong words for a man who breaches boundaries, Grogan." Pa's eyes narrowed, making fear flash down Opal's spine. "Be careful who you insult."

"Some boundaries carry more weight than others." Adam's frown swept away the last of Opal's hope that further ugliness would be avoided. No matter he was right, and if his brother abided by that, they would all be fine.

"Ben's offered no offense," she reminded everyone. "Nor does he intend to."

"Keep it that way," Lucinda snapped, finding her voice when her husband showed up. "We don't want *any* offers from a Speck."

"But we'll make you one," Diggory added, quick to catch on to the problem. "Stay away from our women, and we won't try to claim anything of yours."

"Understood." Pa's jaw clenched so tight Opal couldn't see how the words got out. "And here's the last offer you'll get from the Specks, so listen and listen good. Keep your Grogan carcasses off our land, and we'll keep our bullets out of your hides. Otherwise, you'll be digging graves."

CHAPTER 5

"She's dead." Larry gave voice to the obvious as Adam looked over Sadie's remains.

"Not surprising." He chose his response carefully. "She'd stayed with us longer than we could've hoped, and only stopped producing milk this spring. Not bad for an old gal." Adam patted the cow's side and stood up.

"Wasn't age that took her." Excitement colored his brother's voice now. "Look close—eyes clouded, froth at the mouth, and we both know she hadn't been eating or drinking again."

"Old cattle can get finicky." Noncommittal on the outside, Adam knew all too well what the signs most likely meant—especially given the sporadic losses they'd suffered the past two years.

"Someone poisoned her, and we both know who's to blame!" To a casual listener, Larry's accusation would ring with righteous outrage.

But Adam heard the current of satisfaction and even glee lurking beneath. He knew his brother's itch for trouble had grown to an all-out rash lately, and any pretext to attack the Specks wouldn't be overlooked.

"Assumptions won't get us anywhere." Holding up a hand when his brother tried to interrupt, Adam continued, "Sadie'd been on her last legs long before this, and there's nothing to be served by pointing fingers at our neighbors for what could be a natural death."

"It's not. You know it's not."

"You don't know anything."

Larry flushed, his scar a pale slash against the livid red of his rage. "I know this cow didn't die from old age, and I know you're trying to keep it quiet because you don't want *trouble*."

"Why do you want it so much you create it at every opportunity?" Adam thumbed his hat back. "Couldn't you focus on what's best for the family?"

"What makes you think I'm not? You stare down your nose because you won't grab a gun, but it's just fine to let enemies sneak onto our land, poison our cattle, and get away with it." The words came fast and furious. "Oh no. Big brother *Adam* will be content to wait until Benjamin Speck makes off with Willa or their old man finally settles the score with Pa for good before you get off your high horse and do something!"

"Or we can grab our guns and start a war over an old cow the Specks might not have touched, and be sure that those of us who survive will live with blood on our hands for the rest of our days." Adam jerked the rope off his saddle and flung the heavy coil at Larry's chest. "It's a short step off a steep cliff to go from a sick cow to accusing the Specks of plotting to kill us."

"True." Pa's entrance to the heated conversation took them both off guard, as Adam knew it was intended to. "Swipe the surprise off your faces, boys. An entire contingent could have snuck up while the pair of you went to war armed with nothing but hot air." He unrolled his butchering pack as he spoke. "Least you could've done was string up the carcass to make some use of the time."

"Yes, sir." Larry knotted a noose around the cow's hind legs before flinging the free end of the coil over the sturdiest branch of the closest cottonwood. They joined together in hauling it upright and securing it.

No one spoke, but Adam sent up enough prayers to pepper heaven itself. *Please let Pa see reason, Lord. Don't let him seek revenge or make this feud fatal. . . .*

"So you heard Adam, but I was saying—"

"Heard your bit, too." Pa sucked his teeth as was his habit when thinking. "The thing of it is you're both wrong with a little right mixed in."

Adam held his peace—and his breath—until his father explained. It was too early to be relieved, and far too late not to be nervous about the situation.

"Which is the part I'm right about?" Larry cut straight to the crucial question, as he could be counted upon to do anytime it concerned him directly. "That the Specks poisoned our cattle? That obviously it's the first move and the next will be worse? That we can't let them get away with it unpunished?"

About then he ran out of air, and in the pause for his next breath, Pa went ahead and answered.

"Sadie didn't die naturally and the Specks most likely caused it." His first words brought a self-satisfied smirk to Larry's face before Pa kept on. "Assuming it's part of a grand plan to destroy our whole family would be getting ahead of ourselves, and going after any Speck without solid evidence is a plumb fool move."

Thank You, Lord. Adam felt a knot of tension ease from between his shoulder blades.

"Where's the part when Adam's wrong?" Petulance didn't suit a grown man, and Larry wore it worse than most.

"We can't let this go unanswered." Pa's answer returned the knot to Adam's back, bigger and meaner than ever. "After we butcher Sadie, tonight I'll leave her bones near the Speck place with a note."

"Next time it'll be one of theirs in return?" Glee didn't suit his brother any better as Larry volunteered to take care of things.

"That's right." Selecting a knife, Pa gave a sharp nod. A quick, clean cut to the cow's neck had the blood draining into the large bowl. "Grogans are too smart to start bloodshed." He wiped the blade on some long prairie grass as the stream slowed to a trickle. "But sure as shooting we know to finish it."

～⊙⊙～

"Outnumbered again." Opal bit back a sigh and rolled up her sleeves as the men went out to work the fields, leaving her to face down the mountain of breakfast dishes. She started piling plates.

Sure, her brothers would tease her mercilessly if they heard her talking to the tableware, but they weren't around. Nobody was. *Which is the problem.* Opal scrubbed at the fragments of scrambled eggs with unwarranted vigor. *If I had someone to talk to, I wouldn't bother making the odd comment to the dishes!*

Nor the chickens while she scattered seed, or the cows when she milked every morning, or her bees when she went to the apiary. . . *All right. I'd probably still talk to my bees. But that's to be expected of any beekeeper. In fact,* Opal dried her biggest pan with a flourish, *I defy anyone to hear the welcoming hum of the hives and not want to be friendly in return!*

But maybe she'd make a point of not conversing with the cookery anymore, just to be on the safe side. Things hadn't been so hard before Pete grew old enough and big enough to help work the fields. Autumn brought the harvest, and winter snows imprisoned everyone equally, but it was spring and summer Opal came to dread. The warm months brought sunshine but stole all company and laughter. The only time she saw her family, the men

322

bolted their food or headed for bed.

Opal returned the last dish into its place and pulled the second loaf of bread from the niche near the fireplace. The next slid in immediately afterward. Cooking for Pa, Elroy, and Pete took some doing, but with Ben home, there'd be no time to lose.

She started the stew meat, knowing dinnertime would come as swiftly as the blend of meat and vegetables simmered into a thick broth, and chopped potatoes, onions, and carrots to add in later. Opal readied the potatoes with a generous hand, as the supply held steady even after a hard winter. The carrots, by contrast, she sliced as thin as possible. Until her garden added to the larder, produce was precious.

The smell of warm yeast layered over the tinge of smoke, always managing to elude the chimney to linger in the dark confines of the soddy. No matter that Opal threw the door wide open and pushed back the curtains to their only window, light seemed swallowed by their dark earthen walls. Someday, perhaps, they'd whitewash them. . . .

For now, Opal removed the golden-brown loaf from her baking niche and popped in the final batch of bread with a smile. When this last round finished, she'd be out in the sunshine, free to visit her apiary.

Her broom made short work of sweeping the floor, still a necessary chore no matter the floor itself was hard-packed dirt. Loose dust got on—and in—absolutely everything, a constant battle from above and below when living in a soddy. Opal cast a glance at the ceiling, covered in pages torn from old catalogs she'd coaxed from Josiah Reed when his mercantile no longer needed them.

So long as the pages stayed tacked in place, dirt clods and insects didn't drop onto the table or beds. A few leafs looked to be working free of their moorings, spurring Opal to drag a chair beneath them, climb up, and affix them more firmly.

A woman needed an earthworm to fall in her hair only once in a lifetime, thank-you-very-much. *Actually, I could have done without that even once. . . .*

Her musings ended when the bread finished. After a quick check on the progress of the stew, Opal stepped outside. Spring sunshine spilled onto fresh green grasses bright with new life.

Summer's glare heats the earth in golden browns, making the crops grow. Fire tinges autumn's rays, painting the plants for harvest. Winter nights swallow the daylight too soon, so it shines fierce, blinding white whenever it punches through the clouds. But spring. . .

"I always did like early sunshine best, Lord." She spoke the thought aloud, not bothering to stop and wonder whether it counted as prayer when she talked with God this way. It used to worry her, whether it wasn't respectful enough, but the Bible talked about even rocks crying out to Him. The Psalms, mostly David's thoughts and praises to God, was her favorite book of God's Word. Opal's words weren't washed in poetry like that king's of long ago, but she did her best to put her feelings into words.

"Spring sunbeams are the closest thing I can imagine to the breath of life. If I had to pick a color to represent hope, I'd pick the pale green of a new blade of grass in the soft light of a spring morning."

"So would I." The deep rumble of a man's voice jerked her to a halt.

"Larry?" She held her back ramrod straight against the note of fear her voice betrayed, refusing to turn and acknowledge him. *But it didn't sound like Larry. . . .*

"Adam." The muffled sound of booted steps on moist earth struck no fear in her heart. "I didn't mean to frighten you."

"You don't." Turning to face him, Opal could've kicked herself for the words. "I mean, you didn't."

"Ah." He came to a stop a respectable distance from her, one thumb hooked at the base of his suspenders. "Of course not."

Her pulse, which had slowed after the assurance Larry hadn't made good on his threats to come to the house, picked up its pace again at the half-smile on Adam's face. She frowned. "What are you doing here?" After the scene at the churchyard, the Grogans needed to stay as far away from her family as possible.

"You're not angry." His gaze seemed to take her measure, and Opal squashed the temptation to wonder whether she'd stacked up. "There's still time, then."

"For what?" Anxiety over his purpose, despite it being Adam and not Larry, began to gnaw the edges of her nerves. "And I'm not angry so much as dumbfounded that you'd be so foolish as to breach our boundary with the way things stand."

"Sometimes a little foolish behavior is the smartest thing to do." His dark gaze met hers, drawing her into unspoken questions she couldn't answer.

"That doesn't make a lick of sense, Adam Grogan." She planted her hands on her hips. "And since you don't want to tell me what's going on, you can just scuttle back to your own farm. And stay there so none of my family feels obligated to make things any worse!"

"I'm sorry, Opal."

His apology was the first thing Adam had ever done to frighten her. Everyone knew Grogans didn't apologize.

Her eyes widened as he took a step closer and lowered his voice. "It's too late for that."

CHAPTER 6

"I t's too late for what, exactly?" Amazing how blue her eyes could look against the red of her hair—especially when she widened them like that.

It's too late for a lot of things. Adam blocked that line of thought before it could lead him anywhere worth regretting. He swiftly considered his options once again before arriving at the same conclusion.

When the wrath of the Specks hadn't descended upon them, Pa'd begun to stew about what devious schemes they must be hatching in retaliation for the cow skull and threat Larry left the night before. Larry's lack of concern, however, sparked a different suspicion in Adam—a suspicion confirmed when he'd run into Opal.

Larry didn't obey Pa last night and leave the "message" on the Speck doorstep. He'd done something worse, added an aspect yet to be discovered but sure to provoke fury the likes of which Pa never intended. And Pa'd slept in the room Adam usually shared with Larry to make sure Adam didn't follow Larry and interfere, ruining his initial plan.

So now Adam stared down a fork in the road likely to skewer him. Slink home without finding and fixing whatever Larry had done. . .or enlist Opal's help. That those blue eyes were wide with worry somehow made the choice easier. For as long as he'd been cooling Grogan tempers, Adam had known Opal did the same within the walls of the Speck farm.

"It's too late for me to go back now. There's something I have to do." He drew a deep breath and took a step of faith. "And I could use your help."

"How do we fix it?" Resignation added a grim set to her mouth, darkening the cornflower blue of her gaze and sending a surge of shame through Adam's chest.

We Grogans did that. She doesn't even know what the problem is this time. Just knows it needs to be fixed. And she's the one saddled with it because she's willing to keep a lid on her temper for the sake of her family.

Suddenly his irritation swung right back to the Specks for making Opal shoulder the heavy burden of peacekeeper. Didn't they know it was the man's job to protect, not the other way around? That half the task lay in keeping the weight of worry away from their women?

"Yesterday we found one of our milking cows dead, eyes cloudy, froth around her nose and mouth. Same as has been going on for the past couple of years."

"We aren't poisoning your cattle!" Fire leapt to life in her cheeks. "The Grogans aren't the only family affected by whatever's happening. We've lost three cows to the same thing!"

"Be that as it may—"

"There's no 'may be' about it, Adam Grogan." She flung an arm wide, pointing back toward his farm. "Take your accusations and your uncertainties back where you came from. I can't help you with imaginary issues."

Had he just credited her with keeping a lid on her temper? Adam shook his head and tried again. "Fine. Be that as it *is*," he stressed the word, only continuing after her grudging nod, "Pa believes otherwise."

"You want me to warn my family," Opal surmised. "Done."

"It can't be solved so easily this time." Adam let out a long breath. "Pa sent Larry with a warning of his own last night."

"What warning?" Every line of her body tensed.

"In spite of my best efforts, he sent my brother to put the skull in front of your house with a note inside."

"He'd dare breach the boundary again?" The angry red in her cheeks ebbed, drained by fear. "In bad blood?"

"When your family didn't respond, Pa decided you're all hatching a plot." One look at Opal's face right now would've convinced him otherwise, but Adam didn't have that luxury. "I figure Larry didn't follow orders exactly."

"They're going to kill each other." The realization robbed even her voice of its power, leaving nothing but a whisper.

"Not if I can find his message first." Adam reached a hand toward her shoulder to steady her, but she jerked back.

"Oh, we'll find it." Determination returned the strength to her words. "What do you think your brother planned?"

"Impossible to know for sure, but whatever he thinks would rile your family the most." Adam rubbed the back of his neck. "I thought maybe he'd put the skull in the barn, near your cattle, but it's not there."

"I would've found it when I did the milking," Opal agreed. "Perhaps he unearthed some sense and put it near your boundary line, where a warning would do good to someone about to trespass?"

"Checked there before I came over," he admitted. "Not that I held out any hope."

"Not near the house or the barn, nor the yard. I already slopped the hogs and gathered eggs, so I would've seen it."

"What would be the worst thing he could threaten?" Here's what kept tripping Adam up. The worst aspect of Pa's plan was to threaten the home—Opal's domain. By coming close to her, the move would have been unignorable. Because anyone with a lick of sense could see that Opal was—

Gone?

He watched for a moment as she hightailed it, hiking up her skirts enough to show trim ankles encased in her work boots as she practically flew over the ground. His reflexes kicked in a moment later and he raced to catch up. Somewhere in the back of his mind he hoped none of the Speck men saw him chasing full tilt after Opal.

So why did he want nothing more than to catch her?

Please, no. Oh Lord, please. Opal prayed as she sprinted for her apiary. *Don't let Larry have done anything to my bees!*

She burst through the small grove of cottonwoods to the clearing housing her apiary and skidded to a halt. A swift scan showed nothing wrong. Rows of white frame hives, raised above the ground, stretched before her. No acrid tinge of smoke, no angry drone of outrage greeted her ears, no swarms blanketed the air above.

More importantly, though, was what she could hear. The happy hum of busy workers shimmered in the wind, the same welcome she'd received for years. *Mama's legacy is safe.*

"Bees?" Adam stood beside her, the only unfamiliar element in the tiny world she'd overseen since childhood. "I hadn't thought of Larry putting the message anywhere your brothers or father wouldn't find it first."

"Perhaps that's the point? He knows I wouldn't show them, and your Pa would grapple with the lack of response." She moved among the hives as she spoke, checking to ensure no damage had been done she couldn't see from far away. Now that she'd calmed, she acknowledged that the only thing Larry would've done to destroy the apiary—set it ablaze—would have been detected long ago. Larry didn't know enough about bees to do anything else.

And making the mistakes of his grandfather should be too foolhardy for the greatest of numskulls. But what better to reignite a generations-old feud than fire the rage of such memories?

"Then why bring it at all?" Frustration sounded in Adam's deep voice—far closer than she anticipated. He'd followed her amongst the hives.

He's not afraid of the bees. Opal kept her face turned so he wouldn't see her surprise. Since his grandfather died of a bee sting, the feud had started in earnest. *I thought all Grogans were leery of bees—yet another reason a coward like Larry wouldn't set fire to the hives. He wouldn't risk an angry swarm.* The thought comforted her.

"There." Opal spotted the off-white of the fresh skull, not yet bleached by the elements, resting by the hive closest to Grogan property. *Surprising, Larry came this close.*

"Larry's afraid of bees." Adam didn't bother to hide his astonishment as he picked up the thing. Beneath it lay a curled up strip of parchment.

Opal snatched it before he had a chance and didn't let him get out the protest she could see forming. "I need to know what it says so we can decide what to tell my family. Letting your father stew will just make things worse."

In large, easily legible script, the note read:

NEXT TIME WE LOSE A COW, WE TAKE A SPECK IN PAYMENT.

Opal choked back her rage, narrowing her eyes to make out the addition beneath it.

In underlined, slashing strokes, someone had added a second sentence.

And I got my eye on your only heifer!

She crushed the thin leather in her hand, vowing to burn it before any of her family ever laid eyes on it. Larry knew she'd never show it to them, all right.

"There's nothing I can say to apologize for this." Adam stood as though braced for her anger, hands behind his back. "I heard what Pa planned to write and never wanted you to see it."

"Thank you for warning me." Opal kept a death grip on the message. "I'll tell Pa about your cow and that your pa says the next death will be the end of any peace."

"Larry's trying to end it long before then." Adam peered at her, but for the first time Opal couldn't bring herself to meet his gaze. "I'm still not sure why he put it here."

"To show he wasn't afraid of anything. . .not even the bees?" The suggestion didn't sound convincing, but it was the best she could do at the moment. The knowledge of Larry's perfidy, the extent he'd go to in an effort to show her he'd accept no rejection, stole her wits. *If he'd put this message near the house and Pa saw it. . .* She thought she might be sick.

"Opal?" Did she hear concern in Adam's voice? "What is it?"

"Nothing." But she answered too quickly—Opal knew it as soon as his dark eyes narrowed.

He gave her a long, searching look she forced herself to meet even while she tried to slip the evil note into her pocket. "Oh no, you don't." Adam snagged her wrist, the sudden warmth spreading up her arm making her gasp.

The moment of hesitation cost her dearly as his other hand cupped her balled fist, coaxing her fingers open. She resisted, knowing she made no match for his strength but refusing to give an inch.

"What did he write?" He stood there, his hand grasping hers, not pulling or forcing anything, the warmth of his hold matching the concern on his features. "Larry added something to the message, didn't he?"

She felt herself give the barest hint of a nod before she could guard against him. Opal lifted her chin. "Not that it matters."

"Yes, it does." His already-square jaw hardened. "Give it to me."

"No." The order restored her as nothing else could, making her tug her wrist. To her surprise, she slid from his grasp easily.

Not stopping to consider the differences between Adam and his brother, Opal took the opportunity to shove the note deep into her apron pocket. "I think it's best if you go home now. Tell your father you made sure we'd gotten the message. I'll take care of the rest."

At his nod, she turned to make her way back to the house, where her cook fire could consume the evidence of this morning. *If only it could take away the memory.*

The sigh she bit back turned into a stifled scream as a strong arm snaked around her waist.

CHAPTER 7

I'll deal with the guilt later, Adam promised himself as he refused to let go. While Opal squawked and thrashed—managing to kick him in the shin and elbow him in the gut—he plucked the note from her apron pocket. He'd already started to let go by the time she smashed the back of her head into his chin, sending pain streaking up his jaw.

I deserved that, he reminded himself.

"You deserved that!" The echo sounded suspiciously feminine, an idea confirmed when Opal added, "Stop wincing those big brown eyes of yours and give that back!"

"Big brown eyes?" Affronted enough to speak in spite of his jaw, Adam hoisted the note out of her reach. He'd never been so glad of his height as now, when the little firebrand hopped and still missed her goal by a solid two inches. "What am I, a cow?"

"I can think of less flattering comparisons, if you like." Her mutter wrangled a chuckle out of him as she abandoned the indignity of hopping and crossed her arms.

The chuckle died a swift death as he read Larry's addition to Pa's already awful statement. And reread it. Twice. "I'll kill him."

"Haven't there been enough death threats?" A glint of humor peeked behind the weariness underscoring Opal's words.

It only fueled his rage, making his stomach churn in a sour frenzy as he looked at the woman before him. This brave woman his brother threatened to kill. This woman who, by protecting her family, also protected Larry from the consequences of his actions.

The crunching *pop* of his knuckles told him he'd balled his hands into fists. "Only a coward threatens a woman." *And I wondered why Larry put it by the apiary. I should have known. If he breaks down Opal, scares her badly enough, he'll get the fight he wants.*

"Don't bait me, Grogan." Opal tilted her head. "We're both trying to avoid conflict, so don't make it easy to speak my mind about your brother."

"Who says there'd be conflict?" His growl did nothing to vent his ire. "Just about now we're probably a matched set."

"You can never be sure." Caution replaced humor. "But if you go against Larry, the blame lands right back on me."

"That's not. . ." Try as he might, he couldn't find a way to finish his denial.

"True?" She gave an exasperated huff as she tried to finish his sentence. "You know they'll say I turned you against him. Or were you going to say 'fair'? What about this feud is fair? Or even sane?"

"I don't like it." Larry deserved the walloping of a lifetime, and Adam itched to deliver it.

"Huh." Opal raised a brow. "Not that anyone asked, or that it's for me to say, but I always figured you were the Grogan who put aside what he wanted for the good of the family."

Her assessment caught him off guard, leaving him silent for a long moment. "So that's what you think?" *And what does it mean to you, Opal Speck? That I'm a pushover or that I'm the better man?*

"Yep." She didn't give him another word on the subject.

"Maybe I think you're the same way."

"I should've known we'd come full circle." Opal rolled her eyes, but a small grin played around her lips. "So now that you've gotten back to your 'may be's,' you better get home."

"Yep." He didn't let his own smile free until she turned and started walking away. And still, he watched her go until she stopped and looked over her shoulder.

"And, Adam?"

"What, Opal?"

"Never come back." With that, she disappeared into the trees.

"Stay away from her." Adam's harsh growl raised the hairs on the back of Lucinda Grogan's neck.

Who? She lifted her hand from the door but shuffled a few inches closer—the better to hear her sons' conversation. The glower on her eldest son's face when he'd stormed past the house moments earlier didn't bode well.

"Who?" Larry's slightly nasal tones seeped through the door-frame. "And why should I?"

Don't antagonize your brother. Lucinda swallowed the admonishment. Her middle son sounded defensive, which meant Larry already had a fair idea what—no, make that who—Adam warned him against. *Not good. And it's a woman. The only way this could possibly get any worse would be if Adam named—*

"Opal Speck."

The terse syllables hammered at Lucinda's temples. *No, no, no. . .* She rested her forehead against the door, mind too full of dire possibilities to hold upright anymore. The drag of dismay cost her Larry's response, but years of raising him left her with more than headaches. Lucinda knew her son well enough to guess he'd denied or evaded the blunt confrontation.

"Don't try to sidestep this." Dark determination emphasized

Adam's warning. Never before had he sounded so filled with scarcely contained rage.

Lucinda wondered whether Larry would be wise enough to realize it and drop whatever game he played this time. *Probably not.* Which meant she'd need to corner him once Adam finished.

"You've got us mixed up, Adam. *I'm* not the Grogan who avoids issues or ignores things. That's your domain."

Fool! Lucinda gritted her teeth. If it weren't for Adam's level head, she'd have lost her husband or the fool running his mouth right now a hundred times over.

"No, Larry." Booted steps crossed the room. "*You're* the shame to our family name."

Her hand closed around the doorknob before Lucinda caught herself. No matter Larry's flaws, Adam hadn't earned the right to denounce him on behalf of the family. Especially not after she'd almost lost her middle son to that terrible accident two years ago. *Am I the only one who remembers how blessed we are to still have him?*

"Because I'd rather claim an angry bison than a coward who threatens a woman." Fury seethed through Adam's words, scalding away Lucinda's indignation.

Larry threatened Opal? The bite of shame galled her. *Well, she must have done something to provoke him! What did that vile little Speck gal do this time?*

"Cowards wait and do nothing. I'm a man of action."

"Leaving a death threat aimed at the only female in the Speck family? Making sure she'd be the one to find it, when she's alone? That's the action you're so proud of?" A muffled popping tattled of knuckles being cracked.

Adam's mistaken. Larry hates the Specks for his accident but wouldn't target Opal. Lucinda tried to swallow but found her mouth too dry. *I raised gentlemen! Please, Lord. Let me have that much.*

"I don't know what you're talking about." Fear turned Larry the coward Adam called him.

"When nothing happened, I figured you didn't follow the plan. I went over there and ran into Opal. We found the message. If I hadn't read what you wrote on the bottom myself I wouldn't have believed it."

"Then you know it only said I have my eye on her." The whine destroyed Lucinda's last hope.

"Don't even think about it. And know that the only reason you're still standing is she spoke up against me giving you the walloping you so richly deserve—didn't want things to get any worse."

"No need to get your nose out of joint, Adam. She's grown into a fine woman, and there's nothing wrong with me making a claim—" The sick *thud* of fist on flesh punctuated Larry's mutter before his groan filled the air.

Stomach churning, Lucinda couldn't be sure what sickened her more, that Larry lusted after Opal Speck, that her son would be so vulgar—even though it was just to bait Adam, she was certain—or that her sons were fighting each other.

"If I catch you so much as looking her way, I'll truss you up and deliver you to her pa myself."

Oh no, you won't, Adam Neil Grogan! Lucinda took a shallow breath. *It won't come to that.* Because no matter how awful things were, one truth stood above everything else. . . .

Opal Speck is the one to blame, and she'll be the one to pay. I'll make sure of that!

"I won't allow it." Adam stared at the broken stretch of fence Larry should have mended last week, at the imprints in the softening spring earth, and resisted the urge to throw his hat on the ground.

After all he'd done to keep the peace this week, one wandering dairy cow could destroy them. When Willa confided to him that Marla didn't show up for milking, he assumed she'd gotten lost, maybe stuck in a mud hole. Instead, the oblivious animal ambled right into Speck territory!

Which left him precious few options, and not a single one of them any he'd jump at. Going after the beast constituted trespassing—right on the heels of threats flying thick.

Memories of the day the Speck men came on Grogan land pushed to the front of his memory. *Fences and family—best keep an eye on both of yours, isn't that what Speck warned?* Adam surveyed the ruined fence, fingered the threat still in his pocket, and knew he'd failed on both counts.

"Never come back." Opal's advice from the day before echoed in his thoughts, making the decision simple. Sure, she'd said to stay away, but losing Marla paved the way for Larry to accuse the Specks of thievery. Which made as a good a pretext as any to come after Opal.

"I won't allow it," he repeated, following Marla's tracks until they petered out in the growing grass. An hour later, he'd searched every boundary line, forced to admit he needed to go deeper.

Another hour slipped away under the strain of fruitless searching while trying to find cover where none existed. Typically, Adam loved the rolling flatlands of the prairie, but today he'd trade his back teeth for a forest.

He'd have to check the homestead. The sun scaled the sky, inching toward noon—and dinnertime. Ma's sharp eyes wouldn't miss his absence, but more pressing stood the knowledge that the Speck men would soon converge near the place he suspected he'd find Marla.

Hours overdue for milking and feeding, she still hadn't gravitated toward home. Lately, it seemed the worst possibility proved reality, so he'd believe the contrary cow might have headed for the familiar sounds and scents of another barn. He could no longer avoid entering the hub of the Speck farm.

Adam moved stealthily closer to the barn until he pressed against its side. He edged to the corner and peered in the direction of the house, scanning for Specks on the horizon. The thought drew a grin until something moved by the well.

Opal. Stepping out of the house to fetch some water, she hadn't bothered with the bonnet usually shielding her from the sun. Now its rays played upon the burnished red of her hair, adding glints of gold with joyous abandon until she seemed a living flame. No wonder the sun thrilled to claim her.

"Drop the gun and keep quiet." A firm prod with the blunt end of a shotgun punctuated the hissed order. "Opal shouldn't be involved if Pa decides to kill you."

CHAPTER 8

A vague sense of unease, which Opal firmly told herself she should ignore, stalked her all morning long. No matter how many times she vowed Larry's threat the day before wouldn't affect her, she couldn't shake it. The hollowness in her stomach, the knot between her shoulder blades no amount of stretching could relieve, the heaviness of the air itself—none of it abandoned her until noon.

At that point panic wrapped around her, squeezing away any hollowness and leaving no room for pesky knots. Opal struggled against its tightening grip, searching for something, anything, to explain the inexplicable.

The men hadn't answered the dinner bell.

She rang it twice, racking her brain as she hurried toward the west field where Pa worked today, but no reason presented itself. Pa and her brothers never missed a meal. Pete grew so quick he couldn't spoon food into his face fast enough to fill out, so he most often beat her to the bell.

The only consolations she came up with were that God stayed with them, and that if anyone got hurt they'd have fetched her along with Dr. Reed. Cold comfort, considering the way things stood with the Grogans.

The thought added caution to her steps, making her duck behind the tall windrows of last season's corn waiting to be burnt. Only afterward could the next crop be planted free of any chance of the corn borer.

Clashing male voices revealed their location long before she spotted them. A swift glance showed five men at the far end of the field. *Wait. Five?* Opal crept closer. Pa, Ben, and Elroy stood in a semicircle facing Pete and. . . *Cursed Grogan stupidity!*

She didn't stop to consider whether her prayers for everyone's safety—even the trespasser's—nullified the previous thought. Keeping everybody in one piece mattered too much to get picky about how it got done. Then she caught a glimpse of the Grogan male's profile.

"Adam?" If anyone asked how she got from behind the windrow to the middle of the thick cluster of men, Opal wouldn't have been able to explain. One moment, she'd recognized the man Pete held a shotgun to, and the next, she stood beside him. Fast and foolish as that.

"Opal!" Five voices ranged in depth but matched in consternation made an alarmed chorus before orders came pouring in.

"Get away from him!" Pa wrapped his hand around her elbow and yanked her away.

"What do you think you're doing?" This from Elroy, who tried to step in front of her.

"Stop it!" She wriggled back to the front line by dint of sharp elbows and the tone she used to bully them into washing up before dinner. "Put your guns down and tell me what's going on this instant!"

"You shouldn't be here." Of all people, Adam held the least authority. Which made his statement all the more powerful.

"Even Grogan knows that you should go home, Opal." Ben's gaze bore a steely glint. "This is man's business."

"I'm a Speck. My family, my home, my business, too." She crossed her arms. "Have you taken leave of your senses, Pete? This is Adam, not Larry!"

"Oh, I know it." Pete's brows met in the middle, giving him the look of an angry buzzard. "I'm the one who caught him."

"What are you doing here, Adam?" *After I told you never to come back!* Opal kept the reminder to herself, knowing better than to bring up too many questions about their adventure the day before.

"We lost another cow. Looks like she got through a weak spot in our fence." Misery and resignation marched across his features. "Since we lost Sadie, we can't afford to let this one go."

"You hear that?" Ben burst in. "Lost another cow, he says. After their 'warning' from before. Search him, Pete."

Adam stood stock-still while her youngest brother patted him down, grimacing when Pete reached into his coat pocket.

Pete drew something out, glanced down, and froze. Livid marks mottled his skin. His mouth moved but no sound escaped as he passed his find to Pa.

The message. Opal couldn't even close her eyes against the horror of it, bound by some morbid need to watch her father's reaction to the words. She saw his eyes narrow, a muscle in his jaw twitch when he reached Larry's addition.

"Despite your trespassing and your family's threats, I'd been leaning toward something non-fatal." Her father gave a bark that could have been laughter, but raised the hairs on the back of her neck. "More fool, me, to think any Grogan deserved to live."

"What's it say?" Elroy accepted it when Pa thrust it his way, reading aloud for Ben's benefit. " 'Next time we lose a cow, we take a Speck in payment. And I got my eye on your only heifer!'

Our only..." Disbelief gave way to outrage. "Opal? You came after Opal?"

"No!" Adam shook his head. "I came to find the cow so we would avoid this."

"Then why were you by the house?" Pete's voice cracked. "I found you staring at her while she got water."

"Why would you be looking at me?" Stunned, Opal turned to Adam.

"Why does any man stare at a woman?" Elroy narrowed his eyes. "He liked what he saw."

"Don't be ridiculous." *As though a man like Adam would look twice at someone like me!* "*This* is your reason for brandishing shotguns at him? He probably was waiting for me to leave so he could find his cow."

"The man wasn't looking for a cow. He gawked at you like I'd look at Midge if nobody was watching." Red crept up Pete's ears, but he thrust out his jaw to make up for it. "Only I wouldn't look like I lost half my brains."

"Stop pretending to know what other people think, Pete." Opal refused to so much as glance at Adam for fear she'd get distracted wondering what ran through their prisoner's head. "Adam does not look at me like...that."

"Like a man?" Ben supplied. "He is one, ain't he?"

"No!" She realized her mistake when Adam gave a sort of growl, making Pete bash him in the skull and Pa push in front of her again.

Someday she'd wonder over his ability to take offense at something so paltry when he seemed indifferent to facing death, but for now she didn't have time to dwell on it. "Adam doesn't... I mean, he's"—she huffed as she shoved back into the thick of things—"a Grogan!"

"But still a man. Who ogled my daughter." Pa's tone brooked

no argument. "And even though we only got half the message, he obviously planned what that note said."

"I'm sure there's another explanation." Opal swallowed.

"It's too late for excuses." Ben cocked his gun. "He doesn't leave this property alive."

"But he has to!" Opal looked at the hardened expressions of the men she loved and knew her words fell on fallow ground. "It's murder!"

"Every man has a God-given right to protect his family," Pa informed her. "If Pete hadn't shown up early for dinner. . ." His left eye twitched. "Grogan set his course when he trespassed. He knew what he risked."

Adam stood utterly still, apparently accepting his fate.

Well, I don't accept it. Not Adam. She couldn't give up after all he'd done. "He saved my life two years ago. I owe him."

"You helped save Larry's." Elroy rejected her reasoning on behalf of the entire family, earning a glare that should have left him a pile of ash.

"Dr. Reed saved Larry, but Adam pulled me from that fire." She tried to appeal to their masculine integrity. "Consider it a debt of honor."

"Your honor—and safety—is exactly why I can't let him walk away." Pa wouldn't look at her. "There's nothing in the world that can save him now."

"You kill him, and the Grogans will come for us all." Opal threw herself to her knees before her father. "There'll be more death. Don't do this!"

"If we don't, they'll strike again." Elroy hauled her to her feet. "Run on home, Opal. You shouldn't see this."

"I'm not leaving until you listen to me!" Tears pricked her eyes. For Adam, the only Grogan man she'd call innocent. For her family, who'd turn themselves into killers. Over her. *I'm not worth it!*

How can I change their minds, Lord?

And suddenly she saw the way to save Adam's life. . .if her strength held. Opal felt her tears burst free, washing away any ties to her past.

To save them, I have to betray us all.

Caught gaping like a schoolboy with a crush, Adam had no choice but to let himself be taken to the field where the remainder of the Speck men worked. Only then did he know the identity of his captor—Pete, the lanky boy he'd least concerned himself with.

"What on earth?" Murphy spotted them before his sons, though they followed hard on his heels. "I'd pegged you as the Grogan with half a brain, boy."

"Adam?" Elroy's eyes widened before he lowered his hat brim to hide his surprise. "I could've sworn we spoke with you about your brother trespassing and warned what would happen the next time."

"You did." His only chance lay in appeasing the men his family'd threatened the day before.

"Wait." Ben held up his gun. "Pete, where'd you find him?"

"Skulking behind the barn. I—"

"Adam?" Opal's cry interrupted whatever the youngest Speck meant to say as she rushed into the middle of everything.

Instead of taking advantage of the Specks' distraction to seize the nearest shotgun, Adam joined them in protesting her arrival. Some part of his mind registered that she wore a dress of pale green—the color of hope. It was then he began to wonder whether he had lost whatever sense God gave him.

If I lost it, Opal didn't find it, he fumed as Opal resisted her family's efforts to tuck her behind them and out of harm's way. *Doesn't she know Larry, for one, would've snatched her as a hostage right off the bat?* The woman needed a keeper.

He added his opinion to her family's bluster. "You shouldn't be here." It didn't take much to see she didn't see the value of the comment, but at least the other men backed him up. Adam wouldn't turn down any goodwill at this point.

Opal, of course, didn't budge. If anything, her indignation over his treatment grew. "This is Adam, not Larry!"

Nice to know she appreciates the difference.

His explanation as to why he'd ventured onto their land wasn't met with approval. Though, in light of the message Opal had passed along yesterday, he didn't expect it to be. Another troublesome cow seemed unbelievable.

"Search him." Ben's order made Adam's blood run cold.

Uncertain whether he'd need to show Larry's addendum to Pa at some point, he hadn't burnt the message. Hiding it hadn't seemed prudent, so the incriminating thing sat like a firecracker in his coat pocket. The moment Pete drew it out, Adam knew he might as well have been carrying around his own death warrant.

Opal's reaction told him the instant she recognized what her brother held. All color fled her face, eyes huge and dark against the ice-white of her skin. Her stricken gaze skipped over him to fix on her father's fury as he absorbed its meaning.

Lord, protect my family when this is over. Adam closed his eyes, knowing no words would save him. *Protect Opal from the bloodshed to come. Don't let her bear guilt for what's not her fault.*

Elroy read the blasted thing aloud, disbelieving even in his anger. "You came after Opal?"

"No!" Adam willed her to look at him, to never doubt he intended her any harm. "I came to find our cow so we could avoid all this."

Her slight nod took a weight from him he hadn't known existed. Then her fool of a brother burst out with the news he'd caught Adam staring at his sister.

Now he avoided Opal's glance as she asked why in favor of glowering at Pete. He had nothing left to lose, after all. *You couldn't have just shot me and left it at that?*

"Why does any man stare at a woman?" The disbelief had left Elroy's voice. "He likes what he sees."

"Don't be ridiculous." Opal's scoff sounded genuine.

Wait. Why would that be ridiculous? Adam opened his mouth and shut it again as she said something about his waiting for her to leave so he could find his cow. Not that he believed he'd be getting out of this one, but he wouldn't get in the way of her efforts.

Pete did a fine job of that, for him, as he accused Adam of gawking—and looking brainless while doing it. Yep, the youngest Speck was starting to make dying at peace a real challenge.

Opal, for her part, still protested that Adam didn't look at her like a man looked at a woman, ending Ben's patience.

"He's a man, ain't he?"

"No!"

A growl burst from Adam's throat before he could stop it. Of all the blows that day, this hit the hardest. Worse even than the smash of the butt of Pete's shotgun against his skull in response to his outburst.

Disoriented, it took everything he had to remain on his feet. Feminine protests broke against male pride, and Adam knew it wouldn't be long before he met his Maker. The fog cleared to a vicious throbbing that must have affected his hearing. How else to explain what Opal was saying?

"What?" Four other men exploded with the question he would have asked if his vocal chords cooperated.

Tears poured down Opal's cheeks. She stared at him, imploring him to understand the impossible as she repeated, "You can't kill the man who's going to be the father of my child."

CHAPTER 9

"She's overset—doesn't know what she's saying." Elroy grasped at straws to excuse her declaration.

"I know full well what I'm saying!" Opal also knew full well her face turned bright enough to rival a raspberry. Adam didn't say a word, which showed she'd been right about him catching on quickly. If he'd acted surprised, the jig would be up. Instead. . .

"You die now, Grogan." Pa shoved the barrel of his shotgun in Adam's gut. "Opal, you should've told me the day this filth laid a hand on you. Don't worry about a thing. We'll take care of everything."

"No!" Opal thrust herself between Pa and Adam, dislodging the gun. "How can you take care of it?"

"He took advantage of you, we take his life." Ben tried to pry her away, murder in his eyes. "It's not your fault he forced you."

"Adam would never force a woman!" Indignation on his behalf filled her. "Apologize right now!"

"You—" Pa grappled before abandoning the words. "Willingly?" Disbelief mingled with hope, making Opal realize her father loved her so much he'd rather she betray him with his enemy's son than suffer what he feared.

A fresh wave of tears shook her. "I swear to you he never forced me." She couldn't stand to think what her brothers thought of her now. "Adam wouldn't hurt a woman."

"*That's* true." The emphasis Adam placed on the first word made Opal wince.

"We should still kill you"—Elroy practically shook with the force of his emotion—"for showing disrespect to our sister. Opal deserves better."

"Absolutely." Adam's swift agreement took the wind from her brother's sails for a moment, making Opal wonder.

Does he mean I deserve respect, or is he saying I deserve someone other than him because he doesn't want me—even if it spares his life? Sorrow swamped her at the idea.

"You're sure?" Pa stared at her midriff. "You're going to make him a father?"

"God willing." Opal prayed for forgiveness. She knew where this would lead—and that if she bore children, Adam would be their father. In the strictest sense, she hadn't told a lie. Deliberately misleading her father was more than enough to haunt her. "I'm so sorry, Pa."

"Too late for sorrys." Elroy's mutter sliced through her heart. "What are we gonna do now?"

"Ain't it obvious?" Pa didn't so much as glance at her. "Get the preacher."

"You can't be serious." Midge, realizing her mouth hung open, snapped it shut. Though, come to think of it, she'd never seen Peter Speck look so solemn.

"Pa sent me to fetch the preacher and a witness." He shoved his hands in his pockets, as though bracing for a blow.

"Opal said she's carrying Adam Grogan's babe, and your Pa's got a shotgun trained on him while you bring the preacher?" She wanted to be sure she had the facts right. "*Opal?*"

"You comin' or not?" The ferocity of his question convinced her as nothing else could. Pete nursed a crush on her, so Midge knew it would take a lot for him to bark at her.

"Let me get Clara and Saul." Something didn't add up here, and maybe her adoptive parents could sort it out before someone ended up dead. Or worse—married.

"No." His hand closed around her arm. "I'll hogtie you and drag you back with me before you get another soul involved. Only reason Grogan still breathes is so Opal won't be ruined. Got it?"

"Yep." Bumps prickled along her skin in spite of the warmth of the day. *When did Pete Speck get so forceful?* They walked in silence to the parson's house.

"Pa needs you, Parson Carter." Pete didn't offer any explanations, and Midge didn't add to what he said.

Honestly, what would she say? *Pete tells me Opal says she's carrying Adam Grogan's child and you're needed for a shotgun wedding. I know it sounds crazy, but the whole thing just might be real because I've seen the way Adam looks at her when he thinks no one notices. If she had any other last name, I figure they'd already be hitched. . . .*

Actually, that'd probably do, in a pinch. But Parson Carter's wife might be around to overhear, and Pete had a point about Opal's reputation. So Midge kept her tongue between her teeth while the preacher brought out his Bible and they headed for the farm.

"What's this all about?" Parson Carter's share of courage didn't rank high under the best of circumstances. "Nothing to do with the Grogans, I hope?" He'd practically created a second career of avoiding the confrontations between the two families.

Midge, for one, could have mustered a heap more respect for

him as a spiritual leader if he'd shown more—well, spirit! As it stood, she didn't see much to recommend his faith as having much practical use. Except that people listened to him because he was the pastor. *That would come in handy.*

Pete's grunt didn't reassure their companion any, but from the way he kept looking at her, Midge figured the parson took comfort from her presence. She even understood his line of thinking: If there was blood to be shed or wrongdoing to forgive, Pete wouldn't be bringing her along.

No one would come within ten acres of guessing the truth behind their visit today. When news leaked out, folks would buzz around Buttonwood like vultures around a fallen bison. They'd pick the bones of the story until they had nothing left but sore beaks.

And for once, Lucinda Grogan wouldn't be in the thick of the gossip. Midge wondered how the old buzzard would like being on the rough end of things. The thought shouldn't make her smile, but it did. *I'll take my silver linings where I can find them!*

They reached the end of a windrow, and suddenly, Midge spotted Opal. She sat apart from everyone else—away from where her father held a gun on Adam even. She didn't look up as they approached, but Midge could make out the trails from tears on her friend's face. Her smile vanished.

Ignoring the men, she hurried to Opal's side. Let the Specks explain things to the parson, she'd come for Opal. Midge sank to her knees, enfolding her friend in a hug before she spoke a single word. Not until Opal returned the embrace did she shift back enough to look at her. "So it's true?" Midge let no censure creep into her voice. Not a difficult thing, really, when she felt none.

"Oh, Midge." More tears accompanied Opal's broken whisper. "I've made a terrible mistake!"

"Everybody makes mistakes."

"Not like this. Pa's disowning me. My brothers won't even look at me. They think—" Opal gave a hard swallow. "They all think I'm a hussy."

"Don't say that!" The very word brought back memories Midge couldn't afford. *Not now.* "Give them time to be angry. For now, Adam is the one who matters."

"He's a good man." A sniff, then a garbled, "Deserves better than to be forced into marrying me, but I don't see another way!"

"Hush!" Midge fought back the urge to go smack Adam Grogan. The fool hadn't made it clear he *wanted* to marry Opal? "He's a lucky man, and this is what's best for everybody involved."

"You're right." Opal accepted her handkerchief and mopped her face. The tip of her nose glowed a red rivaled only by her bloodshot eyes. "How do I look?"

"Erm. . ." Midge spotted some squirrel corn a few yards away. "You need a bouquet!" Ignoring the restless movements of the men, she made the short trip, plucked the fragrant flowers, and made an arrangement.

"It's lovely." Opal fingered the heart-shaped blossoms, pure white against the lacy green of the leaves Midge tucked in. "Thank you."

"All right." Midge tucked Opal's free hand into the crook of her arm and walked her over to where the men waited. "The bride is ready."

"Is the groom?" Parson Carter fiddled with his collar.

"He better be." Mr. Speck hefted his shotgun high.

"Then maybe you oughta untie him." The wedding would be memorable, but Midge tried to soften it a little. She hoped Opal didn't notice that Adam looked about as miserable as a man possibly could.

Without a word, Pete flicked open his pocketknife and did the honors before stepping back. Midge put Opal's hand in Adam's freed ones and joined Pete at a distance.

In what had to be the quickest wedding on earth, the preacher hurried through the part where he asked if anyone had a reason why the couple shouldn't be joined in matrimony. All the same, it seemed ages before he finished.

But, finally, they heard the words, "Then I pronounce you man and wife. What God has put together, let no man"—the preacher paused to glower at the Specks until they lowered their shotguns—"tear asunder."

For a moment, all was silence and peace while everyone let loose the breaths they'd been holding. Midge just started to think they might all make it through this when the groom opened his mouth and spoke for the first time since pledging, "I do."

Determination lit Adam's gaze as he pulled Opal close, ignoring the Specks. "Don't I get to kiss my bride?"

CHAPTER 10

Adam heard various shouts as he swept Opal into his arms but didn't care. If they shot him, they shot him. He was done standing around waiting for them to do it.

He'd gotten called out for gaping at Opal. Accepted that Larry's note would get him killed. Withstood Opal announcing to her family he wasn't a man, gotten bashed in the noggin for taking exception to the same, and not called her out on her grand deception to pass off another man's bastard as his.

He'd held her hand, looked into blue eyes awash with tears, seen the pathetic clump of flowers she gripped as though they could save her from being his bride. All told, it was more than enough to make a man reckless.

She didn't resist as he pulled her close. Her eyes widened when he lowered his head to hers, pressed his mouth against lips swollen from crying. Opal went still before melting against him, warm and soft and everything a woman should be.

Everything she's already been to another man.

He ended it, withdrawing so abruptly she almost lost her balance. The bewilderment and wonder on her features could have fooled him into thinking he'd given Opal her first kiss, but given the circumstances, Adam knew better.

Who? The question sank its teeth into him the moment he realized what she'd done and didn't let go as Parson Carter took Midge back to town. *Whose child does Opal carry? Whose child will I raise as my own?*

Because that, of course, was what he'd do. Their hasty marriage couldn't be annulled without physical evidence of nonconsummation. And if he denounced her as a liar, his family would seek vengeance. Their families would battle until blood flowed on both sides.

No, he'd continue the pretense she'd begun. Opal must have seen today as a God-given opportunity, knowing he'd take her as his wife in exchange for his life.

"I always figured you were the Grogan who put aside what he wanted for the good of the family." Oh yes. She'd known he'd marry her and keep her secret, too.

But why hadn't she wed her lover? Adam would find out everything from the woman he'd spend his life with. *She'll learn the meaning of what it is to honor her husband straightaway. There will be no lies between us.*

They didn't exchange a word as everyone walked to the Speck soddy. He waited outside while Opal went in to gather her things. It took only moments for his new wife to emerge with a satchel holding her worldly goods.

"I don't know when I'll be back." Her words sounded dry, as though she'd exhausted all her crying.

"You won't be." The first words Adam spoke to his bride, and they made her shudder.

"He's right." Her father jerked a thumb toward him. "You're a Grogan now. You belong with them."

"Pa!" Opal reeled back at his words as though she'd been

slapped. "You're my family!"

"Not anymore." He didn't look at her as he walked into the house. "Don't forget to move your apiary. No one here will tend it for you. Consider it and all that goes with it your dowry."

Sobs wracked her as she grabbed each of her brothers for a hug when they walked past. "I love you all more than you know."

Each gave her a fierce embrace in return.

"Goodbye, Opal." Ben shut the door behind him, and it was done.

She turned and walked in the direction of the Grogan boundary, making it out of sight of the house before she collapsed. Huddled on the ground, clasping her knees to her chest, with her bag and cloak strewn beside her, Opal made the very picture of desolation.

Adam hunkered down beside her to wait it out. He extended a hand to pat her shoulder, but her flinch made him end the contact immediately. "You were right when you said I wouldn't hurt a woman, Opal."

"I know." Her answer came out muffled. "But you could do worse."

"Your secret is safe with me."

"Promise?" She peered up at him, wary and hopeful. "Pa might forgive me someday if he never knows I lied." Opal's face fell again at the reminder of what she'd done.

"Whatever your reasons, it saved my life."

She gave him an odd look. "My reasons should be fairly easy to understand."

"Pretty much." Since she showed no signs of getting up, he went ahead and sat down beside her. "Why don't you tell me everything."

"Like what?" Opal gaped at him now. "You were there."

"Let's start with the basics." He reached over and enfolded one cold hand in his. "Who's the real father?"

There was a roughness to his hands as he clasped hers, a capable strength Opal found so reassuring it took a moment for the full meaning of his question to take hold.

"The real father?" Repeating the words squeezed no sense from them, unless. . .

A shiver shook her as Opal considered the possibilities. Surely Adam didn't believe her to be with child in truth? Her new husband couldn't think so lowly of her!

"Yes." His steady gaze told her that's precisely what he thought.

"No!" Opal could scarcely gasp the denial as her breakfast clawed its way up the back of her throat. "I wouldn't. . ." She swallowed hard, searching for an explanation and finding none.

"You will." Determination underscored his order. "I need the name of the man whose child I'll be raising."

Dear Lord, how can I convince my new husband I haven't made him a cuckold even before our wedding night?

Wedding night. The very thought drove every other concern from her mind. *I'm a married woman. A wife. Tonight. . .*

Her alarm must have shown in her expression, because Adam's softened. "Whoever he is, it doesn't change things. You don't have to be afraid."

"I know!" *Because I'm not carrying any babe!* Opal realized her hands were tearing clumps of grass from the ground and stopped. How best to tell him?

"No matter your answer, I won't seek to have the marriage annulled."

"Annulled!" The word loomed larger than life, an undeniable threat. If Adam dissolved their marriage, nothing would stop her family from seeking vengeance. "You can't!"

"I know." A muscle in the left side of his jaw twitched. "Without proof of nonconsummation, it's not an option. I understood that when I married you, Opal."

"But you considered it." Her face grew hot enough it must match her hair. "If you had proof?" *If I tell you the truth, will you discard me? Destroy everything I worked for today?*

"I try to consider everything." He smudged away her tears with his thumb.

"Everything?" A huff of laughter escaped before she could hold it back. *You didn't consider the truth—that I'm untouched. That no man before you so much as kissed me!*

"And everyone." He shifted, laying the warmth of his palm against her stomach. "This child will bear no stigma, Opal."

Tears did nothing to cool her shame as she met the gaze of her husband. "You mean it, don't you?" Wonder at his selflessness stole her sorrow for a moment. "You'd take a child you didn't sire into your home, into your life, and stand as father?"

"Yes." He shifted away, doubts rushing to fill the space he'd taken. "I don't like lying, Opal. But I don't see another way to avoid bloodshed. If my family knows I'm not the father, there'll be no stopping them."

"They won't." She wouldn't allow it.

"But I know, Opal." Adam rubbed the back of his neck, staring at his boots. "And for my own peace, I need a name."

"Please don't ask this of me." She closed her eyes. *I can't tell him the truth, but the lies have to end. As things stand, they're piled higher than a windrow.*

"Our wedding was a farce." He clasped her hand in his once more. "Our marriage needn't be."

"I'll be a good wife to you, Adam." The words spilled over from her heart. He deserved so much more than having to settle for lies and a woman he didn't want. *I'll try to make up for it.*

She couldn't ask him to understand. *After tonight, I won't have to. He'll know there is no child. Adam will know I betrayed my family to spare his life. . .and that I betrayed his trust by not telling him the truth.*

"Tell me his name."

Opal swallowed. "I can't."

"Yes, you can." A rumble of anger edged his voice. "You're choosing not to tell me. Not to trust me."

"If I only had myself to think of things would be different." *But I won't risk my family.*

"I know you've more to think of than yourself." His agreement took her by surprise. "Now you have a husband. A husband who's already promised to claim your child as his own."

"Thank you for that."

"Don't thank me." He shook his head. "I don't have much of a choice. But I want to know. . .who is the true father?"

"Ask me tomorrow." She shied away from the question, from another lie.

"Why tomorrow?" Suspicion darkened his gaze. "Why wait?"

"Because. . ." This time her blush had little to do with shame and everything to do with embarrassment. "I know you're a man of honor. You won't even consider setting me aside once we. . ." She couldn't finish the sentence.

"Once we've faced my family?" He let out a deep breath. "I already told you his name won't change things between us."

"Then not having a name won't change things between us." She dug her nails through the dirt she'd exposed by uprooting the prairie grass. "Ask me tomorrow, if you still want an answer."

"Of course I'll want an answer. One day won't change anything!"

"Yes, it will." Opal dug deeper. "One day can change every-thing. Force your family to accept me, avoid a feud, and make ours a marriage in truth."

"You talk in circles. Unless. . ." He stopped pacing to stand before her. "You don't mean a day, at all. You mean tonight."

Her voice abandoned her, leaving Opal with nothing to give but a tiny nod.

"That's what you were saying about my honor." His form blocked the sunlight, casting his features in shadow, but Opal could see the hardening of his jaw. "That I wouldn't seek an annulment after our wedding night."

"Yes." Her whisper scarcely tickled her own ears, but it seemed he heard it. *When you won't be able to get an annulment. When I won't be a maid anymore, but a wife. When my family is safe.*

"Then I'll ask you tomorrow, Opal Grogan." His use of her new last name pierced her heart. "But tonight won't make any difference."

"What?"

"Until you're my wife in trust," Adam reached down to grab her satchel once more as he spoke, "you won't be my wife in truth."

CHAPTER 11

W here is he?" Lucinda twisted a rag in her hands and peered out the window. "Adam's never missed dinner!"

"Maybe he went into town for something and stopped by the Dunstalls' café?" Her daughter's suggestion failed to calm her concerns. "Adam will be fine."

"You're sure he wasn't in the fields?" She turned to her husband and second eldest. "Nowhere on the farm?"

"We checked." Larry's shrug only made his mother worry more. "All we found was that gate needs fixing in the southeast pasture."

"Weren't you supposed to take care of that earlier this week?" Her husband squinted at Larry. "Why does it still need mending?"

"Well"—Larry's gaze shifted away from his father, alerting Lucinda her middle son was doing some fast thinking—"with things the way they've been with the Specks, going near the boundary doesn't seem a good idea."

Since when have you been so preoccupied with what is or isn't a good idea? Lucinda covered her anxiety by fussing with the faded curtains. "Seems to me that's exactly why you'd be keeping that fence in good order."

"Aw, Ma. . ."

But Lucinda wasn't listening to Larry anymore. Her attention focused on two shapes coming closer. "Adam!" *But who else?* She couldn't shake a feeling of doom, despite the surge of relief. "Here he comes!"

"See?" Willa's smile shone through her voice. "Adam wouldn't give us any cause to worry."

"No?" The word came out as a croak, dry and rough as she hurried to the door and rushed out to meet her son. And Opal Speck. Lucinda's years hadn't touched her eyesight, and she hadn't missed the satchel her son carried.

"Adam!" She gave him a swift hug. "Where have you been?" Lucinda's gaze flitted on Opal. "We were worried."

That she blamed Opal as the cause for that worry carried through. It was plain enough in the way the girl didn't move a muscle that Opal was standing on her pride. *As though a girl like that has anything to be proud of.* Lucinda felt the corners of her mouth tighten. *Coming between my sons. . .* The thought brought her attention back to Adam.

"I have some news." Discomfort showed in the line of his shoulders, the telltale way he rubbed his jaw.

"What's *she* doin' here?" Excitement filled Dave's voice. More importantly, the presence of her youngest child alerted them to the arrival of everyone else.

Lucinda looked at the tableaux as though viewing it from a far distance. Willa came to stand beside her, as she always did. A good daughter. Larry stopped just beyond Diggory. . .until her husband's hooded glare and less subtle jab made him fall in line. Dave scampered right up in front of everybody, eyes bright with interest and expectation as he stared at Adam.

Adam. Her eldest. The one who kept them all together.

The one who even now stood beside a Speck.

He opened his mouth, and Lucinda had a wild urge to slap her palm across it and hold back the words to come. With a mother's intuition, she knew as certain as sunrise and as dark as the depths of a moonless night that her family would be changed forever by what Adam had to say.

"You all know Opal." He reached for the upstart's hand, drawing her forward as though presenting someone of importance.

"Yeah!" Dave practically shouted the agreement while the rest of them managed grudging nods. "But what's a Speck doin' here?"

"That's what I need to explain." Adam's gaze sought hers, and Lucinda's hands caught on Dave's shoulders for support as the scene grew smaller, dimmer. "Opal's not a Speck anymore. She's my wife."

Blackness descended, a fuzzy blanket promising to block reality. Lucinda swayed into its softness.

"No!" Larry's bellow dragged her back from the darkness. "It can't be!" It wasn't the outrage in his shout but an underlying anguish that tore into her mother's heart anew.

"It is." Opal's whisper, a pale apology, floated around them for a heartbeat.

"When?" Diggory didn't bother denying Adam's statement. Instead, her husband wanted to know the details. As though his answer could somehow salvage everything.

"Today."

"Then it's not too late! Dave, fetch Parson Carter straight away!" Hope glimmered once more as Lucinda laid out her plan. "You'll get an annulment."

"No. . ." Opal's moan, so desolate and plaintive, would have moved any woman to feel for the girl. At least, it might have if the girl hadn't reached out to clutch Adam's sleeve.

"Don't you touch my son!" Lucinda knocked her hand away.

"Ma!" Willa's gasp didn't spear her half so much as Adam's frown.

He reached for Opal's hand and tucked it in the crook of his arm. "Annulment isn't an option."

"I don't believe it!" Larry's denial came so fierce and furious it took everyone aback. "You wouldn't."

Anyone would think his words were directed at his older brother, but Lucinda noticed Larry's gaze hadn't moved from Opal. The intensity of his stare unnerved her. *What hold does this girl have over my sons? Lord, protect my family!*

"She'll lie, then." Lucinda glowered at Opal. "She'll say an annulment is possible."

"I can't." If the girl went any more pale, she'd turn transparent. "I can't lie that an annulment is possible."

"You will." Larry all but hissed the order. "You'll do it so we don't seek revenge on your family for trapping Adam. I know you'll do it."

"No, she won't." Adam set his jaw. "Opal is with child."

And with that, the darkness won.

"Ma!" Adam barely caught her before she hit the dirt. He scooped her up, noticing for the first time how thin the skin of her face looked. *She's getting older.*

Guilt hit him like a load of rocks. *This will almost be too much for her. But, Lord, what else am I to do? Tell her Opal is my wife and carrying my child? Or tell her the truth, and watch the feud erupt and Pa and Larry get themselves killed? That would be harder on Ma than anything.*

He carried her inside, laying her on the worn sofa before he realized only Dave had followed him. Shouts rang outside.

"Whose is it?" Pa's yell carried best. . .followed by the un-mistakable sound of flesh striking flesh.

Adam raced outside in time to see Pa cup his cheek and step forward, fury in his face. "Stop!" He planted himself between his father and his wife, who'd obviously slapped the older man for his insult.

"How dare you!" Opal's outrage almost fooled Adam, who knew the truth. "I'm not the type of woman to bed one man and pass off his child as Adam's!" She moved forward, casting a pain-and-accusation-filled glance his way. "That you'd ever even consider such a thing. . .you should be ashamed of yourself."

I never would have thought it, Adam agreed. *But here we stand.* His eyes narrowed. She had no right to strike his father, no matter the foulness of his insult, when the offense proved just.

"Wipe that look off your face, son." Pa obviously interpreted Adam's disgust as being aimed squarely at himself.

"You don't talk like that to my wife." He struggled against the urge to defend Opal and the knowledge she didn't deserve it. But he couldn't let his father know that. "Ever."

"Had to ask." After working his jaw side to side, Pa let loose a begrudging shrug. "I won't make that mistake twice."

"Thank you." Opal's regal nod acknowledged the closest thing to an apology Adam had ever heard come from his Pa.

Maybe she knows what she's doing, to convince everyone. The thought didn't make him rest any easier. *How am I to live with a wife who lies so well?*

"I still can't believe it." His brother's bewilderment didn't spark offense as he stared at them. If anything, Larry sounded. . .sad?

"Believe it." He couldn't have anyone doubting his wife or his marriage. "Opal and the child are mine."

Despite the situation, there was something. . .primal. . .about saying that aloud. Something *right*. It was the same sense of calm he'd had when he'd agreed to marry her in the first place.

This, then, must be from God. A peace that passes under-standing. *Because I sure don't understand, Lord.*

"Are you sure?" Now his brother was pushing it, his hoarse query making Opal bristle anew.

"Yes." Adam laid a hand on her arm, feeling some of her tension ebb. "Opal wouldn't tell me another man's child is mine." His words skated the fine edge of truth, when that was exactly what she'd told her father. His peace fled in the face of her grateful smile, a smile pretty enough to make his mouth go dry.

"Not that." Larry peered at Opal, searching out her secrets. "I mean are you sure she's expecting at all?"

"Yes!" His mother's cry made them all look to the house. There she stood, clinging to the doorway as if unable to stand without its support. "It wouldn't be the first time a hussy lied to trap a decent man!"

Opal tensed again, her fingers digging into his wrist, sparking an anger whose power almost overwhelmed him. For the first time, he realized what his wife faced—what Opal knew awaited her when she reached his home.

Far from trap him, Opal's actions spared his life. Sure, she'd turned the situation into a means of saving her own reputation, but she hadn't set out to sacrifice his freedom. Of course she was with child. Otherwise why would she put herself in such a terrible position?

"Opal never sought to trap me." His words came out so low they could have passed for a growl. "Never been more sure of anything in my life."

"I take it her family knows?" Pa got back to the matter at hand. "You haven't run off with her so we'll have a herd of angry Specks on our doorstep?"

"They know." Opal bit her lip but said no more.

"They're the ones who fetched the preacher, aren't they?" Ma all but shrieked the words. "Did they force you to marry her, Adam? Shotgun weddings aren't valid!"

"Yes, they are." Pa rounded on her. "If a man got our Willa in the family way and thought twice about doing the honorable thing, it'd be valid enough."

"*Willa's* a good woman."

"So is Opal." Adam knew the truth of it, despite their situation. "And make no mistake, it was my choice to marry her."

CHAPTER 12

His choice? Opal listened to Adam defend her and wanted to weep. *What choice did he have, Lord? Marriage to me or death?* She looked at the expressions painting Grogan faces.

Anxiety darkened Willa's pretty eyes. Curiosity, avid and eager, kept young Dave's head swiveling back and forth so he wouldn't miss anything. Pride bent to resignation as Diggory acknowledged his son's decision by reaching for her satchel. Larry's fury came off so palpable, Opal wouldn't look at him.

But it was the defeat lining Lucinda's shoulders as she clutched the doorframe that most closely mirrored Opal's heart. Set apart, reaching for strength wherever she could find it, grasping at any hope this could be made right. . .

Oh, how I wish it could be so. But how can you make things right, when you're not the person you thought you were?

Opal balled her fist against the sting of her palm—a fading reminder that she'd struck another person in anger. It didn't matter that Diggory Grogan offered the ultimate insult. That he accused her of sleeping with multiple men before marriage, lying about it, and then passing off an unborn child as belonging to the wrong man in order to trap him into an unwanted marriage. Words paled compared to actions. After so many years of telling her father and brothers that physical violence didn't solve anything, she'd lashed out the first time she found herself alone in her anger.

Hypocrite.

The knowledge stung more than her hand ever could. And the more she thought about it, the more she could add to the list of people who'd believed the worst of her.

After all, Diggory wasn't the first. He certainly didn't rank as the most important, and she should have foreseen the assumptions his family would jump to. Especially when Adam thought much the same thing. The only difference was how much a hussy he thought her. Somehow, that didn't make them any less hurtful.

Even her own family now believed she'd betrayed her raising, their good name, and her family loyalty for fleshly weakness. *The look in Pa's eyes when he said I wasn't a Speck anymore. . .* Another surge of sadness threatened to overwhelm her.

"Opal." Adam stood before her, hand extended.

Not knowing what else to do, she took hold and followed him into the Grogan home for the first time. Oh, she'd been on their homestead before for harvesting, threshing, work bees, and the like to exchange a helping hand.

She stilled at the thought. *Threshing. If I hadn't been here for Larry's accident, I wouldn't have fetched the ice. He wouldn't have thought I harbored secret feelings for him and skulked on our land to act on the supposed attraction.* Her stomach heaved as she followed the progression. *If he hadn't crossed the boundary, Pa and my brothers wouldn't have been so up in arms when Adam came looking for his milk cow. If I'd never stepped foot on Grogan land. . . If I. . .*

She stopped cold, bringing Adam up short. *Oh Lord. I thought I was saving Adam. But really, this entire mess is my fault!*

She lurched away from him for a few steps, turning her back to lose the contents of her stomach in a patch of wild grass. Opal gagged on her realizations until she had nothing left but the hollowness of despair.

"Here." A man's kerchief appeared before her, a warm hand patting her back as though to comfort her. Adam had stayed. His kindness proved the breaking point.

Despite her resolve not to let the Grogans see her cry, Opal felt tears pour free. She stayed bent over for an extra moment, mopping her face clean, trying to gather her composure.

"Well, Larry, I guess now we know Adam's not been hoodwinked. The gal's pregnant, all right." Diggory's laughter stiffened her spine, giving her the strength nothing else could have. If he weren't such an abysmal, callous excuse for a man, she would almost have been grateful.

As it was, Opal straightened up, tucked the soiled kerchief in her apron pocket, and summoned a sickly smile. They'd never know she grinned at the irony of how her sickness over the deception was interpreted as proof of its veracity.

"We've put your things in Willa's room," Adam told her just outside the house, after everyone else had gone inside.

"Willa's room?" She looked up in consternation. *How am I to make an annulment impossible if we sleep separately?*

"Willa's room," he repeated the words with a determined gleam, and Opal knew he'd meant what he said earlier. "Until I can build us a home of our own, I'll stay with Larry in the barn. It's for the best."

"Don't leave me." She hated to beg. Hated that she needed him for more than fulfilling her plans. But the thought of being alone in the Grogan household turned her stomach afresh. If nothing else, she counted Adam as her ally.

"When the time is right, we'll have a house." His gaze held

a deeper meaning than the words he spoke so lightly. "A real marriage."

"When the time is right. . ." She tested the words, certain he meant when-you-tell-me-the-name-of-the-father-whose-child-you-carry.

"I'm glad we understand each other."

"Oh, I understand." She had a husband. Now, what she needed was a plan.

Think, Midge. Think! She rolled over, snuggled into her quilt, and waited for inspiration to strike. A deep breath to calm her racing thoughts didn't do much. Stretching and wriggling her toes, her never-fail plotting method left her without any brilliant insights either.

This is one of those times when everybody else I know would pray. Maybe I should give it a try?

She wiggled her toes some more.

Maybe not.

After all, praying hadn't helped her parents make it past their bouts with influenza when she was little. Praying hadn't helped her sister survive. . . .

No. Not going to think about that.

Midge stopped wiggling her toes. The point was God either hadn't heard or hadn't cared, because prayer hadn't helped her when she needed it most.

Saul had.

Which was the only idea for helping Opal that she kept coming back to—telling Saul and Clara. Oh, Midge knew Opal's reputation was at risk, but she knew firsthand that her makeshift family wouldn't turn their backs on a woman just because of her circumstances.

They were some of those Christians who actually practiced what they all preached and loved folks for who they were—warts and all. Didn't they keep telling her that the beauty of Jesus was that He gave His grace to everyone who accepted it, even though nobody deserved it?

Well, Midge knew she deserved it less than most. She wasn't worthy like Saul and Clara. And Opal, who'd always been so kind and tried so hard to keep her family from fighting with the Grogans, she deserved better than Midge, too. That was probably why Midge's prayers didn't do much, come to think of it.

She burrowed deeper under the covers. *I saw how Adam looked at Opal that day at the smithy.* She tried to marshal her thoughts, sniff out the facts. *I know he saved her from the fire, and any woman would find that romantic. . . . She's so pretty, with her bright hair and blue eyes, it's no wonder he stares. And Adam Grogan's a fine-looking man, even if he is older. Real tall, with lots of dark hair and kindness in his face. Haven't I heard Alyssa say so often enough?*

She didn't spare a thought for her friend, who had a crush on Adam. All Alyssa need do was crook a finger and half the boys in Buttonwood would come running. The other half, Midge allowed herself a small smile, would do the same for her. But none of them could help Opal if she were in trouble.

Opal and Adam might be a good match, but there's something havey-cavey about the whole thing. Opal's not the type to consort with a man. I thought maybe she'd given in to the man she loved because they were separated by family hostilities, but now I know different.

Midge had seen Opal's expression after Adam's kiss. That wasn't the look of a woman who'd been bussed by a longtime lover. Not by a long shot. There'd been no knowing in her reaction. . .just surprise. And enough hesitant excitement to reassure Midge that the marriage still might work.

All hopes aside, though, knowing that Opal wasn't carrying

Adam's child changed everything. It didn't take much to figure out that she'd lied. But why? Because she'd wanted to marry him? Things between the two families were wound tighter than ever, so what had Adam been doing on Speck land in the first place if he and Opal weren't seeing each other?

There were too many questions, not enough answers, and one troubling certainty—whatever caused the wedding yesterday would cause a lot more trouble before this was over. And Opal would be the one to pay for it.

Until she knew more, she couldn't tell anyone. But still, Midge had to do *something*.

CHAPTER 13

W hat?" Adam felt the reverberation from how hard Larry slammed their door through the wall where he hung his hat.

"You heard me, Adam." His brother circled him. "How could you do it?"

"Opal carrying a child out of wedlock never figured into any of my plans." He chose his words carefully—as he had all day. As he'd have to for a long while.

"That's not what I meant."

"You know better than to question why I married her, Larry." Sinking down onto his bed did nothing to ease the weight from his shoulders. "It had to be done." *Just not for the reason everyone thinks.*

"That's not what I meant either." Larry shouted this time but must have realized his voice would carry because he lowered it. "Why *her*?"

"It doesn't matter that her last name used to be Speck." Adam addressed the only other possible cause for Larry's outrage. "Opal's a special woman. God-fearing, kind, smart, pretty—"

"I know that, blast it!"

"Watch your mouth, Lawrence Grogan. There's no cause for cussing."

"Yes, there is." A muscle worked in his brother's jaw. "She was *mine*, Adam."

"No." Bile seared the back of his throat. *Can Larry be the father of Opal's child? My own brother, Lord?*

"Yes," he hissed the word. "She was for me, and you took her. You knew it, and you took her anyway!"

"I didn't know." Adam pushed his hair back. *Didn't I?* A memory fell into place. The day he'd gone looking for the cow skull and startled Opal, hadn't she called Larry's name before she turned around? "This is why you kept crossing the boundary? To see Opal?"

"You read the note." Larry loomed over him. "Knew I claimed her."

"Fool!" On his feet now, Adam looked down on his younger brother by a good two inches. "And if you caught a bullet for your sneaking and started a war? You put us all at risk for an infatuation?"

"And you did any different?" Larry threw back his shoulders. "Don't pretend to be righteous now, Adam."

Red hazed his vision as the pieces fell into place. Larry, determined to cross Speck lines. Larry, eager to start a fight over any little thing as a pretext to go over there. Larry, adding the damning extra lines to Pa's threat. Larry, so preoccupied with Opal he didn't mend the fence he should have. His brother's selfishness paved every step of the journey leading to this impossible situation.

Dear God, what if Larry is the father? What am I to do then? How is it Your will that I'm wed to this woman?

"How did you do it, Adam?" Larry's hands fisted, the most prominent vein in his forehead springing to life. "How did you get to her?" A heartbeat of silence then, "If you forced her, I'll kill you."

"I didn't force her." Even through his anger, Adam could see Larry's sincerity.

"Didn't think so." He lowered himself onto his bunk. "So what was it? What made her choose *you*?"

The crimson halo around everything eased away at his brother's disconsolate look. Larry hadn't been with Opal. *My brother isn't the father.*

For a split second, Adam considered sharing a part of the truth—that between Larry's note and Adam's trespassing in search of the missing milk cow, Opal's interference had saved his life. Just as quickly, he rejected the idea. But how to soothe Larry's pride without making things worse? "I saved her life." *And now she's saved mine, but we're far from even.* Adam's jaw tightened. *She owes me a name, for starters.*

"You used that against her?" Larry's head came up like that of an enraged bull. "Held it up as a debt?" The shove, when it came, didn't surprise Adam. "As though she owed herself to you?"

"No." Adam hadn't toppled from the push, but he planted his feet. "There's just a bond that's formed when something like that happens." *Like the way I never forgot how it felt to hold her, even for a few minutes.* "It's not something I can make you understand."

"You don't have to." Larry pointed at his scar. "Opal helped save my life. It's part of what lies between us."

"Part?" A chill crept up the back of his neck.

"Yes." A fervid gleam entered his brother's eye. "Opal and I were destined to be together."

"You *were* together?" There was a sharp note to his question, but Adam had to ask.

Larry's bark of laughter did nothing to ease his mind. A long silence stretched between them, Larry obviously turning over his answer in his head. A hint of triumph rimmed his response. "What do you think?"

I'd rather be anywhere but here, Lord. Opal swallowed back a lump of grief and scooted closer to the edge of the bed, trying not to disturb Willa.

No. That's not true. I want to be home, Father. I want to be in my own bed, listening to the snores of my family. Pete's nasal whistle, Pa's snorts, Elroy's gusty breaths, and Ben's rusty rumble used to keep me awake. Now I can't sleep without them.

The Grogan house was too quiet. Willa, normally a quiet girl, didn't make so much as a peep while she slept. The luxury of having an honest-to-goodness room for just the two of them, not just a corner of the soddy curtained off, only emphasized how alone Opal was.

Only silence filled this home. . .and it seemed to be waiting for something. The weight of expectation pressed upon her chest until Opal could barely squeeze out a breath. Stillness screamed for truth, and she had to keep that locked inside. Because the facts would unleash the conflict she'd fought to suppress for so long.

If I tell Adam there's no child, he'll seek that annulment. He never wanted me as his wife. Strange how a dull pain spread through her at the thought, an odd accompaniment to the fear that followed. *Pa will take umbrage at the insult to me and determine to carry out the sentence he proclaimed against Adam earlier today. Guns will fire before tempers cool. Even if we all make it through the aftermath alive, Pa will never understand, never forgive me for betraying the family and lying to him to save Adam.*

Obviously, that wasn't an option. She tapped her fingers against the cornhusk mattress, eking some small comfort from the familiar rustle. *If I get up now, slip away back home, and confess to Pa, he'll be so angry.* A muffled sob escaped her. *That I lied to save Adam—that I'd go so far to marry him. He'd see it as putting myself in danger. Then he'd go after Adam for agreeing to it. Even if I explained that the note was Larry's, it wouldn't help. The feud would still start up, and I couldn't protect them.*

No matter how she looked at it, there was no solution. Her mind churned, her mouth went dry as though to make up for all the moisture her tears spent, and still, not even the temporary solace of sleep offered escape.

The blue-tinged light of early morning seeped around the doorframe to find her still awake. Her lips stuck together, and surely some great desert had emptied itself in her eyes to make them so raw. She angled out of bed—already hanging so close to the edge she would've had nowhere but air to roll—and stumbled to the washstand.

A woven rug covered the floor, the chilled softness of its bumpy texture a familiar tickle to her toes. The splintering snap when the thin layer of ice on the wash water gave way seemed overly loud to Opal, but the cold wetness of it quenched her thirst and rinsed the grit from her eyes.

"Good morning, Opal." Willa peered over the edge of the blankets.

"Morning, Willa." She simply couldn't bring herself to call it "good." "Hope I didn't disturb you last night."

"Not at all." Her new sister-in-law swung her legs over the side of the bed. "Though it is strange. . ."

"Yes, it is." Opal didn't ask what the other woman referred to. The sudden marriage? Having her here at all? That Adam chose not to sleep with her? With so many options, and none of them flattering, it served no purpose to speculate.

The two women dressed in silence, preparing for the day ahead.

As much as it's possible to prepare. Opal couldn't quite stifle a sigh at the thought but tried to distract herself by making the bed.

"I wish I could tell you today will be easier." Willa fluffed her pillow and hugged it to her chest, ruining her efforts.

"Easy is as easy does, my mother used to say." *Though I've never seen it done.*

"Do you think anyone manages to do that?" She cocked her head to the side. "Make everything easy?"

"No." For the first time in what felt like years, Opal felt the stirrings of a smile. "It wouldn't be fair to the rest of us."

"True!" Willa's giggle faded all too quickly. "Though—" She paused as she reached the door. "Seems to me there's a lot of things that aren't fair."

Don't I know it. The knowledge doused her rising spirits as Opal followed her sister-in-law to the barn, where cows waited. She had to sweet-talk them, take it slow so they'd get used to her, but it wasn't long before she settled into the ages-old rhythm of milking.

With each squirt into the bucket, a regret tugged at Opal's heart. *It isn't fair to my family that I've abandoned them.* The harsh, metallic ring of milk in an empty pail. *Who'll take on my chores?* One insistent, streaming spray after another as she worked faster. *Who'll make sure they're fed enough. . .and what they eat is worth eating?* Finally, the stifled splash signaling a full bucket. *Who'll take care of Pa and my brothers now that I'm not there?*

After she and Willa toted the fresh milk to the Grogan springhouse, they set about gathering eggs.

"We haven't gotten around to the spring cleaning yet," Willa said by way of apology for the smell around the coop. "They've only just begun laying again, so we haven't turned them loose in the farmyard yet. But we'll leave the coop open when we leave. Today's good enough." Willa sidestepped a cock who'd taken exception to their presence. "Watch out for Jackson—he's a flogger."

"I can't abide a flogging rooster." Opal kept her distance.

"Whenever we came across one, he ended up in a pot."

"Or a frying pan." Willa offered one of her shy smiles. "I love fried chicken. But around here, we find use for floggers."

"What other use can there possibly be for foul-tempered fowl?" Something troubled Opal's memory, but she couldn't quite draw it out. Hadn't she heard the Grogans used chickens—

"To chase cows up a hill when they've got the bloat." There was a forced lightness to Willa's tone.

"I see." Opal didn't say another word. Sick cows were a sore topic. Besides, it seemed as though they were headed back to the house.

Lord, help me. I've always liked Willa, but facing another day with the rest of the Grogans— A thought interrupted her, mid-prayer. *Only it's not a day, is it, Lord? With Adam determined to leave me in the house until I spill my secrets, I'll be facing Lucinda and Larry for weeks, even months....*

And suddenly, Opal's stomach couldn't help but give the Grogans more "proof" of her delicate condition.

CHAPTER 14

If that girl takes sick in my vegetable garden, she'll regret it."
Lucinda knew no one heard her mutter, but it made her feel a
little better to say it anyway.

Who wanted to hear the sounds of someone emptying her
stomach of a morning—or anytime. No matter if the girl was
carrying or not.

I didn't toss my turnips over any of my babies. Just went to show
those Specks weren't made of the same stuff as she—and her
children—could claim. *And if I were of a mind to be generous, I'd
even say I understood why Opal would want Adam. My son would
make any woman a fine husband.*

Pity she wasn't in the mood for generosity. She hadn't raised a
fine boy like Adam to be wasted on the likes of Opal Speck. *And
it's not too late.*

All she needed was to get rid of the girl, and her spawn, before
they did any more harm. She brushed away a shiver of unease at
the thought of the baby.

*Despite her weak stomach and Adam's confidence, I'm not
convinced she even carries a babe.* Her paring knife moved more

quickly, a flashing menace in the morning sun. *Even if there is a child, there's no way to vouchsafe it belongs to Adam. You can't trust a hussy.* She'd make short work of the upstart, just the same as she did these potatoes.

Because she had a plan. For the first time in over twenty years, Lucinda hadn't minded her husband's snores. His wheezy grunts hadn't interfered with her sleep one bit.

No, she'd been wide awake, going over ways to make the Speck girl so miserable she'd hightail it before all was lost. If Parson Carter kept his word—and the man saw the wisdom of not crossing the Grogans, though Lucinda would be paying him a visit that morning as a reminder—they had until Sunday before all of Buttonwood would hear of this disaster.

Which meant she had five days to fix things and keep Adam from being ruined. Keep it contained, erase it from existence, make things right. Five days.

Opal would be long gone by then. Of course, running back to her family would be out of the question. *It's not far enough. If she stays close, Adam will go after her. And Larry. . .* Well, Lucinda had enough to deal with already before speculating on what went through her middle son's head. He fancied Opal, too. That much was obvious. How far he'd go and what it would mean for the family—those were paths she didn't want to tread. *Difficulties I won't have to handle if I get rid of the girl. And it shouldn't be too hard, either!*

After a fitful night full of false starts and impossibilities, the solution presented itself early this morning. With her mother gone so young, Opal had been the only woman of the house for most of her life. And Lucinda had seen firsthand the chit's boldness, the way she tried to make decisions for her family, how she talked back to the Grogans. Hadn't she even dared to strike Diggory the day before?

At the very thought, Lucinda's hand slipped, the knife nicking the fleshy part of her palm.

Now look what the brat made me do! A ribbon of red spooled around her wrist before she staunched the flow with a clean rag.

No matter. Lucinda could handle the hard things in life, but Opal. . .she'd given orders for so long, she wouldn't be able to manage when someone else took over. Oh no, the girl didn't have a meek bone in her body. She wouldn't like it one bit when she didn't have her hands on the reins.

But on the Grogan farm, Lucinda ruled. At least. . .in every way that would matter to Opal.

A slow smile spread across her face as she set the first batch of potatoes in the skillet, hearing the hungry crackle of hot grease. It was one of the little things she enjoyed—the sound of doing something right. Every woman learned, sooner or later, that the little things mattered a great deal.

Lucinda looked up as her daughter and the interloper walked through the door.

It was time to teach Opal Speck just how much those little things could add up.

⁓⟨∞⟩⁓

The next morning's wash water splashed on his face as cold as the reality he awoke to. Adam'd always thought mornings were the best part of day, when the world stretched its legs to see what it could accomplish before the sun sank low.

He fought the impulse to sit this one out. Today would be a gamut the likes of which few men deserved to face. As a matter of fact, he'd be hard pressed to come up with the name of even one man meriting a shotgun wedding to his enemy's daughter who carried another child that may or may not belong to his very own brother.

Though Adam didn't see fit to question God's judgment about the necessity of all this, he took exception to the idea he might be that one deserving male.

Which didn't mean the barn would muck itself, or the cattle feed kindly appear in the troughs. The lump in his brother's bunk told him Larry wasn't going to do it.

Obviously he was taking Opal's marriage hard—much harder than Adam could have foreseen. It would be so easy to shake him awake, demand an answer to the question Larry wouldn't answer last night. *Could you be the father?*

As he stared down at the sleeping form of his brother, rage surged through him. "Get up." No response. "I said, *get up.*" He reached out, grabbed hold of Larry's shoulders, and shook. Hard.

"No."

"Tell me how far things went with you and Opal." He hadn't stopped shaking his brother. "Tell me if there's a possibility you're the father of my child."

My child. The words struck a chord, sounded so right that when his brother shook his head, Adam lifted him from the bed by the front of his drawers. *He's threatening everything, and he may just be doing it out of spite.* "Do you have any claim to her?" Dread ripped the words from his throat.

"Yes." Larry shoved his hands away. "More claim than you. I wanted her first."

I doubt it. He'd always noticed Opal, and it had only gotten worse since he carried her from the flames that threatened to take her life. But these were thoughts he'd squashed, things he'd never said, because they'd only do harm. *Not anymore. I won't keep quiet. She's mine now.* "I doubt it." The words seemed to transfer his animosity to Larry.

"Believe it." If his brother were a dog, Adam would have said he bared his teeth. "Opal always looked pretty, but after she helped save my life I realized what truly lay between us."

"A feud?" Adam considered himself too good a man to put down his brother by pointing out Opal's own worthiness would lay between her and Larry ever being anything.

"Destiny." All but vaulting from the bed, Larry shoved his face too close. "We belong together."

"Parson Carter might say different."

"But would Opal?" The sneer cut down Adam's triumph. "Did you ask her? Did she really have a choice about marrying you?"

"Yes." *More of a choice than I did, that's for sure.*

"You lie!" Flicks of spittle flecked from his mouth. "Opal only married you to avoid a feud! She did what was necessary."

"That's—" *possible. More than possible.* The realization stopped him mid-sentence. *Why didn't I consider that she lied about the baby being mine to save my life and spare her family from Pa's vengeance?* Instead, he'd assumed she didn't want to marry the father, or was unable to. The idea she'd fornicated with a married man sat ill, but Adam far preferred it to this option. Had Opal wed him both to stop the feud and because she'd been unable to wed the father of her child, all right. . .because that father was Larry?

"I went after her first."

Larry's shove caught him off-balance in more ways than one, but Adam held his ground. "I saved her life."

"So she could spend it with me." He moved in for another shove. "You aren't God. You can't give and take away what's mine!"

"Is the child yours?" Adam knocked his brother's hands away. "Tell me now or lose your chance."

"How can any man know he's the father of any child with absolute certainty?"

"Opal wouldn't play a man false!" His defense of her erupted before he considered the ramifications. If only Larry wouldn't catch on. . .

"Then why do you ask if I could be the father?" A crafty gleam lit his brother's gaze, but more disturbing was the wild hope behind it. "You say she wouldn't play a man false. . .then you'd know you're the father if you'd claimed her."

"You're not the father." Adam knew it in the way Larry evaded the questions. Assurance settled over him like a blanket.

"No, Adam"—he rocked back on his heels—"*you* aren't. Opal wouldn't play a man false, it's true. And you wanting to know what lies between us shows there's nothing between the two of you. Release her."

"She's my wife." Adam spoke slowly, letting the words drop like stones. "We'll raise our child together, make no mistake."

"No!" The howl pierced his ears. "It's not too late to let her go." Larry's hands scrabbled at Adam's collar. "Give her back to me. She doesn't belong with you, and no matter what you say, you know it. You can't fool me!"

"I don't have to." Adam turned and headed for the door. "You're fooling yourself if you think I'd set aside my wife." *Not without anything less than absolute proof you sired the babe in her belly. And you want her so badly, you would have told me immediately if that were the case.*

His step lighter, he headed for the barn. But by the time he arrived, not even the familiar scents of animals and hay could lift his spirits.

Larry didn't say he wasn't or couldn't be the father. He said no man could know for sure. . .which would be true if he thought Opal and I were together, as well. He recalled the fervent gleam of hope in his brother's gaze when he noticed Adam's slip. *The triumph in his voice when he announced I wasn't the father. . . Can I really be sure it's not because he just learned the woman he loves hadn't betrayed him?*

And if that's so, can I keep them apart?

CHAPTER 15

"What are you doing here?" Opal could scarcely keep the question in until she and Midge were out of sight of the house.

"Who would believe me if I told them you greeted me at the Grogan farm, and *you* asked me what *I'm* doing here?" Her friend's grin all but demanded an answering smile. "Anyone in Buttonwood would tell me the world's gone mad and taken us along for the jaunt!"

"I'll not complain that our jaunt takes me away from Lucinda." Opal's voice lowered despite the distance they'd covered. "But what did you tell Clara and Saul about where you were headed, and why?"

Does the whole town know of my hasty wedding? Parson Carter promised not to breathe a word, instead allowing the "happy couple" to announce the "glad news" at a time of their choosing, but better plans had failed.

"We need more honey for the store, so I hurried up and volunteered to visit you." Midge winked broadly, with the complete lack of ladylike decorum that Pete swore made her so appealing.

"Can't abide a woman who puts on airs." Opal's heart clenched at

the memory of her younger brother in happier days. Pete probably stayed at home now, saddled with the lion's share of her chores.

"Of course, Clara wanted to come along, but little Maddie's fussy over teething, and I reminded her she'd had a nice long visit with you earlier this week when I was at the Warrens'. So it's my turn." The laughter faded from her face. "She didn't need to know the other part—that she wouldn't find you if she headed to the Speck farm. I know you're not telling folks yet about. . . everything."

A hard swallow and a nod were all Opal could offer her friend, whose gaze held a shrewdness that made her uncomfortable. Midge had never been a typical young girl, and Opal couldn't shrug away the feeling she saw more than she should even now.

"Which is, of course, why I've come."

Because I haven't told you everything? Opal bit her lip. There was no chance she could confide in Midge the full, sorry truth about what she'd done. Her chest ached at her own betrayal. *I can't tell her what Adam thinks I've done, either.* Pain streaked upward, intensifying the ache. *Or what the Grogans think of me.* The heat of anger burned away some of her remorse.

The sight and sounds of her apiary further dispelled some of the gloom that had settled around her heart since the day before. No matter how much it seemed the world had come crashing down about her ears, her bees disproved her self-centered fancy.

All around them, thousands of striped workers went about their business. Springtime meant a flurry of comb-making and scouting, each colony focusing on the home containing its entire existence. Each hive a self-contained, well-run world unto itself.

In those small worlds, so tight knit and busy, everyone had a role to play. Tasks to perform. A purpose among all their relations.

Oh God. The now-familiar thickness of impending tears clogged her throat. The memory of her father denying her, refusing to acknowledge her as part of their family sloughed at her soul. *"Not anymore."* Two words robbed her of her home, leaving her nothing and no one to call hers.

Oh God. Opal couldn't seem to get past the pained cry to the Father she knew hadn't abandoned her. The only one she could still claim. *Oh God. . .* Nothing more came. No way to express the need within her save the simple supplication of calling His name, a constant cry within her heart.

I can't ask Him to take it all away, undo my mistakes. There are so many. Too many. . .

She should have held back after Larry's accident—mentioned the ice to Clara and left it alone. Instead, she'd jumped at the chance to help Dr. Reed. Now look where her foolish hopes that their families could lay aside old differences under new kindnesses had gotten her!

Maybe she could have told Elroy about Larry's increasing attentions, have her brother put a bug in Grogan's ear and keep him away. But she'd been too afraid of sparking the feud.

At the very least, she shouldn't have let Adam keep the threat she'd found in this very apiary. A chill of guilt stole over her as she remembered the moment Pete drew the thrice-cursed thing from Adam's pocket. Resignation dimmed his handsome features. He'd known in that instant, just as she had, that he may as well have been carrying his own death decree.

Why, oh why didn't I insist on burning it immediately? Without that final piece of damning "evidence" against him, Adam might have suffered nothing more than bruises and bluster at the hands of her family for his trespassing. Instead, the die was cast.

Because she'd do anything to protect her family—even marry Adam. And her family would do anything to protect her. *Even if it meant letting me do it.*

If the scenario weren't so dire, the irony would have made her laugh. Even for someone as practiced at finding the bright spot in any situation as Opal, the search turned up nothing to make her smile. The thought flitted across her mind that she'd managed to keep her family safe, but too many threats loomed over that accomplishment like a Sword of Damocles for her to take any comfort in it.

Though Adam didn't know it, he could still annul the marriage. Lucinda, for all her silence this morning, hadn't accepted the wedding yet—her lack of chatter spoke of schemes to instill foreboding. No, the victory she'd won yesterday—if Opal could call losing her family, her freedom, and the respect of everyone she'd ever met in one fell swoop any sort of victory—constituted a minor skirmish.

She looked over her shoulder, knowing she wouldn't see the Grogan farm, nor any of her new in-laws, but unable to quell the impulse. Opal held back a sigh at the thought of battles and ambushes she'd face for years to come.

Oh God, she finally found the words she needed, *give me strength to make it through this war!*

≈≈≈∞≈≈≈

Midge waited. She didn't mind letting Opal sort through her thoughts while they stood surrounded by the energy of the hives. Their restlessness matched something inside her, made her feel like she didn't have to move so much when other critters were so busy.

Normally, though, she wasn't very good at waiting. Anyone who ever met her could tell in a blink that patience wasn't her strongest virtue.

Come to think of it, she wasn't all too sure she showed particular strength in any of the virtues. *No, that can't be right. I'm a good person. There's got to be one. . . .*

Patience got chucked from the list right away, but there were a heap of others to pick from, weren't there? Like peace. Peace definitely ranked as a virtue. *Nope. Sitting still chafes me something awful.* She crossed peace off the possibilities.

Wasn't mercy on there, too? Midge wrinkled her nose. To her way of thinking, justice trumped mercy any day. People lied, cheated, hurt others all the time and got away with it. They deserved to be *punished.* But she didn't remember justice being on the list. As a matter of fact, she couldn't quite recall what the other virtues were supposed to be.

Sure hope memory isn't one of them. I ought to ask Aunt Doreen about it later. I'm running out of options. Funny how that gave her a sinking feeling. *Me not having any virtues fits in with that whole idea I had about my prayers not being good enough.*

But what's the use in being good enough if I can't be me anymore? Saul and Clara kept trying to lead her to God, but something deep inside Midge balked. Because when it came down to it, if she let Jesus in, it sounded like there wouldn't be any room left for Midge. *And it's been real hard making sure I got this far.*

She started pacing. This was why she didn't like staying still— left a body too much room to think about things that didn't do anyone any good. *Seems to me that "not giving up" ought to be on that list of virtues.* She perked up at the thought. *Maybe that's the problem! I'm going by someone else's list. I ought to make my own—just fill in some important things those folks long ago forgot.*

Who knew? Maybe if it was on a list, it would matter more. And then she'd be closer to being good enough....

"Oh, Midge!" Opal's voice jerked her away from the trap of her thoughts. "I didn't mean to ignore you. Here you've been so quiet..."

"We both had a lot on our minds," she shrugged away the discomfort. "You more'n me, that's for sure."

Now that Opal was ready to talk, she wouldn't let a minute

go to waste. "Lucinda has it in for me." Opal settled on the safest topic. "She stayed almost completely silent all morning."

"That's scary," Midge couldn't help but agree. Lucinda Grogan simply didn't do quiet. "You've got trouble on your hands if she's thinking that hard. She's bound to turn up something you don't want her to."

"What do you mean" The quick-fire response told her Opal hid more than one secret.

"We both know your new mama-in-law has a nose for unpleasant tidbits and a habit for sharing them." They strolled through the rows of hives, the whitewashed boxes gleaming in spring sunshine. "You marrying Adam will bring out the worst in her."

"There's nothing she can do about it." The declaration lacked strength.

"Depends on what she finds." Time to put away the kid gloves and work the truth out of Opal. "Folks give away a lot without saying a word, without ever meaning to or knowing they've done it. And Lucinda will be looking."

"What do you think she'll find?" The scoff showed bravado, but her friend's fear seeped through.

"Cut line, Opal." Midge grabbed her hand and plunked down in an inviting spot. "Lucinda will have you under her thumb, watching you squirm until you give up something she can use. And we both know it's only a matter of time because you're too good and too honest to keep up a pretense for very long."

"Pretense?"

"If you're going to dodge reality, do it with someone else, Opal. I know you better, and I know you don't have the time to waste trying to fool me."

"What do you think you know?" Apprehension settled like a death mask across her friend's features.

"You're not going to make Adam a father, for one thing." No sense sugarcoating it.

"Midge Collins, if you even think about suggesting that I'm about to bear the child of another man, you can march yourself straight back to town and. . .and. . ." Tears burbled out the rest of whatever Opal tried to say.

"So that's what Lucinda's been on about, eh?" Midge slung an arm around her friend's shoulders and let out a satisfying snort. "Featherbrain."

"Then you don't think—"

"There's a better chance baby Maddie could sing opera. I should've seen it coming that the Grogans would accuse you of something like that the instant they heard you've a little one on the way."

"Don't care." Opal let loose a long mumble into her handkerchief that sounded oddly like "Schack dig he four sane it."

Which, of course, made absolutely no sense. But when Midge told Opal so, her friend lifted her head with a stubborn glower to declare—quite clearly this time—

"He deserved it!"

"Who des—" and suddenly it fell into place. "You smacked Diggory for saying it!" Midge tried to choke back her laughter but just ended up choking. When she got her wind back, she managed, "Good for you!"

"I shouldn't have struck him." Now that she'd finished defending her actions, Opal looked properly penitent. "He's my elder, and when we're angry, we're supposed to turn the other cheek."

"Oh, good." Midge leaned back and grinned. "I hope he did that, then. That way, you could get him again!"

❧◦◦◦◦❧

"She's got spunk," Pa grunted, raking the dried stalks of last year's corn into windrows. "I'll give your new wife that much."

"Don't I know it." Adam searched for a way to shift the conversation to the topic most on his mind while his father seemed inclined to be amiable and Larry worked clear on the other side of the field.

A devilish grin creased his face. "And you nabbing her has got to be giving old Murphy absolute fits. That's not to be discounted. Especially when the dupe can't do a thing about it!"

"That's not why I married her." He pushed prickly, dried out husks of plants into more orderly piles, trying to organize his thoughts.

"Naw." Pa whipped his hat off and fanned his face with it. "You married her because you found yourself on the wrong end of a shotgun."

"That's not what I meant." *But it's truer than you can ever imagine.*

"Doesn't matter what you meant. Things happen when a man lets a pretty face overrule his common sense." He slapped his hat back on. "I'm sure you didn't mean to get her in the family way either."

Adam held his peace on that one. The truth—that he absolutely was *not* responsible for Opal's predicament—would only get his family hopping mad. Ugly accusations would be flung, honor defended, shots fired. . .and lives lost.

"Didn't think you had it in you, son." Pa resumed raking. "Takes gumption to go after something like that. I'd wondered if Larry's sneaking hadn't been headed that direction, but never so much as suspected you'd be the fox in the Speck henhouse."

"You thought Larry might be after Opal, and you didn't stop it?" Splinters dug into his palms from where he gripped the handle of his rake, but Adam ignored them. "You'd let him prey on a vulnerable woman, just because of her last name?"

"Give your brother some credit. The Grogan men have always had a way with the ladies." Pa straightened. "Glad to see it didn't pass you by, that's all."

"Oh, yeah." He covered his irritation by moving to a new row. "I'm a real charmer." *Can't even get my own wife to tell me the name of her baby's father.*

"Must've been more charming than your brother. He's had his nose out of joint since you brought her back."

But what if I didn't? What if Larry got to her first, and I just stumbled into a wedding? His mouth went so dry, he drained his canteen. It didn't help.

"Of course, that spunk of hers is going to cause problems. She and your ma are going to butt heads like two old goats."

"My thoughts exactly." Adam seized the opportunity. "Ma and Opal will be at each other's throats as long as they live under the same roof."

"We'll manage." Pa gave the refuse a particularly vicious jab. "Somehow."

"I'll need to build us a home. Wood's too scarce, so it'll be a soddy or dugout. The question is where?"

"Your inheritance, you mean?" Pa propped himself up on his rake. "As the oldest, you're supposed to inherit the house. But I'm a long way from kicking the bucket, so you'll need a place to set up for your own."

"Yes. I was thinking the southeast meadow. Make a dugout from that knoll. It'd be the quickest way." Adam laid out his plan. "I wouldn't neglect my responsibilities on the farm."

"Never thought you would." Pa fingered his beard, an avaricious light entering his gaze. "You think we could get the delta land out of Murphy as Opal's dowry?"

"Her apiary is her dowry." He could scarcely get the words out fast enough. The land that birthed the feud would have no part in his marriage. "It's part of why I said the southeast meadow—the far end of it would be a good place to move her bees. The conditions seem about the same."

"Bees?" Pa's swarthy skin lost some of its sun-fed color. "She's bringing her bees to our farm?"

"Yep." Adam appealed to the one thing he knew outweighed Pa's hesitation over the insects—his practicality. "The hives and honey they produce are valuable—good income even when crops fail. And real beeswax candles are a luxury out here, too."

"Once you're situated, just keep them—and your wife—as far from the homestead as possible."

CHAPTER 16

Midge!" Opal gasped at the audacity of such a statement, but a smile snuck toward the corners of her mouth.

"Ah, there it is." Midge pointed, completely unrepentant. "The hint of a smile. That's what I hoped for!"

"Trickster." Her reprimand held no heat. "I should tell you that's no excuse for being so outrageous, but since it worked that would make me a hypocrite."

Hypocrite. The reminder stole away what little merriment Midge brought. *Liar. And so many other things I never would have wanted.*

"I know you're going to feel bad about giving Mr. Grogan what for," her friend's voice called back her attention, "but he had no right—and no cause—to accuse you of tricking his son into marriage with another man's child."

"Didn't he?" *I did trick him. And Adam knows full well I'm not carrying his child. So do I have just cause for my indignation?* "I mean, he doesn't know me." She tacked on this last to deflect Midge's curious glance.

"That's not what you meant."

"Oh?"

"No." Midge shifted, resting back on her knees to look her in the eye. "You meant that Diggory hit closer to the truth than he knew, because you aren't carrying Adam's child."

"How can you say that?" Something tore inside her at her friend's casual dismissal. "I thought you said they were featherbrains for believing that!"

"Listen better. I said they're featherbrains for thinking you might be carrying another man's child." A pause. "Not that they were knocked in the noggins for thinking you didn't have Adam's."

"Oh." The astuteness of Midge's assessment stunned her into silence for a precious moment before she rallied. "Well, that's what they think!"

"Forget what they think. You're trying to distract me from what I know." The younger girl settled back on her heels and crossed her arms. "And doing a poor job of it."

"What makes you think I'm not carrying Adam's babe?" Anger pulsed through Opal. "If you didn't believe it, why didn't you object at the wedding?"

"I didn't know until after, what with the pair of you all set to say 'I do.'" Midge shrugged. "Besides, there was the small matter of four Speck shotguns trained on Adam's head and other vitals. I figured you made up the whole thing to save his life."

"It wasn't fair of me to expect you to try and stop it." Opal rubbed a hand over her eyes, not sure whether to be glad someone saw her good intentions for what they were or be even more sorrowful it hadn't been Adam. "Wait. What do you mean you didn't know until after?"

"The kiss."

"It's normal for a groom to kiss his bride." Opal ignored the heat in her cheeks, focusing instead on the prickle of the prairie grass poking against her skirts. She shifted, trying to evade the discomfort.

"Nothing about that wedding came within an acre of normal. And there you go again, blushing just like yesterday. You looked so flustered at having his arms around you, I'd say it's a minor miracle no one else figured out that you two couldn't be lovers."

"What?" *Adam didn't notice my innocence. Why would anyone else?*

"You're my friend, and you're in trouble." Midge narrowed her eyes. "So stop beating around the bush and admit you're as pure as fresh cream butter."

"Midge!"

"All right, all right." Her friend held up her hands, palms out. "At least you were at your wedding yesterday, even if you're a fully married woman now."

"Stop it." Opal looked away. *Adam didn't want me because he thinks I'm used. And he knows I lied to him, even though he doesn't know which lie.* "Just stop it."

"If you and Adam both agree to say the same thing"—Midge let loose a *whoosh* of breath Opal couldn't miss—"it's not too late to have this thing annulled. People twist the truth all the time for worse reasons. Even if last night—"

"No!" Opal's head snapped back to her friend so fast she heard a faint popping sound. "If we annul the marriage, our families will kill each other. Pa won't take the slur to my honor, and the Grogans will be up in arms over my lying about Adam's character. It's too late to make things right."

Not even Midge had anything to say to that. An uncharacteristic silence fell between them, Opal pondering the impossible situation once more and coming up with nothing new.

"So what's Adam say about this whole mess?"

"Don't ask."

"Too late. I asked." Midge's eyes narrowed. "I'll even ask again, if you make me."

"Adam. . ." Opal couldn't really find the words. *How does a woman tastefully say that her husband thinks she's hoodwinked him into raising another man's illegitimate offspring?* She gave up. "Adam wants me to tell him who the father really is."

"What!" Midge sprang to her feet. "But Opal, this changes *everything*!"

Silence, Midge felt fairly certain, didn't register on that roster of virtues. Good thing, too, because when she got excited, her mind started going a mile a minute. It only seemed natural that her mouth tried its best to keep up.

Like now.

"Of all the addlepated mistakes!" Trampling the earth between the rows of hives set loose an ominous hum, so she forced herself to slow down. "But there's your solution. All you have to do is tell Adam that you made the whole thing up to save his life, and you'll have the makings of a fine marriage. Most women would jump at the chance to have a grateful husband!"

"I can't." The muffled tones of her friend's voice made Midge turn around to see Opal's legs drawn to her chest, her forehead resting on her knees. "Adam took me as his bride, but he hasn't made me his wife."

"Obviously." Midge flopped down next to her friend. "Otherwise there wouldn't be a snowman's chance on a sunny day he'd still think you carried any man's child."

Her friend's ears, the only part of her visible, turned scarlet.

Midge knew from past observation the color stained Opal's cheeks, as well. Another option occurred to her. "Opal, when I said before that you and Adam could get an annulment if you just said the same thing, it's true. You wouldn't even have to tell a falsehood." The rush of possibility carried her away again. "If you're unhappy about this whole thing, I'll never breathe a word. You can prove that the marriage wasn't consummated, and Parson Carter will dissolve it. And you know that for as nice as he is, his liver's whiter than a lily. He won't cross your family or the Grogans. It can be like that wedding never even happened, if that's what you want!"

"No!" When Opal yanked on her wrist, Midge realized she'd started heading toward town. "It won't happen like that. The Grogans will challenge Pa for slandering Adam's good name on my say-so. Not to mention threatening to kill him. The whole thing will backfire."

"And it hasn't already?" Midge shook loose. "You're stuck over there with no one to help you. I always thought Adam was the Grogan with enough brain between his ears to make a respectable rattle, but with him foolish enough to think you're expecting, I'm revising my opinion."

"So long as Pa and my brothers stay alive, I can live with the Grogans." Determination glinted in Opal's blue eyes. "It's more than worth the trade."

"Do you think they'd agree?"

"Pa, Ben, Elroy, and Pete will never find out." The barest breath of a pause. "And I don't care whether most of the Grogans would agree. Adam's alive, and I'll be as good a wife to him as I can—even though he doesn't want me."

"Don't be so sure." Memories of Adam cradling Opal to his chest for a beat too long after carrying her from the fire surged to the front of Midge's mind. "He saved you once, too."

"Because he's a good man." Sadness covered her friend's face like a thick blanket. "He deserves better."

"Good gravy and grits, it must be something catching!" She waved a hand before Opal's eyes as though to test her focus. "One day at the Grogan farm and your wits went dull."

"Stop it." The chide couldn't mask a quick grin.

"There is no better than you, Opal. Adam's a lucky man. He'll figure it out sooner or later, but the sooner the better."

"Any way to help hasten the realization? I'm out of ideas." Her friend gave a gusty sigh. "Though considering my ideas so far, that may be a blessing."

"You'll balk at it."

"After yesterday, you'd be surprised."

"All right." Midge tilted her head so she could see Opal's reaction. "Even if you're not going to go to Parson Carter, why don't you tell Adam the truth about your. . .er, status? My guess is he'll be real glad to hear it, and maybe you two could have a long and happy marriage. . . ."

Midge's voice trailed off as Opal shook her head faster and harder until her bonnet went flying right off. "Impossible!" she gasped. "I can't tell Adam I've never been with a man!"

"Don't get missish on me now." A thump on her friend's back stopped her gasping and started up some spluttering. "It can't be harder to tell your husband you're a good woman than to have him thinking you're some sort of Jezebel."

Midge went quiet after that. Memories of her own past cut off her words like a knife to the throat. Luckily, Opal'd found her ability to speak again.

"I don't mean because it would be awkward!" Her face, a pinkish scarlet, clashed terribly with the fiery wisps of hair dancing around her face. "Even if it would be the most embarrassing thing on earth—and I'm sure it would—I'd get through it if I thought it would make things better. But if I tell Adam I'm still pure, he'll be the one to call for Parson Carter quicker than I can blink!"

"No he won't. He married you and didn't tell his family that the child he thinks you're carrying isn't his. He won't start the bloodbath for the opposite reason."

"You'd think so." Opal buried her face in her sodden hanky. "But he told me on the way to meet his family he'd already considered an annulment, but it wasn't possible without proof."

"So you can't tell him you have proof."

"Never."

At least, that's what Midge assumed Opal meant. Things went pretty watery again. Well then, an indelicate question couldn't make things any worse. "Do you know when he plans to take his wedding night?"

"Yes." A mighty sniff and a few bleary blinks, then Opal got to the crux of the problem. "Adam says he won't make it a real marriage until after I trust him enough to tell him the name of the father."

Well, that's a fine mess.

"And you can't make up a name because it was winter, and there was no one around but the people in town." She turned the problem around in her head. "So you can't tell him the truth, and you can't make up a lie. . . ."

"I'm stuck, all right." Opal patted her apron pockets for another hanky, accepting the one Midge passed her. "And it's only a matter of time before Lucinda, for one, realizes I'm not showing."

"Hmmmm." Midge flipped the problem over and looked underneath for any hidden solutions. There, in the shadows of her past—the knowledge no proper young lady should have—lurked the germ of an idea. "Opal?" She considered how best to suggest the unthinkable.

"What?" A miserable, wet *honk* punctuated the question.

"You only have one option left."

"There's another option?" Opal's eyes widened. "If it's not annulment and it's not slandering the name of an innocent townsman, I'll do whatever I have to do."

Oh, how easily the innocent are led astray. . .but that's exactly what we'll be counting on.

"Neither of those." Midge took a deep breath and summoned a confident smile. "You're just going to seduce your husband."

CHAPTER 17

"There you are!" Lucinda pounced the moment Opal returned from her outing with that uppity Midge Collins. "Should've known you planned to waste half the morning yapping away with your friend when there's work to be done." A broad gesture encompassed her spotless home.

She took pride in her housekeeping, as any good wife and mother ought to, but it didn't serve her plans to flaunt the fact to her new daughter-in-law. A dull pain flared in her midsection, a rejection of Opal's new role.

No matter. She won't be here for long.

"I'll be happy to lend a hand wherever needed." The upstart even managed to say it with a straight face.

Lucinda tucked away the proof of the girl's prowess at lying. "Happy to help, eh?" She drew out the word "happy," as though testing it and finding it false. Which, of course, she did.

"I thought I'd show Opal around today, Ma." Willa's hasty offer earned her a scowl. "Show her where we keep things, how the machines work since there are bound to be differences."

"Perhaps some other time, dear." She casually walked behind

the girls and made a show of looking out the open door. "It's such a fine day. Don't you think it's a fine day, Opal? You've seen enough of it to be certain."

"Very fine." At least the girl knew enough not to argue.

"Well, with a beautiful day and three women working, I'd think it's a perfect time to begin spring cleaning!" She sprang the trap shut with military precision. "Just think how much you'll learn about this household, Opal." With an effort, she kept her smile from being too wolfish.

Oh, you'll learn. You'll learn to rue the day you looked twice at my son. You'll learn that I can make your back ache and your eyes tear and your hands bleed before I'm through. But most of all, you'll learn that there isn't a place in Buttonwood far enough from this farm—that it's best to leave the Nebraska Territory altogether.

"Spring cleaning?" Apprehension laced her daughter's brow. "What did you have in mind, Ma?"

"Whatever needs to be done, I'll see to it." Opal's stiff neck brought her that much closer to being broken.

"Everything calls for a washing, of course." Lucinda started small. "The rugs beaten, the bedding and quilts laundered, the mattresses re-stuffed, and the stove needs a thorough scrubbing."

"Where do you want to start?" The girl's words could have been deferential had they come from another woman. Instead, they sounded a challenge.

"I've dinner going, so the stove will keep until tomorrow." She kept her tone light, trying not to let any triumph creep in. "And, of course, it's too late to begin laundry. Might be a good time to see about stuffing the mattresses."

"With both of us working, we can finish today," Willa offered.

No, no, no. Willa's not supposed to spend time with the girl. This isn't an opportunity to make nice or help her be comfortable. She's supposed to be hot and burdened with the dry, itchy work. "Willa, I'd thought perhaps you could see to—"

"Showing her where we keep the dried husks in the barn?" Willa already headed out the door. "This way, Opal."

Lucinda held her peace as they left. Even with Willa's help, Opal would have to work through the morning and the entire afternoon to see the job done.

Then, tomorrow, Lucinda could begin making the small comments about restless sleep, tossing and turning. About cricks in her back and neck and hard stalks poking her through the mattress—jabs that shouldn't happen if the job were done right. Unless, of course, Opal had meant for it to?

Because working the girl into exhaustion wasn't enough to bring the type of misery Lucinda intended. For that type of despair, she'd need to take away Adam's support of his new bride. Which suited her just fine.

Lucinda shoved away a twinge of guilt.

It's not bearing false witness. I'm just speeding things up so Adam realizes the type of girl he's chained to in time to make a difference. If she stayed, he'd find out that it's all true. He'd just find out too late.

Opal didn't like whiners. Complaining didn't make work any easier, quicker, or more pleasant. It might be good for letting off steam, but the only other thing it accomplished was to make a body seem lazy, weak, petty, snobby, or spoiled. In short, all the things Grogans were raised to believe Specks succumbed to. She'd rather wear shoes two sizes too small than complain. In fact, she point-blank refused to do it.

Aloud, at least.

Within the confines of her own mind, however, she allowed herself to acknowledge her suspicions that Lucinda thought up the day's activity as a punishment for daring to marry Adam. Opal slept on one of these mattresses just the night before and saw no urgent need for re-stuffing.

I didn't actually sleep, her innate sense of fairness pointed out. *But that didn't matter. It could have been a bed made for a queen and I wouldn't have slept last night!*

The edge of the mattress she and Willa lugged outside late this morning had struck her as perfectly comfortable the night before. Together, they managed to heft it in a bulky fold over the Grogans' sturdy wash line. It sagged toward the ground, lumpy as the corn husks inside slowly shifted toward the earth.

"Just a minute." Willa darted toward the barn and came back moments later carrying a horse blanket, which she spread underneath. "This'll make it easier to carry the old out to the compost heap."

"Right." Opal already started cutting through the threads stitching shut the reinforced cotton. In no time they were scooping armfuls of the crinkly old bedding onto the horse blanket.

It took a couple of trips to the compost heap before they'd emptied it completely. Then they turned the entire thing inside out and took turns beating the empty covering until dust and debris danced in the air. By that time, bits of the dried material tickled her throat, scratched her arms, and clung to her dress, but it couldn't be avoided.

Opal didn't hold with vanity but knew full well that she presented a poor picture the moment Lucinda chose to ring the dinner bell. In addition to the dried bits of plant, she'd taken the last shift with the rug beater, so moisture from the heat of the work dotted her brow and made errant locks of her hair stick to her temples.

Willa, having rested for a few moments and even washed up at the well, looked a far sight better as the men came in from the fields. If it weren't so completely absurd, Opal would suspect

Lucinda waited until she looked her worst to summon Adam—to show him what a horror he'd married. *You're just going to seduce your husband.* Midge's brilliant solution of that morning echoed in her mind. As though it hadn't seemed a ridiculous suggestion before.

"I better go see if Ma needs any help." Willa hurried to the house.

Opal put her frustrations into the last few whacks of the rug beater until she was satisfied that the mattress cover, at least, classified as clean. She raised her arm to swipe back a few hairs with the back of her hand.

The Grogan men trouped behind her to the well, the sounds of water splashing intensifying the tickle in Opal's throat. She hesitated to follow, instead hanging back until they'd all gone inside. Then, she made hasty work of rinsing her arms and face, patting them dry with her slightly scratchy apron front before rolling down her sleeves and heading for the house.

It took a moment for her eyes to adjust to the dark interior of the soddy after the bright noon sun. When she could see, Opal paused. Diggory sat at the head of the table, Lucinda, Willa, and Dave to his left, Adam to his right. But Larry sat on Adam's other side, leaving the foot of the table the only open space.

The clear message as to her low status in the eyes of the family carried the extra unpleasant touch of sticking her beside Larry. But more than anything, the fact Adam supported the arrangement left her adrift.

"Looks like she's stopped dawdling." Dave, the young boy who'd spent a lazy morning fishing, greeted her arrival with a scowl that would have made Lucinda proud.

It must have. She wore one to make a matching set. "Now that you've graced us with your presence, take a seat. I'll tell you we won't wait dinner on you again. If you expect to enjoy the bounty of my husband's table, remember that we don't tolerate laziness on *this* farm."

Opal didn't feel the itch of tiny pieces of corn husk in her mouth anymore. Instead, the insistent clawing of hot words tore at her throat. She swallowed them.

"Ma! Opal finished beating that mattress while I came in to help set the table." Willa's unexpected defense soothed her just enough to make speech possible.

"I'll remember." She forced a smile and moved toward Adam. "I know how hard *my* husband works on *our* behalf."

"Larry," Adam all but barked his brother's name, "why have you still not moved?" His words sent hope piercing through her.

"Because he is my son." Diggory's bushy brows now lowered. "And his place at my table won't be usurped. That gal is not a Grogan, and her place is at the foot of this family. She should just be thankful it's not beneath it!"

"You speak of my wife." Adam rose to his feet. "Her place is by my side." Without another word, he plunked *himself* at the foot of the table.

Opal's eyes went wide.

"Adam!" Lucinda all but shrieked. "What foolishness is this?"

"The foolishness of a family who cares more for past grudges than current commitments." For the first time, as Adam set his jaw and glared around the table, Opal acknowledged his resemblance to the rest of his kin. "If you deny my wife her place, you deny me mine. Larry, move up."

Silence stalked every person at the table, from Dave's unhinged jaw to Diggory's too-tight one. But no one made a move.

"Now!" The sudden explosion of Adam's order made Larry jump.

He didn't move much to the side—but it was enough. Opal slipped onto the bench, hanging off it really but seated next to the man who'd made her his priority.

My husband. The thought humbled her. *Perhaps. . .just perhaps, this could work, after all?*

"Don't think I've forgotten," Adam's murmur, so low no one else at the table even heard it, caught her off guard, "that yesterday you told me to ask tomorrow. I'll be expecting my answer."

Though it seemed years ago instead of just the day before, Opal knew he meant to ask her the name of the father. Again.

She stifled a sigh and passed the biscuits.

Then again, maybe not.

CHAPTER 18

Another morning dawned, making Adam a man with a marriage almost two days old—not long by any standards. The measure grew shorter when one considered they slept in different beds. In different buildings. He fought back a wince.

Lord, You know full well why I had to make that *decision. Not only would Ma raise hue and cry if I booted Larry from the barn and installed Opal with me, it'd be akin to a fasting man surrounding himself with his favorite foods. Leaving the temptation untouched, the hunger unfulfilled, would be next to impossible.*

Besides, Adam never intended his wife—no matter how convoluted that story came to be—would live in a barn annex. Shotgun wedding didn't mean slapdash home, and he'd already laid the groundwork for their own place by talking with Pa yesterday. Now, all he needed to do was get Opal to trust him enough that they could move forward with this marriage.

At the moment, he got on with the morning chores. Larry's turn to do the mucking meant he moved forward with the feeding—the far better rotation. He grabbed two big, tightly woven baskets and headed to the silage pit behind the barn. The fragrant corn fodder, chopped up and left to ferment, made a moist and heavy feed the cows loved.

The rich scent of it mixed the sour tang of buttermilk—though none went into making silage—with the sweetness of corn. Adam figured he liked the smell as much as the cows did. But filling the baskets and emptying a hefty measure in the manger before each stanchion left a man with time to think.

And Adam's thoughts were full of his new wife. He'd watched her with Larry the day before enough to be certain Opal didn't return his brother's interest. If anything, she kept as far away as possible. That meant there wasn't any real impediment to the marriage. Sure, his family didn't accept her, but that would take time. *Time, I have.*

Daisy followed him eagerly to the watering tank, the great horse lowering her head to take deep drafts. Water splashed down her long throat, fascinating Adam as it always had.

God's imagination knows no bounds. So the unthinkable to us— that Opal and I should be man and wife—may well be as practical and beautiful as anything else in this world. How am I to know? After all, they'd only been married for two days. Not long enough to make the marriage real, but long enough for Adam to learn a few very important things he hadn't suspected about Opal Speck—make that Opal *Grogan*. He liked the sound of that.

Her temper rivaled any in her family. She just kept better control of it. Opal hadn't come to this farm and set up a sulk, either. She pitched in and, despite the situation, didn't complain. But, other than the revelation she didn't harbor a secret love for his brother, Adam's most important discovery was that his intriguing little wife had a determined streak that could out-stubborn a mule. And she'd focused it on avoiding him.

Oh, he had no questions as to why she kept as far away from him as possible. She'd begun that little dance just after dinner the day before, following his reminder that they were due a certain conversation. Which went to show that forewarned definitely made an intelligent woman forearmed.

How else to explain how Opal, who'd scarcely set foot on Grogan property aside from community events in years past, developed such a staggering specialty in slinking around unseen? Her newfound ability made his father nervous. Adam would have found it amusing, if it weren't so aggravating.

Which, come to think of it, pretty much sums up Opal. Too bad— It's her turn for a little aggravation!

He'd known Opal would be along to help Willa with the morning milking. And now she couldn't hie off or pretend she hadn't heard him call. A slow grin spread across his face when she spotted him and shot a quick look toward the door.

"Mornin', Opal." He banged shut the lid on the oat bin and finished with feeding the horses. "I want a word."

"Oh?" She snatched a three-legged stool and milk pail, making a beeline for the nearest cow. She set them both down, working them into the layers of hay and settling herself on the stool in less time than Adam would have thought possible, given her skirts. "What about?"

"A *private* word." He put a staying hand on her shoulder before she began milking the beast and would have good reason not to stop.

"Willa and I need to do the milking." Her feigned innocence would have put suspicion in the softest heart. "I take my responsibilities seriously, Adam."

"Your first responsibility lies with your husband."

"Go ahead, Opal." Willa's voice came from the next cow, where she sat milking. "I've milked these cows by myself for years."

"But"—his wife's anxiety came across as true—"I don't want your mother to say I'm shirking."

"Then stop dragging your heels." He shoved back a twinge of guilt over how Ma had been treating her. There'd be an adjustment period until he had their dugout set up. "Come on." Adam slid his hand beneath her elbow and braced her until she stood, reluctantly walking with him into the crisp chill of the morning.

He led her a good distance from the barn, making sure no one would overhear their conversation. Every step chafed at him, wearing his patience a little thinner, until he turned to her. He didn't bother wasting a word, just raised a brow, waiting. Now that he'd gotten her alone, she'd have to spit out the truth.

She didn't spit out anything. As a matter of fact, Opal didn't even look at him. Her gaze traced rolling patterns in the clouds, her breath came in nervous little hums he almost found endearing. But not a word crossed her lips.

"Opal. . ." He spoke her name slow and low. It was half invitation to tell him what he wanted to know, half warning if she didn't.

"Yes, Adam?" She blinked, her smile too bright.

"I suggest you start talking, wife."

"Wife. . ." The term seemed to galvanize her. "Yes, husband. We've much to discuss."

At last.

"I've several concerns, Adam." Pain clouded her gaze. "I've no right to ask, but I—" A hard swallow cut off her words, like she choked back strong emotion.

It struck him, suddenly, how fragile she was. Despite her facade of strength, his bride found herself in enemy territory, torn away from everyone she loved, and had given herself—in the eyes of God and man—into his power. Was it any wonder she feared his reaction when she told him the name of her child's father? What the consequences could be?

"Ask." He laid a hand on her shoulder. "What most troubles

you?" Adam waited to hear of her worry that he'd set her aside when she made her revelation. Or her fear that his parents would make the rest of her life miserable, perhaps.

"My family needs me." She fingered the pin she always wore near her heart. "They think I betrayed them. . . ." A tear splashed onto the back of her hand.

"You're not asking to go back?" Something lurched inside him. *She's leaving me.*

"Could I?" Hope, pure and beautiful, shone in her eyes, lightening the blue. "Just some days. I wouldn't neglect my duties here. But Pa and Ben and Elroy and Pete don't have any women—only me. If I could have a baking day, help tend a garden, maybe a little washing. . ." The words poured forth like an overflowing stream, the flood of her heart.

Her concern isn't for her at all. Adam couldn't answer for a moment. Couldn't even listen to the rest of it as she continued. *It's for her family.*

"Only two days out of six. Or even just the afternoons. . ." She didn't stop to draw a breath the whole time she talked. Just stared up at him like he had the power to make her dreams come true.

And what small dreams they were—to do double the work.

"Yes." What other answer could he possibly give? "I'll talk to Ma about which days would be best."

"Thank you." Gratitude lit her face, making her beautiful. "Oh, Adam." She bit her lip. "Thank you."

"Pa's agreed to let you have the meadow bordering Speck lands for your apiary." He couldn't resist the urge to add to her joy. "Let me know about moving it."

"Soon." She fingered her brooch once more. "The meadow is a good place for them—no blockages for the scouts."

"Good." Now that she seemed so much happier—like she didn't dread talking to him—Adam suddenly realized how much he wanted her to want to be around him. But still. . . "Opal, you know I have to ask. You promised you'd tell me who the father is."

The change in her expression came on so sudden, it was like watching a spring storm roll in across a clear sky. "I can't tell you."

"You wouldn't break your word." He refused to believe it. "Tell me."

"I'm not breaking my word." She closed her eyes. When she opened them, pain darkened them once again. "I said I'd tell you if you asked tomorrow." She drew a deep breath and squared her shoulders. "That meant yesterday."

❧

Opal didn't even try to hold her head high after she left Adam and returned to the barn. Sure. . .she'd expressly avoided him after dinner the day before to avoid breaking her word. Never mind she'd assumed he would never have cause to ask the question again. He'd shunned their marriage bed and so still didn't know the dismal truth.

The only thing I've created are half-lies. Opal considered them for a moment. Naming Adam as the man who *would be* the father of her child. Saying she *couldn't* give him a name. Telling him he absolutely *can't* get an annulment. Then telling the Grogans she couldn't *lie* about nonconsummation.

Every single statement skirting truth's edge but dipping into deception because Opal knew how it would be interpreted. She sighed as she helped Willa carry the fresh milk to the springhouse. They lowered the pails into the cool, slow-flowing spring water until only the top third stayed above the surface.

That's how I feel. Sinking so deep, I can barely keep my head above the water, Lord. I'm so busy watching my words, my faults rise higher and higher until they'll wash away what I love. I try to change the things that need changing but make so many mistakes! And what can

I do but wade through them? Even if it takes me deeper still. . .

"Do you want to gather the eggs or go fry the bacon for breakfast?" Willa had the grace to wait for Opal's response before heading to the house, despite the obvious choice.

"I'd be more than happy to gather the eggs and feed the chickens." Better to face a few hen pecks than Lucinda's beak! "The corn sheller doesn't need two people."

So they split ways, her sister-in-law moving homeward and Opal grabbing a basket. She searched the raised lean-to, originally a tool shed, which the Grogans converted to a winter coop first. As it had the day before, the stench of the accumulated winter droppings below made her wrinkle her nose. The coop needed a thorough spring cleaning. Otherwise the daily task of gathering would become something to dread.

She briefly considered offering to take on the unpleasant chore but discarded the idea. Lucinda would probably take offense, seeing it as an implied insult or Opal trying to tell her what needed to be done. If she did the work without asking, her mother-in-law would assume Opal was acting snooty and making decisions about the farm.

After a long, cold jail sentence, most of the hens happily roamed the farmyard, testing their freedom, investigating the offerings of springtime as plants and insects poked from the ground. Only a few kept to the coop, moody clucks who took exception to her search and showed their displeasure with sharp pecks and indignant squawks. Later, more hens would return to the nests, when laying truly began.

Today, Opal left without much to show for the experience but a few scrapes on the backs of her hands and satisfaction in a thorough job. *Now for the real task of hunting eggs.* The sun showed more of its strength as morning aged, brightening the farmyard for her exploration. Left to search around fence posts, beside walls, and beneath mangers, she became familiar with favorite spots of the Grogan chickens. More importantly, she became more familiar with the farm.

She even discovered a well-hidden nest tucked under the corner of the corncrib, with no fewer than four eggs nestled beneath the outraged young biddy guarding them. She puffed up to look twice her size, but Opal won the day, carrying her find to the kitchen.

Considering she'd harvested twice as many eggs as she and Willa managed the previous morning, she felt pretty good about the work. Neither Willa nor Lucinda heard her enter over the sizzle of bacon frying in the skillet, so Opal simply set the basket on the table.

"How are the chickens?" Lucinda somehow managed to make it sound as though her hens would suffer under Opal's care.

"Well enough, though..." She let her words trail off, as though hesitant to say more.

"Though?" An imperious brow hiked toward the older woman's hairline.

"Now that the hens roam free, it might be a good time to have one of the men collect the winter waste." Opal wrinkled her nose for effect. "Not that I envy them, but I know they'll be fertilizing the fields about now."

"True." The speculative gleam in Lucinda's eye before she turned back to the stove told Opal her gambit worked.

I'll be cleaning out that coop before the week is out. Opal shook her head at Lucinda's predictability as she made her way back to the barn.

The Grogans used a different model corn sheller than she'd always operated, but it worked on the same principle. This Rufus Porter design featured a hand crank that looked a lot like a spinning wheel laid on its side and belted to a box where you

419

pushed in the corn up top. Stripped cobs came out the bottom, and the kernels spewed out the side into whatever bag or basket awaited them.

Opal hauled over a bunch of corn, stuffed it into the top, and started turning the wheel. Same as with any machine she'd ever used, starting the thing made for the roughest work. Before long she whirled that wheel for all she was worth, excepting a few stops and starts to put in other loads. It took awhile before she filled the feed basket, but she didn't mind.

The sound of the sheller, the rhythm of the work, the sight of corn kernels piling high were the closest she'd come to home in two days. When Opal finished, she balanced the basket on one hip and headed in the general direction of the coop.

"Chick, chick, chick," she called, clicking the roof of her mouth to catch their attention. When she spotted the first feathers, Opal began the continual process of reaching into the basket, filling her palm with corn, and scattering it along the ground. Hens came rushing around fences and from under haystacks, their thin legs at odds with their top-heavy bodies. Anticipation made them race toward her, causing the slightly hitched stride Opal found so familiar and oddly comforting.

She flung more and more handfuls in wider circles, birds following her like so many eager puppies nipping at her heels. Only instead, they darted their necks down to snatch a morsel of food with their beaks before tilting back their heads to swallow it whole.

The roosters managed to behave as though she bestowed the food upon their harem at their express command, strutting like glossy overseers. From time to time, they'd find a particularly appealing kernel and let loose an imperial "tut, tut, tut," until a group of hens came rushing over to fight for it.

By the time she'd finished, her heart didn't feel so heavy.

The simple chores reminded her that a greater design guided everything, making farmyards and animals and shelling corn the same wherever one went. It was vastly reassuring to find the familiar when surrounded by so much strangeness.

God ordered the world, it wasn't her place to change it, and fighting her circumstances wouldn't do anything but give her grief. Instead, she'd work here, help out back home, and do what she needed to maintain the balance. Because that was a different thing entirely from changing, and peace was worth maintaining.

Opal watched as Adam wiped his feet before entering the house then moved to follow him.

Whatever it takes.

CHAPTER 19

Midge sucked in a breath as she jabbed another finger with her needle. With a glance around, she saw Clara rocking Maddie, listening as Saul read from the Reed family Bible. The Bible where even Midge's name pranced across the genealogy page, despite her not being related by blood.

As that blood, tainted by the past Saul saved her from, welled into a droplet, Midge stuck the injured finger in her mouth. Of all the folks in Buttonwood, only Saul and Clara knew the truth about where she came from.

The first honest, truly honest, people I ever met, and I made liars out of them without even meaning to.

Over two years, and they hadn't breathed a word that Saul hadn't found Midge on the streets of Baltimore. She'd found him while trolling the streets.

But not in time to save her sister. No. By the time Midge brought him back to their alley, Nancy's blood had left her body. *And Nancy left me.*

Midge looked down at the diluted smear around her pricked fingertip and squeezed it until it welled dark red again. She stared at it for a long time. The more of it that gathered, the longer it sat, the darker it became until the red seemed closer to black.

This is who I am. I don't belong with the Reeds any more than Opal belongs with the Grogans. The only difference is I'm lucky. And since I don't deserve my good fortune, and Opal deserves better than her misfortune, I have to figure out a way to help her.

She sniffed, trying to dislodge the lump in her throat. It didn't do much good. But suddenly, something Saul was reading caught her ear.

"Wait a minute!" She sat up straighter. "Can you go back a bit? Reread that last part?"

"Of course." Surprise lined Saul's face, and Midge knew Clara's expression would be the same if she cared to look.

But for now, her attention stayed riveted on her adopted father as he read from Galatians.

"'But the fruit of the Spirit is love, joy, peace, longsuffering, gentleness, goodness, faith, meekness, temperance: against such there is no law.'"

Saul made as though to go on, but Midge cleared her throat to stop him. It would have been disrespectful to outright interrupt a reading of the Holy Book—asking for him to reread part didn't count—but she had a question. They were always encouraging her to ask questions about God and the Bible, so for once she aimed to take them up on some answers!

"Yes, Midge?" Excitement gleamed in Clara's green eyes, making them almost catlike.

"Is 'fruit of the Spirit' another way to say virtue? I mean, I thought there were only seven virtues, but there are two extras tacked on."

"Fruit of the Spirit are traits of good character. You can call them virtues. We all fall short but keep trying." Clara's explanation didn't quite answer what Midge was looking for.

"I think she's referring to the classical virtues." Saul's expression grew thoughtful. "They are both lists of goals for behavior, but they are different. The fruit of the Spirit are spiritual values, Midge. Classical virtues have more practical applications."

Well, that's good. I'm not peaceful, longsuffering, gentle, good, meek, temperate, or someone who shares this faith! Love has to be earned and joy's hard to come by, so those don't overflow from me either.

Midge decided to can the fruit. *Practical sounds more my style.*

"Then what are the classical virtues?" She crossed her fingers behind her skirts. Sure, she knew Saul and Clara wouldn't like the old superstition, but she couldn't help hoping she scored better marks on the next list.

"Faith, hope, and charity are the first three." Clara's comment didn't make Midge feel much better.

Well, I do have hope. . . .

"That sounds a lot alike to me." And her saying so sounded like a grumble, but she wasn't pretending to be longsuffering, after all.

"Temperance makes both lists, too. It's the other three virtues that sets them apart." Saul pinched the bridge of his nose, the way he always did when he was thinking.

"Oh?" Midge inched toward the edge of her chair.

"Prudence, justice, and fortitude." He sounded triumphant that he'd remembered.

"Prudence means wisdom, right?" Midge decided that being able to keep her head in a tough time counted, so she gave herself a check mark for that when Clara and Saul nodded. And hadn't she just thought the other day that she had a strong sense of justice? This was more like it! "What's fortitude?"

"It's—"

"Wait!" Clara hushed Saul before he could make things easy by just telling her. That was the hitch about Clara having taught her to read and write—she kept wanting to make Midge think and learn. "What does it sound like?"

"Fort and attitude put together, so like someone who acts like they can't be brought down." It sounded silly to Midge, and she got a crazy image of someone wearing a little wooden fort and walking around as though nothing could hurt him.

"That's actually very good." Saul's brows went up over his spectacles. "Fortitude is another word for perseverance—a way of saying it's someone who doesn't give up, even when things seem impossible."

Well, what do you know? Midge popped to her feet and went to give each of them a hug. She would've tickled baby Maddie but didn't want to wake her up.

"What's this for?" Clara's smile seemed a touch confused.

"Not much." *I got a solid four out of seven.* Midge scampered up the stairs with a lot of planning to do but decided to let her family know why she seemed so happy. "It just turns out I'm a virtuous woman, that's all!"

But I've still got a few tricks up my sleeves. . . .

"Adam?" The feminine voice called loud to carry into the field and reach him.

Adam pushed on, the steel tip of the plow he guided, breaking thick earth behind Daisy's powerful pull. His wife may have avoided him two days ago, but he hadn't yet found the temperance to hold another conversation with her since the morning before.

His grip tightened on the worn handles as he remembered the way she oh-so-casually walked away from her promise to reveal the identity of her child's father. Literally turned her back to him and walked away as though she owed him no explanations simply because the sun had set and risen.

And I let her do it. Adam pushed harder, and Daisy picked up her pace. *I let her walk away because I was afraid of my own anger. Of what I'd say. Of how I'd make things so awful for her here that she'd run away and the feud would descend upon my family after all. Biding my time is the best choice.*

"Adam?" The voice sounded closer now, slightly out of breath.

"I'll speak with you when I'm good and ready." He bit out the words without so much as looking over his shoulder. "Not before."

"Well, I'm ready now." Now that her breath caught up with her, the woman didn't sound familiar. "And I hope you weren't planning to talk to Opal that way."

"Who are you to tell me how to speak to my wife?" His shoulders stiffened, but he kept plowing forward.

Maybe you need *someone to tell you how to talk to your wife.* A small, too-logical part of him made the suggestion, but he squashed it. He'd been more than reasonable.

"Someone who knows you should at least look a body in the eye to have a civil conversation." Midge Collins bustled into view, walking backward so she could face him. "But maybe I overestimated your ability to *have* a civil conversation."

"Whoa," Adam called the big draft horse to a halt and stared at his unwelcome visitor.

With her arms folded across her chest and freckles marching across her nose, Midge Collins looked determined to have her say. What she had any say in escaped him at the moment, but Adam knew he'd be hearing about it.

"I'm not in a civil mood." He stalked past her to unhitch Daisy from the plow, leading her across that field and the next toward the nearest stream. The sound of Midge's footsteps tracked him. "You don't belong here."

"It's God's green earth, so I figure I belong as much as anyone." A defiant note crept into her voice. "And I need to talk to you."

"You know it's not proper to be alone with a man." *Think, girl. Days past you were at my wedding, the penalty for me supposedly fornicating with a young woman!* He'd always found irony laughable in the past, but this went beyond what anyone could term humorous.

"That's all right." She stopped right beside him as they reached the water's edge. "I'm not planning on a proper conversation."

"What?"

"Go ahead and smile." She tugged at her bonnet brim. "You look like you don't know if you want to grin or try for a quick escape. I'm pretty fast, so my advice is you let out a smile. It'll make you feel better—civil, even. Then hear me out."

"Miss Collins, you have my full attention." Adam kept a lid on his grin anyway. *Not planning a proper conversation. Ha!*

"I'm glad you're not feeling civil. It means I don't have to shilly-shally around things, talking about the weather or," her voice took on a clipped, oh-so proper enunciation, "how pleased I was to attend your wedding." She dropped the pretense. "Sometimes civility can be silly."

"There's a difference between chitchat and civility."

"Not for women."

Silence wound around them while they considered that.

"I think you may be on to something." The thought made him grin.

"You'd be surprised what I catch on to." She reached out to stroke Daisy's mane. "Now, Adam, fact of the matter is, I did attend your wedding because Opal's my friend."

"Don't be so sure." A sudden memory of his bride-to-be's youngest brother ratting him out revived old anger. *He gawked like I'd look at Midge if I thought no one was watching.* Seemed far too coincidental that the witness Pete "happened" to run across was none other than the girl before him. But Adam wouldn't stoop so low as to say so.

"Well, Pete asked me because he likes me." Her matter-of-fact answer gave him all the satisfaction of having taken his revenge on Pete, with none of the guilt. "I went because I care about Opal."

"You two are that close?" Adam trod carefully. *Could Midge tell him the name of any men hanging around with Opal?* If he worked it right, maybe she'd never know what he was angling for. . . .

"Close enough to know that she'll make you a good wife. Then again, I'm not close to you, but I didn't try to interfere with the wedding because I thought you'd make her a good husband." She cast him a shrewd glance. "I caught you gaping at her from the Burns' stable annex while she talked with Brett, you know."

"I don't gape." He bristled at the idea he'd been caught staring at Opal. *Twice. In one week. By two different people.* He stopped bristling.

"Pete said he caught you so easy because you were busy gawking at her on the farm. Do you like that better?" She shrugged. "It doesn't matter. I just figured you were smart enough to realize what a special woman she is and scooped her up."

"She's special, all right." *And driving me mad with her secrets. Mad enough not to trust myself around her.*

"I shouldn't have swallowed the story so fast."

"Story?" It took effort not to shift or make any movements to give away his unease.

Midge, true to her word, still caught on. "You just went still as a statue and twice as stony."

"What story?" *What do you think you know?*

"Now that's the question, isn't it?" She cocked her head to the side. "Some stories, folks carry around until they wear out then patch them up with new material to trot around again. But the most interesting tales are made up out of whole cloth. Like this one."

428

"I'm not here to amuse you." He didn't pretend he didn't understand her direction.

"Never said I was amused by it." Midge's gaze pinned him with the finality of truth. "You never touched Opal before your wedding day, and we both know it."

"Don't make assumptions."

"There's advice you should take to heart." She hadn't blinked in too long. "But anyone who knew Opal, or who cared more about her than their own pride that day to look, could see it on her face that you'd never kissed her before."

Adam remembered the feel of Opal in his arms, the soft look of wonder on her face when he drew back, his initial impression after their embrace. *Midge offers a better explanation than Opal'd never been kissed at all, considering the situation.*

"No need to admit it. You swept her away with that risky move—one that almost had the Speck boys have you leave with a bullet as a souvenir, by the by."

Swept her away, eh? He felt. . .taller. . .at the idea.

"You went still again," Midge's observation broke through his thoughts, "but I'll discount it since that grin takes away the stony look."

"Is that why you came?" He wiped the grin from his face. "To tell me you believe I wasn't her lover?" *And still aren't, but that will change as soon as she coughs up the name of the child's father.*

"That and to see your reaction." Midge started tromping back up the short embankment. "Judging by that grin you aren't sporting anymore, seems I won't need to deliver my warning."

"I trust you'll keep your suspicions to yourself?" Adam wouldn't verify them but didn't want her blabbing.

"Of course." She stopped. "And I'd like to help Opal with her apiary. I know it'll need to be moved, and I'm interested in learning about the bees, if that's all right."

"All right." Not that he'd deny a simple request when she kept such a dangerous secret, but Adam couldn't shake the feeling Midge had another motive for wanting to be around Opal.

"Thanks." Suddenly, without all the spunk and vinegar, she seemed what she'd been all along—a young girl trying to look out for her friend. "No warning, but. . .Adam?"

"Yes, Midge?" He couldn't help but think Opal had chosen a good ally.

"Be good to her. She deserves better than you know."

CHAPTER 20

Waiting made time seem to unwind still more slowly on the Grogan farm. Opal knew she'd angered Adam and didn't want to push him about the times she could go over to her family's farm. If she asked after the stunt she'd pulled at the end of their last conversation, he might change his mind altogether. So she cooled her heels and took whatever task Lucinda shoveled out.

Her new mother-in-law seemed determined to account for every moment of Opal's day, as though in retribution for her very presence on the farm. Little did she know that the constant tasks keeping her busy were also what kept Opal sane.

Even so, she found it hard to hide her smile when Lucinda requested that Opal clean out the "winter accumulation" in the chicken coop. *Lucinda can't know I maneuvered this.* But, Opal reminded herself, no matter how she'd be glad the next time she gathered eggs, today would be far from pleasant.

Armed with her oldest apron, a broom, a scrub brush, thick gloves, a bucket of water, and an empty bucket for disposing of the waste, Opal marched up to the converted lean-to and shooed away the chickens. A cursory check turned up a single egg since she'd looked before breakfast. She set it aside and got to work.

Loading up the old nests, well worn after winter, into malleable bundles wouldn't have been unpleasant if it weren't for the pungent stench and accompanying ammonia fumes almost overpowering the now-empty coop. Opal toted the nests to the compost heap, gulping in the fresh air between. She judged the compost to be the less offensive of the two places.

When she returned to the coop, she stood as near the entrance as possible to wield her broom. Out whisked the old straw, dotted with the distinctive grayish-white of chicken waste, sodden and long overdue for replacing. Opal swallowed back her gags to haul bucketful after bucketful back to the compost heap until she couldn't tell which smelled worse.

Back into the corners, along the shelves, in the crevices of the wood, not a stick of straw escaped the purging. By the time she'd removed everything offensive, she felt distinctly lightheaded. *I breathed in too much of that ammonia,* she decided, turning over the now-empty waste bucket and sitting outside in the shade for a moment. She breathed deeply of the fresh air, letting her head lean against the wall of the coop and her eyes drift shut until the world stopped twirling.

"Enjoying the shade, are you?" Diggory's gruff tone dripped contempt. "Good to see my son married such a *hardworking* woman."

"He did." The criticism stung—both at its injustice and at the core truth she wasn't the woman for Adam. She stood up to face him but moved too quickly. The ground swayed.

"Whoa." Diggory reached out to clamp his hands on her shoulders, keeping her at arm's length but supporting her nonetheless. "Easy there."

When the ground stopped swaying, Opal realized it hadn't been the ground at all. She blushed. "The coop needed cleaning, and I got a little dizzy."

"You stay too long in there the ammonia will do that to you." He hesitantly removed one hand, as though seeing if she'd topple over. When she remained upright, he drew back the other. "Especially in your condition."

The blush grew hotter and, if experience had taught her anything, brighter. "It's nothing, really."

"You were right to take a minute." His voice stayed gruff, but now it held no censure. "I can have Dave finish carting out the old bedding and straw. Plenty of other things for you to do."

"It's already finished." She reached for her water bucket. "I'm ready to start washing it down."

"Good." With that, he left her with her scrub brush. . .and her thoughts.

Opal sucked in a deep breath before ducking into the coop. She stayed close to the entrance, letting the place air out before she ventured to the confines of the dark corners. The top roosts felt the rough swipes of her brush first as she worked her way back then down. Periodic stops to empty filthy water and fetch fresh kept her head from spinning.

Coming this far, and having Diggory see her struggle, Opal refused to leave a single nook not scrubbed. She couldn't poke a broom back and sweep out debris anymore. Only the deepest, darkest, bottommost corners of the lean-to presented her with difficulty. Getting back into the very corners for a thorough scrubbing necessitated lying flat on her stomach and reaching beneath the lowest roost.

She'd just finished the final one when she heard the heavy thud of men's boots race up to the coop. Opal didn't have time to wriggle out and stand up before he came inside and witnessed her indignity.

"Opal!"

Adam's shout gave her such a start she banged her head on the roost. "What?" Scooching backward so she could rise up on her hands and knees to rub the back of her head, Opal eyed her irate husband.

Whatever it is, it can't be good.

~~~

"I know I told that girl we wouldn't wait dinner on her." Ma sniffed and wielded her ladle. "Diggory, why don't you go on ahead and say the blessing?"

"Because I'm going to check on the gal." Pa stood up. "She close to fell over earlier, cleaning out that coop in her—"

The rest of his father's words were lost as Adam vaulted off of his seat and out the door, hitting the ground running and not stopping until he reached the coop. No sign of Opal anywhere around.

He stooped a considerable way to get inside but didn't see more than the outlines of empty roosting shelves after the brightness of outdoors. Adam squinted and made out a figure lying prone on the ground.

"Opal!" It came out as a howl as he hunkered down to help her. His chest constricted so tight, it was little wonder she'd had a hard time catching her breath in the confines of the coop.

Thunk. The lowest roost shook as Opal backed out from beneath it, a scrub brush in her hand and a frown on her face. She scooted back until she could kneel then reached up to rub what would probably be a sizeable lump on the back of her noggin.

"What?"

"You didn't come to dinner." *And I thought you might be passed out in here.* Now that he looked around, he saw that the coop hadn't been this clean since they converted the lean-to from its original purpose as a tool shed. Possibly even before that. In fact, the only part of the whole place anything less than pristine was Opal herself.

She'd shucked her bonnet at some point—a practical decision since there wasn't an overabundance of light in the place. Now the finest pieces of her hair wisped straight up around her face, decorated with the odd bit of straw. A smudge graced her left cheek. Her apron boasted more shades than a painter's palette. Those skirts she shook out stayed rumpled despite her efforts, and her brows almost touched in the middle while she scowled at him for invading her domain. No bows and lace could ever compare.

He leaned in for a quick peck but found his way blocked by a scrub brush.

"What do you think you're doing?" She scrambled to her feet.

How can any woman look that appealing and not expect to get herself kissed? He wanted a chance to sweep her away again.

"Seeing if you're all right." *True. You weren't passed out. Now I'd like a closer inspection.* He took a half-step forward.

She practically backed out of the lean-to. "Just didn't hear the bell from under there." She waved the brush, bristles out, in the direction of the corner. "I'm fine."

"Pa said you felt dizzy earlier." Another half-step brought him the proximity he wanted.

She seemed to realize that backing up would be a mistake. For one thing, she'd fall out of the raised coop. "Only for a moment. It passed." She spoke quickly, making him think his nearness made her nervous.

Good.

"Kind of him to be concerned, though." Opal blinked those blue eyes of hers at him and added, "Nice of you, too."

"I wasn't being nice." A slight shift brought him even closer. "I was being your husband." He leaned closer, his eyes fixed on her mouth.

435

"Good of you!" This time, she stepped out the door and down the step. "Now that I know they're keeping dinner for me, I won't make the family wait any longer!" With that, she hustled toward the well, ostensibly to wash up.

But Adam knew the truth of it.

His wife had flown the coop.

CHAPTER 21

All through dinner, Opal battled a heightened awareness of Adam's closeness. His knee bumped hers beneath the table. His fingers brushed hers when she passed the salt. His smile reached out to her over their bowls.

Ridiculous. Smiles do not reach anything. And of course his knee bumps mine. The closer I scoot to Adam, the farther I am from Larry!

But no matter how she tried to apply logic and reason, her heart still beat in erratic excitement because her husband came to the chicken coop to check on her.

No. He thought I might be ill and he ran to my side. Genuine concern made him bellow so loud when he saw me on the ground like that. Even the indignity of her activity paled in comparison to the significance of his actions. She snuck a peek at him from the corner of her eyes, only to have to ask for a roll when he caught her looking.

Then that look in his eye when he kept getting closer. Almost a predatory gleam, like he was moving in for. . .a kiss? She barely managed to suppress a scoff, knowing it would draw undue attention at the table. Opal'd caught a glimpse of herself in the

437

water before she washed up. Hair sticking straight out as though making a run for it, a smudge on her cheek, and an old stained apron hardly made the image of an irresistible woman.

But what if he *had* wanted to kiss her? What then? Could it mean. . .

Opal dropped her spoon.

Can it mean he's ready to make this marriage real? She ducked her head and focused intently on fishing her spoon out of her soup, then drying it on her napkin. Maybe if she took long enough, her blush would go away.

I've surely done enough turning red to last a lifetime by now. But the thought didn't give her any hope she'd be spared further blushes. If anything, considering what lay ahead, she'd experience them more frequently.

"I like when you blush." Adam's warm breath tickled her neck, his voice a low whisper as he caught her napkin from sliding off her lap. "Makes me want to know what you're thinking." He leaned back, expression as casual as though he hadn't said a word.

Only Larry seemed to have noticed anything as, of course, warmth suffused Opal's face. Adam's brother looked from her to her husband then back, eyes narrowing as she all but scooted off the bench to move farther away from his gaze.

Adam's knee bumped hers again. Or maybe hers bumped Adam's. Really, who could tell? Opal, for one, occupied herself trying to think of chill streams, winter snows, breezy shade— anything that might cool the heat in her cheeks.

Anything that kept her from thinking about whether or not her husband wanted to kiss her. And if he did, if he wanted other things, too. And how if he wanted those other things maybe Midge's suggestion that she lure Adam into the marriage bed to avoid an annulment would be easier than she'd thought.

Unless I get so flustered just by him standing within a foot of me that I run away like a scared rabbit! She sighed into her soup and realized every last Grogan was staring.

"Mmmm, delicious!" She gave another sigh. *I am a ninny.*

"Thank you." Lucinda looked as though she'd searched the compliment for any hidden barbs and come up empty-handed.

"We'll teach you the recipe," Willa offered. "It was Grandma's."

The gesture of acceptance touched Opal. "I'd be honored."

"Don't be. My ma's recipe ain't goin' to no Speck." Diggory shoved his bowl away. "And don't you glower at me, boy. You may have married her, but you aren't living together as man and wife. She hasn't proved herself a Grogan."

"Yet." Larry's fierce utterance took them all aback, but Opal doubted he took note of his family's shock. He didn't so much as glance at anyone but her.

Memories of his advances came flooding back. Larry's hand imprisoning her wrist in the meadow. Larry following her toward the house until Pete saw him and told Pa. Larry's threat on the note that doomed Adam.

His gaze pinned her now, even as his actions had trapped his brother and left her with no options.

Your fault. She thrust her hands beneath the table so he couldn't see how rage made them shake. *This is all your fault, and you dare look at me and all but announce you're not finished?* "How dare you?" She raised her head to look him in the eye.

"Don't take that tone, missy." Lucinda's snap held no sting this time. "My son just stood up for you. He thinks you're not hopeless."

"We can make her a Grogan." The intensity in Larry's gaze sickened her. Whatever the man planned, she didn't want any part of it. Never had.

"You won't make me anything," she vowed. "Adam married me as I am." *He just doesn't know precisely what that means.*

439

"That's right." Adam's arm came around her shoulders, and she leaned into him, grateful for his solid strength. "Opal has nothing more to prove to me."

Because the only thing I have to prove is that I can live on this farm and not tear Larry limb from limb, and Adam already understands that. She closed her eyes. *Understands me.*

It was then she realized her husband was still speaking.

"Opal already *is* a Grogan."

"No, she isn't!" For a split second, Lucinda feared the words boiling in her heart burst from her own lips, but everyone at the table turned to her youngest son.

"Dave!" Willa gave her head a swift shake.

My own daughter, taken in by that Speck tramp. Lucinda bit the inside of her cheek. Speaking against Opal now would only drive Adam further away from the family and closer to the source of all their discontent.

Time is running out. I've only two days until the Sabbath—until Parson Carter tells all of Buttonwood that Adam's shackled to this troublemaker for the rest of his born days. The metallic taste of blood filled her mouth.

"Opal is my wife." Adam spoke slowly, as though every person at the table wasn't painfully aware of the facts, with his arm slung around the hussy. "She carries the next Grogan."

No blushes from his bride this time, Lucinda noted. *The girl's gone red as an apple over anything and everything, but one mention of the child and her face goes pale.*

"The child doesn't change me," the chit remarked. "When I'm not expecting, I'll still be Adam's wife."

I knew it! The Jezebel carries no grandbaby of mine! Otherwise, she'd seize on her claim to Adam with both hands and not let go.

440

"Adam's wife or not, we'll make a Grogan of you." Larry hadn't stopped watching the girl beside him since the conversation began.

His overt, inappropriate fascination made for another mark against the woman whose very presence—no, *existence*—was tearing her family apart.

"Make no mistake, brother." Adam's arm tightened around her shoulders. "Opal is my wife."

"For now." Her middle son either didn't realize or didn't care what he provoked. "Even should you set her aside, she can't go back to the Specks."

Now there's a thought. Lucinda's mind whirled. *Perhaps Adam is convinced the child belongs to him, and he's waiting to claim it? It stands to reason. My son would never abandon his own.*

"I will never set her aside." Adam's declaration shook her.

"No shouting at the table!" She sent him a sharp glance. *You'll set her aside when she reveals her true nature.* "I won't have you fighting with your brothers over nothing."

"I am *not* nothing." Where the girl found the gall to speak stumped Lucinda. Opal looked up at Adam in a nauseating display. "Thank you for defending my honor. I'm proud to be your wife, and though I claim the name Grogan, the Specks are my kin. That can't be changed, and I wouldn't want it to be."

"You speak well of them under my roof?" A vein pulsed in Diggory's forehead. "After we've taken you in?"

"My husband brought me to his home." Unbelievably, the girl kept speaking! "And I'd be a poor daughter and sister to speak ill of my family."

"They are no longer your family." A fanatical light came from Larry's grin.

Lucinda saw where this was heading and couldn't let it go a step further. "Neither are we."

"Yes, we are, Ma." Adam rose to his feet. "You will accept Opal as my wife or force me to make a choice. The Bible is clear to whom I must cleave."

"No." Her breaths came shallow, and she had to grip the table to stand up. "It's not about us accepting her when she still plays Speck games, causing division among us!"

God forgive me for the exaggeration I must use now. Adam won't see the more subtle ways a woman sows conflict within a home, so I have to give him something more concrete.

"What have I done?" Opal played right into her hands.

"As if you don't know." Lucinda suppressed any sign of victory. "Did you think I wouldn't realize the reason for my aches and pains these last two nights? That I'd attribute it to old age and your secret wouldn't be found out? That the Grogans are so foolish we wouldn't notice such a blatant stunt?"

"I don't understand." Her bewilderment came across beautifully—all the better to convince Adam what a liar he'd married.

"My mattress, Opal." Lucinda bit the injured part of her cheek again, letting tears well up. "What will I find if I open the seams?"

"This is nonsense, Ma." Adam's voice held the heat of anger.

"What are you implying?" The ice of winter, a direct contrast to her son, crept into the girl's tone.

"I want the truth, Opal. From your own lips. Confess now and we'll hear no more of it." She moved to slide her arm through Adam's. "For my son's sake, we'll start afresh."

"Cornhusks." Willa sounded confused. "Opal and I put cornhusks in the mattresses, same as always."

"Did seem lumpier than usual." Diggory shrugged. "But not much to fuss about."

"You'd sleep standing up if you had to," Lucinda pointed out to her husband. "Others of us are more sensitive. But, Willa, were you with Opal the whole time?"

She asked knowing the answer full well. After all, hadn't she called her daughter away, asking for help moving the settee so she could sweep behind it? Then asking her to stay for the moment it took for the cleaning, so she could help put it back in place?

"Aside from helping you with the settee." Willa slid a sideways glance toward Opal. "But I'm sure Opal wouldn't do anything wrong."

"This is your last chance. Have the integrity to tell us why you wanted to hurt me." Lucinda bit her lip as though anxious. "Be honest."

"I did nothing."

"So be it." She raised her head high and swept toward the alcove where her and Diggory's bed rested behind a thick curtain. She pulled out the sewing scissors she wore on a chain at her waist and bent to snip the seams along the bottom edge of the mattress. Lucinda guided Adam toward the opening. "Reach inside, son. Let's see what you find."

And she waited as, one by one, he pulled forth the stones she'd slipped inside earlier that very morning. Small enough not to be noticeable when carrying the mattress but large enough to cause discomfort when caught in the rope supports beneath the mattress, where she'd been careful to tuck them.

The gasps around him turned to glares, but Lucinda hardly paid them mind. Her focus was all for her oldest son.

He has to be shown. . . .

CHAPTER 22

The first stone could have been an accident. Easily. The second possibly, if less likely. But by the time his hand rustled through the husks to close around a third rock, they might as well have taken up residence in Adam's stomach.

How could she? He groped for an explanation even as he searched out two more of the offending objects, placing them in a neat pile beside his parents' bed. When he found no more within his reach, Adam stood, walked to the head of the bed, and withdrew his pocketknife.

Swift slices made short work of the tight seam, but Adam didn't kneel to finish the job.

"Opal." For the first time, he looked at his wife.

"Adam." All color had fled her cheeks, leaving her hair a brilliant flame of defiance as she raised her chin.

No need to ask whether or not she'd done it. She made no more protestations of innocence. Only insolence flashed in those blue eyes. Anyone walking through the door of the soddy at that moment would swear she had cause for righteous anger. The kind that swept over Adam as he saw his mother surreptitiously rubbing her lower back.

Sure, Ma hadn't been the most welcoming person in the whole world, but that was to be expected.

Ma's smart enough to suspect I didn't run around with Opal Speck and that the shotgun wedding was a farce. Stands to reason she'd be wary of the woman she thinks tricked me into marriage. He looked at Opal's rigid stance, a slim line soon to swell with another man's child. *Especially since it's true.*

"Come here." Adam stared at his wife. The same woman he'd wanted to kiss earlier that day.

Opal drew closer, not challenging his authority. She stood at the head of the bed, shoulders tense as she ignored Pa's fulminating glower, Larry's calculating air, Willa's betrayed expression, and Dave's angry fidgeting.

"You find the rest." He stepped back and gestured for her to finish the job.

She sank to her knees, spine straight as could be, stiffened by a pride the likes of which Adam never saw before. He waited as she groped around, making the dry bedding rasp and shift until she pulled out first one stone then another. Opal plunged her arm into the mattress again, reached until it swallowed her shoulder, and then gave up. "Seems like there aren't any more." Her voice took on a flat quality he hadn't heard before.

"You'd know." Pa kicked one of the rocks, making it fly and hit her skirts before it bounced off. "Planting these to make my wife miserable, after all she does."

"Rotten thing to do." Willa's admonition took everyone by surprise, since she rarely spoke against anyone.

"Isn't it, though?" Opal agreed with his sister but looked at his mother as though in challenge.

"Why didn't you just confess?" Adam wanted to know. "Ma gave you the opportunity."

"I couldn't." Her tone kept that lifeless luster he found so disturbing. "She knew that."

"Suspected as much," Ma sounded more triumphant than sorrowful. "That she wouldn't give an inch. Hoped I wouldn't risk looking like a fool if my suspicions were wrong, didn't she?"

"I don't like it." Larry looked from Ma, to Opal, and back again. "Don't like it one bit, Ma."

"How could you wish that on anyone?" Adam still couldn't reconcile such a petty act with the woman who'd helped keep peace for so long.

"Didn't." Her gaze stayed fixed on the wall.

"No need to wish when you can make it happen, eh, girlie?" Pa bent over to pick up one of the rocks. "Handy for a stoning. That's what they would've done to a woman like you in biblical times. Not pure on her wedding night—"

"Pa!" Adam clamped a hand around his father's wrist, making him drop the stone. "There'll be no talk of that."

"She must be punished, Adam." Pa wrenched his hand away. "I know she's with child, but you'll have to think of something."

"I already have." He knew what would hurt her most. "Opal, there are seven stones. One stone for each day makes that a full week you won't go to help out on the Speck farm. Aside from church the next two Sundays, you won't see your father or brothers."

"No!" She swung from the wall to fix on him, eyes wide and pleading. "Please, Adam! Don't do this!"

"I didn't." He forced himself to see past her tears to the hard heart behind them. "You brought it on yourself."

"Why?" But she wasn't looking at him. Opal stared at Ma. Her shoulders never drooped, but the one whispered word belied her pose. "Why?"

Ma's gaze went colder than Adam had ever seen. "Because

he has to learn. I won't have my son shackled to a liar." Her voice lowered almost to a hiss. "Adam needs to know what you *really* are."

"Buzzard!" Midge's indignation went a long way toward soothing Opal's own roiling temper. "I wish she *had* slept on rocks. Old besom probably waited until that morning to plant the things, though. Ooooh, I'd like to get my hands on that Lucinda and make her fess up."

"She won't." Opal poured a measure of water in the pie tin beneath yet another hive. "If you waved a loaded shotgun her direction and told her to spill the truth or else, she'd take the bullet."

"Idea has merit." Her friend plunked a few pebbles into the tin. "At least if you won't get vindication, you get a little vengeance."

"And then I'd be known as the woman who smuggled rocks into mattresses and shot her mother-in-law."

"Folk heroes have been made from less." Midge's grin faded. "Still burns my biscuits that Adam didn't think twice before condemning you."

"I shouldn't blame him for believing Lucinda." Opal recited what she'd been telling herself for the past two days. "She's his mama, she put on a very convincing performance, and the evidence was indisputable. Rocks came out of the mattress. Who would believe she put them there just to make me look bad? I shouldn't blame him."

"Just because you think you shouldn't doesn't mean you don't." Her friend took a sip of water. "I would."

"I do." *It shouldn't feel good to admit that.* "It's not fair that I should expect him to trust me over his mother and his own eyes, but I'm angry at him all the same."

"Justice is a virtue, you know." Midge sounded particularly

pleased to tell her so. "Wanting some doesn't make you a bad person. In fact, I'd be worried if you didn't."

"Maybe if I'd yelled and flung accusations at Lucinda he would've thought twice." Opal confessed the other part that still festered. "Instead, I got so mad I shook. Barely managed to choke out a single word once I realized what she'd done."

"If you'd started hollering, they'd have thought you went daft. Now, there's a thought." She came to such a sudden halt, Opal almost bumped into her. "Maybe Lucinda wants to drive you crazy so they can have you put away?"

"Even after two years you still think like a city girl sometimes. They don't have any of those places in the middle of the prairie even if I did start raving. Her plan seems to be more along the lines of making Adam set me aside. Or maybe making me so miserable I head for the hills. She'll learn it won't work."

"Glad to hear it." Midge squinted. "I can understand why the bees need water, but why do we put pebbles in the tins?"

"So the bees can have a place to drink without drowning." *Pity life doesn't always come with a pebble to give you better footing. Just stones planted by devious mothers-in-law.*

"And Lucinda said something about showing Adam what you really are? What do you think she means?"

"A liar." Opal's mouth went dry. "She made up the rocks in the mattress, but I think she knows I'm not carrying Adam's baby. Lucinda just doesn't know how to prove it."

"She won't have to wait long." Midge stuck her finger in the stream of honey Opal poured into a tin and took a taste. "Mmmmm. Everyone will know when you don't start showing."

"By then, the marriage has to be real." Opal dribbled in a little wine and placed the tin under the first of twenty hives, next to the water. "Or Adam will get that annulment."

Midge sprinkled salt on the mixture. "What's this stuff for?"

"After winter, hive supplies run low and most of the workers are busy building combs instead of making honey. So if there's an apiary, sometimes bees will raid other hives to steal food." Opal set down the next tin and moved on. "This way keeps them the most productive. I don't do it for long. . .and not every day."

"They go on raids?" Her friend looked at the hive before her with new respect. "Viking bees!"

Opal laughed for the first time since she'd cleaned out the chicken coop. "Viking bees. . .I like that."

"Yeah, but you've got someone even more ruthless to worry about. I figure you've got a month before your secret's out. A little less with Lucinda so suspicious."

"Less than a month." Opal froze for a second. "I only have a couple weeks to convince Adam to become my husband?"

"No. He's already your husband." Midge nudged her out of the way so she could sprinkle the salt. "You just have to convince him to act like it."

CHAPTER 23

"Tomorrow everyone will find out about the marriage." Opal sounded like she didn't know whether to be afraid or horrified.

Neither. "Good! It's the perfect time to start laying the groundwork." Midge could see that Opal needed some encouragement. "With you two being introduced as husband and wife, it's only natural for you to be looking up at him all admiring, always touching him, whispering to him. . .things that will catch his attention."

"I'm beginning to see why Pete's so obsessed with you."

"Don't be silly." She pshawed. "I don't need to do anything to catch your brother's attention."

"Right. People will think I've anticipated my vows and the marriage was necessary." Opal gave a big sigh. "Which is what the parson thinks, and my husband thinks, and both our families think, so I suppose it shouldn't matter."

"But it does." The very idea of everyone in Buttonwood finding out where she *really* came from made Midge's stomach turn, and the thought of her friend being exposed to the same kind of scorn didn't sit any better. The whispers, the stares, the judgment. . . "You don't deserve that." *I do.*

"I'd rather face gossip than a gunfight." Her friend's tone was light, but she meant every word. "But I feel so. . ."

"Alone?" The thought broke out before Midge could button it up.

"Yes. That's it, exactly. But more than that"—Opal finished pouring the last of the wine into the final tin—"as though I won't be good enough anymore."

"I understand that." Midge flicked the final bits of salt from her fingers and picked at her nails. "Felt like that when I came here."

"I'm so glad you came!" The hug caught her off guard. "Thank you for coming to see me even though I've been disgraced."

"Yours is a fake disgrace." Midge angled out of the hug to grab Opal's shoulders. "Listen to me. I know your secrets, and I won't abandon you or tell a soul, no matter how people treat you. But you have to let me help."

"You're too good." Opal headed for the small grove of cottonwoods bordering the apiary and sat down.

"No." Midge stayed standing when they reached the scant shade, rooted by the enormity of what she was about to do. "I'm anything *but* good. And that's why I can help. Listen, Opal. I have something to tell you, but you can't tell anyone. Only Saul and Clara know. I'm only letting you know because I can't help you win Adam without you knowing why I know some things."

"What's this about?" Opal tugged her hands. "Sit down. I've already gotten the picture that you know more about things no one else notices than I can even imagine!"

"That's because I learned to look." Midge reached down the front of her dress and pulled out the only link to her past. The battered brass locket had to be coaxed open to reveal its tiny portrait. "This here's my mom, but my sister, Nancy, looked just like her. I take after my dad."

"She's lovely." Opal traced the rim of the locket. "They both are."

"Were." Midge snapped it shut and thrust it back down her dress front. "I'm the only one left, that's true. And I met Dr. Reed on the streets of Baltimore, and he did save me."

"Yes, that's what they said. That he couldn't save your sister, but he took you in." Opal frowned. "There's no shame in living, Midge."

"There's shame in *how* we lived." She closed her eyes and could smell the dank stench of the alleyway, feel the cold creeping along the edges of their small fire, taste the terror when Randy looked at her. . . "The fever took Ma and Pa when I was about eleven and Nancy fourteen. I always looked younger, but Nancy seemed older than her years. She got a job at a factory but lost it when the foreman found me in her room. We just about starved until Randy came along."

"Randy?" Sudden wariness darkened Opal's gaze, showing she understood where the tale turned.

"You saw how pretty Nancy was. He turned her head, gave us a home. And in a week, he turned Nancy out. Either she worked the streets and served the gents, or we'd be back in the cold. Nancy refused, but Randy's fists did the convincing his mouth couldn't." Midge shivered. "Randy's fists did a lot of talking."

"Oh, Midge."

Opal reached out as though in comfort, but she jerked away. "I ain't done." She sniffed back tears. "For two years Nancy worked, and I took in odd jobs sewing. I still looked too scrawny to catch a man's eye. Then the day came Nancy's luck and potions failed her. She found herself expecting."

Opal's quick indrawn breath somehow gave her more determination to plow ahead.

"Randy didn't hold with that. He sent for one of the butchers to get rid of the problem. Nancy fought him—and fought hard. So did I, but it didn't do any good. The quack ripped the babe from my sister's belly, but something went wrong. Nancy didn't stop bleeding. So the next day, Randy made me take her place. Dr. Reed was the first man I stopped. Saul noticed the bruises on my neck, how young I looked, and offered to help me find a better life. He even tried to save Nancy, but she'd already passed by the time we got to the room. And then he whisked me away from that place and brought me here."

She spread her arms, palms out, shrugged, and waited for Opal's reaction. Now she'd find out if she'd made a mistake. If she'd lose a good friend and the respect of everyone else in Buttonwood to boot.

"You're amazing, you know that?" Opal's gaze held no disgust, only compassion and—could that be admiration? She reached out to snag Midge's hand and clasp it tight. "I never suspected you'd gone through so much. To think how the Lord brought you here, it gives me hope."

"It wasn't the Lord." Midge snatched her hand away. "It was Saul. Dr. Reed brought me here. God didn't answer Nancy's prayers, and He didn't hear any of mine on her behalf, either. Don't give Him credit for what Saul did!"

"I'm glad Saul came to Buttonwood. I'm thankful you approached him before anyone else." Opal leaned forward. "And most of all, I'm glad you're my friend."

Something hard inside her seemed to soften at Opal's complete acceptance of her. "You're sure? I'm not good like you."

"No. I came from a safe home and managed to spin a web of lies to land myself in trouble. You grew up surrounded by danger and evil and are here to help me." Opal gave a laugh. "We're not much alike."

"That's not what I meant!" But that didn't stop a secret part of her from liking to hear it. "And we're a lot alike. For one thing, neither of us gives up easy."

"True." The light of battle entered her friend's gaze. "Especially when so much depends on seeing something through."

"Tomorrow will be crucial." Midge watched as dozens of bees zoomed around the hives, dipping into the tins of water and honey-stuff they'd laid out. "The ambush yesterday set you back a good deal. You can't rely on Adam as an ally anymore. You've been cast in the role of a sneak, and the way things stand, Lucinda's better at it."

"This isn't helping." She raked her fingernails through a stalky clump of purple buds.

"It should." Midge caught Opal's hand before she could shred anymore of the emerging wildflowers. "You can learn from this— the best kind of sneaking is done right out in the open, so no one suspects it."

"People always suspect things." Her hand clamped tight. "They will tomorrow."

"That's where being sneaky comes in. You have to make them suspect what you want them to." She stood up. "And I'm going to teach you how."

Just in time for church.

Opal marched out the door of the Grogan soddy the next morning girded for battle. As she dressed, she kept in mind the armor of God.

For the breastplate of righteousness, she slid on Mama's pin. She felt that simply going as a Grogan counted as shodding herself in preparation for peace—standing as the link between their two families. The shield of her faith couldn't be seen, but she carried it as surely as she did Ma's Bible—her sword of the Spirit. Her best bonnet didn't quite classify as the helmet of salvation, but it would have to do since no decent woman left her head uncovered in God's house. Which left one missing piece.

Ephesians 6:14 kept running through her mind, mocking her with its impossibility. *"Stand therefore, having your loins girt about with truth. . . ."* Because no matter how she tried, Opal couldn't convince herself she lived up to that spiritual standard. In fact, a virgin trying to seduce her husband to prevent an annulment on the grounds she wasn't carrying an illicit child seemed the very antithesis of truthful loins.

It took all the wash water and a trip to the well to stop her blushes after the realization that her virtue now made her the worst sort of fraud. A *sneak*, Midge called it. *My only chance to keep things together.*

Opal raised her chin high and accepted Adam's arm as they walked to town. *I'll do my part to convince everyone this is a happy marriage, that our families cried peace, and no one needs to get hurt.*

"Adam?" She deliberately slowed her pace until they were a good distance behind the others. Not too far, or they wouldn't arrive together, but far enough for her to speak her piece. "We both know the importance of today."

"Yes." He hadn't spoken a word more than absolutely necessary since handing down his punishment.

"Then you know that standing stiff as a board and looking like you're nursing a sore tooth will make people think you don't want to be my husband." *In other words, they'll catch on to the true state of things.* "My family will see it as an insult to me."

He let loose a drawn-out breath and made a visible effort to relax.

"Better." She swallowed and pressed ahead. "Our families won't be able to hide their displeasure. The town will see it's a mask. But the two of us can show the picture of a happy couple united and uniting others or—"

"Let everyone know we were forced into it and provoke the type of speculation that will cause our families to snipe until they snap." A grim nod. "You're right. No one need know of the shotgun wedding since Parson Carter agreed to simply say he married us in a private ceremony with Pete and Midge as our witnesses. Will Pete pull through?"

"Oh, Midge will make sure of it." Opal gave a small chuckle at the thought of what awaited her brother if he didn't act as though he thoroughly approved the match. "She plans to stay near Pete and make sure he doesn't forget his role and scowl at you."

"Pete doesn't stand a chance." The tight lines around Adam's mouth faded. "I won't forget my part, either."

"Is it such a hard role to play?" A wistful note crept into her voice before she could prevent it. "That you enjoy my company?"

"No." He threaded his fingers through hers. "That's the problem."

Before she could explore that intriguing comment, the clapboard church came in full view. Or rather, they came in full view of the church. And the entire town.

Folks typically gathered around outside, shooting the breeze until time came to shuffle to their seats. Today proved no exception. The Fossets stood chatting with the Calfrees on the left side of the whitewashed building. The Warrens exchanged pleasantries with the Doanes farther right. The Reeds caught up with the Burn men and the Dunstall women front and center.

The parson and his wife stood in conversation with newlywed couple Sally Fosset and Matthew Burn. Young men and women clustered near the well, pretending disinterest in one another while the children of the town made merry mayhem while trying not to dirty their Sunday best. Pa and her brothers headed to meet them, and suddenly it seemed as though the entire scene froze.

Conversations ceased midsentence. Mouths hung agape. Children stilled. And Opal started to pray.

CHAPTER 24

*L*ord, *protect my family. From the Specks.* Adam caught sight of Ma's glower and the bulging vein in Pa's forehead. *And themselves. Don't let any of us do something that lights the tinderbox we stand on.*

"Pa?" The quaver in Opal's voice matched the tremor in her hand. The fabric of her sleeve shook.

Green. The color called forth a memory of her talking to God in the fields of her farm. *"If I had to pick a color to represent hope, I'd pick the pale green of a new blade of grass. . . ."* And she'd worn it today.

What do you hope for, Opal?

The realization that he cared didn't surprise him. He'd wanted her when she was the daughter of his father's sworn enemy. He'd wanted her when she trapped him into marriage. He'd wanted her though she planned to pass off another man's child as his and refused to reveal the identity of the father. Even after she'd stooped so low as to put rocks in his mother's bed to cause petty discomfort, he hadn't even considered washing his hands of Opal.

Shaking her until her teeth rattled, kissing her silly, or sweeping her away so it was just the two of them and nothing else for miles until she spilled her secrets and saw sense—now those, he'd considered. But giving her up now that she'd crashed so completely into his life? Never.

Not while Opal needed him. Not when that child needed him. Whether she wanted to admit it or not, she couldn't do it alone. He'd see through the promise he made to provide for both of them. *For better or worse.*

Adam could wait for the "better" part, so long as Opal wasn't hoping to get out of it.

"Grogan." Murphy Speck didn't even acknowledge his daughter's greeting. The man gave a curt nod and kept walking.

"Opal." Elroy stopped a few feet away, his tone low and urgent. He looked at Adam and back at his sister. "You all right?"

"Yes, Elroy." Opal nestled closer against his side as though happy to be there, but her gaze followed her father's retreating figure. "Adam treats me well."

"Let me know if that changes." The man narrowed his eyes and followed after Murphy, the two Specks cutting a wide swath through the townspeople who didn't make any pretense at doing anything but gawk.

"Of course he treats her right!" Pa's yell jerked them to a halt. "Don't insult my boy by suggesting otherwise or you'll answer to me!"

"Anytime a woman weds, her family keeps an eye on things." Ben, the Speck who'd been gone four years and only just returned, seemed to have donned the mantle of peacemaker after Opal's defection. Whatever else he said got lost in the gasps and sudden swell of excitement as everyone heard him.

His wife shrank into him as though seeking protection. Adam looked down to find her staring up at him, eyes wide, offering a hesitant smile. Before he knew it, he could feel himself grinning back. A fresh wave of murmurs swelled around them.

"I'd say we have plenty of eyes on us." He went ahead and chuckled at the scrutiny, unleashing a townful of titters. But the sweetest sound was the ghost of a giggle as Opal joined in.

Has she laughed once since our wedding? Adam fought to keep his smile.

"Everyone can congratulate the happy couple after the service," Parson Carter called from a safe distance—the church steps. "Let's remember where our attention should be."

Despite the reminder, his flock was slow to straggle into the house of worship that morning. It seemed everyone waited for. . . something.

"Ready, honey?" The endearment came easily, though he hadn't planned it. Adam thought how well it suited his beekeeper as he led her past the avid gazes of everyone they knew and to the bench where his family always sat.

Ben and Pete Speck followed closely, a silent show of support stronger than his own family bringing up the rear.

Adam registered this peripherally, instead pouring his focus into meeting the eyes of every man he passed. Every man in town. It should have been easy to find the man who wouldn't meet his gaze or looked too thunderstruck.

Somewhere among this tight-knit community lurked the scoundrel who'd taken advantage of Opal. Did the man even know of his impending fatherhood? Opal hadn't said one way or another, and Adam hadn't asked. He figured it'd be an issue to take up in person. When he made it clear that the reprobate would never come near his wife—or their child—in the future.

Young or old, tall or short, squat or spare, didn't matter. Adam eyed anyone in britches. And to a man, each eyed him back. Some with speculation; others didn't hide amusement. He might even have caught a flash of pity from one misguided soul.

Even Brett Burn, the youngest blacksmith and the man Adam most suspected, showed only good-natured resignation. If there'd been hostility or even envy, his hackles would've gone up. Instead, even the young man who'd shown an interest in Opal joined the town's main reaction. The great majority seemed to be anticipating something.

Probably for the mother of all fights to break out between our families, Adam guessed. *Truth be told, I'm waiting on that myself.*

If the old adage held any truth—that an overabundance of curiosity counted as sin—Opal hoped all the sidelong glances and outright gapes of disbelief aimed her way were paired with a little shame. The weight of all this scrutiny should splinter the Grogan bench into toothpicks long before Parson Carter finished his opening prayer!

It certainly felt heavy on her shoulders. Or maybe that knot came from her working so hard not to crane her neck to see Pa. Outside he'd acted as though looking at her would taint him. Pain wrapped around her midsection so tight she'd not drawn a full breath since then, and she knew seeing Pa send her one of those special smiles he'd always managed whenever she needed one would make the air right again.

But she wouldn't give anyone in town cause to think she pined to go home. No matter it was truth to rival the Gospels the Parson preached from, she wouldn't disgrace Adam that way. Instead, she kept her spine straight and her shoulders tilted as far away from Larry as possible. Somehow her brother-in-law seemed to take up more space than a body had any right to, making her press closer to Adam than even she'd planned on this morning.

His solid warmth at her side sent a physical message of

reassurance she craved almost as deeply as she needed the parson's reminder of God's sovereignty.

"This morning, I'd like us to think about something we, as Christians, are freely given and called to extend to others. The greatest gift, but we have trouble accepting it and even more trouble offering it to the people in our lives; forgiveness." Parson Carter caught the gaze of each parishioner, but it felt to Opal as though he could see the anger staining her soul.

"Forgiving other people is the step most of us admit we struggle with. When someone wrongs us, it's all too easy to sit on our anger and stew about it, when we're supposed to give it to God and show our fellow man the same acceptance God shows us."

Opal closed her eyes for a moment, refusing to wince at the truth of the message and longing to shut out the realization she needed to forgive Lucinda for the horrible trick she'd played. *Lord, I know I need to. I know I'm supposed to. I know I'm flawed and have no right to judge others because I'm not anywhere near perfect, but at the same time, knowing something and feeling it are very different! I feel she deserves to be exposed for the vicious conniver she is and made to suffer for it. I feel as though she doesn't deserve my forgiveness for what she's done in driving a wedge between me and Adam and keeping me from my family.*

Loneliness crashed over Opal afresh as she sat in the wrong pew, away from the comfort of her father and brothers, with no one beside her but a husband who never wanted her. And, thanks to the machinations of his mother, may never want her. She swallowed a sigh and admitted the worst part of her struggle. *Lord, there's a part of me that is so angry I just don't want to forgive her. It makes me sad to think of how she hates me and how her ploy succeeded to the point it almost overwhelms me. I'm afraid if I give up my anger in favor of grace, I'll be swamped in all the things that weigh me down with nothing to give me the strength to fight it.*

"Our ability to forgive should come not only from knowing that we don't deserve the grace we've been given but also from our certainty that our Lord is just and it is not for us to seek vengeance or hold grudges. He tells us in Exodus, 'The Lord shall fight for you, and ye shall hold your peace.'"

Opal's breath escaped in a *whoosh* as the verse hit her like a blow to the ribs. Strength wasn't supposed to come from anger—it came from resting on faith. Another area she'd failed.

But how do I stop fighting when I'm plunked in the midst of the battle?

Midge struggled to keep her expression calm throughout the sermon. She'd read a description of a heroine in a novel once who'd been serene and liked it. Sometimes words carried flavors for the mind, and Midge figured "serene" tasted cool and smooth, like peppermint.

So that's how she kept her face now. Smooth, as though any hint of a scowl or a frown would wrinkle into a thousand cracks and shatter the mask she'd put on that morning. The mask she always put on before church, where she sat still and quiet as though it came natural to not move, and didn't voice the waves of questions and objections pummeling her thoughts as Parson Carter spoke about the goodness of God.

"How can you do it?" she'd asked Nancy one night, while Randy drank away the money her sister earned from cheap men who dared treat unfortunate women as worthless. "How can you smile and go along when you're screaming on the inside?"

"I smile because it doesn't matter and because I'm not screaming on the inside anymore, Midgelet." Nancy smoothed the hair back from her forehead and tucked her close. "I'm praying."

Her sister prayed for everyone. Even the men who used her

body. Even Randy. Even Midge, when it was all Midge's fault Nancy lost her mill job and ended up in that awful alley in the first place.

Today in church stood Parson Carter, who'd probably never gone hungry a day in his life or seen someone he loved beaten or killed, talking about how God would fight their battles. Problem was the other guys fought dirty, and good people who prayed still died.

So Midge sat tall and straight, screaming silently behind the smile she wore so well.

CHAPTER 25

Lucinda tried to ease some of the stiffness in her neck by turning it first to one side then the next, only to find all of blessed Buttonwood staring at her family's bench! Maybe a few glances darted in the other direction, toward the Speck seats, but Lucinda felt the scrutiny of her neighbors as though pinpricks of fire broke out all over her body. Like a rash.

Of course they stared. Everyone in town knew about the wedding. At least, they knew there'd been one. Parson Carter wouldn't breathe a word about the shotguns that had forced her son into Opal's clutches.

No one will. Adam's honor won't be smirched like that. Oh, people will talk. People always talk. They'll guess there's a child on the way. But the girl will be gone long before she proves them right. Long before she makes Adam known as a fornicator and binds him to her so tightly he'll never escape!

There was time yet, so Lucinda could wait. Hadn't she proven she was good at waiting? Even as young as eleven, when she came to the Grogans, second cousin and poor relation of Diggory's mother, hadn't she laid plans with the expertise of a master mason?

Look at me now. Diggory's wife, just as I planned. Mother of four beautiful children, head of a fine homestead, successful in every way.

Except one.

The Speck gal had more gumption than she'd reckoned on. An entire week's worth of snide remarks, sly jabs, backbreaking work, and deepening aspersions cast on the girl's character hadn't been enough to drive her out.

We'll see how she does after another month. Rocks in the mattress made for a nice start to show Adam his bride's true colors. *Next time, I'll shade them darker. And keep layering things one on top of the other until her character is so blackened Adam can't stand to look at her!*

She curled her fingers around the edge of the bench, welcoming the sharp jab of a splinter poking through her gloves. The minor nuisance fed her irritation over the situation, and she nursed it all through service as she thought up ways to drive the interloper from the ranks of her family. Specks and splinters ruined fine things, but both could be removed with the right technique.

Her thoughts caught her so completely that the closing prayer took her off guard. Service never seemed so short before this morning, but Lucinda offered thanks that the ordeal had almost ended. Whisk the family back to the farm to avoid curious questions, and she'd breathe easier again.

"Before everyone gets up," Parson Carter's voice snagged her when she would have risen and started to make her escape, "I'd like to invite you to a surprise wedding reception. No sense pretending the whole town didn't notice Opal arrived with Adam Grogan, so I'm happy to announce that I married them in a *very* private ceremony early this week. My wife's cooked up a storm and bought out the Dunstalls' café for their ready-mades. It's time to celebrate the joining of two families who've finally laid aside their differences to come together in love!"

Love? Lucinda wrestled with the urge to claw at her bonnet ribbons, which suddenly seemed to choke her. *Lies! Lies of the Specks snaked out to snare my son in this sham of a marriage, and now the parson tightens the bind. But the more taut the rope, the greater the snap when it's severed.*

Lucinda contented herself with certain knowledge that she'd make the Speck girl snap long before the Grogans gave way. But for now, she'd play the part of reluctant mother-in-law of an enamored groom. Anything to preserve Adam's reputation and keep the family as whole as possible.

Standing, she hid her face behind the brim of her bonnet and plucked the splinter from her palm, dropping it to the floor. One step forward, and it crushed beneath her heel, lending her pasted-on smile a measure of sincerity as Lucinda prepared to meet the many well-wishers and scandal-sniffers of Buttonwood.

❧ ∞ ❧

Forgiveness. A concept Christians chased like a cat batting at dust motes glinting in the morning sun. The tantalizing glimmer made them rear up and lunge, only to have what they sought lose the sparkle on those rare occasions they nabbed it.

Because it can't be earned or even caught and held. God's gifts to us can only be appreciated. Adam savored the warmth of Opal pressed close to his side throughout the service. He thought of all the times he'd made mistakes or wished petty things on his brother and knew himself to be no better than the woman he now called his wife.

It wasn't his place to judge her actions or even forgive her for them. Forgiveness wasn't something a man could give—it was a blessing to be shared.

Just one of the blessings I'd like to share with Opal. Lord, I believe You gave me this woman as my wife with the intent that I keep her.

I lay down my anger over the paltry trick she played with the mattress. I want to move on with my marriage. Jesus, please work in her heart so she will confide in me the name of the father of her child so that we can begin afresh and without any looming threats to the life we build.

Parson Carter's announcement of an impromptu dinner came as a surprise. If not welcome, it struck Adam as a good opportunity to solidify their marriage in the eyes of the town and show everyone he didn't regret his choice of wife. When they all stood, it seemed only natural to slide his hand across her back and steer her through the throng of people crowding the aisle.

Opal showed no inclination to stop and clog the narrow passageway to chat. The small church, filled with townspeople for the morning and shut against the chill of the spring morning, began to grow stuffy. Some soul impervious to the curiosity plaguing the rest of Buttonwood had the good sense to throw open the door, sending a welcome breeze through the structure.

Everyone else seemed determined to be the first to reach him and Opal, pepper them with questions, and roast them on the flames of speculation until their lives could be picked apart.

Expressions of disappointment and thwarted determination painted the faces around them as he swept his wife past and toward the open door offering freedom.

They broke through into the fresh air almost at the same time, and for one moment Opal's gaze found his and they shared a smile at their small victory. That smile settled the matter in his mind as they hurried to the open grassy area where they couldn't be hemmed in again. Past mistakes would stay behind them, and they would continue as they were now. United.

He skimmed his hand to her waist and tucked her to his side as the crowd behind them caught up. Her soft gasp at the unexpected closeness made him want to catch her eye again, but he found his view blocked by her bonnet as she focused on a gaggle of women babbling their well wishes to her. Something inside him stretched restlessly as the townspeople kept Opal's attention from him, but the warmth of her waist through the cotton layers of her clothing beneath his palm kept him reasonable.

"Never thought I'd see the day." Old Josiah Reed, owner of the town store, clapped him on the shoulder. "Grogan married a Speck. Took a lot of guts to nab her from her family like that. . . and a lot of determination."

"She's worth even more than that." Adam didn't have to think about his answer before he spoke. *No lie there.* His comment sparked a round of giggles and elbow jabs among the folks clustered around.

"Thank you." With her head tilted back, Opal's bonnet didn't block her pretty face from his view any longer. Genuine gratitude shone in her eyes before she turned to another one of the women. Brim blocked her from him again.

"Snuck in and beat us all." Brett Burn's good-natured acknowledgment confirmed Adam's impression that he hadn't been the man to play Opal false. Some tension eased from his shoulders as he discarded that threat.

"Snuck is right." A grumble sounded from a tight group bunched off to the side of the jubilant crowd.

Adam's eyes narrowed as he surveyed the men and distinguished two distinct knots of fulminating family. The Speck men eyed the Grogan men, with less distance between them than ever before with no bloodshed.

The comment sounded like one that should, by rights, have come from Murphy Speck or even one of Opal's brothers. *Why, then, did that sound like Larry?* Adam shook off the notion. Not even Larry would try to cause problems today.

"Adam is no sneak." Opal's declaration took him off guard— almost as much as the hand she slid behind him to curl around his waist. If a woman could bristle like a porcupine, he got the feeling that's what she'd be doing. It was etched in the straight line of her back, the way the awful brim of that bonnet quivered in outrage. "Our wedding may have been hasty and private due to the tensions between our families, but I'm proud to call this man my husband."

"I gathered the bouquet myself." Midge Collins pushed through the crowd to stand alongside them, dragging Pete Speck in her wake. "Pete and I stood as witnesses, and it's been a positive drain to keep it to ourselves all week!"

"Was it romantic?" A sharp-eyed matron, whose name Adam couldn't recall as she was newer to the town, poked her long nose right in.

"A secret wedding in a spring clearing." Midge waxed poetic to a rapt audience, and Adam had the good sense to let her weave her spell. "I'm sure Parson Carter would tell you it was one of the most memorable ceremonies he's ever performed."

All eyes shifted to the pastor, whose enthusiastic nod sent heads bobbing back to focus on Midge. Adam figured it was time he joined into the spirit of things. He reached up and quickly tugged free the small bow in Opal's bonnet strings with his free hand.

"She wore this same dress, knowing it's one of my favorite colors." He grasped the back of her bonnet and tugged, sliding it from her hair and sending wisps dancing along the breeze around her face. "And no bonnet so I could see her face as we spoke our vows."

A flurry of wistful sighs greeted the gesture, but Adam only cared that his restlessness faded when he could see Opal's face again.

Her eyes widened when the covering slipped from her hair, but the surprise changed to mischief in a twinkle. His bride opened her mouth, and Adam knew he was in trouble.

From the moment they escaped the church into the fresh air and Adam gave her that conspiratorial grin, Opal knew today would mark a new beginning for them. Hope blunted the rage she felt toward Lucinda, who she couldn't profess to have completely forgiven yet, and even muffled the cry in her heart from the way Pa still wouldn't look at her.

The armor of God protected her and held her up, allowing her to accept the greetings and exclamations of her neighbors and friends without arrows of guilt piercing her too deeply. She even kept in mind Midge's advice to make the most of today's opportunity to demonstrate affection.

More importantly, Adam outdid her. Oh, he'd sucked in a breath the first time she'd scooted over and pressed against his side in a bid to avoid Larry's remarkable ability to intrude on her space, but afterward Adam hadn't protested the proximity one bit. Better still, he must have sensed how she dreaded getting trapped between the church benches, caught up in stifling interrogations before she made it outside.

When the weight of his hand settled on the small of her back, the pressure of his palm firmly encouraging her to surge toward the freedom of that open door, she'd felt grounded for the first time since she'd seen him surrounded by her family's shotguns. If a smile could stretch through eternity, Opal would've kept the moment he'd grinned at her as though she were his partner in truth, not pretense.

A mistake, because then she would have missed his arm sliding around her waist, nestling her against his side in the crook of his arm as they greeted Buttonwood as man and wife. She never would have seen the gleam in his gaze when he slid off her bonnet, looking as though he'd uncovered a treasure. And she would have lost her chance to make up for the kiss she'd missed by the chicken coop.

Heat rose from her neck to her ears, and Opal knew that for once her bemoaned tendency to turn red over anything would serve her well. After all, how better to convince the townspeople she was a blushing bride than to blush?

"Midge!" Opal made sure her whisper carried over the bunch of people. "Adam! No one need know any other particular part of the ceremony. Stop discussing the details. Those are"—she met Midge's eyes and nodded meaningfully—"*private*."

Immediately the swarm buzzed, demanding more information, just as Opal depended they would. All the attention increased the heat flushing her cheeks, making her blush brighter.

"She's blushing!" Several people noticed and speculated as to why.

"C'mon, Midge," Alyssa, the sixteen-year-old town belle, implored. "Tell us what's making Opal turn ruby red!"

"Nothing to make her turn red," her friend protested. Obviously, Midge caught on to Opal's scheme to mention the wedding-day kiss, and now whipped the people into an expert froth of nosiness. "Only what's natural for a new bride and groom. . ."

Avid stares heated Opal's blush to boiling, and she began to regret her impetuous course of action. Her boldness fled, her downcast gaze no longer a role to play but a way to avoid meeting her husband's eyes.

"They kissed." Her youngest brother's voice rang with impatience and even a little disgust as Pete sidestepped a sharp elbow from Midge. "No big secret there. Happens at most weddings." His blunt words and obvious disdain did nothing to bring the residents of Buttonwood in line.

Guffaws from the men eddied alongside titters from the women on the afternoon breeze, but a huddle of humanity on the edges of the crowd didn't join the laughter. *Finally, the Specks and Grogans agree on something.* Yet Opal found no joy in the discovery. If all their families shared was rage over this marriage, the tension would escape to consume everyone.

"Kiss her again!" Josiah Reed's voice rose above it all as though on cue. Come to think of it, the man most likely knew exactly what he did, given his history of meddling in relationships. Clara and Saul turned out the better for it, so Opal reckoned she shouldn't complain.

Her thoughts screeched to a halt when Adam's hand moved at her waist, turning her toward him. Her husband didn't waste a word, simply angled his body closer and cupped her cheek with a large, rough palm as he leaned forward.

"I know you did that on purpose." His undertone floated to her ears as though imagined, but Opal knew Adam had figured out her little game. But he kept playing.

Her breath hitched when his lips brushed against hers. Once, a featherlight whisper. Twice, a silky murmur. A third time, and his mouth captured hers for a second of stolen sweetness before he drew away.

When her breath and brains returned, Opal started scheming. She needed another one of Midge's lessons on how to snare the attentions of her reluctant spouse. By sheer force of will, she didn't press her fingertips to the tingle in her lips. *Because next time, I don't want him to stop.*

Adam fought a brief but powerful skirmish with his own unwillingness to release Opal when the guffaw got loud enough to tell him he shouldn't offer any more "proof" of their shared affection.

He'd seen the look in her eyes and known she plotted some

mischief, but never anticipated what she had in mind. In one fell swoop, Adam learned two very valuable lessons about his firebrand of a bride. No matter her determination to lead the town by the nose, Opal's acting skills wouldn't fetch much on the market.

Those overblown protests about Midge revealing the "details" of their wedding couldn't be more obvious. Only her blushes—that becoming rosy tinge creeping up her cheeks as she got the reaction she'd sought—saved her from the whole town catching on to the more important discovery of the day.

Opal wants me to kiss her. The realization rang through him. He planted his boots on the ground and snagged her in his arms. Once he nabbed her, he couldn't resist taunting her with his knowledge that she'd put them in this position on purpose.

But the soft feel of her pressed lightly against him, the warmth of her breath when his lips grazed hers, the elusive hint of honey that hung in the air around her, turned the tables in an instant. Adam snuck a second taste. Then he knew he should let her go—but she swayed into him, and he sampled her sweetness a third time before gathering the fortitude to pull away.

The refreshing breeze that enveloped them when they left the church died away, offering no help to cool the urgent heat racing through his veins. Adam swallowed, trying to make his mouth and mind work as a team again while good-natured friends teased and sour onlookers muttered.

No use. His mind and mouth were hitched in harness to one idea, and wouldn't budge from it. He wanted another kiss.

CHAPTER 26

"Midge Lorraine Collins-Reed!" The hissed whisper offered no advanced warning, as it hit her ears the same moment Clara's hand clamped around her elbow.

Midge might not have minded were it not for a few facts. First, she'd just drawn that selfsame elbow back for a much-needed jab to Pete's ribs when Clara nabbed her. More important, she'd almost forgotten that there'd be a reckoning with Clara once her friend/adoptive mother—although Clara, at only six years older than she, could hardly stand as her true mother—once she discovered the incredible secret Midge had been sitting on all week. Now the skirts of Opal's secret were billowing in the breeze and doing a fine job of exposing what Clara would see as a betrayal of her and Midge's friendship. And last, she hated her middle name. *Lorraine.* Sounded so snotty. Not like her at all.

Midge wrinkled her nose and allowed herself to be dragged a safe—or not-so-safe, depending on how upset Clara turned out to be—distance from where the rest of the town speculated over Opal and Adam's hasty wedding. Raised eyebrows and lowered voices carried theories ranging from star-crossed love to unwanted children, just as she and Opal expected. So long as no one hit on the real reason for the marriage, things would stay manageable.

"I can't believe you kept something this important from me! Did Opal ask you not to say anything?" Clara's large green eyes just about swallowed her face this afternoon, swimming with questions and hurt.

"Pete came to find a witness to the ceremony, and he made me swear not to tell a soul if I wanted to find out what was going on." Midge didn't have to squash any guilt over heaping the blame on Pete. Not only was it true, he'd escaped that second elbowing. "He said Opal needed me, so I gave my word to keep my mouth shut and went with him and Parson Carter."

"You could have trusted me." The protest escaped as though pushed through by a grudge, and her friend showed the grace to look somewhat ashamed of herself for voicing it. "But if you gave your word, I understand."

"I knew you'd understand, even though you wouldn't like it." Midge heard a light footfall behind her and knew Aunt Doreen joined them. "*Both* of you."

"We can waste breath harping on her about why she didn't tell us what happened," Doreen spoke quietly as she came alongside them, "or we can get to the good parts and just ask what happened!"

"Parson Carter married Opal and Adam, and Pete and I stood as witnesses. I couldn't breathe a word because Pete swore me to secrecy." Midge kept it simple, matter-of-fact, and honest. Even if something deep inside her didn't lurch like a drunken sailor at the thought of lying to the Reed women, she didn't want to be scrambling to remember what she said. It's why she'd planned for this moment days ago.

"Obviously." Doreen's keen gaze didn't leave much room to wiggle. "Everyone knows that much. What we want to know is the reason behind the wedding."

"Love." Not so much as a blink while she uttered this proclamation. Sure, she knew Doreen and Clara would think she meant that Opal and Adam were in love with one another, but the wedding went on for the love of their families. Opal sacrificed her standing with her family to avoid a feud and save their lives, after all, and far too much rode on making this makeshift marriage a success for Midge to jeopardize it with something as tawdry as specifics.

"Adam all along! Not even two weeks ago I tried to speak with Opal about Brett Burn, and she went pale as a ghost and said something about ignoring a man who chased after her." Clara practically bounced over the discovery. "Surprised her when she realized I meant the blacksmith. Shocked me she wouldn't tell me who she thought I'd meant but wouldn't say another word about it. Now I know why!"

"Sounds reasonable." *But you're wrong.* Midge started to wonder how much biting one woman's tongue could take. She contributed nothing more than a few absent nods to the conversation.

Adam wasn't the Grogan Opal wanted to ignore. Midge sucked in a breath. *I knew I didn't like how Larry looked at her but didn't know he'd made such a pest of himself. And Opal wouldn't tell a soul, for fear of the fighting between their families.*

The more she fiddled this strange piece of information into the puzzle of Opal's sudden marriage, the more certain Midge became. *Somehow, this whole mess is Larry's fault!*

❦

Lucinda's stomach roiled as she watched her son pull away from Opal's clutches. Adam wore a befuddled expression, as though the hussy addled his brains with nothing more than a smooch.

No. Terrible fairness compelled her to acknowledge that Opal wielded far more than a simple smooch to snare her son. *A kiss marked the beginning long ago. How long?* The questions skewered her. *Weeks? Months? Seasons? When did that baggage first cast her eye on my boy? When did I fail to see the danger?*

She eyed her daughter-in-law's trim middle. *Too trim. Any child far enough along to erase all doubts would begin to show about now.* The back of her throat burned with restrained rage. *Opal lied. She's not carrying Adam's child. He need not have married the scheming whore.*

"You must be soooo proud." Griselda West, overly fancy in her East Sunday costume, sidled up and cooed at Diggory. All that sweetness didn't fool Lucinda one bit.

Sugarcoat a chicken bone and it'd still choke a body, after all. Griselda's avid gaze shone with her true intent. The woman waited for someone to spill even a hint that Adam and Opal weren't a true love match so she could lap up the gossip and spread it across the town.

Choices didn't come easy some days. Champion Adam by making it sound as though he and Opal struck up a forbidden romance, as they spoon-fed to the town, and watch it all come unraveled when her son discovered his wife's lies? Or let it slip that Opal acted no better than she should be, a hoyden with no mother and a godless upbringing, tempting upstanding men into the ways of sin. Adam may seem a fool for succumbing, but most would brush off the lapse with a chuckle at his manly ways—particularly since he'd done the honorable thing and married the chit. This way, when she rousted Opal and got rid of the girl, no one would blame her boy.

"Of course we're proud." Lucinda tilted her chin upward in a haughty show as the newlyweds walked over. "Adam could charm a bird from a tree, but even we didn't know he could manage to woo a Speck from her family loyalty."

A strangled cough rasped from Murphy Speck at that

comment, making the rest of the Speck men go ruddy in fury.

So unbecoming, with all that red hair. Lucinda bit back her first smile of the day, pleasantly surprised with the effort it took once she noticed Opal's reaction. It seemed almost as though the crimson flooding her family's faces leeched all the color from her own, as she went ghostly pale.

The moment passed all too quickly as Parson Carter came and fetched them all to sit at a makeshift table for the celebratory "wedding" dinner. The rest of the town would fend for themselves, more or less. In the end, Lucinda perched on the end of a bench, narrowly avoiding being shoved to the ground by Diggory's enthusiastic shoveling of his food. With all eyes on the "happy" couple, nothing she said made much of an impact.

Lucinda relied on Larry to share her sentiments. Her middle son had always been the one most eager to scrap with the Specks, always the most in tune to her moods. Usually, he took his place at her side, but in the hubbub of Parson Carter's arrangements, somehow both her grown sons flanked her family's intruder.

Adam to her left, Larry to her right, Opal lorded it over the town as though some sort of Buttonwood royalty. She and Adam—acting along—bore the only partially convincing smiles at the table. Murphy and Diggory glared daggers at each other. Lucinda didn't think it coincidence that the Carters settled on serving stew. Spoons made for the least amount of damage in a brawl. Dave sent scowls winging toward Pete Speck, who ignored them in favor of doting on that upstart Midge Collins.

Larry's brows almost met in the middle, disapproval radiating from his every move. Any time Adam or Opal spoke to one another, his lips grew thinner. But Lucinda's brief spurt of pride died into a dry throat when she realized his searing glances weren't directed at Opal. Larry aimed all his fury straight at Adam.

A gust of memory blew away Lucinda's anger over the town

dinner. *Adam and Larry arguing in the barn. Over Opal.* No matter how hard she swallowed, nausea crept up the back of her throat. *Larry saying he had his eye on her. Adam threatening to deliver his own brother to the Specks if he came near Opal. . . I should have known then, but I didn't see Adam's involvement with her.*

As though detached from the scene, she watched Larry angle his arm so his elbow pressed against Opal's arm. The girl's uncomfortable avoidance offered no reassurance. Having lured Adam to her side, that trollop encroached on Grogan land but wasn't satisfied. Now she worked her wiles on Larry.

It's so clear what she plans to do—turn brother against brother and destroy us from within. But this time I see what she's up to. And I'll stop it. Lucinda's knuckles whitened and she felt the metal of her spoon easing from its rigid mold from the pressure under her fingers. *No matter what I have to do.*

CHAPTER 27

Folks filed by throughout the meal, and Adam lost track of how many times men clapped him on the shoulder. He kept busy trying to look every male in the area in the eye, hunting for any glint of anger, regret, or relief to mark the man who'd taken advantage of his wife. *The man who could still lay claim to her.* Mrs. Carter's stew didn't set well at the thought.

As though sensing his discomfort, Opal pressed tighter against his side. The wordless reassurance enabled Adam to keep hold of his grin as Dr. Saul Reed approached. Not that he need have worried about Reed—the man wouldn't have noticed half the townspeople were female if he hadn't been medically trained. That's how strong a bond he'd made with his wife, Clara. Adam didn't fix the label of friend to just anyone, but Reed made the cut.

"Grogan." His friend's grin stretched too wide for show as he hauled his wife and their baby to the table. "You and your new missus proved something I've wondered about for a while."

"What's that?"

"If Clara hung up her matchmaking bonnet after our marriage or if she kept quietly scheming." Laughter greeted the pronouncement, as almost everyone knew by now that Clara had taken a wild bargain and tried to marry Saul off to any eligible woman in Buttonwood two years ago before taking him on as her personal, permanent project.

"Clara didn't plot to bring us together." The supple warmth at his side vanished, replaced by Opal's sudden rigidity as she defended her friend.

"I didn't even know." Clara almost choked on the admission. Surprise, hurt, concern, and suspicion chased each other across her face.

"I'm sorry." The stiffness leached from his wife's spine and Adam felt more than saw Opal slump beside him. The posture of defeat.

It demanded action.

He slid his arm around her waist to bolster her up, jostling her just enough so her head leaned toward him, sun-warmed hair spreading across his shoulder as much as her pins would allow. A small sigh escaped her, but Adam didn't take the time to classify it as sad or satisfied.

"A world of truth survives in silence," Doreen Reed—Clara's aunt and now the wife of Saul Reed's father—intervened. "Kept in quiet and dependent upon discretion."

Mine does. Adam resisted the urge to swallow, all too aware that it would give away his discomfort. *Discretion lays the foundation of our marriage, because if the truth we bury is ever unearthed, our families will destroy one another. Survival itself depends on that silence.*

"Whoa." Dave's nine-year-old voice piped up from down the table. "Somebody real impressive must've said that."

"Thank you." The older woman's acknowledgment made Clara, Opal, and everyone else smile as they realized Doreen hadn't been quoting anyone at all. Just sharing her own insight.

"That was beautiful." Willa's voice, seldom heard outside the family, caught everyone's attention.

For the first time, Adam looked beyond Opal to see where the rest of their families had settled. No surprise to see the Specks to the left of the table and the Grogans monopolizing the right half. Midge Collins made a useful placeholder between Dave and Pete on the opposite bench, but otherwise things had gone awry.

Seated in the center of the bench, Opal should have been the connector to her family, easing tension and uniting what had been antagonistic clans. Instead of this natural order, someone jumbled the arrangement in a way guaranteed to provoke tempers.

How did Willa come to sit next to Benjamin Speck? Adam knew the exact moment Pa and Ma made the same realization. No one blinked. Willa ducked her head under the weight of their stares, obviously regretting drawing any attention to herself.

After Benjamin's ill-advised notice of his sister the previous week—Adam could scarce believe only a week had passed—his effrontery in sitting beside Willa couldn't go unremarked.

"Daughter," Ma's voice sounded thin, as though she spoke from far away, "how did you come to be so far away?"

"Halfway down the table isn't far." Midge's comment, reasonable though it seemed, made no impact.

"Leaving family land to settle with Grogans—that's far." Ben, who Adam noted took care not to let so much as an elbow brush against Willa, kept both his tone and expression even. Nothing to give offense but just enough to show he wouldn't be cowed.

Adam felt Opal go ramrod straight, physically bracing against an emotional blow. His kept his arm wrapped around her, refusing to relinquish his support. Or his claim.

"Just far enough for a fresh start." He gave his bride a squeeze and a smile to diffuse tension. *Today is the most difficult.* He willed her to remember that.

"Says something when a woman needs a fresh start away from her own family."

Adam couldn't say whether Opal's squawk came from indignation over Larry's idiocy or as protest over the way his arm tightened around her in his own reaction. He loosened his grip immediately and started to push away from the table. If he had to knock down his brother to keep up the peace, so be it.

"Don't be a ninny, Larry!" Willa's outburst stayed him. She glowered at their troublesome brother, only the way she wrung her hands in her lap identifying his normally shy sister. "Opal and Adam's marriage means a fresh start for all of us, and we don't want needling comments like yours trying to prick pride and draw blood."

"Well said." Admiration shone in Ben Speck's gaze. More than enough for everyone at the table to notice it.

Pa's eyebrows drew together. Ma reached out a hand as though to snatch Willa to her side then made poor cover of the gesture by reaching for a roll. A sudden jerk from Dave told Adam his younger brother attempted an unsuccessful kick beneath the table.

The Specks showed signs of displeasure as well. Elroy muttered beneath his breath. Murphy gave a swift, short shake of his head. Young Pete looked as though he sorely wanted to make an unwise comment, but a well-timed poke in the ribs from Midge kept his tongue between his teeth.

In fact, the only person at the entire table who showed no reaction was Willa. Having said her piece, she'd ducked her head back down and resumed staring at her hands, oblivious to Ben's all-too-apparent regard.

Well, at least Willa didn't return Speck's interest. Adam rolled his shoulders in a futile bid to relax. They'd still avoid disaster so long as his sister kept her head.

Wait. No. I didn't see that right.

※

Opal felt her eyes widen and didn't even bother trying to fix it. She stayed busy keeping her jaw off the ground as her new sister-in-law gave Ben a timid smile.

Until a fingernail dug into her shoulder blade, an unsubtle signal that Clara wanted to make sure she wasn't missing the byplay. Then Opal's wide-eyed wonder turned into a wince. Her friend needn't have worried. *After spending my whole life trying to keep Specks and Grogans apart, I'm more sensitive to their interactions that anyone in all of Buttonwood!*

The strong hand resting on her waist clenched into a fist, making her amend her thoughts. *Except, maybe, for Adam.* Opal accepted the possibility that her husband made a good match for her in this area, at least. She slid one of her hands atop his fisted one and gave it a light pat to let him know she understood the implications of Ben and Willa's camaraderie.

Strange how this new threat to the fragile truce between their families didn't shake her nearly so much as it should have. Or, at least, as much as it would have before the events of the past week.

Maybe because there's a much bigger threat looming above us. She closed her eyes against misgivings over her hasty marriage. *No. I'd rather think it's because God's brought us this far without bloodshed. Surely another Speck and Grogan getting along will ultimately do good. Like me and Adam.*

Somehow, her fingers had laced with his, and she breathed more easily as she felt some of the strain ease from his muscles. If she wasn't mistaken, her husband had been about to stand after Larry's foolish comment and take care of matters. *Which, of course, would have made everything worse. Lucinda would blame me for turning her sons against each other.*

"Fresh starts are for fools who make mistakes, and there's been enough foolishness to last both our families a lifetime." Diggory Grogan's statement, if retold by a neutral person with a kind voice, might be mistaken as the equivalent of an olive branch offered to the Specks.

But no one at the table, nor any one of the occupants of Buttonwood clustered around it with ears open and minds racing, would interpret it as anything but malicious. Venom coated Diggory's words as surely as the fury in his gaze refused to be held to one person. It spread from herself to Adam, then Ben and even Willa, infecting them all and poisoning all her efforts to keep their families from outright war.

No! The bitterness welled up until it threatened to choke her. *Lord, help me. I didn't betray my father's trust and wed a Grogan only to see it all fall apart now!* The bitterness eased enough for her to draw breath. Even as she asked for strength to fight the hatred surrounding her, Opal knew the answer. Hadn't Parson Carter shared it earlier that morning?

" *'The Lord shall fight for you, and ye shall hold your peace. . . .'* " Fighting only made things worse.

"My father-in-law is right." Opal leaned across the table to pat Diggory's hand, relishing the surprise seeping across his features. "Both Specks and Grogans have wronged one another, made enough mistakes to stop now and never be in danger of committing the blasphemy of claiming perfection." Clara, Midge, and Doreen laughed, and the rest of the town reluctantly joined in. Opal waited for it to die down before she finished. She kept one hand atop Diggory's, anchoring him to her words even as she held her father's gaze with her own. "I'm glad the parson preached on forgiveness this morning. . .so we can leave the past behind and move forward as the neighbors we should always have been."

"Amen!" Parson Carter hastened to offer his support. "The Lord tells us we've all fallen short."

The town erupted into murmurs and even outbursts of hearty agreement as folks besieged the table with congratulations, forcing Parson Carter's hopes of a truce into reality. With the entire town not allowing tensions to break free, and a wedding to cement connection between the families, Opal started to wonder if today might truly be the end of the feud that had threatened her loved ones for so long.

"Well done, girlie." Diggory leaned forward, reluctant appreciation in his gaze as his hand slid from hers. "A worthy move."

"Yes." Lucinda's agreement rang bright and loud before the hissed accompaniment. "Just remember, Opal, that some people fall far shorter than others."

CHAPTER 28

Y ou don't mean it?" Opal's gasp pierced something in Adam's chest.

"A fresh start," he repeated what he'd just told her. "After the way you smoothed the path for our families to reconcile yesterday—especially in the face of Pa's and Larry's aggression—I've decided to put the past away."

"All of it?" Shrewdness sharpened her features.

"We'll forget about the cause for our wedding." *I can afford to be generous when it saved my skin.* "And even dismiss the rocks in the mattress."

Her sudden hug caught him off-balance. Almost literally. One minute his wife stood before him, face bright with hope, and the next instant warm woman filled his arms with softness and his breath with a tantalizing hint of honey. His arms skated around to hold her closer.

It takes little enough to make her happy. Adam didn't even try to dredge up a protest, just savored the sensations. *I'll remember that and be sure to do it more often.*

"Rank ewe." Opal's murmur puzzled him.

"We don't keep sheep." He lost her response when he felt the heat of her breath through the cotton of his shirt. *I'll buy her some sheep if she wants them.*

"Mmffm." Her hands pressed against his arms, pushing the realization that he'd been holding his wife too tightly.

He immediately released her, jamming his hands in his pockets as she took a great gulp of air. Oops.

"Sheep?" She looked confused. "I said thank you."

"I misheard. It's no matter."

"It matters." The shiny happy look came back. "More than you know. After seeing Pa and Ben and Elroy and Pete yesterday, it made me miss them even more. Knowing I wouldn't see them again for so long made me wretched. I can't say how much it means that I can go over there tomorrow."

"I don't want you to be wretched, Opal." *Will she ever look like that when she says my name?*

"Wouldn't have lasted. What really makes me happy is that you're letting us start afresh. Completely new." One smile shouldn't be capable of containing such radiance.

Adam blinked to clear his mind. "Opal, there's one matter that must be laid to rest before we move forward entirely."

"Yes?" The smile faded, though her glow remained. She reached out and clasped one of his hands in both of hers.

"Opal, I know you don't really want to discuss it, but I think we both know that he left town a while ago." He spoke carefully, trying to upset her as little as possible as he broached the topic of the man who'd impregnated then abandoned her. He'd come to the conclusion the day before that the fellow didn't remain in town. "You must have thought he wouldn't come back?"

"There were times when even I began to doubt." Her openness touched him. "But he's a man of his word, Adam. I knew he'd return to us."

Us. She's known she was with child for months now. Opal will begin to show the pregnancy any time. And she still believes he's returning for her and their child? It seemed as though all the moisture in his throat crisped to ice.

"Is he worthy?" *Will you want to leave with him if that day comes?*

"I've never known a more worthy man." The earnestness of her expression felled him. "He'll make a good provider, Adam. You don't have to worry."

"People will talk." He grasped at anything to keep her from slipping away. "Our families will declare war."

"No. Another marriage will only strengthen the alliance between the Specks and Grogans." She squeezed his hand. "Benjamin made a lot of money in the mines, Adam. He'll more than do right by Willa. Your Pa will come around."

"Ben." He all but shouted her brother's name. *How is she talking about Ben?*

"Yes." Opal squeezed his hand tighter, as though to make him focus. Maybe he needed it. "I know you and your family think Ben was flighty for going off to the mines, but he and Pa made the decision together. He always planned to come back. Even if he didn't write as often as I'd like, he tried. You can depend on Ben to stand by Willa, and, like I said, he has the money to keep her more than comfortable."

Her flurry of words penetrated his confusion. *When I asked about the man who'd left awhile ago, she thought I meant her brother?* If biting back a bellow didn't take his concentration, Adam might have struggled against laughter. *I'm trying to coax my wife to confess the name of her lover, and she's trying to convince me that her brother will make a good husband for my sister!*

"No." He placed his free hand over both of hers as the consequences of what she suggested sank in. *Pa will take blood in exchange for his only daughter.* "I can't let that happen."

"What do you mean?" Opal went ahead and asked the question but already knew the answer. As she'd spoken of Ben, she'd watched Adam's expression grow increasingly impassive. *Why did you ask about my brother if you'd already made up your mind?* She wanted to cry out but knew better than to push this new husband of hers.

Already this morning he'd rescinded the punishment for Lucinda's ploy with those rocks in her mattress. Questioning his judgment about allowing Ben to court Willa might set her back more than she could afford.

"I mean that we've more than enough difficulties surrounding our marriage to even consider assisting another one." His hands beneath and atop hers put forth an astonishing amount of heat. "We can't waste our time or energy trying to keep track of Ben and Willa when there's so much riding on our relationship."

"Our relationship." She liked the sound of that far too much, but he said it as though they made a team. *I've always been a Speck but didn't really fit in as the only woman and the one trying to keep everyone from fighting. But Adam's talking as though I could belong.*

"Keeping everyone believing we chose each other. . .it takes a lot of work." His flat comment squashed her silliness.

"Of course it does." She tugged her hands away but only managed to free one. *It's obvious a man like you would never choose a nothing like me unless forced into it. You speak of fresh starts, but really you're just making the best of a bad situation.* Her eyes stung at the thought.

"Especially when we aren't in it together." His grip tightened, as though trapping her.

"What do you mean?" A welcome wave of anger rolled away the loneliness for a moment. "I've stood alongside you to help avert bloodshed from the very beginning. No, even before the beginning. Back before our wedding day. How can you imply anything less?"

The same way Pa figures I'm not loyal to the Specks. The idea floored her. *It doesn't matter how much I do or how many times I prove that I'll sacrifice my own needs for the best interests of others, in the end I'll still be the outsider.*

Sorrow crashed over her, dousing the flames of her indignation. But only for a moment, when she realized Adam was talking about unanswered questions and an uncertain future.

"When you won't tell me who the father is?" he finished as though he'd built up to this last question, though Opal hadn't caught most of what he said.

"You're asking me why you should move forward with this marriage when I can't tell you who is going to be the father of my child?"

"Exactly."

"Perhaps because this marriage saved your life." Opal jerked her hand from his when another light tug didn't immediately free her. "And therefore the lives of your entire family."

"Yours, too." His jaw hardened.

"That's why I'm ready to go ahead." She jumped on the opportunity. "If I'm able to, why aren't you?"

"I'm not the one who would be seen as unfit for society when my babe entered the world without a father." Adam's usual use of diplomacy vanished right along with hers. "You're the one who only wants to go forward so she can leave secrets buried in the past."

"You, you…" Opal clenched her teeth together to keep the words from escaping. *I can't tell him I'm a virgin. I can't tell him my secret is that I have no secrets. If he knows before the marriage is consummated, he'll annul the marriage and get us all killed.* She reminded herself of the facts over and over again. *He only thinks you're carrying a child out of wedlock because you allow him to believe so.*

"I what?" He folded his arms across his chest. "I deserve to know the name of the man whose child I'll be raising?"

"You're a hypocrite!" The accusation bled from her thoughts before she could staunch the flow. "No one forced you to claim me or my future child. You could just as easily have denied me to my family, admitted Larry's guilt in writing the note you should have burned, and taken the penalty. You may even have lived long enough to seek vengeance for the punishment my father dealt your brother. The secrets of which you speak aren't mine, husband." She took a deep breath. "They're *ours*."

"True." Adam closed the space between them. "I don't like it but won't deny it. At least we can share our secrets and the common purpose of safeguarding those we love, Opal."

"Yes." She kept her gaze fixed on his shoulder, knowing somehow that if her eyes met his she'd be undone. "We share those things, if not a bed or a life."

His hissed intake of breath let her know the remark hit home.

"Marriages are based on trust, and trust on truth. There will be truth between us, wife." His forefinger crooked beneath her chin, tilting it upward until she faced him fully. "Tell me his name."

"You're wrong."

She tried to back away, but he held her fast, his thumb coming to rest almost tenderly on her chin.

"How so?"

"Trust is based in honesty, not truth."

"Two branches of the same tree. I'll take either one." The slightly rough pad of his thumb traced her lower lip. "We'll start our marriage in full when you answer. Tell me."

"So be it. Honestly," she closed her eyes against the hot pinpricks of tears as she gave him the only answer she had, "there's nothing to tell."

CHAPTER 29

"Tell me everything." Midge barely waited until they reached the edge of the apiary before demanding information. Opal wore the look of a woman with too much on her mind.

With a fake illicit pregnancy, a hidden shotgun wedding, a pending family feud, and an evil mother-in-law, there's plenty to keep her busy. Even without me asking if I'm right about Larry making a pest of himself and somehow bringing that farce of a wedding on her and Adam. . .

Today called for a tall order of talk, followed by a dose of scheming. *If God really existed, maybe He did well to get me here for Opal, like He put Dr. Reed in Baltimore to save me from Randy.* The thought caught her off guard, so Midge shoved it to the back of her mind. She had more important matters to delve into right now.

"We spoke yesterday after church."

"That much to cover?" Midge gave a low whistle. If Opal's reluctance proved any gauge as to the level of difficulty they could expect, at least boredom wouldn't creep up on her. "And don't try to brush me off. The whole town besieged you and Adam so much the two of us didn't have a moment together."

"Did you bring woolen gloves?"

Opal's question seemed senseless until Midge remembered that her visit bore an actual purpose. Today they had to move the apiary from Speck land to the Grogan clearing Adam marked for it. "Yes. Though leather's easier to work through."

"Not when you're working with bees." Her friend's expression turned serious. "If a bee feels threatened and stings, leather will trap him and he'll die. With wool, he can usually remove his stinger and survive."

"Will you kick me out of your apiary if I say that the bees who sting me aren't my highest priority?" Midge tugged her sleeves down over her wrists.

"I won't, but only because you said 'who' when you talked about them, and that shows you think of them as individuals." Opal passed her a misshapen brown lump. "Put this in your pocket, just in case."

"Looks like tobacco." Midge inspected the texture of the thing then sniffed it. "It *is* tobacco! I don't want this."

"You will if you get stung. It's an old trick my mother taught me. Warm some tobacco in your hand until it's moist then rub it on the site of the sting until the pain and swelling lessen. It works better than even ammonia does and won't take your skin off." Opal passed her a straw hat. "You'll be especially glad since the hotter the weather, the worse the swelling."

"This starts to sound like you assume some bees will sting me." Doubt niggled through her. "They never have before."

"Before, we fed them. Today, we're going to move the hives. They'll see that as an attack." Opal pulled out yards of netting. "It's why we take extra precautions like the gloves and netting and make sure we smoke the hives to lull the bees to sleep as best we can before we start jostling them around."

"Is there anything else I should know?" *Now that it's too late to back out.*

"Keep your ears open. One of the first alerts will be the sound the bees make. When they're making that buzzing hum, they're happy and busy. When they're agitated, it takes on a shrill pitch. That's when they're more likely to sting."

"I've only ever heard them hum, but that's good information to have."

Midge watched as Opal put on her straw hat and began layering netting around her head. Opal wound yards of white netting around her face, covering her head and hair completely all the way to her shoulders. Midge mimicked the motions, insulating herself with the light, gauzy fabric that made the world seem softer. Then they pulled on their gloves.

A brief tutorial on how to handle the smoker, and they cautiously approached the first hive. Movable-frame, Opal had called the 12"x12" boxes. She'd gone on about it being the ideal size and such forth for reasons that seemed too specific to Midge. Right now, though, how to secure the bottom boards and close the openings while smoking the bees definitely seemed important.

They got through the first five hives, loading them into the small wagon with Midge suffering only two stings for her trouble, before they headed toward Grogan land. The mule before them—Simon—plodded as slowly as a creature could move and still count as moving, but Opal said that was the idea. Jostling the bees would upset them and maybe wake them up.

Midge drove Simon while Opal kept the smoker ready to subdue any irritated insects. It was only hours later, when after painstakingly driving over the last of Opal's twenty hives, that Midge found an opportunity to steer the conversation back to personal matters.

With the hives in place and reopened, the contented, buzzing hum Midge found strangely soothing blanketed the new apiary.

She watched as Opal unwound the netting from around her face and followed suit.

"Something like this stuff may work to keep the bees from penetrating your defenses, but we both know I see through such flimsy tactics." Midge handed the netting back to her friend. "You haven't distracted me."

"How do you give the impression your attention is fickle, wandering to new interests before most folks could ever guess, when really you're as single-minded as a bloodhound?"

"Maybe because my fickle attention only wanders when it's not fixed on something important." Midge pulled the loosely woven fabric away and tucked it back in the wagon so she wouldn't have to see Opal's reaction when she said the next part. "You're important to me."

"Oh, Midge." The hug came almost as a tackle. "Thank you for that. I needed to hear it today."

"Why today?" She didn't see any reason to bother with repeating mushy sentiments. Unearthing information so she could make plans, on the other hand, registered high on her list.

"My progress with Adam seems more going backward than anything else." The admission made her friend seem more fragile somehow.

"Of course." Midge snorted. Aunt Doreen's lady lessons sank in deeper than she expected, but sometimes even a lady needed to indulge in a solid, dismissive snort. Quickest way to let someone know she sounded ridiculous. "That's exactly what the whole town will buzz about all week—how you and Adam can't get along."

"We made a good team yesterday."

"You two have made a good team for much longer than that, from what I can tell." Midge scooted her rump back until she perched on the back of the wagon. "It went unnoticed on account of your families, but you've worked in tandem to keep the Specks and Grogans away from the others' throats for years."

"Holding a common cause doesn't make two people a team."

"Call me crazy, but I think doing something alongside each other is exactly what makes two people a team. Some teams are temporary and dissolve after a short task. Some last a lot longer. You and Adam share a burden neither one could pull alone and have for so long you take each other for granted."

"No one wants to marry a horse." Opal sounded positively morose—which meant deep down she wanted Adam to want her. Good.

"Except another horse." Midge gave her shoulder a friendly nudge. "Especially since you two have been hitched together since long before your wedding."

"Maybe you're right." A small laugh burbled from her throat as Opal envisioned her and Adam tied together, each pulling in opposite directions. The laugh died abruptly, as the thought of her husband trying to escape their binds grew more prominent.

"What's wrong?" Midge sensed the change in her mood.

"Hitched together in desperation and driven apart by lies. That's me and Adam." The dark pit of her situation yawned before her, inescapable and bottomless. "How long before the whole thing gets destroyed?"

"Stop it!" Her friend nudged her into the back of the wagon, where Opal sat with little grace. "You're both heading for the same goal, and that's keeping everyone together. So I don't see how you can be torn asunder so long as you keep on that way."

"Lucinda's suspicions and little games, for one." Opal didn't want to think about what her mother-in-law might be hatching next. "Though this morning Adam rescinded his decree that I can't visit home."

"That'll give the biddy more to cluck about." The glee in Midge's voice livened Opal's spirits a little. "And shows Adam's more alongside you than ever. Why so gloomy?"

"Adam asked about two other things this morning, and those didn't go well at all. Since you seem to have all the answers today, you can probably guess." She raised a brow in challenge.

"Ben and Willa?"

"You're downright spooky."

"Nah." Midge made an abrupt gesture with one hand. "That one's obvious. Anyone who went to church yesterday would've come up with it, which means every blessed soul in all of Buttonwood knew the answer."

"Adam says he can't allow it." *As though it's for him to allow.* Opal barely kept the disloyal thought to herself. *Wait. Disloyal? Since when is wanting happiness for my brother disloyal?* Foolish question. *Since I pledged my life to Adam.*

"Who made him king of Buttonwood?" Midge's huff made Opal grin.

It may be wrong for me to voice such things, but that doesn't mean I can't appreciate another person's perspective!

"No one governs the heart, save God."

"Not to argue, but I think we choose who we love. Some people make poor choices is all." Midge shrugged. "Hearts can be won, but they have to be given. If Willa wants to give hers to Ben, nothing Adam can do will stop it."

"He and his family would keep them apart, a big mistake. Even if Ben hadn't returned from the mines with a handsome sum, he bears half of Speck land. The Grogans would have to go far to find another who works half as hard or would do so much for those he calls family. He'll be a good husband and even better father someday." The more she thought about it, the more insulted she became. "Willa would never regret choosing my brother, but the

Grogans act as though he isn't good enough."

"They treat you as though you aren't good enough." Midge's interruption stopped Opal in mid-stew.

"I know."

"You accept that."

"Because I can't change it, and we're supposed to forgive when others wrong us." Opal needed the reminder as much as Midge did. "Turn the other cheek."

"I read that." Her friend absently rubbed her now much smaller lump of tobacco on a small red bump that marked her fourth and final sting of the day. "It makes me wonder, though...."

"Wonder what?"

"How many times?" Past pain shadowed Midge's normally avid gaze, turning it fierce. "How many times do you turn your cheek before it turns you into someone you don't even recognize?"

CHAPTER 30

T hey killed your grandfather!" Ma's voice thinned to a shriek. "Adam, you can't let her bring them here. You can't!"

"Opal won't bring them near the house. Pa and I designated the south clearing for her new apiary." Adam refused to acknowledge Pa's abrupt gesture indicating that he not mention his involvement.

After all, we wouldn't be in this mess if Pa hadn't mentioned Opal moving the apiary today. When Ma commented on her absence at the dinner table, all he need say was that she tended to her bees and mentioned she might run long.

"Diggory Ezekiel Grogan"—Ma rounded on her husband— "you're involved in this?"

"Now, Lucy," Pa used the pet name he only brought out under duress, "you know I'd make sure those bees stay as far away from the house as possible."

"Don't you 'Lucy' me!" Ma clutched Larry's shoulders. "Not when you've put us all in danger. Our children. . ."

"They won't go near the apiary." Pa made it both an assurance and a command for Larry and Willa.

"Opal won't move any of the hives any closer either." Adam joined his father's attempts to placate his mother. "It shouldn't pose a problem."

"Bees killed your grandfather when that cursed apiary remained on Speck land." Ma sank onto the bench between Larry and Willa, an arm around each as though to ward away death itself. "Less distance means more danger."

"Bees didn't fly over here and sting Grandpa." Willa seemed to fold in on herself as she said it, although whether from the strain of using enough nerve to speak against Ma's will or the pressure of Ma's physical grip, Adam couldn't tell. "He went over there."

"They never proved it!" Larry's snarl made Willa shrink even more. "Those Specks could've planned the whole thing and made it look that way. Everyone knows they wanted the border pasture so bad they could taste it."

"Old arguments." *Senseless arguments.*

"Pa didn't get himself trussed up by any Specks." Pa's expression when he spoke of his own father painted a portrait of exasperation and admiration. "Though the bees is what killed him."

"How can you know?" The hairs on the nape of Adam's neck stirred. A piece to the mystery of the origins of the feud lay within his grasp, if he could seize it.

"He told me his plan." A shrug far too casual accompanied the admission. "Specks weren't the only ones angling for that border pasture."

Have the Specks been right all along? Was Grandpa on their land to strike the first blow? Suspicion started to simmer in Adam's chest. "What did Grandpa plan to make the Specks rescind their claim?"

"Burn a few hives, just to show what Grogans are capable of when it comes to protecting what's theirs." No shame shaded the words. "A good plan, if he hadn't been caught."

"Caught." *Just like he told Larry. The problem wasn't in behaving without integrity; it was in getting caught.* "No piece of earth is worth a man's honor."

"He only meant to deliver a warning." Pa's eyes narrowed. "Nothing to harm a living soul, mind. Just enough to send a message to those Specks to keep away."

"Like the message you dispatched with Larry?" Adam's fingers curled around the note he kept in his pocket—a tangible talisman of his wedding. "Not enough harm to prick your conscience but just enough to inflict damage?" *Enough to spark a feud and destroy generations. Enough to trap two people in a marriage neither wanted.*

"Don't start sounding so high and mighty with your morality, son." Pa's jaw jutted out. "Sneaking around behind everyone's backs with the Speck girl. . .what you did far outstrips any note of mine and Larry's they never even found."

"Wrong." Something uncurled within him, smashing against the wall of caution he'd built around every decision he made. "I went over to remove it and had to ask Opal's help with the search. She found it."

"She did." A reptilian smile slithered across his brother's face as Larry processed the news that his note found its mark after all. "Good."

"I took it with me." His hand plunged out of his pocket, revealing the note. "Heaven knows I should have burned it but thought I might need the evidence of Larry's scheming someday. Like his grandfather before him, Larry's message went terribly wrong." He thrust it toward his father. "Read it."

The soddy seemed strangely airless as Pa surveyed the message he'd scripted. The defiant nonchalance slid from his features once he reached the last sentence.

"Larry Bartholomew Grogan, what is this addition?" For once, their father's volume didn't rise.

"Nothing important." Larry noticed the change and registered the inherent threat. He made an attempt to take possession of the note. "Just a last-minute thought."

"You expect me to believe a single thought rattled around in that skull of yours when you wrote this?" Pa's mustache quivered with the force of his inhalation. "Murphy would have the right to slaughter every last one of us for this. Had they ever threatened Willa, they'd not have drawn another breath."

"Opal found it, not Murphy." Larry stood up and took a few steps away. "No harm done."

"No harm." A snort of what might have been laughter, if anything about the situation struck him as funny, escaped Adam. "Murphy read it, all right. That one sentence brought about my wedding, little brother."

"No." The blood drained from Larry's face, and he groped for the edge of the table. "That note didn't force you to marry Opal. You lie."

Lucinda couldn't tear her eyes from the strip of parchment in her husband's hands. That such a small scrap could so thoroughly devastate all she'd built. . .

"Please." Her hand trembled as she stretched toward Diggory, the one word both asking for the note and imploring him to somehow stop a horror already passed.

Her fingers curled around the parchment without conscious decision as Diggory handed it over. Lucinda wondered if she should sit down then realized she'd never stood. She set the fragment on the table before her with great care, splaying her palms on either side to flatten it.

She recognized Diggory in the looping letters of the first sentence. The open lines of his writing betrayed the friendly boy he'd once been, before life and loss taught him better.

NEXT TIME WE LOSE A COW, WE TAKE A SPECK IN PAYMENT.

Simple, fair, impossible to misunderstand. Nothing there to ruin Adam's life. Below, more words seeped into their lives, the ink darker where the pen slashed across the parchment. The angry script could belong to none but Larry.

And I got my eye on your only heifer!

A muffled sob burst from her lips at the irrefutable proof of her second-born's guilt. The only sound since Diggory passed her the note. If Adam said this message caused his marriage, no doubt remained. Only questions. "How?"

"I discovered Marla missing the morning after I retrieved that note and tracked her to a broken fence in the southeast pasture bordering Speck lands."

"'The next time we lose a cow...'" Lucinda quoted, tracing the letters before her. "So you went after it." *Of course Adam wouldn't allow the slightest chance of the threat coming true. He knows it would mean the end of us all.*

"Southeast pasture." Diggory caught Larry by the collar. "I told you to mend that days before! Too busy skulking around the Speck place causing trouble?"

"Stop!" Willa's cry froze everyone. "Let Adam finish. We don't know when Opal may come back. Yell at Larry later, when you can yell at him for everything."

"You know Murphy and Elroy came over the week before to address Larry's wandering. His trespassing increased tensions, so when Pete caught me looking for Marla, the Speck men felt obliged to treat it as a serious matter." Adam kept his face impassable—a sure sign he felt strong emotion. "They searched me and found that note."

"It didn't matter." The shout didn't even sound like Larry, it came out so hoarse. "They'd already decided on their course of action. The Specks planned this from the start!"

"Be quiet, Larry." Lucinda's own voice sounded strange to her ears. "The Specks didn't want Opal with Adam any more than we did. We'll hear no more lies from you."

"When they found the note, they assumed I meant to carry it out and decided they couldn't let it pass. Not when it left Opal at risk."

"Can't blame them." Diggory shook Larry a bit but stopped himself.

Lucinda found herself wishing her husband kept on.

"Opal intervened to save my life." Adam fixed his gaze on Larry. "When logic didn't work, she reminded them I'd pulled her from the fire at Reed's house. When that didn't work, she told her father the only thing that could stay his hand—that I was to be the father of her child."

"Until then she hadn't breathed a word?" Awe underscored Willa's question.

"She never so much as told me." A rueful shake of Adam's head punctuated that statement. "Opal would never have told that to a soul."

"It's true." If anyone asked, Lucinda couldn't have told them whether she spoke the words aloud or simply whispered them to herself. But she knew the truth of it down deep in her bones.

Opal wouldn't let her family feel the bite of betrayal under any but these circumstances. She would have kept the secret of her indiscretion at all costs. No matter if she blamed a man who came through town once. Could even have claimed she was unwilling and her family would keep her. You can't say much for Opal Speck, but she would protect her own.

506

"Larry couldn't have known what one remark would do." If she lost loyalty to her children, she'd lose everything. Lucinda watched the corners of Adam's mouth tighten.

Besides, Adam is the son who took up with the Speck girl, after all. Never mind Larry wanted to. Who knows how many men she's lured with her wiles?

As quickly as that, her perspective shifted. Everything came back into clear focus. *The hussy probably took up with untold weaklings, and I've been right all along. She doesn't carry Adam's babe. She just saw an opportunity to grab a good man and took it.*

Lucinda felt her breath come easier. *Of course my Larry's a victim same as Adam. Opal's the villain here, no matter if she fools everyone else!*

Chapter 31

"Wait." Her sister-in-law's call stopped Opal as she tried to slip from the door of the room they shared the next morning. "Please, Opal. I want to go with you."

What is going on? Since she'd arrived back from moving the apiary yesterday, there'd been a strange mood over the Grogan farm. Granted, Opal thought the feel of the place always seemed somewhat odd compared to the easygoing environment of the Speck home, but even after the usual allowances, things felt different.

"You want to come to my family's farm?" Opal left the *why* part unspoken out of sheer politeness.

"Yes, please." Willa slipped from the bed and hurriedly pulled on a heavy dress. "We both know Ma tries to keep us apart as much as possible, but I'd like an opportunity to talk with you about a few things and get to know you better." As though a speech of this unprecedented length taxed her, the slightly younger girl busied herself with washing her face and brushing her hair, pulling it back in a loose bun.

"I'd like that, too." A surge of warmth toward her sister-in-law had Opal resisting the impulse to hug her.

Willa had scarce spoken a word to her since Lucinda revealed those rocks in the freshly stuffed mattress. This made for a welcome change, even though Opal wondered at the reasons for it. Perhaps Willa returned Ben's interest?

Opal nibbled on her lower lip as Willa laced her boots and fetched her bonnet. Bringing her sister-in-law with her on her first visit to the Speck farm would do wonders to show her family that the Grogans didn't mistreat her. *She'll also get to spend more time with Ben.* A fact that wouldn't go unnoticed by her in-laws. Or Adam.

"Perhaps this isn't the best idea, Willa."

"Ma won't like it, I know." She paused with one hand on the door, a study in solemnity. "It's rare I do anything Ma won't approve of. It keeps things the most peaceful, you see, and I put a premium on peace."

"Then why would you choose this as your chance to do the unexpected?" *When Lucinda will point to me as a bad influence.*

"You always seemed a good person to me." The door opened to let in the weak rays of morning's first light. "Those rocks seemed out of character, but on Sunday the Opal I respected came back. Then, after yesterday, I knew my family has been wrong to misjudge yours. It's long past time for us to be friends."

"Yesterday?" *I knew something changed; I just knew it!* Opal followed her out the door, abandoning the idea of trying to convince Willa to stay at home. "What happened yesterday?"

Her new ally wouldn't answer, just lifted a long finger to her lips and snuck past the house and beyond the yard with quick strides. Obviously, Willa didn't want her mother halting her adventure.

For her part, Opal could be content to wait. Not long, though. Once they reached the fence marking the boundary between

Speck and Grogan lands, she dismissed the easy silence that had accompanied them so far on their walk.

March mornings reminded Opal why spring days fed so heartily on the glory of the sun. Only then did they escape the cold bite of winter that still lingered in the early hours. Snatches of birdsong broke through air thick with moisture and the promise of life. Dew clung to every blade of grass—some cold enough to show touches of ice.

"Ma's scared of your bees." Of all the things Willa might have said, Opal wouldn't have predicted this. "When Pa told her you missed dinner on account of moving your apiary, she went pale as the inside of a potato peel."

"The place Adam selected suits all my needs perfectly." Opal spoke cautiously, sure to praise her husband and clarify that she didn't intend to move the hives closer to the homestead. "The hives will stay on the far edge of the farm, for your mother's peace of mind..." *And mine.*

"Do you know I never stopped to consider you an optimist?" Willa's question left little possibility for reply.

"I give up. Should I take that as a compliment?" Opal doubted Willa would ever deliberately insult anyone, but the thought seemed out of place.

"Yes. Seems I should have noticed it before, since you go out of your way to keep our families from tearing each other to bits. Adam's the same way—always believing the time will come when we'll put aside our differences." Willa gave her a considering look. "You two have a lot in common."

"Don't most people want to keep their families alive and whole?" She kept the words light, but Opal picked up her pace. Suddenly, getting to the house and having things other than Willa's observations to occupy them seemed like a very good idea. "So I should have a lot in common with just about anyone."

"My hinting that you and my brother match each other makes you uncomfortable." A shrug. "Then I'll let it go for now. Would you like to hear about what you and I have in common?"

I want to hear more about what happened yesterday! The desire for a solid friendship won out over impatience. "Yes."

"Both of us grew up with families involved in a feud, though we each refused to take active part in it. Neither of us has a sister who survived infancy." A deep breath braced Willa to keep speaking, leading Opal to wonder whether Willa's silence wasn't actually a preference so much as a habit after being raised by Lucinda. "Men in town won't court us because of our families, and we won't look at men who plan to move away from Buttonwood, so both of us have remained unwed a long time."

"A considerable list." Opal debated for a moment about whether or not to add to it. "Long enough, I think, for me to presume to ask if we share another quirk?"

"Yes?"

"Is there a chance both us may end up marrying the son of our father's enemy?"

<hr />

"No." Adam broke in. "Enough nonsense."

"Adam!" Willa's guilty flush didn't assure him that her answer would have matched his. "You followed us?"

"And we didn't notice?" His wife's incredulous murmur almost made him grin.

"I caught up with you in time to hear that last question. I'd thought to escort you back to Speck land to make sure things went smoothly." *To be there if your Pa hurt your feelings and show him I stood beside you in all things.*

"Didn't realize you planned to do that, Adam." Genuine surprise—even a little bit of pleasure—filled the statement.

"Willa doesn't belong here." He shot a look of rebuke at his sister. "Go home, sis."

"The time has arrived for me to trust my own judgment instead of blankly relying on Ma's or even yours," his sister announced. "At eighteen, I believe it's more than proper for a lady to visit her in-laws in the presence of her brother and his wife."

"That's—" he broke off, unable to finish any logical protest. "Different." Adam squinted at his sister, noticing for the first time how much she'd grown, the calm that surrounded her. *When did this new Willa emerge?*

"Yesterday I came to realize the Grogans aren't always right, in spite of how we claim to be." Her raised brows were mirrored by Opal's. "So I've decided not to let disproven prejudices determine my future."

"What disproven prejudices?" Opal didn't exclude Willa, but her eyes found his. "About my family?"

"Not the time or place." He cast a look around, half-expecting Murphy or Elroy to appear at his side. "Reviving old grudges serves no purpose."

"If I've not shown by now that I don't hold grudges," Opal turned away as she spoke, "you'll never understand." With that, she marched in the direction of the Speck soddy, leaving him and Willa to watch her.

"Poorly done, brother." Willa watched him instead. "Either Opal's earned your trust, or you've grown stingy."

"She and I discussed the matter of Ben. Opal knows I disapprove, yet she went behind my back to encourage your interest." He shook his head. "This behavior doesn't call for trust."

"Did Opal agree with you that I shouldn't indulge in so much as a passing curiosity regarding her brother?" When her pause grew pointed, he shook his head. "Then she didn't break her word or change her stance. Nor, may I add, did she encourage anything.

Simply asked as to my thoughts on the matter. Which"—his sister's gaze saddened—"is more than you took the time to do."

The hurt in her face pinched at him. "Willa, I know you well enough there's no need to ask. You sat beside Ben instead of Ma on Sunday without any reason."

"Another assumption." The words lacked heat but not power. "Ben barely returned home before Opal married you. He tried to sit beside his sister. In part, I think, because he's missed her, in part to make sure she's all right, but mostly to help hide the fact that their father didn't want to because he's too stiff-necked to forgive her yet."

"Why didn't you let him?" *And keep at least one problem off my list. As it is, sounds like you two got awful cozy at that table.*

"Larry shoved his way next to Opal, rude as could be. I saw him eyeing Ben as though considering how best to goad him."

"Likely." Adam closed his eyes. Larry again. *Every time I turn around, my brother creates difficulties.*

"So I politely asked if I could sit between them and did my best to buffer the two." Having finished her explanation, Willa fell silent. She seemed relieved not to have anything more to say.

"Thanks." He figured that part of the conversation ended when she nodded. "Did you come with Opal today hoping to see more of Benjamin Speck?" Aloud, the suspicion didn't sound as ridiculous as he'd hoped.

"I hope to help put the animosity between our families behind us once and for all." With that, his sister followed in the direction Opal had struck out moments before, leaving Adam alone. . .

To notice that Willa hadn't said no.

CHAPTER 32

The nerve of the man, to follow her and Willa, hint about secrets involving her family, then refuse to tell her! Opal all but stalked to her family's soddy. *Oh, very well. I am stalking. But it doesn't make him right. There's a difference between a moment's anger and a grudge.*

Opal didn't bother to hold grudges. For now, though, the anger had her pumping. It carried her into the soddy, where she noticed Pa and her brothers had apparently already left for the fields. The rapid beating of her heart slowed as she surveyed what had been her home for nineteen years.

Father, how can this be the way my family lives?

Dishes slopped over one another across the table, remnants of old biscuits and older gravy crusting them together. Ashes mounded before the fireplace, a source of the dust disguising her wooden cabinets. A pair of empty pants sprawled in Grandma's rocker, mate to the shirt slumped alongside.

A soft keening surprised Opal when she realized the sound came from her. Guilt kept up its assault, only to be driven away by a pair of strong hands clamping her shoulders, bracing her. She drew in her first real breath since stepping past the threshold, the pungent odors of stale coffee and musty clothing strong enough to fell an ox.

"It's not your fault." Adam's whisper made itself felt more than heard. "Things change in time."

"We didn't live like this." She blinked to clear moisture from her eyes, looking up at the roof of the soddy to keep the tears away. Pages from catalogs she'd so painstakingly collected no longer marched in neat rows across the ceiling. Now, advertisements for shoes sagged beneath the weight of debris. Edges of the pages curled down to catch in the hair of those unfortunate enough to wander close. Dark splotches obliterated drawings of bicycles and fanciful dolls.

"This *is* my fault." *For leaving.* The accusation hung everywhere she looked. The entire soddy sat as one dank, wordless recrimination.

Adam nudged the empty pants from the rocker and settled her inside it as though she'd be content to stay there.

The sound of one dish hitting another as Willa cleared the table snapped Opal from her grief and into action. *Face it.* She took inventory of what needed to be done. *I can fix it.* Opal headed for the barn, unearthing the large wooden washtub from the corner and rolling the heavy container back toward the house. *Keep working.*

"What are you doing?" Adam put himself at risk of being trampled by a runaway washtub, planting his feet in her path.

"Washing." Opal rolled around him. *No time to waste.*

"Stop this." He moved as though to block her again, so Opal sped up until she had the tub just between the house and the well. "Let me help you."

"Thank you." Her easy acceptance took him off guard. She could tell by the way he stayed quiet. "If you start filling the tub, I'll help Willa bring out the dishes. Letting them sit in water for a while will make them easier to scrub."

By way of response, her husband began lowering the bucket to the well. No words needed when he showed support. The panic that had gripped her since she walked into the soddy and saw what had become of the place after a single week of her absence began to fade. The alarm served its purpose and got her moving, taking control of things the way she always had.

She and Willa heaped dishes and soap shavings into the rising waterline of the washtub, filling it full. With that done, she took rags from the bin she kept tucked away, intent on attacking the dust and grit built up in her absence. If she could finish the dishes and get everything dusted and wiped down, she could do a week's worth of baking. She'd also make the men a dinner they'd be glad to have in their bellies when they went to work again, with the memory and promise of more to come for supper!

Working felt right. Seeing results made it worthwhile. Having Willa and Adam alongside her, giving their time and labor for her family, made the day precious in a way Opal couldn't put words to. She tried anyway. "You didn't have to—"

They didn't let her get any further.

"I wanted to. How else to repay you for your help stuffing mattresses and cleaning out that chicken coop?" Willa halted briefly when she mentioned the mattress but rallied. "I dreaded that then escaped it entirely!"

Adam cleared his throat at the mention of the chicken coop, his eyes going intense in a way that made Opal wonder whether or not he remembered that day as well as she. Whether he remembered that he'd almost kissed her. . .

She bit back a sigh.

"Opal," a gruffness caught her attention when he spoke her name. "I'll be back before noon. Don't ring the dinner bell before you see me."

Where are you going? She nipped back the question, refusing to be impertinent today of all days. Not when he'd let her see her family. Not when Willa chose now to assert herself.

"Understood?" For the first time, he made it a question. They both knew Adam wasn't offering her a choice, but the acknowledgment made a difference. Somehow.

"Understood." She watched as he exited the darker confines of the soddy and plunked his hat on before heading off.

Lord, what if Pa finds him on Speck land? Or Elroy? Ben won't do much now that he bears interest in Willa, but he'd bring him to Pa for trespassing. Possibilities seared her. *With the town apprised of our marriage, Pa would consider the babe to have a name and respectability, and Adam's death would bring me home.*

Opal made it halfway out the door, lips open to call Adam back to her side, when something caught her.

"Stop." Willa gripped her elbow with surprising strength and pulled her back inside. "If you call my brother back because you're afraid, he'll take it as you doubting his ability to take care of himself and you."

"It's not that I question his manhood. . .but men are mortal."

"Trust in Adam and in God to bring him back this afternoon," her sister-in-law warned, "or poison another part of your marriage."

Opal stilled. *Our marriage scarcely survives as things stand. I can't afford to take the chance.* She turned away from the door, toward the cook fire, and started working.

Keep him safe, Jesus. Please. Oh, please.

⁓◦⊙◦⁓

Adam kept one hand at the pistol on his belt as he made his way through Speck land. He combined a stealthy pace and steady eye to keep away from any sign of Opal's family, not so foolish as to test their tempers so soon.

Soon enough, he passed the fence he'd mended on his wedding night—the fence that led Marla into Speck land and Adam himself into the most muddled marriage Buttonwood would ever see. Back on Grogan land, he usually breathed easier.

Not today.

Not when Opal remained on Speck land, not within quick reach. Her family wouldn't harm her, but Adam didn't like her being so far away. For one thing, the father of her child may return. Where would that leave him?

He walked past the clearing he'd designated for Opal's apiary, giving it wise berth. Adam took note of the twenty hives, placed in neat rows, looking almost as though they'd sat in such an arrangement for years, and acknowledged a sense of satisfaction. Here he saw the beginning, the first outward sign of his and Opal's coming together as a wedded couple ought.

The satisfaction ebbed as he continued on his way. Willa's presence caused both comfort and concern. Comfort to know Opal kept company with someone he trusted. Comfort to know his wife wouldn't run off with some scapegrace under his sister's watch. Comfort to know she would fetch him should anything go wrong. He'd told Willa where to find him. That alleviated some of his concern.

Home. He arrived in front of one of the few large hills on Grogan land, stopped, and surveyed the site. The mound of earth topped him by about two feet—a good size for a dugout. Adam stepped into the depression he'd begun hollowing out days ago. Every moment he could spare from the farm, he came here. This would be the house where he and Opal lived as man and wife, once they'd overcome the most pressing obstacles before them.

Right now, he struggled with the idea of his sister remaining unguarded on Speck property. Willa, determined to stand alongside her sister-in-law in a show of support Adam couldn't bring himself to undermine, placed herself in the path of danger. In the path of Benjamin Speck's all-too-interested gaze.

And in so doing, pitted them all against a threat he couldn't avoid. His formerly quiet sister made that clear enough. The more he protested, the more she dug in her heels. Shotguns and shouts, Adam could hold his own against. But this gentle defiance resisted all weapons in his arsenal.

The rough outer leather of his work gloves faded into pliable softness as he slid his hands inside and grabbed his tools. Time and earth caved beneath the bite of his spade. Each stroke lessened the tumult in his chest and brought him one shovelful closer to building a future.

He kept a close eye on the progress of the sun across the sky. Adam judged it to be before eight when he began digging—a good time. The frost of the morning thawed, leaving the earth moist and soft. As the temperature rose and shadows shortened, he determined it time to head back to Opal and Willa. He planned to make it long before any of the Speck men—the only reason Adam had been able to leave the women for even those three hours was his certain knowledge that the Speck boys would be out working the fields and surely not beat him back. Well, that and the certainty he'd finish the home by week's end. But the main thing was knowing he'd beat the Specks back.

Which didn't make him any less cautious during his return. Adam kept to whatever scant shadows the prairie provided, be they the occasional cottonwood or large rock. Not even the burbling call of a small creek tempted him to halt his progress. Stooping down with his back to the open made a man an excellent target.

Besides, Adam washed up in the stream running close to the site he'd chosen for his own home before he set out. All the same, by the time he got within smelling distance of the Speck place, his mouth watered and stomach rumbled as though competing for attention. Two cold biscuits at the crack of dawn didn't hold a man used to a full breakfast.

"Smells good." He let the compliment precede him, so as not to startle the women as he walked in the door. Adam couldn't even pinpoint what all tickled his nose so well, just that there seemed an array of good things to tempt a man.

Foremost among them stood right next to him. His wife rushed away from the cook fire the moment she heard him, barely stopping before running into him. Adam found himself wishing she hadn't put the brakes on in time. Even in the dim interior of the soddy, her eyes sparkled. "You're back." A smile the likes of which he hadn't seen since before their wedding day lit her whole face. "I'm glad."

"You are?" Not that he doubted her. It just took him off guard to find his wife so pleased to see him. Her blush tattled that the significance he placed on her greeting embarrassed her.

"You're safe." Opal didn't give any more explanation than those two words as she turned back to the table and shifted a few dishes to make room for something Willa carried over.

"I see." And he did. *She worried.* The rumbling in his stomach stopped, despite the wealth of food arrayed before him. The warmth spreading through him left no room for hunger. *Opal cares about me.*

CHAPTER 33

"What on earth is going on?" Pa burst through the door first, gun in hand, scant minutes after Opal rang the dinner bell. His sudden stop just inside the house almost made them pile one atop the other as Ben, Elroy, and Pete skidded to a halt right on his heels.

"Good to see you, Pa." Opal fought back the impulse to rush him with a hug. No sane person rushed a man with a gun—kin or no. Especially when Pa still hadn't shown any signs of forgiving her for her hasty marriage. "Adam thought to let me come over and make you all some dinner as a surprise today." She gestured to where Adam stood at her side, a polite warning of her husband's presence where no Speck had presumed to enter uninvited before.

"Opal?" Pete's voice came through accompanied by hopeful sniffing. "You cooked for us?"

"You don't surprise a man by trespassing in his home, Grogan." Pa raised his gun with more specific purpose. "Dangerous habit you've picked up, boy."

"Pa!" Opal made to step forward and shield Adam, but her

521

husband's hand clamped around her arm and jerked her behind him, next to Willa. "Willa and Adam came in friendship and kindness!"

"Willa?" This from Ben. "Pa, lower that gun and let us inside." He didn't really wait for his father to agree, instead elbowing his way inside. It didn't seem to matter much to him that Elroy and Pete still loitered on the doorstep, but Opal wasn't about to quibble.

"He trespassed."

"Opal invited him." Ben's gaze darted to hers before moving to Willa's. "And her sister-in-law."

"Opal don't live here anymore." Pa's words sliced her soul, and she might have sunk to the floor from the pain of it were Adam not in such jeopardy.

"Would you shoot me, Pa?" This time, she found the power to resist Adam's pull and remain at her place by his side. Her heart couldn't give her voice any more strength than a whisper. "You have my love. If you don't want it, you may as well have my blood. It's the only way to stop me from being your daughter."

"No." Adam stopped trying to force her behind him and stepped in front of her, putting his chest scant inches from the barrel of her father's rifle.

For a frozen moment, no one moved. Opal saw everything from behind the arms her husband spread to cover her, processed Adam's protection, and waited. Pushing him out of the way might startle Pa into pulling the trigger, so she could do nothing but pray.

Lord, please watch over those I love. Don't let them be hurt or killed for my foolishness. Please.

"No." The gun lowered. His face pale, Pa stepped forward and reached out a hand. "Opal, you'll always be my daughter."

A flood of tears broke from her even as Elroy and Pete pushed inside. She squeezed beneath Adam's arm and into her father's embrace for the first time in far too long. "I'm so sorry, Pa." The words came out broken, but it didn't matter. She knew he understood what she meant.

"Me, too." Rough words almost swallowed by her hair, but so precious. When he pulled back, with a suspicious gleam in his eyes, Opal felt better than she had in ages.

The part of her heart that pulsed with hurt since her father turned his back on her began to beat with hope once more. She turned to her brothers and embraced each of them, still able to notice the way Ben went to Willa the first possible moment, murmuring as though to ensure she remained unharmed by the dramatics.

"Speck." Adam extended his hand, and if his gaze seemed a bit wary, none could blame him.

"Grogan." Pa looked down at the friendship offered, glanced at Opal, and took her husband's hand in a firm shake.

Thank You, Lord. It's a start.

"More than a start, I'd say." Midge finished sprinkling salt around the edges of the hives and straightened up. "For more than one thing, even."

"I know." Opal's excitement came through loud and clear as she hastily filled Midge in on the events of the morning. After all, she didn't have much time before she had to get back to where Willa baked on the Speck homestead. If Midge hadn't brought the suppers by, she wouldn't have left. But surely this had to be God's timing? "Pa and Adam can forge peace between our families at last, and maybe Ben and Willa have a chance at a genuine romance. They're good for each other."

"So are you and Adam." She didn't bother to mask her

exasperation. "Why is it you notice all the good in and for everyone except yourself?"

"You know Adam doesn't want to be my husband." The quiet response contrasted so sharply to her friend's earlier happiness, Opal's feelings for Adam must run deep. "Even now he'd annul the marriage should he learn the truth."

"Don't be so sure. He put himself in front of you, shielded his body with yours." She got no reaction. "A man who doesn't care for his wife doesn't offer up his life in exchange for hers without a second thought, Opal!" *Same as you did for him when your Pa aimed the gun at Adam. But I won't point that out just yet.*

"Without thought is exactly right. His sense of honor won't let him see anyone else hurt. I'd make a huge mistake if I thought anything more about it."

"If someone aimed a shotgun at Ben, do you think Adam would step in front of it?"

"Most likely not." Opal's answer came slowly. Reluctantly. Wonderingly. As though Midge got through. Then, "But Adam made a vow to protect me, so that's that."

"What are these?" *Time to change tactics.* Logic couldn't sway the heart, and Midge didn't bother with losing battles. She pointed to the whitewashed boxes they'd tumbrel sledged over to the apiary.

"Supers." She picked up one of them. "We affix one to each of the hives so that the extra bees have space in the spring." She demonstrated how to set it up, and the two of them worked in silence for a little while.

Midge did it intentionally, knowing that working with the bees gave Opal time to clear her thoughts and, more importantly, lower her guard.

"Why are there extra bees in the spring?" She asked only once each hive boasted a super.

"Some die in the winter, but in the spring the honey supply becomes so low, the queen lays up to hundreds of eggs a day so they'll have enough workers to replenish the food stock. They need places to go." They retreated to the stand of three scant cottonwoods nearby, where they always relaxed and talked.

"Then they die?" Sounded like bees used other bees just like people used other people. Midge frowned.

"No. When the hive supply is restored, another queen bee hatches, and the current queen bee flies away. About half the bees follow her and find a new home and start a different hive. It happens in May, usually." Opal clasped her hands around her knees. "You watch for bees to be unable to get inside and hover around outside the hive, especially in the evenings. Then you come early in the morning and try to catch them. I've ordered ten new hives."

"How do you get the bees to choose your hive?"

"You'll see when the swarming starts." Her friend grinned. "For now, I think it's time for you to be teaching me some lessons."

"You did beautifully at church—maneuvering for that kiss..." Midge raised her brows. "I'm glad I caught on to the ploy."

"So did Adam."

"Really?" Midge stopped plucking at the grass at her side. "How do you know?"

"He told me—it's what he whispered right before he kissed me." If her cheeks got any redder, it might be permanent.

"And he still did it. *Three* times." She tapped her fingers together. "Excellent."

"He did it to play along."

"The first time, maybe. Here, you're flushed." Midge passed her friend the canteen of water they'd brought. "The second time would persuade the most stalwart doubters. But the third time, my friend, the third time Adam kissed you because he wanted to."

Glugging greeted her proclamation as Opal all but emptied the canteen in great gulps. When her friend finished, she had to take a minute to gulp in about the same amount of air. At least her flush faded to a dull rose, and determination defended any vulnerability in her gaze. "So what's the next step in seducing my husband?"

"Obviously, he needs to kiss you again." Midge figured she'd need to start out slow with Opal. Her friend may be a farm girl, but her innocence wasn't just physical. "The next time, without an audience."

"Then there's no pretext." Shoulders slumped, her friend exuded hopelessness. "How can I convince him to kiss me without any reason?"

"You *are* the reason, Opal." Shaking the woman would do no good. "You convince him to kiss you because he *wants* to kiss you again. Just like that third time on Sunday."

"Oh." Opal fiddled with the pocket on her apron. "How do I convince him to kiss me the first two times to get him to the third time, then? I can't very well ask everyone to kindly leave after the second try!"

"Stop being silly!" This time, Midge bumped her friend's arm with hers. . .and none too gently, either. "He wanted to kiss you in front of the chicken coop, too. And kissing you after the wedding was his idea. You don't have to inspire an attraction; your husband already fights one. You just have to convince him to stop fighting it!"

"Half the battle's done?"

"The half that can't be taken for granted is over. Now comes the march to victory."

"Sounds promising." The slumping stopped. "How do I march?"

"Easily enough." Midge sprang to her feet and gestured for Opal to follow her. "The first step to master has to do with walking. . . ."

CHAPTER 34

Step, sway. Step, sway. One foot exactly in front of the other. Don't look down any more than absolutely necessary. Shoulders back. Stomach in. Step, sway. . .

Opal kept the litany in her head, wondering whether she'd hear Midge's voice every time she took a step for the rest of the day. Or longer. Oh, she'd laughed when her friend told her she needed to learn to walk. Hadn't she been walking since her first birthday?

Yes, Midge explained. Opal could walk. Serviceably. Which, obviously, would never do. Mules and boots strived to be serviceable. Women needed to embody seduction. At least, Opal did. For now.

Because, Opal vowed, as she placed one foot in front of the other as though walking atop a log, she couldn't manage this seduction business for very long. The very mechanics of it were liable to kill her.

For example, when she stepped forward with her right foot, moving it in front of her left foot, her natural inclination seemed to be to have her hips follow toward the left. But nooooo. Midge instructed that when she stepped across the left, her hip pushed to the *right*. Her friend said it exaggerated the curve and increased the sway of her skirts.

Opal said it increased her chances of falling flat on her face. Although, she couldn't argue with Midge that this gait did make her skirts swing in a saucy fashion she'd never managed before. Between that and holding her shoulders even farther back, the new stride almost lent her a feeling of power.

At least, it would if she weren't afraid of ruining it. She shoved the doubts aside, refusing to let them trip her up—in her thoughts or in reality—and kept on toward where she knew Adam mended fences that afternoon. Yes, he mended fences because fertilizer was setting into the fields, and the smell hardly made for romance, but Opal couldn't afford to be choosy about timing. She could catch him alone now.

There. Not too far away, he bent low, resting on his heels, mending a joint in a fence. No sound alerted him to her arrival. No inexplicable sense of her presence like some couples shared made him look up and send a smile her way. *Because we aren't really a couple. We share no connection save a willingness to pretend at love to save our families.*

She shook off the defeatist attitude, heading toward the first clump of plants that were her pretext for coming here. Opal stooped at the knees, reaching for the bright yellow flowers that already began to close in the afternoon sunlight. Squash blossoms bloomed wide open in the morning and shriveled up as the day wore on—almost the way she felt as she spent time with Lucinda.

Opal plucked the majority of the flowers, leaving enough not to strip the plants, and straightened. A quick glance around showed that Adam moved slightly closer but demonstrated no awareness of her. She took a deep breath and used her new walk to mince toward the next grouping of blossoms, closing even more of the distance between them. She began to stoop and suddenly remembered Midge shaking her head.

"Ladies bend at the knees to retrieve something. It's as demure as a woman can be. Holds all the parts of the body tight together, puts nothing on display, practically begs everyone not to notice that you're there. When you are around your husband, Opal, you don't want him to think of you as a lady. You need him to see you as a woman."

Heat crept up her throat and suffused Opal's cheeks as she realized what she needed to do. Thankful Adam hadn't yet looked up, she slowly bent at the waist, poking her bottom into the air in a shameful manner and stretching her arm out so she could reach the flowers. The first time, she straightened up so fast her head rushed a little.

"If you go up again too fast, the effect is wasted." The caution sprang to her memory a moment too late. *"You lose the appearance of grace and have to start all over."*

She peeked to see whether her husband noted her presence yet. No. Opal breathed a sigh of relief that her clumsy attempt escaped a witness, used her new walk to move on, and tried again.

This time, she decided to get into the spirit of the thing. She put one foot in front of the other—the better to exaggerate any curves—and leaned down with her arm extended as elegantly as possible. After plucking several blossoms, she snagged a final one and, pleased with her success, gave it a celebratory swirl as she gracefully began to rise.

"Opal?" The deep voice right in her ear startled the poise right out of her, making her jump.

Unfortunately, when one leg is crossed over the other and a body is half bent over, jumping is a bad idea. *The only thing I can say for the whole mess,* Opal decided, *is that at least I didn't have far to fall.*

An abrupt movement to the right caught Adam's eye. He reached for his gun and pivoted in one smooth motion to get a clearer view of the threat. Instead, he saw a woman.

Slightly backlit by the afternoon sun, her face obscured by her bonnet, she floated toward him. The vision of femininity swayed a few steps before stopping. Only then did awareness frisson up his spine. *Opal?* Were it not for the calico dress she wore, he wouldn't have recognized his wife.

He opened his mouth to call to her then closed it again. What would he say? More importantly, when would he have the opportunity to observe her when she thought herself completely alone? Adam thumbed back his hat for an unobstructed view as she moved once more, this time the shift so subtle it might not have caught his eye.

A basket half-filled with yellow flowers dangled from one of her arms as she bent to gather more. But she didn't bend as he'd ever seen her. No. This secret Opal, the surprise bride who thought herself far removed from any eyes watching her, moved freely. She folded at the waist, her backside a shapely curve extending into the air. She reached toward the flowers in a smooth motion, long and lithe as she stretched.

He sucked in a sharp breath and found himself at her side before he decided to take so much as a step. From the closer vantage point, he could smell the lingering trace of honey that always clung to her, see small wisps of the red-gold hair that escaped her bonnet to dance in the breeze.

"Opal." This time, he said it aloud.

She offered no soft smile in response. No, this vision of grace, so imbued with the innate allure of woman, gave a strangled shriek and some sort of aborted hop. . .just before she fell right on those curves he'd admired moments before. Which might have done him a great favor and lessened her appeal. If, that is, he hadn't tried to catch her and she hadn't fallen into his knees, knocking him down along with her. They ended in a tangled tumble, her bonnet dangling by its strings, his hat knocked away.

Immediate awareness hit Adam harder than the impact. He lay half atop her, his chest pressed to the softness of hers as she struggled to draw breath. It was her gasp that brought him to his senses. He levered himself onto his forearms, putting some distance between them.

Not enough. Opal's eyes went wide in surprise, her lips parted in an attempt to catch her breath. One of her hands clutched his bicep, another lay flat against his shoulder, but she made no move to push him away. Her warmth seeped into his shirt, beckoning him closer.

"Opal," he murmured her name this time, a one-word question if she was all right.

"Adam?" She tilted her chin slightly, just enough to bring her lips closer. An invitation no man could resist.

He dipped his head to taste her. Softness swept against him, yielding and sweet. *She is mine. My wife.*

She pressed upward, sending heat surging through him, demanding. . .

More. He pulled her bonnet away and sank one hand into the silky strands of her hair. *More.* Adam urged closer, tracing her lips with his. *More.*

"Baby." He no sooner uttered the endearment than he pulled away. *The baby. How could I forget?* He moved back, bent almost double in an effort to keep away from her.

"Adam?" Confusion dampened the dreaminess of her gaze. Her lips full and rosy from his kisses, her hair mussed from his caress, she looked the very image of a woman who'd been thoroughly kissed. And wanted more.

It was enough to drive a man mad.

"Get up." Harsh, shallow breaths made the words rough, but so be it. He gained another measure of control when she sat up and smoothed the wrinkles from her dress, restoring some appearance of propriety.

"I'm sorry." Her lips—still invitingly pink—must have bothered her as much as they did him because she raised her fingertips to them and pulled her hand away as though burned. "I didn't mean to be so clumsy."

"Doesn't matter." The thought she found his kiss distasteful soured his stomach. *What? For a moment did she forget it was me? Did she think it was the real father of her child?* If blood could boil within a man, surely it did now. He thought of the way she'd moved when she'd thought she was alone.

I was wrong. She didn't move in freedom, away from prying eyes. Those were the motions of a woman putting on a performance. Only her imagined audience is long gone, and she's dissatisfied with her substitute.

"It matters to me." Her words verified his thoughts. Of course it mattered to her that she'd fallen into his arms when it was the last place she wanted to be.

"Fine. But I say you can be as clumsy as you like." Adam snatched his hat from where it had fallen and turned away. "So long as you remember not to do it with any other men."

CHAPTER 35

*D*anger. Lucinda's hands shook as she washed the dinner dishes. Dishes used by too few that morning, as Willa abandoned her to join Opal at the Speck place.

Danger surrounded her family, creeping closer every moment. Closing off any means of escape. Tightening the noose. Specks were their greatest enemies. . .always had been. Ever since the greedy gudgeons dared try to claim land Diggory's father staked out.

As though their protests that no markers meant no claim mattered. Everyone knew the land between two runoffs of the Platte could flood. No, instead there'd been bitter battles. Blood and bruises on both sides over a scrap of earth where they'd all end up buried because the Specks wouldn't be honorable.

Lucinda put away another dish and reached for the next. Her mind worked in tandem with her hands, scrubbing circles into the problem in an attempt to shine up a solution. Hadn't Diggory's pa tried to stop the madness? Hadn't he come up with a plan to send a little warning to the Specks to make them see reason and end the fighting once and for all?

Instead Opal's grandma bid her bees to punish him. Lucinda bore the knowledge deep in her heart. *Moving one hive wouldn't kill a man. She must've used some pagan ways to summon the bees from other hives to do him in. I saw it.*

What other explanation for how she'd found her adopted father in that field? When he didn't come back after their secret plan, she'd gone in search of him. And found the horrible truth obvious in his body.

The hives covering every inch of his hands, arms, face, and neck. The terrible way his eyelids puffed up and out. The horror of his swollen mouth and protruding tongue as though screaming even from death for her to run. . .

And so I ran, and never let on that I'd seen. But I didn't forget. I seen the evidence of murder that day, and I won't let it near my family again.

Lucinda looked down when she realized she'd been groping for the next dish for a while. With none left to clean, she hefted the basin of rinse water outside. A few steps around the house brought her to Willa's flower garden, and she flung the water across the carefully cultivated expanse.

Ephemeral bluebells rose to dangle their buds in the breeze, ranging from soft pink to bluish violet. A white blanket of low larkspur provided lovely contrast until the red flowers and notched leaves of bloodroot made an appearance. Star-shaped spring beauties basked alongside white-and-purple shooting stars, the drops of water she'd flung on them catching the sun in a kaleidoscope of colors.

"Too bad Willa's not here to see that." Larry gestured toward the garden of wildflowers. "But it's even worse she's missing it because she's on the Speck farm."

"This will be the last time." Lucinda knew she'd erred in not specifically forbidding her daughter to return, but typically one hint of displeasure sent Willa scurrying in the proper direction. "If it weren't for the influence of that girl, Willa wouldn't have gone today."

"Probably has more to do with Opal's brother." Her son's gaze all but snapped his irritation. "You know how Ben looks at our Willa. It can't go on."

"It won't." Her jaw ached from clenching her teeth.

"She needs to learn she can't disregard the wishes of the family and put her safety at risk, Ma." Larry's expression changed to one of deep concern. He reached out and fingered a damp bluebell. "So many risks around here."

"You know better than to mess with Willa's garden." Some things were sacred, after all.

"She knows better than to consort with Specks." Larry straightened. "Willa's been making those choices, Ma. Choosing the Specks. . .and their bees."

Her throat went dry at the reminder that the hives currently rested on Grogan land, inching ever closer. Making it easier to kill them all.

"Ma, do you know that bees are attracted to flowers?"

"What?" Her eyes fell on the colorful garden she'd been admiring moments before. "No. These are far away."

"Not far enough. I've been reading up." He plucked the bluebell and crushed it between thumb and forefinger. "These could bring the bees. Just like Willa brings Benjamin. And, given a choice, she'd keep things that way."

"Then she doesn't get a choice." Lucinda fell to her knees, blindly reaching among the colorful petals and yanking plants out of the ground in heaping handfuls.

She'll understand someday, my Willa, Lucinda promised herself. *But first, I have to protect her. I have to protect her, so she can learn.*

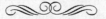

"So old Grogan did mean to set fire to one of the hives." Opal could hardly believe what Willa told her as they headed back from the Speck farm. "All that claptrap about Specks dragging him to be attacked by bees. . . Diggory knew the truth all along?"

"Papa had to protect his pa's memory," Willa said by way of explanation. "He knew Grandpa would turn in his grave if Specks got that land, and Papa wouldn't let him die in vain, so. . ."

"So he's ruined all of our lives, caused bitterness and false enmity for decades?" Anger almost choked the words before Opal forced them out. "Blackened my family's name? Where is the honor in that, Willa?"

"I'm sorry. You know the rest of us only discovered the truth days ago."

"Days ago." *But Adam didn't tell me. Was he afraid I'd be so foolish as to tell Pa? I know better than to give him any more cause to resume hostilities when things are going well!* "And none of you trusted me enough to share this information."

"I thought you should know. I thought. . ." Willa trailed off, and Opal knew her friend was thinking that Adam should have been the one to tell her.

"The hatred between our families ends one way or another, Willa. Pa wouldn't react well to this information, even if Diggory apologized now. It's best to let things gradually mend, as it's begun. With you and Adam reaching out to the Specks, things are bound to keep improving." *I hope.*

"Surely mercy and goodness shall follow us," Willa paraphrased the Psalm with a smile, only to pull up short with a gasp. The smile shrank from her face as she stared before them.

Opal followed her gaze and let out a cry of her own. There, where that morning had stood Willa's beautiful flower garden, sat a bare patch of earth. Completely denuded of its colorful carpet, bald dirt turned raw by the careless piles of uprooted plants scattered around, the sight made her want to weep.

Even worse were the silent tears rolling down Willa's cheeks.

Her friend's mouth hung agape, but no sound emerged. It was as though the new confidence and vitality she'd found had been ruthlessly cut off along with her flowers.

"Now you see?" Lucinda's sharp voice pierced the air. "You see what your new friend did to you?"

She's blaming me. Disbelief washed over Opal. *Just like with the mattress.*

"How could you?" Willa didn't turn, simply kept staring at the destruction of the love she'd lavished on those blossoms.

"Well, Opal?" Her mother-in-law's demand inspired an urge to do bodily harm.

"What's going on?" Adam sauntered around the side of the soddy to get his first look at the damage.

"Look at the trouble your wife caused now!" Lucinda clawed at her son's arm, dragging him farther away from Opal than ever before.

"Opal didn't do this." Adam took one look at the garden and shook his head. "She helped Willa tend it."

"How could you?" Still not facing anyone, Willa stooped to lovingly gather the limp plants into one pile.

"Willa, I didn't." Opal knelt beside the woman who'd become her friend and sister and wanted to weep. "I'll help you replant, I promise. Anything to make it better."

"You can't make it better." The hiss of a snake. "You've made things worse since the moment you married my son."

"Stop, Mama." Willa stood, her arms full of desecrated plants. She extended the corpses of her beloved flowers toward her mother, tears still streaming down her face. "How could you?"

"It's her fault!"

"No, Mama. You did this. Opal and I left and spent the whole day together."

"Why?" Adam put his hands on his mother's shoulders. "Why

would you do such a thing, Ma?"

"It *is* her fault! If it wasn't for her bees, I wouldn't have to get rid of the flowers. Flowers bring bees, Adam." Fear filled the older woman's voice. "I had to protect us all. And Willa has to learn the Specks are dangerous. Don't you see?"

"No." Diggory strode onto the scene and took Lucinda away from Adam. His gestures remained controlled, but that very control bespoke great anger. "You don't punish my little girl like that without my say-so, woman."

"She's consorting with that Benjamin, Diggory."

"Not anymore." Diggory glared at the daughter he'd championed scant seconds before. "Willa, you're not to talk to that boy again, do you hear me?" He didn't even wait for a response before pulling his wife toward the house.

Adam went to put his arm around Willa, leaving Opal reluctant to intrude just to get to the room she shared with her sister-in-law. Instead, she turned and headed toward the barn. The smell of hay and horse never failed to soothe her.

She opened the door and took a deep breath, feeling the weight of sorrow start to ebb. But peace didn't take its place. Instead, a sort of energy crackled, making the hairs on the back of her neck stand up. *Danger.* Opal turned to leave.

Too late.

"Hello, Opal." Larry lounged between her and the door. "Rare to catch you alone these days."

"I'm just heading back." She made as though to step around him, but he blocked her.

"Of course. After we settle a little business between us." He straightened, his body too close to hers.

"We have no business, Larry. I'm Adam's wife."

"Only because of the child." Fury distorted his features. "But if there were no babe, you wouldn't be tied to Adam. Isn't that right?"

"Larry," she could scarcely squeak his name past the terror in her throat. *He can't know. Oh Lord, please don't let him know!* Then the world narrowed to a pinpoint and she doubled over, gasping. Larry pulled his fist from her middle and pushed back her shoulder while she fought to draw breath, desperate for air. He drew back and slammed another punch to her stomach, this time letting her collapse on the floor while he stood over her.

"We can be together now." The smile on his face made her blood run cold. "That should have finished the brat."

CHAPTER 36

Pounding on the barn door woke Adam the next morning. Larry, of course, remained dead to the world—and the knocking.

He pulled on his pants and a shirt, leaving it half unbuttoned in his haste to see what needed attention, and threw open the door with gun at the ready to find his wife, clad in nothing but a night rail and a cloak. Adam reached out and clasped both her arms, pulling her inside. He thrust her behind him and looked to the left and right to find what disturbed her so.

"Willa's gone." Her whisper stopped his search.

No. He shut his eyes against the news, but nothing could shut away the truth of it. His eyes flew open once more when he felt her hands on his chest, doing up his buttons.

"We have to go after her." Opal kept quiet, obviously trying not to wake Larry. "Maybe it isn't too late. I don't know when she left—I slept closest to the wall."

"Put on clothes, Opal." Adam grabbed his boots and sat down. "We'll head over to your family's place, but I'd stake everything I have they're long gone."

She left in a whirl of cotton and cloak, muttering something about having to try.

Opal stood ready in a blue calico dress, still wearing her cloak against the coldness of the pre-morning. Dawn didn't yet lighten the sky as they left.

With Daisy and Dusty as their only draft horses, and mules or oxen notoriously slow, they made their way on foot. Adam's stride ate the distance in long stretches, but it seemed to him Opal lagged like she hadn't before.

"I'm coming," she gasped. One arm curled protectively around her stomach, and it seemed as though hurrying cost her great effort. "Keep on, Adam."

The baby must be moving. Wistfulness panged through him. Any other time, and he would've asked to feel it kicking so he could share part of the joy of their child's growth. *But now. . .* It was all he could do to remain thankful his wife trooped on.

When they arrived at the Speck doorstep, Adam's pounding put Opal's earlier efforts to shame. A bleary Elroy opened the door gun-first.

"Grogan." He peered past them. "Just you and Opal, or the whole clan come for vengeance?"

"Been expecting us, I see." Adam didn't bother to keep the anger from his words. "Only us. For now."

"Let 'em in, boy." Murphy's order came just as Elroy started to open the door anyway. "They're too late to stop Ben and Willa now. Might as well enjoy a visit."

"Might be the last thing you enjoy when my pa catches wind of this." Adam rubbed a hand over his face and sank onto a seat, mind racing.

"Tit for tat." His father-in-law wore the broadest smile Adam could remember since their wedding. "Willa came to Ben, so Diggory's got no call to vent his spleen."

"He will if you can't prove it."

"Willa left a note." Opal reached into the pocket of her cloak, retrieved it, and passed it to him.

My Beloved Family,
I love you all but am tired of living caged by past
disappointments and false discord. Ma uprooted the flowers
and tried to blame Opal, who's done nothing but good since
she married Adam. I don't believe anymore that she put rocks
in the mattress. I've gone to be with Ben. We planned to
elope anyway, but Pa forbidding me to see him hurries things
along. Opal doesn't know anything about this—I go as my
own woman and will return as Ben's.

All My Prayers,
Willa Grogan Speck

"Well, at least this proves she went willingly." Adam carefully folded it and placed it in his own jacket. "Without this note, Pa would've gone after your heads for sure."

"I've been doing some thinking." Murphy leaned forward. "Why don't we come with you to break the news? It'll show we've got nothing to hide. Better yet, I'm willing to agree that the delta land should go to Ben and Willa for them to establish a homestead, if he's amenable. With our families bound by two marriages, it's time to bury the hatchet."

"I'll go in first," Adam decided. "If I think Pa won't shoot first and listen later, we'll all talk like civilized men."

"Best anyone can hope for." A small smile tugged at the corners of Opal's mouth as they all headed back to the Grogan farm.

Adam kept her close as they neared home, wanting to order her back to her room but certain she wouldn't abandon her family under any circumstances. *Not fair to ask her to when I wouldn't either.*

By the time they got back, he found Pa and Larry in the barn. He closed the rolling door behind him, offered a prayer, and cleared his throat to get their attention. "Pa. I need you to hear me out on something. You aren't going to like it, but it's too late to do anything to change it." He took a deep breath. "I already tried."

"What?" Larry's eyes narrowed in that calculating way of his, but Adam simply passed Willa's note to their father.

"No." He crushed the note in his fist, went pale white, then livid purple. "We'll get her before it's too late."

"They left last night. By the time Opal discovered Willa gone this morning, fetched me, and we got to the Speck place, they were long gone."

"Willa ran off with that Speck boy?" His brother surmised the situation. "That girl doesn't have the sense God gave a goose. When we catch up to them, she'll regret the day she ever—"

"We won't catch up." Pa smoothed the note. "By the time we reach them, they'll have reached Ft. Laramie and be hitched right and legal. It's over, Larry."

"Murphy, Elroy, and Pete would like a word about the matter." Adam cautiously laid the groundwork for a meeting. "If you want to discuss it, Pa."

"What's to discuss?" The light of battle gleamed once more. "If those feckless Specks think I'll agree to give Willa a dowry, they've gone mad."

"No, Pa. Actually, they've offered to give Ben and Willa their claim to the delta land, if you'll agree."

"Well, now." Pa stroked his beard. "That might merit conversation."

"You've forgotten how to walk." Midge tsked as she watched Opal's stiff movements. "In less than three days, you've lost everything I taught you. If anything, it's gotten worse!"

"I tried your walk; you didn't warn me of the time limit."

"Time limit?"

"Apparently I can only be graceful for so long before I topple like poorly stacked sacks of grain." The grim tone, coupled with Opal's stiff walk, left no room for doubts.

"Not. . .not in front of Adam, surely?" Her mind started whirring ahead to how far that would set them back.

"Oh no. Nothing so humdrum as falling in front of my husband." Opal waved a hand. "I, of course, fell beside him in such a way I knocked him over as well."

"Wait, this could be good." Midge switched gears. "Did he fall right beside you, or maybe even on top of you?"

"Kind of perpendicular to me. His chest knocked the wind out of mine." The nonchalant tone stayed, but now Opal didn't meet her eyes.

"I hope you made the most of it!" *Well, really, at that point it's Adam who should make the most of it.*

"He kissed me."

"And?" The abruptness of the admission told of things left unsaid.

"Ran his fingers through my hair."

"Good. And?"

"Suddenly stopped and acted like he couldn't stand the idea of being within ten feet of me."

"Wait. What?" This didn't make much sense. At this point, Midge fully expected to hear that Adam wouldn't be able to annul the marriage. Once a man got that carried away, Nancy had told her, he didn't stop.

"He called me baby then just froze." Misery painted the words. "Pulled away, told me it didn't matter, and implied I did such things with other men."

"That's it!" Midge stopped even pretending to pull weeds around the hives. "Baby! It made him think of the one you're supposedly carrying and made him think about the real father, and it didn't sit well."

"You think?" Hope brightened Opal's countenance for a moment then faded. "But I can't fix that until after he beds me, and he doesn't want to."

"He wants to. In fact"—she reached out and grabbed her friend's hand to share the momentous realization—"Adam's in love with you. Otherwise he wouldn't care about the 'father.'"

"No man likes to be cuckolded—even before his wedding."

"Bah. He married you, he wants you, it's time to raise the stakes. I even know how to do it. . .according to the Bible."

"Really?" Her friend stopped working to sit back on her heels and eye her askance. "You found somewhere in the Bible where it explains how to seduce the man you tricked into becoming your husband for the sake of your family?"

"Almost the same thing." Midge held her pause until she could see Opal squirm then still kept quiet.

"Midge, don't make me do something rash!"

"Well, Opal, what do you know about the book of Ruth?"

"The Moabite whose husband died, but she followed God even after his death and stayed with her mother-in-law when Naomi returned to the land of her family?"

"Yes, that one. What *else* do you know?" *The important stuff!*

"She went to glean in the fields to provide for herself and Naomi and caught the eye of Boaz, who owned the field." Opal obviously had a good memory, as she recited the story. "And Naomi told her that Boaz stood as her next relation, which in biblical times meant he could be her kinsman redeemer and wed her. Which he did when she asked, because she had impressed him with her faithfulness and loyalty to Naomi."

"What about the most interesting part?" Midge didn't bother holding back any longer. Folks always tried to hold back the scandalous bits, and they were the best ones! "The part about *how* Ruth asked Boaz to be her husband?"

"She lay at his feet while he slept after the harvest." Opal didn't exactly blush, but a pink tinge crept up her cheeks. "So she could speak to him alone."

"What you mean is she went to his bed."

"He slept on the floor, probably on a pallet. . . ." Opal's protest sounded feeble.

"I used to sleep on a pallet, and I called it my bed. Lots of people have and still do, Opal. When Naomi told Ruth it was God's will for her to seek Boaz as her husband, she went to him in bed."

"You aren't suggesting I go to Adam's bed. . ."The pink turned to crimson. "I couldn't."

"You can."

"No. For now, Adam shares a room with Larry. And you know I can't change that—the man is the head of the house."

"You're forgetting what women do best." Midge allowed herself a wide grin. If Opal spouted particulars, it meant she considered going through with it.

"What do women do best?"

"Men may be the heads of households, but women turn heads."

CHAPTER 37

"Adam." Lucinda stopped her eldest before he left for the fields. With Willa gone, it was more important than ever that she roust the Speck chit and restore order at home. After nights of thinking, she'd found a way to destroy Opal's hold.

"Yes, Ma?"

"Son, there's something we need to discuss." She looked around as though afraid of being interrupted. In truth, she knew Larry left for an overnight hunting trip, and Diggory had gone to look over the delta land he held even more dear now that their daughter would settle upon it. Even Opal made herself scarce on the pretext of weeding around her beehives—as though such a ridiculous thing could possibly be necessary!

"What is it?"

"Come inside." She led him back to the table, where she poured him a cup of coffee and set it before him with a deep breath, as though certain he'd need the strength of it. "A suspicion has plagued me for quite some time, though I feared to give voice to it." She sank down opposite him and lowered her voice. "Now, I'm more afraid not to."

"Suspicion regarding what?"

"Opal's babe." She watched her son square his jaw and knew finding a hole in the wall he'd built around this issue wouldn't be easy. But knowing the particulars of the past paved her way. "Adam, there's no way for you to be certain it belongs to you."

"We've already discussed this." He put down the coffee and started to rise. "Opal's child belongs to me, and that's the end to it."

"But son—" She reached out a trembling hand to stay him. She didn't even have to fake the tremble, anxiety so overwhelmed her. "What if the babe isn't yours but should still bear the name Grogan?"

"I don't know what you mean." Adam's eyes warred with his words.

"Son, think." She shut her eyes as though in horror at the prospect. "We both know Larry skulked around the Speck place—we both saw what he wrote on that note. He's never said a word against her since she arrived but has been terse and tense with you the whole time. What if Opal played you false with your own brother, and he blames you for taking her away?"

Silence stretched beyond her carefully scripted speech. Lucinda waited. If she tried too hard to convince Adam, he'd see it as a ploy. As it was, even she couldn't say she hadn't hit upon the truth. She watched as Adam's eyes darkened, his fingers clamped around the mug.

In spite of what Adam said to her, she considered her work accomplished. She'd sown the seeds of doubt, and it wouldn't be long before they took root.

Kinsman Redeemer. The phrase wouldn't leave her throughout the day. *Ruth had Boaz, I have Adam.* Midge even missed one of the key reasons why Boaz stood in the position to become Ruth's husband. Why, really, Ruth *needed* Boaz enough to creep into his sleeping place and pursue him.

A child. Ruth's husband died without giving her a child, leaving her and Naomi destitute. Her lack of child spelled disaster. And back in Old Testament days, the nearest male relative could be recruited if he met the requirements.

For here and now, Adam is my husband. And my lack of a child threatens to destroy my family, too. Do I have the courage to crawl into my husband's bed?

She pondered this as she made her way to the shielded grove on her family's farm, where she used to bathe on hot summer days. There, in a little crock on a rope, she found the supplies she'd placed long ago. Some of the honey-scented soap she always made, a lump of fired beeswax, and a comb.

She checked to make certain no one loitered nearby or had followed her—though she'd been confident no one would. Midge sent her off to bathe as soon as she'd learned of the possibility, and everyone else expected her to be with Midge.

Opal set the beeswax on a rock to warm while she washed then stripped down to her shift. First, she lathered her hair, luxuriating in the bubbles and rinsing it clean before everything else. It would take longest to dry. Then she made short work of bathing before clambering onto the flat rock where the sun would warm the moisture away from her skin while she worked the comb through her hair.

As a final touch, she took the beeswax and lightly rubbed it over her skin, smoothing it in for extra softness the way her mama taught her so many years ago. By the time she finished, and dressed, and walked back to Midge, her hair dried enough for her to put it back up.

"Ready, then?" Her friend's grin did nothing to calm her nerves.

"As ready as I can get."

With Larry gone on an overnight hunting trip, it took Adam extra time to complete the evening chores. He didn't mind.

Not only did it give him time to think without going mad for lack of something to do, it meant Larry wasn't around. Because when Adam thought about it, really thought back on his conversation with his brother about whether or not Larry'd been with Opal, he couldn't come up with a single solid statement to reassure him.

Only a bark of laughter and his brother's taunt, *"What do you think?"*

Back then, he'd thought Larry'd never gotten to Opal. Now, when he considered his original suspicions, the fact that no other man in town showed any signs of anger or shame at his marriage, that Ma cottoned on to Larry's behavior, he couldn't remember why he'd decided his brother didn't count as a concern.

Tiredness tugged at him by the time he made it to his room, lit a tin-covered safety lantern, and disrobed down to his drawers. But when Adam turned back his covers, he found far more than his pillow.

There, resplendent in nothing but a thin night rail, lay his wife. Her hair flowed down her back and around to cover the curves of her chest like a blanket of fiery silk. Her skin seemed to take on the glow of the scant lantern, a siren's call to make him lean closer. Opal's eyes stayed closed, long ginger lashes giving her an innocence he wished with all his heart she actually possessed as she drew the deep, even breaths of one completely asleep.

She came to my bed. The finality of it staggered him. Everything inside him demanded he slide beside her. That he pull her close, cover her mouth with his, and watch her lashes flutter with awareness at her sweet awakening.

Everything but the warning that his wife might, in reality, belong to his brother. *I should wake her up and send her back to her room.* But all the reason and logic in the world couldn't alter the truth—if he touched her, he'd be lost. If he watched her wake up, stretch, walk to the door in so little, he'd be lost.

So Adam sank onto his brother's bed, wound the covers tight around him, and tried to forget about the woman dreaming only feet away. The woman he'd been dreaming about longer than he'd any right to. The woman who—

The woman who is sliding into Larry's bed alongside me this very moment. Adam didn't move a muscle as his wife snuggled up to him and tugged at the blankets. Didn't so much as breathe when she leaned over and dropped a featherlight kiss on his cheek, sending soft strands of her hair to tickle his neck.

"Adam?" When she couldn't free the blankets or elicit a response, she spoke. "I know you're awake."

"Can't be."

"You are, my husband." Her breath warmed his ear. "And I am your wife."

One man should only be asked to withstand so much temptation, Lord. Adam turned, keeping the covers whipcord tight around himself. "What else are you, Opal?"

He almost would have sworn he saw a flash of uncertainty in her eyes, but she recovered quickly.

"In your bed."

"Wrong." It came out curt, but that suited him just fine. "You're in Larry's bed. Question is, have you been here before?"

"Never." She moved as though to push away from him, but he caught one wrist and kept her connected to him. "Let me go."

"No. You came to my room, you'll answer my questions." He kept his grip loose enough not to hurt. "When Larry kept trespassing onto Speck lands, did he go to see you?"

She swallowed, hard. "I'm afraid so."

Suddenly it seemed as the air turned to lead. Adam fought to keep going. "Do you want to be with my brother?"

"No!" Opal didn't struggle, just stared up at him with pleading eyes. "I'm here to be with you, Adam."

The air thinned slightly, but not enough. He still had one more question. "Has my brother touched you since you married me?"

"Don't ask." A broken sob escaped her lips, one arm curling around her middle as though to protect the babe his brother sired within her.

"Then go." He flung her arm from him and turned his back. "I don't want you."

Opal stumbled back to the room she used to share with Willa and sank down onto the bed.

Lord, what am I to do now? She relived the time she'd spent with Adam that night and saw no ways left to make their marriage work. *There's nothing. If a man won't take a woman who climbs into his bed, he doesn't want her. I should have known that even before he said it.*

After all, Adam didn't choose to marry her. Adam never said he wanted to be with her. Adam didn't arrange for them to room together after Willa left. Nowhere along the way had her "husband" done anything to demonstrate the slightest interest.

She wrapped her arms around herself in a bid to hold herself together and ward away the rejection but found herself wincing once more. Opal lifted her nightgown and peered at the purples and blues smearing her stomach.

At least that's one thing I don't have to worry about—his seeing the bruises and asking what happened. She couldn't work up a smile.

Truth be told, Adam might not even care what happened. *But I care.* She blinked back tears that owed nothing to the soreness in her stomach and everything to the ache in her heart. *I care.*

Adam doesn't want me as a woman, doesn't want me as his wife. He deserves better than to be trapped this way. Now I know Pa will forgive me—he'll forgive me more readily for not having betrayed him the original way. Ben and Willa can be the ones to unite the Specks and Grogans.

Opal rose to her feet and slid her satchel from beneath the bed to start packing.

Tomorrow, I'll see Parson Carter about that annulment.

CHAPTER 38

Adam woke early the next morning. At least, he would have if he'd slept.

In any case, dawn found him already up with most of his chores done and him ready to head to the fields. Which is where he went. Without breakfast. His appetite left at the thought of facing Opal over the table, so he got a great start hand-casting oats.

It wasn't until he ventured back to the well to refill his canteen that he spoke to another living soul. Seemed Pa'd had the same idea at the same time.

"Today another day for Opal to help her Pa and brothers?" The question caught Adam off guard.

"No."

"Must be with the hives, then." Pa closed his canteen and used the tin cup they kept by the well to take a long swig. "We haven't seen hide nor hair of the girl today. With Willa gone and Larry not back yet from hunting, place seems empty."

Unease gnawed in the pit of Adam's belly. "I'll check the apiary to be sure."

A few minutes later, the unease grew to concern when the apiary produced nothing more than humming hives and busy bees. Adam headed back home. He made for the main door but swung around the side, toward the entrance to Willa and Opal's room, at the last minute.

The door stood ajar.

He pushed in but didn't see anything wrong at first. Bed was made neat and tidy, nothing out of place, nothing to cause worry, nothing—nothing. *That's what's wrong.* The realization hit him in the gut. No clothes hung from pegs. No bonnets waited to be worn. No signs told of any woman's presence, save a piece of paper on the writing desk.

Adam walked over to find an already-opened letter. He'd worry about who opened it later. For now, he concentrated on the small, sweet letters whose lines slanted upward at the end.

Dear Adam,

First, please let me apologize for all that's gone wrong. I never meant to mislead you, but when I shouted in the clearing that you would be the father of my child, I chose the words knowing Pa would force a shotgun wedding. I grabbed at my only chance to save your life that day. When you mentioned the possibility of annulment being lost only due to my pregnancy, I knew I couldn't tell you the truth until we consummated our union.

Here, he lowered the letter for a moment, stunned by the revelation. *Does this mean my wife is untouched?* Unable to keep from grinning, he kept reading.

After last night, and in light of Larry's interest, I know we can't be together. By this point, the volatile nature of our

*families' interactions has been largely contained. Ben and
Willa may take up as the new peacekeepers. This sham of a
marriage is no longer necessary to keep bloodshed at bay, so
you may rest easy. Please know that I'm leaving this morning
to speak with Parson Carter about seeking an annulment,
which will certainly be granted upon the supremely provable
grounds of nonconsummation.*

Many apologies for the difficulties I've brought you,
Opal Speck

Adam didn't take the time to fold the letter before heading to
the barn, instead creasing it on the way. He had Daisy saddled—
draft horse she may be, but she pulled double duty in a pinch—
before Ma or Pa could catch up to him.

Opal hasn't been with Larry. Opal never lay with any man. The
certainty flooded him like a song of praise. *She chose to save my life.
She married me because she wanted to.* Memories of all the times
they'd worked in tandem to keep peace jumbled in his mind until
there was only one thing he could keep straight. *Opal and I have
a chance at a real marriage, as long as I can convince her I don't want
an annulment.*

He urged Daisy to move faster as he remembered finding
Opal in his bed last night. *No annulments for us.*

When he arrived at Parson Carter's, the older man hadn't seen
Opal. Adam bit back a grin. Perhaps his wife didn't feel so anxious
to end things as her letter let on. Maybe she waited at the Speck
farm even now for him to show up.

But when he showed up, he found no trace of Opal there
either. Worry clawed its way into a frown, but Adam persevered.
Perhaps Opal had gone back to the Grogan farm, hoping to find
him? He pressed Daisy harder than ever to get home, fighting his
growing unease.

Pa said they hadn't seen her at breakfast, he recalled. *By now she should have visited Parson Carter and been back at the Speck place many times over.*

So it didn't surprise him when he got home and found no Opal. Only his mother remained at the Grogan farm, and even she sat, weeping at the table, raising a tear-stained face to him.

"Oh, Adam," she sobbed. "I think Opal ran off with our Larry!"

Lucinda couldn't stand. She wanted to fling herself at her eldest son, to comfort him over the betrayal of his wife and brother and wring out what comfort she could in return. But instead, she seemed affixed to the bench.

"Why do you think she's with Larry?" His footfalls sounded slow, as though the news weighed heavy on Adam.

"She ran out on her chores this morning. Then Larry came tearing through here like a man possessed." She pushed her handkerchief to her mouth. "He demanded the cashbox, took everything, and left. Said he had someone waiting. I know it's her."

"Opal doesn't want Larry." Certainty rang in Adam's voice. He pushed a letter toward her. "Though Larry wants my wife...badly enough to do something foolish. Which way would he go, Ma?"

Lucinda read the note and had to swallow back the bile that swelled past her throat.

I knew it! I knew that girl didn't carry my son's child. She tricked him into marriage. She threw my Willa at her no-good brother. She turned Adam's head, and now she's addled Larry's wits.

"Ben." She reached past the nausea into her memory for anything useful. "Larry said something about Ben's mine being a good place for a new start."

"I'm going to bring them home, Ma."

"Adam?" Her call scarcely made him pause in the doorway he

was so intent on racing to his hussy. "Be merciful to your brother. Remember your blood."

"Yes, Ma."

Opal awoke to find herself trussed up and slung over a saddle, every step the horse took sending new aches streaking through her bruised middle. She worked her dry mouth and tried to remember what had happened.

The humiliation of last night's rejection rose to the front of her mind until she shoved it down. *I wrote the letter, packed my things, and set out for Parson Carter's.* She strained to marshal her thoughts or even clear her vision but kept seeing spots.

Then it came back. *Larry.* He intercepted her on her way to Parson Carter's and tried to convince her to leave Adam. Hoping to get to safety, she'd told him the truth of where she headed and why, but it backfired. Instead of escorting her to get the annulment, Larry trussed her up like a turkey and went to go read the note she'd left for Adam.

He returned with his whole face lit up, swearing he'd make her happy. But no matter how she played along, she couldn't convince him to take her to Parson Carter's nor her family's farm. The more she insisted, the more he resisted, until he said something about being sorry, but it would be easiest if she slept. Then he raised the butt of his pistol. . .

Which must be why her head throbbed even more than her stomach. She concentrated on drawing a few deep breaths and praying.

Lord, please give me the wisdom to handle Larry and the strength to take whatever opportunities You send. I ask for peace to clear my thoughts so I may be wise.

The one small mercy Larry afforded her had been to not

gag her. Although, having knocked her unconscious, he probably hadn't needed to. At any rate, she tried to use her teeth to loosen the rope around her wrists, contorting her hands and compressing her fingers in a bid for freedom. No use. She decided against trying to rear back and lunge off the horse.

Not only did she gamble a bad fall, it wouldn't do her any good with her legs bound together. At best, the attempt may slow Larry's progress by a few moments. At worst, he might strike her unconscious again. Opal shuddered at the thought and refused to risk it.

But she did try to angle her arms beneath her enough to maneuver her stomach off the horse a little. Not much, just enough to bear some of her weight and relieve the pain. It didn't work, but it alerted Larry that she'd awoken, and she felt them come to a halt.

The saddle leaned as he slid out. His hands sent revulsion up her spine when they settled on her waist and pulled her down, but her much-abused midriff sighed with relief. He didn't say anything, just stared at her for a moment before cupping the back of her head, feeling where he'd bashed the back of her skull. It made her wince.

"I'm sorry, sweetheart." His use of the endearment made her skin crawl. "But I had to do it. I knew you wouldn't leave without saying goodbye to your pa and brothers. Am I right?"

"Yes." The urgency in his voice acted as her cue, even if she hadn't already decided the smartest thing would be to agree with him unless he asked something of her. "I wanted to see them."

"Don't be sad, baby." He smothered her in a hug. "You know if you saw them they wouldn't let you leave with me. I couldn't let that happen." Larry kept one arm around her but pulled back enough to look down at her. "You would've been so upset if they stood in our way."

"I'm sure you would've found a way." She kept the words sounding sweet. *A lying, thieving, sneaking, conniving, abusing, kidnapping, no-good jerk always finds a way to take what he wants.*

"Of course I would've found a way for us to be together." He smoothed her hair back—right over the tender knot that made her wince again. "After how hard I've been working to get them out of the way, you know that. Even if it backfired and you wound up having to save Adam."

"I'm the reason you wanted to spark the feud?" It clunked into place but made no sense.

"Yes. Your family wouldn't let me have you, so they had to be taken out of the picture. We're destined to be together, no matter what I have to do to make it happen." A beatific smile made sinister by the scar bisecting his face. "You know that."

Chapter 39

Adam followed the tracks from the Burn smithy due west. Sure enough, they said Larry'd rented the fastest horse they had. With cash up front.

But that horse carried two passengers, and his trusty Daisy only carried one. Together, they pushed as quickly as possible, the tracks growing fresher the farther they got. Hours of riding saw the scenery change, sending them into a land of reddish soil and spiky desert plants that didn't seem to bear much thirst.

It was here, behind a small stand of bedraggled trees that looked more like twisted bushes, Adam caught sight of his quarry. Lickety-split, he slid off Daisy and snuck closer, taking stock of the situation.

There stood the horse—munching on a tuft of grass so dry it looked as though it would cut a cow's mouth. Larry faced Opal a few steps behind. From this side view, Adam could see that his brother had bound his wife's hands and knees, keeping her completely under his control.

The beast within him that claimed Opal as its own gave a mighty roar when he saw Larry's arm around his wife. When he heard Larry telling her he'd do anything to make them be together, the roaring became louder, rushing in his ears when he saw Opal wince.

"Step away from my wife." Adam gave the order from less than four feet back. He crouched, ready if Larry sprang at him.

"Adam!" Opal made as though to move toward him, but her bindings brought her up short. She fell to the ground with a painful *thud* as Larry released her and turned.

"Brother." The sneer mocked him. Mocked their blood tie. "You read the letter. She's left you. Be gone."

"Noooo. . ." A low moan from Opal negated Larry's taunt.

"Larry, come back home. Opal and I will move out. Things will go back to normal. You'll never go near or even see my wife again." He inched forward, attempting to reason with the unreasonable man. "We'll put this all behind us."

"No. Opal's mine." Larry pulled out a knife. "You tried to take her from me once. You're my brother, Adam, and it took me a long time to figure out how it happened. Now that I know it was a mistake, I can forgive and forget it. But I won't let it happen again. Leave us in peace now."

"Put away the knife and come home." Another step toward subduing Larry. Another step toward saving Opal.

"Get back." His brother waved the knife, moving to stand over Opal. "She and I are meant for each other. Leave us in peace."

"Larry, I have to bring her back. She's my wife. She belongs with me."

"No!" Larry lunged forward, slicing through the air—and a part of Adam's shirt—with his knife. It would've done more damage, but he stepped in some sort of depression in the earth and his balance faltered. He quickly righted himself and attacked again.

Adam grabbed his brother's knife-arm with both hands, keeping it poised away from his body, twisting until Larry dropped the knife. He kicked it far from where they stood, evening the match.

No matter, Larry wouldn't give up. He came after him, fists flying, face full of fury. They had the knockdown, drag-out of the century.

Until Opal screamed.

Larry, as the one closest, processed the problem first. The depression his foot sank in when he wielded the blade hadn't been mere loose earth. While they'd fought, the deadly force he unleashed crept toward Opal.

Each about a foot long, two snakes slithered to where Opal lay, bound and helpless to escape. The yellow background and gray dorsal pattern, with two light diagonal stripes along their faces, clearly marked them as prairie snakes. The usual warning rattle hadn't alerted them, as these youths each boasted only a single rattle, producing a soft sort of sizzling sound to express their anger at having their nest disturbed. Having grown so long, it seemed likely that these two had driven off or eaten most of their siblings.

"Opal!" Adam scrambled to his feet and began to charge for his wife, knowing he wouldn't make it in time.

"Opal!" Larry dove in front of her, directly in the path of both snakes.

Out of the corner of his eye, Adam saw the snakes dart toward his brother while he dragged Opal to safety. He raced to pick up the knife he'd kicked away earlier in the fight, falling upon the creatures still attacking his brother with a vengeance. In seconds, neither snake's head could find its body, but Adam didn't care.

"Larry." Puncture wounds covered his brother's arms, hands, and chest. Young prairie rattlers were known to strike multiple times, with venom more concentrated than that of grown snakes. With two of them. . . Adam couldn't swallow past the lump in his throat as Larry struggled to sit up.

"Opal." His brother's dying request had Adam untying his wife and bringing her to her kidnapper's side. He might have worried that she'd shy away, but not his wife.

"You saved me." Opal dropped to her knees and drew Larry's

head in her lap, her tears falling in a gentle rain. "Thank you."

"See?" A sweet smile transformed Larry into the brother Adam had grown up with. He reached one shaking hand to trace the path of one of Opal's tears. "I was right, Opal." He fought to breathe. "You do care."

His words only made her cry harder and hold on tighter as Larry took his last breaths, his heart giving out from the poison.

Adam didn't move. Couldn't move. Not until all Opal's tears were shed and she stood up. Together, they carefully wrapped Larry in a blanket and tied him to the saddle before setting out for home.

Opal didn't speak and neither did he.

He thinks it's my fault. Opal kept her arms wrapped around Adam's waist to keep from falling off Daisy as they started home.

Oh Lord. After this, there's no chance for me and Adam, is there? The death of his brother. . . He'll blame me. Or he'll blame himself, which is even worse. His parents had barely begun to tolerate me. Now that will end entirely.

Despair bogged her down, rooting her in misery. The best she could hope for now was that their families didn't kill each other over this incident, that Larry's death would be the last. Her thoughts pulled her in so deep, Opal scarcely noticed when the sky turned dark. Not until they came within sight of the Grogan house.

Then she struggled not to tighten her hold on Adam. Funny how she'd thought she'd given him up entirely this morning, but now she felt as though she couldn't let him go. He swung out of the saddle and lifted her down after. She followed him to the other horse, which Daisy had led the entire way, and helped him untie Larry's corpse. Adam carried the bundle inside, where his parents and little brother waited.

"No!" Lucinda's anguished scream rent the night the second she saw Opal walk through the door behind her son and knew the figure masked by the blanket must be Larry. "No!" She grasped Larry's shoulders and sank onto the floor, where Adam carefully placed him.

"What happened?" Diggory's eyes didn't look hard tonight. No greedy glint or angry gleam lit their depths. Instead, his expression seemed strangely flat.

"He kidnapped Opal on her way to Parson Carter's." Adam didn't so much as glance her way as he spoke. "Ma says he then came and took the cashbox, which I assume is still in the saddlebags. Opal didn't go willingly, so he tied her up, which is how I found them."

"Anything you want to add?" Her father-in-law interrupted Adam and turned to her.

"No." Her saying anything would be out of place.

"Tell me everything anyway." Diggory Grogan demonstrated a greater understanding of her than Opal would have credited him with. "Best to have all the details now."

"He knocked me out with the back of his pistol"—Opal flinched at the angry sound from Adam as his hand settled directly on the tender spot at the back of her head—"when I didn't agree that we were in love and I belonged to him."

"Lovesick." Lucinda had freed Larry's head from the swathing and tenderly fixed his hair. "Just lovesick for the wrong girl. That's all he was. He didn't mean no harm."

"He said he's been trying to provoke the feud to kill my family and get rid of any objections." Opal wouldn't meet anyone's gaze as she repeated Larry's words, all too aware how ridiculous it sounded.

"I should've seen it." Diggory lowered himself onto his haunches and looked at Larry's face.

"None of us did." Adam sounded so hoarse, Opal wouldn't have known his voice if she didn't see his mouth move.

He blames me for not telling him. I thought he wouldn't have believed me, but would he? Do such questions even matter anymore? She reached up and curled her fingers around Mama's brooch.

"When I found them, Larry told me to leave them. I wouldn't, so he pulled a knife and sprang at me." Adam recounted how he disarmed his brother, how Larry's step faltered, how the two fought until Opal cried out.

"Tied up, she couldn't get away. Larry threw himself in front of Opal when he realized the situation."

"It should have been you." Lucinda's hiss seemed oddly akin to that of the snakes from earlier as she stared at Opal. "You should be wrapped in this blanket. Not my boy."

"Larry kidnapped Opal, bashed her skull, tied her up, and put her in the path of those snakes." Her husband spoke more loudly now. "It shouldn't have been Opal, Ma. It shouldn't have been anyone, but Larry created the problem."

"No." The hatred in Lucinda's stare made Opal's blood run cold. "*She* created the problem when she seduced you and wormed her way into our household, playing brother against brother."

"Opal misled her family, and myself, into believing she carried a child on our wedding day just to save my life. She's never been with any man, so don't call her a seducer or one who pits men against each other."

"No grandchild?" Diggory's face went duller. "Well, at least we know you got yourself a good wife, son."

"A good wife?" The scream should've brought the town running. "She murdered our Larry and disgraced his name!"

"Larry saved my life." Opal didn't care that Lucinda hated her, but she wouldn't stand by and let her affection for Larry's memory fade to nothing. "I honor him."

"As do I." Adam moved to stand alongside her.

"Same here." Diggory straightened up. "He may have gotten things mixed up, might have caused trouble, but by taking on those snakes, Larry proved himself a good man in the end. I'm proud of him."

"You have reason to be."

"Don't speak about my son." Lucinda lurched to her feet. "Get out of my house. Take her out, Adam. Now!"

"I'll take her home."

Home. Opal bowed her head. *He's returning me to the Speck farm. Of course he is. The only thing that's changed is that his brother died— over me. No wonder he wants to be rid of me.* She followed as he stabled the horse, not protesting when he grabbed her satchel.

Neither one of them uttered a word as they trudged toward the Speck farm.

It wasn't until they stood on her father's doorstep that Adam asked a question Opal hadn't imagined weighed on his mind. "What's wrong with your stomach?"

"Oh." The memory of Larry's fist made her close her eyes, but not before she glanced down and registered that her arm braced her stomach, as it had for most of the walk. "Being thrown over a saddle and jounced around takes a toll."

"No." His eyes narrowed at her shrug. "You hurt before today. I noticed when we went after Willa—but thought it was the baby. Now I know better." He angled closer. "What happened?"

"Doesn't matter anymore." She braced herself more tightly and reached for the door, the obvious escape. "I'll be fine."

His body blocked the door—solid, powerful, and far too close for comfort.

She fell back a step.

"Tell me, Opal."

"Larry."

The *smack* of knuckles splintering wood muffled her husband's curse as Adam gouged her father's doorframe with a vicious jab before stalking off into the night.

Even though the door opened to reveal her entire family, Opal couldn't help but feel isolated. Adam didn't even see Willa and Ben had returned. How could he?

He never looked back.

CHAPTER 40

"W ake up, Lucy." Diggory shook her awake, and for a blessed moment, Lucinda didn't realize why she lay half sprawled on the kitchen table instead of snug in bed.

Then she saw Larry—just as she'd left him when the tears finally carried her to oblivion. Dressed in his Sunday best, arms folded across his chest, freshly shaven, and looking every inch the wonderful son she'd raised. And lost.

She lost the distance she'd gained upon waking, when she'd half risen before reality came crashing back upon her. Knees seemed such flimsy things to stand up to such a blow. But somehow they managed the task when her husband scooped Larry's body into his arms and headed for the door.

"No. . ." The cry emerged as a raspy whisper, her throat too raw from sobbing the night through to manage any volume now. So she followed, stumbling a little in the bright morning light as Diggory carried their son away.

Lucinda blinked away the bleariness by the time her husband stopped—carefully laying Larry in a wooden box he must've cobbled together the night before. Parson Carter stood at the ready, a whole group of people surrounding a fresh-dug grave. *A funeral. Larry's funeral.* Recognition dawned.

An insane urge to throw herself over her son and demand he be given back warred with gratitude toward her husband and friends for arranging the respectful farewell Larry deserved. The battle lasted only as long as it took for her to identify those gathered to mourn him.

"What is *she* doing here?" An aching throat lent itself well to her hiss of rage as Lucinda threw away polite manners and pointed at the Speck Murderess, only to realize the entire contingent of Specks surrounded the dealer of death. "What are *any* of you doing here?"

"Paying our respects." Willa's was the last voice she expected, but her daughter stepped forward, and she realized belatedly that Ben's presence meant they'd both returned. "To my brother."

"So now you remember your family?" Somehow, the words snapped out before Lucinda could snatch them back. Now it was too late to rush to her only girl and envelop her in a hug that would never end.

"I never forgot." Willa didn't recoil or even have the grace to look abashed. Even worse, Ben reached out and clasped her hand while she spoke. "But I remembered that we're no better than anyone else. The Specks are a part of our family now, Ma. Between Ben and Opal, we're joined forever."

"The pair of them aren't worth Larry! The whole Speck family isn't!" Her voice broke through the soreness in a screech. "I won't have it. I won't have Larry's murderer attend his funeral when inside she's laughing at our loss. Willa, come home. Adam's annulling his sham of a marriage. We can all be together again." She stepped forward and reached a hand toward each of her errant children. "Don't let Larry's death be in vain."

"Larry died to save Opal," Dave piped up, walking up to his sister-in-law. "Pa says it was brave."

"It was." The cause of all their woes smiled down at her youngest son, sending a shaft of fear straight through Lucinda's heart as neither Willa nor Adam moved to join her. "I'll never forget Larry's selfless courage."

"No." Lucinda grasped Dave by the soft, fleshy part of the arm, just above the elbow, and hauled him to her side. "I won't lose any more of our family to Speck machinations. Dave isn't permitted to speak to any Speck!"

"Not even me, Ma?"

"You're still a Grogan, sis." Dave wriggled in an attempt to break free, but Lucinda held on tighter. "Ma didn't mean you."

"Yes, I did, Dave. You aren't to visit your sister if she stays with the Specks. Only if Willa comes back home." Willa's gasp sent a surge of satisfaction through her. *There. Let her see what she's given up. Nothing comes without a price.* Lucinda's gaze fell on the makeshift coffin cradling her middle son and fought a surge of dizziness.

"No." Diggory pried her hand off Dave's arm, letting him rush to hug Willa. "Larry died to make amends, Lucy. I won't let it be for nothing. The Specks are here to honor what he done right, and I won't take that away from any of us. Davey can talk to any of the Specks any time he wants."

" 'Hatred stirreth up strifes: but love covereth all sins,' " Parson Carter broke in. "Your son's death epitomizes one of my favorite verses."

"I won't support this." Another sob caught in her throat, swelling until she thought it would swallow her whole. "You know where to find me when you come to your senses." Lucinda headed back to the house, stopping only to plant one last kiss on Larry's cheek before losing herself in the loneliness she'd dreaded so long.

~~~

During his mother's outburst, Adam slid one arm around Opal's waist. It felt right, and her wordless acceptance eased some of the tension from his neck. Opal's nearness affected him that way, relaxed him, put him at peace. Question was, had he discovered it too late?

The night before, when she'd revealed Larry's abuse, he hadn't trusted himself to speak. Hadn't trusted himself to keep from scooping her up and taking her home, where he should have taken her long ago. *But it wouldn't have been right to ask her to be my wife after all she'd been through yesterday.* Instead, he'd gone back to the dugout and thrown himself into the finishing touches. Too little, too late, when he should have protected her all along, but he had to make it perfect before he would show her that he offered her more than he'd given so far.

"Can I have a word?" Her nod had him guiding her across Grogan lands, knowing she expected him to take her to her father's farm.

She hadn't protested when he took her to her father's last night—didn't ask to stay. Why would she? Opal busily did everything in her power to fit in on the Grogan farm, only to have it flung in her face. She'd made every possible move to make their marriage work. . .and. he'd rejected it.

Because I didn't understand. But will such a woman as this give a fool a second chance? God, please help me to do this right.

"I'd like to show you something." He waited for her nod before picking up the pace. Adam knew he shouldn't move faster, shouldn't do anything that could scare her. But his Opal didn't scare easily, and he didn't want her changing her mind.

The dugout looked much like any other hill from a distance. It wasn't until they drew closer to the structure they could make it out for what it was. The hollowed-out hill stood, at its tallest, about eight feet high, with natural earth for three walls and the roof. A stovepipe stuck through the top.

Adam made earth bricks for the fourth wall out of the dirt he'd excavated from the hill. Into this one, he installed the door and covered the window openings with leather flaps until he could order glass.

"Adam?" Her voice made his name a question. "What is this?"

"Home." He swallowed. "If you want it to be."

"You built this?" Her eyes caught the brilliance of the sunlight. "For us?"

Adam couldn't manage much more than a nod. But she didn't say anything either, just stared at the dugout, and he knew now was his last chance. "Opal?" He took both her hands in his. "Now isn't the ideal time, but I'm coming to accept that there will never be an ideal time. And if I don't say something now, I may lose my chance."

"Your chance for what, Adam?" If words could carry color, hers sounded like they'd be the pale green of hope.

He shoved aside the fanciful thought and plowed ahead. "Weeks ago, I didn't choose you to be my bride." He held fast when she made a small sound of distress and tried to pull her hands away. "But I should have seen it as a gift, I should have watched over you more diligently. If you can forgive me for being so slow to realize how blessed I am to have you as my wife, Opal, I ask you to choose me as your husband."

"Truly?" She stopped trying to pull her hands away, her fingers curling around his. "You want me as your wife?"

"I want you, Opal. I want you in my house, I want you by my side." His voice dropped. "I want you in my bed, without any mis-understandings between us. I want what you said that day on your family's farm to be true—I want to be the father of your child, Opal Grogan. What say you?"

"I say..." She tilted her head and bestowed upon him the loveliest smile he'd ever seen while she drew out her answer. "We have a lot of lost time to make up for,"—Opal leaned close—"husband."

"Then let's get started,"—Adam swept her up into his arms and headed for the door—"wife."

DISCUSSION QUESTIONS

1. The Bible specifically calls us to honor our parents, but sometimes parents are wrong. How do you reconcile following what you know is right with the respect owed your elders?

2. Most people will agree that a lie is when you intentionally speak an untruth in order to deceive, but people will also talk about "white" lies or "fibs." Are there gradations to falsehoods? What about when the words you speak, as in Opal's case, are true, but spoken with something vital omitted and the knowledge that others will misinterpret those words? Do you feel there's a scale when it comes to types of lies? Why or why not?

3. No one is perfect and we've all slipped up, but is there ever an occasion where it is all right to lie? Can the good outweigh the bad or the ends justify the means?

4. The way we're raised has a huge impact on who we become and, in many cases, what we come to believe. Can we ever escape what we've been taught and choose another path? At what point do learned prejudices stop being the fault of a family and become personal responsibility?

5. Have you ever done something that changed the way you saw yourself? For example, Opal always took it for granted that loyalty to her family was one of the fundamental parts of her character, yet she found she valued Adam's life more. What would you say to someone who's going through a period where they question who they are?

6. Everyone has things in his/her past to regret, and sometimes we regret things that aren't even our fault. Guilt can be a terrible burden and make us wonder at our own worth. For example, Midge struggles with wondering if she could have done more for her sister, or if she's tainted by her past. Is there anything in your life you're holding on to like this? What if's or regrets burrowing into your heart? What would you advise a loved one to do in that situation? Now, what would it take for you to follow your own advice?

7. The Bible tells us that man and wife are to be as one and husbands are to cleave to their wives, but we all know that sometimes things come between a couple. Both Adam and Opal are pulled away from the other by their families— something that happens even without feuds! How would you keep a marriage partnership the strongest relationship in your life (aside from the one you have with the Lord, of course!) in the face of opposition from loved ones?

8. The inspiring verse for this novel says, "Anger and hatred stirreth up strife, but love covereth a multitude of sins." How do we see that exemplified in the story? What about in your life?

9. Is there someone you've carried a grudge against or someone carrying a grudge against you? When you truly think about it, is the underlying cause more important than the relationship? What can you do to remedy the situation?

10. Do you have a favorite character, scene, or lesson learned from this story? If so, what was it? Why do you think it resonated with you?

THE BRIDE
BLUNDER

DEDICATION/ACKNOWLEDGMENT

For the Lord, who gave me the words to write and the precious friends who encouraged me to do it!

For Aaron, a wonderful editor and exacting historian, without whom this book wouldn't be what it is.

And, most of all, for Steve, who wrote alongside me hour by hour when I thought I had nothing left to say. This book wouldn't exist at all without you. . . .

CHAPTER 1

Baltimore, Maryland 1859

N o." Marge Chandler shook her head, wishing it were so easy to shake away the sudden image springing to life in her mind. "No more bows, Daisy."

"Well. . ." Her cousin nibbled on the edge of her naturally rosy lower lip and fingered the velvet trimmings before her. "Perhaps you're right."

"Nonsense, darling—it's your wedding dress!" Daisy's mother, the aunt who'd raised them both since Marge's parents didn't survive the crossing to America, bustled over and snatched up the ribbons. "Besides, you know better than to ask Marge her opinion on matters of fashion."

True. Daisy should know better by now. A wry smile tilted Marge's lips. *Aunt Verlata will always override me.* Not that it mattered—Daisy could wear a rainbow of gaudy velvet bows and still entrance any audience.

Her smile turned rueful as Marge caught a glimpse of her own reflection in the dressmaker's looking glass. Aunt Verlata's sense of style didn't hamper Daisy's charm, but somehow Marge couldn't manage to carry off the same fussy furbelows with any panache. While feminine touches showcased Daisy's graceful build, her own more generous frame made such flourishes conspicuous. And never before had her relatives indulged in so many fripperies as for Daisy's much-anticipated wedding. Marge's gown for the affair—a light blue silk that had done nothing to deserve such treatment—drooped toward the ground, overburdened with tiers of ruffles.

"They are lovely," she soothed her aunt's ruffled feathers. "But the Belgian lace is so exquisite, I can't imagine drawing attention away from it." *Not to mention the flounces and crystal beading...*

"Well, there's truth in that." The older woman snatched her fingers away from the bows as though they'd attempted to scald her. "It might look overdone."

"There's a possibility of that." Ruthlessly strangling the smile that threatened at her aunt's comment, Marge moved to take the ribbons away. Far, far away.

"Wait!" Daisy surveyed the ribbons then cast a speculative glance at Marge.

Oh no. Closing her eyes couldn't halt the inevitable. She'd learned that when she was six—and they buried Mama and Papa at sea—and kept relearning it every time something came along she desperately wanted to change.

Like Daisy's marriage. Her beautiful, vibrant, loving cousin—the woman who could wed any man in town—had chosen Mr. Dillard. *Trouston* Dillard. The Third. Marge wrinkled her nose. She'd cover every garment she owned in bows if her cousin would choose a man who cared more about Daisy than himself, but she had a sickening suspicion she'd only get the bows.

"Mama, don't you think Margie's dress could do with a few bows? The things she usually wears are so very plain."

"It's foolish for a teacher to dress up, Daisy. My clothes are serviceable, as is appropriate." It was a wonder her cousin didn't mouth the words along with her, the discussion had been so oft repeated.

"Yes, but my wedding will be a good opportunity for you to..." A delicate shrug completed the thought.

"To...?" This wasn't something to let pass by. Daisy never censored herself, so something left unspoken made alarm bells chime.

"Dress up and..." Oh dear, there she went quiet again. This had to be bad.

"And?" Marge didn't miss the furtive glance between mother and daughter.

"And show to advantage, dear." Aunt Verlata lifted one of the bows out of its case and held it up to Marge's bodice. "With Daisy getting married, your time will come soon enough."

"I see." She blinked against a stinging dryness in her eyes. *Now that Daisy's unavailable, the men will have to settle. I have the chance to be someone's second choice.* "In that case, Auntie, by all means, add those bows." *Anything to chase away my cousin's old suitors!*

≈◦∞◦≈

Buttonwood, Nebraska Territory

"It's smoking, son." Grandma Ermintrude's raspy chortle made Gavin Miller pull his hand away from his pocket in a hurry. "You ought to just post it already."

"Next time I'm at the mercantile, I'll pass it on to Reed." He finished his eggs and pushed away from the table. "It's not a pressing matter."

"Men don't bother writing letters if it's not something important, boy. Fact you got an unnatural attachment to this one makes it even more suspicious. Now, drink your coffee before you leave the table." She tapped a gnarled finger on the smoothed wooden surface. "I'm not going to drink it, and no grandson of mine is coward enough to run from breakfast and a few questions."

Gavin raised his mug and scowled into brew bitter enough to strip whitewash. Grandma made her coffee the same way she made her conversation.

And that's a blessing, he reminded himself. If his father's mother weren't such a strong personality, his mother's father wouldn't have sponsored his move west to set up his own mill. Gavin and Grandma Ermintrude got along tolerably well most days, so bringing her along worked out well—most days.

He set down the mug only to have her refill it lickety-split.

"So, who's the gal?"

"What gal?"

"Don't play dumb with me—that's the question I asked you." Her eyes narrowed, the lines spidering around them deepening to webs. "Marguerite."

"Marguerite?" For a fraction of a second, Gavin didn't place the name he'd written on the envelope.

"What'd I tell you about playing dumb? I saw your scrawl on there plain as day—*Marguerite.* No skin off my nose you've swapped sweethearts from that Daisy you used to mention." The things the old woman tucked away in her memory never ceased to amaze him. How many times had he mentioned the woman he'd left back in Baltimore? Twice?

"Marguerite is French for *daisy,*" he explained to forestall any more coffee. "She has her grandmother's name, but no one calls her by it."

"Fancy." She lifted her pinky just so as she took a sip of milk. "And just like youngsters these days to disregard the better choice.

580

Goes by Daisy instead—she must be a plain one, your gal."

"Anything but." Not that he planned to wax poetic about Daisy's fine looks. Grandma would turn right around and accuse him of being blinded by beauty. She did things like that—latched on and poked until she moved things to go her way. Which made as good a reason as any to post the letter today. She'd nettle him about it until he took care of the thing.

"Oh?" When one lifted brow failed to elicit a reaction, the other winged its way upward. "Mouse brown hair, straight as a pin, most likely."

"Black ringlets." *That bob when she walks or tosses her head to laugh.* Her easy laughter had attracted him in the first place.

"Dull, dishwater gray eyes?"

"Green."

A martial glint lit Grandma's eye as she flung more challenges. "Too tall for a woman, I'll wager."

"Petite." The brims of her fanciful hats only reached his shoulder.

"Ungainly shape, lurches when she walks." A smirk brought the closest thing to a smile Gavin typically saw on his grandmother's face as he shook his head. Looked like she was enjoying herself. "Teeth browned and breath foul?"

He couldn't hold back a guffaw at her hopeful tone and the contrast of his memory to the portrait Grandma painted with her words.

"A widow saddled with squalling brats?"

"She's never been wed and is young."

"You're certain about all this?" Her merriment sharpened to a thin edge of a smile at his agreement. "In that case—you have no reason not to send the letter."

Lifting his mug, Gavin took a swig of coffee in admiration of how she sprang her trap shut with the type of precision he prided himself on with his mill. "True."

"Now you're thinking straight." Belying her earlier words, Grandma poured a hefty measure of coffee into the splash of milk covering the bottom of her cup. "After all, besides her saying no, what's the worst that could happen?"

"Daisy, I picked up the post while I was out." Marge tilted her head toward the study as they passed each other on the stairs. "You'll find a few late responses to your wedding invitations on the writing desk, when you find a moment to take a look."

"Thank you, Margie." Daisy gave her cousin a quick hug before continuing down the steps, making a side trip to the dainty escritoire she favored by the study window.

Settling herself on the matching chair, its seat upholstered in her favorite shade of green—to match her eyes, though she would never admit it—she caught sight of a tidy stack of letters. The sight brought a smile to her lips, not only for the basic joy of receiving mail but also for how thoroughly Marge-ish the orderly pile seemed.

Largest letters lay at the bottom, smallest resting atop them, with all the corners squared to make straight lines. Marge supplied a system for everything, created order out of chaos, and made the world make sense down to the tiniest detail. Daisy didn't know quite how her cousin managed these feats, but she long ago accepted it as fact and determined what it meant in life.

Firstly, no matter how hard she tried, Daisy would never be half so capable as her slightly older cousin. Not so clever, not so useful, not so good at making things work the way they should. As her letter opener sliced through the first missive with a satisfying tear, Daisy remembered the time she'd wasted trying to measure up—back when it bothered her that she couldn't seem to be as practical as Marge.

Another acceptance to the wedding. How lovely. I'll have to adjust the reception numbers. . . . She set it aside and reached for the next, allowing her thoughts free rein. Eventually, that whole setup had led to her second realization: So long as Marge made things run smoothly, Daisy didn't need to. Things got done better when Marge did them, and they were both happy enough so long as Daisy did her job—which was, of course, to drag Marge into some sort of social life.

Oh, regrets. . . She set that one off to the other side of the desk and continued going through the letters, putting them into whatever mound seemed appropriate as she thought of all the fun her friends who couldn't attend her wedding would miss out on.

Because, of course, that's what Daisy excelled at. Fun! Always ready to laugh, she loved the social swirl. Her duty, in return for Marge allowing her this carefree sort of life, was to make sure Marge didn't give in entirely to her serious side and experienced some enjoyment of life.

But with Daisy's upcoming marriage, a third realization plagued her. She'd failed her cousin. Daisy would waltz off into a merry marriage with Trouston, whose stolen kisses grew more insistent by the day, and leave Marge behind to a life without laughter or passion. Their whole lives, since Marge's parents didn't survive the crossing to America, Mama had tried to hide the fact Daisy, as her true daughter, was her favorite.

And Daisy had tried to make up for the fact that Mama made a hash of trying to hide something so obvious. She knew her cousin better than anyone alive, and Marge needed a family to call her very own. But if Daisy couldn't find something—and soon—Marge would sink into the role of spinster schoolmarm for the rest of her born days.

With a deep sigh, she sliced open the final letter—addressed ever so formally to "Marguerite." Which must have been why Marge put it in Daisy's pile—wedding responses might be more formal than everyday letters, when most people spoke and wrote to either of them as either Daisy or Marge. It made it less confusing, since they shared their grandmother's name.

Her eyes widened as she read the message. A proposal! From Gavin Miller. . . But Daisy was affianced. And surely Gavin knew. . . . The banns were posted, notices sent. Good heavens, she winged wedding invitations to just about every person she'd ever met. Surely the son of Baltimore's richest miller, who'd been a good friend to both her and Marge, had received one?

She'd kept a list somewhere. . . . A search of all the drawers and cubbies of the escritoire finally yielded the list. Sure enough, Gavin Miller's name appeared. He'd received an invitation to her wedding.

Daisy gasped and jumped to her feet. That meant this letter had to be for—

CHAPTER 2

"Marge!" Her cousin's unladylike bellow brought Marge running full tilt down the stairs at speeds the railroad would be hard pressed to match. "Marge, come quick!"

She almost crashed into her aunt, who rushed toward the hallway coming from the study with a panicked look Marge was sure matched her own. Daisy *never* hollered. Something had to be horribly, dreadfully, unprecedentedly wrong.

Aunt Verlata sailed through the door a scant second before Marge—and only because Marge knew she'd never hear the end of it if she infringed on a mother's right. *No matter that Daisy yelled for* me *at the top of her lungs.* She squashed the thought. It didn't matter once she realized her cousin, far from lying broken or bereaved upon the plush throw rug blanketing most of the study's hardwood floors, was bouncing—yes, *bouncing*—toward them. Daisy was the only woman Marge ever witnessed who could actually bounce as a means of transportation.

"Marge!" Daisy didn't adjust her volume as she launched herself into a smothering hug. "I'm so happy for you!"

Why? Marge winced from the volume, but her hackles raised for an entirely different reason. She'd love to be able to say her Fruit of the Spirit had ripened to such a degree she never begrudged another person any joy. But she and the Holy Spirit knew full well that wasn't the case.

Generally, she'd give just about anything to keep a smile on Daisy's face. But she'd learned the hard way that whenever Daisy felt happy *for* her, trouble loomed. Simply put, the things Daisy felt ought to make Marge happiest bore the uncanny ability to make Marge miserable. Tiers of ruffles and rows of bows on fancy dresses were a minor example.

"Darling, I've never heard you. . ." Obviously Aunt Verlata groped for a term to describe Daisy's earsplitting screeches. "*Yelp*. . .in such a manner. You caused no small amount of alarm. Marge and I both thought you were in some pain."

"Far from it." Daisy unwound from about Marge, her more sedate tone underscored by an odd crinkling that hadn't been noticeable before. "It's just so exciting!"

"What is?" For the first time, Marge noticed Daisy held a letter—now abused and rumpled—tight to her chest. She instantly surmised this to be the instigator of Daisy's outburst.

"He's on the list!" Her cousin thrust another paper, this one clutched in her hand, toward Marge. "Gavin Miller."

"Gavin. . ." Marge's breath caught at the mention of her old friend who'd gone westward. She and Daisy hadn't heard from him since he left—a niggling source of upset she'd refused to acknowledge. After all, she'd pinned no hopes upon the handsome, determined, talented man who'd actually taken the time to speak with her as well as Daisy.

Liar. Her conscience pinged at her attempt at self-deception as she smoothed what she now recognized as part of Daisy's pages-long list of invited wedding attendees.

"Here!" Her cousin's perfectly coiffed curls blocked her view for a moment before a buffed nail tapped the paper just above Gavin's name. "See? He's on the list, Marge!"

"So he is." *Of course he is. I put him there, hoping he'd show up.* Marge blushed as the first hint of excitement welled up. Perhaps Daisy knew of her little infatuation for their friend? "Did he respond? Is he coming for the wedding?"

"No–o–o–o." The drawn-out response doused Marge's new-found anticipation until Daisy thrust the second sheet of paper—the one she'd cradled against her chest—into her hands. "Better! Read this, Marge!"

Marge accepted the note, slipped her spectacles onto her nose from where they hung on a slender silver chain around her neck, and could practically feel the breath of her aunt upon the page as she set to read. On the pretext of wanting more light, she moved toward the window, making certain to turn slightly to provide more privacy.

Smoothing the crinkles, her fingertips brushed over the lines Gavin wrote, the teacher in her noticing the thick strokes of his penmanship, the ink-filled hollows of his vowels, the friendly way his words leaned to the right. She allowed herself a small smile before she scanned the greeting.

Dear Marguerite,

"This isn't for me, Daisy." She whirled back toward her cousin. It says 'Marguerite.' No one calls me that."

"No one calls *me* that either." A truculent expression set her features. "And it *can't* be for me. Keep reading."

She turned back to the window, shoulders rigid, and read once more.

Dear Marguerite,

I know no one calls you by your Christian name, but a man only does this once in a lifetime—I hope—and I want to do it properly. We've been friends for years, and it can come as no surprise I've admired you during that time but wanted to prove myself before coming forward. I think fondly of our conversations about the adventure of making a life out west.

Marge's vision blurred for a moment, her head dizzy with a sudden hope that could never be. She closed her eyes until she felt steady, one palm flat against the warmth of the sunbaked windowpane. The heat calmed her, enabling her to read on.

Now my mill is running well, I make a good living, and I'm in the position to provide well for a wife on my own terms. Would you do me the honor of becoming my bride? If so, my father will see to your travel arrangements to join me in Buttonwood.

Hopefully yours,
Gavin Miller

Marge read it again before resting her forehead against the heat of the window. *It can't be. He must mean Daisy.*

"Marge?" The weight of her aunt's hand descended upon her shoulder, concern evident in her voice. "Are you all right, dear?"

"It's for Daisy." Marge straightened and thrust the letter toward Aunt Verlata. "Not me." She couldn't even look at her cousin, lest her disappointment spill into bitterness.

"No, it isn't." Daisy edged toward her with far more hesitation and tapped her list. "Gavin knows I'm affianced, Marge. He received a wedding invitation."

A pure, sweet note of hope rang in her heart. "Did he respond?"

"Well, no..."

"Bachelors seldom do, unless their mothers do so for them." Aunt Verlata passed back the letter. "Mr. Miller has no mother to do so. And what is this mention of conversing about westward adventures?"

"That was you, Marge." Daisy's subdued reminder, so different from her natural exuberance, gave it more credence.

"We spoke of it, but Daisy was there."

"I nodded, but I was bored. You were the one talking about homesteads and townships and articles you'd read and making history." Daisy wrinkled her nose. "I like *shops*, Marge. They don't have those in the wilderness. Everyone knows that!"

"That is"—Marge paused—"true." *And logical. What has happened that Daisy is being the logical one?* Her mouth went dry as a desert. "You remembered the conversations about westward expansion, and *that's* why you looked up the list, isn't it?" Her cousin never looked anything up. But she'd deemed this important. *Because she knew I wouldn't believe Gavin meant me.*

"Yes." Daisy waved the list. "And it's right here!"

"Thank you." Marge buried her in a hug. *Gavin asked* me *to marry him. He wants* me, *not Daisy.*

"So"—Aunt Verlata slid her arms around them both, making it a group hug as she joined in—"you know what this means, don't you?" If the other two women hadn't been holding her, Marge held a strange certainty she'd float.

"Yes," Marge and Daisy chorused.

I'm getting married! Marge would have shouted her answer aloud, but Daisy beat her to the punch.

"Now we need to buy *two* trousseaus!"

He spotted her doing it again. Midge Collins headed his way, bonnet forgotten as usual, sun bringing out the red tones in her mahogany hair, only to change course as soon as she caught sight of him. This time, she darted behind the smithy.

Amos didn't plan to let her get away with it. Moving around the far side, behind the attached stables, he could cut off her getaway route. Stepping around the corner, that's exactly what he did. With one shoulder rested against the structure and the bulk of him leaning in her way, he made her pull up short in a hurry. And not just because she was a petite little thing.

He got the impression most folks forgot what an undersized woman she really made, because the rest of her came out so big. Some folks had that way—a smile, a sharp wit, a way of holding themselves that made them ten times their natural sizes. They learned it out of necessity, though—and that was just one more mystery to add to the pile that made up Midge.

"Miss Collins." He tipped his hat.

"Mr. Geer." Her nostrils flared at being thwarted, making some of those freckles dance. Cute. "If you'll excuse me, I—"

"Nope." He crossed one booted foot over the other and got comfortable. Time to enjoy himself.

"What?" Her brows came together in obvious frustration, not going upward in astonishment as she begged his pardon, like most ladies would do. He liked that.

"I said, 'Nope.' I'm not of a mind to excuse you, Miss Collins." Amos unleashed his grin. "See, we need to have a discussion on why you've been avoiding me."

"Who says I've been avoiding you?"

"No one says it. And no one else has noticed. But I have, and

I want to know why."

She looked at him for a long moment, as though measuring him. "You know, if you keep asking questions, you might run across an answer you don't like."

"Try me."

"All right, how's this?" She leaned closer, close enough for him to catch some sort of light, flowery scent. "You want to know why I avoid you?"

He took his shoulder off the wall and leaned closer to hear her lowered tones. "Yep."

"Well, Mr. Geer. . ." Quick as a deer, she slipped between him and the wall and scampered off, calling out her answer, "You can't always get what you want."

Amos chuckled as he watched the edge of her skirts swish around the building. *We'll just have to see about that.*

CHAPTER 3

"Y our pacing won't make the stage get here any sooner." Grandma Ermintrude's amusement came through loud and clear.

"It'll come this afternoon," Gavin conceded. "And Daisy will be on it. . . ." He walked faster.

"So you want to wear a hole in the floor to welcome her?"

"You want to change your mind about coming to the café for dinner and waiting on the stage?"

"To sit and twiddle my thumbs until her highness arrives and I can *ooh* and *aah* like a yokel?" No one could snort like Grandma. "If I don't like her, do you plan on sending her packing?"

"Daisy's easy to like." He pushed aside a pinch of misgiving. Grandma wasn't so easy to get along with, but Daisy charmed everyone. People got along like millstones—too much distance didn't do any good. Too close, and everything jammed. In time, they'd find the right balance.

"Just the same, I'll wait until you bring her here. No sense making the private into a public matter. You two are wise to spend some time before having the ceremony." She jerked her head toward the mill. "Did you set up your bunk?"

"All set." Gavin had decided not to whisk Daisy to the altar immediately upon her arrival in Buttonwood, thinking it best for her to get some rest and settle into town life first. With Grandma to make it proper, he'd bed down in the mill for a few nights until Daisy knew for sure she'd be willing to make a life in the Nebraska Territory. "If you're staying, I'm heading on to town."

Daisy grew up sheltered, surrounded by fine things. Her romantic outlook of the West might not last long enough for her to make a go of it. Lovely and lively though she may be, Gavin didn't intend to chain her to him and a way of living she'd resent. Best to think things through and not collect regrets.

The wagon ride to town did nothing to clear his thoughts or siphon away his energy. Easy enough to figure out why. . .if he were man enough to admit it. This restlessness didn't come purely from excitement. No, an underlying nervousness picked at him. Questions about whether Daisy would be happy to see him, if she'd like the town, if the house he'd built near his mill were good enough—they swirled together in his brain to form a mass of unknowns.

Lord, I prayed to You before coming out here, and You gave me peace. I prayed before writing the letter, and You gave me peace. I prayed before sending the letter, and that very morning Ermintrude gave me the kick in the pants to move things along. So, no matter what happens when she steps off that stage, please help give me the peace to know it is Your will.

"Mr. Miller!" The warm greeting of Mrs. Grogan stopped him in front of the mercantile. With a toddler on one hip and another child obviously on the way, Opal Grogan seemed a woman who'd taken well to motherhood. "Good to see you."

"Miller." Her husband, Adam, gave a friendly nod. Adam was one of the most prosperous farmers in the area, the Grogans having been in Buttonwood since the town began in one of the rare fertile pockets alongside the Platte.

"Today's the big day." Another feminine voice had Gavin angling so he didn't block Mrs. Reed, who'd come up behind him. "Stage ought to be in soon."

"That's right." Midge Collins joined them, shaking her head. "So let's hope the rest of the town is a tad more subtle about their intent to watch for a glimpse of Mr. Miller's bride-to-be."

"We like to be welcoming," someone—Gavin couldn't tell who—protested. "Good to be friendly and introduce ourselves."

"Well, Grandma Ermintrude wasn't feeling up to making the trip to town, and I'm sure after a long stage ride, my bride-to-be, as you put it, will be worn out." Gavin silently blessed Grandma for her wisdom in avoiding a spectacle. "So the introductions will have to wait a little while."

"Sounds like a glimpse is all you'll get." Miss Collins sounded amused, but Gavin didn't mind. She'd been helpful, pointing out something he was now determined to avoid.

"Everyone knows the wedding isn't today." Adam Grogan made a show of male support. "And he's right to take her to get to know his grandmother before making the town rounds."

"Glad you understand." Gavin decided on the spot to charge Adam only half rate for the next load the farmer brought to his mill. You couldn't put a price on easing a man's way, but you could show gratitude. "When the time is right, you'll all be glad to have her as part of the town."

"There's bound to be curiosity about her." Mrs. Reed's pale green eyes danced with it even as she spoke. "But it's not bad. We don't let any of the gossips grumble about her staying with your grandmother until you wed. It's known you've made arrangements to sleep elsewhere."

"Miss Chandler won't be looked down on," Mrs. Grogan chimed in, and for the first time, Gavin realized he was catching a peek into the power structure of the women of the town. How things ran. It seemed Opal Grogan, Clara Reed, and even young Midge Collins carried considerable weight.

It made sense, considering their connections. Mrs. Grogan linked two previously feuding farms—Specks and Grogans, the two most powerful properties in town. Mrs. Reed and Miss Collins were related to the town doctor and owner of the only mercantile. Not to mention they were all young and friendly.

Daisy would do well to make friends of them. She'd feel more at home with companions her age, and they'd ease her way.

"Thank you. She has a real heart for others, and it will do her good to know she already has friends in Buttonwood." That did the trick. The married women beamed at him, and Miss Collins quirked a brow in acknowledgement. Gavin felt his first smile of the day tug on the corners of his mouth.

"If you'd like, we could make up a small dinner party," Mrs. Reed offered. "Myself, Saul, Midge, Opal and Adam, and, of course, Josiah and Doreen." She listed everyone present, plus the owner of the mercantile and his wife. "Something private to ease her into things before church on Sunday perhaps?"

"That's a wonderful idea!" Mrs. Grogan chimed in. "Or even afterward, to get to know her better. Whenever she's comfortable."

"We'd like that." Gavin barely got the acceptance out before he spotted what looked like a brown cloud on the horizon. The stage was coming—an hour early.

Now, Midge wasn't a great believer in the loving-kindness of the Almighty, but she didn't question His existence. And she'd hatched a few theories of her own over the years.

One of them was that every single person got a gift at birth. Not the myrrh or frankincense or gold mentioned in the Bible for baby Jesus—although gold *would* have been nice, mind—but a different sort of gift. A talent, perhaps. Whatever gifts people received got pointed to the sort of things they'd think were important.

Midge even extended her theory to the realm of matchmaking. People's talents had to match up—not be the same, but they had to mesh right or a couple wouldn't work out. Adam and Opal— both peacemakers, but neither of them weak enough to be walked over. That worked. Clara loved on people once they got close. She matched up with Saul, the healer who provided a different sort of care. Doreen, who could say the right thing, went well with Josiah, who had the uncanny way of knowing what someone needed at what time.

As for her, Midge's flair was for observation. She watched, she listened, she *noticed*. In short, she spotted things people didn't want others to guess at. She read expressions, registered changes in stances or gestures, wondered about things that were none of her business because she learned long ago that a girl never knew when something might *become* her business.

It pays off to pay attention.

And right now, from her vantage point a few paces away—out of sight of Mr. Amos Geer—Midge couldn't help but frown. Mr. Miller seemed like he was holding back his excitement before, but now that the stage arrived—the top loaded down with more luggage than she could've dreamed up even with her considerable imagination—his posture tattled of surprise.

He'd reached up to help down a woman, smiled in a friendly but not loving way at her, and asked something to make her shake her head slightly. Why was he glancing back in the coach? And there. . .the stiffening of his shoulders as he signaled for the luggage to be brought down.

Mr. Miller didn't look excited anymore. His smile stretched tight instead of wide, his movements went jerky, like a body's does when doing something under protest.

Midge looked at the new lady, Miss Chandler, who seemed vaguely uncertain and massively overdressed. *No. . .something is wrong here.*

She watched Mr. Miller take Miss Chandler's elbow—touching her as little as possible as he helped her into his wagon. *Very wrong, indeed.*

All too aware of the town's scrutiny as the stage pulled up, Gavin took a deep breath. It didn't matter what anyone else thought although Daisy's charm and looks would win over the stodgiest grump in no time flat. But it did matter if she felt uncomfortable the moment she stepped foot in town.

The stage stopped a few feet in front of him, making him walk to meet them. He pulled down the folding steps as the dust settled then straightened up to open the curved door. A mass of lavender skirts floofed into view before one dainty hand, clad in soft tan leather, reached toward him.

Daisy. He enfolded her tiny hand in his, stepping back as one small foot extended toward the steps, offering a glimpse of polished black boots whose endless buttons encased tantalizingly trim ankles. She descended, gaze lowered to watch her step, her hat blocking her face until they moved a short distance from the coach. It was only when she raised her head to smile at him Gavin recognized the woman before him.

"Marge?" He clasped her hand in both of his for a moment. Unexpected it might be, but it was a pleasure to see his old friend. Daisy should have told him she'd brought her cousin for companionship on the journey. "So good to see you!"

"Wonderful to see you as well"—a faint blush colored her cheeks before she added—"Gavin." Her use of his given name sent an odd, though not unpleasant, clench to his midsection, but he brushed it off. They were soon to be family, after all.

He peered past her. "Where is Daisy?"

"She couldn't accompany me, I'm afraid." Marge lifted her chin. "With her wedding date so near, she couldn't leave, and Aunt Verlata and I determined it wouldn't be overly improper for an affianced woman to travel alone." A teasing smile tilted her lips. "Daisy told me to be sure and mention how put out she is that you didn't RSVP to her invitation."

"The invitation. . ." The echo came out choked as the stagecoach driver began tossing down Marge's luggage. *Daisy is to be married. . .but why is Marge here? Marge. . .* All at once, the missing memory slammed into place with the finality of a nail in a coffin. Marge. . .named for her grandmother, just like Daisy.

I got the wrong Marguerite!

CHAPTER 4

Marge perched atop the wagon seat, right hand curled around the rough board to help keep her balance as they rolled toward Gavin's mill. After days on end in the stagecoach, jouncing along rutted dirt prairie roads was nothing new. Her backside could attest to that. No matter. The journey paled in comparison to what she found at its end.

Gavin.... She snuck a sideways peek at his profile, gaze traveling from the sweep of his sable hair to the firm set of his jaw. Back home, the family encouraged friends and close acquaintances to call her Marge, and Daisy by her favored nickname. Having two "Miss Chandlers" created far too much confusion. So Gavin had been using her given name for quite some time, but today marked her first use of his. He'd seemed surprised, though not displeased—a reaction that reassured her of her new place in his life.

He hadn't said much, but Marge found that reassuring as well. What words Gavin did give were enough. *"So good to see you!"* Simple, warm, and welcoming—genuine. Her fiancé remained the man of her memories, which meant they'd have a good marriage. Solid. Comfortable.

Marge peeped through her lashes at him once more, drinking in the way hard work beneath the sun had bronzed his skin since last she saw him. His lips formed an almost-straight line, swallowing the slight fullness she remembered. It looked as though he was thinking. . . .

As though sensing her perusal, he turned his head. His dark brown gaze searched her face as if seeking answers to some unspoken question.

The sudden intensity of it warmed her cheeks in what she knew to be a blush. . .although Marge wasn't in the habit of blushing. Blushing, she'd always maintained, was for two types of girls: silly wigeons who didn't realize that it was whomever spouted the drivel who should be embarrassed, or those naturally charming women like Daisy whose blushes meant she was enjoying herself. Marge didn't fit either category.

Which meant Gavin's scrutiny had turned her into a temporary wigeon.

She silently blamed Daisy even as she offered him a smile and he returned his attention to the road. *This behavior is all Daisy's fault! Nattering on and on about how romantic it was that Gavin nursed an affection for me but never spoke up until the time was right, then brings me across the country to be by his side. . .*

All right. Perhaps it wasn't *entirely* Daisy's fault. Marge thought the same things, let the knowledge fill her with delight until it seemed nothing and no one could make her frown. What she could—and would—lay at Daisy's door were the ridiculous fantasies she'd indulged in throughout the long journey. If her cousin hadn't filled her head with ludicrous scenarios of her grand reunion with Gavin, she wouldn't feel self-conscious now.

But truly, she'd known full well there'd be no overblown display of passion. She hadn't expected him to sweep her into his strong arms the moment she stepped off the stage and declare how very much he'd longed for her arrival. Such behavior wouldn't be in keeping with the reliable, steady nature she so valued in her groom-to-be.

Marge Chandler wasn't a woman who expected or even sought a grand passion. Such theatrics wore thin over time and flaked away to reveal the tawdry substance beneath. Like gilding atop plaster—it wouldn't last. No, she looked for something simpler and sturdier, and Gavin Miller provided exactly what she'd always dreamed of.

He chose me.

A gentle breeze pushed away the last lingering bit of warmth from her blush as the mill came into view. It didn't seem to be running, but she hadn't expected it to be, with Gavin not there to attend it. The slightest shift or stress in the workings could set off a reaction to ruin the entire operation, so a mill required constant vigilance.

Much like a classroom.

She smiled at the connection until a small twinge of regret chased it away. Married women weren't permitted to teach, and she'd miss it sorely. But now wasn't the time to think of the students she'd left behind or the injustice of how men could work and support families and women weren't allowed to teach. . . . No, now was the time to begin her new life. As a bride. As a wife.

She stifled a groan of frustration as the blush returned. *Wigeondom awaits.*

Instead of dwelling on the thought, she inspected the structure before them. Three stories high, the stone building reached toward the sky like a beacon, breaking the relentlessly flat stretch of prairie, despite the manufactured hill built behind it for the millpond. The source of the mill's power looked placid but slightly murky—typical for water of the Platte River. A thick millrace connected the pond to the waterwheel standing upright alongside the building, easily reaching the second story.

"It's beautiful—easily as fine as any big-city mill." She craned her neck as they rode by toward a modest, two-story, whitewashed house beyond.

"I like to think so." Pride colored his voice as Gavin hopped down and came around to lift her out of the wagon. Broad hands closed around her waist, sending heat skittering up her spine until he set her on the ground. "After I put Smoose in the barn, I need to start her up. Would you like to see?"

Smoose? Marge eyed the massive draft horse, decided it did rather resemble a moose in horse form, and gave an enthusiastic nod. "I couldn't tell whether the overshot wheel had buckets or paddles."

"Paddles. Buckets don't keep the pace as steady, in my opinion, and paddles are simpler to replace." His appreciative glance made her glad she'd read up on gristmills. A short walk to the small stable and they headed onward to the mill.

The manufactured hillside made easy access into the second story, where the millstones and housing dominated the center of the floor. A wooden grain chute slid from the ceiling to just above the large receptacle above the stones.

"This is the hopper." Gavin pulled a lever and the chute opened, allowing grain to fill the hopper. When he was satisfied with the amount, he closed the chute. "The grain will funnel down through the hole in the top stone and be crushed beneath and come out here." He touched various parts of the machine as he spoke, and Marge could see the loving familiarity even as she knew he was giving an oversimplified explanation.

"The gears are housed on the bottom floor and have to be turned by the wheel—which you noticed earlier. Now that there's grain to be ground, we're ready to get her running." Marge followed Gavin to a door at the far end, which opened to a wooden walkway of sorts above the end of the millrace.

"The sluice gate"—he crouched and gestured to the mechanism as he spoke—"adjusts to different heights, depending on the amount of water speed and pressure needed to turn the wheel at any particular time." He raised the gate, releasing a gush of water that steadily streamed down to hit the flat paddles of the overshot wheel, pushing them downward until the wheel caught the momentum in a constant, smooth turn.

"It seems so simple, but it's not at all. So much thought and time and precision to make it run..." When he smiled at her musings, Marge decided to make a request. "Sometime, after I meet your grandmother, I'd like to see the gears and learn more."

"I'd like that." He took her arm and led her back outside. The pleasure of showing his mill faded from his expression. "Let me tell Grandma Ermintrude you're here then bring you to her." With that, he released her arm and hurried into the house ahead of her.

Blinking at the sudden change and odd behavior, Marge followed at a slower pace. Why wouldn't he simply walk her inside and introduce them when the old woman knew she would arrive today? A jumble of voices, a sound of exasperation—surely that came from Gavin—began to raise doubts.

"*Marge.*" She heard him stress her name but didn't catch the lady's reply. Unwilling to eavesdrop, she halted a few feet away and tried to calm the tumult suddenly arising in her stomach. Something didn't feel right....

Somehow, Gavin had to figure out what he was going to do before the gnawing numbness wore off. Shock, folks called it. Sure, it'd seen him through a cursory round of introductions in town, loading up the wagon, and the ride home. He'd even managed to put it all aside for a few moments because she seemed so interested in the mill. But now he had to take her to the house.

And Grandma Ermintrude.

Shock couldn't save him there. Everyone else only knew his bride-to-be's name as Marguerite Chandler, as was proper. Grandma, on the other hand, would immediately try to gain the upper hand by calling her Daisy. *And then the secret would be out—that I sent away for a bride and got her cousin by mistake.* My *mistake.* He winced.

The farce unfolded without him knowing until it was too late to prevent disaster. He forgot Daisy and Marge were *both* Marguerites when he wrote the proposal. They received it, knew he'd been sent an invitation to Daisy's wedding, and logically assumed he'd been sending for Marge. So here he sat, driving the wrong bride back to his home—and she had no idea about any of it. This was the sort of situation that could drive anyone to abandon civilization and make like a mountain man.

But he couldn't do that. He had Grandma—and now Marge—to think of. *No Daisy.* That hit him hard. If she'd refused the proposal, he could've taken it. But thinking she'd consented to be his bride and he'd have the wife he wanted for the rest of his days, only to be disillusioned later?

Lord, I prayed over this and trusted in Your will. . .and You sent me Marge? Now I know how Jacob felt when he got Leah instead of Rachel. A dry swallow didn't make the knowledge go down any easier. *Except Jacob still got Rachel after a few years, and I'll never have a chance with Daisy. The only way I can figure is to marry Marge and never let her know of the mix-up. I sure as shooting can't tell her she's the wrong one. . . . Besides, I sent for Marguerite Chandler as my bride, she arrived, and I need to follow through on that commitment.*

It didn't make doing the right thing any easier though.

With a mishmash of half-formed thoughts clashing in his mind, he told Marge something about telling Grandma she was here and rushed off. It didn't come across as gentlemanly, but when a man had no options, he couldn't be choosy.

"Grandma." He burst through the door and plowed into the parlor. "Marguerite is here."

"I would hope so. Not at all good manners to leave your bride in town." She raised her head slightly, in the manner of a fox trying to catch the scent of new prey. "Don't leave her outside. Bring her to me."

"In a moment." His mind raced madly. Telling Grandma Ermintrude about the mix-up would be the fast way to ensure Marge got beat over the head with it. Gavin wouldn't allow that. So, the only thing left was to say, "I made a mistake." *Did I ever.* "She goes by Marge now. Don't call her Daisy."

"Not Daisy?"

"Marge." He waited for her nod before dashing back out the door to fetch his bride.

And face his future.

CHAPTER 5

"She's ready." Gavin emerged from the house with a smile stretching his face—but that's exactly how it looked. Like a painful stretch.

Marge's stomach clenched still more tightly. *Just how difficult could one old woman be?* She straightened her shoulders. *No more difficult than a room full of students. God brought me here. He'll see me through whatever lies ahead.* She accepted Gavin's hand and returned his strained smile as they walked inside her new home.

Grandma Ermintrude waited in the parlor, posture ramrod straight, back not conceding to so much as touch the back of the settee. Steel gray hair trapped in a bun topped a face etched with a hardness to rival that of any metal. Eyes narrowed, lips thinned, hands folded and clenching the top of a cane—Grandma Ermintrude could easily have descended from a Gorgon.

So Marge did what every brave woman did in the face of imminent threat—resorted to pleasantries. "Lovely to meet you, Mrs. Miller."

The woman didn't respond at first beyond a further narrowing of the eyes and what Marge could only deem an indulgent harrumphing. And quite a harrumphing it was. Ermintrude Miller made it not only a sound, but a physical expression of disdain, as her shoulders raised and her chest puffed in indignation before finding relief in that not-so-genteel snort.

"We'll see about that." One wizened hand lifted from atop her cane in an imperious motion. "Come over here so I can get a good look at you."

Gavin seemed reluctant to release her, a sign Marge couldn't read as positive or dreadful, but she moved to stand before her would-be grandmother-in-law.

"Take off that hat. My eyes aren't what they used to be."

Somehow, Marge had a feeling that the woman before her remained as sharp as ever, but kept her tongue between her teeth. She untied her hat and slid it from her hair, resisting the urge to smooth back any wisps that might have escaped. Preening would be a mistake—and a useless one, at that.

Another harrumph. "You're not what I expected, girl." The inspection shifted from her hair, to her eyes, then swept down to the tips of her toes. "Taller, for one thing."

"To be fair, you aren't what I expected either." Marge imbued her shrug with a nonchalance she was far from feeling. "Although you didn't ask, my journey went well and I'm pleased to be here. I trust your day has been pleasant so far."

"Well, she has a mind." A cackle accompanied the comment directed at Gavin. "That's better than I hoped, although she's not as pretty as I pictured."

Marge sucked in a breath at that but held on. "Pretty is as pretty does, they say. I always say you can judge a person based on his or her decisions."

"Interesting." Two eyes sharpened upon her like knifepoints.

"And you've made quite a few decisions recently."

"Yes." She smiled at Gavin, although his face could have been etched from the same stone he'd used to build his mill. "And I stand by them."

"So tell me, Miss Chandler. . .when did you decide to stop going by Daisy?"

"Grandma, don't—" A sort of fear flashed across her fiancé's face at the evidence of his grandmother's lapse. Men never dealt well with seeing weakness in their loved ones. Marge had seen it before.

"It's all right." Marge put a hand on Gavin's forearm when he moved forward. "It's easy enough to get confused, and Grandma Miller never met both of us, after all."

"No." Gavin shook off her hand and looked severely at the older woman. "She needs to remember herself."

"I haven't forgotten." A smile multiplied the grooves bracketing her mouth as she ignored her grandson. "*Both* of you, you say?"

"Yes, ma'am." Marge struggled to reconcile Gavin's harshness with her image of him, choosing instead to focus on Ermintrude's turnaround. "Daisy is my cousin, you see."

"Is she, now? Marge—short for Marguerite, yes?" A raspy laugh greeted her nod of acknowledgement. "Would this cousin of yours happen to be. . .oh, at a guess. . .a petite, green-eyed charmer with black ringlets?"

"Does it matter?" The angry burst from Gavin sent the fine hairs on the back of Marge's neck prickling.

"I'm not sure." Suddenly, it felt as though Marge were watching herself speak from over in the corner. "Why did you ask me where Daisy was after I got off the stage? I assumed you thought she'd accompany me, but that's not the reason, is it?"

The look on his face provided all the answer she needed. Shame, disappointment, anger—they chased one another across his features until they burrowed their way into her heart.

"I did say she had a mind." Ermintrude's voice bore into the descending blackness. "I'll bet Marge here is a better choice than that Daisy you wanted in the first place."

∾∾∾

"Marge!" Gavin slid one arm around her surprisingly slim waist and cupped her too-pale cheek with his free hand. At Grandma's words, she'd closed her eyes and swayed slightly.

"Ooh." A small moan, almost a whimper, broke through her lips—lips that bore the only color in her face aside from the dark fans of her lashes.

"Don't faint." He put the words to the panic gripping his chest. What would he do with a fainting female?

Her eyes flew open, two small palms pressed to his chest, and she pushed him away with a strength belying her sudden pallor. "I am not," she seethed, "the type of ninny who faints."

"Bravo!" Grandma Ermintrude thumped her cane in a show of approval. "I've seen enough ninnies to last a lifetime."

"Well, the world has seen enough liars." Hazel eyes suspiciously bright, Marge made as though to push past him and out the door.

"Where are you going?" He caught her elbow to bring her up short. It wasn't as though she could just flounce out of his sight and march back home.

"I need some time." She jerked her arm away. "To think."

"That's the one problem with those gals who have minds. They think on things." Grandma's delighted commentary made a muscle in Gavin's jaw twitch.

If the old bat had kept her mouth shut, I wouldn't have this problem.

609

"There's nothing to think about. We'll get married as soon as you're ready."

"Ready?" Her eyes grew even brighter as a strange, flat laugh hitched from deep inside her. "You'll have a long wait for that."

"You changed your mind?" The hot sting of wounded pride whipped around his throat, making the words tight.

"You change yours?" She tossed the challenge over her shoulder as she sailed out the front door.

"No." He stalked after her, anger fueling his steps so that he caught up to her just outside the mill. "I set out to marry Marguerite Chandler, and that's what I intend to do." He snagged her wrist this time, and the force of her halted momentum made her turn to face him.

"You set out to marry *Daisy* Chandler." Those long eyelashes of hers had gotten darker—and belatedly Gavin registered they were damp. Her eyes went so shiny because she held back *tears*.

The breath left him as fast and painful as if he'd been kicked in the gut. *I made her cry.*

Hurt angled her brows as she whispered her question. "And you weren't even going to tell me about the mistake?"

"Marge. . ." He wanted to say something to make it better but couldn't. "I didn't want you to know."

"You would have made me live a lie!" Fury blazed away the tears—a welcome change from where Gavin stood. Anger, he could deal with.

"I—" The loud groan of stressed oak poured through the mill windows, warning of calamity. "Stay here. I'll be right back." He sprinted to close the sluice gate, reaching it just as a great, splintering *crack* rent the air.

The water flow trickled to a stop, the wheel halted its turning, and all sounds of the running mill ceased. Somewhere down below, on the ground floor, he'd find a broken runner on a gear wheel. But now wasn't the time to inspect it. He had a bride to take care of.

Hustling back, he turned the corner to where he'd left Marge… and found no one.

His bride had vanished.

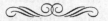

Amos Geer had been staring at her again. Midge shivered and picked up the pace, heading for the spot that never failed to calm her down.

When Gavin Miller and his new woman drove off, she'd stopped concentrating on figuring out what seemed a bit askew between those two and had looked down to gather her thoughts. Then she looked up to find a pair of blue eyes, so dark they seemed stormy, peering directly at her from behind a shaggy lock of corn-colored hair in desperate need of a trim.

Looked like she'd found a fellow watcher.

Not good.

Even worse, it looked like he'd found her…first.

Midge let loose a huff as she pressed onward. Living in Buttonwood for the past four years must've made her turn soft. She'd have to work on that with another watcher around. The last thing she needed was someone paying close attention to the life she'd built in this small—although much larger than when she'd arrived—town.

She remembered the week before, when Amos blocked her escape behind the smithy. Yes, she'd been avoiding him since he first showed up in her town. It'd taken no more than a minute to sum up that the man was too confident, too perceptive, and too curious to be anything but trouble. But when he confirmed that he watched her as closely as she watched everyone else, she'd sealed her verdict regarding the tall newcomer.

Dangerous. He'd turned that considerable curiosity on the mystery of Midge Collins—and she'd spent years guarding those secrets. Nothing could persuade her to leave it to chance that Amos would not remember their encounter from four years before.

The more distance she put between them, the better she felt. Just as she went around the millpond, the point where she breathed easier knowing the apiary lay not too far ahead, something snagged her.

The sound of boots thudding against earth, still audible despite the muffling layer of thick prairie grass, gained urgency as someone came up fast from the left. Midge whirled around, instinctively crouching in a defensive stance, making her vitals less accessible to any attacker.

A flash of violet through the scrawny scrub oaks caught her attention just before Mr. Miller's bride-to-be came tearing full tilt around the millpond. Skirts streaming behind her, chignon bobbing precariously without the covering of any hat, Miss Chandler presented a picture of panic.

"Marge!" A deep yell from around the other side of the mill provided all Midge needed to know. Somehow, Mr. Miller scared this woman—and men who frightened women didn't deserve them.

Women on the run from such men, however, unquestionably deserved her help. Midge burst into a sprint, helping close the short distance between them, and grabbed Marge's hand. The other woman raised glistening eyes to meet her gaze but only faltered for a moment when Midge matched her stride.

They dashed past the scrub oak, past the border of Miller's land, and didn't stop running until Midge found the familiar grove of black walnut trees bordering Opal's apiary on Grogan grounds. Marge matched her pace—an impressive feat, and something more to respect in a woman who had enough sense to find the road when a man found his temper.

Neither of them spoke for a few moments, both too preoccupied with drinking in great gulps of fresh air laced with the faintest hint of honey. As their breathing calmed, the merry *buzz* of hundreds of worker bees busily zooming in and out of the dozens of wooden movable-frame hives in the meadow before them became discernable.

At least Midge could make it out in between the hitched, sniffle-laden, quickly-stifled breaths of her companion. Miss Chandler dabbed at her eyes and nose with a pressed linen handkerchief, tucking it into a pocket in her skirts before looking up. The mop-up job hadn't done much to hide the fact she'd gone on a crying jag. Red nose and watery eyes tattled on both her upset and her inability to play a good damsel in distress. That made her more likeable in Midge's book.

"You don't have to go back," she piped up once the other woman seemed ready to hear her out. "We'll get you taken care of. Now, what did he do?"

"It's a mistake." Miss Chandler's lips moved almost too slowly for the words she spoke. "A terrible mistake."

"Don't you worry." Midge reached over to give her a soothing pat on the back. "We'll make sure you get home again, safe and sound. No woman need put up with a man who done her wrong." She heard her molars grind in the silence as she waited for her new project to confide in her.

But this woman managed a rare feat—she kept her lips buttoned and her thoughts sewn up. She simply looked to the right, off to the distance, as though trying to make a plan, and periodically shook her head as though to clear it.

"Did he hit you?" Midge couldn't see any marks.

"No! Gavin would never do such a thing. How could you say that?" In an instant, the sorrow and uncertainty gave way to bristling indignation. "He's a good man."

"If you're so fond of him, I don't know why you were dead set on running away from him. I suppose that's your business, but seeing as how I thought he'd done you wrong and tried to lend a hand"—Midge worked what scant angles she could—"maybe you could see your way clear to explaining why you don't want to marry the man?"

"If only it were that easy." The tears came back. "I'd rather no one saw me like that, but I needed some time to think on my own."

Obviously this would take some additional needling to get any useful information. Midge used another tactic. "Understood. I'll just wait here while you finish thinking about the reasons you don't want to marry such a fine man."

"Simple. He doesn't want to marry *me*."

CHAPTER 6

If she had her "I'd rathers," or *druthers*, as Aunt Verlata termed them, Marge wouldn't be confiding in this piquant girl who'd whisked her away from the mill. Proclaiming aloud that Gavin didn't want her did nothing to ease the heart-hollowing impact of its truth and only served to broadcast her shame.

Contrary to what she'd told Gavin's grandmother, she'd done an excellent ninny impression when she hied off like that. Fainting ninnies, at least, held no control over their unfortunate reactions. Unless, of course, they were that vile breed of fake-fainting ninny, whose real classification became far less pleasant.

Marge would have said she didn't believe in fleeing one's troubles but rather standing one's ground and confronting them head-on. Putting off an issue didn't make it go away, after all. Yet when things became unbearable and granted her a moment to make a bid for freedom, she ran.

She ran away from going back in the house to face Awful Ermintrude. She ran from seeing the man she'd rejoiced to marry tell her he didn't want her but would take her on as an obligation.

Most of all, she'd run until her heart had no room to feel anything other than the threat of bursting through her corset in overexertion.

What she hadn't expected was running into the woman before her. A woman who'd seen her, upset and fleeing, and not wasted time asking questions but rather taken her hand and led her to what must be a safe place. A woman who now thought the worst of Gavin. . .because of Marge.

"Not to be combative," the younger—she looked younger, at least—girl began, signaling an oncoming disagreement.

"Wait." Marge held up one hand, palm outward. "Whenever someone says they don't intend to be combative, or argumentative, or disagreeable, or any such thing, it is a sure sign they are about to be. So I will restate that the cause of my distress lies in a mistake and nothing more, in the hopes you will not question my word when I say that Gavin does not want to marry me."

"Ah." The other woman, who Marge suddenly noticed wasn't wearing a bonnet or hat any more than she was, seemed to be fighting a silent battle. Her lips twitched. "Easy to see you don't know me. I'm Midge Collins."

"Marge Chandler." She barely caught herself before adding how lovely it was to meet her—entirely inappropriate in this situation.

"I know." Miss Collins lost the battle and a wide smile won out. "I also know that Mr. Miller wrote, sent for, and brought you here to be his wife. So I doubt you have any cause to worry about him wanting to marry you."

"You think me a lackwit, and I can't say I blame you. What bride, newly reunited with her groom-to-be, runs from him as though chased by the hounds of hell?" Marge pinched the bridge of her nose, hoping to ease some of the tension throbbing behind it. "But a terrible mistake has been made, and I am not the bride Mr. Miller hoped for."

"Hogwash. You're Marguerite—Marge, if you prefer—Chandler. The woman he's told everyone he's going to marry. The woman he picked up at the stage and brought home to his grandmother. There is no mistaking that." All merriment faded from her features. "If he's threatened or harmed you, don't try to protect him. It will only get worse."

"You almost have it right, Miss Collins." Marge could see there was no recourse but to tell this woman of the mix-up. Otherwise, Gavin's reputation would be forfeit. "I am Marguerite Chandler, who goes by Marge. Gavin Miller did set out to marry Marguerite Chandler. The problem, you see, is that he wanted my cousin. We're both named after our grandmother, but she goes by Daisy."

"You're putting me on." Suspicion slid into the set of the other girl's jaw. "Two Marguerite Chandlers, and you're the wrong one?"

"Precisely." Despite her best efforts, the hot salt of tears pricked her eyes, and her breath hitched once more. Marge fumbled for her handkerchief, barely registering as her newfound confidant flomped onto the shady bit of grass before them.

"Well, that's about as crooked as a snake in a cactus patch. Oh, and it's Midge. Any woman who can keep up when I'm racing down the plains earns that right."

"Thank you, Midge." The unspoken offer of friendship eased some degree of the isolation that washed over her in encroaching waves. "Please call me Marge."

"Do you know," her companion offered, drumming her fingers against one knee as she thought aloud, "I never did like daisies. They look nice, but I can't say I care for the smell."

The random nature of the comment did the trick, forcing a chuckle despite the circumstances. "Marguerite is French for *daisy,* and my cousin always smells very nice."

"I'm sure she does, but this situation you're in puts off an awful stench—and Ermintrude Miller isn't going to make things any sweeter." Her friend stopped drumming her fingers. "You can stay with my family until you go home, if you like."

"Go home. . ." Her knees suddenly shaky, Marge decided to sit before the ground rose up to meet her.

Oh, Lord. . .give me strength. If I go home, everyone will know. Half of Baltimore knows of my engagement to Gavin, and none of them will be surprised to learn he wanted Daisy instead. I'll be a laughing-stock. Daisy will be wracked with guilt. Aunt Verlata will pity me and trot me in front of prospective suitors until my eyes cross. . . .

"No." The horror of such a future flashed before her with such agonizing clarity, Marge's stomach lurched. "I can't go back."

~⚬⚬~

"That gums up the works." Midge chewed on her inner lip. It was clear as fine crystal that it would do no good to ask why her new friend didn't want to go home.

Because that's the way reality stood. Marge blanched when she thought it over, but the fact she thought it over at all meant returning to Baltimore—if memory served, and memory always served Midge—remained a possibility. An unattractive possibility, judging by how pale the other woman had gone, but that could be due to any number of things. Like pride. Best tread lightly on that one.

"If it were me, I wouldn't be in a hurry to let everyone know either. How much time do you reckon you have? Can you stay until Daisy arrives?"

"Daisy won't marry Gavin. She's to be wed this very month's end—Gavin's father didn't take that into account when he purchased my stage tickets and couldn't transfer them." A gasp of mirthless laughter escaped Marge. "Otherwise I would have waited a little longer before coming here. As it stands, I'll miss my cousin's wedding and have none of my own."

"Little wonder you two thought he proposed to the Marguerite without a fiancé." The words came out with a wince hard on their heels. *Could've been more sensitive there.*

"We'd even sent him an invitation to Daisy's wedding." The beleaguered bride-to-be busied herself trying to find a dry spot on her handkerchief. "I feel such a fool!"

"You are not." Midge rummaged around in her own pockets until she found a rumpled but serviceable linen square and passed it over. "Proposing via letter to Marguerite without clarifying which one seems a numskull thing to do though. Since we're assuming he thought you were both unattached."

"A mere oversight. . ." The rest of the mumble went to the handkerchief.

"A whopping great oversight, if you ask me. More to the point, when he realized what happened, he shouldn't have told you."

For this, at the root, is what had her hackles in a rage. No matter Gavin Miller got the wrong woman, his trap should have stayed shut. He sent for a Marguerite, he received a Marguerite, and he had no business making her feel unwanted. Real men followed through on their commitments. Just look how much he'd hurt poor Marge.

"He didn't tell me." A delicate blow punctuated the confession. "Grandma Miller asked why I didn't go by Daisy anymore, and I figured it out."

"Then he plans to marry you anyway?" *Well, a point to the miller then. At least he had the right idea, even if he didn't carry it out well.*

"That's what he says." A slightly less delicate blow.

"I take it you're less than thrilled."

"You could say that." A downright honk.

"Bully for you. Women aren't interchangeable, and I wouldn't give him the satisfaction of my hand when he didn't bother asking for it properly in the first place either." Midge leaned back. "He's going to have to court you now."

Marge's hiccup of laughter didn't bode well. "Gavin doesn't want to marry *me*, and he won't. At best, he doesn't want word to get out that he's stuck with the wrong bride." She groaned. "Folks around here will find out soon enough. Is there an inn nearby? I need a place to stay until I can sort out a plan."

"No inn, but you're more than welcome at the Reed house—which is my family. I'm adopted, in case you're wondering." Midge hopped to her feet and dusted off her backside. "What sort of plan do you think you'll come up with, a single woman on her own?"

"Surely I can find work as a teacher out west. I have experience and letters of reference." Her new friend followed suit in brushing dust from her skirts. "Never thought I'd need those letters, but I always feel it's best to be prepared. It pays off."

"You're a teacher?" Midge barely held back a whoop. The town council had been looking for someone to take on the local children as soon as they finished building the schoolhouse, and one too many of them had broached the subject with her lately. If they didn't scrape together enough sense to see she'd make a poor schoolmarm, she'd have to find another solution. "Looks like you're an answer to prayer, Marge. Buttonwood needs a teacher."

"That would be. . .ideal." Hazel eyes blinked in disbelief. "Do you think the town council would consider a woman for the position, or are they solely looking for a schoolmaster?"

"No need to worry about that." Midge started trekking back toward the mill. "My adopted father and grandpa are on the council.

So is the husband of a close friend. None of them would look down on a woman, and all of them would support you on my say-so—especially once Clara and Opal weigh in."

"I met them briefly before Gavin and I left town."

"Yes, you would have. They like to meet everyone new. Clara would be the green-eyed blond, Opal the blue-eyed redhead. Clara is married to Dr. Reed, the man who took me in."

She hurried, pleased when Marge increased her speed to match. Midge did so as much to gloss over the topic of her informal adoption as to get to the mill faster. Much as she liked to ask questions, answering them didn't sit well.

As they rounded the millpond, Marge's steps slowed. "Gavin should be relieved to be well rid of me." A forced smile accompanied wistful words.

Midge shook her head. "If I'm any judge of men and their mettle—and of this there is no doubt, although you don't know it yet—Gavin will not let you leave him so easily."

"He cannot stop me from teaching."

"I did not say he could or would." She caught sight of her friend's fake fiancé as he rounded the mill like a charging bull. "But, at a guess, I'd say you underestimate his determination to wed you."

CHAPTER 7

Gavin circled the mill. He searched inside the mill—all three stories. Twice. The barn yielded no sign of a bride on the run either. No woman of sense would go back in the house with Grandma Ermintrude, and Marge always struck him as the practical Marguerite, so he resorted to hollering like a madman.

No results.

In scant moments, his bride-to-be had become a bride-already-gone. With nowhere to run, what strange thoughts crashed in her mind? The most illogical option—returning to the house to throw him off—brought him nose to nose with Grandma.

"Never got the bride you wanted and already lost the one you found?" Sounded like she'd been waiting for him since he'd bellowed for Marge. "You've got a real touch with the ladies."

"I take it she didn't come back here then."

"Told you that one had brains to rattle betwixt her ears. No woman with sense or pride stays where she's unwanted if she has the slightest choice." Grandma Ermintrude cocked her head. "Not that this one has a choice. She just needs time enough to think it through and she'll be back.".

"I *told* you not to call her Daisy." Gavin gave vent to the ire that continued to mount, swelling with each moment he couldn't look after Marge. "Why couldn't you leave well enough alone?"

"Why couldn't you tell me the truth?"

"You would've used it against her." She wanted truth? He'd give it to her.

"Never." A long-buried pain rose from the depths of her gaze. Grandma's voice went soft. "I'd never do that to another woman."

"Grandma?"

"Now *you*. . ." Her customary sharpness returned in an instant. "*You* I would've taunted with it, and that's a fact."

"Then don't ask why I didn't spill the whole story with her waiting out front." Anger at himself for how he'd handled things and at her for how her quarrelsome ways influenced him made his tone harsh. "You gave me cause to doubt the way you'd react."

"Blaming others for your mistakes makes for more mistakes to come."

"I'm sure there will be." With that, he headed back to the mill. Until Marge returned, he'd busy himself repairing the gearwheel mechanism that gave way earlier. He set to work, restless in the silence. No turning wheels, no sounds of water churning, gears turning, and grain grinding accompanied him this afternoon. No cheerful *tap* of the damsel against the shoe as grain worked down the hopper between the millstones. Only stillness.

He stopped every so often to go upstairs and outside, checking to see if she'd returned. No such luck. Three times he repeated the process, but it wasn't until he'd replaced the splintered tooth entirely and did several test runs to assure himself of the integrity of the piece that he spotted someone approaching.

No, not *someone. Two* women skirted around the millpond toward him. One wore the purplish color Marge arrived in, so Gavin abandoned his post and hustled to meet them. When he drew closer, he identified her companion as none other than Midge Collins—one of the women he'd hoped Daisy would befriend.

Relief at Marge's safe return crashed against rage that she'd ever left. Regret joined the other two emotions when he saw her reddened nose. *Has she been crying this whole time?*

"Marge—we were worried about you." Somehow it didn't sound like the reprimand he'd intended or the half apology he almost felt appropriate. He sounded stiff.

"Were you?" Miss Collins noticed his voice sounded off. Her very posture spoke of disapproval and suspicion.

"Thoughtless of me to disappear like that." The mumble hardly sounded like Marge. "But in times of trouble, I find it best to collect one's thoughts and determine a course of action." This last sounded more like her.

"I already determined what we'd do." He kept it vague, uncertain how much Marge told Miss Collins. The less anyone else knew about the problem, the better.

He could already hear the gossip if word got out. *"There's our town miller—such a fine head on his shoulders he can't even propose to the right girl!"*

"Your plan is unacceptable." The red all but left her nose. "Thankfully, I ran into Miss Collins here, and we've devised a better one."

"This is none of Miss Collins's affair." With great effort, Gavin kept from shouting. "You are my bride. This is a matter between us."

"Ah, but that's just the problem, isn't it, Mr. Miller?" Miss Collins stepped forward. "Marge is *not* your bride."

⁓⟨∞⟩⁓

"She will be." Gavin's jaw thrust forward in an expression of such determination Marge could almost have believed he wanted to marry her.

Almost.

She opened her mouth to reply, but another voice sounded.

"Would you all get inside this house"—Grandma Miller's caterwaul belied her age—"so an old woman can hear what's going on?" Standing on the front stoop, cane planted in the dirt one step down, she glowered at them all from a good distance away. Such a distance, it was a wonder she'd managed to know there was anything going on at all—particularly with the sound of the mill running.

"*Another* watcher." Midge's mutter made absolutely no sense, and Marge didn't bother asking. "Do you know, I always thought of her as a cantankerous woman, but I'm starting to think she's got spunk. Why don't we all go inside?"

Because you were closer to the truth with cantankerous? She bit her tongue, instead admiring the way Midge managed to work her way inside the house in spite of Gavin's obvious discomfort. All three of them trouped in to follow the old woman's command—although Midge was the only one to manage some semblance of enthusiasm.

Grandma Miller inclined her head in a manner fit for royalty. "Miss Collins, how do you come to join us this afternoon?"

"I ran. . .across"—Midge's choice of words would have amused Marge at any other time—"Marge as she sought some time for private reflection. I'm afraid I drew some faulty conclusions regarding Mr. Miller." Here, her gaze flicked to Gavin. "So Marge explained your predicament to make it clear he'd done her no wrong."

"Thank you for not letting the townspeople of Buttonwood think I chased you off." Gavin's dry tone strengthened Marge's resolve.

"So you should thank the gal." Grandma Miller chose to speak up on her behalf. "If she let Miss Collins think you sent her running off like that for any reason other than the truth, you'd sorely regret it. As it stands, this couldn't have been an easy thing for Marge to divulge. It doesn't reflect well on either one of you."

"It's hardly Marge's fault, from where I sit." Midge demonstrated a friend's loyalty already. "But broadcasting she wasn't the woman your grandson wanted will hardly enhance her standing— or her options—in Buttonwood."

"Options?" The word came out as a muted roar. "What options? Marge will marry me, as planned."

"I most certainly will not." She didn't even care that she sounded waspish. "As I said, Midge and I made other plans."

"Have you?" An old woman's head truly ought not swivel so swiftly nor so far as Grandma Miller's managed during this conversation. "Things grow more interesting by the minute."

"No, they haven't."

"Yes, we have. Marge mentioned she's a teacher," Midge cut in, refuting Gavin's denial. "Buttonwood needs a schoolmistress, and I'm willing to speak on her behalf. It all works out."

"You see?" A hard swallow cleared her throat enough to allow the words through. "I don't have to marry you."

"You don't have to marry me, but you will." Gavin crossed his arms over his chest. "As planned."

"You didn't plan on wedding me, so it's moot."

He took three large steps closer and peered down at her. "I plan on it now. I planned on it since you alighted from the stage and

I knew why'd you'd come. Make no mistake, *Marguerite* Chandler, before long, you will be Marguerite Miller."

His stressing of her formal name, far from driving home the point or underscoring any commitment, incensed her afresh. "Marge." She poked a finger into his chest with each word she ground out. "Call—me—Marge."

"Good point. If you'd called Daisy, well, Daisy, she wouldn't be here in the first place." Midge made herself comfortable in a wing-backed chair. "Although I, for one, am quite glad Marge came to Buttonwood. We need her."

Suddenly, Marge realized she'd just prodded a man. Who wasn't her fiancé. In public. She felt the blush heat her cheeks even as she balled her hands into fists and pushed them deep into the pockets of her lilac traveling ensemble. *Running like a hoyden, confiding in strangers, putting my hands on a man. . .what am I coming to?*

"You mistake me. I said *Marguerite* because I proposed to her as such, and she accepted that proposal. We are bound by that agreement, and she needs reminding."

"Fools don't grow on my family tree. He gets that from his mother's blood. My son didn't pass on the type of addled thinking that would make a man keep mentioning he didn't specify which woman he was proposing to." Grandma Miller made this general announcement while Marge headed straight for her reticule, opened it, and withdrew what she sought.

"Reminding everyone that this whole mess is all his fault won't do him a lick of good." Midge sided with the old woman. "Marge, what are you up to over there?"

"Here." She moved to Gavin's side and slapped the money onto his palm, folding his fingers over it. "You did not propose to me. You proposed to Daisy. A misinterpretation doesn't bind me to you, although I do owe you something. This is for the stage fare."

"I don't want your money." He made as though to return it, but she backed away. "I want your hand."

"Do you?" Someone else spoke the question on Marge's heart, and it took her a moment to realize it was Midge.

Lord, I already know the answer. Please give me strength to move forward. I trust it's Your will for me to teach the children here—that there is a reason and a purpose for this horrible misunderstanding. Otherwise, it would simply be too cruel to leave her standing here, staring at the man she'd been so delighted to marry, waiting for him to say—again—he didn't want her.

Gavin didn't answer immediately, a blessing and curse, in that it showed he was taking time to truly consider the question. His perusal took her in from the top of her head to the tips of her toes before he uttered one word. "Yes."

Air became unbreathable for an instant. Until she saw him open his mouth and knew the next words would somehow ruin it.

"She is mine."

Something primal rippled up her spine, but her mind and heart rejected it. "I don't *belong* to you, Gavin Miller."

"He already said he wanted her." Seemed like Grandma Miller, along with Midge, was enjoying the show. "What more is she after?"

"Tell him, Marge." Midge cheered her on. "Tell him what he has to do if he wants you."

"I won't play out this farce." Her nose prickled, signaling another onslaught of tears.

"Marge..." Gavin's request cut through her confusion. "Tell me."

"All right." *The worst that can happen is he doesn't do it, and that's already where I stand.* "If you want to marry me, Gavin Miller, you're going to have to do one thing."

"Which is?"

"Prove it."

CHAPTER 8

"Prove it?" Gavin echoed the challenge she'd thrown down like a gauntlet. "Doesn't me saying so and asking repeatedly do that?"

"His mother's side, I tell you." Grandma Ermintrude couldn't seem to hold it in. "If he only took after my son, he'd cotton on far quicker."

"I'm inclined to believe you, Mrs. Miller." How he'd ever thought that Collins girl would be helpful stumped Gavin at the moment. It must have shown, because she addressed her next comment to him. "From where I sit—quite comfortably, I might add—you have a lot of proving to do. For one thing, I haven't heard you ask Marge to marry you on one single occasion. You do, however, demonstrate a distinct talent for giving orders."

"Now *that* he gets from me." Leave it to Grandma Ermintrude to make a man proud.

"You're both wrong. I didn't issue orders. I stated facts." If he had to stand trial, he'd provide a solid defense. "Marge will marry me. It's the obvious decision based on what she's already done."

"Forgive me for failing to see how my refusals would make

630

marriage a foregone conclusion."

"A man proposes to be sure a woman wants to marry him." Gavin didn't know how women managed to get these things so twisted around, but he'd straighten them out. "I know Marge wants to marry me. She wouldn't be here otherwise."

"You think...that's why...ooh. Wrong!" The woman he'd just proclaimed wanted to marry him spluttered the most vehement denial he'd ever heard.

"If you didn't want to marry me, you wouldn't have left your home and family and come here as my fiancée." He could be patient, even understand that her position made her vulnerable. But the woman had to see reason. "I'm not wrong."

"That proposal theory of yours was." Grandma Ermintrude shook her head. "A man doesn't only ask a woman to wed him to see whether or not she wants to."

Miss Collins simply glowered at him. "Her wanting to is only half of it. A man proposes to demonstrate to his woman how much he values her."

"The mere act of asking implies that." Three women in the house were two too many. Possibly three too many, but that wouldn't help Gavin win a bride.

"And you haven't asked." Marge recovered her ability to speak. "You asked Daisy. You've proven that you want to marry *my cousin*."

All of a sudden, the problem became clear. *Easy enough to get that bee out of her bonnet so we can get married and move on. Marge will be a good wife, and no one need ever know things weren't planned this way.*

He closed the short distance between them, dropped to one knee, and took one of her hands in both of his. Looking up into hazel eyes wide with surprise, Gavin gave his future wife the one thing that would make all the mistakes better—a proposal. Better yet, a proposal before witnesses.

"Marge Chandler, will you marry me?"

Her lips parted, her eyes searching his, she held perfectly still for one spellbound moment. Then she snatched her hand from his grasp and backed away. "No!"

"What do you mean, 'No'?" He lurched to his feet and tracked her. "You said prove it." She scuttled farther back when he came within reaching distance. "You said a man proposed to demonstrate how much he valued his woman."

Their deranged dance continued—his stalking closer, her scooting backward around the room in a bid to avoid him. "I proposed. I proved I valued you." With his final point, he backed her into a corner. Literally.

"I mean, 'No, I will not marry you.'" She lifted her chin, defiant despite being caught. "Or, if you like, 'No, you have most certainly not proven yourself.'"

"I don't like it." He leaned closer, deliberately placing one palm against the wall. "You can't change the rules."

"Don't accuse me of cheating." Sparks of green blazed in the honey brown of her stare—he'd never noticed that before. "Yes, a man proposes to show he values his woman." She reached up and pushed on his elbow. When it didn't give way, she ducked beneath it and made an escape. "But the problem is you can't skip the steps that come before."

"You made no mention of other steps." He looked at the space where she'd been so neatly sandwiched a scant moment before. A faint scent of something. . .clean. . .lingered. He liked it. "What other steps?"

"I'm not *your* woman." She'd taken refuge between Miss Collins and Grandma Ermintrude, of all people.

"You will be as soon as we're wed." Confound her circular logic.

"Wrong way around." The ever-helpful Miss Collins poked her nose in again.

"I didn't have to prove she was my woman when she first came. Why now?" *And how?*

"Before, everyone thought she was the woman of your choice. That was enough." An exasperated *thump* of Grandma's cane sounded. "Think, boy. How do you win a woman?"

Gavin swallowed a groan as the answer hit him like a pebble between the eyes. . .with enough force to fell a lesser man. "You three are saying I have to court my own mail-order bride."

"I think it's best you stay here with Grandma Miller while you teach"—Miss Collins directed the statement to Marge—"rather than come home with me, after all. Seems only fair to allow Mr. Miller the opportunity to"—she turned to give him a meaningful look—"get to work."

<hr />

Hard work was to be met head-on. *"And whatsoever ye do, do it heartily, as to the Lord, and not unto men. . . ."* Amos considered the verse in Colossians a daily challenge. Fulfilling it meant food on the table for Mother and his six siblings, a sense of satisfaction in a job well done, and a well-earned night's rest.

It also, he reflected as he sat on a church pew on Wednesday morning, brought with it the benefits of clean living. The Geers hadn't set up in Buttonwood for much more than a month, as of yet, and already people took notice of a solid work ethic. With the mill finished—though he'd only been around to help put on the final touches—the town council contracted him to build a schoolhouse.

Perfect timing, since he and the family arrived too late for spring planting on the homestead and a paying job came as nothing short of a blessing. Amos went ahead and stretched his boots beneath the pew ahead of his. Might as well get comfortable—his presence was more of a formality than anything else.

It wasn't as though he had much to say in the hiring of a new schoolmarm. He hadn't been in town long enough to bear any right to vote on anything so important. No, Parson Carter and Josiah Reed—minister and mayor, or Field Mouse and Fox, as Amos privately dubbed them—requested his presence so that they could all discuss the progress on the schoolhouse. Ostensibly, if they hired on the new woman, she might make some requests and such forth.

No matter. He'd adjust whatever they liked. Today's meeting caught his interest for a few reasons—that he had four school-aged brothers and sisters didn't even make the top two. A few questions rustled around in the files of his mind, so Amos made sure to show up early. Good call.

The council filed in and took chairs at the front of the church. Then in walked the two points of interest. Amos stopped slumping and sat up straight as Midge Collins strolled in alongside Mr. Miller's new bride.

Just as I suspected. Only one new woman got off that stagecoach—but married women don't teach. Here then lay an entire collection of questions waiting to be answered. Amos couldn't help but notice Mr. Miller didn't join his bride-to-be for the interview this morning. *Never a dull moment when one pays attention.*

Especially when Midge Collins made an appearance. Amos's focus slid to her and stayed put—with good reason. Now there was a woman to work for. She knew it, too. Had half the pups in town sniffing after her skirts but knew better than to go twitching them at anyone. Every man alive heard of women who played hard to get. Well, here he'd found a woman who meant it.

He never could resist a worthwhile challenge, and it didn't

hurt that this one came wrapped in a petite package with that saucy smile and a few freckles. *Always had a soft spot for freckles.*

But the one girl Amos fixed on talking to went to extreme lengths to avoid him. *I wonder if she remembers our encounter four years ago. How long can she hold it against me for "manhandling" her?*

He'd find out soon enough. Until then, Amos fully intended to enjoy the view. So he watched and listened as Midge explained to the council how Miss Chandler came to them highly qualified, with letters of reference, and would like to help them set up the Buttonwood school.

More importantly, he listened to what Midge avoided saying. No mention of how it'd been rumored she herself was to be given the post. Not a word about Mr. Miller and Miss Chandler's impending marriage. The unsaid attracted more and more attention.

"Miss Chandler, your references exceed expectation and your experience speaks to your ability." Saul Reed gave a satisfied nod and fell silent amidst nods of agreement.

"There is an issue left to address." Frank Fosset, a short, jovial man who sold and traded oxen to wagon trains heading to Oregon, apparently hadn't gotten the same information as others on the council. "Miss Chandler, it is my understanding you came to Buttonwood to be Mr. Miller's bride. As you know, married women find themselves carrying many responsibilities that preclude them from teaching. I apologize for asking a personal question, but it seems the council has forgotten to look into this matter of your marital plans. Are you getting married or not?"

"Eventually." Marge refused to slouch. "I plan to marry in the future, but Mr. Miller and I have yet to determine absolute compatibility and set a date."

Despite Midge's efforts on her behalf, Marge knew there'd be questions. This council meeting would only be the beginning of the queries, speculation, and downright gossip about her and Gavin.

Gavin. Strange how she couldn't re-erect the barrier of his name in her mind. After calling him "Gavin" in her mind for when she claimed him as her fiancé, then for a scant hour in person, she couldn't convince her head or heart to reclassify him as "Mr. Miller," as was proper. Oh, when she spoke to others she could adhere to social convention easily enough. But in private. . .

They always say you're at your truest when no one else is watching. Marge didn't want to think about the things she hid within, the things she allowed no one to see. *What does that say about who I am?*

"The Grogans, my son, and I are aware of the. . .uncertainty regarding Miss Chandler's arrangements with Mr. Miller." Josiah—at least she thought that was his name—Reed, owner of the mercantile and mayor of Buttonwood weighed in. "Until such a time as the matter is settled, we understand she is to live with Ermintrude Miller, while Gavin takes up temporary residence within the mill itself."

"While Miss Chandler and Mr. Miller go about reacquainting themselves," Dr. Reed—Midge's adoptive father—added his voice, "she is applying for the position of schoolmistress. Should she wed, obviously another candidate would be needed."

"Which would leave us in the lurch." Mr. Fosset seemed unlikely to cave to popular opinion. "We need some sort of stability or contingency plan if we're to take on such a poor risk." He belatedly realized how that sounded as he added, "No offense, Miss Chandler."

"None taken." *Though I'm not half so poor a risk as you might think. Have they not noticed Gavin didn't bother to accompany me this morning? In all likelihood, I'll be a schoolmarm until I can no longer remember the subjects I teach.*

"We'd be no worse off than before." The farmer, Mr. Grogan, held true to Midge's prediction.

"No. I remember us discussing Miss Collins as a possible candidate for the position."

Marge held back a sigh. Normally she didn't like to judge. But to her understanding, Mr. Fosset dealt in oxen. Perhaps that was the source of his bullish obstinacy?

"I don't believe I'd make a good candidate." Midge didn't mince words. "Besides having no experience, patience isn't my strongest suit. Everyone knows that."

Guffaws met her admission.

"What if we compromise?" Parson Carter leaned forward. "Hire Miss Chandler to help set up the school and keep her on so long as is possible, but with an added provision."

Hope, vibrant and welcome after the flattening revelations of the day before, fluttered to life. "What provision?"

"Miss Collins trains alongside you as your successor." The parson couldn't look more pleased as the rest of the council nodded in agreement.

Marge stood in no position to protest, although one look at her friend's face told that Midge felt just as she had when she realized Gavin didn't want her.

Trapped.

CHAPTER 9

Peace and quiet. That's all Midge really wanted. Complete silence. A place with no one and nothing but utter stillness. So she could shatter it by shrieking.

Instead, she got a guided tour of the new schoolhouse-in-progress. Led by none other than Amos Geer. Amos. Geer. The very reason—aside from her total lack of patience and inability to remain still indoors for any significant length of time—she balked at becoming a teacher.

The moment they contracted Amos Geer to construct the school, Midge decided to have nothing to do with it. Folks were always saying to "listen to her gut," and that man made hers grumble. Not in a sour milk sort of way, but in a keep-your-distance type of warning.

A warning she'd done her level best to heed until a scheming town outmaneuvered her. All because she'd tried to do the right thing for a fellow outsider. *The old adage is true—no good deed goes unpunished.*

She scarcely refrained from aiming a kick at the stray rock

in her path—that would have been childish. Instead, she played a little game as the three of them trouped toward the building. A game of how-many-things-about-Amos-are-unattractive. Midge prepared to create a long list.

Four years ago, that incident at Fort Bridger, for one thing. He most likely didn't even remember it. *But I do.*

Then there was the sad matter of his overconfidence. His walk alone should be a source of shame. That stride, legs swallowing the distance as though it was nothing, shoulders relaxed as though completely at ease.

Why couldn't he slouch, stoop, strut, swagger, or go stiff in the neck like every other man in town? Those men had the sense God gave a goat and knew full well that everybody had something to cause a hitch in their get-alongs. Any man unaware of his flaws made for a fool.

And any man who could hide his so well became a threat.

"Here we are." An obvious statement—and another thing to add to her list of things to dislike, since people who said obvious things lacked ingenuity, as Amos gestured to the already-laid foundation of the schoolhouse. "You can see it'll be a good size, but plan for the walls to be thick."

"It's larger than the schoolroom I managed in Baltimore." Marge seemed pleased, at least. "Why will the walls be so thick, I wonder?"

"Council batted around a few ideas when I came up with the building materials' cost. Wood's scarce around these parts, so we'd have to ship in whatever we used. It's not the best insulator against weather. Would need steady upkeep and repainting, too. But the main argument against it seemed to center around the issue of safety."

"Fire." Midge fought to keep from going pale. Amos would

notice—and it made her freckles stand out.

"Yep." His nod didn't seem to notice anything unusual. "Some folks saw a wooden schoolhouse full of boisterous children and a stove as a catastrophe waiting to happen."

"Not worth the risk." She let them both know she agreed with that opinion. "Brick is a better choice."

"Expensive." Marge frowned. "Wouldn't the money be better spent on books, slates, ink, and paper for the children to use?"

"They balked at the high freight cost, but I found a substitution." He made his way behind a cornerstone and lifted a piece of canvas to reveal an orangish red block far larger than a normal brick. "This is made from a type of red clay found not too far from here. It holds up well to wind and water, and the thickness of the blocks will keep the building sturdy enough to withstand the worst storms."

In spite of herself, Midge crouched, stripped off a glove, and ran a hand over the block. A fine layer of soft reddish grit dusted her fingertips. She rubbed them together. "Little red prairie schoolhouse—not brick and doesn't have to be painted. Ingenious."

"I can see now why the walls will be so thick," Marge commented. "We'll be glad of it in the heat of summer."

"This will make the place dark." The very thought of it—forced to stay cooped up inside in a dim room with thick walls—made Midge's toes twitch with the need for a quick escape.

"We've ordered a total of six windows." Amos pointed first to the length then to the breadth of the foundation. "Each side will have two, so you'll get light in morning and afternoon. The third pair is slightly smaller, to bracket the entrance."

"Glad to hear it." Her toes stopped twitching, at least. Well. . . mostly.

"Will I need to speak with the council about ordering a

blackboard, desks, and supplies?" It seemed Midge wasn't the only one who made mental lists, as Marge began rattling off things like primers and hornbooks. "Or has that been seen to?"

"The blackboard and desks, they're ordered. I couldn't speak as to the rest." Amos stepped up onto the foundation, walking to the very center. "This is where we planned to put the stove so it'd heat most evenly come winter. If you ladies approve that, then there's not much else to discuss."

"I approve." *Time to leave Mr. Geer behind. . .far, far behind. So I don't have to consult with him again.* Midge looked expectantly at Marge.

"The council mentioned a bell?" Her friend's question may have been reasonable, but Midge didn't appreciate it all the same.

Especially when they all walked back to the general store and Amos Geer pointed up a narrow flight of stairs. "It's up there. You can't miss it."

Marge started up without a moment's hesitation. Midge, however, balked when Amos stepped back to let her go ahead.

"I've already seen it, thank you." It would take far more than a bell to make her waltz up those stairs, knowing her rump would be straight in his sight line.

"Good." A wide smile revealed that the slight gap between his front teeth hadn't completely closed in the past four years. He moved in such a way to block the stairs. "Now you can explain why you've been avoiding me."

Amos didn't bother to hide his amusement as his quarry looked to the left then right for avenues of escape. Let her look. He'd chosen well—with Josiah Reed at the far end of the counter, clear at the other end of the mercantile with another customer, Midge couldn't pawn him off on anyone.

At the same time, if she tried to go out the door, the bell would jangle to catch everyone's attention. He already blocked the staircase, and good manners dictated she wouldn't abandon Miss Chandler in any event. All he needed was time.

"Miss Chandler?" He pitched his voice to carry up the stairs but not across the store.

"Yes, Mr. Geer?" The miller's would-be-wife peeped over the top of the stairwell. "Will I not be able to find it?"

"I'm sure you will. It's to the left." A smile would reassure her—and concern Midge—so he flashed one. "Mr. Reed might have mentioned a crate of primers up there, if you'd like to look for a moment." He heard a quick exhalation from the woman at his side, the type of sound that could only be called a huff. His grin grew.

"He mentioned no such thing," Midge spoke through gritted teeth. How anyone could call her something so stuffy as Miss Collins escaped Amos's understanding.

"I said he *might* have."

"We both know better."

"Then tell me something I don't know." He really shouldn't be enjoying this so much. "What did I do to set up your back?"

"What makes you think you're of any concern to me?" The imperiously raised brow could have fooled someone who hadn't watched her systematic avoidance over the course of weeks.

"Speak plainly. Are you in a sulk because you think I don't remember you?" He deliberately provoked her, intent to see whether she knew what he meant.

"Sulk?" She latched on to the word and ignored the question. "Grown women don't indulge in sulks."

"A girl I met once did—at Fort Bridger." Amos saw the flash

of recognition in her eyes and felt a surge of satisfaction. *She remembers.*

"Did she? If I had to make a guess, I'd say you deserved whatever she threw at you." Her studied nonchalance missed its mark only because it was a shade *too* studied. "For amusement's sake, why don't you tell me about this so-called sulk."

She wants to know how much I remember. That boded well. For the first time, he caught a glimpse of the curiosity she kept contained around him. The curiosity that shone from her whenever she spoke with just about any other soul in Buttonwood—only to shutter when she glanced his way. *Why?*

"Scrawny gal." He saw her eyes narrow at that. *Good.* "Thought her to be about eleven when I first caught sight of her poking her pretty little nose where it didn't belong. Not time enough to shout a warning and be sure she'd hear me—much less heed it if she did—I ran up and pulled her away from the door."

Midge opened her mouth, obviously fixing to interrupt, but he held up a hand to stop her. She'd asked him to tell the story, and he'd finish his version before she got her say.

"You see, my brother Billy almost died in that room just a few days before, and it hadn't been cleaned out. That nosy little girl could've died if I hadn't saved her. But did she thank me for my troubles?" Amos shook his head mournfully as Midge's glower grew still more fierce.

"No. Instead, she stomped on my foot, elbowed me in the ribs, and threatened me with a bloody nose. That little girl sure lucked out that I had a soft spot for freckles."

"You grabbed me from behind with half the force of a freight train and no word of warning!" she burst out in rebuttal the moment he stopped. "Then had the nerve to tell me it wasn't manhandling. Any male who sneaks up on a woman deserves whatever he gets—including that bloody nose you escaped." Midge drew a breath, still visibly livid. "And you're wrong. I did thank you."

"But you didn't apologize." Suddenly he recalled that she had thanked him after he explained about Billy.

"Did so."

"Only for stomping on my foot—not for elbowing me in the ribs. Now that I know you remember Fort Bridger," he said, shifting closer and lowering his voice, "you still owe me an apology."

"You won't get it."

"Looks like you're lucky." Amos heard the unmistakable sound of feminine footsteps on stairs and got in the last word. "I *still* like freckles."

CHAPTER 10

Gavin dipped his hand in the half-full sack of flour, knowing by the feel of it in his palm it was wrong. *Wrong, wrong, wrong.* Everything he'd turned out that morning either went to scrap feed or had to be put through again with exacting adjustments to fix what should have been right the first time.

Lord, is this Your way of telling me I should have gone to the town meeting with Marge? Part of wooing a woman is supposedly being supportive, but how does it help my cause to support her means of being independent? To encourage her to push farther and farther away from me?

To be sure, although he already knew exactly what he'd find, he rubbed the forefinger of one hand in the small mound of flour covering the opposite palm. Small grits tattled of stones set a hair's breadth too far apart. He let it fall back into the sack with a dismal pale *poof* and went to shut the sluice gate. If a miller lost his touch, he lost everything.

Same could be said of a man and his temper. In fact, that's where Gavin suspected the real problem lay. If he looked hard enough, he wouldn't find the flaw in the grain, or the gears, or in his knowledge or finely cultivated instinct for grinding and tending the mill. He would admit it came from his sudden sense of dissatisfaction.

If idle hands did the devil's work, distracted ones opened the doors. With a mind full of Marguerites, precious little focus remained for the mundane. Not when at that very moment, Marge stood before the town council, revealing that she most certainly did not plan to marry him.

An impossible situation. Go, and appear to endorse her decision to refuse him. Or stay, and seem to sulk at her defection. Either way, he'd be the butt of every joke in town until he got her stubborn self to the altar—*where she belongs.*

How to get the job done presented a problem. Particularly when he wanted to ask the woman what in tarnation she was about, broadcasting their business to everybody like this. Tempers didn't tempt anyone, so he'd have to keep a lid on his.

He could do that. Anger provided a poor way of life, and Gavin didn't hold grudges. However, holding grudges didn't match up with bearing responsibility—and he didn't hold all of it in this situation. *Marge needs to meet me halfway.*

"I came all the way to Buttonwood." A surprised voice behind him made him realize he'd spoken aloud. . .and Marge had returned. "That's more than halfway."

"Not what I meant." He kept the exasperation from his tone and turned to find her silhouetted in the doorway. For the first time, Gavin looked at her as the woman he would wed—the woman who would stand and sleep alongside him for the rest of his life.

With strong shoulders for a woman, trim waist, hips round enough to bear a man several sons, Marge wasn't a woman he would have overlooked had she been standing beside anyone other than her cousin. Better yet, right now, she looked amused.

"This morning I came back to the house from town, and when Grandma Miller said you were here, I met you at the mill." Was that a teasing glint in her eye? Had Marge ever teased him before?

"Come a little closer," he invited. To his recollection, Daisy was the cousin with a ready smile and easy laugh.

"Said the spider to the fly?" She finished the first line of the nursery rhyme and shook her head, bonnet bobbing. The motion carried subtly through the lines of her body, making her skirts sway.

"I thought the spider said, 'Step into my parlor'?" At her nod, he held up a finger. "You forfeit a penalty then. One step."

"Mills have no parlors." She still gave him one step and held up two fingers. "Your penalty."

"So be it." He liked this side of her. "Now give me another, as a toll for entering my mill."

"You wouldn't demand such a thing!" Her overdone gasp amused him. "Besides, the miller himself bid me enter."

"That he did. He wanted his toll."

"Very well." She slid forward a few inches. "But the forfeit for churlishness is three full steps."

"Woman!" Three steps brought him far closer, but he managed to drum up a scowl. "You cannot penalize a miller for seeking his due! Three steps for impertinence!" Her three steps would have made but one of his, and they both knew it. His scowl lost some of its pretense.

"He overcharged." The merriment left her face. "Four steps from the man who asks too much."

"Then I'll grant two, for I seek what's right." His footfalls sounded heavy. "And take two from a woman who gives too little and then fines the miller for wanting more."

647

"I'll give no more until he proves himself worthy but penalize him further for the way he believes he's entitled to what he wants." Her eyes blazed with indignation. "Remember that, Gavin."

"So long as *you* remember I'm willing to pay for what I want." He gestured to the now-scant distance between them. "In time, I'll earn my prize."

"Prize, indeed," Marge muttered to herself as she made her way toward the house. "Consolation prize, more like."

"Hmph." The pronounced snort warned her of Grandma Miller's presence too late for her to keep her thoughts where they belonged—inside her head. The old woman seemed to be on her way back from the necessary. "Airing woes, are we, missy?"

"No, ma'am." She held the door open for her companion and followed her inside. "Just repeating something your grandson mentioned." *And adding the part he left unsaid, to remind myself of the true state of things.*

Just because Gavin grinned in appreciation at her good mood and little game didn't mean he truly enjoyed her company or wanted a lifetime of it. He'd made his choice—although he'd not received it. Now Marge made hers. If she didn't keep a tight hold on her emotions and plans, she'd unravel.

"You can peel those potatoes while you tell me all about it." Grandma plunked herself down at the table and began making short work of a mound of turnips and carrots. Venison already roasted in the stewpot atop the fancy modern stove Gavin had ordered for his wilderness home.

The stove he planned to have Daisy fix him meals on for the rest of their lives. A smile tickled the edges of her mouth at that thought. No matter how modern, a stove couldn't work miracles and cook for her cousin. Gavin might be disappointed to know Daisy couldn't so much as boil water....

But no. It served no purpose to mention such a thing. And Marge wasn't so vain as to point out her cousin's lack of skill in hopes Gavin would appreciate the woman who'd come to Buttonwood to wed him. That would be folly.

"We lose folks to lots of things—time, sickness, heat, drowning, animal attacks, wars..." The slightly croaky voice of her companion pulled Marge's attention away from her musings. "With all those dangers, seems pure foolishness to lose yourself in thought."

"If people thought more, many tragedies could be avoided." She set down a peeled potato and reached for the next in the pile. "I daresay fewer would be caused in the first place." *Like misbegotten, accidental proposals that seem cheery and full of hope but snatch away everything just because no one stopped to truly think about what was going on!*

"Unpleasant situations like proposal letters gone awry?"

Thunk. Her blade chopped off a large hunk of the potato she'd been peeling. It seemed rather pointless to feign nonchalance after that telltale move, but Marge gave it her best. "Perhaps."

"Perhaps a thoughtless mistake will turn out for the best. Sounded to me like that cousin of yours was all smiles with no spirit to back it up."

"Daisy is full of spirit." The knife met the table as she lost her concentration again. "My cousin is a force unto herself—something no one who's not met her can possibly appreciate. And there's no one who doesn't like a good smile."

"True. Maybe you'd best stop scowling."

"I'm not scowling!" Marge glared at the mangled potato before her for a moment before realizing it. A grudging chuckle escaped her at her own ridiculousness.

Grandma Miller added an approving cackle. "Good to see you have a sense of humor. I started to wonder. More to the point, you'll need it if you're going to wed that grandson of mine."

"Oh, but I'm not going to wed your grandson." Slow, careful strokes of the steel knife sent peels curling toward the table. "I'm going to teach here in Buttonwood. Eventually things will be settled enough I'll not stay here any longer, and Gavin can find a new bride." *One he wants.*

"He already has Daisy's replacement. Why would he need anyone else?"

"It's not a matter of need." Another perfect, methodically peeled potato joined the pile. "It's a matter of what your grandson wants in a wife. I am most assuredly not that woman."

"A man wants a woman. Plain and simple." For all the bluntness of the words, the older woman's gaze stayed fixed to the table. "One who'll put supper on the table and babies in his nursery. You'll do quite well."

"No, I won't." *A man has to choose that woman.* "I won't be second choice to my cousin."

"I can understand that. Maybe even respect it. But if you think half as much as you seem to, take some advice from an old woman." Grandma Miller raised her chin, eyes blazing with some old ember of memory. "No one wants to be second choice to another woman. But it's worse to be a slave to your own pride."

CHAPTER 11

"Don't you love me?" Trouston looked up from where he'd been nibbling—in slightly slobbery fashion—behind her ear.

"You know I do, darling." Daisy gave one of his perfect curls a playful tug in hopes the gesture would distract him. Of late their stolen moments seemed to become more and more awkward. And if Trouston's urgings were anything to judge by, it was a good thing they'd be married before week's end.

"Sweetikins, we've discussed this." He drew back, cupping a protective hand over the back of his skull. His glower told her the petty gambit worked beautifully in shifting his attention. "You know it takes Richards far too long to see my hair properly done. I won't have you messing it up."

"Sorry." She tried to look penitent even as she shifted forward from the half-reclining position he'd pressed her into on the settee. "Your valet does work wonders." She suppressed a disloyal spurt of amusement at her fiancé's vanity. Valets for men had gone out of fashion decades before, after all.

"Where are you going? There's no rush, my dear. Your mother

won't expect me to bring you back for hours yet."

"Mmm. . ." She sought a reason for her conspicuous movement. "Suddenly I'm parched. With no servants here, I meant to go find a glass of water." A bright smile hopefully covered her sudden discomfort.

Leaving the Brodington musicale a bit early under pretext of a headache seemed a fine idea when Trouston whispered it to her after that dreadful performance by one of their daughters. No misgivings fluttered in her stomach when he drove her to the two-story townhome he'd purchased upon their engagement, telling her he wanted to give her a private tour before the servants took up residence the next day.

But now. . .now the faint chimes of muffled good sense thumped unpleasantly in the back of her mind. Proper young ladies simply did not disappear into empty houses with a man.

Even an engagement didn't excuse such laxness.

"Allow me." Without a moment's hesitation, Trouston left the room, his lanky frame angling out the doorway as though eager to fulfill his mission.

That's my Trouston. At his show of devotion, the alarms stilled. After all, Trouston could be depended upon to uphold respectability. She trusted him with her hand, her heart, and her entire future—of course she could rest easy for an hour or so in his company! There'd be an entire lifetime of such evenings to look forward to.

She waited for the ballooning sense of elation to overtake her, as it always did at the thought of being Mrs. Trouston Dillard III. And waited. . . The usual ebullience escaped her, leaving an oddly deflated sort of feeling she most emphatically did not wish to dwell upon with scant days to go before her wedding.

"Darling! Thank you!" His return spared her from the uncertainty, giving her good reason to push away any doubts and glide across the room to meet him. She accepted the proffered glass and took a deep draught without bothering to so much as glance.

"Easy, sweetikins." His warning came too late, as the pungent brew burned its way down her throat, leaving her spluttering. "I thought we'd toast our upcoming wedding with some particularly fine Scotch."

"Trouston!" She coughed up his name, wishing she could cough up the vile brew currently snaking its way down to her stomach, trailing a discomforting heat in its wake. "You know I don't imbibe!" Daisy blinked, trying to hide how her eyes watered—something he would surely disapprove of.

"I'm disappointed. This is one of the finer things in life, Daisy. I thought to share a sophisticated pleasure with you, and you cavil like a schoolgirl."

"No!"

"Give me the rest. I won't have you waste it." The sharp lines of his jaw seemed brittle as he nodded at her glass. "If you won't toast our happiness with me, I'll take it back."

The burning sensation faded, leaving a dull warmth at odds with the chill of his words. "Take what back?" *Our happiness?* Her fingers curled protectively around the sapphire ring he'd given her to mark their engagement. "No."

"You'll drink it?" Triumph gleamed in his eyes as he raised his own glass. "That's my girl. To my beautiful bride and all the happiness that awaits us."

"To us." Daisy lifted her own glass and took a tentative sip. This time, the heady mixture swirled against her tongue before sweeping its scalding path down her throat. She allowed only the smallest gasp to betray her discomfort.

Disapproval clouded Trouston's gaze when he saw how much still sloshed in her cup. "I've seen more enthusiasm from you over a new pair of gloves." He looked pointedly from his empty glass to hers. "You only ever get one husband."

"I'm overcome." Her laugh sounded shrill to her own ears, so she raised her glass once more, this time holding her breath for a deep swallow. It didn't burn so badly this time, although it still stung. Whatever the case, now so little swirled at the bottom of her glass—a heavy silver piece she knew was never typically used for spirits—Trouston couldn't scowl when she put it down. Which she did. Immediately.

"Come with me. I wish to show you the rest of the house." He took her arm, leading her through the places she'd already seen. Parlor, sitting room, breakfast room, formal dining room, kitchens, pantry, music room. . .and by then she couldn't quite remember why she'd ever been uneasy about spending time with her fiancé in their home.

A heady warmth suffused her stomach, her head felt light with hopes as they climbed the stairs and he showed her the nursery, the guest rooms, and, finally, the master bedroom. It was here he swept her into his arms and began pressing urgent, moist kisses on her lips and neck.

She giggled and wriggled away, spinning to look at the decor. The colors blurred a bit. . .cream and purple. . . "Lovely," she pronounced.

"Yes, you are." He guided her to the bed. "You seem a bit unsteady, sweetikins. Why don't you sit down?"

"Just a moment." She settled on the down mattress and gave an experimental bounce. "Comfortable."

"Yes, it is." He sat beside her, pulling her close for one of those deep kisses that always made her nervous and thrilled. He held her fast when she tried to tug away. "Easy, little one. Nothing to be afraid of. This is our home."

His smile coaxed one from her in return.

"Now, sweetie," he murmured, trailing a finger along the edge of her bodice as he spoke, "you're going to show me just how much you love me. . . ."

❧⁓ⴕ⁓❧

Marge stared at the sheet of paper before her in a mixture of rage and dismay. Another stage would come through town tomorrow… and folks back home would be expecting word from her about how things progressed.

Daisy would be waiting eagerly for news of Gavin's romantic tendencies. Descriptions of longing glances, fulsome words, and extravagant gestures the likes of which her cousin had been treated to since she first learned to bat her lashes at men. Somehow, a wry retelling of how Gavin's grandmother spilled the beans that Marge was the wrong woman wouldn't measure up.

On the other end of the scale, Aunt Verlata would be wearing a path in the carpets, fretting that something had gone awry and Marge hadn't made the splendid match they'd all gloated over. Her concern would be made up of one part horror at the idea of facing society should Marge have bungled things and become, in the eyes of civilized folk, a ruined woman with no prospects, and one part concern for Marge's safety.

Daisy may be the apple of Aunt Verlata's eye, but her aunt still cared for her a great deal. In truth, Marge only put concern for her safety as a secondary concern because she liked to think she'd proven herself to be highly capable. Capable enough to mitigate some of the worry that would plague her family if word about this little fiasco ever got out.

Which brought her back to the letter she needed to write. One page, filled with words to alleviate worry when, of course, anyone with a modicum of sense and the slightest inkling of the true state of things would be filled with misgivings. So Marge couldn't let them know. And she couldn't lie. That didn't leave much to say, and they'd know in an instant things weren't well if she didn't fill the entire sheet. Confound her hate of waste. Now they'd expect a page filled with news and descriptions of her new home.

Marge stared at the desk in front of her before finally standing up, walking over to the imposing collection of luggage dominating her room, and unearthing the trunk she sought. The sheer volume of bags, valises, trunks, and crates she'd dragged to this small town provided irrefutable proof of her foolishness. If hope sprang eternal, Marge had packed for it.

When she'd prepared a list of things to bring, she'd thought long and hard about what she'd need for a lifetime in a small frontier town. What her family would need, and since she'd always been a big believer in being prepared for anything, the list took on a life of its own. Now, as she dug her travel writing desk out of the trunk in question, Marge couldn't help but feel struck by the irony.

I prepared for everything except reality.

She couldn't muster even a tiny smile at that, no matter how she tried to appreciate the wry humor behind the situation. Instead, she took the wooden box over to the bed, plumped up the pillows, and settled herself comfortably. Only then did she unfold the box, on its well-oiled hinges, revealing a sloped writing surface inset with stiffened leather.

She lifted out the leather, withdrawing the smallest sheet of paper she could find before unstopping the small bottle of ink nestled snuggly in the carved-out niche of the corner. With her favorite mother-of-pearl dip pen in hand and a prayer on her lips, Marge set to work.

Dear Aunt Verlata and Daisy,

I trust this letter finds both of you doing wonderfully, as usual. As for myself, I'm very pleased to see the end of my journey westward. Days on end cramped inside a stagecoach wending its way over every rut along the Oregon Trail gave me a newfound appreciation for the everyday freedom of walking about on one's own feet, breathing in air that hasn't been mixed liberally with dust.

It's beautiful here in Buttonwood. Remember the time we spent trying to imagine what it would look like, Daisy? It's green, rolling grassland as far as the eye can see. I'm told as summer heats up, the green will turn golden, but for now it seems lush with wildflowers. The sky stretches almost end-lessly above from horizon to horizon, largely unmarred by any buildings. No smoke fogs the air. The town itself is tiny, though with enough amenities to make it feel homey.

I've not yet had the chance to meet everyone—that will come on Sunday, after church. For now, I've made a friend of a young woman named Midge Collins. She's a lively sort and chosen to be Buttonwood's schoolmarm. I've been enlisted to step in and help set up the school as soon as the building is finished, which makes me feel like I'll be part of the town in no time.

Gavin is just as we remembered. Charming and hand-some as ever, if a bit sun-bronzed, which looks quite well on him. His grandmother is a woman of great spirit and looks to make for some lively conversation, to say the least. The house and mill are beautiful and thoroughly modern, I must say. I'll go into detail in my next letter, as it seems I've quite run out of room and my candle begins to gutter. Tomorrow evening there is to be a dinner party of sorts to ease me into knowing some of the more prominent people in town, so I need to get a good night's rest and make the best impression possible!

All my love to you both,

Marge

If she pressed the nib of her pen particularly hard as she signed her name, she didn't think anyone could blame her. It was all she could do to leave it at "Marge." As it stood, though, they might suspect not all was as well as her letter portrayed if she added "Not Marguerite!" at the end of her signature. . . .

CHAPTER 12

Were it not for the sound of birds chirping a merry song, Gavin would have had no way of marking the arrival of morning. The bottom floor of the mill, built into the side of a man-made hill alongside the millpond, was designed to hold the gear housings and insulate against moisture.

He'd chosen to set up his temporary residence down here for practical purposes, not comfort. Customers saw the main floor and the storage area above it, where they placed the grain they brought for him to grind into flour. Gavin couldn't have a pallet and sundry items laying about the business. Tucked into the corner farthest from the gears down here, no one saw. The lack of light helped with that, of course.

Down here, no windows invited cheery rays of sunshine to brighten the darkness. Morning arrived unheralded by anything but the call of birds as they swooped around the millpond, scouting for insects and even fish. Normally Gavin loved that. Liked to think of it as just another way the gristmill served as a hub for the community and helped provide a steady food source.

This morning, the bird cries sounded shrill to his ears, as though determined to prey upon the unsuspecting. With the way the past two days had gone, he found himself missing the house more than ever. Waking up to a windowless, dank room seemed worth it when a man knew he'd have a bed—and a wife to share it with—in a matter of days.

Now that he could rest assured of neither wife nor bed in any foreseeable future, Gavin didn't have to guess why his outlook took a turn for the worse. A long stretch led to a series of not-unwelcome pops along his spine, loosening up his muscles for the day ahead.

Aside from a full day's work, he had that dinner party at the Reed place to look forward to this evening. Rolling over and punching his pillow did little to unleash the surge of outrage the thought provoked. Just before Marge stepped off the stage, he'd agreed to the meal as a sort of informal introduction to Buttonwood society—such as it was.

He'd thought it a chance to show Daisy a good time and show off his lovely bride-to-be in what would hopefully be the first of a string of social engagements befitting their status. Now, instead of bringing his prize, he brought an unending stream of questions. Even worse, a lot of those questions numbered as ones he couldn't answer.

Yet.

Gavin sprang out of bed. He didn't have much time. Questions demanded answers, and Marge needed to give him a few before the day began in earnest. More importantly, he needed to hear those answers before their plans that evening. He dressed hurriedly, sneaking into the house to wash up. No matter how skilled the man, anyone needed good light to shave.

By the time he got to the breakfast table, he saw Marge and

Grandma Ermintrude putting platters of bacon and biscuits down. His stomach let loose a growl he could only hope neither of them heard. A rough night's sleep left him with a hearty appetite—and Gavin planned to eat enough to give him plenty of strength for what lay ahead.

Taking his place at the head of the table, he folded his hands and waited for the women to follow suit before asking a blessing over the meal. The warm, doughy scent of the biscuits rose beneath the heavier smell of fresh bacon and pungent coffee. Gavin waited for his stomach to still so as not to have his attention divided.

"Dear Lord, we come before You this morning and thank You for the food on our table and the company at it." He ignored Grandma Ermintrude's amused snort and kept on, "We ask Your guidance as we move forward, putting the past behind us and fixing our eyes upon the future You've placed before us. Amen."

"Amen." Marge didn't meet his gaze as she passed the biscuits— perhaps a sign that she was considering putting past mistakes behind them?

Gavin grabbed three and handed the basket over to Grandma, helping himself to a hearty rasher of bacon. His fork split the first biscuit without any difficulty, letting him spread a large gob of butter across the surface with ease. *I wonder whether Grandma made these or if Marge did?* He couldn't recall whether or not his bride-to-be knew how to cook.

That's the sort of thing a man should know about the woman he intends to make his wife. A big, buttery bite went a long way toward soothing his discomfort. *Although, I can be forgiven for not knowing whether or not Marge can cook. Originally it was Daisy I proposed to.*

He pushed away the sudden realization that he had no idea whether or not Daisy could cook. All women should be able to—and Daisy, always the epitome of everything feminine, surely wouldn't disappoint. Marge, however, with her more practical, bookish nature might have overlooked the domestic skill.

"Mmm." He decided a compliment might be the fastest—and most diplomatic—way to discover the truth. He polished off the first biscuit and began slathering another as he spoke. "This is delicious."

"I'm glad you like it." Grandma Ermintrude's amusement didn't help him one bit. "Been awhile since you've been so enthusiastic about breakfast. I wonder why that is?"

"Flattery?" When her eyes widened, he could see more of the green flecks livening the amber. Marge's lips twitched slightly—only once, as though holding back a smile. "Are you assuming I baked the biscuits, Gavin?"

"As a matter of fact, I am." Well and truly caught, he had no choice but to brave it out. His hopes for a response came to nothing as both women looked at him in amused silence. "Am I wrong?"

"Often." Marge's pert reply let loose the smile she'd been holding back. "Though I doubt that's the answer you seek."

A chuckle escaped him. "Hardly."

"Does he know whether or not you can cook? Or is he fishing to find what skills his surprise bride brings to the table—or doesn't, if it turns out that I made the biscuits?"

"I don't believe your grandson and I ever discussed my culinary skills, Mrs. Miller."

"Ermintrude." Grandma's bark took Gavin aback—the old woman rarely gave anyone permission to use her Christian name. "If all goes well, you'll be the next Mrs. Miller."

"That remains to be seen." The smile fled Marge's face at the first outright mention of the marriage question that morning. "Although I did bake the biscuits."

Is the thought of wedding me so awful? His food lost its flavor at the strength of her reaction. *I'm the same man she came all the way out here for. What am I supposed to change to make her want to be my wife again?*

<hr>

"How are things going?" Midge darted around the corner of the house and whisked Marge aside before she so much as reached the door. "Tell me everything!"

"Not much to tell." Her shrug should, she felt, say it all.

"Pishposh. You can tell me what he said when you came home from the meeting yesterday and told him you'd be teaching, for starters." Her friend's eyes glowed with expectation.

The memory of their little game in the mill brought warmth to Marge's cheeks. She'd been playful with him—at a time when she should have been telling Gavin that she'd successfully received the teaching post and he wouldn't be stuck with her.

"You're blushing."

"Nonsense." Marge scowled. "Actually, Gavin and I didn't discuss it. He seemed to take it for granted that I'd be given the position and didn't so much as ask me how it had gone." A spurt of indignation overtook her. "He could have at least pretended some interest!"

"No, it seems that's not his way. Mr. Miller is pretending the teaching position is a whim—a sidelight, something that won't truly get in the way of what he wants." The younger girl rocked back on her heels. "Good. That means he does want you. Otherwise, he'd be anxious to hear all about the arrangements you made, when they'd take effect, and so on."

"Considering the schoolhouse isn't yet up, his asking about those sorts of things would seem overeager." The good mood that had buoyed her spirits on the walk to town abandoned her now. "Gavin's always been polite."

"Don't you think it would have been polite to escort you to the meeting and show his support of your ability?" Midge gave voice to one of the doubts that pestered Marge. "Or at least show some interest in how it went once you returned? No. . .if he's ignoring the whole thing, that's as good as trying to wish it away. He doesn't like the idea that you have options other than marrying him."

"Some men like to exert control. Gavin always seemed the type to have a good grasp on what went on around him." Marge shifted her sewing kit from one hand to the other. "Which must make this entire situation even more distasteful to him." *Makes* me *even more distasteful to him. A man used to making his own decisions and ordering his life just so—and he gets me instead of the woman he's handpicked as his perfect bride.* She indulged in a small sigh.

"Don't tell me you're going to be melodramatic or make a bid for martyrdom." Her friend's eyes narrowed. "You didn't strike me as the 'oh, woe is me' type. I've never liked that type, to tell you the truth."

Nettled, Marge lifted her chin. "Neither have I, though I've inclined slightly toward the mopes since I found out my groom isn't really mine at all. Difficulty deserves recognition just as do the kinder things in life. I won't pretend I'm pleased with the way things turned out."

"Mmm-hmm. Thought so." Midge made a show of walking behind Marge. "Yes, there it is. A bona fide spine. I'm glad to see you're making use of it again."

A short burst of laughter escaped her. "You'll make a far better teacher than you give yourself credit for, Midge Collins. Some people are born with a knack for passing out lessons."

"Not all of us have the patience to plan them."

"You strike me as the type to always have a plan or two. Speaking of which," Marge continued, lowering her voice, "was it your idea to invite me for a sewing circle this afternoon before the dinner party. . .or do I have someone else to thank for that?"

"Not my idea. That would be Clara—and she plans to sniff out why the miller's bride petitioned to become the schoolmarm. A few hours of cozy time with nothing but women, tea, and sewing would be enough to make anyone crack."

"It stands to reason they have questions." *No way to avoid that.*

"Questions abound." Midge gave the deep, satisfying sigh Marge held back. "But it's the answers that always cause trouble."

CHAPTER 13

Trouble walked through the door just after Mr. Miller and just before dinner. Midge stopped a very pleasant round of self-congratulation—a brief, private celebration that she and Marge managed to get through the sewing circle that afternoon without giving away too many personal details about her sticky situation—to gape.

Her mouth, like the door, hung open for a moment in what promised to be a highly unattractive manner. She snapped it shut as Amos Geer strode into the parlor, looking for all the world as though he'd been invited to join everyone for dinner. As Clara took his coat, the suspicion sneaked over Midge that that's precisely what had happened.

When did Amos Geer wrangle an invitation into her home? And when had she become so lax in her watching that she'd not noticed until it was far, far too late to stop or even minimize the damage? Such thoughts screeched to a halt as she painted a pleasant smile onto her face. After all, he was doing the very thing that made her want to avoid him at all costs. . . .

Amos Geer was watching Midge. Again. With an intensity she could scarcely believe went unnoticed by her family. Although, if she thought about the matter, she most emphatically did not want them noticing his interest. So that was for the best. For a brief moment, she considered how nice it would be if she didn't notice him either.

Him watching me. She shook her head once to clear it. *If I didn't notice the way his eyes follow me around, I wouldn't have to deal with him at all.* Flawed logic, but it did seem that the more she attempted to avoid him, the more determined the man became to catch her off guard. Midge rather hoped after the interrogation he sprang on her the day before he'd become bored. Now that he knew she remembered him—she quelled a spurt of satisfaction at how well he remembered her—he could stop wondering and move along.

Except he was moving along into the parlor. Straight toward her. Midge fancied he could hear her molars grinding, and that brought the ridiculously warm smile to his face. *Contrary man. Well, if cornering me makes the game fun for him, I'll take away the thrill.*

"Why, Mr. Geer!" She came forward to meet him, her smile growing as his faltered. "I didn't know you were joining us this evening." A swift, accusatory glance at Clara got her nowhere. Her adopted "mother" busied herself trying to coax information from Mr. Miller—who Midge believed would be no more forthcoming than herself or Marge.

"Miss Collins." He gave a shallow, almost imperceptible bow. "Mrs. Reed invited me. When I heard of the plans for a small, intimate dinner among friends, I couldn't resist getting to know some of the most fascinating people of Buttonwood a bit better."

"A wise choice." She kept her smile in place and didn't kick him, although she noticed the faint emphasis he'd placed on the word *intimate*. "I do wonder what other. . .surprises. . .Clara has in store for us this evening." She made a show of looking at the door as though hoping for additional guests.

Amos surveyed the rest of the party, seeming to take some sort of head count. "Traditionally, the hostess makes sure numbers are rounded out." A wolfish gleam lit his gaze. "I do believe I'm intended to be your dinner companion."

The nervous burble of laughter died as Midge looked around. Aunt Doreen and Uncle Josiah. Saul and Clara. Adam and Opal. Mr. Miller and Marge. *He's right.* She stifled a groan. *Clara did invite him to even out the numbers—the perfect reason for him to stick to me like a barnacle for the entire evening!*

"Excuse me; I need to check on the food." More accurately, she needed to check on the stove, but she certainly didn't plan on explaining that to Amos. As things stood, she beat a hasty retreat and headed for the kitchen without waiting for his response. He'd have to find some way to amuse himself other than pestering her with his laughing gaze and knowing grin.

Midge couldn't help but notice the differing reactions on the faces of her loved ones as she made her way through—an approving nod from Saul, the welling of compassion in Opal's gaze. . . though she wouldn't admit to it, a shrug of acceptance lifting Aunt Doreen's shoulders, and the exasperated shake of Clara's blond curls. This last caused a twinge in her breastbone—Midge knew full well Clara thought her preoccupation with the kitchen wasn't healthy.

But of all the people in the house, Clara should be the one who most understood. To be really fair about things, Clara ought to be the one most concerned about another fire. She'd been the one to live through the first one, after all. She should be at least as vigilant as Midge about making sure it never happened again.

Instead, Clara chalked it up to God's will—that classic Christian catchall that seemed to Midge a sort of spiritual "oh, well." Seemed to her that God got a pretty nice deal—praise for anything good and respect for anything unpleasant. She paused in the kitchen doorway, scanning for signs of any sparks or small, telltale curls of smoke anywhere they didn't belong. First glance showed nothing out of the ordinary.

An enormous pot of stew simmered on the stove—any larger and Midge would call it a vat. Whorls of fragrant steam rose from within, but no smoke. She ventured over and opened the oven, which kept an already-cooked beef roast tantalizingly warm. The baking compartment groaned with its load of corn bread—three pans stacked atop each other to retain their heat until serving. Seemed as though all was as it should be.

Just the same, Midge took a towel and ran it around the farthest edges of the stove to clear away any bits of food that might spark later. Then she noticed someone had left the broom leaning on the wall a bit too close. She returned it to the corner, where it belonged. Finally satisfied no sudden blaze would consume the house and everyone inside it on her watch, Midge turned around. . .to find Amos Geer loitering in the doorway.

"How long have you been there?" She sounded snappish, but then, she felt snappish.

"Pretty much since you checked the stew." He braced one broad shoulder against the doorframe in what Midge was swiftly coming to recognize as a favorite posture of his. "Long enough to know you didn't hear me say I'd like to see the kitchen."

"You followed me." *Again.*

"Yes. I planned to see more of the house—I've an appreciation for architecture." That made sense, considering he'd helped build the gristmill and now worked on the schoolhouse. That might have put Midge at ease, if he weren't looking her up and down and still talking. "Turns out, I got to see far more than I planned on."

~~◦◦~~

Amos watched her fight the flush rising on the crests of her cheeks. The rosy glow somehow made her freckles brighter. He liked that. He also liked the way he managed to discomfit her—the girl was obviously far too used to being the one with the upper hand. It'd do her good to have that turned around.

"You saw me straightening things up and checking on supper." Her nonchalant tone warred with the flush she finally wrestled under control. "Nothing interesting about that."

"I beg to differ." Not that he planned to mention just how interesting he'd found the view when she leaned down to peer inside the oven.

Her spurt of laughter caught him off guard. "Odd. You don't strike me as the sort of man to beg for much." With that, her mask fell back into place. Gone was the flush, the flash of hesitance in her gaze that let him know he got under her skin. Before him stood the composed, confident woman with a mischievous streak that promised to liven up the dullest days.

But he already knew that Midge. Everyone knew that Midge. Amos wanted to see more of the woman she kept hidden so well—plumb the depths of the tiny cracks in her fearless facade. For now, it didn't matter why he wanted to. He just did. "You're right—I don't beg. But I do differ."

"Differ as much as you please. I still say there's nothing of interest in spying on me doing my chores."

"Spying?" He noted the way her eyes narrowed infinitesimally for a scant moment, an accidental acknowledgement that she'd revealed more than she intended. *She feels exposed. . .as though I've intruded on something. And she knows she just gave it away.*

"Spying, lurking—whatever term you prefer." An airy gesture to brush away her discomfort. "Truly, Mr. Geer, you should find a new hobby."

"And if I like lurking?" He allowed his amusement to show.

"It still doesn't get you very far."

"I'm not planning on going anywhere, so that's not a problem."

"You should plan on rejoining the others."

"We will." He didn't budge an inch. "As soon as you tell me what made you so afraid of fires."

Her mouth opened and closed twice before she managed a single word. "What?"

"At first, I assumed you wanted a reason to avoid my company." Amos ignored the slight inclination of her head at that statement. "Because your aunt Doreen had just come from this direction a few moments before you took off. Now I know better."

"I'm glad to hear you acknowledge that I didn't lie. Now that we have that settled, we can get back to the party." She took a step forward—the first time she'd ever voluntarily moved toward him. Obviously she wanted this conversation to end.

Which made him want to pursue it all the more. "Either you're excessively neat and overly conscientious—which strikes me as out of character—or you're afraid of a fire."

"I hope I'm not excessively anything."

"Oh, you are." *Suspicious, for one thing. Secretive. Clever. Appealing. . .* "But that's a topic for another time. Right now, I want to know why everyone seemed to expect you to go to the kitchen almost as soon as your aunt left. Why you stopped in the doorway and looked over the room as though searching for something. Why you checked every nook and cranny of that stove and oven then cleaned it and inched back a broom that was several feet away to begin with."

A succession of emotions flickered across her gaze. Anger, fear, and longing dazzled him with their swift intensity before she schooled her features to reveal nothing. She didn't say a word—didn't acknowledge his observations.

"I'm right." He left the doorway to stand before her as something else fell into place. "You're afraid of fire. You're the reason the council decided to make the schoolhouse out of brick, aren't you?"

"It's a wise decision." The protective glint stayed long enough for him to truly appreciate it this time. "One I support wholeheartedly."

"You more than supported it." Another step closer. "You insisted. Admit it."

"There's nothing in the world I could insist on that would make a difference if the men in town leaned another direction." Evasive and overly modest, the answer struck a false chord. "Insisting doesn't make much of a difference in anything." That statement rang true.

"Fair enough. You're too clever to outright insist on something, but you suggested and persuaded until you got your way." *No wonder, with those big eyes. . . . A man would have to be made of stone to hear her pleading about her worries over a schoolhouse fire and not do what he could to alleviate them.*

"I like to think logic holds sway when presented properly."

"Indeed? Then surely you know I will persist in my questions until you explain the reasoning behind your impressive vigilance against any wayward sparks in the kitchen." Ah, but he enjoyed matching wits with her. Not only did he relish the thrill of the challenge—and such challenges came by only too rarely—he reaped the additional reward of seeing her discomfiture as he undermined all her arguments.

"Persist as you please. It will do no good."

A pretty face and a sharp mind made for an intriguing combination. Add in some mystery, and Amos saw opportunity for entertainment long into the future.

"Oh, I don't know about that, Miss Collins." He let her step around him toward the door. "You're right—lurking becomes tedious. I should thank you."

She stopped and looked over her shoulder. "For what?"

"Don't you know?" A grin spread across his face. "For providing me with a new hobby. This one should be far more interesting. . . ."

CHAPTER 14

"Oh no, you won't catch me tagging along to a dinner party." Grandma shook her head. "Fodder for gossip is all anyone will want. The conversation cuts through folks the same time the knives slice through the meat."

No matter how Gavin insisted she wouldn't be tagging along—or coaxed and even hinted that surely Grandma could more than hold her own in any discussion—he wound up heading over to the Reed household alone. Not that it came as a surprise. Grandma refused the day before, and he'd had to mention to Dr. Reed that the old woman wasn't feeling overly sociable these days.

Not that Gavin could call to mind a time when Grandma ever seemed overly sociable, but the point still stood. Well. . .maybe that afternoon when Marge arrived, ran off, and returned with Midge Collins in tow. Grandma Ermintrude seemed downright gregarious when surrounded with so much conflict. Though she may just have seemed more companionable than Marge, who bristled so pointedly at him once she'd learned of the mix-up.

He wouldn't have minded having his relative along this evening to help monitor the conversation and put in place any noses that started poking about in his business. Honestly, Gavin wondered if it wouldn't do Grandma good to get out and about more. If some friends wouldn't improve her outlook and give her something to look forward to beyond sneaking in those little barbs whenever they spoke.

Not that he could manipulate her into coming. He'd thought perhaps the lure of Miss Collins's company, along with witnessing firsthand how he and Marge handled their foray into town life, might convince her. With that failing, he had no choice but to arrive on the doorstep with nothing but staunchly suppressed concerns about how much Marge mentioned during the sewing circle she'd attended that afternoon.

"Mr. Miller!" Clara Reed opened the door and took his coat, peering behind him as though expecting someone else.

"Grandma didn't feel up to coming—I mentioned to Saul that might be the case." It seemed an explanation was needed.

"Oh, Saul told me." She still held the door open. "Mr. Geer, welcome!"

"Thank you, Mrs. Reed." Amos appeared in the entrance right behind him, making Gavin marvel at how silently the other man moved. "Glad to be here."

"Good to see you, Geer." He nodded in acknowledgement as Mrs. Reed took their coats to some closet or another.

"And you." The other man's gaze skimmed the room, coming to rest on where Marge and Miss Collins stood chatting. A slow smile spread across his face. "I met Miss Chandler the other day. Buttonwood has a lot to thank you for."

"No thanks required." Gavin didn't like the way Amos Geer peered in the direction of his woman. Nor the way he addressed Marge—not "your fiancée" or "your bride-to-be" or even "your

Miss Chandler," as would have been appropriate. No, Geer left it at a simple "miss," as though Marge might still be available. Gavin forced a chuckle. "My reasons for bringing her here are entirely selfish, after all. Excuse me."

Without waiting for a response, he headed straight for Marge. "Good evening, my dear." He cupped her elbow in his hand and angled close. Almost immediately, he felt calmer.

"If you'll excuse me. . ." Miss Collins murmured some pretext for politely making herself scarce. Her thoughtfulness raised his opinion of her a notch—though it would take a lot more for him to be glad of her budding friendship with Marge.

"Gavin, how was your day?" She must not have realized she used his first name—no blush stained her cheeks.

He wouldn't mention it. If she continued the familiarity, he'd have good reason to call her Marge as he was used to—a clear signal to any upstarts who thought "Miss Chandler" might not be firmly attached. Besides, he liked the sound of his name on her lips.

"Well enough, though much improved now that I can enjoy your company." Ah. . .here came the first faint stirrings of that blush. Excellent.

"I see you're continuing where we left off this morning." Her pause didn't elicit the reaction she sought, because she clarified. "More flattery?"

"You insult me." He steered her over to a sofa and sat down next to her. "Flattery means you think the statement false."

"Perhaps not false. . .but certainly overdone." She scooted away a little bit. "Thank you, all the same."

"You're more than welcome." Under the pretext of making himself comfortable, he sprawled more—taking up every inch of space she'd just put between them. "I think you underestimate how much it means to a man to have something to look forward to at the end of a long day's work."

"Mrs. Reed will be delighted to hear you think so highly of her dinner party." Her smile brightened as Opal and Adam Grogan approached them.

Gavin sat in silence for a moment before exchanging greetings with the Grogans. They took a few chairs nearby and began the meaningless chitchat always present at such occasions—the sort of conversation that encouraged a man's mind to wander. Particularly when he had a lot to think about.

He watched Marge smile and speak, noticing how animated she was—the way she used her hands and leaned toward whomever she spoke with. His bride-to-be really was an engaging little thing, but she wasn't proving easy to catch. The ease with which she deflected compliments created an unforeseen challenge. *Daisy always took them as her due. Why doesn't Marge?*

⚬◦⚬

Gavin kept staring at her. The more she tried to ignore it, the more the awareness grew, until it curled up into a tight, nervous bundle of uncertainty ricocheting within her ribs.

Why is he staring? What is he looking for? Is he comparing me to Daisy? Is he looking for flaws? These she almost understood, but it was the last possibility that made her want to weep. *Is he trying too hard to find something he might like—to convince himself he hasn't made such a bad bargain if he marries the other cousin?*

The entire time she discussed modern farming methods with Opal's husband, she could scarcely concentrate on recalling all the facts from the journal articles she'd read. Honestly, while she realized how important developments in steam-driven threshing would be to agriculturalists, Marge's interests were taking a decidedly self-centered turn.

Am I boring him? Is he thinking how horrible looking and dull I am compared to Daisy? She shoved the doubts away and tried to focus on the conversation. After all, Mr. Grogan appeared fascinated by her comments. Hopefully Gavin noticed that. . .and it pleased him.

Not that she set out to please him. Marge fell silent as the two men began discussing the relative merits of steam versus water power for various aspects of cultivation. *Daisy would be bored to tears.* Even Opal, who had the same vested interest in farming machinery as her husband, seemed less than entertained.

She gave the other woman an understanding smile. "That's a lovely brooch you're wearing, Opal."

"It belonged to my mother." Her hand fluttered up to touch the long, thin pin adorning her collar. Studded with seed pearls and the faceted shine of marcasites, it glimmered in the lamplight.

"She always wears it." Her husband slid his arm around her waist, pulling Opal—and the chair she sat in—closer. "Opal's very loyal to her family."

"Mama's brooch and my wedding band." His wife thumbed the thin circle of gold adorning the ring finger of her left hand.

"That's better than all the finery I saw in Boston." Marge leaned forward for a closer look. "What you have there are true treasures."

"Exactly." Opal's blue eyes shone with the sparkle of joy. "I'm so glad you understand." Impulsively, she reached out and clasped Marge's hand. "And I'm glad you came to Buttonwood."

"So am I." Gavin's deep rumble spoke her thoughts before Marge so much as opened her mouth.

"Are you?" It took incredible effort to keep the words light and teasing, but Marge turned from the Grogans to search Gavin's expression while he answered. *Are you really?*

"Of course he is!" Mr. Grogan stepped in, but not before Marge caught the flash of uncertainty in Gavin's eyes. "He hardly spoke about anything but your arrival up until now!"

"I very much doubt that." Hopefully a gentle smile hid the sorrow behind her reply. *Because Gavin wasn't talking about me at all—he was talking about Daisy the whole time. Two days in my company won't have changed his choice.*

"Mr. Grogan exaggerates," her fake fiancé murmured.

"Somewhat," Opal admitted. "Though Mr. Miller did speak quite highly of you. It was plain to see how much he anticipated your arrival, Marge."

Clara bustled up. "Perhaps it's not the best of manners to mention it, but it's easy to see Mr. Miller is pleased to have you here. He can scarcely keep his eyes off you!"

Ah ha! So it's not simply my imagination. Marge could feel the heat of a bright blush sweeping from her cheeks down her neck. *Gavin is staring.* Now the only question was why she seemed embarrassed by the fact when he was the guilty party?

"Why would I want to?" He lifted a brow. "She's so animated it's easy to get caught up in what she's saying."

"Isn't it though?" Clara perched on the last seat in the arrangement. "Forgive me for my absence; I was just checking on Maggie. But the important thing now is that I noticed the same thing earlier. Even with her hands busy sewing, Marge is an energetic speaker."

"Something her students will appreciate." Adam Grogan's words made Gavin stiffen beside her, but certainly no one else noticed. "I must admit, when Midge first came to us asking that we hire your Miss Chandler on to help start the school, I had my doubts. Now, I'm more and more pleased by the decision."

"*Your Miss Chandler*"? Marge's spine straightened to match

Gavin's. The last thing he needed was for the townspeople pressuring him into marrying her. True, Mr. Grogan didn't know the details of their situation, but those types of comments would steer Gavin down the aisle whether he wanted to go there with her or not. And Marge didn't see any way to stop it, short of confessing the whole sorry situation.

Which meant she and Gavin would continue to play this infernal game of cat and mouse, as he toyed with her before swallowing his pride and his hopes and settling for a poor imitation of what he'd really wanted. Unless she stayed strong and saw through his ploys long enough to set them both free from the entire tangle.

"Marge will be a wonderful asset as she helps set up the schoolhouse." Gavin placed an emphasis on "set up" that no one could mistake. "I understand Miss Collins is to be the regular schoolteacher, after the initial starting up period?"

"It's far too soon to discuss timetables." She somehow managed to keep from glaring at the man. "I'll very much enjoy working alongside Midge to implement a curriculum and workable schedule that best suits the needs of the children. Without the building and without having met the students, obviously it's impossible to judge what will be needed."

"You give yourself too little credit." Gavin's smile suddenly looked predatory. "I'm certain it won't take you long to have things in order."

"We'll see." Marge kept her tone noncommittal, but inside, she stewed. How dare he interfere with her livelihood in a bid to maneuver her in front of the altar? Had the man no sense at all?

Chapter 15

"Daisy, he's here!" Mama poked her head through the door.

"I'll be downstairs in just a moment." Daisy forced a smile until Mama shut the door again. Then the smile fell from her face. *I should be relieved. No. . .I should be excited.*

Yesterday had marked the first day since their engagement—and, if she were to truly think on the matter, long before even that—Trouston hadn't called upon her or escorted her to some event or another. An absence made all the more conspicuous considering what had happened the night before.

I don't want to think about that. She shook out her skirts then smoothed them nervously. Daisy didn't recall absolutely everything from that night, but any time she started to remember, she pushed the thoughts away. They were too shameful, too embarrassing, too. . .unpleasant. And now, for the first time, she didn't want to see Trouston.

Yes, you do want to see Trouston. She looked at her reflection, dismayed by how wan her cheeks seemed. Daisy gave them a quick pinch. *He's your fiancé, and you'll be wed before the month is out. Anything that happened isn't important because you'll be together.*

Except. . .except that she had the nagging sense it was important. That the way he insisted she drink the Scotch. . .how his hands went everywhere. . .the way he demanded things he didn't have a right to yet. . .Somehow, all of that did seem important. But it was too late now. No changing her mind, no changing the past, and no changing the fact that he was waiting for her downstairs.

She put an extra bounce in her step as she reached the small parlor—her favorite room in the house. Here, the lighting was best, the seats were coziest, and even the rug seemed most plush. It never failed to lift her spirits to entertain a close friend in this little jewel box of a room. Until today.

"Trouston?" Her step faltered at the look on his face.

"Miss Chandler." He gave a scarce inclination of his head.

"Why are you calling me that? You've called me Daisy for ages." She looked and saw a new hardness bracketing his mouth, a stiffness to his neck, a disdainful glint in the eyes that before had so openly adored her. Her heart fell to the toes of her embroidered slippers. "What's happened?"

"I think you know."

"You are. . .displeased with me." Her fingers curled around the back of a chair. *Shouldn't he be sweeping me into his arms, vowing his eternal love? Telling me how much my trust means to him, how sorry he is that he hurt me?*

"Oh no." His gaze raked her with an appraising leer she would have protested under any other circumstance. "You pleased me all too well, *Miss* Chandler."

The memories she'd stomped down welled to the surface, searing the back of her throat with the acid taste of bile. "I told you we shouldn't. . .that I wanted to wait."

"But you didn't. And, while I enjoyed the experience, I have to say it's not worth taking a strumpet to wife."

She recoiled as though he'd slapped her across the face. "What are you saying, Trouston?"

"That's Mr. Dillard to you." How had she never before noticed how sinister his sneer was? "And obviously, I'm saying that I won't bind myself to soiled goods. You're no better than you should be, which makes you not good enough to be my wife."

"But you love me." She blinked back tears, but they spilled down her cheeks anyway as she walked up to him, hands outstretched. "I know you do. I'm your sweetikins."

"I enjoyed what you had to offer." Another smirk. "Now you can play 'sweetikins' to another man. You still look the part of the innocent, my dear. I'm certain you can trap some poor, unsuspecting clod before he realizes the truth."

Something inside her gave way the moment her slap cracked against his curled lip. "You insufferable—" Her voice broke before she could utter a word that should never come from a lady. She lifted her hand to strike again, blindly seeking to vent the rage and hurt he'd inflicted upon her.

"Easy now." He caught her hand with ease. "I'll allow the first one—it's little enough compared to what I took. Any more and you'll have me rethinking my decision to be generous with you." Trouston's fingers—cold, always so cold—clamped around her wrist in an ever-tightening vise.

"I don't want anything from you," she hissed, trying to yank free. Daisy bit back a cry when he wrenched her wrist in a cruel motion and tried to beat him off with her other hand.

"Oh, I think you do." He caught her other wrist and yanked her close, the reek of his cigars washing over her. His mouth clamped over hers, cutting off her breath in a slimy assault.

Struggling only brought her closer against him, so finally

Daisy stilled, sensing somehow that's what he wanted.

"Good girl." He was breathing hard. "If I'd suspected you had such spirit, I wouldn't have ended things so swiftly." Trouston let go of her right hand, wrenching his family engagement ring from her left. "As it stands, you're too popular for me to enjoy anything more than what I've sampled."

"You'll get nothing more from me." She jerked away, retreating behind the settee. "Don't fool yourself."

"Don't fool yourself, Daisy." He lingered over her name, making a mockery of the way he'd wooed her. "If I chose, I could demand more of your delightful. . .company. . .in return for my silence regarding your wanton behavior."

Her gasp made him grin.

"As it stands, I'm giving you a choice. Either you cry off the engagement, giving the standard reason that you've decided we shall not suit, or I'll break it off publicly and you'll be ruined."

"No." Daisy's knees wobbled. "Miss Lindner?" A horrible certainty swamped her as she recalled the way Trouston's previous fiancée suddenly cried off their engagement, leaving him heartbroken and dashing when he started to court her. "You've done this before."

"A gentleman never tells, my dear." Trouston headed for the door, opening it, and looking back one last time. "Unless, of course, you make me."

"Don't make me ask what happened last night." Ermintrude pounced the moment Marge showed her face downstairs the next morning. "I won't ask, you know."

"You just did." She shook her head at the older woman's blatant attempt to extort all the details without making a request.

"Leaving off the question mark doesn't make it less of a request, you know.

"I know no such thing, nor do I care to. What I do care to know is how you held up in the face of all that curiosity last night. It was the first time I felt tempted to attend something other than church since we got here."

"Then why didn't you?" She led the way into the kitchen.

"The drawbacks outweighed the lure. As time passes and the disappointments of decades etch themselves into your mind and flesh, you'll learn to avoid as many as possible."

Marge halted, eyes fixed on the older woman as she bustled forward in a pointed show of ignoring any reaction to the words she'd just spoken. She noted the slight stoop to Ermintrude's back and suddenly wondered if it tattled of the weight of regrets. *How long has she lived this way—expecting so little that she makes no concessions for others?* Pity welled up, unbidden, at the idea. *And she expects I'll become the same?*

"I hope not."

"I know better." Ermintrude lifted her cane and poked it toward the pantry. "Fried ham and flapjacks this morning, missy." She moved to the shelves and picked out a large mixing bowl, bringing it over to the table. Setting it down heavily then settling herself before it, she waited for Marge to bring over the flour, sugar, crock of butter, and oiled eggs. "We'll need milk, so you can gather your thoughts and try to refute me when you get back."

"Very well." Rolling up her sleeves both to prepare for battle and to draw up the large bucket dangling in the well, keeping the milk cool and fresh, Marge marshaled her arguments. She marched back to the kitchen with milk in one hand, a pail of water in the other, and plan of attack at the ready.

"Heh. You've got a fire in your eyes and a set to your jaw to tell me a good conversation is in the offing." Ermintrude cracked an egg on the edge of the bowl with a deftness that belied her age. "So tell me, Marge-not-Daisy, how is it you foresee so clearly that you won't seek to protect yourself from disappointments as years go by?"

She set down the bottle of milk with a *thud*. "A low blow, mentioning Daisy." Marge swallowed any hurt the reminder caused and focused on the injustice of her opponent's tactics. "To resort to such tricks so soon smacks of desperation."

"Not at all. You're a teacher—easy to see you'd be inclined to make any debate an academic one." She splashed milk into the batter. "Academics aren't my style, and you'd best be prepared to deal with the school of experience." Ermintrude thrust a wooden spoon and the mixing bowl toward Marge. "No one escapes it."

"Why escape it," Marge countered as she fit the mixing bowl into the crook of her left arm, "when you can shape it?"

"Quick. I like it." The gleam of appreciation gave way to discomfort as she lurched toward the stove to start water boiling for morning coffee. "Even if it is just like a teacher to think she can control what life hands to her or what other people do. It never works that way."

"It's foolish to think one can control another person." She plunged the spoon into the bowl and began mixing, her arm moving faster as the words came pouring out. "No matter how much we may wish we could order what other people want or think, it's impossible."

If it were possible, everything would be different. Gavin would want me for his wife, we'd be getting married tomorrow, and everyone would be happy.

"It's stirred enough." The older woman tugged the bowl away, making Marge realize she'd absentmindedly mixed the batter until bubbles were forming. "Avoiding disappointments is far easier than taking them out on flapjacks, Marge."

"You're focusing on the wrong thing, Ermintrude, by thinking only of the negative. I choose to focus on my response. And I choose not to pull away from everyone and everything because I'm afraid of being disappointed."

"Now we come down to the meat of it. The way a person has to respond to disappointments. Well, I hate to tell you this"—it didn't sound as though the older woman hated to tell her so at all—"but there's only one thing that people do consistently when they can't have what they want. The same thing you'll do once you set aside your pride."

"I'm not a proud woman." A twinge told her that might not be entirely true.

"That's why you'll do what I did—what Gavin is already willing to do."

In spite of the churning in her stomach warning her against it, Marge gave in to curiosity. "What's that?"

"Settle."

CHAPTER 16

Seems a fine-looking woman," a voice Gavin couldn't quite place emerged from the smithy. All the Burn men sounded alike, and with three of them, all talented smiths, it made for some confusion unless a body stood right in front of whoever was speaking. "Can't have too many of those around."

A few appreciative guffaws competed with the heat of the forge to fill the air while Gavin stepped inside. The father, Kevin, and his younger son stood by the water barrel. "Afternoon." He spoke loud enough to let them know he was there.

"Your ears must be burning." Kevin sauntered over. "I just told Brett there that I looked forward to catching sight of your bride at church tomorrow." The grizzled blacksmith gave a broad wink. "Don't blame you for keeping her under wraps this week."

"I told Pa she's a fine-looking woman." Brett—Gavin would be sure to remember the name, since this was the unmarried brother—headed back toward his anvil. "Never enough of those to go around out here."

"So long as you remember Marge is spoken for." No sense

taking any chances. "Just giving her time to settle in to Buttonwood before making her my wife."

"What brings you here today?" The older Burn wisely changed the topic. "Can't imagine anything we made for that mill of yours would be giving you problems already." A displeased frown at the idea of anything he or his sons worked on being below standard birthed a deep furrow between his brows.

"Not at all." Gavin disabused him of the notion immediately. "Though the mill's easily gone through half again as much work as it typically would. Lots of grain stored up in these parts, lots of need, lots of work, so there's a good bit more wear than I'd usually see."

"Stands to reason." Relief relaxed the other man's features. The Burns, like everyone Gavin dealt with in Buttonwood, took pride in their work. "What do you need?"

"Mill pick. The one I ordered from a catalog isn't balanced right, and my old one is too worn down to sharpen and keep using." He produced the old one, its wooden handle worn smooth from years of use. "I doubt you can affix a new metal chisel piece to this one—wood's already been soaked to swell around this one—else I would have brought it to you before."

Wordlessly, the master blacksmith extended a massive paw, palm up, to receive the implement. When Gavin handed it over, Kevin Burn didn't grasp it. Instead, he kept his palm flat, fingers open, and tested the heft of the tool. Then, with his right forefinger, he nudged the wooden handle so the pick pivoted on the worn metal head. He ran his fingers over the chisel piece then shifted and got a grip on the handle, his large hand dwarfing the piece.

Finally, he nodded. "You're right—trying to affix another head piece would weaken it or ruin the feel." He raised it to eye level. "For the new version, I assume you'd like the same style handle? I've not seen this type before, with the slight bend, but it makes for a more secure grip. I can see why you got so much use out of it."

"Yes, make it as similar as possible." That the blacksmith inspected it so thoroughly and noted its distinctive traits made Gavin rest easy. "It's obvious you appreciate quality."

"Of course we do." A mischievous smile lit Kevin's face as he tucked the pick into his work belt. "In tools and women. So why don't you tell me about this fiancée of yours?"

"Now I know why he's been so closed mouthed." The younger smith edged closer. "He didn't want any of the other men gearing up to swipe his bride-to-be before he got her down the aisle. I caught a glimpse when she stepped off the stage, and it's easy to see he has good reason to be worried."

Gavin's eyes narrowed at the threat. It might be spoken in jest, but it hit too close to home for his liking. "You don't know Marge. She's not the sort to flit from one man to another."

Daisy is. The sudden thought took him off guard, but he couldn't deny the truth of it. That's part of why he'd been so surprised and relieved when he thought she'd accepted his proposal—he'd gauged the chances of her having found another beau to be most likely. *And I was right.* His frown deepened. *No chance I'll let Marge slip through my fingers, too.*

"A steadfast woman's worth her weight in gold. If she wears a pretty face, so much the better."

"She wears a pretty face, and she was wearin' pretty clothes to make a pretty li'l picture when I spotted her, Pa."

Little? Gavin paused to consider. *Daisy's the tiny one.* "Marge isn't overly petite, and you're in no position to judge how pretty she is." *Sure Marge is pretty. In a quiet sort of way someone has to get close to her before being able to appreciate it.* "You shouldn't be gawking at a woman from across the street and deciding she's to your liking." *You shouldn't be looking at all.*

"I don't see the appeal of doll-like females. There should be enough to a woman for a man to appreciate." Brett let loose a wolfish grin. "Everyone will get a close enough gander after church tomorrow to see that I'm right about her looks."

"Remember yourself, Burn." Gavin took a step forward. "More than one look and we might tangle."

"I'll remember." The burly young blacksmith crossed his arms and waggled his brows. "But you remember something, too, Miller. Spoken for ain't the same as taken."

Midge woke up early—even for herself—that Sunday.

Usually, the darkness around the edges of her window curled back beneath the insistence of morning light before she arose. Even then, by the time she washed and dressed and pulled back the window sash, the town buildings just began to glow with the rosy oranges of sunrise.

Today, she scarcely knew she'd opened her eyes. To be sure, she shut them, noted that, yes, everything did get darker, and opened them again. This time she could make out the hazy, indistinct borders of her window, where the very first blush of light barely began to appear. She lay there, watching it take on more space, more dimension.

Most folks she knew said darkness grew deeper and light grew lighter. Midge held the opinion that light had every bit the depth of dark—more, as a matter of fact, as it possessed the power to plumb every crevice and make anything visible. To her way of thinking, the world needed more light.

But they weren't going to find it in church.

She groaned and let her head fall back on the pillow. *Today's Sunday*. Which meant hours stuck indoors, sitting on hard pews, listening to that Parson Carter drone on and on about the light no one could see. *So how does it do anyone any good?*

Unable to remain still for another second, she rolled out of bed and tromped over to her water basin. Mind churning over other things and eyes having to navigate more shadows than usual, she knocked her shin on the small wooden trunk beside her washstand. Hard.

Amazed the resounding *thud* hadn't woken anyone else, Midge perched atop that selfsame trunk, hiked her nightgown around her knees, and poked at her bruised shin to determine how badly she'd gotten it. Starting where she figured it'd be a good distance from the main bruise, she still sucked in a breath. Yep—it'd be a good one. Probing closer to the bone, her fingers hit a warm wetness—blood.

She curled the stained fingers upward, swung that hand over, and gave it a good dunking in the washbasin. Then, making sure she held her nightclothes away from the injury, she lit an oil lamp on her dresser and peered down to get a better look. Crimson welled from a gash about four inches above her ankle, right where she'd made contact with the metal trunk latch.

Little red streams raced down her leg toward the bare wooden planks beyond the edge of the rug. Midge caught them with one swipe of a clean washrag, dabbing the cut and squinting to try and determine whether or not she'd have to tell Saul about the mishap. Having a doctor adopt you came in handy, but he also tended to overreact about minor scrapes, pulling out witch hazel and whatnot at the slightest provocation.

Hmm. . .deep enough to consider bothering him but minor enough to manage on my own. She pressed the rag down hard, drawing in a hissing breath at the stinging sensation, but she kept pressing until she counted to one hundred. Cautiously, she lifted the rag. Sure enough, the bleeding slowed to almost nothing at all. She'd had worse.

A surge of memories made her drop the rag. The crushing pressure of having her hand caught in one of the mill machines when she was seven—she lost three fingernails and her thumb snapped before the foreman had it shut down. That's when Nancy stopped letting her work. Her hand healed, the throbbing ache replaced by hunger's gnawing insistence as she hid in her sister's room. Until the foreman found her and kicked them out.

Midge drew her knees to her chest. *My fault.* She'd accidentally caught her almost-healed hand in the drop-front desk and let out a small cry. Not much. Just enough for them to find her and fire Nancy. That's when they moved in with Rodney—Nancy's beau. Midge began to rock back and forth.

*The sharp pain of every breath after Rodney knocked me across the room for talking back to him that first week. . .*what she now knew to be the symptom of a broken rib. The constant bruises she and her sister wore as they struggled to eke out a living, until Rodney put her sister on the streets as a common prostitute. Until the night he chose to end the life of the child Nancy had conceived and took both of theirs in the doing.

Her eyes fixed on the deep black-red of her own blood on the rag, remembering her sister's blood-soaked pallet. Remembering Nancy's waxen face as Saul Reed checked for signs of life and found none, telling Midge God had taken the last good thing from her life.

Her beautiful sister, so good and kind that she prayed even for the men who used her body and belittled her for the privilege, ripped from this world. Nancy could have none of the things Midge got to enjoy now—a fine bed, plenty of food, lovely clothes, friends who'd never know the things she'd done in the past. Everything Midge had, Nancy deserved—but Nancy was gone forever.

My fault. She stopped rocking and rested her forehead against her knees. *I'm as old as Nancy was when she died for what I did.* Midge stuffed half her fist in her mouth to muffle the broken sobs. *And nobody knows it but me.*

CHAPTER 17

The scrape of the straight razor may irritate some men, but Gavin found it calming. He peered in the mirror, lifted his chin a fraction of an inch, precisely positioned the blade, and used deft strokes to finish the job. When he concluded, he rinsed his instruments, put them away, patted his face dry, and gave himself one last look-over in the mirror.

Let that hulk of a blacksmith try to outdo me this morning. Gavin straightened his collar, knowing his Sunday best to be better made than most garments in town. Whistling, he headed down the stairs, only to pull up short at the vision awaiting him in the parlor.

Ermintrude had donned her most gaudy ensemble for the occasion—a burnt orange monstrosity he'd attempted to "lose" during the move out West, but somehow it always reappeared. Awful as that sight may be, it wasn't what made him stop. No, he reserved that honor for his fiancée.

Marge must have plotted with the older woman, for she looked some sort of fashion-plate apprentice in a peach-hued dress and fur-trimmed frock. If the color weren't objectionable enough, Gavin grappled with the fact she looked good in it. Downright delectable, if someone put him under oath.

He didn't like it one bit.

Somehow, the peachy tint brought out a becoming color in her cheeks he hadn't noticed before. The rosy pinks she'd worn alongside Daisy made her seem good and sallow. Back then, Marge had weighed down her outfits with layers of ruffles and poufy sleeves until a man could see her coming from a mile off. He'd sort of noticed since she came to Buttonwood that all the bows and flounces seemed to have vanished, but this morning he missed them. *She shouldn't look so slim and elegant.*

"He looks like he swallowed a porcupine." Grandma Ermintrude's gleeful observation told him he needed to better keep his thoughts from his countenance. "Told you he hated orange. I can't tell you how many times he tried to get rid of my favorite dress. Or how many times I thwarted him." She ran a loving hand along the line of her skirts.

"Surely you didn't try to throw away your grandmother's favorite dress?" Disbelief didn't quite conceal Marge's amusement. "Such a thing would be wasteful—and rude."

"I've offered to replace it thrice over."

"Style may change, and I wouldn't mind updating it, but I doubt I'd find the color twice."

Exactly. "Surely something would please you."

"We both know better." His grandmother's comment was thrown down like a gauntlet, but Gavin knew better than to remark upon it. When he simply walked over and offered an arm to each of them, she gave a resigned sigh. "Didn't rise to the bait."

"Nope."

"Wise move." Marge's laugh sounded suspiciously like a

giggle, but Gavin had never heard her giggle before. "For what it's worth, I told her she should've taken you up on the offer. Three dresses in a variety of colors makes for a better deal."

"I thought so." He almost suggested she select a softer shade—like the one Marge showcased—but didn't want his fiancée to know he liked it. *The less she wears this one, the better. At least*—he allowed himself an appreciative glance—*until we're safely married.*

"Three times the opportunity to wear one-of-a-kind creations you'll disapprove of!" When she bit her lip, a dimple peeked from her left cheek. "So Ermintrude just might change her mind, after all, and your grandmother and I will shop."

"I am ever in your debt." Gavin replied as expected—with wry humor—but inwardly chuckled. Marge's smiles were worth the joke at his expense. Besides, no matter her threats, nothing they came up with could be as bilious as that vile burnt orange. Particularly considering Marge's newfound sophistication in her own dressing habits. . .

Which he had cause to deplore as they came within sight of the church. Or, more accurately, within sight of all the townsmen waiting to catch a glimpse of his intended bride.

The intended bride who he hadn't really intended to marry but now did—as soon as he convinced her to agree. The intended bride he couldn't truly lay claim to despite everyone's understanding of the situation. The intended bride who looked far too becoming in her simple peach dress this morning.

Gavin didn't miss the way Brett Burn's eyes widened when he got a good, long look at Marge. Nor did he miss the way folks whispered and elbows burrowed into ribs. Looked like his fake fiancée was the roaring success he'd predicted Daisy would be. . . and she hadn't even uttered a word yet.

His spine stiffened as the Burn men broke away from the crowd and headed over, masculine appreciation written plain across their features.

Gavin glanced at Marge, who blushed becomingly at the certain knowledge she held everyone's attention.

He started plotting ways to get her back into fussy pink dresses—immediately.

She'd never been so thankful to slide onto an uncomfortable pew in all her born days. Marge stifled a sigh of relief at having made it through a throng of gawkers and well-wishers to take her seat in church. For the next few hours, at least, the attention would be where it belonged. On God.

After the service, she'd be in the midst of things once more, but she'd use the time to collect herself. Marge well knew she'd be nothing more than a nine days' wonder in Buttonwood. Once everyone discovered she didn't hide any deep, dark secrets or reveal any exciting talents, they'd lose interest. Waiting for the newness to rub off would take only a little bit of time. So lost was she in the comforts of these thoughts, she missed the hymn the parson named for the start of service.

Yet as the familiar words rose around her, Marge swiftly recognized it. Not a hymn of lilting praise nor a slow acknowledgement of the suffering the Lord underwent on their behalf, this less-oft heard song struck a chord Marge would rather have left alone this morning.

"Father, whate'er of earthly bliss
Thy sovereign will denies,
Accepted at Thy throne, let this

My humble prayer, arise:
Give me a calm and thankful heart
From every murmur free;
The blessing of Thy grace impart,
And make me live to Thee."

Nevertheless, she joined in the singing of it, knowing the words to be true. Knowing that the very way her heart ached at speaking them meant she needed their message more than ever.

As the hymn continued and Marge sang along, she added a private prayer to the worship.

Lord, lately it seems as though You've tantalized me with certain promises, only to pull them away. It's not my place to question Your will, but I can't deny how my heart aches to know Gavin wanted Daisy. How Ermintrude's caution about settling rings in my ears every time he smiles at me. I care for him and always have—enough so that a part of me wants to marry him and take what happiness I can. Help me be strong and follow Your will, Lord, even if it denies me marriage and I am to teach for the rest of my days.

She blinked back tears as the hymn and her prayer came to an end, waiting to feel as calm and thankful as the song promised. But she didn't. Marge shifted on the wooden bench as Parson Carter prayed then began the introduction to his sermon for the morning.

"Today I'm delving into the book of the prophet Jeremiah, who I think really gets into the heart of the way we follow God." Parson Carter, a tall, spare man with spectacles and tufts of white hair over either ear, looked every inch the mild scholar. Even his skin had the look of aged parchment—at once tough but vulnerable to the wear of years of demands made upon it. "Chapter seventeen discusses more than the more common issue of what we do to follow Him. Verses seven and eight, particularly, deal more with the *why* and *how*."

Marge made an effort not to shift restlessly. Honestly, she was as bad as some of her former pupils! But the reason believers followed Christ was simply because He was God, and she expected more from a sermon than a restating of this. She needed a deeper understanding, something to take away from church that she didn't already know, or at the very least, a reminder of something she hadn't considered in a long time.

The parson's voice recaptured her attention as he began reading directly from the Word. "'Blessed is the man that trusteth in the Lord, and whose hope the Lord is.'"

Oh. Shame washed over her at her arrogance. *I shouldn't have assumed I knew what the message would be. He's speaking of following the Lord in trust, not following facts.* She closed her eyes at her mistake. *Although. . .we do put trust in facts. We do trust Him because He is. So, in a way, I was right. But trust goes so much deeper—the heart can know what the head cannot.*

Her gaze slid to the man beside her, who listened intently as the parson kept reading, describing the man who trusted in God as a tree planted by a river, nourished and fruitful even in times of drought.

My heart tells me that Gavin is such a man. My head tells me I was a fool to ever imagine he wanted me.

She listened to the parson speak of the link between trust in God and putting one's hope in Him.

Did I put my hope in God when I came to be Gavin's bride? Was I hoping that He'd answered my prayers for a husband and trusting this was His path—or was I putting my hope in Gavin?

Marge didn't like the questions that were starting to spring up. Not the ones about what brought her to Buttonwood and not the more urgent ones she couldn't seem to stomp down as the parson talked about anticipation for the future. With supreme effort, she tore her gaze away from Gavin.

What is it you're hoping for now, Marge? God's will—or your own?

CHAPTER 18

Midge sat on an unlined pew, her back not touching the wood rest behind her, posture rigid as a poker stick as she listened to Parson Carter speak about trust and hope.

She chewed the inside of her lip until it made her wince, realized that would give her away, and forced herself to stop. Still the man kept yammering on and on, misleading the entire town as everyone around her sat there, lapping up the lies as though they were soul-saving truths. Midge switched to a new little game to keep herself from bursting out with her opinion and disgracing the family who'd done so much for her.

Not for all the satisfaction in the world would she embarrass—or worse, hurt—Saul, Clara, Doreen, and Josiah Reed. So instead, she listened to Parson Carter like she never had before. Tuning out everything else, she raised her boot heel and tapped the fresh cut on her leg every time he said "hope." It kept her grounded, gave her something to focus on. It wasn't until she felt a wet warmth around her toes she realized she'd opened it again. . . and that, perhaps, it was deeper than she'd originally thought.

No matter. Small wounds stung, bled, scabbed, and healed. It was the deeper ones a body had to watch out for. The ones that made people with sense want to cover their ears and race away when folks proclaimed how good and great God was. Only Midge knew He had her trapped now. So she went ahead and considered the problem that had plagued her since Dr. Saul Reed swept into her life.

Which one's worse—me or God? God, for knowing everything but not paying enough attention to listen to Nancy's prayers but granting mine when I begged for a different life? Or me, for forgetting to ask that Nancy could come with me?

The searing, dry, scratchy feeling clawed its way up the back of her throat to her eyelids until the heat of tears stung the dryness away. Midge willed the tears away, digging her fingernails into her palms in rhythmic squeezes until it seemed the series of red half-moons would never fade. They would. They always did.

But for now, the important thing was that they got rid of the tears so no one would know how much she hated sitting here. How much she hated pretending to belong next to the Reeds, how much she wanted to scream at them all to wake up—that they deserved better than a God who wouldn't come through for them when they most needed Him. Midge knew it—she'd lived it. Her sister lived it...then died from it. And all the pretty praise songs in the world wouldn't change it.

So she went back to the circle of questions she'd chased since she first realized they were chasing her back. *I'm worse—Nancy was my sister, and it was my fault we got kicked out of the textile mill and she fell in with Rodney. It fell to me to protect her, and when I couldn't do it in life, I absolutely could have in my prayers. I deserved to be punished for being so selfish.*

Only, there was a problem with this answer. The same problem she'd come up against for the past four years. Did Midge deserve to be punished? Without a doubt.

But Nancy didn't. Nancy deserved all the wonderful things in the world, and instead God gave her sorrow and pain and death. So either He wasn't paying close enough attention, because He got the wrong sister, or He knew hurting Nancy would hurt me most. She sucked in a sharp breath.

Because the cycle didn't end there. Four years ago, when she first came to Buttonwood, Midge had been convinced prayer didn't work. God either didn't hear them or didn't care. The reason why prayer proved ineffective didn't matter so much as the fact it was. Back then, Midge was still stuck on the fact she'd asked for a better life, and she hadn't realized she only assumed God would know that included Nancy.

At one point, Clara almost had her convinced she'd gotten it turned wrong way around and she needed to add more praise to her prayers and less requests. So after thinking on it, Midge decided to give it one last try—and thanked God for the one solid thing she couldn't help but be thankful for. She praised him for the fine house that kept her and the new people she cared about safe and happy.

The next day, it burned down—almost killing Clara and Opal in the process. As she looked at the ashes, Midge knew that something had gone wrong. Either she'd messed up her prayers somehow, or God had botched up again. Whichever way, it was a pattern she didn't plan on repeating.

But even as she sat on that stiff pew in the middle of church, vowing once again not to get caught up in that same problem, Midge couldn't help but make one small comment—and if God heard her, so be it.

All right, maybe we both messed up. But only one of us is supposed to be perfect. . . .

Amos sat beside his mother and the oldest of his younger brothers in church, enjoying what he found to be a first-rate sermon. Church was the one time Midge didn't command his attention—even though she always fidgeted the whole way through. But by the end of today's teaching, he'd cast more than a few concerned glances her way.

Her face—more tan than just about any other woman's he'd ever known, since she hardly ever wore her bonnet—went oddly white. It made her freckles stand out more, but for once Amos didn't find it entrancing. Something was wrong—and he wanted to know what it was.

No, he admitted to himself, *I want to take care of whatever the problem is and bring back her smile.* Not that he had any right. Or even that he should want to take such a role in her life. *But I do. Midge Collins caught my attention four years ago, and when I saw her again in Buttonwood, it seemed she'd never let go.*

So Amos had done a fair bit of praying, talked it over with Ma, and made his decision. His fascination with this woman hadn't ebbed—so it stood to reason God was pointing him in her direction. *She's running away from me just as fast, but it's been a steady pull, and the Lord will have His way with us both.*

At the conclusion of the service, while everyone clustered around the miller and Miss Chandler, Amos hunted down a few folks who wouldn't need today's introduction. It took a little doing, but with the right maneuvering, he managed to get Dr. Saul Reed, the doctor's father, Josiah, and both their wives on the far side of the church. Away from everyone else.

Not a one of them said a word—he wouldn't have if he were in their boots. All four looked at him expectantly—unblinking. If he didn't find it so amusing, it would be downright eerie. As it stood, he got the impression they already knew the general reason he'd snuck them over for a private conversation.

"Afternoon, Reeds." He gave a respectful nod—directed mostly toward the men. "I appreciate you coming over to talk with me on such short notice."

"So talk." From anyone else, the words might have sounded short, but Josiah Reed had a smile on his lips and a knowing look in his eye that told of a good nature.

"Don't rush the man, Josiah." His wife, an even better-natured woman by the name of Doreen, if Amos recalled rightly, shot her husband a warning glance before fixing her gaze on him once again. And again, forgetting how to blink.

"No rush at all. I want you to know I've taken my time about this, brought it before the Lord before bringing the matter to you." Approving nods—and restless fidgeting from Dr. Reed's wife— met this pronouncement. "Normally, I'd just speak with Dr. Reed about this matter, but your family is as close as mine, and that's something I respect. So I stand before all of you this afternoon, seeking your permission to court Miss Collins."

"I knew it!" Clara Reed burst out. "Knew it at the dinner party. You have my approval, Mr. Geer."

"Same here." Josiah added his two cents. "Now that you spit it out." A wink softened his gripe.

"Well, aren't you two quick to agree?" Dr. Reed raised his brows at his wife and father. "Traditionally, the man explains what he has to offer the girl and why he's interested."

"That's when he's asking permission to propose," his wife reminded. "Mr. Geer only asked about courting."

"I knew right off Clara was the match for you," Josiah reminded his son of a fact Amos hadn't even known. "Maybe someday you'll learn to trust my instincts."

"Midge trusts her own instincts." The elder Mrs. Reed's quiet voice cut through the chatter. "And she avoids Mr. Geer." Her brows drew together. "I'm not entirely certain that's a bad sign, but it's by no means something I assume to be good. So I'll leave it at this: You've my approval to spend as much time with Midge as she'll allow. If you're the right man, you'll convince her to see things your way."

"She avoids you?" The good doctor seemed to be tabulating something in his head.

"Yes." Bad as it sounded, Amos wouldn't lie. "I disconcert her. She seems rather used to getting her way and winning most battles of wit or will."

"You've answered my next question—whether you know her well enough to be sure you want to court her."

"Well enough to want to know more—though I've a question I'd like answered, if you wouldn't mind." Amos jumped on Dr. Reed's statement. "Something I surmised, but Midge won't admit or explain. I'd appreciate it if you'd shed some light on the topic."

Uneasy glances and surreptitious head shakes had him wondering what the Reeds feared he'd ask. "We'll try," seemed the best he could hope for.

"The night of the dinner party, I noticed Midge seemed unusually preoccupied with keeping order in the kitchen. I think she hides a fear of fire."

"No wonder she avoids you—you pay such close attention." Most people would have missed Doreen's comment beneath a flurry of explanations, but Amos heard it loud and clear.

That means Midge hides more than one secret. I wonder what they are? He tucked the intriguing question away to play with later.

For now, he listened as Clara Reed's voice won out and she

started over again with an answer to his question. "Four years ago, we had a house fire. Opal Speck—Grogan, now—and I were inside, and we almost didn't make it out. Saul and Adam pulled us to safety. Ever since then, Midge has become very vigilant about keeping watch over the stove...even though it was a fireplace that caused the problem."

"I see. It makes sense now."

"She's very protective of those she loves." A smile spread across Dr. Reed's face. "Midge needs a strong man, and so far none in Buttonwood have been able to match her." He stuck out his hand for a firm shake. "It's settled. You have our blessing."

"Thank you." Amos moved along to shake Josiah's hand. "You won't regret it, I assure you."

"Of course not, Mr. Geer." The older man shook his head. "We just can't promise you the same thing."

CHAPTER 19

Daisy, darling, I'm ever so sorry for you." Cornelia Walthingham poked her snub nose in the air and looked down it. "You must be perfectly devastated that he's dropped you."

"She cried off, you silly goose." Alice Porth, a girl Daisy privately used to consider too plainspoken for her own good, came to her defense. "He didn't drop her. No man would!"

"I'd never say such a thing." Daisy managed a small, secretive smile, which dissolved the instant her teacup reached her lips. *Not out of modesty, but because it's not true. Cornelia has it right—Trouston dropped me. And I was wrong about Alice.* She set down her cup with an uncharacteristic *clink*. *She's perfectly lovely.*

"Terribly conniving of you to suggest otherwise, Cornelia. It smacks of jealousy." Daphne Kessel joined the ranks of friends supporting Daisy in her time of need. "Particularly considering the way Trouston carries on about the whole thing."

Dread clutched her stomach, making Daisy reach for yet another pastry as she tried to seem carefree. "Whatever do you mean? I've not seen him, of course."

"Don't you know? He's crushed by your defection. Claims he'll never love another." Alice swiped the last cake from the tray, so Daisy rang for more. "He's gone so far as to don a black armband to signify that he's mourning your loss."

"Ridiculous." Suddenly she lost her appetite. The very idea Trouston made such sport over the way he'd used her and ended their relationship, making a show of himself to draw attention and pity, it created a swell of such rage, even shopping couldn't possibly cure it. "Pure theatrics. It's one of the reasons I came to see we wouldn't suit."

"He swears you'll come back to him." A jealous gleam lit Cornelia's gaze. "That no other woman can capture his attention and he won't leave off until you're his once more."

"Trouston will persist for precisely so long as it takes him to realize black armbands, when worn consistently, stain certain fabrics." Daisy knew she made her ex-fiancé sound petty, and perhaps sounded rather low herself, but she didn't care. "He's exceedingly conscientious about his appearance."

"Not so conscientious he wouldn't fight for you." Daphne gave a little sigh. "It's positively romantic the way he's threatened any man who so much as looks at you to a duel."

"What?" Daisy's posture, already held straight by her tightly laced corset, became even more rigid.

"Mr. Dillard says he simply can't abide the thought of you with another man, and thus he won't allow one anywhere near you." Alice leaned forward. "Haven't you wondered why none of your old beaus have come to renew their suits?"

"I presumed they were exercising judicious manners and allowing a respectful period of time to pass so as not to offend me or Mr. Dillard." Daisy delivered the line just as she'd rehearsed, for of course she'd wondered. *Though I assumed that somehow men possessed an uncanny ability to know when a woman had been despoiled and would no longer be of interest to them.* "It never occurred to me that Trouston was making threats to hold them at bay. Of all the nerve!"

"Every woman appreciates a man who knows what he wants. When will you put him out of this miserable waiting period and take him back?"

"Yes, when?"

"Can you arrange for us to watch the reunion?" A flurry of exclamations greeted Mama's question.

"Mama, I already made it clear. I won't take Trouston back." *He doesn't want me to. It would ruin his scheme to play merry bachelor for the rest of his born days, leaving a string of heartbroken women in his wake.* The thought lent a very convincing sniff to her own performance.

"But you must! You simply must." The torrent of feminine cries blended into one shrill babble, making Daisy wince.

"It's so dashing, the way he's working to win you back." Alice, in particular, refused to drop the matter. "You'll seem a horrid, hard-hearted tease if you refuse him."

"*'Playtime is over, Daisy.'*" Trouston stopping her when she tried to ease some distance between them. . . "*'You belong to me, and no man likes a tease. . . .'*" Another piece of her murky memories from that night rose to the surface, making her gasp.

"I'm not a tease." Tears sprang to her eyes. *If I were, this wouldn't be happening. I'd still be engaged, not knowing what an awful man I chose, instead of sitting here in polite company, pretending to be one of them. Pretending I'm not base and ruined and not worth their time or friendship.* "Excuse me, but I'm afraid I've come down with a megrim."

"You do look frightfully pale." Mama frowned. "Go rest for a while. I'll check on you in a bit."

Placing one hand to her temple, Daisy skirted around her friends and various pieces of furniture until she reached the hall. The moment she slipped from sight, she sagged against the wall, drawing in a ragged breath. *It's only a matter of time until they see what I've come to. Lord, I can't go back and fix it. I can't remake myself into what I was before I erred so badly. . .and all the wishes in the world can't make it better.* She swallowed a sob.

"She did not look well." The words were proper, but Cornelia's tone carried no concern. Instead, a malicious hint of satisfaction underscored her observation.

"Daisy simply hasn't been the same since she threw over Mr. Dillard." Daphne drummed her fingernails on the rim of her saucer as she always did when unsettled. "I worry for her."

"As we all do."

"If she doesn't recover her composure soon, it may be too late for her to find someone else." The satisfaction sounded even more pronounced now, and Daisy determined to have nothing more to do with Cornelia. "If she's truly foolish enough to let a prize like Mr. Dillard slip away."

A prize he's not. She didn't want to hear any more. Placing one hand on the banister, Daisy headed up the stairs on silent slippers until she reached her room. *But slipping away. . .if only I could manage to. Everything would be better.*

Eschewing the bed, she reclined on the divan near her dressing room and thought of how much she wished her cousin were there. *Marge wouldn't have left me alone with Trouston. And Marge would know what to do, now, after. . .* The tears she'd held at bay rolled down the bridge of her nose. *I wish Marge were here, instead of out west. Or that we could change places and I could be far, far away from Trouston and all the mealy-mouthed misses still besotted with him.*

She sat bolt upright. *What am I thinking? I can be far away—it's the perfect solution.* Her first real smile in days tugged at the corners of her lips, and she gave in to an unladylike grin. *I'll surprise Marge with a visit!*

≈≪⬡≫≈

The way Gavin saw things, ladies liked surprises. So long as they weren't creepy, crawly, slimy, dirty, or involving hard work, women couldn't get enough of the unexpected.

All right, if I'm going to be out here almost before the sun decides to rise, I may as well be blunt about the matter. Ladies don't like surprises—they like gifts.

Well, who didn't? Gifts showed a woman she was being thought of. Cared for. Appreciated. No souls on earth could deny wanting those things—not without lying through their teeth, at least. Presents made for tangible expressions of the things people had a hard time talking about.

In other words, a present made the perfect way to further his case with Marge and speed up this courting process. She wanted him to prove his desire to marry her—and asking didn't suffice. Showing her off to the whole town and laying claim seemed to backfire. Brett Burn hadn't been the only one whose eyes lingered too long. Nor had Gavin missed the way they all seemed to find reason to chat with her whenever he escorted her into town these days.

Gavin pulled his hat brim lower and squinted, trying to make out the different low-lying plants hidden by prairie grasses. He didn't make a habit out of hunting plants, but exceptions existed for every rule. It didn't matter if he had to tromp around for miles before he'd found and gathered enough of what he'd come looking for. Gavin didn't intend to show up at breakfast empty-handed this morning.

Prove it. Her challenge rang in his ears as he spied the first of his unofficial harvest and fell to with a vengeance. If words didn't prove it and standing beside her didn't prove it and respecting her wish to help set up the school didn't prove it, Gavin had one more weapon in his arsenal to show a woman that he valued her. He'd prove it with a strategy so well laid even Marge Chandler couldn't deny it.

And she'd like it.

With a resolute nod, Gavin stepped over the area he'd stripped bare and moved on. *More.* A handful wouldn't be enough, and a man only got one chance to pull off a grand gesture. Repeating a failed attempt just looked foolish—and he wasn't a man to play the fool. Nor was he typically a man to play the romantic, but Gavin had already lost one bride. If a little show of finer feeling netted him another, at least he'd keep his pride.

Show me a man who won't tromp over ten miles of prairie gathering wildflowers to salvage his pride and earn a bride, and I'll show you a liar or a lout. Though not every man could put a personal twist on the exercise—a sweet sentiment designed to win a woman's heart.

Not only would he earn favor by presenting Marge with flowers, he upped the ante in several ways. First, by gathering them himself, which meant he put out effort, as opposed to the way things were done back in Baltimore where a man purchased such things. Then, he'd remembered her favorite color—purple—and only chosen flowers of that shade. *Good thing the strange breed blooms around here. . . .* As the crowning touch, he brought Marge a bouquet of no flower but wild daisies. . .same as her name.

This was the type of thing women went wild for. Romance, thoughtfulness, individuality, a creative flair—all told, he should have her consent to wed him before the week ended. They'd stand before Parson Carter, with the entire town looking on and wishing them well, next Sunday.

Three days is short notice. Best make it some day next week. I'll let Marge decide, to keep her happy. Good to make the little woman feel as though she's involved.

By the time he'd gathered a huge bouquet and made his way back to the house, Gavin felt better than he had in over a week.

Time to win a wife!

CHAPTER 20

The days settled into an easy pattern. Too easy. Marge awoke the following Thursday feeling as though something had changed. She lay perfectly still beneath the warm weight of the bedclothes, trying to determine the difference. When she couldn't, she closed her eyes. *Lord, what new thing awaits me this morning? I try to put my trust in You—though I'm afraid my hopes still lie with Gavin. Whatever the day holds, help me trust in You, and help me put my hope where it belongs.*

Upon opening her eyes again, Marge suddenly knew. The icy misgivings that she'd clenched around her heart since the moment Ermintrude first mentioned Daisy's name now thawed. All the concern and hurt and disappointment hadn't melted away, but the unrelenting, pinching pressure of it lessened. She pushed the covers aside and hopped out of bed, eager to get downstairs for her morning debate with Ermintrude as they prepared breakfast.

I'm trying, Lord. Thank You for seeing that and helping.

She tackled her long mane of hair, amazed to find her brush sliding easily through the thick strands. Since her first night in

Buttonwood, she'd slept so restlessly it'd become a morning battle to untangle night's knots. As a result, she beat the older woman downstairs and had the milk and water already inside by the time Ermintrude showed up.

"Either you're rising earlier, or I'm sleeping later. I choose to believe it's the former."

"I agree."

"Now *there's* a pleasant surprise." Ermintrude's brows winged upward until they almost touched her hairline. "I take it you've grown tired of losing our little arguments every morning and decided to take the easy way out from now on?"

"Hardly. I enjoy our *discussions*." Marge emphasized the final word in that sentence. "Arguments indicate a sort of bitterness and a cyclical futility I don't believe describes the way we converse."

"That's more like it." She thumped her cane on the floor in approval. "Glad to see you've not lost your spirit."

"On the contrary, it grows stronger by the day."

"Then Buttonwood must be doing you some good." The deep timber of Gavin's voice in the doorway caused them both to turn around. He stood there, one arm behind his back, a broad smile brightening his face.

"You're early, too." Ermintrude's grumble sounded genuine, and Marge softened slightly at the idea the older woman felt cheated of their debate time.

"We'll continue our conversation later today. Don't think you've escaped." Her jest had the intended effect, making her opponent straighten up at once in anticipation.

"You'll be the one wanting to escape!"

"No." Gavin crooked a finger, still keeping one arm behind his back as he called to her, "Marge wants to come over here."

Instantly suspicious, she didn't budge. "We've played this

game, Gavin. I said I'd give no more steps until you proved yourself worthy." It didn't help the situation that Ermintrude watched them both with avid curiosity.

"That's what I'm trying to do. We were far closer at the end of that round. Give me that, at least."

Against her better judgment, her curiosity guiding her, Marge shuffled until only a few feet separated them. "This is as far as I go." *Physically, at least.* Her heart and dreams drummed onward, until her hopes placed her firmly in his arms. *He says he's trying to prove himself—Lord, let him succeed! Please, please let this be the end of the difficulty and that be the reason I felt better this morning.*

"I told you I'd earn my prize." His stare caught her, held her fast. "You told me to prove myself. I've spoken the words, shown you before my peers and been proud to claim you, treated you well as the woman in my home." Here, he ignored a faint squawk from Ermintrude, though it sounded more like a reminder of her presence than any true protest. "I've proven myself in all the ways I know how, save the traditional courting gifts."

"Oh, Gavin." Shame flooded her even as something softened at his determination. Could it be that Gavin truly wanted to wed her for reasons beyond duty or guilt at his mistake? "No gifts. It was never my intent for you to purchase anything."

"They say the thought matters most." He pulled a massive bouquet from behind his back with a dramatic flourish. "I bring these to you and hope you read my thoughts and find all the proof you seek." He held the bunch of flowers in front of him, his expression gleefully expectant.

Marge stared at the overlarge clump of daisies he thrust toward her, mind working furiously. Smashed together, the blossoms wilted, bent, leaned at unnatural positions. Leaves trapped between the stalks poked through Gavin's thick fingers as though trying to escape confinement. All told, the flowers looked about as manipulated and abused as Marge felt.

"Thank you." Somehow she choked out the expected phrase. *He's trying. He brought you flowers. He picked them himself. They're even your favorite color—not that he remembers that. But he's trying, at least.* Some logical, optimistic part of her mind sent a litany of cheery thoughts in an attempt to mitigate the crashing disappointment, but it was no use.

Daisies. Daisy. The cousin he wanted but didn't get. He promises to show me his true heart and prove he wants me but brings the only thing he could possibly find to symbolize the bride he cannot have. Rigid cold spread its fingers through her chest once more, stretching their reach beyond where they'd dipped the first time she'd seen Gavin's heart.

"Aren't you going to take them?" Two lines furrowed between Gavin's brows as he inspected his offering. "You seem overcome?"

The statement sounded like a question as Marge started to raise one hand to accept his gift then dropped it back to her side. "I can't accept these, Gavin." She took a step back—a larger step than normal, though she doubted he'd notice. "I appreciate what you're trying to say and the thoughtful manner you chose to do so. Thank you."

"If you don't like them I can pick something else." His grip tightened, forcing the poor plants into even more contorted positions. "Your cousin only likes violets and roses, but I thought you'd appreciate these."

"You still think of her often?" Marge let loose a humorless rasp of laughter. It was either that or allow the parched ache in the back of her throat to bleed into dry sobs. "You can't have Daisy, so to tell me you've made your peace with your second choice, you bring me her namesake?"

"What?" Astonishment blanketed his features. "No. Marguerite means *daisy*. These are your namesake, Marge, every bit as much as your cousin's."

"I don't identify myself with the flowers."

"But. . ." Frustration brought his brows together entirely, and she could practically see him turning over her interpretation of his gift in his head, unable to argue with it. "Grandma, didn't you tell me these aren't even real daisies? They're Tahoka daisies—a sort of wild version. Different." He beamed as though that made everything better. . .instead of worse.

"Uu–u–g–g–h–h." A *thud* punctuated Ermintrude's moan.

Marge couldn't be certain, but she suspected the older woman dropped her head onto the table. Heavily. Which meant that Ermintrude, at least, saw the reason why Gavin should have kept this little fact to himself.

"I see." She stared at the increasingly bedraggled grouping as though it threatened to bite her. "So they're *fake* daisies?"

Marge saw the moment he realized where he'd gone wrong—he caught himself midnod and started shaking his head vehemently.

Too little, too late.

Where did it all go wrong? Gavin knew well and good he didn't have the time to hammer out when his scheme turned rotten, but the entire thing carried the flavor of an ambush. *When I realized she objected to the idea of my giving her daisies, I shouldn't have tried to soften it by backtracking on what sort of daisy they were.* That much, he should've seen coming.

Now, she'd stepped back from him. Not a small step, or even a series of hesitant shuffles, but one great big decisive step that showed he'd well and truly damaged his chances this time. Worse, no matter how fetching she looked with her eyes that bright, Marge seemed to be gaining more steam than she let off.

"Imposters, I suppose? Like myself?" Her voice rose with each question, gaining volume but losing fullness, as though getting louder somehow stretched it out.

"No. Absolutely not. Marge, that's not what I meant at all." He moved to close the distance she'd increased, but she backed away more with every move he made, until the kitchen table sat between them, with Ermintrude right smack in the center of it all. "You're taking this the wrong way."

"Since you asked me to read your thoughts by your gift and you brought fake daisies for the imposter who arrived in place of the Daisy you sought, I'm taking it rather well."

"If that's the way I meant it, you would be." Frustration started to seep through into his own tone. After all, he'd made a real effort here. *Even if I botched it.*

"Man finds himself in a hole, best thing to do"—Grandma poked him in the side with her cane to let him know she wasn't making a general observation, as though she ever just made general observations—"stop digging!"

"I thought you'd like them, so I went and got them for you. Being wrong about your reaction doesn't change the reason I did it." A muscle ticked in his jaw. "Purple is your favorite."

"You knew that?" His fiancée's stance relaxed slightly.

"Yes. You said so on the day you came to town—your dress was your favorite color." He scowled at the thought she implied he would lie about such a thing. "Easy enough to remember."

"But not everyone would." She softened a little more.

"I did. And I remembered that you're a flower every bit as much as your cousin. But when I picked you a bouquet, you looked at it like I insulted you." He stared down at the pitiful, if still enormous, lump of flowers in his hand. Suddenly he didn't want to be in the house anymore, standing in front of the woman who kept refusing him, holding a clump of mangled blossoms as though still hoping she'd accept them.

"Call when breakfast is ready." With that, he stalked outside, going a few paces before flinging the daisies into the dirt.

This is why men don't make grand gestures very often. When they fail, the blast knocks us back farther than we can afford. Now Gavin had to come up with a new plan.

Just as soon as he decided whether or not he really wanted to.

CHAPTER 21

I don't want to ask him. Midge grappled with the issue, livid at how well Amos had played his hand. Somehow, the man understood that the one thing she couldn't stand—aside from someone hurting any of her people, a depth to which Amos would never stoop no matter how badly he wanted her attention—was awareness of her own ignorance.

She took pride in knowing things no one else did—noticing what others didn't bother to look for reaped many rewards. So she didn't often find herself the last to know something. And it was driving her up the wall—or at least as close to it as physically possible.

The agitation provoked by Amos's secret, which everyone stayed cursedly closed lipped about, took her all over town. Clara beamed at her in the kitchen but wouldn't spill whatever Amos told them. So Midge hied off to Saul's office, waited for him to finish treating a patient, and launched into an interrogation he withstood with good humor—but no information.

Which took her to Josiah, in the general store. Midge made

herself pleasant and useful, but her adopted grandfather didn't return the favor. He'd outright laughed at her attempts to nudge anything out of him and directed her to go ask Amos.

When Midge tracked down Aunt Doreen helping the Dunstalls with an afternoon of baking at the town café, she'd heard the same advice.

An exhausting day of fruitless attempts to coax anything from her loved ones brought Midge to the edge of becoming cranky. She squashed her irritation and made a fresh try the next day. And the next. Now, after a week of trying to wear down any of the adults in her makeshift family and failing to elicit anything but amusement, Midge needed a new strategy.

Pretending she didn't care wasted time. Not only did all the Reeds know better, Amos suspected her true reaction. If he didn't give her so much grief, Midge might even have given him some measure of respect for his clever scheme. She avoided him whenever he came near—so he'd thought up a way to make her come to him. A grudging appreciation for his shift in tactics didn't bring her any closer to thwarting him though.

She scowled. *If I could somehow let it go—not care about whatever he trumped up to manufacture a senseless conspiracy—that would show him how far above his silly games I am.* Midge gave a resolute sniff, turned on her heel, and headed back toward the house.

Or my apathy will provoke him to new heights. Her steps slowed. *I can't maintain the pretense of disinterest in the face of a continual onslaught. And the longer I hold out, the more humbling it will be when I finally ask him for something.* She halted in the middle of the street, debating.

Only a fool persisted in winning minor battles if it meant losing the larger war. *It's been five days—near enough to a week to show him he can't pull my strings so easily. If I wait longer, he'll know how much I fought against my curiosity.* Somehow, she'd almost arrived at the site of the schoolhouse before making the decision to go there. *So now is the best time to face him—beard the lion in his den, so to speak.*

Come to think of it, *lion* proved an apt association for him. The afternoon sun gleamed gold on his sandy hair, darkened at his temples from perspiration. As she drew closer, Midge watched him draw a large handkerchief from his back pocket, her gaze following the motion of his hand upward. Vaguely she noted that he wiped his brow, but Midge's attention caught on the breadth of his shoulders.

At some point during the day, as he shaped clay, straw, and water into the thick sun-baked bricks to build the reddish schoolhouse, he'd abandoned his coat. The loose white lawn of his shirt caught whatever scant breeze chanced by, the wind playing a happy game of hide-and-seek with his chest as it alternately pressed then lifted the fabric away. Dark suspenders outlined the broad V of his back as he mopped his neck and returned the bandanna to his pocket.

Midge sucked in a breath. No matter how devious his mind, there was no denying Amos Geer cut a fine figure of a man.

At least, he did until he turned to give her one of those slow, infuriating grins of his.

"Like what you see?"

His question made her throat go dry. "I suppose." Midge framed her answer cautiously. He'd snagged her staring, and it wouldn't do to pretend not to know what he meant. "Though the view improves with distance."

"Odd. The walls aren't tall enough to be seen from far off." His brows knit as though considering her words, and Midge realized her mistake.

"It's easier to imagine," she hastened to cover her mistake. *Amos didn't see me looking him over.* Relief tingled all the way to her toes.

"Now that's the first smile I've seen from you in a while." He tilted his hat back atop his head. "Pretty sight."

"I smile often." She stopped herself midglower and gave an overly sweet simper. "Interesting you see otherwise."

"Well, every minx needs some time to sharpen her tongue. I assume you credit me with the ability to withstand your practice."

Midge strangled a laugh at the quick brilliance of his riposte, instead focusing on her response. "Is it any wonder I lose my habitual good humor around you?"

"Wonders abound." His gaze grew more intense. "Although you don't seem the type to lose much."

"Oh?" *If only you knew.* "You might be surprised."

Amos watched the mirth fade from her features and could have kicked himself for whatever he'd said to provoke the signs of sorrow that stretched soul deep.

Fool. The Reeds took her in—obviously she's lost much. It was just too easy to forget that in the face of her vibrancy.

"What have you lost?" He wanted to step closer but sensed she'd see it as a violation. Instead, he held his ground.

"No less than anyone else." Sadness sifted into wariness. She must have realized too much of her thoughts showed.

Amos found himself torn between wanting her to stop throwing up barriers and donning cheerful masks and hating to see any glimpse of suffering in this indomitable woman. "Most likely, you've lost more than many."

"I do fancy myself to be exceptional, but in this case I'd gladly forfeit my status." An impish grin told him she'd recovered from whatever regrets tugged at her heart moments before. "Seems I'm doomed to lose many things."

"Such as?" He followed the prompt of her exaggerated sigh.

"Push buttons. I lose track of time when I'm enjoying myself. My temper, when I'm not." The grin grew shrewd. "But most of all, it seems I can't keep hold of my patience."

He burst out laughing at her display of wit. "So now we've come down to it—the reason for your unscheduled visit to the schoolhouse site?"

"You dance well, but I lack grace. Mr. Geer, you know full well why I've come here today."

"Ran out of the last drop of your limited supply of patience but have a surplus of curiosity?" Amos hazarded a guess and was rewarded with her grudging nod. "You held out longer than I'd anticipated."

"What? I wasn't holding anything."

It was almost too easy, but he couldn't resist prodding her. While she'd been refusing to come ask him what he'd spoken with her family about, he'd cooled his heels waiting on her pride. He raised his brows in a credible imitation of surprise. "Then you've lost more than your patience. What were those other things you listed—track of time? Must be the reason you've dawdled so long before coming to talk to me."

"Dawdled?" Scathing tones made the echo blister, but she hushed and didn't continue with whatever she'd almost set loose. Which, of course, made it all the more interesting.

Luckily, Amos knew well and good what she'd been up to for the past five days. Midge Collins didn't dawdle. She asked, interrogated, wheedled, and downright demanded information, but she'd kept busy trying to ferret out information for the entire week. Amos knew, because he'd kept himself entertained watching her venture all over town trying to run her family members into the ground. Apparently none of them had broken their promise not to reveal what he'd asked. Doreen even went so far as to commend his strategy.

"Your family wouldn't explain my request, I take it."

"Not so much as a peep." This was the closest thing to an admission of trying to discover what he'd said to them that Midge was likely to make. Yet she didn't come out and ask him.

"You're adorable when thwarted."

"I," she seethed at his compliment, "am *not* adorable."

"*Cute* describes children, and *pretty* is too common." He crossed his arms and made a show of looking her up and down. "We both know, Miss Collins, that you're anything but common."

"I'm many things." She looked somewhat mollified in spite of herself. Irritation turned to expectation, and she lifted a brow to prompt him. "Right now, I'm waiting."

"And I'm considering the minute possibility I was wrong."

"Of course you are." She shifted her weight from one foot to the other. "About what this time?"

This time. Ha. Her attempts to goad him affected him in exactly the opposite way. The more she opposed his attention, the more firmly he fixed it upon her. "If I am wrong in this instance, you bear the blame."

Triumph flashed in her eyes before wariness dampened it— she was too clever to think she'd won that easily. "How so?"

"If you aren't adorable, it's only because you won't let yourself be adored." He finally took the step he'd been denying himself, closing the distance between them. "*Now* tell me I'm wrong."

She stared at him in a silence that brought him more satisfaction than all the sparring he'd enjoyed before. "No."

728

"No?" He noticed she didn't step back. Whether she simply stood her ground out of stubbornness or didn't mind his nearness was hard to tell. Except he remembered their first meeting and knew Midge wouldn't put herself within arm's reach unless she felt good and comfortable there. "I want you to."

"But you're right. Adoration isn't for me. I don't look for it and I won't inspire it." She tilted her head a notch to look him in the eye. "So for once, we agree."

"In that case"—Amos reached and tweaked a strand of hair that escaped her bun, fingering its softness before tucking it behind her ear—"I intend to prove us both wrong."

CHAPTER 22

Flummoxed. Midge could find only that single word to describe what Amos had done. She couldn't quite manage to get past it. And he knew it, too. The knowledge danced in his eyes and the slightly lopsided tilt to his smile.

He flummoxed me. She waited for a tart reply to spring to mind, but none did. Midge blinked. *Why? What is it about this man that he unsettles me?* She fixed on that lopsided tilt, refusing to look away but unable to meet his expectant stare. *Is it simply because he wants to?*

"Have you gone mad?" The very idea that Amos Geer succeeded in making sport of her brought Midge to her senses.

"Not at all."

She waited for an explanation, but it seemed she'd wait in vain. Meanwhile, his smile didn't diminish one bit. *He can't be serious. A man like Amos Geer, adoring a girl like me?* She didn't have to fake the snort of laughter that erupted from the very thought.

"What's so funny?"

"You." She took a savage satisfaction in watching his smile slip a notch. "You almost sounded serious."

"I am." Nothing in his face indicated otherwise. No laughter, no anger at hers—just an intensity that made her mirth dry up in an instant.

"You can't be." *Not me. Not the real Midge Collins.* She stared him down right back. *If you knew even a hint of the truth, you'd see why I laughed.* She took in a gulp of air. *And why I'm not laughing now.*

Truth be told, Midge knew as deep down as a body could that she wasn't a good woman. Oh, she tried to be. Four years with Saul and Clara taught her a lot about the way people should live and love, and she'd come a long way from the bitter child Dr. Reed plucked from a back alleyway. But lessons learned late in life only sank so deep. No one could wash away the sort of filth that seeped into a person's core early on.

Lucky thing of it was most folks didn't look that deep. Didn't care to and didn't know how. So Midge got by on being friendly and clever and following the rules. Well, most of them, anyway. Someday she'd marry a man who didn't look too closely and would never realize the taint she carried—and she'd make sure he was happy.

"Ask me what I spoke with your family about, Midge." The deep timbre of his voice caressed her name, luring her closer.

"What did you speak with my family about?" It didn't count as obeying orders, since she'd planned on asking him long before her feet brought her here.

"I wanted permission to court you." With that, he closed the door on any doubts about his sincerity.

But Amos Geer was a rare one. Before her stood a man who wouldn't just look into the heart of the woman he chose, he'd demand she give it to him entirely. If he glanced her way much longer, he'd see what she hid. Which, come to think of it, might be the easiest way to convince him he didn't want her.

Midge ignored a pang at the thought. Fact of the matter was she'd fought too hard to make it this long and still be Midge. She didn't plan to make a lot of changes or give up everything she'd built for the sake of a man—no matter how clever or handsome he may be.

"They approved." It wasn't a question. They both knew he wouldn't mention the matter if he hadn't received permission.

He nodded anyway.

"Well then"—she indulged in a sigh—"I suppose you'd best walk me home."

"I'd be delighted." His smile returned as he offered his arm, not in the least bit put off by her easy capitulation.

So he's not solely interested in a challenge. She watched him from the corner of her eye as they walked along in silence. *No matter. All I have to do is be myself and I'll chase him off in no time. It's for his own good—because spending time with Amos Geer doesn't appeal in the slightest.*

She kept walking, ignoring the silence. Ignoring the stares of the townspeople as they passed by. But most of all, ignoring the tiny voice in her head that got louder with every step.

Liar.

If she heard it again, Daisy very much feared she'd scream right there in the middle of the soiree. As things stood, she scarcely kept a hold on her temper. But truly, even the most well-bred of women had her limits.

"Daisy!" She didn't even see the woman's face before she found herself swept into a matronly hug. "I'm so sorry. . . ." Mrs. Such-and-Such, whose name escaped Daisy at the moment, blathered on about broken hearts and their more horrifying counterpart—broken engagements.

She didn't really listen. The vibrations of her teeth grinding genteelly behind a grateful nod blocked out most of the speech. Not that it mattered—she'd already said *it*. The phrase Daisy now loathed with every fiber of her being. She'd heard people say often enough that no one wished to be pitied, but she'd never experienced the humbling nature of it before.

Outings used to be marked with smiles and laughter, chitchat and flattery, admiring glances and merriment. Now, that single, awful phrase eclipsed it all.

"I'm sorry. I'm so sorry. I'm *so* sorry. I'm so *sorry*." Even the overblown "I'm *so sorry*." All winged their way in an attack to make Grecian Harpies proud. No matter if and where the speaker placed the emphasis, the syllables remained the same. And so did their effect.

"I must go." With a cursory nod, she abandoned the mouthy matron in the midst of her monologue and took a turn about the room. *To Buttonwood, to be exact.*

She'd looked into taking the train, but as she should have remembered from earlier conversations with Marge, the train didn't go through that area. The stage wouldn't leave for a couple days and would take a frightfully long time—if Daisy were so foolish as to think she could manage traveling alone.

Marge handled such things with aplomb, but Daisy didn't. *Just look what happened the last time I was unchaperoned for any length of time.* She shoved the thought back to the dark recesses of her memory, back where she could almost convince herself it was forgotten.

Mama would stop her if she knew her plans—though Daisy fully intended to leave a reassuring note behind if her new scheme worked. She'd hatched it up upon arriving with Mama this evening and spotted Miss Lindner and her brother exiting their conveyance at almost the same time.

Mama insisted on following fashion, so the Chandlers rode about in a sprightly landau—only good for light town driving. The Lindners didn't seem to have time for fashion. To be honest, everyone seemed surprised when Trouston began calling on the quiet, bookish Elizabeth. Their very differences made them a striking couple, or so everyone exclaimed. She was pretty enough, with that black hair and pale skin—similarities Daisy ignored when Trouston came calling on her—but they shared no interests.

Daisy wished she'd paid more attention—now that she knew her ex-intended's dastardly game, she noticed Miss Lindner more. Tonight, she noticed the Lindner coach. A private coach—well sprung, expensively made, designed to stand the test of time and use. The sort of conveyance one could take long distances, if need be.

Well, I have need, and Miss Lindner should have understanding. Daisy remembered how Elizabeth disappeared for almost the entire winter after she dropped Trouston. Of course she'd feel natural empathy with Daisy's need for solitude and escape.

Which was why Daisy watched the other woman like a veritable hawk the entire evening, waiting for just the right moment to snag her elbow and draw her into an abandoned sitting room. It worked beautifully, save the complete dismay painting her new friend's features as they faced each other.

"My apologies." Daisy refused, absolutely refused, to ever say "sorry" again unless forced to do so. "We don't know each other very well, but I've a desperate need to speak with you."

Miss Lindner didn't nod or say anything encouraging but neither did she sidle toward the door. Surely that meant something good?

"I believe we have something in common, you and I." Daisy walked over to a sofa and took a seat, patting the cushion beside her in an invitation Miss Lindner could choose to refuse.

"It is my fervent hope you refer only to our good sense in not marrying Mr. Dillard." She walked to the door, and Daisy's heart sank at the thought she'd lost her chance. Instead, Elizabeth closed the door and joined her on the sofa.

"Mostly." Now that the moment arrived, Daisy found she couldn't mention her disgrace. Their disgrace. It was all just too... disgraceful.

"I see." Her companion's eyes went soft but somehow angry. "Though I hope our reasons differ somewhat?"

"I—" She couldn't hold back a telltale sniffle as the enormity of the situation crashed over her once again. "I'm afraid not, Miss Lindner."

The other woman didn't say a word, simply passed a perfectly pressed handkerchief and took one of Daisy's gloved hands in her own. This show of sisterhood, after being without Marge during such a confusing and important time, proved Daisy's undoing. Tears ran down her cheeks and dripped from her nose.

"I need to leave." She barely got the words out between sobs. "My cousin went out west—I miss Marge. I thought, of all people, you'd understand." Daisy dissolved into tears once more.

"You've no idea just how well I understand. I went to Vicksburg to visit my grandmother for a few months after..." A fluttery hand gesture finished a sentence neither of them could speak aloud.

"Will you help me, Miss Lindner?"

"It's Elizabeth, and of course. Any way I can."

Swiftly, Daisy outlined her plan—Marge's home out west, Elizabeth's carriage to take her there safely. When she finished, silence stretched between them.

"It belongs to my brother—you'll have to convince him. I'll do my best to help." Her new friend rose to her feet. "Take a moment to compose yourself while I find him," she advised as she slipped through the door.

Daisy wasted no time blowing her nose and drawing a few deep breaths to restore her color. To gain an extra moment between tears and facing Shane Lindner—an imposingly clever man who never failed to make her tongue-tied—she kept her back to the door. She heard it open and closed her eyes for a quick prayer that things would go well.

"What have we here?" Trouston's voice oozed across the room. "A pretty little flower—already plucked but still fresh enough to enjoy."

She sprang from the sofa and faced him. *I won't let it happen again. I won't. I can't let him drag me further away from the person I'm supposed to be—the Daisy people think they see when they look at me.* Remorse somehow lent her strength. "Leave."

"No." He unbuttoned his coat, revealing the waistcoat beneath. The motion made Daisy's stomach churn in remembrance. "You've disappointed me, holding private conversations with my other forgotten fiancée." A cold gleam lit his gaze as it traveled over her. "And I'm of a mind to teach you how to behave."

CHAPTER 23

I'm not yours to teach." She all but spat the words as he advanced. Torn between fleeing and launching herself at him, nails digging into his face, Daisy stood her ground. *My gloves would make it useless anyway.*

"You're mine, all right." Instead of respecting her newfound courage, he advanced. "Mine to teach. Mine to touch."

"No!" She backed away a second too late as his arms caught and drew her to him in a heavy clasp.

"Yes." Trouston seemed amused by her determination to keep him at bay as she straightened her arms and leaned as far back as possible to avoid him. He snagged both her wrists in one hand and jerked her close. "Mine to take, whenever I choose."

Pulling back one foot, regrettably clad only in a satin evening slipper rather than a pair of sturdy half boots, she delivered a vicious kick to his shin. A cry of pain broke from her lips as her toes took the brunt of the assault meant to cripple *him*, but, incredibly, he was letting her go. . . .

Daisy took advantage of his distraction to scamper toward the door, realizing the moment she got underway that it hadn't been her kick that stopped Trouston. Shane Lindner held him by the scruff of the neck. Odd, she'd never realized that his remarkable height lent him enough strength to lift a grown man off his feet.

But that's exactly what Shane did to Trouston now—if only for a moment. Abruptly, he released her attacker, letting Trouston fall heavily on his feet. Not that he stayed there. Shane's swift right hook sent him sprawling across the carpet. Trouston didn't get back up.

"I always thought he had a weak chin," she marveled, looking at Mr. Lindner with new respect. "Thank you for putting it to good use."

"My pleasure, Miss Chandler." A reluctant smile lifted his lips, though he tried to repress it. His efforts only brought out a well-hidden dimple Daisy never noticed before. "Now, I hear you need some transportation?"

Marge stared at the drop front desk in the guest room—a luxury this far west. Gavin ordered, transported, and implanted beautiful things. He surrounded himself with only the best.

I need to remember that. She stayed seated on the bed, fisting her hands in her lap, riveted by that desk. *I don't belong with the fine things he brought to Buttonwood. He made a home to showcase his finest prize: Daisy.*

It would be so easy to pretend it all away and act as though Gavin wanted her. If she chose, Marge could walk down the aisle with her head held high, her future assured, and no one the wiser. One of her favorite verses came to mind. *"When I was a child, I spake as a child, I understood as a child, I thought as a child. . . ."*

She'd grown up long ago, surpassing the point of make-believe and happily-ever-afters. Deep down, she'd known Gavin's letter for what it was—a tantalizing glimpse into a life not meant for her. Only, she'd wanted it so badly, she seized hold and rode out to meet it. Reality won.

Mostly.

Marge couldn't take it any longer. She rose from the bed, crossed the room, and laid one hand atop the desk front. Sliding one finger along the groove, she unlatched the hinged compartment, cradling it so it wouldn't stress the chain meant to hold it up as a writing surface. It opened to reveal the secret within.

Purple daisies, once crushed, wilted within a crystal vase. Deprived of sunlight and fresh air, they faltered far faster than they would if Marge bore the courage to display them on her night table. Instead, she hid them away. *"For where your treasure is, there will your heart be also."*

Perhaps she hadn't outgrown childish games entirely. Marge reached out to finger the soft, fragile petals of one blossom. After Gavin stalked out, she'd seen him hurl the flowers in the dirt, and something inside her howled at the sight. She'd resisted the urge to run out and gather them all up, instead biding her time until Gavin stayed at the mill and Ermintrude rested her eyes for a while.

Then she'd ventured outside, carefully selected just enough of the flowers to fill the crystal vase she'd brought from home, and snuck back inside. Unearthing the vase took longer than she expected, and once she had them properly placed, Marge realized what she'd done—what it would look like to Gavin or Ermintrude if they saw her keepsake. She'd seem a lackwit.

So she kept them closed away in her desk, companions to the words Gavin sent burrowing into her heart after she'd challenged his choice of daisies. *"Purple is your favorite. . . . You said so."*

Yes, she said so. Gavin thought it important enough to remember though. That meant something. It didn't mean a passionate, undying love. It didn't mean he'd been expecting Marge to step off that stage. But it still. . .counted.

"You're a flower every bit as much as your cousin." This is what made her sneak out to save some of those daisies. The sound of his voice, so earnest as he said sweet words. Not flattery or compliments or a calculated bid to earn her favor. No, these were sweet words uttered in exasperation. *True words.* She turned the vase slightly as she deconstructed that lovely sentence for the hundredth time.

The teacher in her couldn't resist diagramming it—pulling out the root sentence. *You're a flower. You are a flower.* Without bothering with grammar, she replayed the meaning of it. Flowers were known for color, scent, texture—sensory appeal. It took time for them to blossom, time for them to be appreciated.

I am a flower. No wonder she couldn't stop smiling whenever she opened her desk. Even better, he'd compared her to her cousin and found her equal. *Every bit.* He hadn't said, "just like." Otherwise, Marge would have discounted the entire comment. She and Daisy weren't alike. Flowers were unique—no two the same—but they could be equally attractive. *If only I knew how to thank him and apologize for how I interpreted things. . . .*

"That's a big sigh."

Marge slammed the desk shut at the sound of Ermintrude's voice. She turned to see, and sure enough, the older woman stood in her doorway. Who knew how long she'd been watching Marge moon over a stray sentence? Her only hope lay in the idea that her body blocked the flowers from view. Surely Ermintrude hadn't seen the vase.

Lord, this is the type of thing I pray about without thinking—

asking Your protection and strength. This time, I can't. My treasure and my heart aren't supposed to be of this earth, much less locked away in a drop front desk, hoping for the love of a man who wants someone else. Please help me control myself and follow the way You set out.

"Big sigh then holding your breath?" Ermintrude made her way into the room, apparently finding an invitation unnecessary. "Thinking about how much luggage you brought, wishing you'd shown a little restraint?"

"It won't do me any good cluttering the place and waiting to be repacked. I tried to hope for the best and pack for the worst." Marge eyed the mountain piled against the far wall, sprawling out into the surprisingly large room, and started to wonder where she'd put everything once she took up her official post as teacher.

Settling herself on the bed—and managing to look exceedingly comfortable—Ermintrude fixed her attention on Marge. "It's not doing you any good all boxed up."

"Yes, but it doesn't make any difference." Marge couldn't keep herself from admitting the sad truth. "Nothing I brought will help with the contingency of my groom expecting another woman."

"There's much to be said for versatility. You've been debating for days about the uselessness of hiding from disappointments."

"I'm not hiding from my luggage." *Though there are some things I don't want to unearth.* The very notion of seeing her wedding gown proved enough to make her sit down. Honesty compelled her to add, "Most of it, anyway."

For an uncharacteristic moment, Ermintrude held her peace. Stillness reigned for an endless moment the likes of which teachers dream about often. How many times had she faced a classroom of students, or her overly enthusiastic cousin, and longed for silence only to be given none? Now she had quiet so fresh it crept through the room—a crisp, intoxicating delicacy.

One Marge suddenly lost her taste for. *Why did I never realize silence simply offers an invitation to be filled? If not with sound, with the thoughts one wouldn't care to speak aloud. The sort that plague a person, preying on dreams and surfacing doubts until one realizes just how lonely quiet can be.* She blinked suddenly stinging eyes. *I miss Daisy.*

"You don't like it either." Ermintrude ended the episode. "Let me tell you something, Marge. It gets worse as you grow older. The hopes filling the silence now slowly fade into memories and regrets."

A shiver ran down her spine at the truth she sensed in the warning. *Lord, don't let me become bitter.* Immediately she felt better—good enough to challenge a prickly old woman whom she'd come to think of as a friend. "If you don't like silence, why do you shut yourself up in it? You don't attend town functions, invite people into your home, or accept invitations when they're offered. Why punish yourself?"

"I don't. I don't have to. Life's done enough of that." A pause told Marge Ermintrude realized how snappish she sounded. "No, I keep to myself because the contrast of company makes things worse when the silence returns. This way, things stay on an even keel. But on to the matter at hand." She gestured to Marge's trunks. "'Waste not, want not.'"

Inspiration struck, and she offered a bargain. "If I accept your version of the homily, will you accept mine?"

"You'll unpack a bit and settle in if I do?" A shrewd light lit the old woman's gaze, her capitulation too easy. At Marge's nod, she didn't hesitate. "Agreed."

Marge wondered for a moment if Ermintrude was so set on her unpacking because she thought it would be another step toward making Marge stay. *She's lonely.* . . . "You're going to start attending functions then."

"How does that have anything to do with my adage? 'Waste not, want not' refers to using what's at hand."

"Town events are close at hand, and I said you'd abide by *my* version." She bent to open the first trunk, drawing out a beautifully worked starburst quilt. "Too late to change your mind now."

"What is your version?" Curiosity overpowered the irritation in her friend's question, and Marge knew she'd won.

She eyed the small trunk in the corner, knowing she wouldn't open that one but still wishing she'd have reason to someday. "Want nothing, waste away."

CHAPTER 24

The day proved particularly difficult. But then, the two days since he'd tried to give Marge those daisies seemed filled with small difficulties. He needed that mill pick—the grind of the flour became progressively rougher, and he had to rerun entire batches. Not only did the process waste time, it took intense concentration to adjust the distance between the stones and judge the length of time needed.

Waiting became tedious as he hovered in the mill, keeping a vigilant ear for any problems once he had each round going smoothly. By the fourth time he emptied the hopper, Gavin's restlessness proved his undoing.

Reading my Bible isn't an option. Even if it were something I'd try to undertake with only half my attention, it would draw me in until I might miss a signal something's gone wrong. Pacing wasn't enough. He'd already smoothed, oiled, straightened, swept, and done every bit of maintenance possible. *I'll try my hand at whittling again.*

It's what his father used to do on days like this, but Gavin usually didn't bother with a pastime he didn't excel in. Anything he attempted to carve wound up slightly awkward or downright unrecognizable—somewhat like his attempts at courting Marge.

Maybe I should carve something for her. He grinned as he walked toward the house for his whittling knife—far more light-weight and easy to wield than the blade he always carried. *Then she'd appreciate the flowers more.* The grin faded.

Things had grown. . .stilted. . .since that morning. The easy conversation between Grandma and Marge dried up when he came to the table. More than once he'd caught her eyes on him, asking something of him, but he didn't know what. Jokes fell flat. She'd started retreating to her room in the evenings rather than reading alongside him in the parlor.

Strange that he hadn't noticed how much he enjoyed her quiet company until she took it away. If he could unearth a way to ask her back without sounding either demanding, or worse, foolish, Gavin would see her in the matching armchair across from him that very evening.

He liked how comfortable she always looked. It made him feel like he put her at ease, and that, in turn, made the place seem more. . .well, homey. There was something homey in the way she curled her feet up beneath her skirts and nestled in to enjoy something edifying or entertaining.

But the very best part, the part he missed the most, was something Marge probably wouldn't believe. She only wore her spec-tacles while reading. The first time she'd tugged them from a case in her pocket, looping a fine chain about her neck and slipping the delicate golden frames atop her nose, Gavin sat transfixed. Only one night since had he missed that moment—when Grandma asked him to fetch some water. Otherwise, he cast furtive glances over the top of his own book until the time she transformed.

Because that's what happened. Marge unearthed her spectacles, and somehow, they unearthed something hidden about her. They made her face softer, drew attention straight down her pert little nose to the way she absently nibbled her lower lip while she read or parted them in surprise and delight—depending on what she found between the pages.

The best part about the whole thing? Gavin felt fairly certain no other man ever witnessed this nightly revelation. Just him.

Except he hadn't seen it the past two nights either. *I'm losing ground instead of gaining it.* This sort of situation made a man reevaluate, and the more he looked, the less Gavin liked what he saw. A couple short weeks ago, the stage brought him a bride. An inconsequential error—a mere technicality—robbed him of the possibility of a union once she discovered the truth. And in trying to change her mind, he'd forfeited even the simple pleasure of companionship.

The more he thought about it, the angrier it made him. *Aside from labeling that letter ambiguously, I've done everything right. How long is she going to let stung pride get the best of her. . .of both of us, Lord? Or is it just that she doesn't appreciate any of the effort I've made? Did learning I'd proposed to Daisy first harden her heart so much she can't be reached?*

He ignored the sound of feminine voices coming from the guest room. *Her* room. If Marge passed the afternoon talking with Grandma, that meant she wasn't reading, and nothing short of her spectacles could lure him closer than necessary for now.

It took him a few moments of digging through the chest at the base of his bed, where he kept odds and ends, before he unearthed his whittling knife.

I haven't used it since I moved west. The realization didn't surprise him. What with building a house, reshaping the land, forming a millpond, and building the mill, he'd had precious little time for anything but work. *I sent for her as soon as I got everything ready.*

"Stop shaking your head and say hello to your grandmother." She called orders from where she half sat, half lay on the bed, surrounded by an assortment of girly things. "Marge needed to. . .step out. . .for a moment."

"I see." It felt strange to step into her room, take in telltale signs of unpacking. *She's settling in?*

"She's kept everything boxed up this entire time, so I convinced her to at least sort through."

Neat piles of clothing covered the foot of the bed; a sewing case leaned against Grandma's hip while she perused an album of tintypes. "Quite a collection." Most of all, though, he saw books. Marge's Bible lay on her nightstand, but another Bible, this one looking to be written in French, now lay beside it. Stacks of volumes marched along the floor in orderly lines. The collected works of Shakespeare held vigil next to a complete set of McGuffey's Readers. The travels of Marco Polo vied alongside *Gulliver's Travels*, outgunned by sets attributed to Dante and Milton.

"If you wondered what she packed in all those trunks of hers, now you know. Marge brought a library along with her."

"I believe it—would have believed it without seeing them. It's Marge all over." Words, wisdom, and wonder—that's what books offered. And Marge knew they were rare out west. "Back in Baltimore, we spoke about the lack of education and availability of reading material in the territories." The memory took him off guard.

"Looks like she aims to fix that."

"She's passionate about books." Surely Grandma didn't hear the disgruntled note that entered when he said "books"? *No helping it that I want her to be passionate about more.*

"Paper." Grandma's gaze went sharp as the razor Gavin used,

but the hint of a smile deepened the grooves bracketing her mouth. "I need a bit. Get me some from the desk, would you?"

It wasn't a question. Gavin pressed the latch, folding down the drop front to look for some paper. He stopped looking when he caught sight of what else the desk held.

A crystal vase, filled with fresh water, cradled a few slightly wilted purple blossoms. Tahoka daisies, to be exact. Gavin shut the desk, apologized to Grandma for not finding any paper, and made his way back to the mill, mind spinning.

She snuck outside and saved some. It made no sense. It didn't have to. *Marge still feels for me. It's not too late to win her back.*

It seemed so early to retire to her room, yet since the day she'd made a hash of accepting Gavin's gift of the wildflowers, Marge hadn't mustered up the courage to sit across from him in the parlor reading, as they'd settled into.

"Give him time to let that temper of his cool off. . .and then give him an extra day to help him realize what he's missing," Ermintrude had advised after her grandson stalked out that awful morning. She'd also muttered something about a healthy change in perspective for mule-headed women, but that, Marge ignored.

It's been a few days now. Perhaps enough time passed that Gavin's temper cooled and he wouldn't dislike company this evening? The spark of hope died a swift death. *He's scarce looked at me since that day, much less spent a moment alone.*

Refusing to let her shoulders slump, Marge snuffed the lamp in the now-clean kitchen, preparing to follow where Ermintrude had gone upstairs a scant hour before. *Well, here's proof that it's men, not children, who age women before their time. How many seasons have I spent in a room of youngsters without ever turning in early, only to change my habits after mere days living around a man!*

Her head turned toward the parlor as she passed, despite her determination not to peek in. Truth of the matter was Marge couldn't pass up the opportunity to see Gavin relaxed at the end of a long day—even if she simply snuck a glance on her way to self-imposed exile. Evenings showed Gavin in a different light—not just the literal lamp glow either—than his busy days.

He rose with the sun and seemed determined to out-busy it. Sure, the sun shone all day, illuminating the entire world. Gavin put it to shame with his constant motion. After all, everyone knew the sun remained stationary. End of day proved the only time the miller stayed still, dropping into an armchair scarcely large enough to accommodate his width.

Not because Gavin ran too large. Simply because his broad, strong frame dominated furniture. He sat down, settled back, propped his booted feet on an ottoman, and sank into a relaxation so complete it only lacked a sigh of satisfaction. Of course, a sigh might ruin the entire masculine appeal he presented so effortlessly.

He should make things easier on me and start sighing. She felt the wry twist to her lips and knew the idea counted as unreasonable. *I don't care. If Ermintrude is wrong and his temper hasn't cooled. . .and he doesn't miss me, the man needs to demonstrate the courtesy of being less fascinating. That's the absolute least he could do.*

"Marge?" His baritone, rumbling right beside her, made her realize she'd loitered at the base of the stairwell for far too long. "Are you all right?"

An unbecoming flush surely painted her cheeks. "Wool-gathering. If you'll excuse me. . . ." She made for the stairs, mortified to have been caught daydreaming. *Did he see me stare at him?*

His hand caught her elbow, blocking her bid for escape. "Wait."

Even if she'd wanted to leave him standing there, it wouldn't have been possible. Not when he asked her to stay. Not when he stood so close. Not when warmth spread from his fingertips to rush up her arm, five streaks of heat to rival the strength of her blush. For a heartbeat—no, several. The sound of her own thundered in her ears loudly enough for her to know, after all. For a brief moment she stayed still as a statue, waiting.

"I hoped you would join me this evening." Gavin inclined his head toward the parlor but didn't move his hand.

"Oh?" If the word came out a bit squeaky, Marge could do nothing to help it. *He's asking to spend time with me!* Swiftly on the heels of that thought came one slightly less welcome. *That makes Ermintrude right—I'll never hear the end of it. No matter. It's more than worth the price to have Gavin seek my company!* She beamed like a fool.

"Yes." Now he removed his hand, taking away his warmth.

"I'll just be a moment." She turned to the stairs again, her step light. "Let me fetch my book."

"Of course. Oh, and Marge?" His smile brightened his tone— she could hear it even with her back to him. "Don't forget your glasses."

CHAPTER 25

Had it been over a week since he told Midge he intended to prove a man could adore her? Amos could hardly believe the time went by so fast. He made a point of seeking her out every day and was gratified when she rarely declined a walk or a meal with his family. In fact, the only two days they hadn't spent time together had been the past two Sundays.

She doesn't seem herself on Sundays. The thought plagued him. Amos found it increasingly difficult to keep his mind on the sermon when he noted so many signs of Midge's discomfort without even bothering to look. A simple glance or the number of times her shifting or fidgeting would catch the corner of his eye told a story plain as day. *But what story? And why am I so drawn to it, Lord?*

He'd hurry to catch up with her after church, but she either surrounded herself with friends or hied off like a hunted hare. If she spoke with friends, she smiled too brightly and laughed too hard. If she disappeared, it seemed to serve none of the purpose Amos had come to expect of anything Midge did. So even as he spent time with her and enjoyed more of her wit, humor, and the heart she hid beneath them, Amos discovered more distance lay between him and the girl he'd chosen.

Even now, while he waited for Josiah Reed to finish his short speech marking today's occasion, the puzzle of how to bridge the *Midge gap*, as he'd come to call the problem, tickled his mind. There she stood, beside the Reeds, smiling as her grandfather/ uncle turned to face him. It had taken Amos awhile to understand precisely why Josiah Reed could claim either title, but now he knew Josiah was father to Saul and husband to Doreen, Clara's aunt, so he stood as adopted grandfather and great-uncle to Midge. Amos snapped to attention as the mayor of Buttonwood motioned him forward.

"Here's the man who's brought us this far along. The town council felt they'd found a good man for the task of building a fine schoolhouse in the middle of the Oregon Trail, and Mr. Amos Geer didn't disappoint. When the scarcity of wood made it pro- hibitively expensive, as did the freight cost of brick, it was Amos who suggested using clay from the Red Basin not overly far from here."

"At least," Amos interjected, "not far compared to big cities like Baltimore or Independence."

"So he fetched the clay, made the bricks, and built up the walls a ways to show us how it's done. Now it's our turn for a school- house raising the likes of which the West has never seen!" Cheers filled a brief pause. "We're going to finish these walls and raise the roof, including the bell tower, today."

"This morning." Amos didn't mean to interrupt, exactly, but with the large, thick bricks already made and dried, fitting them in place and mortaring them together shouldn't take too long. "Work gets done fast with the whole town to help—yes, the ladies, too.

The men should admit we wouldn't be so willing to do this without the promise of the fine dinner we know you're all preparing while we build." Laughter and agreement greeted his acknowledgment, but Amos watched Midge, whose slow smile was all the approval he needed.

He swiftly divided the townsmen into four teams, one for each wall, as the women dispersed. For each team, he selected a foreman. Adam Grogan, Gavin Miller, and Saul Reed joined him in organizing their crews and getting work underway. Soon they had things up and running in a rhythm Amos hoped would keep on until they finished the walls.

The *glop* of mortar plunked atop set bricks, followed by the *slap* of the next thick brick hefted in place, and then the relentless scrape of trowels removing whatever excess oozed between the layers. Multiply it by the many men working, square it to take into account the four walls, and it formed a symphony of sound the likes of which Beethoven never dreamed.

Amos loved it. The echoes of efficiency provided a sort of workingman's music to the sight of an entire community coming together for the best reason he could imagine—their children. He rolled up his sleeves and got his hands dirty, reveling in the different scents and textures as he always did when working with his hands, particularly whenever he worked in the great outdoors.

The rich, gummy smell of wet clay skimmed over the lighter scent of sun-warmed stone as a soft sandy silt covered his hands and had him breathing in the earth. Amos kept on, working until his crew needed to use one of the pulleys he'd rigged to swing the huge bricks into place on the top of the walls.

With the work slowing, he looked around to see the other teams matching him, or close to it. The sun hadn't reached its height. His optimistic prediction might come true, with their completing the bulk of the work before breaking for dinner.

A glint of red caught his eye, and he turned to see Midge watching him. A smile, a wave, and she turned back to the children who tugged at her skirts in an obvious demand for attention. With the breeze in her hair, a smile on her face, and children gathered around, Midge looked to be in her element. It made Amos think something that had been cropping up more and more as he watched her interact with his brothers and sisters.

Midge will make a good mama. . . .

❦

I'm going to be the world's worst mother someday. Midge tramped around with an entire herd of scapegraces aping her every move. *Mothers are supposed to be stern, supposed to be genteel, supposed to teach little girls how to be little ladies.*

Midge, for her part, far preferred playing with children to raising them. All the fun, very little of the responsibility—if it weren't for the fact she so badly wanted a little girl to name Nancy and give all the things taken away from her sister, she'd be content as Auntie Midge for the rest of her days.

Auntie. *Not* Teacher. *Teacher* implied responsibility and living up to standards Midge couldn't aspire to. *Even if I could stand and sit still in a classroom all day long—even so fine a one as Amos is having built—I'd make for a poor role model. The children don't seem to mind, but I know better.*

The question is. . .why don't their parents?

A frown creased the space between her eyebrows; she could feel the wrinkle forming. Worse, the kids noticed it.

"Miss Collins," Annie Doan, a bright, outspoken girl of about eight who reminded Midge of her own younger self, spoke up on behalf of everyone. "Did we do something wrong?"

"Of course not." Her smile felt forced, so Midge quickly turned it to one of exaggerated suspicion. She narrowed her eyes in a dramatic scowl and raised on eyebrow. "Did you?"

"I asked if we could play at dodging?" Billy Geer, Amos's younger brother—and the one he'd pointed out to her as having had diphtheritic croup four years ago at Fort Sumter, and the reason he'd tackled her to keep her out of the sick room—carried a leather ball and eyes full of hope.

With his sandy hair and brown eyes, he was the spitting image of how Amos must've looked at that age. The thought of his almost dying made her heart squeeze up so tight it was hard to get words out, so Midge just nodded. *Thank God Saul came through when he did to save Billy. Otherwise, so much might be different. . . .*

She took a stick and drew a large circle in the dirt, an impromptu playing field for a game of dodge the ball, but stopped once she realized what she'd done. *Thank God?* Shaking her head didn't do much to clear it. *Thank Josiah for sending for Saul. Thank Saul for going and caring enough to be a doctor to help Billy. Thank Amos for pulling me away so I didn't catch the sickness. Thank any and everyone involved, but God had precious little to do with it!*

No. People looked after other people. At least, the ones who cared did. Folks like Saul and Clara were the first she'd met, aside from her own sister. The longer she stayed in Buttonwood, the more people she counted as genuine and caring—what Aunt Doreen would call the "salt of the earth." She didn't even have to explain that one—Midge understood the instant she heard the phrase back when she was thirteen.

Salt of the earth. . .salt was good for two things, flavor and preservation. If someone added something enjoyable to a life and helped preserve or further the good in and around it, the person was like salt. If someone managed that for just about everyone he or she knew, Midge could see a sort of domino effect where the whole world was kept from the decay of people just using each other for momentary wants.

The way people treated Nancy. The way people used to treat her. The way Midge tried never to treat anyone, no matter how despicable. And the way she most deserved to be treated.

Thud. The muffled declaration of a leather ball striking shins through layers of cotton skirts and petticoats came at the same time as a forceful knock to the back of Midge's knees. She faltered, almost corrected herself, but jerked back when little Sadie Warren darted just in front of her. Then it was all over.

Midge went down, hitting the hard prairie earth with a jarring impact. Her ankle bent at an awkward angle beneath her, a by-product of trying to avoid Sadie. Aware that every child froze the instant she met the ground, Midge pushed herself into a sitting position and tried to reassure them.

The way children handled an upsetting situation said a lot about the type of people they'd grow into, and Midge got a chance to witness firsthand the foundation of Buttonwood's future. Not many could say they saw so far when their rumps hit the ground.

Most of them fretted, asked if she was all right, hovered anxiously. One excitable five-year-old burst into tears and ran for his mama, while a seven-year-old ignored the entire mess and chased down the renegade leather ball. In spite of the usual reactions, a few young ones stood out right away.

Maggie Reed, Midge's three-year-old sister, scampered off in a flash to go fetch her pa the doctor, while her best friend, Tessa Burn, trundled over to offer more immediate comfort. Popping her thumb in her mouth and her favorite doll, Bessie, into Midge's lap, she half sat, half tumbled to cuddle at her side.

Annie Doane announced it was Roger Warren whose throw

had gone awry and watched the older boy like a hawk. She gave the impression of a girl ready to haul a criminal to justice the moment he made a false move.

Roger Warren, for his part, mumbled apology after apology, squatting back on his heels and reaching for Midge's hands to help her up. Of course, she couldn't accept his gallant offer with little Tessa tucked at her side, but Midge could tell the ten-year-old had the makings of a fine man. Someday. In fact, Midge wouldn't be surprised if he and Annie were casting more appreciative glances at each other in another five years.

But it was Billy's course of action that most ruffled Midge. At twelve, the boy should know better than to run tattling to his older brother over the slightest mishap. Not that Billy seemed to have learned the value of discretion. Instead, he trotted back toward her with his brother overtaking his pace in long strides.

Midge stifled a groan. *He had to fetch Amos?*

CHAPTER 26

"Mrs. Miller, so good to see you!" "Glad you could join us this morning, Mrs. Miller." "Wonderful to have you up and about, Mrs. Miller, why don't you sit by me?"

Marge watched and listened as the women of the town did precisely as she'd hoped and fussed over Ermintrude. Not only did the divided attention serve her well in helping foist off questions about her interest in teaching when she *must* plan to start her own family soon—the warm welcome went a long way toward putting her friend at ease.

Oh, Ermintrude hadn't said a word about it, but Marge knew she feared she'd avoided the townspeople for too long to be truly accepted so much later. Not that Ermintrude hadn't said a word about anything and everything else having to do with her first forced social interaction in years. But no matter how she grumped, threatened, or harrumphed, the old woman kept her bargain and joined Marge at the site of the schoolhouse raising.

"You put them up to this." The mutters went largely ignored. "Don't think I don't know you told them to make nice to the old curmudgeon who's been making you miserable."

"Don't think I don't know you're intentionally trying to make me show disrespect to one of my elders by giving in to the temptation to tell you to hush." Marge nudged Ermintrude toward a large table. "I did no such thing, and you don't make me miserable except when you're trying to take credit for such an outrageous accomplishment."

The resulting harrumph wasn't up to Ermintrude's usual standard, a sign she enjoyed herself more than she wanted to let on. "Going to deposit me at the biddy table and scuttle off to join your friends now, are you?" Behind the challenge lay a glimpse of the older woman's true worry.

"Not at all." Marge settled herself across from Ermintrude. "Aren't you used to peeling potatoes with me by now? Soon someone else will come to join us. It'll take a lot of mashed potatoes to go around when everyone in town wants a serving!"

"You have no idea." Opal Grogan slid onto the bench beside her. "I'm so glad Adam had them set up these tables beforehand. It will make preparing and serving everything so much simpler. Good morning, Mrs. Miller. It does my heart good to see you. I've been a poor neighbor, I fear, not stopping by more often."

"Not at all." Ermintrude waved her paring knife in as magnanimous a fashion as a knife could possibly be waved. "You've a little one tugging on your skirts and another soon to follow. Before your new-addition-to-be made his presence known, you stopped by a few times. I should've returned the favor but didn't want to impose."

"Impose?" Opal's laughter matched her looks—fiery and full of life. "It'd be a respite to visit for a while."

"I'd thought, with your family and your apiary, you kept as busy as those bees of yours." Ermintrude's peeling picked up the pace, a barometer of her opinion of the conversation.

"Never too busy for a new friend, Mrs. Miller."

"Oh. You have time for new neighbors but can't be bothered to bring Rachel to visit her grandmother?" A sour-faced frump whose name Marge couldn't recall at the moment flounced up to the table and planted her hands on her hips. "I'm sure Mrs. Miller here wouldn't approve your choice."

"Considering you've scarcely bothered to speak two words to me since I came to this town, I doubt you're in any position to speculate on what I do and do not approve of, Lucinda Grogan." Ermintrude's swift reply supplied the name Marge needed.

Ah, yes. This is Opal's mother-in-law. She took the opportunity to look over Lucinda as the woman made a show of settling wearily onto the bench beside Ermintrude. Deep bitterness dragged gray brows to a habitual scowl over a face aged beyond its years, thin features wreathed in the wrinkles of a perpetual frown.

I never would have remembered—much less guessed—this to be Adam's mother. Though, if I think back further and remember that this is a woman who helped keep a feud going, it makes more sense.

It took all Marge's effort not to shoot Opal a commiserating glance. Such things were too often misinterpreted, and Opal, while showing the promise of a good friendship, didn't know her well enough to read her intent. Besides, she might have a soft spot for the unpleasant woman haranguing her and take exception to anything that could be seen as negative.

Although, Marge admitted to herself after catching a glimpse of the grin on Opal's face as Ermintrude took up the cudgels on her behalf, *that doesn't seem likely.*

Ermintrude, who, with at least a dozen years on her new bench mate, put the younger woman to shame as her pile of potatoes grew by leaps and bounds. For that matter, she put them all to shame. Marge figured it was safe to assume her friend was enjoying herself.

"You're mistaken, Mrs. Miller." A disdainful sniff that would have been more in place coming from one of Daisy's snobby town friends punctuated Lucinda's response. "I speak with everyone. If you've chosen not to engage in conversation when the opportunity presents itself, you've no one to blame but yourself." She left unspoken—barely—the obvious truth that Ermintrude had avoided contact with everyone.

"I'm not the one mistaken, Lucinda. You see, I've been watching the way things are done here, getting the lay of the land before joining in, so to speak. You don't talk *with* everyone." Ermintrude paused in her peeling as though savoring the moment. "You talk *about* everyone."

Amos looked over Midge's raggedy retinue then met her exasperated gaze with an amused one of his own. "Children, why don't you run along while I make sure Miss Collins feels all right?" Several were slow to leave, until finally only Tessa and Billy remained.

"I'll go tell Doc you've got it under control." Billy must have been trying to make amends for fetching Amos, because he headed over to the far side of the growing schoolhouse, where several of the men had gone for some water before they started putting up the roof.

"It appears you've been abandoned." Amos hunkered down to be at eye level. "Except for the sleeping beauty there, who almost puts you to shame."

Refusing to rise to the bait, Midge looked down at where Tessa lay curled against her side, thumb still in her mouth. A little one like this could make the hardest heart melt. Sally and Matthew had a lot to be proud of in their firstborn.

"You're right." She craned her neck as though trying to look beyond Amos. "Those Burn men do make some beautiful babies...." She knew every bit as well as he did that Brett Burn, the youngest of the blacksmiths, wanted a wife.

In fact, Brett had started edging closer ever since Pete Speck relinquished his claim on Midge and began courting Amanda Dunstall instead. The gossips said all sorts of things about Pete's defection, but when he and Midge remained close friends, folks started accepting something that looked more like the truth: Midge saw Pete more as a brother than anything else, and she'd finally managed to convince her friend of the fact.

"That's the Fosset side in her." Amos referred to Sally, Matthew Burn's wife and Tessa's mother. He almost managed to sound completely unbothered, but Midge saw the slight lowering of his brows before he caught himself. "Anyone can see that."

"Really? What else can anyone see?" Midge stroked the tips of her fingers through the baby-soft curls covering Tessa's head. To her way of thinking, plenty of things went not only unnoticed but completely unsuspected by the majority of people.

Take her and Pete, for example. Most came to understand the two of them weren't meant to be more than friends, despite the giant-sized crush he'd nursed for a couple years. Yet no one—or hardly anyone, since Midge sometimes wondered whether her friend Opal bore an inkling—so much as guessed Midge sent Pete to Amanda because he was too good for her and deserved better. Midge liked Pete too much to marry him, plain and simple.

Brett, on the other hand, she avoided for less altruistic motives. While all the Burn men worked hard, smiled often, and more than earned their good standing in town, blacksmiths possessed certain traits Midge preferred to grant wide berth. Barrel-chested men with ham-sized hands couldn't be controlled by any measure of quick wit or careful cajoling.

Hadn't she and Nancy learned that years ago, when Rodney's deep chest held an endless well of rage plumbed by huge hands turned to solid fists? No, Midge wouldn't choose a big, beefy husband, no matter how jovial or kind he may seem. Rodney charmed her sister into a life of degradation and filth with such pretense....

The flutter of a breeze on her petticoats made Midge shift, both her feet and her attention. A momentary fear she'd been sitting there with a leg exposed by her little scrape swiftly subsided into astonishment as she watch Amos inch her petticoats and skirt above the line of her lace-up boot.

"What are you doing?" She hissed the question, trying to keep quiet and pull away without waking Tessa or drawing undue attention from any of the rest of the town.

A devilish grin lit his face. "Checking your ankle, something not just anyone—like Brett Burn—can see."

"Neither can you!"

He caught her hand, impeding her progress in tugging the hem of her skirt to cover her ankle. "Billy said he saw you twist it. Let me make sure you're all right."

"It's fine. Really." The concerned determination in his eyes made her hesitate for a split second too long. He had a grip on the layers of cloth again when she tried to shift away, the end result exposing her calf almost to her knee. "Stop it!"

"What's this?" One large hand—large, not heavy or thick knuckled—clamped to hold her skirts at her knee as Amos squinted at the ugly, puckered pink marking her shin. "What did you do?"

"It's nothing." She tried to wriggle away, only to be held fast. Not by force, but by the tender way he used one fingertip to trace around the healing gash. Midge knew it would scar when she had reopened the wound two weeks ago in church, but scars faded. Right now, the mark flushed a deep, angry pink.

"It's not healing well, so I'm assuming you didn't tell Dr. Reed when it happened." He released her knee, his refusal to drop a question Midge couldn't answer making her agitated beyond belief. "That's *not* nothing."

"We just have different definitions of the word." Midge levered herself onto her feet, cradling the heavy weight of the sleeping toddler as she stood. "The fall was nothing, the scrape was nothing, and so is this conversation."

CHAPTER 27

Billy's a good brother. Amos watched his sibling saunter off to leave him alone with Midge. Or, at least, as alone as a man and woman could be with the entire town less than an acre away and a sleeping toddler snuggled against her side. *Lucky toddler.*

Since Midge seemed unharmed, a little teasing was in order. As expected, when he named Tessa her rival, Midge joked back. What Amos didn't expect was the searing shaft of envy that struck him when she seemed to be looking around for Brett Burn. For a wild moment, he considered sweeping her off the ground and hauling her in front of Parson Carter right then.

She wants babies? I'll give her babies. Some of the unreasonable jealousy leaked away at the thought. *Any child of Midge's will be beautiful. Our family will be blessed.*

But he couldn't say something like that aloud. Midge would bolt like a frightened rabbit. Amos knew full well she'd seen this courtship as a farce from the outset. Otherwise, his freckled firebrand wouldn't have capitulated so easily to the idea. If she had an inkling he seriously intended to make her his bride, Midge would no longer play this little game of trying to wait for him to grow tired of her saucy ways.

Instead of voicing any of these thoughts, he ignored her compliment to the Burn men and gave credit for Tessa's cuteness where it belonged, with her mother. As he anticipated, Midge snapped out a response without batting a lash.

"What else can anyone see?" The dry question demanded a comeback, but Midge drew away from him even as Amos sat before her. She traveled somewhere in the landscape of thoughts she didn't care to share, didn't even enjoy having, and Amos couldn't journey with her.

The sparkle in her eyes grew shuttered. The pert tilt to her mouth flattened. Her breaths went shallow then deepened into an occasional sigh sad enough to rend him. There was only one thing to do—jolt her back from whatever memory caught her.

So Amos took advantage of the pretext of her fall to nudge her skirts above her boots. If nothing else, the action would grab her attention and put it back where it belonged—them. Now.

Obviously, Amos acknowledged as the ruffled hem of her petticoat fluttered to reveal slim ankles encased in tightly laced leather, the plan held other rewards. Besides, it worked.

"What are you doing?" If she hadn't been trying to avoid a scene or waking up Tessa, or maybe both—Amos couldn't be certain which reason guided her—Midge probably would've screeched instead of squawked. As things stood, she kept fairly quiet while trying to wriggle away and tug her hem back over the tips of her boots.

As though a glimpse of her boot laces might give him ideas. Amos would've laughed at the thought, if her concerns weren't so well-founded. One peek had him plotting ways to unlace those boots. "Checking your ankle, something not just anyone—like

Brett Burn—can see." *A twisted ankle surely needed to be examined more closely. Yep. That boot is coming off.*

"It's fine. Really." Midge's assurance came too late.

Amos made a plan and intended to see it through. Trouble came in when Midge decided to impede his progress by shifting away, inadvertently revealing a length of smooth leg almost up to her knee.

The sight of that fair skin, covered only by the sheer silk of her stocking, just about poleaxed him. He could find no other reason for his ungentlemanly gawking. Amos might have remained speechless for a good while longer if it weren't for the angry pink of a still-healing wound glaring up at him midway between the top of her boot and the bottom of Midge's knee.

She must have seen him notice, because she redoubled her efforts to pull away. He put a hand on her knee, ignoring the intimacy of the action to focus on her injury. "What did you do?"

"It's nothing." For the first time, Midge sounded uncertain. She stopped trying to shift back, and Amos could feel her gaze following where he traced the area around the gash.

His fingertips, made rough from working all day with the bricks, snagged at her stockings, but Amos felt the warmth of her skin and the heat of her embarrassment with far more strength. And interest. *Midge isn't clumsy. Even her fall today came from being hit with the ball.*

"It's not healing well, so I'm assuming you didn't tell Dr. Reed when it happened." He removed his hand before he did something foolish. "That's *not* nothing."

"We just have different definitions of the word." Midge stood up, keeping a firm hold on Tessa so the toddler lay cradled in her arms. "The fall was nothing, the scrape was nothing, and so is this conversation."

She didn't want to discuss whatever caused the cut, or why she hadn't told Dr. Reed about it. *Which means either she's embarrassed, or...*

"Who hurt you?" He ground out the words, making it a demand for information more than a simple question. Amos felt his pulse kick into high gear as she paused, seeming to debate whether or not to answer at all.

"I struck my shin on a chest in my room." Midge's explanation held the ring of truth, but her flat tone told Amos more lay behind the story.

"Let me know if you need someone to chop it up." He knew his little joke was the right response when some of the stiffness left her spine.

"No, thanks." She jostled Tessa in her arms, repositioning the little girl so she'd sleep more comfortably. Then she spoiled the mature, maternal image by looking up with a mischievous twinkle. "It's a good reminder that things keep me on my toes when I least expect it."

Amos escorted her back toward where the other women worked and gave her a pointed look. "I know exactly what you mean."

❦

Rage soured the air Gavin breathed as Lucinda Grogan opened her mouth to snipe about Marge's intent to teach and what it meant to their marriage—as though it made any difference to her. He hadn't dealt much with the woman, but he'd heard and noticed enough to take her measure long ago. It was part of the reason why, once the walls were up and most of the men took a short break before beginning work on the roof, he'd headed over to where Marge and Grandma sat with the bitter busybody.

He'd also thought to head off Brett Burn and enjoy Marge's

company for a stolen moment or two, but there was no denying Lucinda's tart tongue made for the most pressing reason to stand at her side. Or behind her, as the case may be.

"You're assuming marriage and teaching are mutually exclusive." He didn't even fight to keep his tone even, instead letting the honest irony of his comment fill his words with dry humor. *So does Marge, but we've not discussed it.* Too bad. Now would be as good a time as any for him to point out a compromise that seemed obvious to him.

"They are." Scorn smeared the certainty of Lucinda's statement. "Everyone with a lick of sense knows that."

"We already know your own children don't ascribe to your theories, since two of them wed the children of your sworn enemy, so I suppose we should be thankful you didn't bother with any teaching once you got Mr. Grogan down the aisle." Grandma sharpened her wits on the gossip, and although Gavin knew it wasn't very godly of him, he couldn't help but be glad of it.

If Lucinda didn't watch herself, she'd wind up looking like that pile of potato peels—sliced down and laid bare by Grandma's finest blade—her tongue.

"You know nothing of the situation." How the woman made a sentence sound like a hiss with so few *s*'s was beyond Gavin, but somehow the elder Mrs. Grogan managed quite well. "People shouldn't give an opinion on anything they don't understand."

"Well I, for one, would like to understand more about Mr. Miller's views on married teachers." Opal Grogan stepped in to calm troubled waters, an admirable trait Gavin suspected she used often considering her in-laws.

"Yes, Gavin." Marge tilted her head back at what had to be an uncomfortable angle to see his face. "Explain to the ladies just what, exactly, you mean."

If he detected any challenge in her invitation, her curiosity so vastly overshadowed it. Gavin figured this opportunity could be golden. *After all, one of the things Marge wants is to be appreciated for herself, and teaching is so much a part of who she is....*

"God gave Marge a passion for teaching, and any child who studies under her will be glad of it. I see no reason why our children"—he gave her shoulder a slight squeeze—"should be the only ones blessed by her gifts."

"Thank you." Marge's smile, he'd come to realize, held the key to another one of her intriguing transformations. Not the small, tight smiles she gave when uncomfortable, or the overly wide ones that tried to mask when she didn't want to smile at all, but the wholehearted ones. The ones that spread all the way to her eyes and made the flickering green glow bright against their amber background.

He put his free hand on her other shoulder in a sort of bracing half hug. "You're welcome. I know how important family is to you, Marge. Ours will never lack just because you answer a calling outside our home."

"See that?" Grandma jerked her head toward him. "He gets that from my side of the family. I've made it a point to try to teach the boys to appreciate more about a woman than the children she carries." An uncharacteristically thoughtful pause followed. "You know, Lucinda, it's a lesson you'd do well to apply to your daughter-in-law. Opal seems a rare woman."

"She is." Marge spoke up almost before Lucinda opened her mouth to respond. Almost, but it looked to Gavin as though she ignored the viper's glower. "Opal manages to be a wife, a mother, and a businesswoman. Apiaries don't run themselves."

"Oh yes. That's the whole problem, right there." The older Grogan refused to back down, despite the good sense behind

Grandma's advice. "Opal keeps my grandchild from me because she has too many demands on her time."

"You're welcome to visit whenever you like." The words bore the flavor of having been oft repeated, as Opal Grogan didn't even look up from the potato she grabbed. "It's your choice."

"Maybe I would, if you weren't such a busy little bee."

Gavin decided he'd had enough of hearing the woman sow strife. "It's good to fill one's time. Keeps folks from more troublesome things." *Like making everyone else miserable.*

"I'm sure I don't know what you mean. I have plenty to keep me occupied."

"What my grandson means, Lucinda," replied Grandma, putting down her knife as she spoke, the pile of peeled potatoes before her larger than any other on the table, "is that it's better to be a busy bee than a busybody."

CHAPTER 28

Our children. Marge kept hearing Gavin say the words, feeling his hand pressing in silent promise against her shoulder, long after he left to rejoin the men. *"Blessed. . ."*

It seemed to her as though her heart could double as a spare bellows for the smithy, the way it expanded many times past its original size, fighting with her every time she tried to close it back down to something manageable. The struggle played out again and again, and each time, Marge lost a little more ground to the swelling happiness when Gavin did something thoughtful or kind or. . .even. . .just spent time with her.

She'd snapped the feelings shut once she learned about his original intent to marry Daisy, determined to contain the damage and never again let false hope buoy her spirits. Because at first, she'd seen no way Gavin could be pleased with her as a substitute bride. Midge's challenge that he prove he genuinely wanted to marry Marge seemed an impossible one.

The entire situation seemed a veritable Pandora's box. So Marge let out the hurt, confusion, and disappointment by refusing to marry a man who didn't choose her. She poured out her heart in prayer, on the pages of her journal, doing her best to rid herself of the anger and upset. The only thing she didn't let out was her hope—the foolish, forlorn hope that somehow Gavin would come to want her. And prove it.

That stayed locked away. Marge knew about the hope, knew it didn't shrivel up or waste away. Felt it grow stronger with each gesture Gavin made. The daisies. His asking her to read with him in the parlor. And now. . .his telling the town gossip how much he respected her judgment and ability. And mentioning, for the first time, the children that would complete their family. . .

It was that confounded hope that swelled her heart until Marge could barely sit still. It seemed she floated through the rest of the day. Had anyone asked, she couldn't have recalled the details of Ermintrude's and Lucinda's constant sniping. Wouldn't be able to describe the food she helped prepare, much less what any of it tasted like. Only two things would mark the day in Marge's memory.

Gavin, and the children.

Not their own. Though the thought made her giddy, it was the children of Buttonwood—her future pupils—who wrested Marge's thoughts away from romance and made the day of the school raising something even more special.

At the beginning of the day, Marge felt the need to stay close to Ermintrude and make sure her friend felt comfortable. Not that she needed to worry, as Gavin's grandmother waded into the social waters of Buttonwood with the bravado anyone who'd met her would come to expect. Marge didn't worry about whether or not Ermintrude would seem at ease. . .but she watched carefully to see whether or not it was all show.

After dinner, when the dishes were cleared and the men were

back to raising the schoolhouse roof, Marge decided Ermintrude carved out a splendid niche among the other older women of the town. Save Lucinda Grogan, of course. But in a strange way, Marge would have guessed that having a sparring partner to enliven things is what made Ermintrude feel most at home. After all, there had to be something satisfying in finding an adversary when someone loved to debate as much as Ermintrude.

So with her friend settled, Marge took advantage of the opportunity to join Midge. She'd noticed her friend and coteacher watching over the town's children while the other women got things ready for the massive dinner. Now, she hurried over to the group of youngsters before anyone stopped her for more chitchat.

"Miss Chandler!" Midge greeted her in the same type of loud voice Marge herself used to get the attention of her students during recess. "Glad you could join us."

The controlled flurry of activity around the two women ground to a halt. Older boys looked up from a game of marbles; older girls stilled their jump ropes. Squares of hopscotch scratched into the earth were abandoned; the thin, piping voices of younger children called their friends back from games of hide-and-seek or sardines. In no time at all, Marge found herself surrounded—and stared at—by a group of about twenty youngsters.

"Good afternoon." Marge made a point of smiling at each and every one of them—even the toddlers too young to attend school. Then, especially, the ones who looked old enough they might be needed at home or choose not to attend or do so sporadically.

"Good afternoon, Miss Chandler." The slightly singsong cadence of the classroom greeting started at different times, but all the children ended together. A good sign.

"I look forward to getting to know you." Nervous glances met her pronouncement.

"Why?" A little girl, looking to be about eight years old, cocked her head to the side like a curious little owl.

Marge chuckled. "Because you're each worth knowing."

The other children watched this girl's reaction. She blinked, as though thinking it over, before breaking into a wide grin. "Yeah, we are. Most of us, at least."

"Some of us, you might regret." A towheaded boy who looked to be older than the girl puffed out his chest.

"Speak for yourself, Roger!" Some good-natured jostling looked like it might devolve into shoving, so Marge cleared her throat. Immediately the children stopped fussing.

Midge raised a brow, a silent acknowledgement she was impressed, and if Marge didn't miss her guess, a warning that the children wouldn't always be so easily reined in. That was par for the course—students always trod lightly in the beginning, growing bolder as time passed.

That's when things got interesting. For now, though, Marge would take advantage of the sweetheart period to establish ground rules of order and get to know the children.

"For teacher." A small girl—most likely the youngest who would go to school—shuffled forward, a slightly wilted ringlet of flowers like the one Midge wore clutched in her hand. The shy offering obviously came not only from the little one but from the group of girls encouraging her to step forth.

"Thank you." Marge stooped, untied her bonnet, and took it off so the little one could rise up on tiptoe and crown her. "It's lovely. What's your name?"

"Rachel." She looked up. "I wanna go to school, but Mama's not sure I'm old enough."

"How old are you?"

"She's five." The curious girl, Annie, spoke up. "And smart,

too. I'll make sure she won't be any trouble if you let her come."
Her face, Marge realized, was an older version of Rachel's. The
two must be sisters.

"Five is a fine age to start learning. Rachel is welcome." A swell
of murmurs and giggles made Marge look up from the littlest one's
beaming face, to realize almost every child wore a matching grin.

Obviously they approved of her decision. It looked like an
extremely well-established group, everyone friendly despite the
disparity in ages. Their closeness would be both a blessing and a
challenge as she sought to keep discipline, but Midge would be a
help there.

It wasn't until after Midge introduced each child then sent
them off to play that the two women had a chance to discuss their
pupils.

"They're a handful, but good kids." Midge looked fondly over
the entire group. "Do you usually have so many?"

"Yes. Baltimore is a large city, so there are plenty of children.
They aren't usually so close as these though."

"I see." Her friend seemed to be considering something.
"Before we talk about the school, I've been itching to know how
things are going with Mr. Miller."

"Oh." Marge felt her smile grow wide enough to make her
cheeks ache. "Don't worry—he told Lucinda Grogan today that
he doesn't see a reason why I can't be a wife and a teacher, so long
as the town approves."

"Good." Relief, almost palpable, made the one word a sentence.
"So then, it sounds like you're thinking about being his wife?" She
cast a glance back toward the schoolhouse, obviously trying to pick
out Gavin from among the men working.

"After today, I've pretty much made my decision."

Midge's gaze whipped back. "Which is?"

She drew in a deep breath. "The next time Gavin asks me to marry him. . .I'm going to say yes!"

～◎～

Another week passed almost before Gavin could reconcile the passage of time. The town council had scheduled school to begin two days from now, and in the week since the schoolhouse raising itself, he'd gone out of his way to spend more time with Marge before teaching took her away several hours a day.

Well, no. . .he hadn't gone out of his way. More like he'd made sure his way coincided with hers at as many points as possible. Mealtimes simply didn't offer enough time to spend in her company when he'd be missing the opportunity so soon. The time they spent in the parlor reading helped, but Gavin somehow fixed it in his head that if he couldn't convince Marge to become his wife before the start of school, he'd never manage it. And that was a lesson he refused to learn.

Their days fell into a sort of a pattern he wouldn't have expected. He woke up earlier these days—perhaps a side benefit of sleeping on the bottom floor of his mill with the gear housings. The windowless room that used to bother him since he couldn't tell what time it was, and whether or not night ended unless birds heralded the arrival of morning, became a blessing. Without light to tell him when to wake up, he naturally seemed to err on the early side, which gave him more time each morning.

Time he used to go to the house, slip upstairs, and shave every day so he looked his best. Not that Marge ever commented on it, but Gavin knew she noticed by the small, secretive smile he saw tilt her lips once he started coming down freshly smooth. Just one more thing to appreciate about Marge—the way she valued little things.

He even liked shaving more these days, because he could hear Marge and Grandma poking around the kitchen downstairs, smell the enticing aromas of breakfast, and know it all awaited him once he finished. Besides, while Gavin didn't stoop to eavesdropping, the two women sometimes grew animated enough in their conversation for him to overhear parts of it.

Agreeable arguments—that's what Grandma handed Marge every morning. Not because of her agreeable nature, but because of Marge's. That is to say, Marge had an agreeable nature, but she gave as good as she got each and every day, refusing to let Grandma plow her into a corner and get the best of her. Easy to see that they both looked forward to their morning debates.

Not quite so easy to admit Gavin looked forward to them, too. Particularly when he couldn't let on that he listened in to what they said. That would be rude. But he liked what he heard. He liked the way Marge turned things back on Grandma, challenged her to get out and interact more with people in the town. Gavin didn't spare much thought on the matter before he heard Marge point it out, but Grandma kept to herself too much. Besides, when she talked more with other people, she seemed in better spirits.

Best of all, she made better coffee.

At some point, Marge started joining him after breakfast for the morning ritual of opening the sluice gate. She didn't say much, but he could tell by the way she leaned over the railing to watch the water turn the wheel she enjoyed the power and precision of it. Something they had in common.

There was a beauty to the way the rushing water spilled over the wooden slats, pushing them down and bringing the wheel round and round. Everything a set motion, everything a shared purpose as it brought the mill to life. Shared purpose and appreciation is what made things work well together, after all.

It's what would make his and Marge's marriage such a beautiful system.

She sees it, too. I know she does now. That's why she's going to say yes when I propose this afternoon. Again.

Gavin didn't say much over dinner, too busy planning the proposal that would win him Marge's hand once and for all. The smile that took up constant residence on his face fell away for a bit as he pondered. He knew it not because he felt it, but because of the concerned glances Marge kept sending him.

She knows me. She notices my moods. I notice that she notices. Lord, You sent me the right wife. Thank You for not allowing my plans to ruin our lives. And now that I appreciate what You've brought me, I ask Your help in keeping her.

CHAPTER 29

After dinner, Gavin asked Marge to take a turn around the millpond. As he'd pretty much expected, she readily agreed.

Wonder if she knows I'm going to ask her again. I wonder if she plans to say yes. He tucked her hand in the crook of his arm, pleased to note how well her height suited him, how he didn't have to make a conscious effort to slow his steps to accommodate her. *We match—surely she sees that. . . .*

He turned to look at her, drinking in the lines of her profile for the scant second before she turned a piercing gaze upon him.

"What's wrong, Gavin?" Concern shaded her features. Concern and something else—something he couldn't put a name to.

"Nothing's wrong."

"You hardly spoke all through the meal." The other emotion strengthened until he could identify it as anxiety.

She may not want to, but she feels for me. "I keep thinking about the way nothing's wrong—everything feels right, Marge." He heard the sound of a large wagon coming toward the mill but ignored it. The customer could wait while Gavin attended to the

780

important things in his life.

"Oh?" A flash of understanding replaced the anxiety.

"Yes. We get on so well—things have never been better. I know you wanted me to prove my desire to build a life with you, and I think we're already creating one."

"What do you mean?" She stopped walking, but it didn't pull him up short. Like so much with Marge, it seemed natural.

"The time for wondering and waiting is over. Marge," he murmured, clasping one of her hands in both of his as he spoke, hoping that her sudden paleness boded well, "you must know what I want."

"Daisy?" She whispered her cousin's name, a faint question calling into doubt the outcome of his proposal.

"How could you think that?" A swell of anger almost kept him from noticing that she didn't look him in the eyes. Almost. "Look at me, Marge!" He dropped her hand, reaching to brace her shoulders.

"No." She stared past him as though fixated. "It's Daisy." A few swift blinks, and she shrugged his hands away, stepping past him.

It was only when he reached for her elbow to stop her from leaving that Gavin saw what Marge had seen moments before.

The sound he'd heard wasn't a wagon. Their visitor was no customer. Instead, stopped before the mill, sat a grand, glossy black coach the likes of which didn't belong on the prairie. And beside it stood someone who belonged there even less.

"Daisy?"

Dusty. Dry. Desolate. These were the words Daisy would use to describe the great mythical American West. *And really, that's a shame, because so many people are going to be disappointed when they get here.*

781

She alternated between peering out the coach windows and keeping them closed so as little dirt as possible clogged the stuffy air within. *Worse, all those words start with* D. She frowned. *D was her favorite letter, after all. Why did I never notice how many dreary words begin with it until now?*

Dreary. Oh no. There's another one. Between what Trouston had done, days on end with no one to talk to, and the mounting suspicion that her escape would be rather disappointing, Daisy felt dangerously close to the doldrums. *Now that I've started thinking in* D*'s, I can't seem to stop. How depressing.* But the more she tried to stop, the more she noticed it until it became a sort of awful game.

She had a small notebook in her reticule filled with words starting with *D* now. If nothing else, it helped pass the time when the ruts in the earth grew too bothersome to allow her to doze off. Yet all the way through, she clung to the hope that Buttonwood would prove some sort of shimmering oasis on the Oregon Trail—a haven for weary travelers where she could anticipate lively entertainment and the bracing sympathy of her cousin while she recuperated from Trouston's abuse.

But Buttonwood, when they finally pulled up to the town, was just that. A town. To be sure, it boasted more than any other outpost she'd seen for days, complete with a church, smithy, general store, café, and what looked to be a schoolhouse. All in all, quite adequate if someone wanted to. . .subsist. Or carve a niche in the unforgiving prairie. Daisy wanted neither.

Actually, at the moment she wanted two things: a good chat with Marge and a bath. *Although*—Daisy wrinkled her nose as she stepped from the coach into the dry heat she should expect by now but always hoped against—*perhaps the bath should come first.*

Nevertheless, she pasted on a bright smile for the driver, as she always did, and looked around. A three-story building—the mill—dominated this area. She'd seen a nice little house when they drove up, too, so perhaps Mr. Miller created a corner of civilization here. But the best thing in sight was the figure staring at her from the far side of the millpond.

"Marge!" Daisy didn't waste another moment. She grabbed handfuls of her sea green traveling costume to lift the hem out of danger and started to run. "Marge!"

Odd that Marge wasn't moving. *Must be shock. She and Gavin are so surprised to see me!* It didn't matter. Once she'd gone about halfway, her cousin came to her senses and started rushing to meet her. Gavin stayed where he was, but Daisy liked that. Her sister's husband didn't really belong in the moment of their reunion, after all. *Good for him for realizing that!*

Then the time for thinking mercifully ended, and she met Marge's embrace. Folded into the familiar comfort of her cousin's hug, Daisy took the first deep breath she'd managed in weeks. It smelled faintly of lemons. *I forgot that Marge always smells like this. Fresh and new—just what I need.*

She clung to that hug for longer than perhaps she should have, but Daisy needed a moment to collect herself. It simply wouldn't do to face Gavin with red-rimmed eyes. Already she'd arrived unannounced, and while Daisy knew Marge would welcome her with open arms, uninvited houseguests weren't the most beloved individuals in the world. Weepy ones sank to the bottom of the list, so she took a few more of those wonderful deep breaths before letting go of Marge.

Strange. Gavin only now began to approach them. No smile warmed his face. Unease twinged between Daisy's shoulders. Or perhaps that was one of the side effects of traveling so long? In either case, the sensation didn't strike her as pleasant.

Worse, Marge didn't look overjoyed either. Oh, her cousin smiled, obviously pleased to see her; but something shadowed the hazel of her eyes. Since Marge didn't make a habit of pouring out her heart and seeking comfort for whatever troubled her, Daisy knew she'd have to pry it loose.

But then, it might be good to focus on someone else's problems for a while. Heavens knew she'd gotten far too much time to ponder her own, trapped in that coach. *Time to move on.*

"Marge?" She reached out and grabbed one of her cousin's hands. "What's wrong?"

What's wrong? Marge blinked, trying to process her cousin's sudden appearance, still attempting to understand what it all meant. *You're here. . .for starters.*

But she couldn't say that and hurt Daisy's feelings. It sounded all wrong, because the truth of the matter was Marge wanted to see her cousin. *Sort of.* Admittedly, now didn't rank as the best timing. *Or does it?*

She resisted the urge to glance back toward Gavin, whom she knew hadn't yet joined them. Somehow she always knew where he stood—how far away, what direction, and so on—without needing to actually see him to verify it. If he stood directly behind her, waiting for a turn to greet Daisy, Marge would feel a pleasant prickling along the back of her neck.

Instead, an ominous churning in the vicinity of her stomach told her Gavin still hadn't recovered from the surprise of her cousin's arrival. *Is he happy to see her? Glad she showed up before he proposed again?* Because if Marge didn't miss her guess—and, after all, she rarely allowed herself to be mistaken—that's what he'd been building toward when she caught sight of Daisy.

Lord, does he still want her? Is he looking at the pair of us, even now, remembering why he chose Daisy in the first place? Seeing her delicate beauty and realizing anew just how far short I fall of her standard? I'd hoped. . . Oh, Father, why did You bring her now? Why not in a few days? After—

Suddenly other troublesome aspects of Daisy's appearance hit her. Not just the repercussions for her and Gavin, but the timing. What it meant. Marge craned her neck, realizing Aunt Verlata should have joined them by now. But no one else emerged from the coach. No one.

"I should ask you that same question, Daisy." She searched that beautiful face, noticing much later than she should have the tension drawing Daisy's forehead too tight, the slight puffiness around her eyes, the darker imprint along her lower lip that tattled of her nervous nibbling. . . . "What's wrong?"

A pronounced sniff preceded the answer. "I *missed* you, Marge." But Daisy's green eyes looked downward as they always did when she tried to hide something.

"I've missed you, too." Marge's reassurance won a far-too-brief smile. "But where is Aunt Verlata? Where is your fiancé?" *Why are you here, when you should be in Baltimore preparing to become Mrs. Trouston Dillard III?* Questions crowded her mind—all of them suggesting a scenario Marge didn't want to contemplate. "You're to be married this weekend! How are you here?"

Only two possibilities presented themselves. Either Daisy hied off, abandoning her engagement without a word to Aunt Verlata or Mr. Dillard, deciding to avoid the unpleasantness of breaking it off, or Daisy had already married him and found she disliked the company of her husband.

Lord, help me, I hope it's the second. If Daisy's in a sulk over married life not being as grand as she'd hoped, I can handle that. Soothe her ruffled feathers and send her back. But if she's run off, I can't salvage her reputation or engagement.

Which would mean Daisy was single. In Buttonwood. Right under Gavin's nose.

CHAPTER 30

There she stood, looking like she'd stepped from the pages of a *Godey's Lady's Book* his sister used to be so fond of. Daisy Chandler stepped from that glossy black private coach looking fancy enough to call on the queen.

Well, perhaps not, but that green fabric—and it sure looked as though they'd used an awful lot of it to make one dress for such a small woman—had to be expensive. Lace decorated the sleeves and collar, matching ribbons fluttering along the brim of her hat. Except some of those ribbons kept snagging on something that looked like, of all things, a bird's nest perched among them.

Other than that, though, Daisy Chandler looked perfect, from her perfect black ringlets down to the tips of her black boots that kept their shine despite the dust her coach kicked up. Perfect, and perfectly out of place.

Gavin kept his distance as the two cousins embraced, trying to marshal his thoughts. Not so much thoughts but questions in a quantity to clog the gears of his mind. *What brings her here? What am I supposed to do with two of them? Where is her aunt? Her fiancé? Isn't she supposed to be married this week?*

Suspicions rode hard on the heels of those questions. *Did Marge write to her and tell Daisy of the mix-up?* Despite the heat of summer, cold swept down his spine. *Is she here to take her rightful place as my bride-to-be, when I've been courting Marge this whole time?*

But no. Even if he didn't remember Marge's sudden pallor when she spotted her cousin, one glance at the confusion and concern on her face now told him she didn't expect Daisy any more than he had. It didn't solve everything, but the realization made it possible to walk over and behave with some semblance of normalcy.

He approached slowly, giving the women a moment to themselves—and himself an extra measure of time to decide how to handle this new development. Gavin knew full well he couldn't go stalking up and demand to know why Daisy had come.

Thankfully Marge asked for him. Oh, she did it as a concerned cousin and in a way that couldn't possibly offer any insult—in short, far better than he would have managed—but she still got the question out at just the same time he joined them.

"I *missed* you, Marge." A forlorn answer, in keeping with Daisy's downcast gaze, spawned a new set of suspicions.

That can't be all there is to it. Not when she arrives alone scant days before her wedding. Gavin tugged the brim of his hat both as a gentlemanly acknowledgement of her arrival and to hide the way his eyes narrowed.

He needn't have bothered. Daisy didn't so much as glance at him. She seemed too busy processing the volley of questions Marge lobbed at her. Gavin grinned for the first time since their unexpected visitor showed up. Leave it to his Marge to ask everything on his mind. All at once.

"Mama and Mr. Dillard remain in Baltimore, of course." She still didn't meet Marge's gaze, instead turning her smile on him. Dazzling and full of charm, Daisy's smile could blind just about any man.

Gavin knew—he'd been one of them. *How did I not notice how empty it is? How practiced?* Because the sad truth staring him in the face was that Daisy's smile was just for show. It didn't reach her eyes or light up her face the way Marge's did.

His lack of response—teamed with Marge's waiting silence— must've made Daisy uncomfortable. All at once, a flood of words poured from her mouth. A garbled explanation of words stumbling over each other, blocking one another, stopping anything from making sense as she kept piling on more explanations.

At some point, Gavin tuned it out in favor of waiting for her to finish. Watching the two women, he couldn't help making comparisons. Not because it was fair to do so, or even right to, but because he couldn't help himself.

There stood Daisy, resplendent and picture perfect, ringlets bouncing, hands waving, eyes widening and mouth going a mile a minute. She looked gorgeous, as always, but her blabbering made her far less attractive than Gavin remembered. He also noticed that in what he could catch from what she said, she didn't ask anything about how Marge fared.

Everything about Marge seemed simple by contrast. From the slim lines of her deep blue skirt and crisp white blouse, the mother-of-pearl buttons its only decoration, to the way she held still, tilting her head to take in her cousin's words, Marge exuded calm and caring. No ringlets bobbed around her face. She secured her chestnut waves in a practical bun at the nape of her neck. Dust speckled the tips of her brown boots, silent evidence of the walk they'd been enjoying before Daisy descended upon them.

Gavin liked that dust. Liked walking with her. Would have liked to finish that conversation. Instead, here he stood, waiting for an unwelcome visitor to finish speaking her piece so he could have Marge translate what it all meant. He waited a long time before Daisy wound down and Marge looked up at him.

"What?" He didn't need to be more specific—Gavin knew Marge would understand exactly what he asked.

"Daisy decided she and Mr. Dillard wouldn't suit and broke off the engagement, and he's made a spectacle of the entire thing to punish her." She glanced at her cousin, who nodded in a way Gavin would have thought overly eager for such a glum topic, but he didn't pretend to understand women.

"So she decided she needed a change of scenery and came to visit—without Aunt Verlata's agreement or knowledge." Marge's voice took on the sharp edge of remonstrance—as well it should. "You know she'll be worried silly."

"I left a letter." Daisy wrung her hands. "Like I said I did. And at the last opportunity I sent a telegram letting her know nothing befell me. Mama won't worry overmuch."

"Yes, she will." Gavin didn't know Verlata Chandler too well, but she doted on her daughter—which might be partly out of necessity as well as devotion.

"Not once she knows I'm safely here with you and Marge." Nothing there to misunderstand. "Mama knows she can trust Marge, and there's nothing to damage my reputation while I stay with my cousin and her husband."

Gavin shot Marge a glance she didn't meet. Obviously Daisy didn't have the slightest idea of the true state of things.

Husband? He let out a grin. *Marge can't wiggle out of this one.*

Once Daisy knows the state of things, she'll help me get her cousin to the altar. . . .

"But, Daisy. . .I'm not her husband."

～ⓒⓒ～

"I'm not her husband." Gavin's words struck her with the force of a physical blow, but somehow Marge remained standing. His grin as he informed Daisy he was still a bachelor sent secondary ripples of pain skittering across her bruised heart.

He discovers Daisy's available, and his first step is to reassure her that he is, too. Marge closed her eyes, though no tears threatened. Strange how the ache seemed too deep to provoke tears. *She got here just in time. Even one day later and I would have accepted his proposal. . . .*

Now the pain rose to claw at the back of her throat, stinging behind her nose. *Because Gavin meant to ask me today. Just now. And I would have said yes.* Shame over her foolishness burned back some of the sorrow. *I believed we'd reached a point where we'd form a solid marriage. Convinced myself I could make him happy. . .*

But one look at the grin stretching across his face as he told Daisy he hadn't married her put an end to that notion. It couldn't be more obvious what truly made him happy.

"Marge?" Her cousin sounded somewhat shrill, the way she always did when forced to repeat herself. "I asked if this is true. You two haven't married yet?"

"It's true." *Not yet. Not ever.*

Daisy looked from one of them to the other, confusion showing in her pretty pout. "But. . .why?"

Because I'm not the woman he wants to marry. Marge wanted to shout the words. Wanted to burn them and bury the ashes of their truth. *You are.* As things stood, the confession stuck in her throat—a raw lump she couldn't dislodge. She might well have stayed that way, frozen in a morass of self-pity, but for her cousin's reaction.

"You!" Daisy rounded on Gavin, indignation drawing her up to her full—if not imposing—height as she whipped off her gloves and advanced. "What—did—you—do. . ." A stinging patter of blows rained upon a bemused Gavin as Daisy flailed her gloves at his shoulders and hat, her voice rising to a screech as she continued. "To—my—cousin?"

"Daisy!" Marge ripped the gloves from her hands. "Stop that this instant!"

"Give them back, Marge." Her brows almost touching in the middle, chin set in an expression of absolute rage, Daisy extended one hand. "I'll take care of this."

She kept a firm grip on the gloves with one hand and snagged Daisy's elbow with her other to make sure her cousin didn't launch another attack. "Take care of what?"

"She's berating me for not having married you yet." Gavin, for his part, hadn't lost his grin. Obviously the wretched man found the entire scene hilarious—the woman he'd actually proposed to giving him what for over not marrying someone else.

"If you want him, he'll marry you." Daisy jerked her elbow from Marge's hand but didn't move otherwise. Her voice went so low Marge almost couldn't hear her. "If he's done anything to change your mind, you don't have to."

"What?" Gavin asked the question echoing in Marge's mind.

"I said," Daisy repeated in an exaggerated voice, "if she wants you, you'll marry her. If she doesn't, we'll go home."

"Daisy, you don't understand." Marge realized she had to tell her cousin the truth. Immediately.

"Yes, I do." Her scowl remained. "It's plain to see you're not happy, Marge. We're leaving."

"No." Gavin moved to stand directly in front of Daisy when she would have swept past him, a determination such as Marge had never seen hardening the lines of his jaw. "You're not going anywhere."

CHAPTER 31

Y ou can come with me or you can stay here, but I've a mind to visit Marge." Midge recovered her wits the moment the black coach drove out of sight.

It'd stopped at the smithy for just a moment—not even long enough for the dust to settle—and then taken off in the direction of the mill. Since nothing else lay that way, and it branched off the Oregon Trail, nothing could be more obvious but that the driver had asked directions and intended to take his passenger to the mill. To Marge, if Midge didn't miss her guess.

And, of course, she aimed to find out that she hadn't.

"Visit Marge or follow that coach?" Amos knew what she intended and let her know it.

"Both. Will you escort me?" He had her hand nestled in the crook of his arm, where, Midge admitted to herself, it felt quite comfortable. So long as it stayed there though, they remained attached—a problem, since Amos showed no signs of moving in the direction the coach had taken.

"What if I don't want to encourage you to be nosy?"

"I'd be forced to remind you that hypocrisy makes men far less attractive." She gave him an arch glance. "And considering the way you kept asking questions about me when I showed no interest in answering, you've a good dose of nosy in your own makeup."

"I don't indulge in nosiness." His brows rose so high his hat brim went up. "When I have a vested interest in matters, I may, however, investigate."

"Very well." Truly the man deserved no end of teasing for his wordplay, but time wasted while they wrangled. "I've a vested interest in Marge's well-being and would like to investigate. Either turn me loose or accompany me, but make your choice, Amos Geer."

"What makes you think whoever rides in that coach might present a threat to Miss Chandler's well-being?" He began walking. Slowly. Far, far too slowly for Midge's liking.

"An instinct, you could say." *That, and the fact I know far more about Marge than you do but can't tell you any of it. Because if I don't miss my guess, Marge's relatives have come to visit. . .and might ruin everything!*

"Not reason enough." If possible, he slowed his pace.

"I'm privy to more than you are when it comes to my friend," Midge reminded, plowing forward as though sheer determination would force him to move faster. "And if her visitor is the woman I suspect, things might become very difficult for her and Mr. Miller in short order."

"That's their business." He stopped altogether, his hand clamping down upon hers to ensure she stopped alongside him.

Midge glowered and tried to pry herself free. "She might need me. I won't leave her to deal with a shock like this all on her own."

"She's not alone. If, as you suspect, it's her family in the coach, she has them and Gavin." Amos showed no signs of budging.

"Besides which, it's not your place to pop up every time trouble comes calling. Even your closest friends have to learn to stand on their own feet."

"People shouldn't have to stand on their own."

"We never do. The most important support and best friend Miss Chandler can call on is always available."

She gave a mighty tug but didn't gain so much as an inch. "Not with you keeping me in town!"

"Silly." His fond smile might have charmed her at any other time. "I meant the Lord. He's with them at the mill, His hand is upon them, and it's not your place to intrude on whatever family matters unfold there this afternoon."

"You're serious." Midge held stock still. "That's your answer when a friend faces trouble—prayer?"

"Absolutely. Better yet, I add my prayers to theirs."

Prayer. Midge swallowed a sneer. It always came back to prayer with the good folk of Buttonwood—talking with Someone who either couldn't hear you or only listened enough to get the wrong idea when He bothered to help at all. Why hide behind something as insubstantial as prayer when a body could do something in the here and now?

"Be practical, Amos."

"I am." Something in her tone must have grabbed his attention, because his smile vanished. "You don't see prayer as being practical in nature, Midglet?"

"Midglet? What is this?" The man chose a strange time to create an endearment.

"Little Midge. . .Midglet."

"It sounds like *piglet*." She couldn't let him know she liked the name—not that easily. Not when they were about to argue. Not when she probably wouldn't hear him say it again.

"I like baby pigs, and I like you even better. Now answer the question." The teasing faded away, leaving him serious. "You don't see the use of prayer?"

"No." And no amount of cute nicknames could change her mind or make her cushion the truth of how she saw things. Even if it did make her wish he'd either started calling her Midglet earlier or never started. For him to show such affection now, when he was about to decide not to spend time with her anymore, seemed an awful sort of joke. "Prayer isn't practical at all."

"You think God asks us to do something without purpose?" If his brows raised his hat brim before, now it rested so low on his forehead it almost hid the intensity of his gaze.

"I don't pretend to know God's purpose, Amos."

"What do you know?" No teasing lightened the words, but neither did belligerence underscore them. Amos sounded thoughtful, hesitant, as though treading lightly.

That I don't want to talk about God. Midge sighed. "I know that I want to go visit Marge, and you're stopping me."

"You can't keep her here." If the man didn't move, Daisy would shove him out of her way. She'd made the decision after her last encounter with Trouston that no man would bully her again—and that went double for Marge.

The very thought that he'd lured her cousin here with the promise of marriage only to keep her trapped in the middle of nowhere with no wedding and no hope for escape enraged Daisy beyond all measure. She hadn't intended this visit to Buttonwood be a rescue mission, but obviously that was precisely what was called for.

Pity Gavin Miller has such a strong-looking jaw instead of a weak chin like Trouston. I might be tempted to try that maneuver of Mr. Lindner's. . . .

"He's not holding me in Buttonwood against my will, Daisy." Marge's dry tone went a long way toward convincing her. "There are stages coming through here regularly—I could have chosen to return at any time."

"Looks like Mr. Miller disagrees with that assessment." Daisy shouldn't have had to point out the forbidding expression overtaking the man's face at Marge's mere mention of leaving, but something told her it was important.

"I do." He crossed his arms. "I brought Marge out here to be my bride. She can't just run off at the first sign things won't be a fairy tale."

"Surely you aren't referring to me?" Daisy matched him glower for glower. "I didn't run away from my fiancé, Mr. Miller."

"Sounds like it."

"Gavin"—Marge moved forward—"we don't know what happened with Daisy and Trouston, but I would think you'd be glad to see her." A strange look Daisy couldn't quite interpret flashed across Marge's face. "I, for one, never cared for the man. And I told her so."

"I should have listened." One of those pesky waves of regret threatened to swamp her. "But I didn't run off, Mr. Miller. Trouston Dillard drove me away. There's a difference."

"Makes a man wonder if Mr. Dillard sees things in the same light." Disapproval radiated from Gavin so strongly, Daisy almost wondered whether he suspected the truth of the matter.

She sniffed. "Of course he doesn't, though I wouldn't believe a word he says if you ever have the misfortune of speaking with him."

"It does seem men are not inclined to admit when they've made a mistake." That time, the look Marge threw Gavin spoke

798

volumes. Perhaps Marge didn't want to flee, but her fiancé still had a lot to answer for.

And Daisy aimed to make sure he did.

"I've owned up to my mistakes."

"Privately, perhaps." Something glinted in Marge's eyes, but Daisy couldn't tell for sure whether it was moisture or determination. "Publicly makes for another matter, doesn't it, Gavin?"

Daisy sucked in a breath. *Some mistakes should never be made public. Not when there's nothing to be done about them. . .*

"Some truths serve better as secrets. It protects people." His explanation almost echoed Daisy's own thoughts.

"From embarrassment?" Marge gave no quarter. "Things will be worse now for having waited to tell everyone about the mix-up. They'll wonder why we didn't say something from the start. Why—" It seemed as though her cousin caught herself just before she spilled the most interesting bits.

She always does that.

"They won't wonder about a thing. There's no need."

Marge's head snapped back. "I know they won't wonder why once they see Daisy. It's obvious why a man would want to be her fiancé. They'll wonder about the reasons things didn't work out."

"Do folks here know about Trouston?" Her heart fell. *So many miles away, and I still can't escape the past? Are gossips truly that effective even out in the wilds where they have no telegraphs, railroads, or newspapers?*

"That's not what I meant—"

"I know," Marge outright interrupted Gavin—his mouth was still open and everything—"but Daisy doesn't know what you're talking about. She thinks we're discussing gossip about her leaving her fiancé in Baltimore—not the situation right here in Buttonwood."

"What situation?" Daisy got the distinct feeling she'd missed something. Something important.

"Marge," his voice came, holding a warning Daisy, for one, would have been too cowardly not to heed, "don't."

Marge always had been the brave one. Pain and pride warred in her cousin's eyes. "The reason Gavin and I aren't wed, Daisy, is that I'm not the Marguerite he wanted."

"You mean?" She gasped and stared from Gavin to Marge and back again. "The letter. . ." Daisy wouldn't have believed it to be possible, but suddenly she felt even worse than she had before.

Marge blinked, and Daisy knew with bone-deep certainty the glint had been tears all along. "Gavin doesn't want me."

"No." His growl went ignored by Marge, but Daisy heard the vehemence in it.

"Yes. He proposed to *you*."

CHAPTER 32

Amos Geer didn't consider himself a coward. Far from it. When trouble reared its head, he faced it. When his family needed something, he set out to get it. When tragedy struck, he called on the Lord and plowed ahead until he overcame the challenge or learned enough from it to make it worth the trial.

But for the first time since Pa's death, Amos found himself tempted to avoid something, ignore the warnings clanging in his mind. Wish it away, or at the very least, borrow an ostrich's trick of burying his head in the sand until trouble passed on.

I could do it, Jesus. I could set my feet to walking, take Midge to the mill, and leave the questions knocking on the back of my brain right here on the road. All it would take is not asking anything more. Not taking the chance that I'll hear what seems most likely, given everything Midge tells me so far.

Only problem was he couldn't. Lead might as well coat his feet for all they moved. It certainly felt as though something that thick and heavy clogged his chest, strangling the contentment he'd enjoyed the past week as his courtship progressed.

You don't give us a heart of fear, Lord. But then again, You haven't given me the wife I desire either.

He looked at her, reading the obstinance and impatience dotting her thoughts as clearly as those pert little freckles sprinkled her nose and cheeks. *I assumed she belonged to You.*

Please, please don't let me be wrong this time, Lord.

"Well?" She huffed the word out. Midge obviously didn't want to speak about the important things any more than he did. Most likely, they both knew where such a conversation would lead.

Can it be that my prickly little Midglet doesn't want to divide us any more than I do?

Some of the weight eased from his chest, though not much. "Let Marge handle her visitor as she sees fit. This is more important." He walked her over toward a bench outside the church.

"What is?" The closer they came to the church, the heavier her steps became. "Amos?" Fear didn't color her voice, but hesitance shaded each syllable, telling him as clearly as if she'd shouted it that she didn't want this conversation.

He sat her down on the bench, noticing she sank onto it as though relieved. *Relieved I didn't take her inside the church?* His suspicions solidified more with each passing moment, coagulating into a clot of foreboding.

The way she fidgeted through every sermon—even more restless than usual. Her constant moodiness on Sundays. The way he'd never heard her refer to God, never seen her volunteer to pray, never spotted her with Bible in hand. Everything pointed to the one thing he'd never thought to see, never thought to look for in a woman raised by such an obviously religious family. *But the Reeds didn't raise Midge, they adopted her.*

"You're right." Amos didn't sit beside her, instead standing in front. He had two reasons for the posture—first, it kept her attention on him, making it overly difficult for her to hop up and rush away, and second, he knew good and well he couldn't sit calmly with his thoughts in such turmoil.

"Of course." She raised a brow as though prompting him to continue. When he didn't, she sighed. "About what this time?"

"I was nosy when it came to learning everything I could about you. Whatever watching couldn't tell me, I tried to pry out of you. If that didn't work, asking others usually did."

"No need to admit it. I already knew."

"The thing of it is," Amos continued, pacing a few steps away and back as he tried to best phrase what wore at his mind, "I never thought to investigate the most important aspect of your character. When it came down to the crucial matters, I made assumptions. Assumptions I'm starting to think were wrong."

"Dangerous things—assumptions." She reached up and fiddled with the battered locket she always wore. "I suppose now that you've spent time with me, you've found flaws in my character that lead you to believe I would make you a poor wife?"

"Dangerous things—assumptions." He managed a small smile. "I've not unearthed any flaws to make me stop courting you, Midglet. But questions have risen to the surface, and I can't ignore them or pretend the answers won't matter."

"If you've not found the flaws, you've not looked hard enough." The slight movement of her jaw told him she ground her teeth in between sentences. "It's only a matter of time, so perhaps the wisest course of action would be to part ways now?"

"Fatalism is every bit as unattractive as hypocrisy."

"Seems to me fate's never been pretty." She stood, her nose almost touching his chin when he didn't step back. "So there's no reason for you to be surprised."

He put a hand on her shoulder and pressed her back onto the bench. "Why don't you let me be the judge of that?"

～◎～

"Me?" Daisy's squeak made Marge wince.

Well, if she felt like being completely fair, it wasn't so much the squeak as the reason for it. But Marge didn't feel like being fair. *Honestly, what's the point of it anymore? If I spend my time trying to give everyone else a fair shake, I'm the only one who winds up exhausted and with nothing to show for it. In the end, being fair doesn't end up fair at all!*

"Yes, you." Since Gavin seemed to have decided not to say a word, Marge confirmed the awful truth.

Awful to her, at least. Not so awful for Daisy, whose charmed life showed no signs of slowing down. Lose a fiancé, come to visit her cousin, find one she didn't even know she had. . . .

I wonder what it must be like to have so many options. A rueful little bubble of laughter swelled up, but Marge didn't let it out. If she let out any emotion, everything might come pouring forth in one massive flood.

"But I had already accepted Trouston's proposal!" Daisy protested as though tacking on some facts could possibly change others. "You couldn't mean to propose to an engaged woman."

"I didn't know you'd accepted another proposal." Gavin's annoyance came through loud and clear. In fact, even though he didn't roll his eyes, Marge could see his resisting the impulse.

She almost didn't blame him. At least, she wouldn't blame him if the entire wretched mess wasn't *all his fault*! Imagine proposing to a woman using a name she shared with another single woman in the same household and expecting the occupants to read his mind as to which woman he wanted.

Except I did know which woman he wanted. From the very start. That pesky propensity toward fairness wouldn't leave well enough alone. *As a matter of fact, Daisy thought the same thing. Why else would she tear apart her desk to unearth the list of wedding invites and make sure Gavin hadn't been writing to her? We both knew which cousin would be his first choice. . . .*

She closed her eyes, hoping to blot out the truth. Or, if not the truth, at least the appalled look on Daisy's face.

"Oh, Marge. I'm terribly sorry." Her cousin's voice sounded. . . defeated. "I'd so hoped one of us would find happiness with our fiancés. Instead, neither of us will be wed."

"Let's not be overly hasty." Gavin cleared his throat. "While you have my. . .condolences. . .that things didn't work out with Mr. Dillard, that by no means invalidates my engagement."

"But. . .we aren't engaged." Daisy's blink might as well have been a hammer's blow to Marge's heart. "I never accepted you, Mr. Miller. Marge did. Mistakenly, but. . ."

"Mr. Miller's proposal wasn't mine to accept." *Really, this conversation is worse than a Cheltenham tragedy—or a farce.*

"Marge, we've discussed this." Gavin sounded as though he scarcely held on to whatever thin layer remained of his patience. "I used your name, you accepted, I accepted your acceptance—no matter the technicalities of intent, you remain my fiancée."

"We have discussed this." She snapped out the words, refusing to pretend a calm she didn't even remotely feel. "Intent comprises far more than a technicality when it comes to a proposal. Daisy was your intended fiancée."

"This is why you haven't married him?"

"Yes." For once, she and Gavin had the same answer—at the same time.

"Yet you still offered to wed her, once it became clear what happened?" Daisy's mouth hung open in what, even to Daisy, classified as an unappealing manner. She probably realized it, because she closed her jaw after just a moment. "Why?"

That did it. *Even my cousin can't fathom why Gavin would make such a sacrificing gesture?* "Thank you." She kept the irony from her response and straightened her shoulders, ignoring Daisy to look Gavin in the eye. "I've been wondering the same thing for weeks and am no closer to understanding it."

His roar was immediate—and deafening. "Have you both gone daft? Do all women lack sense, or is it limited to those bearing the name Marguerite?"

"Well, we Ermintrudes happen to be renowned for our good sense." She half stalked, half hobbled into their midst, making Marge wonder how she hadn't noticed the old woman's approach. "But on behalf of womankind, I'd say it's men who bellow insults at the two women to whom they've offered proposals who may just be lacking their wits."

A spurt of laughter escaped Daisy, though she quickly stifled it. "I agree, and though it didn't seem to be the case, I meant to ask Marge why she refused to wed you. Now, of course, I needn't ask. You're not nearly so agreeable as I remember!"

"I presume that you, of course, are Daisy." Ermintrude glanced from the newcomer to Marge as though looking for similarities. She'd find precious few, Marge knew.

"None other. I'm pleased to make your acquaintance, Mrs. Miller." Daisy bobbed an informal curtsy. On the prairie. For the grandmother of the man who'd mistakenly proposed to her cousin. The same grandmother who now eyed her as though she were a prime candidate for Bedlam.

"Afraid I can't claim the same, missy. Your arrival throws a spoke in the works." As usual, Ermintrude didn't stop to sweeten her thoughts with a coating of diplomacy. "My grandson made great strides with that one"—she poked her cane toward Marge—"until you showed up. Now that's all gone out the window."

Somehow Marge managed to keep her expression impassive, while on the inside she vehemently agreed with the old woman who'd come to be her friend. *Absolutely. Now that Daisy's here, things can be rectified. Gavin will court the woman he always wanted, and I'll gracefully bow out and focus on teaching.*

Never mind the streak of pain that came every time she imagined Gavin speaking the wedding vows to her cousin or the dull, throbbing ache that seemed to have taken up permanent residence in her chest. That would ease in time, as did the pain of every sort of loss. Yet there seemed to Marge an odd creaking from the vicinity of her heart as all three of them made their way toward the house.

It wasn't until after they'd given the coach driver something to eat and sent him on his way that Marge managed to identify what it was.

Pandora's box. . .with Daisy here, even hope has left me behind.

Chapter 33

"Why should I let you decide?" Midge sat down despite the defiance of her words. *Why wait for the inevitable?*

"Because we don't always make the same decisions, you and I." This time, he sat beside her, his knees angled toward hers in a silent display that he didn't intend to leave just yet. "You might like mine better."

"I'm used to depending on myself." *Which means I shouldn't like the fact you're still here. It shouldn't matter.*

"Most people admire self-reliance."

"Not you?" She raised a brow. "Strange, since you seem remarkably self-reliant and capable in most things you do."

"Ah, but that's not true." He leaned back, but somehow his shoulders filled even more space.

"I've watched for long enough to know."

"Depending on yourself again? What you see and what you hear shapes everything you believe?" Amos held himself too still to be as comfortable as his stance indicated.

"What I see, hear, touch…everything I experience. The things that happen around me, things people do to show who they are. I watch and listen and learn." The more tension he exhibited, the more comfortable Midge felt. "And you do the same thing. It's part of why I avoided you for so long."

"Afraid of what I'd see when I looked at you?" He pinned her with the question—asked in his words and his eyes.

"Not afraid." *Uneasy, yes. Uncomfortable, yes. But afraid?* Midge Collins was no coward. "Just. . .aware."

Amos kept silent precisely long enough to make her wonder if she'd won that easily, only to come back with the last thing she'd expected. "Aware of me, but not aware enough to know what I truly rely on?"

It fell into place so swiftly Midge felt as though she should hear a *thud*. "God. You're going to say that you rely on God more than you rely on yourself. Am I right? Is that it?"

Of course it is. That's what all Christians say, even while they do all the day-to-day work of taking care of themselves and their loved ones. God doesn't do it, and they don't expect Him to. People see to the details of life. I do. Saul does. Amos does. The only difference lies in who gets the credit. I don't give mine away.

"Yes."

This time, Midge let the silence spin out between them, deepening, widening until it became a heavy, noiseless gulf. An uncomfortable ocean she didn't have the means to cross, because she didn't share his belief in the benevolence of a God who let people suffer every day. Even good people who deserved better. Maybe even especially the good people who deserved better.

"What are you thinking?" Amos broke through the barrier she could not, for all the good it would do.

"You don't want to know." Midge gave him the truth and waited for him to refute it, insisting that he wanted to hear whatever she preferred not to reveal.

"There's some truth to that. No one wants to know things that make someone special seem farther away." Somehow his acknowledgement of what was happening helped bridge the gap.

Midge looked at him for a long moment. "Then don't ask."

"I already did."

"You already know the answer."

"It's not the same as hearing it from you, Midge." He seemed determined to make this as difficult as possible.

"Fine." The fact she sounded like a petulant twelve-year-old gave her pause, so she modified her tone. "Fact of the matter is I don't believe in prayer because it's never worked for me, and I've seen it fail the people I care about. Logical people form theories based on observation."

"Now you sound like the daughter of a doctor." His wry grin salved some of the sting from his words.

Though, in truth, the sting came not from his opinion that she sounded like Saul's daughter but from the irrefutable fact she wasn't. "I'll take that to mean it sounds like good sense."

"To an extent, but it leaves too much unaccounted for when you rely on your own sense. Or senses, as the case may be." He stretched his legs out as though settling in for a long conversation—which, come to think of it, he most likely was.

"Personally, I prefer to leave things unaccounted for, with room for potential error, rather than assign credit where none is proven due."

"You speak of faith as though it's a fallacy."

"Do I?" She leaned back against the bench, resigned to following the conversation all the way through to its natural end. To their natural end. "Although I never thought of it that way, it's a good way of putting it."

"No, it's not." He straightened up, planting his boots in the dirt. "You're discounting the way faith has different roles to play, Midge. Faith doesn't merely exist to serve."

"Did I say such a thing? Faith offers comfort to those who can't or won't understand the true nature of the world around them, Amos. False comfort. I want no part of it." There. She said it. Any moment now he'd stand up and walk away, just like she'd always known he would.

Sure, it had taken him longer than she expected to realize the truth about her, but he'd figured it out. Eventually. More importantly, his newfound realizations would prove her right. . .again. Amos would lose interest in her and prayer didn't work—two different things he wouldn't have agreed with, but Midge knew better.

"So it's not just prayer you don't believe in. It's God, too?" If words could drown in sorrow, his would.

"Don't be ridiculous, Amos. Of course I believe in God. Any reasoning person with the eyes to see the world has to know it didn't just sprout up willy-nilly or by chance. Complex systems don't simply appear, and there's far too much order to the natural world for it to be accidental. God exists."

Confusion beetled his brows. "Then why don't you believe in prayer, Midge?"

"I didn't say I don't believe in God, Amos. He simply hasn't done anything to justify having faith in His goodness." She stood up and started to make her way back to the house. *I'll visit Marge tomorrow. He may have a point about her having to handle things on her own.*

"In a nutshell, you've decided God exists but that He's not worth having faith in?" Amos's voice called after her, letting her know it had begun. He wasn't following anymore.

Midge wondered why she felt none of the grim satisfaction she'd been expecting. "Exactly."

~⊚~

"What are you doing?" Gavin waited until Daisy excused herself for a "private moment" before pulling Marge aside. As things stood, the only way he caught hold of her alone was lying in wait in the hall for her to wander back from showing her cousin to the necessary.

"I assumed Daisy and I would share the guest room." She stared at him with a blankness he found unnerving. "It simply wouldn't be proper for one of us to sleep in the master bedroom—even while you continue to bunk in the mill."

"That's not what I meant." Although for a fleeting moment the thought crossed his mind that with Daisy there as an additional chaperone, it might be possible for him to move back into the house without provoking undue gossip. "What were you thinking, telling your cousin I meant the letter for her originally?"

"I thought it best to tell the truth. After all," she declared, closing her eyes and pausing before continuing, "you're the one who told her we aren't married. Surely you knew she'd ask why?"

"Yes, but we could have told her the same thing we told the rest of the town—that we waited until you felt comfortable and certain you wanted to make a life here in Buttonwood." That sounded weak when spoken aloud, but Gavin couldn't very well take it back now. "Or that until you had the school up and running, that took the bulk of your focus."

"She's my cousin, I'm tired of half-truths, and this concerns her directly."

Her remonstrance hit the mark, making him uncomfortable with the way they'd been deceiving everyone in town. "Half-truths are better than whole lies, particularly when one works toward making them more and more real."

"I'm finished fooling myself, Gavin. Whole truths are best." Marge made as though to move past him and return to the parlor.

"Wait. If you wanted to tell Daisy the whole truth, why did you leave out the most important part?" Her expression told him plain as daylight she didn't know what he meant. "You left out the fact that I'd proposed to you since we discovered the switch. You told Daisy all about the way I'd originally written to her but didn't say how I've courted you ever since."

"She knows you offered to go through with the arrangement. Don't worry. Daisy doesn't think poorly of you for not marrying me. She knows you tried to stand by your word, even when you hadn't given it." The confusion cleared from her features, replaced by that dull, vague look he found so disturbing.

"That's not the same thing, and you know it."

"What do you want from me, Gavin?" For a split second, the blank mask fell away, revealing the conflict raging beneath. Fierce, proud, despairing—she embodied all these things and more as she rounded on him, enough to drive away a man's breath.

His lack of response settled her back to impassivity, making Gavin wish he'd thought more quickly.

"Daisy knows you initially proposed to her. She knows that once you discovered the mistake you stood prepared to do the honorable thing and marry me to uphold your word." It sounded almost as though she ticked things off some sort of mental list. Knowing Marge, she most likely was. "She sees the house and mill, knows you from back in Baltimore, and understands that I wouldn't let you marry me out of a sense of duty. That doesn't reflect poorly on you."

"None of that matters." He reached for her hand, but she

shoved it into one of those ever-present pockets hiding within the folds of her skirts. "What matters is that she doesn't know how I've pursued *you*, Marge."

"That doesn't signify." She shook her head, her smooth bun scarcely moving at all with the motion. "She needn't hear my tales of your thoughtfulness, Gavin."

"So long as you remember them, I'm satisfied."

"You owe me nothing." She straightened her shoulders as though brushing away all his efforts, an impression verified by her next words. "You're free to woo Daisy, as you always wanted."

CHAPTER 34

Marge almost made it past him when his hand closed around her forearm. *Why won't he let me go? I've not harmed his chances with Daisy. Does he want my promise to put in a good word, help his cause?*

The ache in her chest echoed at her temples as the thought hammered home. *Daisy changes everything, except the parts I most wish she could.* Her cousin's vivacious beauty snatched attention, admiration, and the marital aspirations of the one man Marge wanted. It seemed a cruel hoax that, in spite of everything taken away, Marge was left with the regrets and disappointments of all that came before.

"How can you think I'd transfer my attentions to your cousin so swiftly?" Gavin's grip tightened a fraction before easing, as though he fought the urge to shake her.

Marge put her hand over his and pulled his fingers away. For once, the contact didn't send spirals of warmth cascading through her. If anything, she felt colder once he let go.

"Why wait, Gavin? You planned to be married to her weeks

ago. Don't postpone things for the sake of pride."

"Pride?" A muscle jumped in his jaw. "You think I choose not to pursue your cousin out of misplaced pride? You sell us both short, Marge, if you can think of no other reason."

"Some of the members in town will think you fickle." The admission brought a kick of vindication she carefully didn't show. "Until we explain what happened. Then no one will see you poorly. I'll make sure they have no questions about your integrity, Gavin. I promise you that."

"What of your integrity, Marge? As far as everyone is concerned, *you* are my fiancée."

"Oh." *He's worried about my reputation.* She dragged in a deep breath. "There are some who will be unhappy, maybe even hurt I didn't confide in them, but Clara and Opal will forgive me in light of the circumstances."

"That's not what I meant." Anger marched along the set of his jaw as he stared at her.

Lord, how is it that I'm reassuring the man I thought You'd sent me to marry that it's perfectly all right for him to abandon me? No, I know why. I know it's the right thing. But my heart doesn't understand why You've let me go through all this, if the outcome is so harsh.

"Midge already knows the truth, as does Ermintrude. The town council has been aware from the beginning that we might not become man and wife. In fact, this makes me a better choice for schoolmarm in a lot of eyes." If Marge could have dredged up a smile, she would have, but it proved an impossibility.

He stepped forward, his boots brushing her skirts, his head tilted so she couldn't avoid his eyes or words. "Forget the rest of the town, Marge. They don't matter. What about you?"

Her heart clenched and collapsed at the intensity she read in his face, at how fiercely he asked after her well-being. *Why, oh why couldn't he want me? Why is he only worried or showing any sort of tender feeling now, when it comes down to his ability to leave me behind?*

"I don't blame you, Gavin." She took a step to the side, pressing against the wall to sidle past him to the safety of the parlor... of Ermintrude's company.

"You shouldn't. I tried my best to make it work. You're the one sending me to your cousin." The more softly he spoke, the deeper his voice became and the darker his mood sounded. "If you've anyone to blame, Marge, it's yourself."

She froze. "What?"

"I didn't say anything, Marge." Daisy breezed through the door. "Though I am a bit tired after all that traveling. Would it be too terribly selfish to ask to be shown to our room for a little rest before supper?"

"Not at all," Gavin answered for her, turning on his heel and stalking into the parlor. "Marge will be happy to show you. I'll let Grandma know before I get back to work."

Marge watched him go, fighting the urge to stop him and demand what he'd meant by blaming her for anything when there was no possible way for her to be more understanding. *What good can come of it?* She tamped down the newfound spring of resentment and led Daisy up the stairs to the room she'd come to view as her haven.

Another thing I can't think of as mine anymore. Shame flooded her. *It's little wonder hope left me—I don't deserve it. Gavin needs a better wife than I can be if I've become such a bitter wretch I begrudge my cousin anything. Daisy is the sister of my heart!*

But no sooner did she open the door to the room than a traitorous voice added the sort of thought she most needed to avoid. *And going to be the wife of the man who holds that heart. Little wonder you're not as pleased to see her as usual.*

"How charming!" Daisy stood in the center of the room and did a little twirl. "Small, though I'm sure we'll manage."

"It's a good-sized room when not filled with luggage." Marge didn't just mean her own; for a girl who'd snuck out right beneath Aunt Verlata's nose, Daisy managed to pack an astonishing amount. "Between the two of us, we must have brought half of Baltimore to Buttonwood."

"Good." Daisy bounced onto the bed. "From what I've seen, the place could use a few more touches of civilization!"

"If by civilization you mean crowded streets, air filled with soot, and the smells of far too many people packed on top of each other, I far prefer the wild West." Marge sank onto the chair positioned before the drop front desk that hid a few now-drying purple daisies.

"Don't be so negative. I'm talking about paved streets, shops and businesses, parks, and the like."

"The general store here is enormous, and whatever they don't carry one can order via catalog. With the mill, the smithy, a church, the new schoolhouse, and even a café, Buttonwood has everything we could need. Besides"—Marge gestured toward the expanse of land and sky shown through the window—"the prairie puts any park to shame."

"No dressmakers or cobblers or haberdasheries or confectioners or lending libraries..." Daisy frowned. "I'm glad you're content with so little, Marge, but you'll not convince me a place like this is any match for the comforts of home."

"But...you just learned that Gavin proposed to you." A faint flutter signaled the return of a hope Marge began to feel she was better off without. "How can you decide against staying when you've only been here an hour?"

❧❧❧

"Don't be silly, Marge."

"When have you known me to be silly?"

That brought her up short. Daisy thought for a moment, and probably would have thought long and hard, but it seemed too important to waste the time on something as trite as thinking. "Never. So don't start now. Gavin might have written that letter to me weeks ago, but we both know I'm not the Marguerite he wants to marry anymore."

Marge blinked but didn't say anything, which could be a good sign or a terrible one. To tell the truth, Daisy never saw Marge speechless, so she couldn't say for certain which way it went. She decided to be optimistic.

"We just have to make sure he realizes it."

"Daisy, Gavin wanted *you*. He got the surprise of a lifetime when I stepped off that stage, and while he's acted nothing but a gentleman and offered to do his duty"—her cousin grimaced, and Daisy couldn't blame her—"by marrying me, I turned him down. That means he's more than free to pursue you. Since you're no longer engaged, it's the perfect situation."

"You can't be serious." *She isn't serious. That's all there is to it. Marge isn't offering me the man she wants to marry—the one she got so excited about building a life with she wrote endless lists of what to bring to the wilderness. The only thing that ever inspired her to care about what dress she wore. She isn't trying to convince me to take her place?*

Belatedly, Daisy realized Marge had been talking the whole time she'd been lost in thought. *Oops. No matter. Whatever she said doesn't change the fact that, deep down, Marge wants to be Mrs. Miller. And I don't.* Guilt and shame tugged at her stomach. *Even if I did, I couldn't. . .now that I've been ruined.*

"I cannot believe you're trying to convince me to spring from one failed engagement into the midst of another failed engagement, Marge." When all else failed, Daisy learned long ago that tears worked. That proved fortunate, since they sprang up so very easily these days. "You and Gavin didn't work out, so you're trying to foist him off on me, when I'm still recovering from what happened with Trouston?"

"Oh, Daisy." Marge got up from the spindly desk chair and walked over to sit beside her on the bed. "How thoughtless of me. I'm sorry. Tell me all about it."

In an instant, Daisy realized her mistake in bringing up the fiasco that had been her abandoned engagement. She'd known Marge would ask about her reasons for breaking things off with Trouston, but she hadn't planned on bringing it up directly. Avoidance would have been best for as long as possible. Especially since she hadn't yet decided how much to tell Marge.

"It's just all so upsetting." She indulged in a satisfyingly loud sniff. All right—a great galumphing snort of a sniff. The likes of which would horrify her mother, who wasn't here to remind her to be ladylike at all times. *Perhaps there are benefits to the West, after all.* The thought cheered her, but she refused to smile. If she did, Marge would expect her to be more forthcoming

"You used to be so devoted to him. Is there. . .is there any chance you're put out with him now but you'll forgive him later?" Marge spoke slowly, softly, as though testing the waters.

"No!" Daisy's response came out sharp enough to make her cousin jump. "Absolutely not. I'll never go back to him, no matter what he says or does or promises."

Marge slid an arm around her waist and rubbed her back. "I've never seen you so. . .put out. What did he do?"

Her cousin's kindness proved Daisy's undoing. Everyone else had demanded to know, or asked in such a way as though making her out to be some sort of flighty chit out for attention. Not Marge—Marge understood just like she always had.

"You wouldn't believe it." The tears burst forth—not gently sliding down her cheeks anymore but pouring out in great gushes that had her going through both their handkerchiefs in minutes. "He pretends to be such a gentleman, so upstanding, so considerate and attentive, as though he'd make a perfect husband. But it's all an act, Marge! If you knew what he's really like, how terrible a monster lurks beneath what he shows everyone else, you'd be positively horrified by how close I came to marrying the man. I know I am." *And you'd be even more horrified to know that it's my fault for letting him ruin me.*

"He's a fraud then?" Marge's tone indicated that she'd suspected as much.

No. . .I'm the fraud. But so was Trouston. In fact, hadn't Marge warned Daisy Trouston seemed too good to be true?

"I believe it. He seemed something of a ladies' man, but it looked like you had him in your pocket."

"You're right." Daisy seized on the opportunity to explain the problem without revealing her own lapse. "He's the most horrid womanizer, Marge. I can't live with that."

"You don't have to. We should have known, Daisy. Trouston was too smooth and polished to be anything but a slippery eel."

"A trout." Daisy wallowed in the most gratifying blubber of her life. "Did you ever notice it's what his name sounds like? And sort of how he looks, if you truly think about it." She gave a vindictive *honk* into her third handkerchief.

Her cousin didn't hesitate for an instant. "With his pale skin, thin whiskers, and the way his eyes bulge out when someone surprises him? Yes, I noticed, but you were so taken with him it seemed petty to point it out at the time."

"Don't forget his weak chin." She fought a smile at the memory of Trouston crumpling to the ground beneath Mr. Lindner's fist. "Surely that contributes to the entire impression of fishiness."

"Without a doubt." Marge handed her a fourth linen square, although Daisy didn't think she'd be needing it.

"I feel much more myself now." She let out a small smile. "Coming to Buttonwood was the right choice."

CHAPTER 35

"So you figured it out." Dr. Saul Reed ushered Amos into his exam room and diagnosed the trouble in one glance. "I wondered how long it would take. You strike me as highly observant."

"She's not a believer." He walked in but didn't take the seat the older man indicated. "That's not the sort of thing I expected to discover, Dr. Reed. It is the sort of thing I would expect a man to reveal to another man who asks permission to court his daughter."

"As you pointed out at the time, when I remarked that it seemed like a conversation you should have broached with me in private, you weren't seeking her hand." Reed raised a brow. "You sought permission to spend time with her and grow to know her well enough to determine whether or not you'd be a good match. Rest assured, had things progressed beyond this point, I would have made certain you knew of her beliefs."

"Or lack thereof." Now, Amos sat. "I doubt most of the town knows that she attends church more for your benefit than her own?"

"Very few are aware of where Midge stands spiritually. Her

heart and the way she treats others speak for themselves in most instances, and folks take her at face value."

"You mean they assume, as I did, that she believes in the Lord based on the way she lives."

"Midge puts many Christians to shame when it comes to carrying through biblical precepts in daily life, though she doesn't realize it." Reed took a seat across from him. "She is, however, all too aware of the hypocrisy of many Christians."

"I see." *Then the problem has more than one facet. The human witness and the divine evidence both present challenges to her.*

"Do you? I'm not sure how much of her past she's discussed with you, Mr. Geer, but the Lord is working mightily in Midge's heart." Dr. Reed leaned back. "And He has been for the four years since He entrusted her to my care."

"We've not discussed her past. Any hint that the conversation headed that direction, she shut it down or changed the topic." Amos bent forward to rest his forearms on his knees. "Nor did I suspect her lack of faith. Although once she mentioned her views on prayer, it seemed so obvious I couldn't believe I'd missed it."

"We frequently miss what we don't look for. Midge counts on that to maintain her place in this town and protect my standing. It's what I believe Doreen referred to when she mentioned it being a good thing Midge attempted to avoid you. You see more than most."

"Not enough."

"Not yet. But you care enough to keep asking. That's good." Dr. Reed rose to his feet. "I begin to think you might be the match we've prayed for."

"I won't be unequally yoked, Dr. Reed." Following the older man's cue, Amos stood. In truth, Dr. Reed didn't even have a decade on him, but his profession and his family lent him an undeniable maturity. "Midge's disbelief is an unanticipated obstacle."

"Obstacles are created to be overcome." The doctor opened the door. "The only question is whether or not you feel the reward is worth the undertaking."

Amos didn't hesitate. "Undoubtedly. I take it." He eyed the door as he asked, "This means you don't intend to enlighten me about Midge's past?"

Dr. Reed shook his head. "It's not my story to tell, and I won't do you or Midge the disservice of interfering in that way. Best you find her and convince her to confide in you."

"I will." Amos walked through the door and took his hat from where it hung on a peg in the hall. "You can be sure of that."

"You want to come with me to visit Marge?" Midge gave Amos a dubious look the next morning. "Why?"

"To be honest, I'm more interested in having this sack of grain ground up." Amos gestured to the bag on his shoulder. "I'll leave the socializing to you."

She ignored the appealing grin. "Why are you here, Amos?" They both knew he couldn't be unequally yoked—that is, married to a woman who didn't share his belief in God. "I thought we decided I was a waste of your time."

That doesn't sting. I won't let it sting. If I'm not enough for a man on my own, then it's his loss. The bravado sounded hollow even in her head. *All right, it does sting. But I knew from the start I wasn't good enough for a man like Amos Geer, so I've no one to blame but myself.*

"Midglet"—his use of the endearment tore through her—"you're never a waste of time."

"Don't call me that." She started off toward the direction of the mill. "And if you haven't realized I'm a waste of your time, it's only because you don't know me well enough."

He fell into step alongside her. "I'll agree that I don't know you well enough, but I'm trying to fix that."

"You've seen all the good, and it goes downhill from there. It's best to cut your losses, Amos."

"The only way I can lose out is if I let you go without learning everything about you." His words drove sharp spikes of dread and longing through her core.

A broken laugh seeped through her defenses. "Everything?"

"Everything." No doubt clouded his answer. Just certainty, as pure and whole as the man himself—the opposite of anything Midge could offer.

"How about I sum it up for you?" She veered to the right, where she knew she'd find a grove of wild black walnut trees in a few moments. "Follow me and I'll show you exactly what you need to know about Midge Collins. *Everything* you need to know."

He didn't say a word, simply increased his pace to match hers as she hurried to get this over with. What went through his mind she couldn't begin to guess, but before long he'd understand that he should keep far, far away from her.

"Here." She slowed as they reached the trees. These were the oldest, largest plants in the area—just about the only trees aside from a few scrub oaks and cottonwoods. The only reason they'd been left standing rather than harvested by some pioneer for lumber was the walnuts they provided each fall.

"What?" Amos set down his sack of grain, peering around as though waiting for something to become clear. "All I see are walnut trees without any walnuts."

Midge pointed to a stump on the far left, where wind and locusts did their damage until Uncle Josiah chopped it down and carted it away. There'd been no other method of saving the other trees. "That one. You like to observe and investigate. Look closely and tell me what you see, Amos. Everything."

He made his way to the sawn-down tree, crouching before the barren stump and passing his hand across the weather-worn surface. "It's a stump. Walnut tree, same as the others, but one of the oldest—or would have been if it hadn't been cut down. Looks like the roots go deep, and whoever bothered to haul it away saw no need to remove the rest. It's sat here like this for a couple years, at least. The dark marks show folks have put walnuts here during fall harvest."

"True. All true. But that's not the most important part." Midge moved to stand beside him. She reached out, took his hand, and laid it on the dead bark roughing off in brittle flakes along the outside. "Locusts infested it, so they had to cut it down to spare the others."

"This has nothing to do with you, Midge." He started to straighten, but she put a hand on his shoulder.

"I'm explaining." She guided his hand from the bark to the flat surface. "See how worn away, decayed, corrupted the outside is, but the farther inward you go, the more intact it becomes?" She slid their hands toward the center. "The evil attacked and destroyed the outside, making it ugly, but when they cut down the tree, they showed what was good and right went all the way through to the core."

"Now I see." He turned his hand in one swift motion, threading his fingers through hers. "You both have good hearts. Midge, I didn't need to look at a tree stump to know that."

"No!" She yanked her hand from his, but he didn't turn loose. All she managed was to throw herself off balance, so she sat heavily on the stump she'd brought him to. "You didn't let me finish,

Amos." She swallowed back the anger and pride and sadness over how obtuse he insisted on staying—that he forced her to spell it out.

"Finish then." He stayed crouched before her, his thumb rubbing circles at the pulse point on her wrist, making her want to lean forward and get away all at once.

"I'm nothing like this tree. I'm its exact opposite." A ball of heat settled at the bridge of her nose, pressing against the backs of her eyes. "People can't tell when they look at me. I seem all right on the outside, but on the inside, I'm not like the others. They can't remove me or reveal me for what I really am, because it would destroy the Reeds. So instead of taking out the part of the group that's rotten, I stay."

"Midglet, that's a lie." Anger tightened his grip on her hand and deepened his voice. "A foul lie you're far too intelligent to believe, much less expect me to."

"It's the truth." To her horror, the hot ball broke into drops of salty tears she couldn't blink back. "I'm rotten on the inside, ruined by the bad things of the world early on. The pretty parts and smiles are just for show, Amos. Most people just don't bother to look closely enough to notice the truth."

"No one's looked as closely as I have, and I'm telling you you're wrong." He braced his free hand on her other side, closing her in. "The way you see yourself is wrong. No one who's been corrupted and lives with a decayed soul is able to love others the way you do, Midge. . .is able to swallow back her feelings every Sunday and sit in church for the good of her family. Everything you do shows that you care about other people more than you care for yourself, and that makes your core beautiful."

"Sin leaves stains same as the hulls of black walnuts." She lifted her knees into the space between them, braced her heels against the surface of the stump, and pushed back out of his reach, standing up and hopping down as swiftly as possible. "And I already know the way you Christians think, Amos." She kept walking toward the mill, knowing he'd need to go back for his sack of grain before catching up to her.

"You don't know everything, Midglet." He spoke quietly enough for her to pretend not to hear, but his persistence in using that nickname balled her hands into fists.

"You only think a heart is beautiful if it belongs to God. . .and mine doesn't."

CHAPTER 36

Is that cousin of yours still in bed?" Ermintrude looked up from her embroidery when Marge came downstairs with her set of McGuffey's Readers after putting away the breakfast dishes.

"It's been a long journey for her, and she's not used to dealing with anything so taxing." Marge fought off the feeling she was making excuses and sat down in her favorite armchair.

"Of course sitting in a luxuriously cushioned private coach for days on end must be absolutely exhausting."

"She's also nursing a broken heart." *And keeping secrets, which Daisy's never been able to do well.* Marge kept the second part to herself.

Until she knew the full and precise reason why Daisy broke off her engagement to Trouston Dillard III, she refused to speculate or pressure her cousin to accept Gavin's suit. A gnawing worry pressed against the back of her throat every time she remembered the look of panic on Daisy's face when she'd asked what went wrong.

"A broken heart, unlike a broken limb, does not leave a body bedridden." Ermintrude's snort almost sparked a smile in response, but Marge was in no mood for merriment.

"Daisy's accustomed to town hours, where she stays up late into the night and doesn't rise until long after the sun."

"Foolishness and unnatural. I notice you come from Baltimore—on a hired stage—and didn't indulge in such behavior." Approval rang in her friend's voice. "I say the right bride arrived in Buttonwood the first time. Furthermore," she went on, raising her voice when it became apparent Marge intended to interrupt, "I believe my grandson shares my opinion."

Marge decided to ignore the last part altogether. "Since I've always taught school, even in Baltimore, country hours aren't a switch for me. It's not fair to judge Daisy by my schedule."

"Going to avoid the important statement, are you?"

"I'm going to find the story I mentioned to Midge the other day. After church tomorrow is the field day celebration to mark the start of school on Monday. She should be here any time to go over our lessons." With that, Marge buried her nose in a book. The familiar page before her went unread as her mind churned with a thousand things.

"Difficult to read without turning pages."

"Planning lessons requires thoughtful consideration." Her retort to Ermintrude's prodding lacked conviction—mostly because she hadn't been reading or planning lessons at all.

Truly, she'd brought down the books so she'd have them on hand when Midge arrived and only opened them to avoid an uncomfortable conversation with Ermintrude. Obviously she needed a more clever ruse if she wanted to fool the old woman.

"If you can concentrate on grammar when you think you've lost my grandson, then you never deserved him."

"You know me too well for such a short period of time."

Snapping the book shut, Marge set it aside and rose to go stand beside the window. "On the bright side, that means you must know I don't wish to discuss the possibility of Gavin courting my cousin, much less marrying her. At any rate, it seems such things will be placed on hold until such a time as Daisy's heart recovers from the disillusionment she suffered at the hands of her last fiancé."

"Why put them on hold? Let your cousin sleep the days away, recovering, while you marry my grandson." Her rocking chair creaked at a faster pace as the old woman laid out her plans. "Then we'll all be happy, and Sleeping Beauty needn't be disturbed. No delays required."

Thankfully Midge came into sight at that moment, allowing Marge to excuse herself without having to tell Ermintrude precisely how ridiculous she sounded. After all, she'd been raised to respect her elders—even when those elders didn't show much respect in return.

"Midge!" Marge rushed out the door and met her friend several yards from the house, thrilled to make her escape. Thrilled, at least, until she caught sight of Midge's face up close. "Why have you been crying?"

"Amos." She reached up and swiped angrily at her eyes, making the red even more pronounced. "That man simply doesn't know when to accept defeat and call it a day."

"I know a few people like that." Marge led Midge toward the barn, not wanting to return to the house or, worse, venture near the mill. . .where Gavin spent his time. *I wish Gavin wanted me that way—that he chose me, settled on me, and refused to give up until he won me as his bride. But look where my hopes have gotten me so far. I'm better off without them.*

"Hurry." Midge cast a disgruntled glance into the distance behind them, where a figure approached at a rapid pace. "He's catching up and I'm in no mood to speak with him now."

"Here." Marge ducked behind the mill and made a straight path to the small barn, where Gavin kept two oxen to pull his wagon and one milk cow for Ermintrude's sake. She remembered thinking how sweet it was for him to have purchased that cow and taken the time every day to milk it simply because his grandmother favored fresh milk and wanted a regular supply. But those were happier times, when she'd first arrived. When she'd still thought things might work out. She blinked and pointed to the ladder leaning against the hayloft. "We can talk up there for a while, and no one will think to come looking for us."

"Good." Midge scampered up ahead of her, settling into the sweetly scented, slightly prickly hay. "Now, I hate to be nosy. . . ." she started, making Marge laugh for the first time since Daisy arrived the day before.

"No one hates being nosy. People just hate being thought of as nosy." She shook her head. "Since I want to know what Amos did to upset you, I'm just as guilty as you are. Go ahead."

"The beautiful black coach that came through town yesterday headed this direction—everyone will be asking you about it tomorrow at church." Most people's eyes grew red after they were exposed to bunches of loose hay, but on Midge it seemed to have the opposite effect. The signs of her tears all but vanished as she waited for Marge to explain.

"Daisy."

"I thought so." The two of them sat in silence for a moment. Midge understood the magnitude of what Daisy's arrival meant for Marge and her budding relationship with Gavin without Marge needing to expound upon it or bemoan the change. "You would've said if she'd arrived with her fiancé. . .or her husband. I forget when her wedding date was supposed to be."

"Today." Marge closed her eyes and didn't add to the damning nature of that one word.

"Ah." If a mind were a maze and thoughts traveled through, the map of their course was printed in the lines on Midge's forehead. Her brow furrowed, lifted, crinkled, smoothed, and creased as she attempted to solve an impossible quandary. Finally her friend shrugged and said the last thing Marge could have expected.

"Amos knows now that I'm not a Christian, and he doesn't want to marry me anymore."

~~~⚬~~~

"Where is she?" Amos Geer stalked into the mill with a bag of grain on his shoulder and a scowl on his face.

"Which one?" Gavin muttered the response before considering that Amos had no way of knowing about Daisy's arrival.

"Midge, of course." He dumped the sack onto the floor, where it slumped as though dejected to be left there. If a man could resemble a sack of flour, Amos fit the bill as he slouched against one of the mill's wooden support beams. "She won't listen to reason."

"She's a woman." Gavin tied off the bag of flour he'd just filled, adjusted the opening to the fresh one, and tested the grind between thumb and forefinger. *Perfect.* "They don't seem to be in the habit of listening to reason. At least, not around here. Sounds like things aren't much different for you."

"Midge decided I don't want to marry her."

"Marge decided the same thing." Gavin straightened and returned Amos's confidence with one of his own. It felt right, considering they found themselves in the same boat. "Wonder if it's a stubborn schoolmarm characteristic?" They shared a rueful laugh at his joke, despite the fact it wasn't funny at all.

"I could use some wise counsel, and you're about the closest I've come to a friend I can trust since I came to Buttonwood." Geer's admission didn't surprise him.

"Makes sense. Pretty much the same thing here." Since Amos had been the one to help with the mill, Gavin spent enough time with him to trust the other man had a good head on his shoulders. "Both been too busy with work to do much gabbing like women make time for. Marge's only been here a few weeks, and she's already got a gaggle of friends."

"Women manage that. Women and children." They stood in silence for a moment, wondering at the parallel but refusing to say another word about it.

"So what seems to be the trouble with your Miss Collins?" Gavin recalled the night of the dinner party at the Reed place, when everyone welcomed Marge to town, and how he'd disliked the way Geer's eye fell on Marge. Later he'd come to realize the other man's interest lay in Marge's friend—something he was only too happy to support.

"Understanding it goes no further than this conversation." The other man waited for his nod before continuing, "Midge isn't born again. She knows I won't be unequally yoked, and she's decided this means I can't see anything of interest in her."

"She's not a believer?" Gavin heard the astonishment in his own question but didn't try to soften it. "I never would have guessed. Miss Collins attends church regularly. . . ."

"Church attendance and belief are not one and the same."

"True. But usually you see things the other way around." Gavin wiped the flour from his hands on a spare rag. "There are plenty of people who attend church and claim salvation but don't live it out. Miss Collins lives as though she believes, but if what you're saying is accurate, isn't saved. That's surprising."

"I know. At the same time, it shows that her heart's in the right place." Frustration coated the other man's words. "I'm not wrong in the choice of the woman. It's the timing I have to wait on."

"When the heart's good, the soul follows. I'll keep it in prayer, my friend." Gavin bent down and grabbed the fifty-pound sack of grain.

"Thanks." Geer followed him up the stairs to the storage room, where they poured the contents into the bin leading to the hopper.

"This won't take long once I finish Speck's last batch down there."

"Good."

They tromped back down to the main floor. Amos took up his post by the support beam, and Gavin checked the progress of the flour.

Sure enough, the batch had just about finished running— the mill capacity ran at three hundred pounds per hour, after all. Gavin pulled the lever to release Geer's grain into the hopper. He needn't adjust the distance between the stones, and the type of grain hadn't changed. Fine white flour coated his hands and shirt, settling in his hair as it always did when he bent near the output, but he didn't mind.

Breathing in air mixed with flour made it seem as though all was right with the world, even when it wasn't.

Just as the thought crossed his mind, an ominous scrape sounded, simultaneous with the searing flash of burned powder as a spark ignited, setting the mill aflame.

CHAPTER 37

To say the earth shook with her pronouncement might be somewhat of an overstatement, but not nearly so much as Midge would have liked. No sooner did she get to the bottom of what ate at her than a horrendous, grating scrape, followed by a sort of booming explosion, shattered the stillness of the prairie.

If it hadn't been for the fact Marge sat in her way and beat her to it, Midge would've been down the ladder and out the barn door before the sound stopped echoing in her eardrums. As it stood, the two of them raced outside, with Midge pulling up alongside Marge in a desperate rush for the mill.

"Gavin!" Her friend's gasping scream sounded the note of desperation thumping in Midge's own heart—though the name differed. She reached the door the same moment as Midge, her hand closing around the handle with the thoughtless determination to yank it open.

"No!" Midge threw herself between her friend and the door. "Like this!" She pushed them both to the side, behind the wooden barrier as she opened the portal—the only way to offer some scant protection against the possibility that fresh air would make a raging fire belch out the door in new fury. She hadn't spent so much time reading about fire safety only to let Marge succumb to unnecessary injury now.

No flames burst out, reassuring Midge that the tan stone of the mill had done its work in minimizing the impact of the blaze. She looked around the door, felt the heat, and smelled burned flour and something worse, something stronger than the singed stone around them as Marge pushed past her.

"Amos!" Smoke blanketed the room, blinding her for a moment. Flames licked greedily up wooden supports to the beams bearing the floor of the next level above. *If this continues, the upper story will collapse upon us all.* "Amos!" She screamed his name, hearing Marge call for Gavin—hearing Gavin respond.

Cold clutched her in a tight fist when Amos didn't call back or come to her. *No. God, no. Don't let him be hurt.* She didn't care if she was praying. Didn't care if her asking for Amos to be spared meant God might decide to let a burning beam fall atop her. *It doesn't matter, so long as he and everyone else are all right. Do You hear me?*

"Over here!" She followed Gavin's voice—the wrong one, but the only lead she had—eyes tearing from the smoke and her fear. Midge felt more than saw Marge move to the right, and she followed, avoiding the large dark shape that must be the millstones in the center of the building.

"We need to get him out of here." Gavin could only be talking about Amos. He came into view, crouching low over a prone figure.

"Amos?" Midge fell to her knees, scooping her hands beneath his underarms as Gavin picked up his ankles. "Wake up, Amos!" Even as she spoke, she knew it would be best for him to lie still while they moved him. But so long as he remained still, dread clawed at her that the life had already left him.

A low moan, raw and filled with pain, brought a new flood of tears. "He's alive!" Together the three of them lifted him, carrying him around the millstones and out the door.

Eyes streaming, Midge didn't see Amos's face until they got him a good distance clear of the mill. The skin on his cheeks, forehead, and chin burned a livid red beneath blackened streaks of burned powder—at least, what Midge assumed to be burned powder. Flour. His eyes, closed, looked bare without their thick dusting of sandy lashes and unkempt bushy brows above.

Blackened holes tore through his shirt, displaying more burns beneath. His hands, where they rested at his sides, already showed signs of blistering. But he breathed steadily in and out, and his pulse, when she found it, beat strong and regular beneath her fingertips. "Oh, Amos." She smoothed a hand through his hair, wincing at the crisp of the locks up front.

It was only then she realized Marge and Gavin had left—most likely rushed back to extinguish the flames devouring the wooden structures inside the brick building. For a brief moment, she wrestled with the question of whether to go help them. But it was no choice—not with Amos lying helpless and unconscious before her.

"Midglet?" His eyes opened for a moment, dazed but determined. "Heart—" He sucked in a breath and shut his eyes. "Beautiful."

"You'll be all right." One of her tears trickled onto his forehead, but she knew better than to wipe it away. She gulped back a sob as he slipped back into unconsciousness. "You have to be."

"You aren't going back in!" His yell came out more like a croak, courtesy of the singed flour coating his throat, but that didn't diminish Gavin's determination as he halted Marge outside the mill door.

"If you're going, I'm going."

"No time to argue." He shoved—yes, shoved—her out of the path of the door, slid inside, and slammed it shut, barring it from within to keep her from danger. If the woman wouldn't listen to good sense, he'd see to it she had no choice but to abide by his decisions. *Effective—something I'll apply to other areas of our lives when this is over.*

For now, he rushed right, where the second water barrel stood waiting. Thick smoke clogged his vision and filled the room, relieved only by the sinister orange of the flames climbing up and across the beams to his ceiling, sliding their way to the grain stored above. He grabbed hold of a cotton blanket kept immersed in one of the fire barrels, the fabric made heavy with water as he flung it around the top of a wooden pillar, its weight and the force of his throw wrapping it around the top.

Gavin tugged it downward, smothering the flames on that brace, then rushed to repeat the maneuver. Smoke crept into his lungs, tickling his throat, teasing forth coughs he didn't have time for as he hauled soaked fabric back to slap at the wooden ceiling above him time and time again.

If he'd been able to leave the door open, he might've had more air. But Gavin breathed easier knowing he'd made sure of Marge's safety. The door to the sluiceway stood open, letting out some of the smoke, at least. Until the scant sunlight permitted by that opening became blocked by something. Someone.

A woman, moving slowly, as though encumbered by extraordinarily heavy skirts, headed for another water barrel. "Marge!" As Gavin watched, she lifted a bucket and splashed its contents on the rafters, ignoring him as she focused on the flames. He wasted precious seconds trying to determine how she'd gotten there, and deciding he wouldn't be able to force her out, he got back to fighting the fire with renewed desperation.

It wasn't just about saving the mill anymore. *If the building goes down, I lose Marge.*

They worked in silence, soaking and smothering every hint of flame and fire before Gavin took the time to reopen the main door. He would have done so far sooner had he not feared taking the time away from subduing the blaze. It was then, surveying the smoldering wreckage of every bit of wood in the room from the decimated gears and millrun to the now nonexistent hopper and the charred remains of the supports leading to the upper floor, that another heat unfurled within him.

She tried to muffle a cough, but it did no good. He heard. How could he not? How could she think he wouldn't know exactly how blistered, raw, and aching her throat felt? That knowing she experienced such a thing didn't make it worse by tenfold?

Gavin reached out, snagged her hand—a hand made rough with minor burns and scrapes coated with soot and burned flour, a hand he remembered as being soft and sweet mere days before—and led her outside. He dragged in a deep breath, ready to vent the rage of unrealized fears, only to pull up short when he realized he didn't have all the facts. "How did you get inside?"

Black streaked her cheeks, locks of hair wisped free from her habitually tidy bun to wave fiercely around her face, and her chin thrust forward in defiance. "I waded over and climbed the brace to the sluice gate walkway."

"You waded through the millpond and climbed up the walkway?" He wanted to shake her. He wanted to yell at her until she never put herself in danger again. Gavin looked at her, proud and disheveled and irresistible. *I want to marry her.*

But she wasn't looking at him. He turned to see Midge Collins kneeling at his friend's side, Dr. Reed next to her with his trusty black bag. Obviously the girl had run to fetch her adoptive father. Amos rested in the best of hands now.

That meant Gavin was free to confront Marge with the consequences of her actions.

As soon as Daisy released his fiancée from a hug that looked likely to strangle her, that was.

He coughed into his already-soiled handkerchief as Grandma approached, hoping to stave off the inevitable show of affection. It did no good. Before he could do a thing about it, Grandma had him and Marge in a clasp that would have done a jailer proud.

By then, he couldn't wait any longer to hear how Amos fared. Gavin walked over to confer with Saul Reed as the women held their own impromptu meeting, with Midge dispensing information.

"He'll live," Dr. Reed offered. "Good vital signs, and the burns aren't nearly as severe as they could have been, given what I suspect happened." Reed's words went a long way toward relieving Gavin's mind. "So long as we keep infection at bay and he doesn't succumb to lockjaw, Amos Geer should make a full recovery. Although I do wonder what we'll discover when he regains consciousness."

"What do you fear, Doctor?"

"Depends on what happened in there." Saul Reed jerked his head toward the still-smoking mill. "I've read that rye powder can be ten times as explosive as gunpowder but hadn't credited the rumors until Midge ran to fetch me and described what she knew, though she didn't witness the actual incident." There was no mistaking the look of relieved gratitude on the man's face.

"I've not had the opportunity to investigate, but this sort of thing happens when a small piece of metal finds its way into a sack of grain and feeds through the hopper. It sparks against the millstones, ignites the powder lying thick in the mill air, and flashes into an instant explosion." Gavin closed his eyes at the memory of the intense white light.

"So it is a flash burn. Then it's likely Mr. Geer will suffer blindness." The doctor held up a hand. "In most cases, it's temporary rather than permanent. But forewarned is forearmed. I'll bandage his head and warn him as soon as he awakens so he isn't alarmed that he doesn't have his sight. That would be. . .disconcerting."

Gavin nodded. He could only imagine the sense of panic at losing his vision without warning.

"Although you seem not to have borne the impact of the explosion to the same extent as Mr. Geer, the fact that your vision remains unaffected beyond the effects of the smoke is highly encouraging."

"The circumstances of this accident are somewhat unusual. I expect to find that the piece of metal at fault is rather large— the scraping sound tells me the top millstone was knocked from the runner. I happened to be kneeling over a sack of flour at the time of the incident—judging by the location of the flames in the mill, at about the place where the stones collided once dislodged. It would have acted like a sort of barrier, guarding me from the brunt of the explosion."

"And directing it toward Mr. Geer?" The doctor caught on fast. "In that case, I won't make any expectations based on your condition, Mr. Miller." At that point, he turned his attention toward examining how Gavin fared after breathing in so much smoke, and repeated the inspection on Marge.

"Here." Dr. Reed gave him a rinse for his stinging eyes and a packet of herbs to make into tea. "This will help soothe the raw throat. You're both breathing fairly well. Don't try to stop the coughing. It's your body's way of getting out the soot." With that, he and Gavin loaded a still-unconscious Amos into the doctor's wagon, and he and Miss Collins took him back to town for further treatment.

"Marge, I don't know when the next stage comes, but I guarantee that we'll be on it," Daisy's voice rang out, shrill and demanding in the stillness left behind doctor and patient. "You don't belong in this forsaken place, full of dust and danger and...and..." She plucked a small notebook from the pocket of her full skirts and rifled through it before adding triumphantly, "Dilapidated machinery leading to explosions!"

"Gavin's mill isn't dilapidated!" Marge's outburst matched his thoughts exactly. Well, almost exactly.

"If you want to leave, be my guest, Daisy." Gavin slid an arm through one of Marge's and began walking, forcing her to keep pace alongside him. "But Marge stays with me."

Chapter 38

Let her go, you. . .you. . ." Daisy rushed after them, searching for the right word. "Bully!" She reached over and tried to wrench his arm from Marge's but couldn't budge it.

"I'm no bully." He kept a firm grip on Marge's hand. "Tell her, Marge."

"You can't order someone to say you aren't a bully! Only bullies do that!" Daisy knew she was shrieking but didn't care. If her voice happened to be the only weapon at her disposal, she'd wield it until Gavin Miller let go of her cousin and clamped his hands over both ears to block her out.

"Marge?" He ignored her entirely, focusing on his captive.

"Do you know, Gavin, she makes a good point. You've issued a lot of orders lately." Marge attempted to tug her hand free but had no more success than Daisy had on her behalf. "That's a very poor record for someone who promised to meet his bride halfway. Particularly when he can't seem to decide which bride he wants."

"Not me!" Daisy vented her ire by whacking him on the head

845

with her reticule, which startled him enough to allow Marge to pull free. "He doesn't want me, that much is certain."

"Agreed!" The brute reached for Marge again. "Now that we've settled that much, you can leave us in private while your cousin and I come to an understanding about what the future holds."

A private moment? "Never!" Daisy refused to remember the private moments Trouston insisted they share. "An unmarried woman should never be left unattended."

"I'm her fiancé!" Far from cowing her into obedience, his roar strengthened her resolve not to leave Marge alone.

"No, you aren't." Marge stepped beside her—away from him.

"You aren't anyone's fiancé, Mr. Miller." Daisy linked arms with Marge to point out the way they stood together—against him. *Me and Marge against overbearing men. . .*

"I will be, if you'd stop poking your nose where it isn't wanted." His scowl left no doubt in Daisy's mind that her cousin had managed a very narrow escape from a lifetime under the thumb of an overbearing ogre. "Marge and I have things to discuss."

"Marge needs a bath, some of the tea the doctor prescribed, and lots of rest." Daisy started toward the house, tugging her cousin along when she hesitated. "A certain miller lured her out into the middle of nowhere, toyed with her affections, and almost got her killed battling a dangerous fire today."

"She snuck back in!" His protest made no sense.

"I wouldn't have had to if you hadn't locked me out." Some of Marge's old spirit flickered to life again. "You can't control everything, Gavin Miller."

"Come back here, Marge."

"No." Now it was Marge sweeping Daisy back toward the house. "Because most of all, you don't control me!"

Burning. Heat claimed his face, his chest, his hands—a blazing pain sinking deep past the surface to set his very nerves aflame. Amos shifted, trying to escape, only to send a fresh wave of knife-like heat surging through his skin.

He held still, waiting for it to subside before opening his eyes. *Darkness.* He blinked, trying to dispel whatever blocked his vision, only to find no relief. Without conscious thought, he raised his hands to his eyes, sucking in his breath at the searing sensation caused by the movement.

"Don't move." Midge's voice came to him, cool and soothing. Close. "It'll make your burns hurt, though I'm sure you've discovered that."

"Burns. . .the mill." The memory of a blinding flash and intense heat knocking him against a stone wall came rushing back. He sat up and immediately wished he hadn't when discomfort churned to nausea. "Is Gavin all right?"

"Yes—lay down." He felt the pressure of her hand against his shoulder. Somehow, it seemed she'd found the one place that didn't hurt. Or maybe it didn't hurt because she touched him. Amos couldn't say for certain which was true, but he sank back slowly, trying not to trigger any more bursts of fiery punishment. "You've probably discovered that you can't see. Saul bandaged your face and eyes."

"Bandages." Relief coursed through him. "Thank God."

"God didn't put them there—Saul did. Dr. Reed, if you prefer." Her words sounded more clipped, controlled. "But if you're thanking the Almighty that it's bandages blocking your vision," she continued, her tone gentler, "you need to know that's not entirely the truth, Amos."

"Explain." He swallowed, unable to brace himself any other way as he felt her weight sink onto the corner of the bed beside him. "The bright flash of light—how bad is it?"

"We expect you to remain unable to see for a while, even without the bandages, but Saul says blindness caused by flash burns almost always corrects itself in a matter of weeks."

"Blindness." Amos blinked several times, as though to push away the darkness. Foolish, he knew—it gave him reason to be glad the bandages hid the desperate act from Midge.

"*Temporary* blindness." Her emphasis somehow made it more palatable. "You're young and healthy and may recover in as little as two weeks." The smooth rim of a glass pressed against his lips. "Drink this."

He swallowed. It took an effort to answer "yes" instead of nod when she asked if he was comfortable. It would serve no purpose but to set off the system of painful alerts warning against any movement. Not that he would be comfortable for a long while, but he knew that she meant it in a relative sort of way. "And the burns?"

"Not nearly as severe as they feel. Your hands took the worst of it and will be slowest to heal." She lightly touched his wrist as she spoke, the featherlight brush of her fingers affording a unique comfort. "You will heal, Amos."

A catch in her voice caught his attention. "There was doubt?" *And you care. Deeply.* He kept the observation to himself, but some of his restlessness eased away.

"You didn't answer when I called for you—lay so still when we carried you out of the fire. . ." Memories tinged her words with fear relived. "At first I didn't know if you'd survived." A ragged breath was drawn in quickly so he wouldn't notice—but it was too late. He'd heard it.

"Don't worry, little Midglet." He wanted to see her, reach out, hold her—but could offer nothing but the truth. "God watches over His own, and He kept me safe."

"Safe?" Her weight suddenly lifted from the bed as she jumped up. "*This* is how God watches over His own, Amos? *This* is the way He answers prayers for protection? *This* is what you offer me as proof of His love and grace?"

"No...what happened today makes one example out of many." He listened to the staccato clicks of her boots as she paced along the hardwood floor and surmised he must be at the Reed house.

"You're burned, blind, and could have died!"

"Exactly." He smiled and found the expression barely stung. "I'm here, not even badly burned, and only temporarily blinded according to all reasonable expectation. Things could be so much worse—how can I not be grateful?"

"Things could be worse." Exasperation underscored each word. "This is the basis for your faith? Things could be worse? Amos, what about the reverse side? Things could be so much better. Things *should* be so much better, if God really cared and protected His children as you claim."

Lord, guide my words to best reach this woman You've brought into my life. We've finally come to it—the real reason why she turns from You. Help me show her. . . .

"Why?" He waited one beat, then two, eventually counting out seven long breaths without any response from her. Even more telling, her skirts hadn't so much as rustled, telling Amos Midge hadn't moved a muscle since he asked the question.

"Why what?"

"Why should things be better, Midge?" *This would be so much simpler if I could see her face, Lord. If I could gauge her reactions and adjust my approach—temper my words to best reach her. Remember the tree? She thinks she harbors a heart of ugliness and corruption, not knowing the beauty within is only missing the fulfillment of accepting Your promise.*

"What sort of question is that?" Midge still didn't move. "It's what we always work toward—to make things better."

"Exactly." A rhythmic tapping let him know she'd begun to fidget. "We work to make things better. We earn the good things we attain—and that's as it should be."

"God could make everything so much easier. If He wanted to—if He loved as deeply and fully as He's supposed to."

Anger veiled the true motive behind her words, and if he'd been able to watch instead of rely solely on listening, Amos might have missed the deeper vein running beneath. The hollow note of betrayal burrowed beneath Midge's rage, eating away at the foundation of faith.

"We don't appreciate things that are given to us easily, Midge. It's the process of improving ourselves and the things around us for the people we love that makes us more worthy." He listened, realizing she'd gone still again.

"God judges the heart—sees deep inside who and what a person is, and what he or she can become based on that." She started pacing again. "He doesn't need proof of whether or not we can be worthy—He knows it already. He knows what we think and what we need and when and how we hurt. . .and He lets it happen."

"We learn through our mistakes, Midge."

"What mistake did you make today, Amos?" Her steps moved farther away, until he heard the sound of a door opening. "What were you supposed to learn?"

"I don't know." His admission stopped her cold.

"Well, at least you know you don't have all the answers." She shut the door and walked back to his bedside. Looking down at him lying there, propped up against pillows, his face swathed in bandages, Midge felt rage rise up once more. "You didn't need to learn anything, Amos."

"There's a change I didn't expect." If she didn't know better, Midge would swear he smiled under those bandages. "A day or so ago you would've told me I have a lot to learn."

A grudging grin tugged at her until she realized he couldn't see it if she let it out. So she did—and it felt good. "That's not what I meant."

"You can't have it both ways, Midglet." His voice went deeper, his speech starting to slur from the medicine she'd given him to help him sleep and ease the pain.

"Neither can God." She sank into the chair at his bedside, suddenly weary beyond memory. "He can't have a reputation for being loving, forgiving, and all-knowing but turn around and let the entire world stumble and struggle and suffer. That's the worst sort of hypocrisy I can imagine, Amos."

Worse, even, than the men who abused my sister then demeaned her for it.

"But that's not God—that's Satan." It looked as though he fought to remain awake. "Midglet, don't ever forget we live in a war...." With that, sleep claimed him.

War? Midge left him to sleep. To heal as best he could. *What does God have to do with a war?*

CHAPTER 39

She'd won a battle against her own heart that afternoon, but Marge knew the victory to be hollow. Even now, she lay in bed beside Daisy, hearing her cousin's mutter in her sleep, as she always had; and her thoughts wandered to Gavin.

Lord, help me, please. I walked away this afternoon. Please help me give him up. Give me the strength to follow the path You put before me and be content with whatever I find it to be. Let me stop wondering what he would have said to me had Daisy not followed. Take away my worries about whether or not he's positioned his pillows just right so he breathes easiest after all that coughing.

"Not until we're married." Daisy threw out a full sentence before lapsing into incoherence once more. It sounded as though she were remembering fending off Trouston's overeager advances.

Marge wondered whether she should awaken Daisy or if it was best to let her sleep. She still hadn't decided when Daisy spoke loudly enough again to be understood.

"You promised...." Even in sleep, this sounded forlorn. Small. It made Marge frown and listen more closely.

If this counted as eavesdropping, she'd disregard it. Daisy hadn't explained the complete reason behind the abrupt end to her engagement, and obviously something deeply troubled her typically happy-go-lucky cousin.

More mutterings sank into silence. Then, "Can't leave me now!" The wail burst out so suddenly, Marge almost rolled out of the bed. "How could you?" This came so quietly, she could almost believe she'd imagined it. "Ruined. . ."

Ruined? Marge gasped. *Surely she can't mean what I think she means!* Yet no matter how intently she listened, Daisy would only repeat that one word every so often, as though unable to move past it.

"Ruined. . ."

If Marge had fallen asleep first, as she had the night before, she wouldn't know. *I shouldn't know now. Daisy didn't tell me.* Sadness shafted through her. *I didn't ask; I was too wrapped up in my own troubles to truly take note of how much she hurt.* She kneaded her pillow, trying to vent her guilt.

It didn't work. She lay there, turning the problem over in her mind, again and again, examining it from all sides. The facts didn't change. If her suspicions proved correct—and she held out little hope they wouldn't—Trouston had coerced or forced her cousin into giving him what should only be given to a husband.

"Ruined. . ."

Which means she'll have a difficult time finding a husband who accepts her past. Daisy wasn't the sort of woman to find her own way or push through on determination or grit. The simple truth of the matter came down to a bald fact: Daisy needed someone to watch over and provide for her. In short, Daisy needed a husband.

And Gavin needs a wife. Resolve flooded her, sweeping away most of the regret she should feel at the new plan working its way through her mind. *Lord, can it be You orchestrating this so my cousin wouldn't be left to fend for herself after her parents' deaths? If You mean Gavin for Daisy, I can accept that.*

She didn't like it. She didn't want it. But when faced with her cousin's need and God's will, Marge knew she could bear it. Even if the small box in her heart gaped wide open, the hope seeping away in small puffs of necessity, seeming to echo the one word on Daisy's mind. . .

"*Ruined. . .*"

The next day's sermon passed with agonizing slowness. With Amos laid up downstairs, Midge thought she'd found the perfect reason to avoid attending church. . .only to be outmaneuvered.

"I won't be the reason you don't go to church." Amos spoke up the moment she entered his room, somehow knowing it was her despite his inability to see. "Dr. Reed and I agree on that much, Midglet. I'll be fine for a few hours."

Maybe he's fine, she pondered, scowling as Parson Carter showed no signs of slowing down, *but what about me?* The longer she sat in that pew, the more Midge stewed. *Last night, Amos mentioned being in the middle of a war. He's about to learn how right he is. . .and that he picked the wrong opponent!*

Then something Parson Carter said caught her attention—something about fire. "Mr. Geer's accident brought to mind a verse that used to be one of my father's favorites. And while we keep Amos in prayer today, I'd like to read from Isaiah 48."

Midge sat up straighter, listening carefully so she could pass along Parson Carter's message when she got home to Amos. But when the parson finished reading the verse, she felt so astonished she could scarcely credit it.

After entering her house following the service, she found herself stopping to pick up the Reeds' Bible and take it with her to Amos's room so she could read it and verify the message.

Amos still slept when she entered, but he must have sensed her presence, because no sooner did she begin turning pages than he stirred. "What are you reading, Midglet?"

"Searching for a verse Parson Carter read today." She could tell by his silence Amos wasn't sure how to respond. "In your honor. I think I must've heard it wrong, and I want to get it right before we talk about it."

"What's the verse?"

Midge consulted the scrap of paper where she'd scribbled the attribution. "Isaiah 48:10." She kept turning the thin, fragile leafs of the Bible as Amos lay there, waiting. When she finally found the right page, she traced one finger down the column to settle on the exact verse and read aloud.

"'Behold, I have refined thee, but not with silver; I have chosen thee in the furnace of affliction.'"

To her surprise, she made it about halfway through before Amos began reciting the verse as she read it. "You know this verse? By memory?"

"Until you began reading it, I wasn't sure I had the right one in mind." He lay unmoving, a live corpse before her save the movement of his mouth. "But yes, I know it. And others that refer to the same idea."

"This is what you talked about yesterday—having to earn things and prove ourselves worthy. And today Parson Carter chose it because your ordeal reminded him of being put into the furnace of affliction." Midge stared at the verse until it became a jumble of letters. "As though it makes sense you needed to be tested like a precious metal to be found pure."

"No, Midge, put through trials to become refined into something more than the base metal I began with." His bandaged face turned toward her, and she clenched her hands to keep from ripping the coverings from his eyes. "The challenges we overcome shape us and prepare us to deal with those that await."

"I understand that." She shut the Bible and laid it on the bedside table. "I even respect it, Amos. But I don't see why God puts us through all of that if He's supposed to be perfect in His mercy."

"Free will, Midglet. God gives us the choice and asks us to choose Him rather than succumb to the lures of Satan and live in selfishness. Many choose wrongly, and the world becomes a constant battleground."

"The war you spoke of?" She thought of it. . .examined what Amos was telling her, poked at it in an attempt to find a weak point—but it made sense.

"We fight for those we love, we fight to do what's right in the name of the Lord, and we fight against the parts of ourselves that want to stop fighting and indulge in all the things that look so easy or enjoyable." He lifted his hands then lowered them again as though anxious to enjoin battle once more. "That is our war—and one we wage so long as we value God's gift in letting us choose how we live out our days."

"No." She didn't bother to explain why that didn't work— hadn't figured out how to put it into words just yet—but knew enough to go ahead and refute what he said.

"No to what part? All of it? Some of it?" He raised his hands and spread them wide in a questioning gesture.

"The last part, mostly." If she thought about it, Midge could get behind the stuff about fighting for loved ones and battling against taking the easy way and doing wrong. "All that about the Lord giving us the gift of freedom. He's all rules and impossible standards and demanding you give yourself up."

I've worked too hard to keep myself together to do that.

"We need things to aspire to—you've already agreed to that. And God doesn't ask you to give yourself up. You're looking at it the wrong way."

Tears pricked her nose and eyes, clogged her throat, and made her breathing harsh. "What's the right way, Amos? He loves me in spite of the fact I lived in a back alleyway and Saul only just barely saved me from life as a prostitute? He loves me even though He let my parents and sister die?" She took in a great gulp of air and waited.

Now he knows the truth about my past. Now he won't want to talk to me or think I'm worth saving anymore.

Amos stayed quiet for a long time. "Jesus didn't condemn the fallen, and God sacrificed His only Son for our sakes." His words surprised her enough to dry up the tears. "You are precious in His sight, Midglet."

Midglet. He still calls me Midglet. But no more tears came. Instead, an odd calm descended upon her. "If He loves me so much and plans for me to keep my freedom, what does God want?"

"The same thing any of us want. Stands to reason, since we were made in His image." Amos shifted in the bed, turning his face just slightly so that it seemed as though the bandages stared straight through her. "He wants you to accept Him."

"As I am, He wants me?"

"To choose to accept Him. Yes." Every line of Amos's body seemed tense—with a hope Midge could understand.

"But it's my choice? I stay myself and gain an ally in fighting for what's good?" She waited for Amos's nod. "You're sure He already accepts me?"

"He already loves you, Midglet." She could see Amos swallow.

"In that case. . ." Midge got up and perched on the bed beside Amos, resting her head against the shoulder that hadn't been burned. "It's not hard at all for me to accept Him."

"And me?"

"Don't be silly, Amos." She smoothed his hair back. "I chose *you* ages ago."

"Good, because there's only one thing I want to see when my sight returns, Midge Collins."

"Oh?" Her hand stilled. "What's that?"

"You should've guessed." His smile made a mockery of the bandages swathing his face. "Freckles."

CHAPTER 40

Grandma cornered him a few days after the mill fire, while Daisy paid yet another visit to the mercantile and Marge ruled over the new schoolhouse. "Have you decided whether you take after my side of the family yet, or do you fancy the flibbertigibbet who pulled in here last week?"

"It would help if you let me know whether you leaned toward one or the other." Gavin kept a straight face as he answered. "Unless, of course, you bear no preference."

"Very well." The old woman chuckled and wandered over to her rocking chair. "If you've brains enough to be smart to your grandmother, I trust you've sufficient intelligence to choose the right Marguerite." She paused long enough to make Gavin wonder whether or not she'd leave it at that. "*This* time, at least." The final jab, when it came, earned her a smile.

"You can be sure of it, Grandma. I know how fortunate I am that Marge misread the letter and came here. I don't plan on letting her leave." With that, he grabbed his hat and headed toward the schoolhouse.

Truth of the matter was, he couldn't blame Grandma for starting to wonder which cousin he'd decided to wed. Marge avoided him like the plague, whereas in direct contrast, Daisy seemed to pop up everywhere. Like a weed. It'd become ludicrous, the way he'd hunt out one cousin only to wind up stuck with the wrong girl.

The girl I thought I wanted to marry. Gavin shook his head. *Lord, I was blinded by a pretty face and cheerful laugh, when the true value stood right beside. Thank You for giving them the same name. I praise the day Marge stepped out of that stagecoach instead of Daisy.*

He wasn't sure he'd timed it right to arrive at the schoolhouse just as Marge let class out for the day, and as it turned out, he was early. Gavin glanced through the open door at the twenty or so students sitting inside—boys and girls ranging in age from five to about twelve—and decided to wait outside. Going inside would just disrupt things, and he didn't want a single thing to go wrong this afternoon.

Wandering around the side of the building, he heard Marge's voice through an open window and stopped to listen. It took him all of a moment to figure out she was reading a story to her students. Gavin rested one shoulder against the reddish brick of the schoolhouse and settled in to listen.

Marge spun the story of a boy named Henry Bond, whose father died and whose mother struggled with the cost of sending him to school. Her voice grew sad, her pace slow as she told of how Henry needed a grammar book but his mother couldn't afford one. A note of hope entered her reading, which picked up speed, as Henry woke to find freshly fallen snow and took the initiative to clear paths for his neighbors until he'd earned enough money for his schoolbook.

Satisfaction shimmered in the syllables as she read the end

of the tale. "'From that time, Henry was always the first in all his classes. He knew no such word as *fail*, but always succeeded in all he attempted. Having the will, he always found the way.'"

Just as I've the will to find my way into marriage with a certain schoolmarm.

Gavin straightened up as he heard Marge tell her students she would read a section of a poem to them and then they'd be dismissed for the rest of the day. Her voice took on a lilting cadence as she recited the first stanza to a familiar rhyme.

"'Tis a lesson you should heed,
Try, try again;
If at first you don't succeed,
Try, try again;
Then your courage should appear,
For if you will persevere,
You will conquer, never fear;
Try, try again.'"

"Now remember, students, you can't expect to learn everything all at once. Sometimes you'll forget, sometimes you'll make mistakes, but that's all right so long as you do your best and don't give up. I'll see you all tomorrow!"

Gavin watched as the children filed out the door in clumps of two and three, some lingering far too long for his liking, before finally they'd all left. Only then did he venture inside the schoolroom, where he found Marge wiping down the blackboard at the front of the class. He walked up behind her and waited.

"Gavin!" The little shriek and hop made him smile. "You startled me!"

"I'd apologize, but the truth of the matter is I enjoyed it." He waggled his brows. "I've never seen you jump before."

"Sneaking up on someone tends to have that effect." With her surprise fading, she became all brisk and businesslike—as though brushing him away. "What brings you here, Mr. Miller?"

"I should think that would be obvious, Marge." For the moment, he ignored the way she'd reverted to using his proper name. Perhaps it had something to do with their standing in the schoolhouse. "I came for you."

"There's no need to walk me back to the house." Marge fiddled with the stack of readers on her desk, stalling for time. *Why is he here now? How do I talk to him about Daisy?*

"I want to." Somehow, his broad-shouldered frame swallowed all the space inside the one-room schoolhouse that managed to accommodate twenty children. "It's been difficult to spend time with you these past few days."

"With the start of school and Midge busy caring for Mr. Geer, there's been much to keep me busy." She skirted around the far edge of the desk—away from Gavin. "Besides, you've been repairing and replacing things as needed for the mill and haven't had much time to waste standing around talking."

What little time you've had, I've done my best to make sure you spend with Daisy. Thus far, however, Marge saw no signs that her plotting bore any fruit. For a man who'd written and sent for Daisy to come out west and marry him, Gavin showed precious little inclination to woo her cousin. When it came right down to it, he showed no interest whatsoever. Marge fingered the chain to her glasses.

"You wear them when you teach?" His voice interrupted her thoughts, and it took her a moment to realize he referred to her spectacles.

"Only when reading." She snatched her hand away from the chain. *How many times has Daisy told me not to draw attention to my spectacles, not to wear them unless absolutely necessary? Men find them off-putting.* Except. . .Gavin didn't seem put off by her glasses in the least. Even now, he looked at where they hung near her waist as though wishing she'd don them.

Surely that can't be so. Marge blinked. *Even if it is, it shouldn't matter. Not anymore.*

"I've got a question for the teacher." A mischievous smile played at the corners of his mouth. "Will she explain something I've been wondering about for a while?"

"I'll do my best." It took a moment for her to identify the tingling feeling in her stomach as nervousness.

"Why is it," he began, tapping one knuckle on her desk with each word, making his way toward her while he asked his question, "that every time I turn around, you're foisting me off on your cousin?" By the time he finished, he loomed directly in front of her, brows raised in expectation of her answer.

"Foisting?" she squeaked. There really wasn't another word for it. "I don't know what you mean."

"Wrong answer." He took a step closer—a step she couldn't afford to give him without retreating a small measure herself. "Try, try again, Teacher."

She gasped. "You heard my reading to the children!" Heat swept up her cheeks at the idea he'd been watching her without her knowledge. It seemed so. . .intimate.

"I was waiting on you." Gavin ate up the step she'd retreated. "I still am."

"Daisy's the Marguerite you want." Marge couldn't believe she had to spell it out for him. "She doesn't think she wants to stay in Buttonwood, but you can change her mind."

"Who says I want to change her mind?" This time, he didn't move forward. He looked. . .puzzled. "Daisy's not the wife I want. You should know that, Marge."

The faint flutter of hope reborn made her giddy. And nauseated. *Not again. I can't keep going through the disappointment, Lord.* A dismaying notion chased away the other feeling. After all, he and Daisy had been spending more time together the past few days. Had her cousin confided in him?

"Is this because of what happened with Trouston?" She blurted out the horrible suspicion before considering the ramifications if he didn't know. "Because—"

He rested a work-roughened finger against her lips, effectively hushing her. "This is because of what happened with you, Marge. I don't want Daisy. I want the Marguerite who came to Buttonwood to meet me more than halfway."

"Daisy's in Buttonwood." It emerged slightly muffled, the words working around his finger before Marge tilted her head back. "Surely that counts for something."

"I'm not interested in counting. I'll leave the arithmetic to your students." One giant step on his part had her backed against her desk. "I care more about other things."

"Such as?" She found it difficult to breathe all of a sudden.

"Reading." He reached between them, plucked her spectacles from the clasp at her waist, carefully unfolded the wire frames, and set them upon her nose with a tenderness Marge never would have expected. "I want you to read my face and see clearly which bride I want."

"No." She shook her head, spectacles sliding down her nose until he pushed them back into place with one finger. "You can't have changed your mind, Gavin. I'm—"

"Godly, kind, intelligent. Brave and foolish enough to wade

into a millpond and scale sluiceway braces to stand at my side and fight a fire." His gaze didn't leave hers, staring with an intensity that gave the eerie impression he saw beyond her glasses and all the way through to the woman beneath. "You're many things, Marge. It shouldn't have taken me so long to see it."

She blinked. *Daisy is the beautiful, vivacious one every man wants.* "But I'm not—"

"Mine." He braced his hands on the desk, bracketing her. "Not yet." Then his lips found hers, warm and firm as they silenced her doubts. His hands slid from the desk to curve around her back, holding her close. When he finally let her go, he rested his forehead against hers. "Marge, I've only one more question to ask."

"Hmm?" She really ought to gather her wits, but they'd scrambled beyond repair anyway. "What is it?"

"How much longer will you make me wait before you become my wife?"

Her smile started slowly and spread until it felt as though every inch of her glowed with it. "Exactly as long as it takes for you to arrange the wedding."

"Done." Gavin angled his head for another kiss. "You'll be mine before the week is out."

CHAPTER 41

"I love weddings." Midge sat stock-still in the pew beside Amos, waiting for the ceremony to begin.

"Good." His smile could almost convince someone who didn't know him better that his eyes saw more than the varying shades of gray lightening the absolute black he'd walked in for a few days after the incident at the mill. Darkness still dodged his steps, but now Midge knew it wouldn't last.

God is faithful. She would've squeezed his hand but knew the burns there hadn't healed nearly so quickly as those on his face, so she settled for patting his shoulder.

"So do I." Daisy Chandler, the cousin who Midge could scarcely believe was related to Marge, much less shared her name, giggled from directly behind them, where she sat beside the Lindners. Midge didn't know precisely why the Lindners followed Daisy to Buttonwood, but if the admiring glances Mr. Shane Lindner cast in Daisy's direction were anything to go by, she'd assume he had marriage on his mind.

Parson Carter cleared his throat. "Before we begin the vows,

Marge and Gavin have chosen to add something of their own. So bear with us as they do something they want to call "Meeting in the Middle."

The entire town started murmuring when they realized Gavin and Marge both stood at the front of the church—on opposite sides of Parson Carter's pulpit.

"She's wearing sky blue silk with simple lines—none of that overblown, fancy nonsense." Midge whispered the details so Amos wouldn't feel left out. "She's standing to the far right of the pulpit, he's to the far left, and they're looking at each other instead of walking down the aisle."

"I said I wanted a wife who'd be willing to meet me in the middle," Gavin spoke loudly enough to hush the crowd, "but the man is head of the household, so I take the first step." With that, he took a giant step toward the center of the church.

"For a man who's willing to give as much as he receives, I take another step." Marge's gown shimmered as she moved. "And add a second one in faith that he will match me."

"Two steps make a small price to pay when the reward is a wife who will stand by my side for the rest of our days." Gavin moved forward again, reaching the pulpit as he spoke. "And I add a third in thanks she's come this far."

"One step to tell you no thanks are needed, only a promise to continue as we've begun." Marge's smaller stride meant she lagged slightly farther behind. "And three more to represent the three members of this marriage. Myself." She stepped forward with each name. "My husband." Another step, and she almost reached the pulpit—and a waiting Gavin. "And the Lord, who brought us together." The final step brought her to her fiancé's side, before the man of God.

"And so we meet in the middle." Gavin beamed as he spoke

words that must have a special significance to the couple.

Midge thought about how lovely the whole thing was as they exchanged more traditional vows, waiting until Parson Carter pronounced them man and wife before whispering to Amos once more. "I'm sorry you couldn't see it."

"I liked what I heard." He shrugged. "Besides, I'm only concerned with seeing one wedding."

"Are you?" Midge couldn't tear her eyes from him even as Marge and Gavin rushed down the aisle. "Which one?"

For the first time, he slid his arm around her shoulders, keeping her in the church for a moment after everyone else followed the newlyweds outside. He leaned forward, and even without the benefit of being able to see, unerringly found her lips with his in a brief, sweet kiss before answering her question. . . .

"Ours."

Without another word, keeping his arm looped around her shoulders, he guided her outside. "I want to hear this surprise you've been working on with the children."

"All right." Midge called them all around. "Is everyone ready?" She waited for them to nod, knowing that this would be their present to Marge every bit as it was her gift to the town—a way of sharing what filled her heart since the day Amos led her the last bit of the journey to Christ.

After all, she wouldn't have been on the path without Saul, Clara, Opal, Adam, and all the friends who'd prayed and showed her Christian love for four years. Their patience still astounded her, now that she knew the peace they'd wanted her to share. But if they'd pushed, she wouldn't have stayed.

Wouldn't have been here when Amos came calling.

Wouldn't be here now to listen to the students she shared with Marge recite the prayer she'd found in one of the McGuffey's

Readers. Their voices blended in a celebration of the wedding, of the town, and most of all, of the Lord who watched over them all. When the townspeople insisted on an encore, Midge mouthed the words along with her pupils.

"'When the stars at set of sun
Watch you from on high
When the morning has begun
Think the Lord is nigh.

All you do and all you say,
He can see and hear:
When you work and when you play,
Think the Lord is near.

All your joys and griefs He knows
Counts each falling tear.
When to Him you tell your woes,
Know the Lord is near.'"

"We know the Lord watches over you, Marge and Gavin"— Midge tucked one arm through Amos's—"so you'll have far more joy than tears." She couldn't hold back a tiny sniff as she leaned close to add something only Amos could hear. . . .

"And so will we."

Discussion Questions

1. The two Marguerites in this novel have a bit of a rivalry going. How does this shape their relationship? Have you ever been consistently compared to someone else or competed with another person? What is the biblical perspective on that?

2. In the novel, Marge is angry but doesn't want to admit it, because she considers anger to be bad. She's angry at Gavin for his foolish mistake, and later, angry at Daisy for her selfishness in coming to town. Have you ever been angry and unwilling to admit it? How did it affect you? What would have been a better way of dealing with it?

3. What character did you most relate to in this story? Why is that? Is there something you wish he/she had done differently? If so, what would it be and why? How would changing that thing impact everyone else and the story itself?

4. Gavin feels cheated out of what he most wanted when the wrong bride arrives. Have you ever felt like you didn't get what you deserved? Did you really deserve it? What is it about mankind that makes us feel as though we're entitled to what we want—and why is that something Satan can use against us?

5. Gavin feels cheated, but by the same turn of events, Marge feels unwanted. Disappointing someone we care about is always difficult to take—how does Marge deal

with it? How have you dealt with it? How should we respond to circumstances that make us feel bad about ourselves without becoming angry or depressed? It's so hard to do. . .what do we need to remember?

6. What was your favorite scene in the book? Why? What made it special to you?

7. Midge struggles with whether or not to believe in the Lord and His offer of grace. How would you approach someone like her today? If you've read the Prairie Promises series in its entirety, how have you seen Midge change since the 13-year-old living such a hard life?

8. Amos wants to marry Midge but feels strongly that he can't wed a woman who doesn't share his faith. How does he handle this? Do you think he's right—both in his point of view and in how he approaches Midge? What advice would you give a believer who loves a nonbeliever today?

9. Daisy's keeping a secret from everyone. How does the truth affect her relationships and impact her spiritually? Is she right or wrong to stay silent? What spiritual foundations support your answer?

10. If you had to choose just one message to take away from this novel, what would it be? Can you give examples of how you found that message expressed in the novel? Do you agree with it? Why or why not?

KELLY EILEEN HAKE is a reader favorite of Barbour Publishing's Heartsong Presents book club, where she released several of her first books. A credentialed secondary English teacher in California with an MA in Writing Popular Fiction, she is known for her own style of witty, heartwarming historical romance.